WAR FOOTING

THE CHAMPIONS OF 1941

KENNETH TAM

WAR FOOTING

THE CHAMPIONS OF 1941

KENNETH TAM

ICEBERG

Published in Canada by Iceberg Publishing, Waterloo

Library and Archives Canada Cataloguing in Publication
Tam, Kenneth, 1984-, author
        War footing : the champions of 1941 / Kenneth Tam.
ISBN 978-1-926817-59-0 (pbk.)
        I. Title.
PS8589.A7676W37 2013   C813'.6   C2013-906814-7

Firebox (ebook) first published in January 2013.

Grand Banks (ebook) first published in March 2013.

Elspeth (ebook) first published in May 2013.

Mandarins (ebook) first published in July 2013.

Dragons (ebook) first published in September 2013.

War Footing (print omnibus) first published in November 2013.

Cover Photography: Olivia Witzke Photography
Cover Design: Kenneth Tam

Iceberg Publishing
171-55 Northfield Drive East
Waterloo ON Canada N2K 3T6
icebergpublishing.com

For my grandfather
Richard Joseph Barron.

And for my father, Peter Tam.

ACKNOWLEDGMENTS

It's been an exciting year with Alex, Stephanie and Strong, and as we reach the end of their adventures for 1941, it's my privilege to share their stories in this omnibus edition. Before we get to the action, though, many thanks must as usual be given.

To begin, I must single out Mike Strong himself — or as many people know him, Mark Kipper. One of the members of the Canadian Military Heritage Society who joined us back in 2007 for the beginning of *His Majesty's New World*, Mark has remained a fine friend and generous contributor. Along with his son Matt, his wife Anita and his daughter Christine, his efforts have helped make this series look truly great — and Mike Strong personally owes him a lot. Mark, as ever: thanks.

Speaking of the look of the series, I remain indebted to the team behind the cover photos that have given *Champions* such a powerful — indeed, award-winning — visual presence. Fashion and editorial photographer Olivia Witzke's excellent shots have given us the best covers this genre may have ever seen. Models Lizz Caston and Kris Scalisi — both trained as artists — brought Alex and Stephanie alive in fine form, and were ably styled by hair and makeup artist Amy Bridger. Not often do authors get a chance to see their characters realized in real life, so to all the excellent people involved, I offer my continued thanks.

Moving from the images to the words: I benefitted greatly from the expertise of a variety of people while researching these stories for 1941. In particular, I'd like to single out world champion pistol shooter Julie Golob, for her assistance filling in some details about Stephanie Shylock's exceptional shooting abilities. Armed with Julie's insight I felt much better prepared to follow our American Lieutenant into the fray.

Closer to home, I must as usual thank my old friend Mikael Christensen. Originally in the field with us for the *His Majesty's New World* photo shoot in 2007, he continues to be the first person I call whenever we need to round up re-enactors and send them into the field. I only wish that happened more. Mik, I'm perpetually obliged.

Finally, as ever, I close by acknowledging my partners in Iceberg Publishing: my parents. Eleven years of this madness and they refuse to quit and always insist on doing things better. There would be no stories... no *Iceberg*... without their dedication, and I could not be more grateful for the example they have set throughout my life. Thank you, guys... the adventure continues!

A quick note to readers: most weekdays from September to June, the Iceberg writers post 'Author Notes' at icebergpublishing.com. *If you're curious to learn more about the inner workings of series like* Champions *or* His Majesty's New World, *go online and check them out.*

"The world has long stood in awe of the resources made available to our Empire by the new world, but no resource has created such envy as these children of the savages. For centuries to come, it will not be the minerals, the timber, or the treasures about which people whisper; it will be these children. The responsibility therefore falls to us, and to our cousins in the United States, to wrap around these young people a strong and stable structure; to give them responsibilities and expectations, so that they can become truly worthy of the stories that will one day be told of their deeds."

– Baron Julian Byng of Farpoint, addressing the House of Commons after the tabling of the bill that would usher in the 'Byng Policy', in 1924.

ESSENTIAL TIMELINE OF NEW WORLD HISTORY

1881 | Explorers in the Rocky Mountains on either side of the Canada-US border discover gateways that transport them to another planet. This new world teems with riches, and the United States and the British Empire partner to begin colonization.

1882 | Early new world explorers find local inhabitants, who appear outwardly to be human but behave like feral animals. These creatures possess incredible strength and speed, and are viciously carnivorous, indiscriminately eating men, women and children. They are labeled 'savages', and their existence begins to dictate settlement of the new world.

1919 | After nearly four decades of human colonization, the Royal Newfoundland Regiment is dispatched onto the grasslands of the new world, to escort Lady Emma Lee and Miss Kara Lynne in search of the source of savage strength. They discover the presence of an alien race, the Hubrin (then called 'blue men' or 'Martians'), who have genetically modified humans to become attack animals for their military. Emma Lee (more properly known as Emily) is discovered to be a daughter of these savages, who was rescued at an early age and thus developed as a civilized human being — with extraordinary physical abilities.

1920 | The Royal Newfoundland Regiment frees members of the alien Saa race (then called 'dragons') from a Hubrin prison camp and forge a partnership with these more agreeable creatures. After an incident that led to her death, Miss Kara Lynne (more properly, Caralynne) is captured, resuscitated, and genetically altered by the Hubrin, giving her the enhanced physical abilities of the savages. She is rescued when humanity and the Saa join forces to capture the Hubrin capital on the new world. During this battle, the Royal Newfoundland Regiment is almost completely wiped out, but thousands of savage children are freed at an age young enough to allow them to mature as civilized humans.

1924 | The Byng Policy establishes the protocol to be followed by the British Empire and the United States in integrating the children of the savages into human society as 'Champions'. The Lady Emily Academy for Champions is established in Newfoundland, and the Colonel Robinson Champions Institute is established in Virginia. When they reach puberty (and their abilities begin to manifest) young Champions will be sent to one of those schools for training.

1928 | The first class enters the Lady Emily Academy, comprised primarily of young female Champions.

1929 | Lady Emily and her son, Robert, disappear from their quarters one evening. After months of fruitless searching, Caralynne assumes control of the Academy.

1935 | The first Champions graduate from the Lady Emily Academy, and a special military unit is formed to support their efforts to police the British Empire, under the command of the Viscount of the Grasslands, Lord James Devlin. The United States creates a similar unit.

1940 | See: *Whitecoat: The Champions of 1940.*

1941...

THE CHAMPIONS OF 1941 PART 1
FIREBOX
KENNETH TAM

PROLOGUE

Burying her bare feet in the snow always settled Alex's mind.

Whenever she was able to wiggle her toes in fresh powder, she felt oddly like she was taking a swim in her beloved North Atlantic. The icy white crystals would press against her arches and heels, melding to every inch of skin and applying a refreshing firmness that was familiar but unique... like walking barefoot on a rocky beach *while* swimming in cold water. Who wouldn't love that?

Well, most people.

But then, most people would have suffered more than Alex had they tried. It was a bit of an old song now, though that didn't make it any less true: she was a Champion with some odd ways of bonding with her native Newfoundland. Alex loved to bury her bare feet in cold snow, and whether ordinary people could do the same (without losing their toes to frostbite) wasn't her concern.

She had other things to worry about. Like nightmares.

Annoying, persistent, silly nightmares.

As much as she loved the snow on her bare skin, Alex wouldn't have been sitting on the front step of her house in the middle of the night if she'd been able to sleep. The next day was slated to be busy: she and her friend Stephanie, her Sergeant Mike Strong, and her mother Caralynne, were due in Virginia for joint training with the senior class of United States Champions. That was important work, and as one who'd never excelled at all-nighters, she figured she should have been getting some sleep.

Unfortunately, the subject of the two-day training visit had led to the resurgence of a nightmare that had plagued the young whitecoat since August. Alex was meant to teach the soon-to-graduate Americans how to survive an encounter with a rogue Champion — Emily — while Stephanie and Strong were to teach some American soldiers the new 'firebox' tactic, which was an ordinary person's best hope of capturing a savage-born Lady.

To accomplish their assignments, Alex and her friends would have to relive and relate their experiences from the previous August, when Emily had led them on a chase around St. John's and up Signal Hill in the dead of night. It had been a defining experience for Alex, then fresh in her white coat. She'd nearly ended up shot by the end of it.

Hence the nightmares.

Those dreams were always the same: the young whitecoat was on a darkened Signal Hill, trapped by a smiling Emily and a Browning with a failed magazine safety. She ended up shot and left for dead. Admittedly, her subconscious wasn't being particularly creative as it posited that outcome — it seemed to have decided that showing Alex the most realistic fate was scary enough.

It was right.

But the worst part of the dream was never being shot. It was the feeling that filled her when she lay alone on the mossy ground, cold and wet as her blood turned her beloved coat red, and no one came for her — because she'd run away from Stephanie and Strong, and in the nightmare, they didn't find her. It seemed her subconscious wanted Alex to understand that leaving her friend and her Sergeant so she could carry out an impetuous chase was dangerous. Dying was bad, but dying alone as she pleaded with the empty night for someone to keep her company... that was the worst.

Alex figured she had digested that lesson and didn't need more reminders, but her subconscious didn't know how to quit lecturing her.

Strong had promised the nightmares would stop eventually, and indeed, Alex had thought she'd seen the last of them sometime before Christmas. But now, just a few days after new year's, they were back. She supposed they'd returned refreshed from their holiday, and were eagerly looking forward to spending 1941 interrupting her beloved sleep.

Kind of them.

Fortunately, the Newfoundland winter was on Alex's side. Breathing deeply of the icy air, she felt her core temperature continue to drop. She'd had to change after sweating through her nightclothes — not exactly a pleasant experience, for her or the clothes — but now that her fresh pajamas were suitably icy, and her body was appropriately chilled, she'd hopefully be able to sleep again.

If not, she'd sit outside until the sun came up, and the American students could deal with her being tired (or more precisely: cranky).

"You wouldn't want me to be rude to a bunch of students, would you?" Alex asked her brain. "That wouldn't be fair to them. So clearly you have to let me get some sleep."

Strangely, her brain didn't answer. Someone else did.

"You're talking to yourself. Good sign."

A body settled down beside Alex, and just as the Champion frowned and wondered precisely how she'd missed the sound of her friend opening the door behind her, Stephanie Shylock yawned.

"Sorry," the Lieutenant said, "I yawned. Continue."

The American girl noticeably didn't put her feet — which were wrapped in heavy socks — in the snow. She'd also pulled a coat over her pajamas, and a scarf around her neck.

Alex decided to do up the top button of her pajama shirt in solidarity, since apparently it was cold. She then answered casually: "I was just explaining to myself that it's important to sleep before trying to mentor the Americans. You know how touchy Americans can be."

"I do know," Stephanie nodded, since she was aware of her own nationality. "And we often think people who sit with their bare feet in the snow in the middle of the night while they talk to themselves might not be, in the strictest sense, sane."

"Americans are so close-minded," Alex shook her head with completely legitimate disappointment.

"Fortunately we compensate for that by always being right," Stephanie replied with totally genuine seriousness.

Alex shrugged slightly, "Americans are also so delusional."

"We are. And we tend to pick the weirdest best friends," Stephanie's retort was gentle, and then with a slight smile she let that joke freeze — which to her seemed like the natural fate for anything spending time outside on a night like this. It was *cold*. The new world where she'd been raised was known for mild, rainy winters — no snow at all — and while three years in Newfoundland had helped her grow accustomed to the local climate, she was hardly immune to it. Not like her eccentric friend.

But even Alex wouldn't be skipping sleep without a good reason, so Stephanie took a deep breath of the cold air and let her chin dip, "Any new additions tonight?"

"Nope," Alex answered immediately, knowing precisely what her friend meant.

Stephanie knew all about the nightmares, and hers were similar. Of course, she hadn't fought that duel with Emily, but her subconscious happily scolded her some nights, by making her feel the terror of not being able to find Alex once they were parted... or being completely helpless against Emily if battle was joined. Both were entirely realistic possible outcomes of the encounter they'd shared in St. John's. Both were terrifying because of their sheer plausibility.

Like Alex, Stephanie had seen little evolution in her own terrors over the past few months. They were less frequent, but always the same. Perhaps that consistency made it easier for both of them to get over the fear they brought... because controlling such fear was important. Neither girl tried to pretend the nightmares weren't happening — denying them would have been silly. But they were both determined not to be trapped by them.

Others had suffered much worse that night against Emily — lives had been lost, and both Alex and Stephanie had been fortunate to survive. As Alex's father had told them, it was natural to worry about the what-ifs, and to be anxious or afraid of what might have gone wrong. But it would have been the height of self-pity for either girl to allow herself to be crippled by such fears. They both had to learn to set such feelings aside — especially since it was likely they'd see much worse, some day in the future.

"I hope when we come up against something more worthy of terror, we get new nightmares," Alex said eventually with a sigh. "Be nice to have a little variety."

Stephanie nodded with some confidence, "I'm sure we'll be able to schedule a whole lineup of nightmares, one for each day of the week."

"Alternating terrors on Sundays," Alex sounded hopeful.

"Something to look forward to," Stephanie agreed, and then she fell silent.

They both did, and for a moment they just breathed the cold air and stared out at the dark woods that surrounded the Smith house. Had they been younger and more innocent, the nighttime forest — and all the monsters it inevitably contained — might have seemed scary. Now it was just pleasantly, perhaps slightly hauntingly, still.

"Well," Stephanie spoke up eventually. "You think you've negotiated a truce with your subconscious? Though I enjoy freezing to death slightly more than the next girl, I'm sleepy."

Alex took another deep breath, then closed one eye as if that'd help her figure out what was going on inside her head.

"I'll chance it," she said after that diagnostic.

"Good," the American girl got to her feet first, then offered her friend a hand. "And don't be cranky tomorrow. Americans are touchy about things like that."

Alex shrugged, "At least they're always right."

"No, they're just delusional."

"I'm not going to complain about that," Alex frowned. "If they weren't, I wouldn't have a best friend."

"Aww you," the young Lieutenant put an arm around her friend at the words, but then released her immediately. "I can feel how cold you are through my *coat*. This can't be healthy."

With a jaunty shrug and flip of her partially-frozen hair, Alex led the way inside, "You're just jealous."

"That literally does not even make sense," Stephanie followed.

Watching from the woods as the door shut behind them, one of the forest's monsters shook his head.

"I suppose I was that young once. But I certainly didn't talk to myself," he said, without a hint of irony.

CHAPTER I

There was no snow on the ground in Virginia. That wasn't unusual for January — winters at the American Champions school were seldom as trying as those at Jimmystown.

The milder climate suited Corporal Vanier Cross just fine. He hailed from Georgia, a state with no real notion of winter, and he found the temperatures took some getting used to whenever duty led him north. How people lived in a place where snow could pile five feet high was a question he simply couldn't answer... but they did, and they were welcome to it. Meantime, he was on his way to his Fort Eustice duty station, his hands thrust deeply into his pockets against the almost-freezing air. It was as much cold as he wanted to deal with.

The sun was far from rising as he made his way to the Fort's Headquarters building — the location of the Americans' Saa screen, which he helped monitor. Vanier was one of twenty trained operators stationed at the Fort, and he worked hard to make sure he was one of the best. The competition wasn't exactly fierce. Many of the members of the Saa screen team were political appointees — working with dragon machinery was a prestigious job for a young army officer, so many politicians and captains of industry pulled strings to have their sons included.

Those sons weren't all as bad as their career paths might have implied, but plenty of them were accustomed to easy lives, and they didn't make the efforts necessary to excel at their jobs.

For obvious reasons, Vanier came from the opposite end of the spectrum. He was the lowest-ranked man on the team — a mere Corporal in a room full of Lieutenants and Captains — but he'd earned his place through sheer aptitude and determination. Three years in, he was almost starting to become comfortable with his position, and some were even suggesting promotion might be in his future. But he didn't care about that. Rank meant nothing to him: Vanier just wanted to spend time with the beautiful machine.

The alien-manufactured screen was like an incredibly intelligent living creature. At the press of a key, it could paint text, photos, and moving pictures on its massive glass-like face... predict what a user needed and help him find it... organize and remember more data than the most brilliant humans in the history of either world. Working with it was a unique privilege for a boy who'd grown up reading stories about the Saa dragons, and tinkering with machines (until he got caught).

He'd relish the post for however long it lasted.

On this particular morning, he was getting a relatively early start. Many of the politically-placed officers on his team had yet to return from their lengthy Christmas leaves, so the men who'd stayed on the base over the holiday were working extra shifts to maintain normal operations. Some of the officers grumbled about the work, but Vanier basked in the extra time. He'd even worked all through new year's night, allowing his comrades to get out on the town with their girls, and him to explore new sections of the screen's database that no other American operator had yet delved into.

So while it was cold, Vanier Cross was quite happy to march across his slumbering base in the pre-dawn light. Thrusting his hands deeper into his pockets, he turned up the path that led towards the Headquarters building, and enjoyed the silent base around him.

Fort Eustice had been established in 1918, specifically located to make it a good training facility. Sitting alongside the James River, it had access to all manner of Virginian terrain, making it a logical place to stage exercises for regular infantry and artillery, and the absolute ideal location for Champion development. It was also delightfully close to Washington, which was helpful for politicians seeking publicity.

Directly attached to the Fort was the Robinson Institute for Champions — the parallel to Lady Emily's Academy, just as Fort Eustice was a match for Fort Waller. Vanier had never been to the British counterpart facilities — never been further north than Toronto — but he had a hard time imagining they'd be superior to the Virginia base.

"Vanier!"

Corporal Cross' musing was interrupted by a familiar voice, and he slowed and looked back over his shoulder just in time to watch Constance Cormack emerge from the darkness behind him.

Though she was six months away from graduating into the title of 'Champion', Constance already struck him as one of the finest of her kind. Of course, he was prejudiced — he'd known her much longer than anyone else in the Fort, or the Institute, and had a unique appreciation for her.

Now she glided up behind him and offered him a big smile, "You couldn't sleep either?"

He blinked, then frowned, "I've got an early shift. Half the screen team is still on leave."

Constance's expression sobered just slightly: "Oh."

That was all she said, but the look that crossed her face was one he was familiar with; he was supposed to ask what she was so excited about.

"So...?" he put the question to her, and her smile broadened again.

"Lady Alex and Lieutenant Shylock are here today! Remember?"

Vanier hadn't remembered... but then he did. Information about the visit had passed through the Saa screen weeks earlier — a quick forty-eight hour visit arranged by Colonel Adams, to take advantage of the holiday quiet to schedule exercises for soldiers from the 25th United States Infantry. Those men would never be allowed to utilize the training facilities when the base was more densely populated.

The senior class of Champions would be training too, he recalled, which explained why Constance had turned into a morning person. That was not her style — she was a habitually late riser.

"You even going to be awake by the end of the day?" the Corporal asked.

"I had four cups of coffee already!" she answered with an even bigger smile, and Vanier's eyes narrowed.

"I'd make a joke about you climbing the walls, but..."

"Climbed the library already! Twice!" Constance assured him.

It appeared that she was, perhaps, excited. And wired on coffee.

But of course she was, because Lady Alex was a hero both to her and to many soon-to-graduate Institute students. Just days after picking her distinctive white coat, the Newfoundland Lady had survived a duel with Emily. And for Constance it was even better, because she and Alex were reportedly the same height — shorter than the average Champion.

Plenty to be excited about, but Vanier remained serious.

"Try not to scare them away, alright CeeCee?" his tone was fraternal, and Constance wanted to hug him. Of course she couldn't — it was dark and they seemed to be alone, but it would have been foolish to risk it.

"I'll be good," she assured him, and then the need to do something else really exciting to eat up another few minutes before her heroes arrived from Newfoundland got her twitching. "See you tonight?"

"I'm done at 1730," Vanier nodded. "Domino Club?"

"Yes!" Constance nearly levitated at the prospect of dancing. Of course, it was likely she'd pass out from exhaustion before that 5:30 appointment, but they'd figure that out later. "See you then!"

With that she was off — a blur as she disappeared into the darkness. Taking a deep breath of icy air, Vanier watched her go, then smiled as he turned back up the path towards Headquarters. Constance was as irrepressible as ever.

It took another minute for the Corporal to reach the massive Headquarters building and climb the steps to its entrance. Once past the sentries inside, he descended to the basement where the Saa screen was installed, and headed down the long, barren hallway to the operators room.

Captain Fischer and Lieutenant Clarke were inside when Vanier opened the wood-and-glass door, both men standing and clutching coffee as they carried on a deep conversation. Based on what Vanier was able to hear, their topic was clearly one of great importance to the security of the United States.

"She has a bitchy face, though," Clarke was saying. "And not much meat on her bones. I'd certainly go for a ride, but I like my girls to be better endowed."

"I didn't think you had the luxury of choosing," Fischer shot back. "But if you don't want her, then I'll have her. I love girls who look aristocratic. They usually have something to prove... or a lot to learn..."

Vanier really did try to get along with men like Fischer and Clarke — both were sons of wealthy industrialists — but when they talked about women, it was difficult for a boy raised by his momma in the Church to take part. He just hoped neither of them ever noticed Constance.

"What about it, Vanier?" Fischer detected that a possible tie-breaking vote had arrived, and he sought to include the Corporal. "If you could convince Lady Alex or Lieutenant Shylock into bed, which would you have?"

"They're both adventurous types, by all accounts," Clarke added with a grin. "I'm sure they'd love to love a strapping negro prince like yourself."

Vanier's default response to such banter was simply to smile politely: "I'm no prince, sir. And they wouldn't have eyes for a Corporal, with all the eligible officers around."

"You're too humble, Cross," Fischer smiled and shook his head.

Clarke just chuckled, "Just as well, though. Imagine the sensation of a black cavorting with a Champion? The world isn't ready for such sights!"

Of course it wasn't, Vanier knew. Fischer nodded at the words too, though he didn't seem to appreciate them — to the Captain, every man (regardless of color) seemed to possess the right to chase any woman, regardless of color. Rumor was he'd even had some flirtations with black girls since he'd come to Fort Eustice... but of course, he could. A white officer and a black girl was, at worst, an unsavory entertainment. A black enlisted man and a white Champion? Vanier would be lucky if he was the only one lynched; his momma and the rest of his family back in Georgia would have a very difficult time.

None of that mattered, though, because while Lady Alex and Lieutenant Shylock might be due at the Fort this very day, his duties were with something less controversial: "I'll take over now."

The words were all business, and with a nod, Fischer waved his coffee cup in the Corporal's direction, "There's a good man. See, Clarke, we should really follow his example."

"And yet, we won't," the Lieutenant grinned.

Of course they wouldn't, but that was fine. Vanier Cross was the only black man to ever be granted access to the Saa screen, and he was only too happy to operate it alone. He moved to his desk, pulled out his chair, and settled in for a day of work. Behind him, his two officer colleagues continued to speak about the girls who were coming to Fort Eustice that day.

CHAPTER II

Skycruisers traversed the air with the same grace and power that great luxury liners employed upon the sea. Massive vessels built for humanity by the Saa dragons, the heavier-than-air craft could fly to the very outer reaches of Earth's atmosphere, accelerate to many times the speed of sound, and then land on a dime — no runways required.

All without so much as a jolt.

Indeed, having breakfast in *Major George Tucker's* dining room was such a civilized affair that fine china could be used... though that china was, admittedly, stored in special padded boxes when not in use. The skycruiser could do most of its fantastic feats in a stable fashion, but violent emergency maneuvers could unship things, just as a storm at sea could toss a liner.

Fortunately, this early morning called for neither violent maneuvers or stormy weather; as the sun rose over the horizon beyond the dining room's big windows, Alex, Stephanie and Strong sat around a completely stable table, digging into the ample breakfast that had been provided by the ship's cook.

And it was *ample*.

"Think they have any more bacon?" Alex hadn't finished chewing the bacon she was already eating when she asked that, and Stephanie looked up at her with a raised eyebrow.

"You single-handedly want to make pigs extinct?"

"No," Alex shook her head indignantly. "I'll happily accept help in making them extinct."

Strong perked up at that, "So I can have more bacon?"

Alex shot him a look that conveniently reminded the Sergeant that he was already full, so he smiled and sat back, "Sorry, I just realized I've had sufficient."

The Colour was in a particularly good mood this morning, and his good humor was not lost on either Alex or Stephanie. However, since neither girl had slept well, they were both determined to take on more fuel before they dared trigger any more explanations regarding his enthusiasm.

It wasn't as though he hadn't told them already. A dozen times. And once in a poem. Which had been awkward.

"You sure are filling up... didn't sleep well?" the Sergeant laced his fingers together and laid his hands on the table, and as he looked from his Lieutenant to his Champion and back, it was the American who answered (because her mouth was less full).

"Nightmares," she said. "We were up in the middle of the night."

Strong didn't like the sound of that, though the fact that it was admitted so easily impressed him. He'd known many men who had spent years not owning up to the scars their war service had left on their minds... himself included. Admittedly neither Alex nor Stephanie had seen much real horror — yet — but the fact that they were shepherding their current woes so responsibly boded well.

Though some of their practices did seem strange...

"Wait, barefoot in the snow again?" the Sergeant looked at his young whitecoat, and she shrugged.

"You sound judgmental."

That earned her a frown, and the Colour corrected her misapprehension, "No, I'm *protective*. Particularly of your toes. You don't want to lose your toes, do you?"

"I'll tie strings to them next time?" Alex's reply was in the form of a question, and it made Strong shake his head.

"You'll be the death of me," he muttered the traditional Newfoundland oath, then realizing he'd tempted fate, he unlaced his fingers and rapped the wooden table with his knuckles. Just in case.

By now Stephanie had finished her plate — she only needed one — so as she sat back and grasped a cup of tea, she decided to divert her forlorn NCO: "So tell me again who you're going to introduce us to?"

That was it: the dam of stories from the new world was about to open its gates.

Mike Strong had been with the Royal Newfoundland Regiment on the new world in 1919 and 1920, and he'd marched alongside the black soldiers of the 25th United States Infantry on two occasions:

during the dangerous mission to a forlorn place called Promised Town, and then in the brutal engagement on the Badlands, where most of the American regiment had been destroyed.

The survivors of that last fight had gone home to the United States as heroes, and had cemented their regiment's reputation in American military lore. Now they were the guardians of Fort Eustice and the Robinson Champions Institute — the latter campus bearing the name of the Colonel who had commanded the 25th out to Promised Town, but who had been a politically-appointed fool, right up to the moment he'd been killed by outlaws.

Though Strong hadn't seen men of the 25th in years — and the last time only at a commemorative ceremony in Toronto — he still held them in high regard, and spoke of them with the reverence natural to any old soldier reflecting on hard days gone by.

"Well, Colonel Adams of course," the Sergeant began. "But you know him."

That was true: the black commanding officer of the regiment was known to both Alex and Stephanie, because he traveled more than his men, and he was often a guest of Lord James Devlin in Jimmystown.

"But it's the NCOs... the old soldiers from the ranks. Sergeant Major Turner... well, you know him too... but Marks and Preston, they'll still be around..." flopping back in his chair, Strong involuntarily found himself smiling, and his gaze drifted away as he thought about those men.

The names were familiar to Alex and Stephanie, since their families both had plenty of history with the 25th. The black soldiers had twice saved Mister Smith, Alex's father... and on one of those occasions, they'd also saved Stephanie's clan, and Stephanie herself.

"They're all good men," Strong caught himself before getting too lost in nostalgia — the flight to Virginia wouldn't be long enough to allow him much daydreaming. And he had certain priorities too: "Oh, and if you happen to notice that there are some big strapping handsome fellows in their regiment, you just be sure to behave."

Alex had just begun collecting scrambled eggs with her fork when he said that, but as the words processed she looked up, "Did you say... handsome?"

"You mean, we could find husbands?" Stephanie keyed in on her friend's intended joke, and made sure she sounded like a secondary character in a Jane Austen novel.

"Maybe I could have two? A spare could be very handy…" Alex sat up taller in her chair, locking eyes with her friend.

"Why not one for each day of the week?" Stephanie replied.

They shared a smile, and then looked wickedly to their Sergeant.

He raised an eyebrow, "You're not very funny when you haven't slept properly."

"I'd contend we're not very funny *ever*, Colour," Alex shrugged, then went back to her eggs.

"Not humorous funny, anyway. Strange funny perhaps," Stephanie suggested, and Alex nodded as she took another bite.

"Mmmhmm," she agreed.

"Keep telling yourselves that," Strong shook his head. "And if any handsome man down there takes a look at either of you, I'll… I'll…"

His threat ground to a halt as he realized he wasn't sure what he'd actually do. Punching out a soldier from the 25th would be bad form. Obviously he wouldn't kill such a man either. And saying he'd do either wouldn't be right.

"You'll what?" Stephanie sounded genuinely curious, and Strong met her inquisitive eyes with his stern — sorry, protective — ones.

"Just you wait and see," he copped out, and Stephanie smiled, then glanced back to Alex.

"That's how you know it's serious."

"Mmhmm," the young Champion agreed, and continued to eat her eggs.

While *Major George Tucker's* dining room was right out of a Cunard cruise liner, its command deck was like something from an H.G. Wells story. Caralynne Smith was generally impressed as she stood with folded arms at the rear of the stateroom-sized compartment, watching the five-man flight crew operating the ship.

But all the blinking lights on the consoles — and there were many — aggravated her headache. It was another migraine, not as bad as some but still powerful, and it was going to make the next couple of days more trying than she'd have liked.

Still, she was used to such headaches now; they seemed to be the worst side-effect of the Hubrin treatments that had made her a Champion, all those years ago when she'd died. Once at a dinner party, when a particularly daft man had suggested that they were a terrible consequence of her ordeal, she'd assured him that she preferred being alive with headaches to being dead. He had conceded the point.

Still, on days like this migraines were inconvenient. Colonel Adams had called in a favor to get this visit set up, and owing to her long history and friendship with the man, there was no way Caralynne could say no... or let her daughter travel to Virginia alone.

There had been no sign of Emily since August — not even a hint — but the elder Lady Smith had nevertheless kept her daughter close, ostensibly so she could be part of the Jimmystown Champion contingent, and help create and teach new doctrines like firebox. Sending her to America with just Stephanie and Strong, even for forty-eight hours, was a bit more than the mother could tolerate.

Of course the time would come when Alex had to leave Caralynne's protective sphere, but after missing the fight on Signal Hill due to a moose collision, mother was going to remain protective a while longer.

That meant flying with a migraine, and glad-handing with whatever political appointees were at Fort Eustice when she arrived. Adams had promised that the base would be largely quiet — American officers liked very long Christmas leaves, apparently — but there was always some politician's son who expected attention.

She'd figure it out. For the moment she waited for *Major George Tucker's* Flight Captain, Levi Boguraz — a survivor of Russia's vicious post-collapse pogroms — to finish coordinating with his second in command, Flight Lieutenant Ted Hong, an Australian-Korean.

"We'll be landing in the guest slot right between their two cruisers," the Flight Captain confirmed, his words barely reflecting a Russian accent.

Hong's Australian accent was sharp as he replied, "We'll show 'em how she's done."

Such were the details they had to worry about, and Caralynne let them finish up. Once they'd fallen silent, she advanced towards the pair, who occupied the two front seats on the command deck, and had wide consoles wrapping around them.

Getting closer meant stepping nearer to the bright light that was beaming in through the massive canopy they faced, but with a squint, the elder Lady Smith bore the discomfort, "What are the security plans when we're on the ground, Levi?"

The Flight Captain hadn't noticed her approach, and he looked back with surprise, "Oh, M'Lady, good morning. We will be keeping the ramps shut at all times, and use the watch cameras for any signs of danger. All men confined to the ship."

"A shame, I've heard there are good clubs in Newport News," Hong grinned, and then looked up at Caralynne.

She didn't exactly glare back at him, but it was close, so he sobered, "But we're not going to find out. M'Lady."

"Just be careful, please," she said far too gravely.

Her head was hurting tremendously, which she supposed accounted for her growing feeling of unease, but it seemed caution was warranted. What if Emily took this chance to come after them? There was literally no reason to expect such an assault, but... but...

"We will not take our safety for granted, M'Lady," Bogoraz was far less jovial than his Flight Lieutenant, and his gravelly words of reassurance helped.

With a slow nod, Caralynne decided she'd made her point sufficiently, "Thank you, Levi. Ted. I'll go take some breakfast before we land."

"M'Lady," Hong nodded back, and then the two returned to their duties.

Turning away, Caralynne made for the command deck door, and then moved on towards the dining room. Given the pain in her head, she wasn't certain she'd be able to eat anything, but that was fine. She'd cope.

As she went to join her daughter, *George Tucker* crossed into American air space, bound for Virginia.

CHAPTER III

Vanier Cross was sure he'd done something wrong.

Staring at the Saa screen with a deep frown, the Corporal keyed the board at his desk, driving a page of text down, then up again, wondering if something had gotten stuck. But it hadn't — the pattern remained.

Which made no sense.

Unable to explain the error, he navigated out of the registry window he'd been checking, then re-entered the database. But the problem was still there. Had he accidentally overwritten some of the registry archives? And if he had... *how* had he managed to do it?

Sitting back in his chair and pulling his hands away from the console in front of him, the Corporal took a moment to breathe and assess. His momma had always told him that when confronted with a confusing situation, he just needed to step back and make sure he could see the whole picture, so he could understand what was wrong.

In this case, that didn't take much time: the registry entries for twelve hours of the previous day's work on the Saa screen had been overwritten. He'd never seen such a thing happen in three years of working with the screen, though to be fair, he'd only started examining the registry a year earlier.

What could have caused it? He didn't think he'd miskeyed any commands so far for the morning... there was no reason for him to expect anything he'd done could have disrupted the normal workings of the system. That suggested, then, that someone might have intentionally changed the registry. But who, and why?

It was a critical question, and one that could conceivably have sinister implications. The screen was the most powerful piece of Saa technology in the United States, so if someone had wanted to gather secret intelligence about American forces, or the Champions, or even about the British and their Lords and Ladies, it would have been a treasure trove.

But it was also constantly under guard. For someone to have successfully snuck into the screen room and accessed its technology seemed almost impossible. And for that person to have then gone ahead and overwritten the registry — effectively erasing all trace of the files and databases they had consulted — suggested a particular level of expertise with the screen and its systems.

So the sinister possibility wasn't too hard to divine: someone from the screen team might have been nosing around where they didn't belong, and then decided to clear their tracks.

Coming to that conclusion, Vanier folded his arms and let out a long breath. It could be very dangerous... or it could still be a glitch. And he wasn't exactly sure what to do about it. That uncertainty wasn't helped by him being alone in the office, either — Captain Fischer was supposed to be on duty with him, but the officer had gone out for more coffee forty minutes earlier. Presumably he'd be back soon, but even if he returned, Vanier wasn't sure what to say or do — what if Fischer was responsible?

Or worse, what if he assumed Vanier was?

It was a difficult question, and unfortunately, the Corporal had no time to step back and examine it.

"Something wrong, Cross?"

Fischer had come through the door jauntily, but his mood shifted immediately as he read the Corporal's body language. Looking over his shoulder, Vanier realized he'd have no choice but to own up to what he'd found — if he said nothing while clearly looking at the anomalous records, it might seem as though he were somehow responsible for them.

"Have a look at this, sir," the Corporal came to his feet, then rounded his desk and advanced towards the screen. "The registry overwrote itself yesterday. Twelve hours identical to the day before."

Fischer slowed and frowned at the explanation, then raised his coffee and took a sip before shaking his head, "You sure? They might just be similar..." His question trailed off as his eyes scanned the text on the screen, "But Willis was out with his girl yesterday."

He was referring to one of the registry entries for Captain Fred Willis that was dated for the previous day... when he'd been in a seedy hotel in Newport News.

"Exactly, sir," Vanier nodded as he arrived at the screen, then pointed down to one of the lower lines on the list. "And here's the entry from the day before... same time of day, exact same duration and file path. It's clearly been repeated. We just... don't know why."

As he stared intently at the screen, Fischer's expression grew tight, and without much thought he moved sideways to his own desk. Laying down the coffee cup, he keyed a couple of his controls without sitting. The screen rolled up, then down again — the Captain was trying the same fix that Vanier had attempted, with the same result.

"That's... that's either a glitch in the system, or someone did it for a reason," the Captain said quietly. "You didn't accidentally overwrite it, Cross?"

The Corporal felt a little heat flash to his cheeks, but he shook his head, "Don't think so, sir."

"No, it wouldn't be you," the American officer agreed. "You don't make those mistakes. Others might... God knows, some of the politicians' sons here are too stupid to own money. But you realize it could be something serious?"

"Yes sir, I do," Vanier confirmed with a nod. "What do we do?"

That was a good question, and Fischer didn't have an immediate answer. Still, he grasped for something, and the chain of command seemed like the most comfortable solution: "We report it. And we make sure... we make sure no one from our team is in here alone. We'll all be suspects."

The thought of being blamed for something he didn't do was, unfortunately, not a new one for Vanier Cross. His uncle had died for similar reasons, though at least at Fort Eustice, a torch-carrying mob wouldn't be determining guilt.

Hopefully.

"Let's... um..." Fischer was far more shaken than his black counterpart. "We'll find the Commandant."

"He's not back yet, sir," Vanier shook his head. "Neither is Brigadier Walker."

"Right," Fischer nodded, remembering that the base's two senior soldiers were still away for Christmas leave. That left the Colonel of the 25th United States Infantry in charge... Adams would have to do. "Let's go find your Colonel, then."

The prospect of being able to explain this to Adams was good, Vanier decided. Hopefully together they could find a way to get to the bottom of the mystery.

Locking the screen, both Captain Fischer and Corporal Cross thus left the room — and locked the door behind them.

Though Fort Eustice and the Robinson Institute were conjoined in much the same way Fort Waller and the Lady Emily Academy were, the relationship between the two facilities was somewhat different. Eustice was, depending on who explained it, either a more comprehensive facility, or a less capable one.

Much of this disagreement came from the fact that its landing field lay within the perimeter of the Fort — a parade ground had been converted to house the two American skycruisers, *Major Ernest Krazakowski* and *Captain Arnold Koster*, as well as any visiting ships. Unlike Torbay airport, though, this field could not accommodate man-made aircraft; the United States Army Air Corps and the United States Naval Air Corps both operated squadrons in the Hampton Roads area, so having another airstrip had never seemed to make sense.

Standing on the edge of the skycruiser park, Colonel Robert Adams, the commanding officer of the 25th United States Infantry and the single most consistent figure of leadership either the Fort or the Institute had seen, was satisfied with that arrangement. His men were expected to manage the security of both installations, and the Champions who trained at them. That complicated their lives enough; having to worry about a squadron of pilots would have stretched their meager resources even further.

Proud though he was of his men, Adams was distinctly aware of their limits... and indeed, his purpose for being at the skycruiser park was, ultimately, to push those limits.

Glancing at his watch, Adams predicted that *George Tucker* had to be nearby — hopefully on schedule, so that he could have some time with its passengers to explain to them what to expect. He hoped that Caralynne in particular would understand the realities of the new 25th United States Infantry — she'd visited Fort Eustice enough over the years to have some idea — but Alex and Stephanie had never served in any capacity alongside the black soldiers. If their expectations had been formed by the stories of the past, or even by the reputation Adams' men projected, they might be sorely disappointed.

It was an unpleasant, even *embarrassing* thought for the Colonel who had been with the glorious 25th at Promised Town, and the Badlands, and ever since. But the truth was simple: his regiment today was barely fit for guard duty, and what soldiering abilities it did possess were confined to the hundred men in its ranks who had seen those battles on the new world.

Particularly with the new threat of Emily, it was vital his troops started learning more about real soldiering — learned to be like the hundreds of men Adams had marched with in the Philippines, and then in Pacifica. Bringing in mentors from Newfoundland for just forty-eight hours was the first step in that process. The Colonel just hoped it wasn't the last.

The gloomy thoughts compelled the black officer to sigh heavily, and the exhalation was timed just right to spur a response.

"This will help the men, sir."

Regimental Sergeant Major Eric Turner had arrived beside his Colonel, and with those words the veteran provided reassurance. Turner and Adams had been together since 1915, and they'd been through a lot. On one occasion, Turner had even been captured by the Hubrin, along with none other than Mister Smith, Alex's father. He was no less saddened by the state of the regiment to which he'd remained bound, but he could never allow his officer to see that disappointment. As RSM, he had to make the soldiers of the 25th the best they could be, up to and including their Colonel.

Letting Adams stew wouldn't be good for anyone.

Now the black officer shook his head, then reached up and adjusted his hat against the cold, "I'm trying not to get my hopes up."

"You just say how high you want the hopes, sir, and I'll get us there," Turner sounded unflappable, and that did actually help.

With a thin smile and shake of his head, Adams nodded to his old friend, "Thank you, RSM."

Turner didn't answer; together the two veterans simply waited for *George Tucker* to appear in the sky.

"How's your head?"

Caralynne heard her daughter's question through a slight fog, and only realized after a moment that she needed to make eye contact and try to answer. She was squinting when she did, which didn't reassure Alex at all.

"That good?"

Waving a dismissive hand, the elder Lady Smith replied, "It's fine."

"You're such a good liar, mother," the young whitecoat's tone was stern. "Promise me you'll come back here and lie down if it gets worse."

It was the sort of maternal instruction that only a daughter could offer her mother, and lacking the energy to argue, Caralynne nodded. With a last glare, Alex turned away to join Stephanie and Strong, both of whom were waiting at the edge of *George Tucker's* landing ramp. The skycruiser was just settling onto the ground at Fort Eustice's field, so they would disembark momentarily.

"Listen to Lady bossy-coat," Strong was smiling as she arrived, and that earned him a glare too — though, as ever, he found glares from girls to be more encouraging than anything else. "Makes you wonder what she's going to do when she gets in front of a class full of upstart Champion kids."

Looking away from the Colour and purposefully turning her nose up slightly, Alex squared her shoulders and then shrugged just a little, "Oh I don't know... what would Mike Strong do?"

"Oh — *oh!*" Strong perked up instantly, then raised his hand so Alex could high five it. She did so, without looking at him or changing her expression.

Standing on her white-coated friend's other side, Stephanie's expression remained sober, and then just in case anyone had missed it, she pointed out the obvious: "That wasn't funny."

"Which is why it was *amazing*," Strong explained.

Thank God the intercom sounded before that could lead to any discussion. It was Hong on the speakers: "Now hear this, we have touched down. Ship will remain at security condition one for the visit, no foolin' around. Landing party, prepare for ramp drop."

As soon as the Korean-Australian's words stopped, a bell rang on the landing deck. Seconds later, the motors hummed, and the ramp began to lower — proving that Virginia was indeed beneath the skycruiser's hull.

The fact that there had been no sensation of landing, or even touching dirt, was still mildly disconcerting to Alex — Saa technology meant *George Tucker* basically had its own gravity. But that somewhat strange reality wasn't something to dwell on now; with a look back to make sure her mother was moving, the whitecoat led the way onto the lowering ramp, so she could reach its end just as the lip dug into the field.

"We look completely awesome when we do this," Strong ruined the moment with his observation, but then, saying it looked pretty impressive didn't actually change the fact that it did. In a dramatic line abreast, the trio and the senior Lady they were escorting walked down the broad ramp even as it lowered beneath their feet... and then as soon as it touched grass, they stepped off.

A perfect arrival, which surely would have set the crowds cheering.

But there were no crowds, just two men.

As the quartet came to a stop in front of Colonel Adams, the American officer frowned, "Doesn't protocol require you to wait for the ramp to completely lower before walking down?"

Alex took offense: "Well, doesn't protocol forbid me hugging the commanding officer when I arrive?"

That was pretty silly, and since he wasn't expecting it, Adams didn't answer... or at least, not in time to prevent Alex blurring forward and wrapping her arms around him, "Happy New Year!"

She did know Adams well enough to get away with such an unbridled greeting, and shaking his head with a smile, the Colonel hugged her back, "Good to see you too. Looking fine in white."

Alex was smiling as she withdrew, and then she played bashful, "Why thank you, Colonel Adams. Sergeant Major?" She held her arms wide towards Eric Turner, but that just got her one of his cool stares.

"M'Lady," he said, keeping his arms behind his back.

She grinned at him, "One day, Turner. *One day.*"

With that threat delivered, she turned in time to see Stephanie approaching the Colonel a bit more sheepishly, "I really can't hug now, can I *sir*?"

Of course she couldn't; she was a Lieutenant, and officers hugging wasn't really done. Probably. Well, Adams had a solution: "Handshake, then."

"Handshake," Stephanie agreed, and so they did shake hands — more warmly than most Lieutenants would ever shake hands with most Colonels. Because, of course, Adams had been part of

Stephanie's life since nearly the beginning — he was essentially an uncle to her and Alex both.

"I'm hugging everyone!" Strong declared as Stephanie shook Turner's hand, and managed to coax a slight smile out of the RSM.

But then Caralynne intervened, "Let's just quit the hugging, Colour. Robert, Eric, so good to see you... if I avoid eye contact, it's just the migraine."

She was shaking their hands too as she explained her affliction, and that sobered Adams slightly, "Sorry to hear that. Well, the consolation is there are so few officers here, I think you might actually get to take it easy."

"Promises promises," she smiled wryly in reply. "How are Eadie and the girls?"

Adams' wife and daughters were two of his favorite topics, but before launching into any tales from home, he nodded up the path in the direction of Headquarters, "Let's walk and talk. Hope you're hungry, the cooks are doing up a special breakfast for you all. Lots of bacon."

Alex had just rejoined her friend and her Sergeant when she heard the words. Her head climbed upward immediately, her chin rising above her collar as though she was a turtle stretching extra-far out of her shell. It was also possible that she began to levitate.

"Actually, we just ate on the—" Strong started to speak, but then his instincts detected danger, and he looked to his white-coated Lady. Alex's eyes were far too wide to be healthy, and her jaw was clamped shut.

Looked rather intense... so the message was clear.

"Yes," Stephanie said for her friend. "We would love to have a delicious breakfast."

Looking from Sergeant to Lieutenant to young Lady, Adams smiled, "And it's a buffet."

For some reason, all eyes turned to Alex at that last word, and with a shrug, she played it as cool as she could: "I'm going to try really hard not to think of the next few minutes as a race to the dining room. Because if it was a race, I'd beat you all. Badly."

"Your restraint is an example to us all," Stephanie said most earnestly, and Alex nodded.

"I know."

With that established, the four guests and their two hosts set off for Fort Eustice's Headquarters, passing the American skycruiser *Captain Koster* on the way. Behind them, *George Tucker's* ramp began to close.

CHAPTER IV

"The Colonel's not in his office, Captain…"

Captain Wendel Fischer had blazed into Colonel Adams' outer office without so much as a word of introduction, but as the black orderly who'd been behind a desk in the dignified chamber came to his feet, the officer stopped and turned, "Where then, dammit?"

Vanier arrived just after the words, having struggled to keep up with the urgent steps of his white counterpart. Apparently Fischer was very worried about the screen situation and he was doing his duty, trying to make certain his screen was protected, or that any misdeeds were found out. He was also conducting himself with the brusque determination that only a white officer from a wealthy family could enjoy.

No one would suspect Fischer of wrongdoing. He was one of the boys, who chased women and drank heartily at social functions. Vanier, on the other hand, would naturally be treated with suspicion, and could be a perfect scapegoat for whatever had happened, since many people would simply assume him to be villainous.

Fischer could thus chase around with as much enthusiasm as he liked; Vanier would hang back and, at the very least, make certain he put due thought into how he presented the situation.

Adams would be a reasonable audience, of course… but if this was serious, and it seemed likely that it was, then the story would be told over and over again, to ever more senior people with ever fewer reasons to believe a negro Corporal. That story couldn't change anywhere up that chain, so Vanier had to make sure he had it right from the first.

"Where is the Colonel?" Fischer repeated his question, turning on the orderly, who didn't seem impressed with the tone.

Still, he had to answer politely: "He was receiving the guests from the Lady Emily Academy, sir. I believe breakfast is being served in the guest mess."

Fischer blinked; the visitors had dropped from his mind as soon as this breach had appeared, but now the significance of their presence, and the timing, seemed evident on his face. He turned to Vanier: "That's not far from here. We should hurry."

Of course it wasn't far from the Colonel's office — it was two floors down and in the opposite wing. Knowing as much, the Corporal nodded, and then Fischer dashed from the room.

Waiting a few seconds, Vanier shook his head and then looked at the orderly, "Something serious. We'll tell him direct. Sorry about... *that*."

It was all he wanted to admit just yet, and with some sympathy the orderly nodded. Vanier was pretty well known among the men of the 25th — he was technically one of theirs, just seconded to the Saa screen team. His accomplishments and responsibilities earned him a lot of respect, but plenty of the black men on base knew it also put him in danger. Being so close to something so important was asking for trouble, and on the bare face of it, Fischer did look like he was bringing trouble along.

Perhaps he was. Vanier would soon find out.

The Headquarters guest mess was one of Fort Eustice's more unique facilities. Designed in recognition of the number of visiting officers who would come through the base on a regular basis (and thus not have a barracks or mess of their own), it was ostensibly a place to relax. Because of the number of politicians who came to the Fort for tours, it was also very well appointed, and particularly well-staffed.

The cook, for example, was a veteran of American embassies all around the world, and had prepared food for royals, premiers, presidents and ambassadors. In spite of that rarified air, he seemed most pleased with Alex when he came out from his kitchen, and discovered the young Lady had thrown her white coat over the back of her chair, and was digging into a second plate of his breakfast omelets.

Spotting the man with his distinctive chef's hat, she tried to offer a smile, but it was hampered by her ballooning cheeks. Instead she gave him a thumbs up, which he actually returned before beaming and then disappearing again.

"Think you just made his day," Stephanie was sitting beside her friend, and much as she would have liked to eat in solidarity, she'd stopped after a small share of eggs and bacon. Champions might be able to burn food like a speeding battleship burned oil, but she was just ordinary.

Alex shrugged at her friend and, once she was able, added: "It's important he knows his work is appreciated."

Her enthusiasm for good food was incomparable, but it was only a diversion. That in mind, she turned her attention to Adams — sitting right across from her at the round table they'd taken over — and smiled, "Sorry, I think you were talking about things that matter."

The Colonel was sitting back in his chair as he watched Alex with a smile. She was as irrepressible and enthusiastic as he'd ever seen her, the sort of woman he hoped his daughters would take after. Now she wore a Champion's coat, and was very much coming into her own...

He hoped she and Stephanie would be able to help his men.

Reluctantly, he turned back to that more sober line of thought, "You'll have the senior Champions in class this morning. Stephanie will be in the field with 'A' Company and Captain Lowestoft. This afternoon, you're both out with the senior class and 'C' Company. Now all 'C' Company's officers are still on leave, but the NCOs are veterans. And then tomorrow it's 'D' and 'B'... and... but..." he trailed off at that point, because he was struggling not to say exactly what he needed to say — and it was showing. He had to be direct, he knew, so he suspended his pride: "You need to understand, it's all going to be *basic* instruction."

Alex was digging into her omelet again as she followed the schedule, but Adams' growing unease drew a frown to her face. Stephanie picked up on the same, and she cast a quick glance at Strong, then Caralynne, before deciding she'd been nominated to speak: "So, you just put a lot of emphasis on the word *basic*."

Mike Strong hadn't attempted a second breakfast — he didn't want to overdo it when he knew he was going to spend the morning running around a field — but that freed him to support his officer: "Yes, Colonel. Even with officers on leave, your men will be fine..."

Caralynne's expression suggested the same sentiment, though she elected not to comment. So with four sets of eyes converging on him, and Turner having excused himself to check on the day's arrangements, Colonel Adams felt awfully alone. He'd have no choice but to be explicit, he supposed. His smile faded, and he leaned forward to put his elbows on the table.

"This isn't the same... well. Sergeant, the men you and I marched with in the old days are still good, just as you are. And the men who've come since are good too. The best to get this post. But..." he trailed off for a moment, and the obvious direction of his comments forced frowns onto the brows of all his guests. With a sigh, he continued: "It's ridiculous. We guard the most important training facility in the United States, but forty-five weeks a year, we don't have a chance to get near any of the training grounds. Most of my men fire live rounds *twice a year*, on range proficiency days. They get twenty rounds each to prove they can hit a target at *thirty* yards. None of the new men have seen combat. And I can only get them out for field exercises at times like this, when more *worthy* regiments don't have the grounds booked."

It all spilled out of the Colonel rather more candidly than he'd have liked, and Alex stopped chewing as she listened. Of course she couldn't say anything to reflect her surprise while her mouth was full, but she looked at her mother and discovered Caralynne's expression was almost identical (evidently that's where Alex had gotten her 'shocked face').

"I hadn't thought it was that bad," the elder Lady Smith said simply, quietly, and Adams could only shake his head.

"We don't exactly advertise it. And the assault companies in the Champions Regiment are good... but we're just the base's guards. You've only ever really seen us on parade, or at ceremonies. Up until last August, that was all we were expected to deal with. There didn't seem to be any reason for the War Department to give us training resources — no threat here, and even if there was, we had at least three assault companies based at Eustice. But now all those men have been deployed to protect more valuable targets, and we're expected to make up the difference. But my men... good men... don't have the training for it."

He didn't like the taste of the words — no commanding officer would. To speak ill of his own regiment, which he had served in his whole career, and had marched with against the Hubrin... it felt like betrayal. But to say nothing for sake of pride would have been worse.

"One session with you probably won't make a huge difference,"

Adams shook his head. "But it's a start. If it goes well, I might be able to beg more training time out of the Commandant... but right now, I just have to try anything I can. So I impose on you. Sorry."

Leaving it at that, the Colonel sat back, and his guests remained silent for a moment. Apparently the day would be more serious that they'd anticipated.

"Well," Alex pushed her second cleaned plate away and sat back too, "glad I had two breakfasts."

"Honestly, it was more like four," Stephanie offered that correction quietly, but then shifted her attention to Adams. "We'll do our absolute best."

"I know, that's why it had to be you," the Colonel said, and then he fell silent as a new man came through the mess door. All of his guests immediately noticed the abrupt change in Adams' expression — he seemed even more serious, which given the previous subject wasn't easy. With a nod, then, he called out a greeting to the newcomer: "Major Travis."

It was not a name familiar to Alex, Caralynne, Stephanie or Strong, so they all simultaneously turned in their chairs to face the door. The man striding into the room in a rather slow, deliberate fashion appeared to be in his thirties. He was a veritable giant — six feet and six inches at least — and somehow wore his uniform severely. He was United States Army... and based on the flashes on his shoulder, he was with the Champions Regiment.

The well-trained Champions Regiment, that supplied assault companies and lances, and monopolized all the field time the 25th wasn't getting.

As the Major approached the table, his cool eyes remained on Adams for a moment, then traversed the guests, "Our friends are here."

He had an accent, though Alex was terrible with them — she couldn't tell if it was more southern or western. Either way, he sounded like he'd come from the American frontier, and he bore a sturdy, unapproachable air. Different than her father, who always projected humanity.

"Yes, I'm just briefing them over breakfast, Major. Care to join us?"

It was obvious to everyone listening that the offer was not one Adams wanted to make... and fortunately, it was not one Travis wanted to accept, "No. I'll take another table."

No courtesy, or explanation with those words — the Major seemed effortlessly rude. Alex wasn't impressed.

"I didn't catch your name," Caralynne was even less approving, and she laced her words with some aristocratic disdain, just to make sure the Major got the message.

But if he got it, he ignored it, "Sheldon Travis, ma'am. Major in the United States Regiment of Champions. Without an assault company here, as I was away when mine was sent overseas."

His words were so staid, and he seemed completely unaffected by Caralynne's tone. His cool edge sat wrong with the guests and the table, so Stephanie took her turn: "Why don't you go join them?"

Travis turned his cool stare at his fellow American, "Orders. *Lieutenant.*"

Right, he expected Stephanie to respect his rank, owing to the uniform that she wore. A defiant fire started up in young Lieutenant Shylock's belly at that tone, but — perhaps fortunately — she didn't get the chance to do anything with it.

Two more men burst into the mess, set eyes on Adams, and hurried over to the table.

The pair's officer, a white Captain who appeared out of breath, saluted immediately, "Colonel, Major, Corporal Cross and I have found something you need to be aware of."

The interruption was jarring, but welcome, and as Alex twisted in her chair to look at the newcomers, she found herself staring up at a tall, uncomfortable-looking black soldier. For a second he looked down at her, their gazes crossed, and then his eyes turned to the white coat draped over the back of her chair.

As soon as he put two and two together and discerned her identity — which took just a second — his eyes darted away, as if he wasn't allowed to make eye contact.

Fun.

"What is it?" Adams was beginning to ask, rising with a frown at the apparent urgency of the interruption.

Looking to Stephanie, Alex just pursed her lips and then started drumming her fingers on the table. At least she'd finished eating breakfast before the friendly mood of the morning was derailed...

Well, fourth breakfast. She probably couldn't complain too much.

CHAPTER V

Though Caralynne refused to admit it to anyone, her headache was strengthening — and the arrival of the Saa screen operators with a warning of a possible security breach only made it worse. There was no option to slow down, so as she, Adams and Travis followed Captain Fischer and Corporal Cross down to the screen room, she set her jaw and focused on keeping her strides steady and even. She wouldn't want to go all wobbly now...

"So we don't think it can be a glitch, sir," Fischer was continuing to explain their discovery. "And I can vouch for Corporal Cross, I definitely can't imagine it's something that would have happened by accident. He's our best operator."

The white officer was doing all the talking — frankly, a bit too much talking. He clearly lacked experience with stressful situations, and like a child trying to make sure he wasn't blamed for a problem, he was spilling *everything*. The black operator with him remained silent, which made sense to Caralynne. She hadn't even known the Americans had let a black man at their screen, but whatever his story, she expected he had to be worried about the state of affairs.

"Thank you, Captain," Adams was trying to cool Fischer's anxieties, and because they were almost to the door of the screen room, he rightly figured they could wait for more exposition.

Caralynne paid close attention to the corridor as they covered the last dozen yards; the screen was in the basement, presumably for added security against air raids, but there were no sentries posted. That surprised her, given its obvious importance, but then it was inside a Headquarters building that was guarded at every entrance.

The screen in Jimmy's office back at Fort Waller had been similarly unguarded... until Emily's recent visit. Now it was under double guard. And the other screens in Jimmystown were all protected by secrecy… perhaps more guards were necessary here.

That was what the elder Lady Smith was thinking as Fischer led the way into the screen chamber, "Now we switched off and locked before…"

He jolted to a stop, forcing the rest of his group to do so. Caralynne was last in line, behind the massive Major Travis, so she couldn't see what had surprised them. Then she realized there was more light in the room than was probably provided by bulbs alone, and she side-stepped so she could have a look: the screen was on, not locked or shut down, and a man was sitting at his desk, operating.

"Clarke, what are you doing?" Fischer sounded incredulous as he stormed across the room, and the Lieutenant at the desk looked up with only partial interest, until it registered that it wasn't just his fellow operator who'd joined him.

"I thought I'd get… more work done…" he trailed off and frowned as his audience became apparent. "Where were you?"

"You idiot, we locked this down for a reason…" Fischer dropped into the chair at his own desk and used the controls to freeze the screen. The Captain's level of tension was growing higher still — this was undoubtedly a nightmare scenario for him, and he didn't know how to cope. "Cross, be a good man and get up to the screen so we can show Colonel Adams what's happened."

The Corporal did as he was told, and as he advanced towards the screen, Clarke rolled back from his desk and the base's senior officers moved in for a better view. Caralynne remained nearer the door — even with a migraine, her Champion eyes could pick up the details on the screen with perfect focus. And right now she was more interested in reading the body language of the men in the room with her.

"What's… happening?" Clarke sounded properly confused, but Fischer lacked the patience to explain.

"Just watch," he said, then tapped a few controls and pulled the registry log up on screen. "Look."

Cross had arrived beside the huge glass display just in time, and turning back to his audience, he set the context: "I was reviewing the registry this morning… it's like a log book that tells what operators have been in the system, at what time, for how long, and doing what. When I looked today, though, I found that yesterday's log was an exact copy of the previous day's log. That's not possible, because different men were working each day."

He summed that up very well, and for a second Caralynne wondered why they'd felt it necessary to actually haul officers down to the screen room to explain... but given Fischer's anxiety, it was likely just a desperate attempt to make sure the 'parents' saw everything — no hint or notion that the truth was being hidden.

"Here," Cross continued, gesturing to a line of text near the top of the screen, and one nearer the bottom. "At 1124 each day, Captain Willis apparently did the same exact thing in the system."

"But yesterday he was out with his girl, sir," Fischer continued, though some relief started to creep into his voice now that his discovery was off his chest. "This has been duplicated. And while it could be an error in the machine, we thought it was suspicious. Especially since it happened the day before Lady Smith and her daughter arrived."

Right. For all the things competing for Caralynne's attention — her migraine, her assessment of men like Fischer, and Cross, and even Travis — that last statement stuck in her head. A security breach the day before they arrived here... it was either a most unlucky coincidence, or something much worse.

"Who could have altered the registry?" Adams asked that logical question first, and Fischer turned his chair away from the screen, his eyes almost absurdly wide.

"It would have to be one of us, sir. Unless... unless someone from the outside with sufficient knowledge managed to break in."

Adams' chin dipped slightly, and even from behind it looked as though weight had been added to his shoulders. Caralynne wasn't sure which option he'd have preferred — a criminal in his midst, or an intruder having found her way onto his base. Either option was a disaster.

"Does Emily have the knowledge to do this?" the Colonel asked simply, looking halfway back towards Caralynne.

Shaking her head, the elder Lady Smith answered honestly: "Not when we saw her — she was trying to force Jimmy to get the information she needed. Though she could have learned more since then."

Adams nodded slowly, then fell silent, his mind clearly working over the various possibilities, and implications. Action needed to be taken, of course, but how much was a good question — and how obvious? He needed a moment to assess it all…

"Colonel," Travis interrupted the silence with that single word, and Adams looked up sharply.

"Major?"

Travis was staring at the black officer, clearly with an agenda of his own, though Caralynne wasn't certain what his specific aims were. Adams seemed to understand, and he looked back to Fischer, "You men stay here, all three of you. I'll send guards as well, and summon the rest of the operators to join you. I want you all here until we learn more."

That made sense — if there was a traitor among them, he'd be powerless to further cover his tracks when surrounded by all his peers. But it was only the first step, and with that in mind Adams nodded towards the door, "Join me outside, Major?"

Travis didn't nod; he simply followed as Adams led the way. Caralynne waited for them to exit before looking over the three shocked faces in the room one more time, then stepping out as well.

The argument had already started when she got through the door.

"…and this base is still under my command until the Commandant or your Brigadier return, Travis," Adams was keeping his tone cool and low, because sound would undoubtedly carry quite a distance in the empty hallway.

"I will not question your orders," the tall Major's reply was equally contained. "But if this is a serious danger, your men need to be stood up and we need to get started on a proper investigation."

"That is obviously my intention," a layer of defensiveness crept into the Colonel's reply. "I'll have Sergeant Major Turner look into it personally. But I do not want to call an alert and drive a possible spy to ground. If someone here is breaking into that screen, for *Emily* or for anyone, we need to capture that man."

"And if it's Emily herself? Or if Fischer is right and the timing has something to do with the arrival of the Ladies Smith? We need to have men ready to respond. Or we need to send them home," Travis' tone remained low and firm, and to his credit he wasn't speaking nonsense. There was a real potential danger.

The question was how to deal with it, and ultimately that came down to the discretion of the commanding officer — Adams.

"My regiment is rotating through exercises all day, so we'll have a good excuse to have them armed, without raising suspicions," the black officer said, then spotted Caralynne standing back from the discussion. "What about it, M'Lady. Do you want to withdraw now, or have your daughter under guard?"

It was a loaded question — not one Caralynne actually appreciated in that sense — but she could sympathize with Adams, so she shook her head, "I'll warn Alex, Stephanie and Strong to be on guard. But until we know more, we can wait to sound the alarm. As long as we know more *quickly.*"

Adams nodded, "Good. I'll get Turner on it right now."

As far as the Colonel was concerned, that was the end of the discussion, so he turned back to Travis, "Of course I'll keep you informed, Major."

The white officer blinked in surprise, "I can help Turner."

"We'll handle it," Adams shook his head. "That will be all for now."

With that dismissal, Adams turned towards Caralynne, leaving the tall Major behind wearing a cool look of surprise. He paused for a moment, then decided to deliver the parting shot: "I'll scrape together what men I have for some impromptu training of our own."

Adams closed his eyes when he heard the words, then tilted his head, "Suit yourself. And be sure to call your friends in Washington, too, Major."

And that made things even tenser. Almost as though it were a sixth sense, Caralynne found her migraine pounding hard — warning her that an explosion was imminent. She turned her eyes on Travis, and expected the political-appointee to be shivering with rage.

Instead, some of the tension seemed to have released from his expression, "I don't have any friends in Washington, Colonel. That's why I'm still here."

With that, he turned and strode down the corridor.

Once he'd turned the corner and disappeared, Caralynne approached Adams, "Wise to be excluding him?"

Adams opened his eyes and shook his head, "If there's a traitor on the base, literally the only thing I can be sure of is that it's not Turner. I don't... I don't know what any of this means, but I'm not going to have him forcing some spy into taking drastic action, especially with you and the girls here."

There seemed to be some logic in that, though Caralynne had

other questions...

The certainty on Adams' face forced her to temporarily abandon those.

"Let's get Eric, and warn your girls," the Colonel said. "Don't worry about my babysitter for now."

"Travis?"

Turning and gesturing for the Lady to begin moving, Adams nodded, "They never let a colored Colonel command this base without an officer here to keep an eye on him. This year Travis drew the short straw."

That dismissal of the tall Major seemed a little too easy for Caralynne, but then she hadn't been under the boot of a segregated army for two-and-a-half decades. Still, there seemed to be more to the man than just a political babysitter...

For now, that wasn't relevant. She did need to get to her daughter, Stephanie, and Strong, and let them know what was going on.

"Think it's actually something serious... or did someone just forget a triplicate signature?" Alex was sitting on the Headquarters building's front steps, her elbow planted on her knee and her chin resting in the palm of her hand.

She might have looked slightly bored, but she made sure to smile at every passing American, most of whom seemed confused by her rather un-Champion-like posture.

Leaning against one of the big stone posts that held up the railing at the edge of the steps, Stephanie had folded her arms and was looking similarly uninterested, "I don't know, they clearly thought it was serious."

"Headquarters types often get worked up about little things," Strong was standing higher than either of his charges, his hands stuffed in his pockets as his eyes scanned the base.

Of the three of them, he was most disconcerted by Adams' revelation that the 25th had deteriorated. Perhaps, as a wise old soldier, he should have known better... but all the regiments he'd known from the Hubrin War — the Newfoundland Regiment of course, as well as the Canadian Rifles, the Princess Patricias, and the Voltigeurs — had maintained their training in the years since. To be barred from proper war training because of color... well, Strong didn't like it.

Still, he could be part of the solution, and that counted for something. And perhaps — perhaps — the men wouldn't be as green as their Colonel seemed to think. They'd soon find out, as they were due on the training field.

"What company are you with first?" The question wasn't expected, and as soon as he heard it Strong turned towards the Headquarters door. Major Travis was putting his hat on and descending the steps at the same time, though when no answer came he stopped. "Sergeant?"

Strong blinked, "They said 'A' Company, sir."

Travis' expression tightened very slightly, "Lowestoft is younger than any of you, and his men have no experience. What about this afternoon?"

The warning meant little to Strong — or to Alex or Stephanie for that matter — but none of them liked the idea of a Major coming along and prejudging men of another regiment. Again, Travis seemed both aware of and indifferent to their feelings, "What company this afternoon?"

"'C' Company," Stephanie answered, sounding as impressed as she was. "Sir."

Travis' eyes shifted to his fellow American, and lingered on her for just a moment, "Good NCOs in that company. No officers back from leave, though…" He trailed off, then shook his head. "Be careful today."

And with that cryptic warning, he nodded to Stephanie, Strong, and finally Alex, then descended the Headquarters steps and hurried off. The trio watched him go, none of them quite sure what to say about the frontiersman's manner.

"Well," Strong tried, but gave up.

"Exactly," Alex agreed. "I was thinking the same."

They'd have to see what the day brought.

CHAPTER VI

Alex had never quite felt at home in a classroom. It wasn't that she didn't appreciate learning — far from it — but where Stephanie had always possessed a certain thirst for sitting and absorbing lectures, time spent sitting more or less still at a desk, hadn't been terribly appealing to the young Champion.

Perhaps that was her father's influence; no one would call Smith an ignorant man, but most of the knowledge he'd picked up over the years had been learned on the move — riding a trail, working with someone on something... by *doing*. Alex was a bit like that too, and though she was fortunate to have a brain that seemed to absorb facts and figures relatively well, she'd rather not have done so in a classroom.

That being the case, her first steps into one of the Robinson Institute's classrooms were not enthusiastic ones. Her mother's explanation of the possible security risk on the base was still ringing in her ears, and her Browning — retrieved from the skycruiser since danger was possible — was digging into the small of her back. The gun was too long to carry concealed comfortably, but she didn't want it visible on her hip inside a class building. All things being equal, she'd much rather have been out helping search for Emily, or whoever had manipulated the screen.

But Colonel Adams was adamant that they proceed normally. Normal, in fact, had been his very word. And Alex's argument that being in a classroom wasn't 'normal' hadn't flown.

No escaping it, then: others would investigate, while she taught some American students — most of whom were probably only a year her junior — how to survive a crisis. Like the one that *might* be happening on their very base, that very day...

Realizing she probably needed to stop allowing herself to be distracted, Alex blinked a couple of times and took a breath. She'd entered the lecture hall and nodded to the instructor — an ordinary woman who she didn't know — and now she turned to face the eager students.

The first thing that struck her was how few were present. This was the senior class of Champions — the ones whom, within a year, would be picking their coats — and yet there were only around fifty. At the Lady Emily Academy, the same class numbered closer to 100, but even that was a massive decrease from past years.

Fewer and fewer children of the savages were being found and rescued on the new world — as settlement spread, savages were gradually wiped out, and while that meant more safety for settlers and their families, it meant fewer additions to the ranks of the Champions. Perhaps a few hundred new children being rescued each year, as opposed to the thousands that were found in 1920 and 1921.

The trend would turn around when those thousands of Champions — people like Lord Grey and Lady Winter — started having their own children, but until then, every Champion in school became disproportionately more valuable. They all had to be kept as safe as possible, and that meant Alex had to share her wisdom.

Right.

At least they all seemed receptive: all eyes were on her, and their expressions reflected eagerness. That was... good? Alex didn't know. She just hoped they'd be receptive and cooperative... and not require too much attention. Just in case something untoward was actually happening.

"Seniors, this is Lady Alex Smith from Newfoundland, and as promised, she's here for the next two days to take us through the firebox technique," the instructor came to her feet from behind her desk, and her introduction was particularly soft — even a little meek.

Alex didn't know what to make of that, but it was irrelevant: she raised her hand and waved to the students, "Um. Hi."

Great start — and in recognition of her amazing grasp of rhetoric, the room actually exploded in applause. The young Champions-in-training were excited to see the whitecoat who they believed had bested Emily in battle.

They had a lot to learn.

• • •

"This is a Jeep!" Stephanie declared enthusiastically as the open-topped olive truck rolled fast down a road into the woods east of Fort Eustice.

The soldier behind the wheel — a black Private who couldn't have been older than seventeen — wasn't sure if the exclamation was meant for him, but he thought it better to actually answer his passenger, in case she wanted him to comment.

"Um. Yes ma'am."

"Not a Land Rover," she persisted, then glanced back to Strong, who was riding in one of the back seats, and wearing a studied expression.

Caralynne's orders to act normally weren't really working on the Colour — he was much too preoccupied with the implications of a security breach, questions of who might be responsible, and what dangers might result. Stephanie was assuming the guise of an enthusiastic eccentric with more ease, and now she needled her Sergeant to play along.

"Not a *Land Rover*, right Colour?"

He blinked, then nodded, "Correct. This is a Jeep. Capital 'J'."

The soldier behind the wheel still didn't know what the conversation was supposed to be about, but he tried to take part, "You don't have Jeeps up in Newfyland, ma'am?"

His indulgence was helpful, and Stephanie smiled at him, "We have Land Rovers, which are not *Jeeps*. Different patents, but very similar in their abilities. I've just learned to drive them, actually... so my compliments on your very smooth driving today, Private."

She wanted him to say his name at that point, and he got the hint: "Wells, ma'am."

"Good driving, Private Wells," she declared, and because her compliment sounded genuine — if a bit over-enthusiastic — the young soldier smiled.

"Thank you, ma'am. It's mostly the road... the ground is all frozen, so the dirt track is smoothed. This road is our back way out of the Fort, though... so during the spring and the fall, when it's wet, the mud and the ruts can get bad and bumpy. Because we uses it a lot."

There, she'd got him talking — the surest way to make someone think everything was normal (or indeed, going well) was to start him talking about something he took pride in.

"I'm sure you drive well in all conditions, Private," she paid him that compliment honestly, and then subtly went after more information. "So this training ground... how far is it from the base?"

"The one we're going to? Just about two miles, ma'am. Nice big open field, running up to a ridge. And on the other side of the ridge is a sheer drop into the river."

Interesting — sounded like a good place for live-fire training, with a backstop... but it also sounded isolated. Stephanie wasn't sure if that was going to be a concern.

"How near to any facilities... an armory, for instance?" she pressed the question, even though it was a bit more conspicuous.

Wells seemed not to notice, "Oh they truck all the guns out here for training, or the men bring them along. No one else around for miles, ma'am."

For better or worse, Stephanie decided. Glancing back at Strong, she found the Colour had been listening too, and his expression reinforced her own feelings: it'd be wise to be cautious today.

"Well, this shall be fun," she said carefully to Wells, and then she just managed to keep her hand from unconsciously settling on her Browning's holster. She was glad she had it with her, and that Strong had picked up his Thompson. Just in case.

It was a few more minutes before the Jeep veered off the dirt track and onto the grassy shoulder. Stephanie watched as a hedge that had run alongside the road dropped away, and revealed exactly the sort of ground Wells had promised: grassy, a few times larger than a football field, with a ridge rising on the opposite side to serve as a backstop against live fire drills. Before the base of that slope, a rough-looking train car had been placed — a training aid for units trying to practice the scenario Champion Marcus Steele had encountered at Penn Station in New York.

And arrayed in the field were nearly 200 men, all in long winter coats against the cold, and carrying their rifles — all Garands from what she could see, though she hoped some would have Thompsons too.

"Here we are, ma'am," Wells smiled as he shifted out of gear. "I'll be waiting for you, so I get to watch."

Stephanie looked back to the driver with a smile, then shrugged, "Well if this was a Land Rover, we could drive right down there into the field. Want a little adventure?"

Wells' smile got bigger, and he nodded, "Yes, ma'am."

Strong leaned forward at this point: "Really?"

"Just want to make a good impression," Stephanie glanced back, then grabbed the frame of the Jeep's windshield and levered herself up onto her feet, so she could stand dramatically.

"Hold on," Wells didn't sound like he was actually worried when he said it, and then he cranked over the wheel to turn the Jeep off the shoulder and down the gentle grade into the low lying field. As he did, all the soldiers waiting turned to watch the arrival, and they were greeted by a magnificent sight: Second Lieutenant Stephanie Shylock standing up in the passenger's seat, as though she were George Washington crossing the Delaware.

Strong got to his feet less eagerly, and scanned all those faces for any sign of experience amongst them... but even the Sergeants he saw looked impossibly young. Perhaps Adams was correct. But then, young didn't mean incapable — if it had, a lot more men would have died fighting the Hubrin.

One of the youngest faces he spotted was a white one, belonging to an officer who had to be Captain Lowestoft. As the Jeep rolled to a stop beside the first group of black soldiers from 'A' Company, it was that man who hurried up to the vehicle, came to attention, and saluted Stephanie Shylock with great earnestness: "Captain Stephen Lowestoft, ma'am, presenting 'A' Company of the 25th United States Infantry!"

Stephanie knew she was basking in the glow of her arrival a little too much, but this greeting helped shake her mind into reality. She looked down at the Captain, then glanced back at Strong, who shrugged. A very gentle frown then creased her brow, and she wasted no more time in hopping down to the ground.

There was a satisfying crunching sound as her boots hit the frozen grass, but she ignored that as she slowly approached the young man. He was very skinny, and his skin was still spotty — he was perhaps nineteen. And yet, he was a Captain.

"Um," she lowered her voice and leaned close to him. "Captain Lowestoft, I'm junior to you. I should be reporting to you."

Strong hopped from the Jeep as she spoke, and his eyes swept the entire scene: a lot of young black soldiers were just barely containing smiles at their officer's foolishness. Perhaps he would have done the same, were he in their position, but something struck him as wrong about the whole scene. These were men wearing the same regimental flashes as the men he'd fought with on the new world — most of whom he'd seen buried in the badlands. For them *not* to be good soldiers was not acceptable.

"Company," he barked. "Attention!"

He wasn't supposed to be able to order another army's company to attention, but he was a Sergeant — even a good one, when he stopped pretending not to be. It appeared that these men could use one.

Humor seemed to fade, but the men didn't immediately respond — until their Captain looked from Stephanie to Strong in a slight panic, and repeated the order, "Company Sergeant, attention please!"

The Company Sergeant repeated the order, and men came to attention. Strong glared at all who could see him, then reached back into the Jeep and grabbed his Thompson, just to emphasize his coarse mood.

Getting the sense her Sergeant felt discipline was needed, Stephanie decided to play along with protocol as best she could. Coming to attention, which she rarely ever did, she snapped a good British Army salute — long way up, palm forward, "Second Lieutenant Shylock, reporting for training with Sergeant Strong, sir."

Lowestoft was beginning to realize his error, so now he tried to correct himself, "Uhm, thank you Lieutenant. Welcome."

He lowered his salute, and then stepped closer to her as she did the same, "I'm so sorry."

His words were fortunately low, and Stephanie managed not to react to them. She could instantly peg the young officer — he was not a natural soldier, and he didn't seem to have the respect of his men. But he was not on Christmas leave, probably because he thought it more important to actually spend time with his soldiers. It was only a first impression, and Stephanie knew those could be wrong, but she believed he meant well.

He also made her feel rather more authoritative that she normally considered herself. She was no proper officer herself, but her experience and upbringing made her closer to the genuine article, she supposed.

Well, whatever the case, she'd do her absolute best — just as she'd promised Adams.

"Thank you, Captain," she replied loudly enough for men

nearby to hear, and then she reached out and shook his hand. "Not to worry."

He seemed relieved, and that was good... though as he took a step back and aside to present his company, Stephanie found herself staring at 200 men who she had no real idea how to teach. Well, she and Strong would figure something out. At least they could rely on each other.

CHAPTER VII

"So it's like the name... firebox..." Alex felt surprisingly alone standing beside the blackboard at the front of the lecture hall, a piece of chalk in her hand as she sketched an admittedly amateurish diagram of the tactic she'd come to teach. It didn't help that the room was hot — she hadn't taken off her coat because she didn't want anyone to see her Browning, but if somebody didn't open a window, she was bound to start sweating.

No matter: she had to tough it out.

"We shoot over her head," Alex tapped the diagram as she persisted, indicating a dashed line drawn over the head of a stick figure meant to represent Emily. "Then we shoot to either side of her." She tapped the dots to the right and left of the figure. "So she's boxed in by fire from above, and fire from the sides, and... well, the ground boxes her in under her feet, but you get the idea... that's why it's called 'firebox'."

The explanation wasn't as eloquent as she'd imagined it, and as she scanned the lecture hall for reactions, she found herself confronted by an array of numb expressions. It probably didn't help that her diagram was just a crude version of the one they'd all seen already — a pamphlet with the technique had been printed and circulated the previous autumn.

No, the real point of her visit to Virginia was not to lecture these students about a theory, but to train with them in the field. That was what she wanted, and they wanted, and she decided there probably wasn't any point to denying it.

"So," she said, laying the chalk down on the board and dusting off her hands, "that's what we're here to learn. Review. Probably more of a review. And we'll be in the field this afternoon practicing."

Those last words caused more of a stir, as students perked up at the prospect of being handed guns and told to jump around. Alex could sympathize.

"Any questions?" she asked — foolishly, because she expected none.

One hand went up immediately: a boy who was probably only a year her junior, sitting in the second row.

"Yes?" she pointed to him, and the corners of his mouth turned up a little at the attention.

"Why aren't we out there this morning, M'Lady?"

Alex blinked. Apparently it was because Adams didn't think 'A' Company was ready for joint training with Champions, but she could hardly say that to a room full of students. Instead, she hedged — and hedged badly, "Review first, then practice... what was your name?"

"Todd Randall, M'Lady," he said, almost sounding as if he expected her to know who he was. Alex didn't want to make any assumptions, but he did have a slight air of being pleased with himself.

"So it's not because that's 'A' Company out there, and they don't know how to shoot straight?"

Alex's eyebrows rose instantly, and as a ripple of laughter filled the back half of the lecture hall, she glanced at the instructor. That ordinary woman remained silent, which made no sense, since she was a *teacher*. But perhaps she was just a substitute, and the real instructor was still on leave, like just about everyone else from the base...

Well, Alex wasn't quite as hot-headed as Stephanie in racist situations, but she could certainly give someone a talking to...

"You need to learn when to shut up," one of the girls in the front row was ahead of her — a shorter student who'd been beaming even during the worst of Alex's mangled explanations.

"Get off it, runt," was the comeback, and then other voices joined in.

Instant mayhem, as Alex stood there and watched. What the hell did the Americans teach their Champions?

It didn't take very long to break 'A' Company into squads, which actually surprised both Stephanie and Strong. Perhaps years of parade and guard duty had made them good at formation, but it was immediately obvious from the way men started handling their rifles that few knew much about how to wield them.

Time for lessons to begin.

Stephanie had moved up to the train car at the head of the field, and deciding altitude would favor her again, she climbed up into its doorway and turned to look out over the men, "Alright, we're going to be training today with the firebox tactic. Captain Lowestoft has been telling me about the instruction you've received already, so I'm looking forward to getting off to a fast start."

Standing on the ground just below and to Stephanie's left, Mike Strong watched the reactions of some of the men who were standing nearest the train; they seemed more impressed by Stephanie's figure than her words, and he marked certain fellows for some recalibration.

"Would anyone like to tell me how your squad fire plan is shaped in an encounter with a Champion?" the Lieutenant asked next, sounding a bit more like a schoolteacher than Strong would have advised.

Captain Lowestoft was standing with his men, and despite Stephanie's supportive comments, he still looked stricken. It didn't help when none of his men answered — as the silence lengthened, he started to go red.

Stephanie spotted this, and then glanced quickly at Strong. There were two paths to follow now: intimidation or charm. The latter seemed a better starting point, because it would make the former more dramatic if it became necessary.

Smiling in a manner that she had, on occasion, used to charm men for various purposes, Stephanie held onto the rails on either side of the train door, and leaned forward, "How about you, Corporal. You want to tell me what firebox is?"

She made eye contact with one of the soldiers who seemed a bit too smug for his own good, and as soon as he realized she was talking to him, he grinned, "Want me, ma'am?"

Strong began to bristle, but before he could bark at the brat, Stephanie rocked forward in the doorway playfully, "Depends, soldier. How good are you with firebox?"

Smile broadening, the man stepped forward, "I'm good with it. *Real* good."

Wait. That sounded like a double entendre. A doubly-inappropriate double entendre.

Creeper.

Now Strong was really ready to do some yelling — funny how

easy his old Sergeant's instincts came back — but Stephanie was already hopping down from the train, and advancing on the man. He stood waiting for her, his Garand in hand, finger on the trigger.

Though the loss of altitude made it difficult for all the men of the company to see Stephanie, she figured this was best anyway. Approaching the man with her smile intact, she tipped her head girlishly, "So how do you do it, soldier?"

"The right way," he said again, liking the proximity far more than he should have.

Stephanie's smile grew, "Now you need to tell me what it says in the firebox pamphlet. Feel free to ask your friends. Don't make me wait."

Fine, he'd play along — he turned so that he could look back to the men in his squad, and as his body direction changed, the muzzle of his rifle went with it. Fortunately, a hand stopped him from completing his turn — a hand on the foreguard of the Garand.

"You know why you're out here with no Champions, while the rest of your regiment gets to train with them?" Stephanie's tone was suddenly very sharp, and the Corporal's head whipped back.

"What?"

"Take your *finger* off the *trigger* of your rifle, *now*," her eyes were ice the moment he met them, and her tone was entirely unsympathetic.

"You heard the Lieutenant, get your finger off the trigger, you sorry excuse for a soldier!" Mike Strong surged into the picture with a bellow only real Sergeants could produce.

The sudden onslaught of terror convinced the young soldier to let go his rifle entirely, which was probably for the best. Since her hand had been on it already — keeping it from inadvertently being pointed at any of the men of the company — Stephanie took it up, turned to the train, shouldered it and squeezed the trigger.

A nice hole appeared in the side of the car, and was accompanied by thunder.

"This man very nearly swept the muzzle of his rifle across his squad. Do you understand what that means?" Strong grabbed the Corporal by the collar of his coat and half-threw him back to the side of his colleagues.

"He had his finger on the trigger of his rifle," Stephanie's yell was less terrifying than Strong's, but it still carried. "Most of you know that my godfather was a gunfighter called Cameron Kard.

When I was shorter than this rifle, he taught me never to point a gun at anything I wouldn't be willing to shoot, and never to put my finger on a trigger unless I intended on shooting."

"By that definition, this man *wanted* to shoot his friends, Lieutenant," Strong followed up. As he spoke, Stephanie locked back the bolt of the Garand and leaned it up against the wheel of the train, then hopped back up into the doorway, this time with an icy smile.

"Well if that's the case, he's under arrest, isn't he, Sergeant?" Stephanie declared.

"Right you are, ma'am!" Strong barked back. "Unless he admits he's a damned fool. Then maybe we could be lenient."

By now the soldier in question was moving from surprise towards indignance… but the force of Colour Strong was staring him in the face, warning him not to allow his wounded pride to manifest.

"What about it? You all think he's a criminal, or are all of you just too convinced that you're gunfighters to listen when your Captain tries to teach you things?" Stephanie was going to try to preserve Lowestoft in all this, though it wouldn't be easy. "He's the only reason you're out here at all. Unlike all your other officers, he's not on Christmas leave. He believes in you so much that he convinced us to let you train. But we knew this was what you'd do, so we refused to let you train with the Champions. We leave that for *real* soldiers."

It was not really true, of course, but Stephanie was willing to be a bit dramatic for a good cause.

Strong went further: "In case none of you know who I am, I am Mike Strong, one of the Royal Newfoundland Regiment. That means I served with men from your regiment in the Hubrin War. They were good men. The *best* kind. You are a disgrace to them. You are *not good men*. Not yet. You can try to blame that on being black men in a white army, but those men were black men in an even *whiter* army. So no excuses. Listen to your Captain. Listen to us. Then next time we come, you'll get to play with the Champions."

Stephanie closed it off: "And gentlemen, if you don't cooperate, you will die. You will either kill each other like fools, or you will be killed when a rogue Champion comes here looking for secrets. You *will die*. Clear?"

Yes, it was pretty damned clear. She let her cold proclamation hang in the air, and knowing the effect it would have, Strong held his tongue, allowing the silence to endure for a long moment. Stephanie Shylock hopped down from the train, took a deep breath, drew her Browning, and then approached Captain Lowestoft. They had much to fix.

At first, Alex had assumed the motivation behind the young man's comment had been one of race — that Todd Randall, the awesome Champion-in-waiting, was saying the men of 'A' Company were no good because they were black. But the argument within the classroom had quickly revealed that color wasn't the issue: Randall, and many of his friends, simply didn't like ordinary people.

"Look, some of them are good," he was backpedaling a little now, because the 'runt', Constance, had just put him on the defensive. "That's fine, but we have to put our lives in the hands of whatever ordinaries are assigned to us. Look how that worked out for Steele. Emily didn't kill him, his own Sergeant did. Some old fat soldier who thought he was better than us shot Steele in the back because he didn't know how to hit what he was aiming at! Now if I get a reject like that, what good is firebox? He'll shoot me by accident!"

There were murmurs of agreement from the youngsters behind Randall, and the boy shook his head and folded his arms, "You're too much of an idealist, Constance. Not everyone is like your precious Vanier."

That volley delivered, eyes turned back to the girl in the front row. She was under a thundercloud now, and though Alex didn't know who 'Vanier' was, she supposed he was ordinary. Perhaps invoking his name was meant to destabilize her, but it didn't work.

"We're going to be assigned lances whether we like it or not. We have to train with them, Todd. Otherwise they *will* shoot us by accident."

It was a perfectly practical argument, and Alex approved. It also seemed a natural moment for someone like the teacher to interject and stop the verbal scuffle... but she was just sitting at her desk, staring at her hands. The whole notion of such an argument in a classroom was alien to the schooling at the Lady Emily Academy, but at least it was over now...

"They won't shoot you if you're sleeping with them, maybe," Todd Randall said, and a few people giggled. Alex blinked, realizing she'd been foolish to think it was over, so she held up her hand and took a step forward. Not fast enough.

"I don't sleep with soldiers," the boy then declared, seeming to imply that Constance did. "Well, not unless I get Lieutenant Shylock!"

A few of the schoolboys — and despite the fact that they were only a year younger than Alex, that's clearly all they were — started to laugh, before the dominating presence of the whitecoat at the front of the room made them think better of it.

Alex simply blinked. Randall started to pale as he realized he'd sprinted quite a ways across the line, but his voice failed him as his mouth worked to backpedal again.

It wouldn't have helped, even if he'd been able to. Alex let her eyes settle on him, and then she shook her head, a sad smile turning up the corners of her lips.

"Well," she said. "You've just said something very wrong about my friend, Mister Randall. And you know it. What you don't know is how wrong it is. Or why. And perhaps that's my fault. I came here and was distracted, and drew a silly diagram, and I didn't stop to explain to you *why* firebox matters."

The room was silent, and as Alex noticed that she sighed, "I still have nightmares about that fight with Emily. Actually, I had one last night. The very night before I was supposed to come here to talk about surviving Emily, I had a nightmare in which I was more or less killed."

She paused, then her sad smile twitched, "More or less. You can only *more or less* die in a dream. But it's frightening. Terrifying."

On that note she turned away from the class, then strode towards the blackboard and waved at her mangled diagram, "Everything we've trained for, things like firebox, will keep you moving in the moments when your mind locks up. You can train your body to do these things automatically, and later you'll realize you did them. And when you do realize, it might scare you. You might start counting your bruises in the mirror and realize you got them without thinking. You can be proud of yourself for being able to do what you did, but when you realize it was all automatic, that you weren't really thinking for any of it... that's when you'll start to question. What would have happened if my training hadn't been good enough? What if it broke down?"

Turning back, she zeroed in on Randall, "That's something that gives me nightmares, Mister Randall. And it will give you nightmares, if you're lucky enough to survive. But if we lucky few Champions with all these talents face such fears, imagine for just one moment what it must be like for the ordinary people who serve with us. At least you and I know that we're stronger and faster than almost everyone who might want us dead. Those people volunteering... actually *fighting for the chance* to serve with you... how does it look to them? They're ordinary men, and yet they're willing to follow you into whatever trouble you find."

Coming to a stop, Alex shook her head, "Those ordinary people are braver than we are. They have to be. Maybe some of them aren't the best. I grant that. Maybe some of them need more training. I know. But if they're risking their lives because they *want* to be there in the moments we need them, what do we do? What do Champions do? I can't believe we just dismiss them. I don't think that's what we are. Or if it is what we are, it's not what we should be. I think we have to work together, and train together, and fight together."

Randall's eyes fell, which was probably a sign that he was at least listening. At that point Alex let her gaze wander across the rest of the class, and her words grew sadder, "And maybe we all die together. Maybe, no matter how good we are, we all die together. That's scary. But listen, me dying isn't the real reason my nightmares *are* nightmares. What makes them terrifying isn't Emily, or the mistakes I made fighting her. The terror comes because, in every single one, I am alone. However scary it was to face her, it's more terrifying to imagine how it would have gone if my friends hadn't been with me. My ordinary friends."

Taking one last deep breath, Alex shook her head, "We are special. Don't believe differently. But that does not make us demigods. That does not force us to be alone. Loneliness like that can be corrosive. Don't divide yourselves from the people who want to help you. That's what Emily did. It's actually what she said to me — that I should *not* trust ordinary people."

With a last scan of somber faces in the room, Alex shrugged, "But I trusted them, and I still do. That's why I only died *more or less*... and only in my nightmares."

Such was the end of young Lady Smith's sermon, and as she realized she'd done a bit of a monologue, she felt slightly sheepish. Perhaps yelling would have been more appropriate, but Alex was very much her father's daughter — and Smith had never raised his voice, in all the time she'd known him. He spoke plainly, and said what he meant. He'd have been proud of her speech now, and with that certainty to hold to, she didn't turn red.

She just hoped the message had gotten through.

"Listen, I'm done," she said after her pause. "Go get lunch early. I'll see everyone on the training field this afternoon, with 'C' Company. You won't be live-fire training until tomorrow, so don't try to draw pistols from the arsenal. Just get yourselves there, and be on time. Go on."

They needed some coaxing to leave — perhaps she had actually engaged them and they wanted more, but Alex was fresh out of prose. She watched them go, nodding to a few, noticing others who conveniently managed not to make eye contact. Randall was one of those.

Eventually the room emptied, save for Constance herself.

"Thank you, M'Lady," the American said, though she seemed a little nervous at the prospect of one-on-one conversation with the white-coated Lady.

Not liking the idea that anyone would feel nervous talking to her, Alex tried to be disarming: "You said my name wrong. You were going for 'Alex' but it came out 'M'Lady'."

Constance was tense — naturally, after the bout she'd had with Randall — but those words seemed to bleed a little of the stress from her expression, "Sorry about that. Obviously I get a lot of things wrong."

That sounded a bit defeatist, but Alex decided not to launch into any sort of 'believe in yourself' lecture. She'd come too close to eye-rolling idealism already — at least by her own estimation.

"So we're the same height, we both get a lot of things wrong… you're like my American sister," she said instead, hoping that would help.

Surprisingly, it actually did; Constance smiled, "I thought that was Stephanie."

"Hm. She is very possessive, and slightly crazy. Cousin, then?"

Constance clearly knew she was intentionally being reassured, but she still smiled, "I'll take that, thanks, M'Lady."

"Did it again. No one listens," Alex shook her head and sighed. "Come on. I'm getting lunch, so sit in and I'll give you a talking to."

It was a lunch invitation, which for a second didn't seem to register with Constance. Then, as her smile widened and she nodded, Alex decided she'd done okay. Turning back to the wayward instructor (still sitting at her desk), the young Lady Smith waved, "Bye now, thanks for the help."

When she didn't get an answer, she shook her head and nodded towards the door, "So they call you runt? We're the same height."

Constance frowned, "Well what did they call you?"

"You're making me wonder," Alex replied, and they left the classroom.

CHAPTER VIII

Vanier Cross sat silently at his desk, and refused to become involved in the arguments breaking out in the screen room. All but one of the operators currently on base had been delivered to the chamber by Regimental Sergeant Major Turner, and now two men from the 25th were guarding the door to make sure none of them left.

Such confinement — and the implications of possible guilt on the part of someone in the room — led to a considerable amount of tension, and unfortunately few of the men present were good at dealing with such stress in a reserved fashion.

"I don't care, obviously *I* didn't do this," Lieutenant Shane Gallagher was the loudest, and probably the most offended at the notion that he might have betrayed his nation. Of course, Gallagher was going to be a future president, and he intimated that fact to everyone he met on a daily basis. His family was wealthy and important, he was working on the Saa screen because he was brilliant, and ultimately, he would rule the country — if not both worlds.

Modest fellow, and this potential danger to his stellar trajectory was insulting.

"Shut up, Gallagher," Captain Hind was a more level-headed sort, but Gallagher refused to listen.

"I clearly didn't do this!" he shouted again. "Why am I here?"

"We're all here," Fischer tried to interdict with reason again. "We all *could* have made the changes to the registry."

"Not me, I wouldn't know how!" Gallagher protested, apparently oblivious to what his comment implied about his own competence.

It was all a bit more than Cross wanted to put up with, but he had no choice. He simply kept to himself, and wondered whether this would somehow be blamed on him. And if it was, how he would deal with that fate.

Difficult to predict, and perhaps not worth worrying about, but he did — and as he shook his head at Gallagher's persistent laments, Fischer noticed the black Corporal sitting mournfully at his desk.

Taking advantage of the cover provided by an explosion between Clarke and the future-president, the Captain rolled his chair over to Vanier's desk, "You doing alright, Cross?"

Surprised at the arrival, Vanier looked up and shook his head too quickly to seem genuine, "Fine sir, just... thinking."

Fischer wasn't daft, so he read through the poor front, "Don't worry, this is just a formality. They'll know it's not you, and if someone tries to drop this on you, I'll testify on your behalf. You very probably have saved us all from something much worse... you won't suffer for that."

It was an uncommonly kind thing for a white officer to say, at least in Vanier's experience. But then Fischer was right: if this breach was serious, then the discovery might indeed be significant to their ultimate fates. Having the Captain — and his wealthy family's contacts — on side would give the young Corporal some hope if things came to a head.

But he remained skeptical. Warm words counted for little, even if they were genuinely meant.

Those thoughts were crossing Vanier's mind as the doors to the screen room opened, and Captain Oldman was escorted in by Sergeant Major Turner.

"Wait here, please, sir," the RSM said to the officer, and with some consternation, the man nodded.

"Sergeant Major. I expect we'll have updates soon?"

Turner paused at Oldman's question, then looked between the officers already confined in the screen room — the heated atmosphere was impossible to miss, and it probably needed to be defused.

"Colonel Adams and Lady Caralynne are looking into this right now. They'll want to speak with each of you individually, find out what has gone on. For now, just keep an eye on the screen for more trouble," the soldier said sternly, and then without ceremony he departed.

As the door shut, Oldman shook his head, "What the hell is going on?"

"One of us is a traitor," Gallagher declared. "And it's not me."

Suspicious glances were traded again, but Vanier simply stayed below the fray. There had to be a way — some way — to figure out who had changed the registry. He tried to concentrate, but in the loud room it wasn't easy.

Caralynne was shading her eyes with her hand as she sat in Adams' office. The midday sun outside was sending bright rays through his large windows, which were none too kind to her migraine. Other things were unhelpful as well — particularly the ten files that were spread out on the Colonel's desk, splayed open as they tried to sift through them for hints.

"I don't know most of these men personally," the 25th's commanding officer was explaining. "They report to the Commandant. I know Vanier — he came up through our regiment, and got moved over thanks to a wealthy friend. I trust him, but I don't know about the rest — not even Fischer."

Nodding, Caralynne looked at the file for the white officer who'd brought the news, "He did seem nervous when he was explaining things, but that could just be natural."

At that moment there was a knock on the door, and before Adams could answer, it opened. Turner let himself in, then closed it behind him, "They're all down there now, under guard."

Adams nodded, "Good, thanks."

With that the RSM advanced up to the desk alongside Caralynne. She nodded briefly to him, but they shared no words — they didn't really need to. Since 1919, these three had known each other, and their relationship had grown strong enough over the years to allow them some silent shorthand.

For a few moments, they considered the various members of the screen team. Then it was Turner who produced the first idea: "It could also be someone who's on leave, who snuck back on base. He'd know how to get around with a low profile, and he'd have a good alibi."

"True," Adams agreed. "We'll have to keep an eye out. But… working with what we have… I think we'll just let them all stew down there for a few hours."

"They're getting tense already," Turner observed. "A little stewing might make the spy panic."

As ever, Adams was on the same wavelength as his RSM, "And if we have them all together while Corporal Cross starts going through the evidence on screen, one could incriminate himself." It was the sort of gambit one might find in a detective novel, but it had some merits, and it answered one practical question. "Whatever we do, we actually need someone to dig into that screen. If no one admits to this, we'll need some way to learn what happened."

Turner nodded, then folded his arms, "Wait for the rest of their team to come in off leave?"

"I'm just worried something happens before then," Adams shook his head. "I think we should take some guards down to the room and force them to figure something out. If they can't... we follow Travis' recommendation and go to full alert."

"We could do that now," Turner said. "Start the interrogations with the base locked down, be certain we don't get any surprises."

That was a good point, and pausing thoughtfully, Adams turned to look out his window. It was a clear day, and from his office, he could see most of the way across the Fort, and out to the training grounds beyond. An alert would give them certain advantages... but it would also deny his men the training that Caralynne and her daughter had come to deliver.

"If there's another spy out there, or whoever did this has some plan in motion, an alert will either disrupt it, or drive it underground," Caralynne weighed in for the first time. "Maybe go halfway: put guards on important assets — the skycruisers, your Champion residences and class buildings — but don't actually sound the alarm."

It seemed a fair compromise, so Adams turned away from the window and nodded, "Yes, let's do that. And if we don't get an answer by... say, 1500 hours, we'll go on alert tonight. If there's some sort of mischief planned, I don't imagine it'll happen in broad daylight."

A safe enough assumption, but not wanting to test it, Caralynne added one more point: "I'll get back to *George Tucker* and talk to our shipboard engineers. One of them might have some idea how to get in... and I'll call back to Jimmystown. George Devlin is a guru with Saa technology. He might be able to tell us what to do."

Two good ideas that neither Turner nor Adams had considered — they weren't entirely accustomed to having such support available.

"That'd be excellent," the Colonel nodded, then frowned slightly as Caralynne's hand descended further down to cover her eyes. "And maybe you should take a break."

"I'll be fine," she shook her head, but neither soldier at the table was convinced.

"Mister Smith wouldn't think well of me, not respecting his wife's head," Adams said evenly. "If you call in to Jimmystown, it'll probably take an hour for them to get back to you. Why not just rest until you have an answer to bring back?"

That was logical enough to overcome Caralynne's natural resistance. She took a breath, then conceded, "Just a long lunch, then."

"Good," Adams agreed immediately. "You head off, Eric and I will start deploying men quietly... and then this afternoon we'll all get down to the screen room for an interrogation."

That seemed to settle everything, so with a last nod to each of the soldiers, Caralynne departed. For a few seconds, she allowed herself to hope that rest would ease the pain stabbing through her head... but as soon as she indulged in that self-serving thought, she drove it back in favor of a more practical one: she needed to get advice from Jimmystown, and needed to remind her daughter to be especially cautious.

The day was far from over.

CHAPTER IX

"They knew we were here for two days, so they put aboard enough food to feed an assault company. Eat lots, and don't be shy," Alex summed up her philosophy on life (and specifically, eating) as she grabbed a plate from the stack in *George Tucker's* dining room, then proceeded down the buffet line to begin collecting her lunch.

Constance Cormack was still in a minor state of shock about the whole situation — she was aboard the British skycruiser with her personal hero... and they were eating from a *buffet*.

"But... who did they prepare the buffet for? All this food?" she asked, still not quite grasping what was going on, so Alex stopped and turned back with a smile.

"No, see, this ship is based in Newfoundland. The Captain is a Russian Jew, and the second in command is a Korean-Australian, but the ship is from *Newfoundland*. That means they will always prepare a lot of food, and it will all be good, and when you have the metabolism of a Champion, you will be expected to eat as much of it as you can. So, like, enough for six people."

Standing back from the line for a moment, Constance could only shake her head, "You... you really are my hero."

Alex shrugged, "You're catching me on a good day. *Four* breakfasts. How can you beat *four breakfasts?*"

The answer was simple: you couldn't. Recognizing that fact, Constance picked up another plate and then joined the buffet line — just in time to see the ship's cook emerge from the galley, "Oh, a friend, M'Lady?"

"One of America's future Champions, I'm just introducing her to the ways of the world," Alex replied with a smile, and the man grinned.

"Does that include dessert with lunch? I have a cake."

Lady Alex Smith stopped in her tracks, then looked back at the American she'd invited aboard, "You see? Anyone who ever says a bad word about ordinary people, you ask them who makes cakes for lunch. Just ask them."

Constance could only nod — she still wasn't quite keeping up with the whirlwind.

Turning back to the cook, Alex bowed, "You, sir, are a gentleman."

"Aw love, you'd don't have to insult me," he waved his hand. "I'll bring your cake."

With that, he disappeared through the galley door, and Alex collected the last of the food she wanted from the buffet, before choosing a table. Soon the American followed, and as the Champion-in-training settled down opposite the Lady, she shook her head.

"This is... amazing. Is it always this... amazing?" she sounded star-struck, which Alex supposed was rather her fault. As she dug into her pasta, the young Lady Smith tried to answer honestly.

"We always have good food aboard ship," she said between bites. "We can't take it everywhere with us, though. I haven't done any deployments to inhospitable places yet, but I'm betting they aren't as cozy."

"Still," Constance shook her head, "when you know you have this to come back to. I guess I wish I was British."

"Newfoundlander," Alex corrected gently, and Constance nodded as she began to eat. Again. After another bite, the white-coated Champion decided to pry a bit more from her guest: "So, if you had to estimate, what percentage of your class would side with Randall? I could make a pretty good guess, but you know them better."

It was a testament to the good food that Constance's mood didn't sour at the question, "A little over a third, I think. They... some of them just don't get to know regular people much. They grow up sheltered with wealthy families... their fosters give them a sense of superiority, and it doesn't stop when they come here and are treated like royalty."

"But not you," Alex observed, and Constance shook her head.

"My mother is a good southern lady. She inherited a nice estate, but she believes you have to earn respect."

Well that didn't sound bad to Alex, so she pressed on, "Where from?"

"Georgia," Constance answered with just the slightest hint of longing. "Augusta is our home."

It was encouraging to hear a savage-born girl — one whose actual biological parents would have been cannibalistic beast-humans shot down by soldiers when she was a baby — identifying strongly with the foster who had taken her in. Alex was obviously fortunate to have known both her biological mother and father; she didn't envy the Champions with anxieties about their origins, because there weren't really any easy answers about how they'd come to be.

But some Champions seemed unbothered by those details, and Constance was one of them.

"Leave a boy back there?" Alex turned the conversation in that direction — an unusual path for her, but one prompted by Randall's charge from the argument that she was sleeping with an ordinary person.

Smiling a little more, Constance shook her head, "Brought a boy with me. But... it's not like people think. He's..."

"Ooh, guest!"

Stephanie Shylock won the award for the most perfectly-timed interruption of the day, as she strolled into the dining room with a look of distinct satisfaction. Alex glanced back over her shoulder to her friend, then waved, "I left food, and there's cake coming!"

Stopping with a frown, the Lieutenant turned back to Strong, who was also just arriving, and asked the obvious question: "Dessert at lunch?"

"Don't be close-minded," Alex scolded her.

Taking the invitation to revisit their unfortunate humor from the middle of the night, Stephanie lamented: "But I'm an American."

No, it didn't make sense to anyone else, but that was fine — Strong grabbed his plate and hit the buffet, while the Second Lieutenant approached the table for a quick introduction to the unexpected guest, "I'm Stephanie."

Standing quickly and extending her hand, the Champion-in-training replied: "Constance Cormack. Really pleased to meet you."

"That's the opposite of how people usually feel about meeting me," Stephanie said with a smile. "You must be strange."

"I must be," Constance couldn't quite keep up with the wit, but her efforts were appreciated.

As the younger American resumed her seat, Alex questioned her friend, "Sounds like you had a good morning?"

"I yelled a lot, and taught some soldiers a bit of respect," Stephanie's smile grew. "It's nice telling people off now and then — as long as they deserve it. And they did."

That wasn't exactly what Alex had been expecting to hear, but she supposed it added up — Adams had been worried about his men's lack of experience, and even Travis had been critical of 'A' Company.

"They needed a boot up the backside," Strong confirmed as he arrived at the table with a hastily-assembled plate of food, and laid it down in the spot beside Constance. As he pulled out the chair and settled in, he didn't look at her immediately... and then he stopped and very specifically caught her eye. "Hello there, young lady. Did you say your name was Constance?"

Surprised by the, er, charm, Constance nodded, "I did say that. Is that okay?"

"Perfect," he smiled. "My name is Mike Strong. Heard of me?"

"Yes," she answered immediately... which threw him off.

"Wait, you have?"

"Yes," she repeated her answer, then clarified: "You have a reputation."

"And she was just telling me about a boy from Georgia, so back off, Colour," Alex interdicted.

With that bad news in hand, Mike Strong proved he was gallant even in pretend-defeat, "He is a man of great fortune, to have the affections of such an admirable young lady."

"Oh dear God," Stephanie took the seat on the other side of Constance. "He never says nice things like that about me."

"Only because we work together, dear Lieutenant," he persisted, and Stephanie smiled without taking her eyes off her food. Strong didn't linger long on the dangerous subject; he turned back to the morning, "No, 'A' Company was a mess. Well-meaning Captain, but they ran roughshod all over him, and didn't know much about soldiering. Good that we didn't have Champions out with us — I'd have been worried about someone getting shot."

Alex was in mid-chew as he spoke, and instantly she stopped and looked up. Constance caught the same irony, and her eyes met young Lady Smith's. Slightly awkward, of course, given their recent argument with Randall.

"Well," the lady in white said, "we had a big argument in class...

a third of the students were resistant to training with ordinary troops because they feared exactly what you describe. So... let's not bring that up when we're out there this afternoon."

Strong frowned, then looked from Alex to Stephanie and back, "Sounds like we all had interesting mornings."

"But Constance, you weren't against training with ordinary folks like us, were you?" Stephanie turned that question to the guest, presuming she knew the answer — there was no way Alex would invite an ignorant girl to lunch.

"I was on the other side. I like ordinary people," the Champion-in-training confirmed, and then almost blushed for some reason.

"Her mother's from Georgia, a real southern lady," Alex added, and Stephanie nodded approvingly.

"Raised me on her own, with the help of her help of course," Constance continued, and her pride was obvious — she clearly thought well of her mother, which again was refreshing to see from an adopted Champion child.

"Very good," Stephanie approved wholly.

As did Strong.

"So," the Sergeant paused, "You're saying your mother is single?"

"Dear God, he's in fine form," Alex looked up at the Colour, and Stephanie could only shake her head.

"Been putting up with him all morning."

Constance looked from the Sergeant, to her hero Lady, to the Lieutenant, and then back down at her plate. She really had no idea what she was doing in *George Tucker's* dining room, but if the life she was soon to embark on was anything close to this warm, she had much to look forward to.

Unfortunately, there were two sides to every coin.

As the ramp rose behind Caralynne, she could smell food and hear laughter coming from the dining hall — even though it was one deck up and a few corridors away. Not only were her Champion senses particularly fine, for better or worse today's migraine had magnified just about all of them.

Alex had clearly come back for lunch. She'd have to be briefed... but first, a call had to be placed to Jimmystown, so a request for ideas about the Saa screen registry could be routed to George Devlin. He'd probably need at least an hour to reply — time during which the elder Lady Smith could speak to her daughter… maybe even lie down, though she was still trying to resist that notion. How could anyone lie down with all this going on?

That question in mind, Caralynne took a deep breath and then raced at Champion speed from the ramp to the command deck. She found Lieutenant Hong had the watch.

"I need to send a message to Jimmystown," she declared as she came up alongside his chair, and looking up in surprise — she'd been fast and silent — he stammered before answering.

"Um… oh yes. Sorry, M'Lady, you just came out of nowhere."

Without delay, he reached out and flipped a couple of switches, then turned his chair and pointed to one of the banks of consoles further back in the chamber, "Just take Sol's chair, it'll be up on the screen in a moment."

Caralynne did as she was told. Lowering herself into the seat — which felt disproportionately comfortable, largely because it meant getting off her feet — she let her head sag, then reached up and covered her eyes with her hands. That provided a bare hint of relief, and also interrupted her view of the screen in front of her.

"Caralynne?"

She dropped her hand as soon as she heard the question, and found herself looking at Lord Jimmy himself, standing in his office in his Headquarters, "Oh, Jimmy. I thought I'd get the other screen."

He shrugged, "I was doing paperwork."

Right — whenever the Viscount of the Grasslands was doing administrative work, he tended to set his office screen to accept incoming messages, which could serve as distractions. She wasn't sure if that was actually helpful just now, but no matter: she began to explain the situation, and whatever Jimmy had been working on fell away.

"I'll call George," he said after a moment, picking up his telephone.

"We get to ride in a Jeep to get out there," Stephanie sounded rather enthusiastic about that, and as she led Strong, Alex and Constance towards *George Tucker's* ramp, she turned around and walked backwards just to make sure she emphasized the fact: "Not a Land Rover, a Jeep!"

"You really are American," Alex shook her head slowly.

"I'm coming late to this American joke, aren't I?" Constance interrupted at that point, her first time attempting to slide into the repartee shared by the friends.

"Never assume what they're saying is supposed to make sense," Strong leaned closer to her with the advice. "It will drive you insane."

"Aw Colour, we had such a good morning together," Stephanie rallied to her own defense. "We really were a great team, browbeating and scolding and telling it how it is..."

Fond memories, to be sure, but as she got caught up in them, she inadvertently backed right into Caralynne. Fortunately, no one was harmed.

"Oh... oh sorry!" the American Lieutenant turned with the apology, but Caralynne was already holding up her hand and trying to smile. That last part didn't work particularly well.

"Don't... it's fine," she said, then let her eyes move to Constance. "Oh. Hello there."

An abruptly pregnant silence followed that greeting, because for the first time it occurred to Constance that the legendary Lady Caralynne wouldn't necessarily have known she was aboard.

"I'm... Constance Cormack," the young American said quietly. "I just... sorry... I..."

Caralynne realized she must have sounded more angry than curious, so she corrected the misapprehension, "Oh, no, it's fine you being here. I just have a migraine, and I need to speak to these three. It's... nice to meet you."

That corrected the misunderstanding, but sounded hurried — Caralynne's head was pounding so bloody badly it was the best she could manage. Fortunately, Constance was quick on the uptake, "Oh. Then excuse me. Nice to meet you!"

She hurried past Stephanie towards the ramp, which began to open, and then Caralynne nodded to the nearby door that led to the armory. Strong led the way in, and then Stephanie entered last, shutting the hatch behind her.

Again wasting no time, Caralynne kept her explanation short: "We're thinking security breach. I called Jimmystown... George is working on a way to track who did it, but until we know more we're increasing security at key locations here. Colonel Adams is worried something might happen tonight, but we really don't know. If any trouble starts, just use your best judgment."

The words came fast, and there was no questioning their seriousness. Alex's fine mood began to fade, and as she took a heavy breath and looked across at her best friend, she saw Stephanie sobering in a similar fashion. Fun time was over.

"We'll take care," Strong replied for them all. "You do the same."

Caralynne nodded, and then waved towards the door, "I'm going to wait for George to get back to me. Might lie down. And then Adams and Turner and I will be trying to get the truth out of the screen staff. If you need us, we'll be at Headquarters. Or here."

That made sense to everyone, and since she had no appetite to linger, the elder Lady Smith nodded towards the door, "That's it. You should go."

It was both abrupt and concise, but that was probably for the best. Still, as they filed back out into the corridor, the daughter stopped and gave into the urge to quickly hug her mother.

"Have a good afternoon," Caralynne said as her arms closed around her white-coated Lady.

"You too," Alex answered.

Then they parted ways, Caralynne turning in the direction of her stateroom while the trio headed for the ramp. It was down by the time they arrived, and Constance was already standing at the bottom, beside the Jeep driven by Private Wells.

Somehow, another attempt at a Jeep joke didn't seem right, so Stephanie, Strong and Alex simply hurried down to the ground and hopped aboard. It was a bit tight in back when Constance climbed in, but they made room. Then, as *George Tucker's* ramp began to rise, they rolled off.

As they went, two Jeeps with stern-looking men from the Champions Regiment in their seats, and .30 caliber machine guns mounted in their backs, rolled past in the opposite direction. Increased security indeed…

CHAPTER X

Adams emerged from his office just as a slightly out of breath black soldier arrived at his orderly's desk, carrying a piece of paper.

"Sir!" the soldier turned immediately to his Colonel, and the urgency in his voice drew a frown to Adams' face.

"Private?"

"Sorry, sir. I was posted over at the motor pool, but Major Travis came through about twenty minutes ago. He was looking around for a few minutes, then he came up to me with this and said I had to get it to you as fast as I could. I ran over here."

He held up the piece of paper as he finished his explanation, and Adams grabbed it, opened it and read it on the spot:

Adams —
> *Have found equipment and vehicles missing. Meet me at the motor pool immediately. Bring Turner.*
>
> *— Travis*

The message was cryptic and confusing — why would the Major insist on Adams going to the motor pool, instead of posting guards there and coming back to Headquarters himself? Had he found something that couldn't be moved... evidence of the spy? It was difficult to predict the white officer's intentions — even to those he was friendly with, the tall Major seemed distant. And he certainly wasn't friendly with Adams.

But nothing could be ignored just now. Looking quickly at his watch, the Colonel decided he had sufficient time before his planned interrogation of the Saa screen staff. He crumpled the paper in his hand and stuck it in his pocket.

The soldier who'd carried the message had just managed to catch his breath, so Adams looked to him, "Sergeant Major Turner should be at the arsenal posting guards. Find him there and tell him to meet me and Major Travis at the motor pool, quick as he can."

Of course that order meant more running, but the man had no choice but to obey.

"Yes sir," he nodded, then turned and hurried out of the office.

Adams watched him depart, then took one step after him before stopping. He didn't have any idea what to expect at the motor pool, but given the circumstances, it seemed unwise to travel unarmed. Returning to his desk, he drew his Colt 1911 and holster from one of the drawers. He strapped on the sidearm — the very same gun he'd carried at Promised Town and the Badlands — and headed for the door again.

"If Lady Caralynne returns, let her know I'm at the motor pool," he instructed his orderly, and then he was gone.

The Jeep rolled down the narrow track towards the training field. Alex found the ride was actually rather pleasant, but she didn't say as much because such a comment might have been contrived as some kind of admission, and the mood of the afternoon was too serious to permit such diversions.

Instead, she kept her eyes moving back and forth, from one side of the road to other. The Virginia wilderness was rather different than Newfoundland's — the trees and underbrush seemed less severe, and the meadows far less boggy. Pleasant enough, though Alex remained loyal to her home.

The training field appeared to the Jeep's left after a few minutes, and as Wells arrived he glanced at Stephanie, "Straight in, ma'am?"

He asked it with a smile, and the Lieutenant matched his expression, "Your discretion, Wells."

"I think I know what that word means," he grinned fully, then cranked over the wheel. "Hold on!"

Alex's eyes widened slightly, but she got her hands around the Jeep's frame just in time to support herself as it bounced off the road and down the gentle embankment onto the grassy field. It figured that Stephanie would insist on a bit of off-road driving... though again, the ride wasn't as bouncy as the young Lady Smith had expected.

No matter; the vehicle rolled to a stop, and Stephanie swung her legs over the side and hopped out. Constance leapt out quickly too, and then the Sergeant and his Lady brought up the rear. As they all got their boots on the crunchy frozen grass of the field, they were confronted by quite a sight: 200 men, only a few of them wearing coats, and fifty Champions-in-training, all of them wearing the khaki short field jackets issued to students of the Institute.

"You need your coat?" Alex realized she'd abducted Constance without thought of her proper gear — the girl was in shirtsleeves.

"I'd just take it off anyway — gets too warm when we're training," Constance shook her head as smiled back, then nodded towards the other students. "I'll go join them?"

"If you must," was Alex's answer. She actually regretted the young student's departure just a little. She'd apparently taken a liking to Constance, and this felt like a small goodbye.

Constance seemed pleased enough; she skipped off to rejoin her friends, pointedly ignoring the glares of students like Randall — the sorts who'd think she was some kind of teacher's pet, riding in with Alex, Stephanie and Strong in their Jeep instead of running to the field like everyone else.

Alex ignored those people too, because a new figure arrived to distract her: the Company Sergeant from 'C' Company presented himself in front of Stephanie, then saluted, "Afternoon, ma'am." Then he looked past Stephanie to Alex and nodded, "M'Lady."

Seemed a nice enough hello, but Mike Strong took offense, "Look at this rogue. I thought you'd be dead by now."

"A lot of us hoped the same about you, Strong," he replied without missing a beat. "My sister still asks about you."

"She clearly has good taste," the Colour advanced towards the American, but the black man stood his ground.

"I love her, but she's never had good taste," he replied, and Strong came face-to-face with him at that point. A manly staring contest resulted, and as Alex advanced to Stephanie's shoulder, she frowned.

"I think they know each other," the whitecoat observed.

"Maybe they want alone time?" Stephanie suggested.

Strong raised an eyebrow and glanced at his charges, "This man, here, is the worst kind. Present yourself to my ladies, Frank. Admit who you are."

"Fine," he agreed, then turned back with a slight smile, "Company Sergeant Frank Preston, ma'am, M'Lady."

It only took a second for Alex to put the man's name, his rank, and his age together. Then she said: "Oh!"

Stephanie glanced at her, frowning, "Preston... that's one of the sharpshooters your dad talks about?"

"I think so. Right, Colour?" Alex turned to her trusty Sergeant for confirmation, and Strong raised his eyebrow.

"I don't know what your dad talks about, but this man here was part of the best sharpshooter team the 25th has ever had. And he did save your dad twice."

"Once at Promised Town, and once outside the hotel room I was hiding in as a very little girl," Stephanie added the context, and Preston acknowledged by letting his smile grow a little bigger. He was a big man and a well-presented soldier... and the Garand rifle slung over his shoulder looked well cared for.

"Where's Marks these days?" Strong put the question to the man, and Preston nodded his head back towards the Fort.

"Company Sergeant for 'D'. You'll see him tomorrow," he replied, but then he turned his attention to the girls. "So I feel as though I know you both a little, ma'am, M'Lady. Sorry if that's presumptuous."

Alex found that charming, "Well, since my dad wouldn't be alive and I wouldn't exist if it wasn't for you, I think you're allowed to presume."

He was, and then she stepped forward to extend her hand to the man.

Stephanie followed, "Surprised we haven't met somehow before now. But I guess you guys don't get out much?"

As soon as the words were out of her mouth, Stephanie realized they could be misinterpreted. Fortunately Preston understood her intent, "That's what we're hoping to change. Should I form my men for inspection? That's what our Captain would normally do... but he's not here."

With a shake of her head, Stephanie looked to Alex, "No?"

"Don't see how it'd help," she agreed. "Let's just go say hello... and I have to talk to the students."

That sounded fine, so Preston nodded and turned back towards his men. With Strong in step beside him, he led the two girls further onto the field. All the soldiers seemed decidedly more professional than the men of 'A' Company, and while some looked awfully young,

Stephanie approved of the directions in which their rifles were pointed — all slung, safely pointing up.

A few of them were also handsome, which provided a perfect opportunity to needle Strong.

"What do you think, a few husbands here?" Stephanie asked her friend, not-quite-quietly enough to be missed by their illustrious Colour.

"Let's see how good they are at taking orders," Alex reminded her friend severely.

Strong didn't even look back over his shoulder at the pair, which was disappointing.

"Not even paying attention," Stephanie lamented.

Ahead of them Preston looked at Strong, "Keeping them out of trouble must be interesting work."

The Colour grinned, "Who says *they're* the troublemakers?"

Adams didn't want to look as though he was in a hurry, but as he crossed his base towards the motor pool, he found his patience under strain. He needed answers soon — whether from Travis or the men in the screen room, he needed a better sense of what was happening. There would be no ease until he had some clarity, and then, depending on the nature of that clarity, things could well be worse than they already were.

But such thoughts were getting too far ahead of the game; the Colonel needed to focus on the immediate — on why Travis had summoned him so cryptically. Vehicles and equipment missing... it sounded dangerous, but many things sounded worse than they were when someone communicated them with such brevity.

Whatever the case, at least security was being increased. It was subliminal in many respects, but as he crossed the base, Adams could see a few reassuring signs of Turner's guard deployments.

The skycruisers were coming up next — *Captain Koster* and *Major Krazakowski* flanking *George Tucker*. All three of those ships were named for men the Colonel knew from the Hubrin War, and who had died on the Badlands or later. Adams remembered Koster's demise clearly — remembered a savage leaping out of a cloud of red dust, landing on him, dragging him over a cliff in the midst of a hot battle while the men of the 25th were retreating towards a mesa held by the Newfoundland Regiment and the Sikhs.

Koster had been a good man, as had Krazakowski, and of course Tucker. What they would have done in the midst of threats like these, Adams didn't know, but as he passed the first of the skycruisers that bore their names — *Arnold Koster* — he was glad to see that a Jeep carrying a .30-cal machine gun had been posted at the bottom of its open ramp.

He approved of that sight and kept walking.

Then he stopped.

There were no men in the Jeep, and the skycruiser's ramp was down. It was standard procedure to keep ramps closed while a ship was on the ground, and there was no way Turner would have allowed anything different. Clearly he'd sent protection to the ships, so if the guards were missing from the Jeep, and the ramp was down...

Adams' thoughts began to accelerate as he held still. Who could have taken out a Jeep's crew without a shot fired? Who could want to go aboard a skycruiser?

Was it Emily?

The Colonel's hand dropped to the holster on his belt, and he looked down the path towards the other Jeep parked a couple of hundred yards away, in front of *Ernest Krazakowski*. It was similarly abandoned, and the ship's ramp was also down.

At least *George Tucker's* ramp was up between the two... but for two machine gun Jeeps to be abandoned in front of unlocked ships, under the present circumstances...

Opening the flap on his holster, the Colonel let his fingers slip around his pistol's grip. His eyes traversed the ground nearby, looking for any of his men — indeed, any men at all — to summon for support, but none were in sight. How was that possible? It didn't matter, he had to do something.

Adams looked back towards the open ramp of the nearest American ship, fearing he'd see Emily, but it turned out his anxiety was premature. A frowning Sergeant, two Privates and a Captain were hurrying down the ramp. Each wore the flashes of the Champions Regiment on their shoulders, and they were carrying their weapons at the ready. Adams didn't recognize any of them — they were undoubtedly Travis' men — but they were coming straight for the Jeep, which suggested it was theirs.

"You men," Adams called. "We need to keep these ships buttoned up, and make sure to keep a man with your Jeep at all times."

His call drew their attention, and simultaneously they all fixed their gazes on him. As their cold stares locked on, every instinct Adams had developed over twenty-five years of soldiering told him something was quite wrong.

He began to draw his 1911 from its holster.

But they had four guns to his one — three Thompsons along with something the Colonel didn't immediately recognize. And they were already prepared.

Colonel Robert Adams felt nothing as he watched the world topple in front of him. It took him a second to realize that his hand was no longer on his gun and that he was on his back on the ground. When he tried to lift his head to look down at his chest, he couldn't. He thought his face felt wet, but he'd had the wind knocked out of him. His legs didn't feel like anything.

He coughed when he tried to breathe, and that wet his face more. What had happened?

A shape loomed over him — it was the white Captain — and then a pistol Adams didn't recognize swung into view. No, he did recognize it: a Luger. A German gun. How had an American Captain gotten hold of a Luger?

Adams had been shot by a German gun. He put some of it together in that flash, and then he saw the muzzle stare at his face.

He tried to gasp *no*, because it didn't make sense to die now, in this place, without being able to see his wife or daughters again. Their images flashed before his eyes, and then he was back on the Badlands, with all the other men from his regiment who'd died fighting savages and Hubrin.

As he saw the muzzle flash, he knew he'd rejoin them presently.

He would not, perhaps fortunately, witness the destruction of his base.

CHAPTER XI

Alex liked the men of 'C' Company. It was clear they had good NCOs, because their habits as soldiers were solid — they had clean equipment which they knew how to carry, they were smiling but not disrespectful, and they seemed to look to each other for guidance and support, even in the small things.

Certainly they might lack experience, but they were a world away from what Stephanie had described with 'A' Company, and that was good. Perhaps the Champions they'd be training with would learn something.

Having made the rounds and quickly met the Sergeants from Preston's company, Alex turned to those students. Randall was near the front of the group, a cluster of his supporters around him, and they all looked at her with icy glares. That was fine; Alex would make sure they got a workout to warm them up—

Gunfire.

It was an unmistakable sound, and Alex froze and frowned as she heard it.

On a training base, the report of submachine guns and pistols was hardly rare — it was indeed expected. But the shots sounded as though they'd come from the direction of the Fort, not the training grounds.

Another single shot snapped the air. This one sounded very different... the report of a gun she wasn't at all familiar with. She knew Colts, obviously knew Brownings... but this gun hissed more softly, so quietly that, had she not benefitted from a Champion's ears, she wouldn't have heard it.

None of the men or Champion students on the field seemed to pay much attention to the noise, but with an intuition that came with years of friendship, Stephanie spotted her friend's distraction and hurried over, "What?"

Alex blinked and looked to her friend, "I thought I heard shooting at the Fort."

Stephanie frowned, then turned her eyes back towards Preston and called: "There any rifle ranges between here and the Fort?"

The NCO was chatting with Strong, but stopped midsentence and answered immediately, "No, ma'am."

Looking back to Alex, Stephanie's frown only deepened, "Shots in the Fort could…"

She didn't get to finish.

The flash and fire was the first thing Alex saw — two bright explosions erupting simultaneously, visible over the trees to the west. Then the roar hit, and the ground shook, and pieces of debris were suddenly hurtling up into the air.

Alex's jaw dropped just as the bone-jarring thunder slammed into her, and everyone else in the field. It was a louder explosion than she'd ever heard in her life, and she was miles away.

Then she clearly made out the shape of a skycruiser engine as it hurtled through the air before dropping out of sight behind the trees again. A sheet of flame tore into the air after it landed — then more thunder.

No one could speak. No one knew what to say.

But part of Alex's mind managed to grasp what was happening, and those thoughts forced a single word out of her mouth: "Mom…"

Caralynne had not been sleeping — one rarely can with a migraine — but resting her eyes in the darkened stateroom had marginally reduced the anger of her pain. By the time George had an answer for her, she'd hopefully be in slightly better condition.

Then the ground bucked violently, and *George Tucker* jumped as though it had been hit by artillery. The only real noise she could hear inside her stateroom was that of metal twisting and groaning in the skycruiser's hull, but it was more than enough for the elder Lady Smith to realize something serious had happened.

They were too late.

Her head could pound all it wanted; Caralynne threw her legs out of bed and grabbed her coat and gun from the nearby chair as she hurried — staggered, really — out the door. Smoke was starting to billow into the corridor as she moved, and that was obviously not a good sign. She tried to ignore it as she moved up the hall, turning one corner, then the next towards the command deck.

The second corner revealed three of *George Tucker's* crew hurrying somewhere with a fire extinguisher, bellowing something to each other about the port engine and shrapnel. None of the men seemed to notice Caralynne as they passed — they had a singular duty to their ship.

As she kept pressing on, the sounds of twisting metal were soon overcome by the whine and hum of the skycruiser's engines firing up. Were the pilots trying to take off? Did that mean an attack?

It wasn't much further, and with all the effort she could muster, Caralynne hastened herself to Champion speed. Within seconds, she opened the command deck hatch and stepped through, then gritted her teeth against her migraine as the bright lights from the main windows stabbed at it.

Her eyes refocused. She was able to see Hong and Bogoraz working madly at their controls... and through the command deck windows, huge amounts of fire and smoke blotting out the afternoon sky.

"What... *what...?*" Caralynne tried to ask, but it was no good — even if the two officers heard her, they were much too busy to answer.

"Still nothing from the port engine," Hong's voice was cool, despite the haste with which his hands were moving.

"We'll go with one," Bogoraz answered with equal calm. "Full thrust, get us up."

The words were mechanical, but effective; *George Tucker* began to climb from the ground. It was unsteady compared to one of the skycruiser's usual takeoffs, but as the smoke began to blow away from the command deck windows, and the deck vibrated beneath her feet, Caralynne knew they were moving...

"Excuse me, M'Lady," one of the other flight officers was hurrying between panels, and Caralynne realized she was right in his path. She strode forward quickly, to get out of the way and get a better look.

"Get us to 10,000 and we'll orbit," Bogoraz continued his smooth orders, and Hong nodded.

As the ship started to find its feet in the air, Caralynne put a hand on the back of the Captain's chair and used it for stability as she leaned forward. There was still too much smoke obscuring the ground below to figure out what was happening.

"At least one of the American skycrusiers just blew up, M'Lady," Hong didn't make her wait. "Maybe both. No idea how."

Bogoraz then added: "We don't know how, but if it's an attack we're not staying on the ground. One engine is out, we think due to shrapnel, but we can fly without it."

"Good," Caralynne nodded, her mind truly not catching up to the implications of what was being said. Then something clicked: "Orbit towards the training fields. Alex is out there with the students."

"Yes, M'Lady," Hong nodded, and his hands danced over his control board.

"What the hell is that?" one of the Champion students was the first to blurt out the obvious question, but Alex didn't have an answer.

At least, she didn't think she did. Somehow she still spoke: "Explosions at the Fort. Looks like two skycruisers…"

As she automatically narrated the sight, her ears somehow began to pick out the sound of a skycruiser's engines, and then she watched one rise from between the pillars of flame… *between* the pillars, hopefully meaning it was *George Tucker*. Smoke was billowing out of a nasty gash on the ship's port side, but it was climbing determinedly… running from an attack?

"Are we under attack?" Preston asked the question urgently, but didn't wait for an answer as he turned back to his men, "Load up, *now!*"

He had one full company of infantry, and while the black men had limited experience, they had no choice but to rally to the defense of their base.

"Any other aircraft up there?" Stephanie was already turning and scanning the sky in different directions. Pillars of fire could mean bomb strikes, but there was no sign of attacking planes.

How would enemy aircraft have managed to get into this airspace anyway — the Navy and the Army patrolled the skies with Mustangs and Bearcats, planes that were years (if not decades) more advanced than anything a rival power could put into the air, thanks to the contributions of Saa technology.

"I don't see anything…" Alex answered her friend, turning

away from the Fort just long enough to scan the sky for any signs of intruders. Then she shifted her gaze back to the flames, and the skycruiser climbing above them. "No. It must have been from the ground... there was gunfire... an attack with explosives?"

She was piecing it together as best she could. Stephanie was processing with similar speed, and her next conclusion was the most pertinent one: "If someone got through security to blow two skycruisers, they might still be out here... that road is one way out of the Fort."

Remembering that fact from her conversations with Wells, the Lieutenant pointed at the frozen dirt path that had taken them to the field. It could prove important — a back way out for attackers... and a way for Preston's company to move in to support the base.

"We should get back immediately!"

That rather confident remark came not from a soldier, but from one of the Champion students — the *unarmed* Champion students. Of course, Alex shouldn't have been surprised that it was Randall, but she was so focused on trying to figure out what was happening, her more nuanced observational skills were on hold.

She hadn't seen him puff up — or noticed the look of eagerness on his face. Because, of course, here was an opportunity for him to prove himself.

"Wait," she made the order simple and direct, then turned to Stephanie. "This road is the back way out of the Fort?"

"So says our driver," her American friend confirmed. "And here we are, positioned to block it. Or... we can go in."

"We go *in*!" apparently Randall didn't understand the word 'wait'. Alex tried to ignore him while she considered the two options — be passive or chase into a maelstrom of fire...

Just to punctuate the thought, another explosion shook the ground and unleashed a hellish roar. Whether it was a new blast or a secondary explosion from one of the previous ones, she just couldn't tell...

"We'll go, you wait here!"

At first Alex didn't quite believe she'd heard that. Clearly it had been Randall's voice, but such defiant words had no place coming from a student. She turned as they started to sink in, but already the boy and a dozen of his friends were separating themselves from the group, heading back towards the Fort.

"What are you doing?" Constance was the first to call after them.

"Randall, get back here!" Alex hit him with the most authoritative yell she could manage while surprised.

He looked back at her, then shook his head and waved a dismissive hand before sprinting for the road. His friends went with him.

"Dammit," Alex slammed her palm into her thigh, then shook her head. "Idiot."

Perhaps that was too strong a reaction — perhaps him running towards the Fort was no different than her chasing Emily. But if anything, that just made it less intelligent.

"Every other student stay exactly where you are," Alex whirled on the rest of the group, and her own voice was suddenly like thunder. She then turned back to Stephanie and Strong, "Let's get a look at this road."

With a nod of agreement, Lieutenant Shylock waved to Preston, then her driver, "Sergeant, with us. Wells, bring the Jeep."

Together, they hurried up the slope to the road, the Jeep bouncing after them.

"Stabilizing at 10,000," Hong sounded slightly relieved to deliver that news, but the vibration running through *George Tucker's* hull prevented anyone feeling too reassured.

"Flight systems normal... but two is down and I can't get any response from the auto-starter. I'll get down there for a visual," one of the engineers to the rear of the command deck reported, and with a wave from Bogoraz, he departed at a jog.

Caralynne was still trying to stay out of the way, but she couldn't afford to withhold her questions: "Are we alright to stay in the air?"

The Flight Captain might have preferred not to have had to answer such basic questions, but he didn't sound impatient when he replied: "With one engine we are still fully flight capable, M'Lady."

"We just can't maneuver much," Hong added quickly. "Up, down, forwards — that's what we can do."

That still sounded like plenty... but the posh-cruise-liner feel was gone from *George Tucker*. Drifting eastward under half-power, the ship was clearly an instrument of war.

The road might have taken twenty minutes for an ordinary human to walk, but for a Champion to run it took barely any time at all. Randall and his team of seniors — all the best of his class, as far as he was concerned — were barely 200 yards from the base's outermost buildings when they slowed for the sound of approaching Jeeps.

Holding up his hand, Randall stopped his group as the pair of fast-moving machine-gun carriers hurried onto the frozen dirt road. Frowning at their haste, the Champion-in-training waved to stop them. The driver of the leading Jeep hit his brakes first, and as the vehicle skidded and drifted at an angle, the one behind nearly banged into it before they both ground to a halt.

All the men aboard the two Jeeps looked stern but anxious, so Randall figured they had to know what was happening. He asked: "What are the explosions? Are you securing the perimeter?"

He expected an answer immediately — sure he was a student, but he was a *Champion*, and these men appeared to be from the Champions Regiment. But instead of speaking, the men behind the two .30-caliber machine guns looked at each other, then glanced down at their Captain. That officer waved his hand over his head, and the gunners nodded.

Randall didn't understand. Then the shooting began.

Both .30-cals roared, streaming lead over his head, but he still couldn't comprehend what they were doing. His mouth worked to try to form words even as he heard screams from some of his classmates, and then he realized the men in the Jeeps were leveling Thompsons at him.

His heart started to pound — he could even hear it over the guns — and as the first Thompson lined up on his chest, instinct took over: he leapt up for safety.

The ceiling of the firebox cut him nearly in two.

Another unthinking Champion student was similarly killed, while the rest stayed down and darted left or right... running into walls of Thompson lead as they tried to breach the firebox walls.

Three made it into the ditch beside the road unharmed; four others got there with just wounds. But they were all helpless where they lay, and with a wave of his hand, the Captain directed both .30-cals to cross their bodies. The screaming did nothing to abate the flow of lead.

The Jeeps rolled along moments later.

CHAPTER XII

"I have a ground view now, M'Lady," Flight Sergeant Sol Barrister was one of *George Tucker's* command crew, and as he summoned the elder Lady Smith to the chair from which she'd previously called Jimmy Devlin, he pointed her to the screen that was now lit up with a magnified view of the ground beneath the ship.

"You pan around using these dials," the Flight Sergeant indicated the controls, and with a nod she settled in and started scanning the road leading towards the training field.

The two fast-moving Jeeps caught her attention immediately — they were running away from the base at high speed, and had the ground not been frozen they undoubtedly would have been churning up a great deal of dust.

Where had they come from? Caralynne took hold of the control knobs and moved the lens of the scope back towards Fort Eustice, looking for any sign of—

Red stood out on the frozen ground. A great deal of red. Dear God. At least a dozen dead… Champion students. Those Jeeps had just passed them, meaning they were chasing the killers, or they were themselves responsible. Either way, Caralynne knew where she needed to be.

Turning away from the screen, she couldn't control her volume as she yelled to Bogoraz, "There are two Jeeps running east, we have to get over them!"

The Flight Captain again probably had plenty else to worry about, but he remained calm — and better, he didn't complain, "Understood. This will be… bumpy…"

With that warning, Hong hit a switch and activated *George Tucker's* intercom: "This is Hong, we're about to get low on one engine. Secure anything breakable, including yourselves."

Sergeant Barrister dropped into another chair on the command deck, then belted himself in. Caralynne didn't have quite that luxury, so she got to her feet: "I'll be at the bow ramp. If you can get us stable at a hundred feet or less, I'll jump."

"M'Lady, I can guarantee you we *cannot* get stable at low altitude. We'll have to land," Bogoraz continued to sound impeccably calm. "I'll get you in front of those Jeeps, and we'll land."

It sounded like it would take longer, but the Flight Captain's voice was firm enough to convince Caralynne she had no choice. Her daughter was out there, but she'd have to look after herself until *George Tucker* could set down.

"Wells, get your Jeep up here, put it across the road," Stephanie called to the driver, and he nodded immediately, clearly trying to swallow his anxieties. The Jeep rolled up the embankment seconds later, leaving Stephanie, Strong, and Alex standing with Preston on the shoulder of the dirt track.

"So we'll have a block here," the Lieutenant repeated the conclusion of their quick discussion, and Alex nodded.

"Make sure no one gets past us this way, and then I'll go find that brat Randall," the Lady said sharply, looking in the direction of the Fort. She could have sworn she'd heard machine gun fire moments before, but there were so many secondary explosions at the base now, it was impossible to know.

Her preoccupations were different than Stephanie's; though the American girl had never held any real designs on becoming a proper soldier (her uniform was mainly a tool to keep her beside Alex), she knew now she was in charge.

And, strangely, the thought didn't quite panic her. Perhaps the lessons learned in August would pay off: "Preston, your best platoon should go into these woods, and your next-best platoon should get into those ones..." she gestured to the thick trees on the opposite side of the trail first, then to the woods alongside the training field.

The Company Sergeant simply nodded, "Ma'am."

"Your other two platoons need to look after the Champion students. Find somewhere safe for them all..."

"That thicket halfway along the base of the ridge, there," Strong suggested helpfully, pointing to a wide patch of trees and bushes that led into the woods on one side of the training field.

"Perfect," Stephanie agreed. "Make sure every man is ready to shoot, but they'll need to wait for orders — there could be a lot of panic, and we don't want any accidents."

She sounded like an officer — a proper officer, with combat experience — and as much as that might have surprised her, it reassured Company Sergeant Preston. Lieutenant Shylock was in command.

"Yes, ma'am!" he answered her with a nod, then turned back towards the field, where his men and the Champions were still waiting — all kneeling down on the cold ground, because standing up in the midst of explosions just seemed unwise. "Sergeant McCoy, take Second and Fourth to that thicket. Bill, Sam, get your men up here now!"

He was presumably giving the orders he needed to, and as he did Alex realized she needed to give directions to the students. She began to turn in their direction, and even spotted Constance, who had hurried up towards the road in anticipation of instructions... but the sound of two approaching Jeeps stopped her.

With all the men moving in the field, and the rumble of fires and explosions still sounding from the Fort, no one else seemed to notice, but Alex looked back down the road just in time to see the two vehicles round the corner at very high speed.

They both had machine guns mounted in their backs, and they were being driven by men in uniform, so there was no reason to expect either vehicle was dangerous to the group. But Alex felt the hairs on her neck start to rise, and she wasn't alone. Now that they were in sight, Stephanie and Strong both sensed it too.

Something... was wrong...

Unfortunately, none of them could put their finger on what until the first machine gun opened up.

Private Wells had finished putting his trusty Jeep across the road, blocking the way of the speeding gun-carriers, and was shifting out of gear when .30-caliber lead pounded through him. He didn't even know what killed him.

The roar, and the sounds of tearing metal, alerted anyone who hadn't been paying attention to the arrival of the fast-moving vehicles. In the field, men from 'C' Company raised their weapons, and Champion students tensed for action.

But the machine gun from the second Jeep cut loose, streaming lead over all their heads and forcing them down to the frozen ground. Even as it shot at the training field, the lead Jeep's gun traversed, its operator wanting to sweep the dirt road clear ahead of him.

Alex's hand had been on her Browning, and the pistol was suddenly out from under her coat. She could feel the air over her head starting to churn — she wasn't sure if there was lead up there already, but she knew jumping would be wrong. So she crouched low and started to run for the trees on the opposite side of the trail.

As she went, Stephanie raised her own pistol and moved in the opposite direction, back towards the training field. She had no time to aim, so she began simply point shooting — something she'd never do if she had the chance to be deliberate.

Strong moved more slowly, but the lack of speed had nothing to do with his age. His Thompson was immediately at his shoulder, and as his sights aligned with the Jeep, he exhaled and squeezed the trigger. He was still in the middle of the road — he just dropped to one knee to stay below the machine gun fire. His job was to protect his girls, and if that meant he had to be the obvious target, he'd do it without a thought. Literally.

Sergeant Preston was every inch the veteran Strong was — he'd fought savages and Hubrin, even been captured by the Hubrin alongside RSM Turner, and Alex's father. Now he was cool under the threat of fire, and he swung his beloved rifle to his shoulder with the ease of a veteran hunter.

He didn't even crouch; he just peered through the peep sight and fearlessly stood tall, aimed, fired.

The head of the driver of the lead Jeep received Preston's first shot — if anything, the Company Sergeant was a better marksman now than when he'd been a younger man. Strong's Thompson bursts crossed the man in that vehicle's passenger seat... a severe white man in a Captain's uniform, whose chest burst... and then the vehicle went out of control — the wheel cranked hard to the left, one of the tires rolled off its rim because of the violence, and it keeled over and tumbled to a stop.

To anyone watching, those two Sergeants in the middle of the road had stopped a speeding Jeep in seconds.

Unfortunately, there were *two* Jeeps.

Stephanie got to Constance's side just in time to dive into the young Champion-in-training. Had she taken any longer, a stream of lead from the second machine gun would have cut her down; the fire had lowered, no longer seeking to be the roof of a firebox, but instead determined to kill the men with guns in the field.

"Cover the students!" one of the Sergeants from 'C' Company ordered, since there was nowhere for them to hide. While Champions-in-training fled behind them, those brave men started to die as powerful fire punched through their bodies.

Stephanie and Constance were protected only by being on the reverse slope beside the road — too close and too low for the gun to depress to catch them. Strong was out of ammo; changing magazines, he dashed off the road and slid onto the grass not far from his Lieutenant.

Preston shot the two survivors in the first Jeep as both of them struggled for their guns, and kept firing at the second vehicle until his Garand pinged, ejecting its spent clip. Then he retreated towards Wells' mangled Jeep to try to reload as well, but four men were in the approaching vehicle, all but the machine-gunner aiming for him.

Stephanie still had half a magazine. Her heart was pounding, everything seemed in slow motion. She kept one hand on Constance's back, signaling for her to stay down in the frozen grass, and then adjusted the position of her feet so she could rise. If the second Jeep had to slow down to get around the wreck of the first...

Strong was thinking the same, and as he slammed home his fresh magazine, he concentrated on his breathing, instead of on the number of blessings he'd undoubtedly used up staying alive during the first five seconds of the shootout. He had more work to do.

The Jeep was coming... slowing...

And then it was tipping.

The pounding in Alex's chest was familiar. She knew it not only from her fight with Emily, but from every nightmare since. It bothered her. Really. But didn't stop her.

From the trees she watched the second Jeep begin to slow, and all its attention was towards the training field, where men were dying. As she listened to the cries of the wounded, she realized dead men made no sounds.

All the men in that damned Jeep were looking the other way, save for the driver, who was paying attention to the road. So Alex pointed her Browning at that man, aimed carefully, and shot him.

She was aware, in some way, that it was the first time she'd ever shot a man — indeed, killed a man.

Because of the roar of the .30-cal, the other men in the Jeep didn't hear the shot that killed their driver. And their focus on the training field meant they didn't see Alex either.

Still following her training not to go high into the air, young Lady Smith drove straight out of the woods, leading with her shoulder. She ignored the explosion of pain as she collided with the vehicle's front fender. She had hit it too high, but still with enough force for the Jeep to tip halfway. As it bounced back down onto its wheels, the gunner was knocked off balance.

Alex turned on him, ignoring the pain in her shoulder as she raised her Browning, aligned, fired twice — two rapid shots to make sure he was dead.

Strong and Stephanie burst from the slope on the opposite side of the road, and knowing they'd need clear lines of fire, Alex fell back and dropped into a low crouch. The two other men who'd been in the Jeep were turning in her direction — they could only process so many threats at one time, and she was the most recent they'd become aware of...

Tracking only one target wasn't exactly a mistake, just a limitation, Stephanie supposed. She too had never killed a man, but long ago Cameron Kard had told her one thing: when someone's life is on the line, you have to shoot. Worry about the rest later.

The man who was turning a rifle towards Alex received three bullets in his chest because of that advice. Stephanie stopped shooting and stood still, looking down her sights at him as he gurgled a last breath. She was aware of Mike Strong blasting the last gunman with his Thompson... and then she slowly lowered her pistol. Partway.

Silence settled over the ground. Even the cries of the men wounded in the field seemed to stop. Stephanie breathed once, and a second time, and let her gun drop to her side. Strong was beside her, his Thompson smoking hot as he used it to cover the Jeep. He was saying something to her, but she didn't hear it.

Preston came from the shot-up Jeep and the body of poor young Wells, his rifle also ready, and his eyes fixing on Stephanie and Strong. The young Lieutenant was aware of his attention, but didn't know what his expression meant.

And then Alex appeared on the other side, Browning down, her left arm bent as she rolled it at the shoulder. That made it seem as though she'd hurt herself, but her coat was bright white, and her expression was cool. She hurried around the front of the shot-up machine gun Jeep, stood beside her friends, and said the first thing that Stephanie actually seemed to hear: "Who the hell were they?"

No one had that answer. They were all dead.

George Tucker definitely gave the sensation of landing as it touched down on the training field. Waiting at the top of the ship's ramp, Caralynne was able to keep her balance, but the half-dozen crew members with her — two with guns, and the rest getting ready to check the damage from outside — all had to hold onto railings to stay on their feet.

There was no delay, though; as soon as the skycruiser landed, its ramp began to drop, and Caralynne leapt through the opening.

She'd watched from high altitude as her daughter stopped the Jeeps. It had been the most terrifying experience of the elder Lady Smith's life — more frightening than dying, or being revived. Even more terrifying than being delayed on the way to Signal Hill — at least then her daughter's danger had been unknown. Had she been forced to watch Alex be gunned down while she circled helplessly above...

But Alex had survived — had done amazingly well in fact — and now Caralynne had to see her.

The younger Lady Smith knew that her mother would come straight from the skycruiser, and want a hug. She was still on the road with Strong, Stephanie, and Preston, inspecting those they'd shot just minutes before, but she turned towards the landing ship just in time to feel her mother's reassuring embrace close around her.

"Mom," was literally all she could say.

"Twice," Caralynne gasped back, and they both knew what she meant — her lament that this was the second time she'd been just out of reach at the most dangerous moment.

"It's okay," Alex promised into her mother's shoulder, and then she let go her grip. It took Caralynne a few seconds more to do the same, but she did. Her daughter was safe. Thank God.

"I saw from above... you handled it perfectly," the elder Lady Smith shook her head quickly, then she glanced at the American

Sergeant who'd been with them. For some reason seeing who it was made her feel a bit better.

"M'Lady," he nodded. "Tell your husband I said hello."

It seemed an odd time for such a thing to be said, but Caralynne understood the meaning: Smith would know that the same man who'd saved him twice had now protected his daughter. Whatever the state of its new recruits, the veterans of the 25th United States Infantry were still excellent shoulders, and Caralynne was grateful. But she couldn't dwell on that; as Stephanie came close enough for a quick one-armed hug, and Strong nodded to her, Caralynne started to focus on the dead men before them.

They were all wearing the uniforms of the Champions Regiment.

"A group of students headed back towards the Fort before we could stop them," Alex said quietly. "Did you see if they ran into these guys?"

Caralynne blinked, then looked down at her daughter. The fact that she didn't respond immediately, or at all, was answer enough, but then she said, "Firebox... works."

Alex swallowed, closed her eyes, then shook her head, "What the hell is going on?"

"I think we need to find out," her mother answered, then looked back towards the field. "Let's get people aboard *George Tucker* in case we have to escape... then you and I will sneak back to the base for a look."

That sounded logical, and Caralynne said it with the sort of authority that Alex wished she possessed... perhaps did seem to possess when she wasn't thinking about it. Well, she realized, at least she wasn't crashing the way she had on Signal Hill. The benefit of four breakfasts, and two lunches...

"I should come with you," Constance Cormack sounded wary as she arrived beside the much more experienced people on the road, but her voice wasn't wavering. "I know that base better than you do... I can help..."

She made a good point. With a glance to her mother, and a slight nod of endorsement, Alex supported the idea. Caralynne took a breath and agreed, "Alright. Just you... we'll get you a gun. Everyone else secure this area, in case more comes our way."

With that direction, everyone moved off the road, leaving behind three shot-up Jeeps and nine dead men.

CHAPTER XIII

They purposely avoided Randall and the dead students on the way in — both because they didn't want to see the carnage, and because there was no time to waste. Led by Constance, who seemed more comfortable now because she was armed and doing something useful, the trio of Champions made their way into Fort Eustice.

The whole base appeared to be on fire.

"The arsenal and the fuel depot both went up," Constance had to yell to be heard over the rumbling, but as she pointed to two pillars of smoke she helped clarify the devastation.

Men were running in all directions, without apparent leadership or clear purpose. Black or white, none of the soldiers or instructors from the Institute seemed to know what to do. The fires were spreading, chaos reigned... if this was the prelude to an attack, there seemed no hope.

As the trio proceeded towards Headquarters, hoping to find Colonel Adams, they came upon the skycruiser field... found the craters where the two American ships had been.

"Holy God," Alex didn't moderate her reaction. The blast sites looked like nothing she'd ever seen, and the craters had to be four or five yards deep. "How did *George* survive between those two?"

Caralynne didn't know — she could only credit the quality of Saa construction. But the fact that the Newfoundland skycruiser did survive led to one conclusion: "It rules out the possibility that one was hit and set off the other. Someone specifically targeted those two... must have used explosives. It wasn't an air attack."

As if to emphasize that point, two planes slashed by overhead — Bearcats from the nearby Naval air station must have finally arrived to provide cover. Whether they had been summoned or simply responded to the evidence of the fires, it was impossible to know.

"We should keep moving," Alex finally said, drawing a nod from her mother. They set off again. Headquarters wasn't far.

Vanier Cross simply didn't understand. He was in line behind Fischer as men from the Champions Regiment herded them down the steps from Headquarters, but all around them — in every direction — were fires. They'd heard thunder from inside their basement office... the ground had shook... but beyond that they'd been cloistered until white soldiers burst into the room and ordered them to follow.

Now... now the world was on fire.

"Jesus Christ," Fischer could barely keep his breath. "Were we bombed...?"

One of the Champions Regiment men nearby shook his head, "This all was done by someone on the ground, Captain."

Vanier felt ill. The breach in the screen... that registry overwrite... had been hiding *this*? He felt the urge to hurry off into the chaos — to find someone he could help, to put out a fire... to seek out Constance... but though the men from the Champions Regiment were being mostly polite, the Corporal got the distinct sense that they wouldn't allow any man to run.

Confirming that sentiment was Major Travis, who Vanier quickly spotted at the base of the stairs. The officer had a pistol in hand, and was waiting beside a big army truck — one large enough for all ten of the screen operators.

Looking around for a familiar face — Adams, RSM Turner, anyone — Vanier was quickly disappointed. He was going to be taken away, held somewhere while they sought answers. It was a cold realization, and as he finished descending the stairs and found himself near Travis, his unease must have been clear on his face.

The white Major stared at the black Corporal for a second, then nodded to one of his men, "Get them loaded up, Sergeant."

"Sir! Come on, gentlemen, we need to get out of here..." the soldier continued to be reasonably cordial, but the shock of the burning all around was keeping some of the men from moving.

And then there was another interruption.

"Vanier!"

It was Constance's voice, thank God, and before any of the men guarding the screen team could catch sight of her, the young

American Champion-in-training had blurred between them and thrown her arms around the Corporal. It didn't matter who could see; Vanier had to hug back as soon as he felt her.

Major Travis held up his hand to stop his men reacting, and watched impassively for a moment as the youngsters embraced. It was impossible to discern his thoughts from his expression, and irrelevant; more pressing matters appeared right behind the young American.

"What's going on here, Major?" Caralynne slowed to a visible pace with her pistol down at her side, and Alex appeared behind her mother, then immediately stepped far out to one side so she could better cover the dozen Champions Regiment soldiers she was facing.

Men wearing the same flashes as those from the Jeep. Her heart rate began to climb again, and she kept her Browning at the ready.

Turning to the new arrivals, Travis remained cool as ever, "I'm trying to get these men out of here before something else blows. Have you seen Adams anywhere? I sent for him but he never arrived, and then things started exploding."

It was more than Caralynne expected the man to say, and it did nothing to defuse her suspicions, "You know that eight men wearing uniforms from your regiment just killed a dozen Champion students, and seven men from the 25th?"

There was no way Travis could have known that — unless he was involved — and his genuine-seeming surprise was reflected in the seconds it took for him to respond, "What? Dammit."

The first emotion Caralynne or Alex had seen from the man came as he pounded his fist into the fender of the truck he stood beside. He then looked knowingly at his Sergeant, who wore a grave expression, "That's where they went."

"Were they in Jeeps with .30-cals?" the Major asked, shaking his head.

"They were," Caralynne answered, though she wasn't completely convinced by the man's apparent anger.

Whether she believed it or not, Travis persisted, "We found equipment missing, and two Jeeps. Dammit all. A dozen students, you said?"

"And seven men killed from 'C' Company. Eleven wounded," Alex added, her words sharp. "And you're surprised by this?"

Travis didn't catch her implication immediately, but when it sank in he blinked, then looked from Caralynne to Alex and back, "You're…"

He stopped himself, and it looked like that took effort. His eyes went back to his Sergeant, and Alex could see that man nodding very subtly to his men. It was warning enough: she raised her Browning and trained it on the Major.

"You might not want to have your men try anything feisty," she said coolly, and Travis met her glare with a cool stare, before looking back to Caralynne.

"These men here are from my regiment, and they're the only ones I can trust right now. We're going to get these screen operators to some place safe, because one of them either did all this, or can help us find who did. And then we're going to get reinforcements to put these fires out, and find Adams. That's what we're going to do, unless you stop us."

He sounded firm, and that basically meant they were in a standoff. Caralynne hadn't raised her pistol, but she knew Alex had her covered, and now Constance was stepping back from Vanier, lifting her borrowed Browning as well.

"We have no reason to trust you," Caralynne's observation was direct.

Travis could only shake his head, "I can't help that. But I won't have my men shoot at you if you try to stop us, because that's the opposite of our job. We *protect* Champions. Which is why I'm going to suggest something else."

Alex kept her eyes moving between the soldiers, who were watching her with their weapons down. They didn't look to her like the killers she'd helped stop on the road — the longer she watched their faces, the more and more they looked like honest men. But that meant nothing…

"I have no organization here. I don't know where the 25th is. I can't protect the rest of the Champion students on this base. You have your skycruiser flying? You get all the students aboard it and you get them to Newfoundland. Make sure they're safe. Because if this is just the first attack, I can't protect them."

Caralynne blinked — the suggestion hadn't occurred to her, and it disrupted her train of thought. She looked quickly to her daughter, and Alex's eyebrows were up. Then she looked to the men from the screen room, most of whom seem terrified.

"If we're taking the students, why not them too? We have more resources to secure them than you do right now."

A good question, but Travis seemed to have an answer. Moving slowly — obviously — he stepped closer to the elder Lady Smith, then lowered his voice, "And if one of them is responsible for all this... for the explosion of our skycruisers? You want to risk taking him back to your base?"

A very good answer. Caralynne still couldn't read Major Travis, but the man was talking sense. She paused for a few seconds, forced her still pain-riddled mind to reconsider what he was saying, and then nodded, "Fine. Go."

Alex lowered her pistol immediately — to the apparent relief of the soldiers she'd been covering — but Constance was less convinced, "But... I can vouch for Vanier. Can we take him?"

It was a plea that cut into Caralynne — clearly the girl cared for the black Corporal — but as she looked to Alex, she knew it was too much of a risk. Perhaps he was the culprit, it was impossible to know. For now, the rest of the students had to be the priority.

"No..." the elder Lady Smith said slowly. "I'm sorry, but not now."

Constance bit her lip, but held her tongue — she clearly wasn't used to this sort of moment.

"It's okay," Vanier tried to help matters. "Get the kids to safety, I'll see you when things get settled..."

With that, Travis nodded to his men. They began calling politely for the screen operators to move, Vanier among them. With a last nod to Lady Caralynne, the Major then climbed up into the truck's cab.

Constance stood and watched as her big brother was taken away. Moving up alongside the young American, Alex pocketed her Browning so she could put one arm around the student's shoulder.

"You know how we get cake for lunch?" the white-coated Lady asked quietly, and Constance closed her eyes before Alex continued: "When we're not doing that, sometimes we're doing *this*. I wasn't lying about the nightmares."

As the men finished climbing into the truck and the back was pulled up, the engine switched on. Travis looked out his window one more time, nodded to Caralynne, and then the vehicle rolled off — going rather fast as it headed for the main gate.

Constance and Alex watched it go, and as it turned away Vanier Cross was visible through the open back flap. He waved to Constance, and she watched until he was out of sight.

For a moment, then, she just stood there silently, and Alex and Caralynne allowed her that pause. Then they began to discuss their next problem: whether to bring the Champions to the skycruiser, or the skycruiser to the Champions. They'd spend nearly an hour moving people, while all around them, a leaderless Fort Eustice burned.

No one knew where Colonel Adams was. No one knew he had died.

EPILOGUE

Champions-in-training, most of them terrified, were crammed into every compartment aboard *George Tucker*. With only one engine functioning, carrying so many people was less than ideal, but Flight Captain Bogoraz hadn't complained — he'd simply nodded and said, "It will be bumpy, but we will get home."

Now, after three choppy hours in the sky, they were most of the way to Newfoundland, where Lord Jimmy's Special Service Regiment and the Royal Newfoundland Regiment, were locking down Jimmystown for the arrival. Bearcats from the United States Naval Air Corps had escorted *George Tucker* much of the way; now RAF Spitfires from Torbay Airport had taken over.

Sitting at one of the tables in the skycruiser's dining room, Alex watched those camouflaged planes flying elegantly alongside, their formations having no trouble keeping up with the wounded ship. It was some comfort.

With her at the table were Stephanie and Strong, and both were silent as they stared at the cups of tea the galley had provided. Alex looked from the planes beyond the window to her two friends, then down at the full cup of tea that was sitting in front of her. She didn't even like tea — she didn't know why she'd let the cook pour it for her.

She wanted to say something — wanted to speak in recognition of what had happened. She had, for instance, shot two men. Stephanie had shot one. They'd never killed before today, but now they each had deaths on their conscience.

Were they supposed to feel guilty? Did they feel anything at all? Alex didn't know, because it was too soon. But she hadn't crashed, or gone all wobbly after the shooting. That seemed like... progress.

Strong had been a real hero, as usual, by shooting up that

first Jeep. And Stephanie had been so good as a leader, giving 'C' Company some certainty at a very uncertain moment.

Much they could discuss, and yet Alex had no words at all. She sat in silence, looking out at the Spitfires, then back at her tea. She wondered if she'd have new nightmares, like she and Stephanie had callously joked about the night before. She wondered how many dead had been left behind, and whether Adams was among them. She wondered if Constance would see her handsome black boy again, or if Travis was a villain.

So many questions left unanswered, both inward-looking and outward-focused, and Alex had no idea where to begin. Eventually, she looked to Strong, and found enough air in her lungs to ask, "What do we do now, Mike? We haven't crashed."

The Sergeant had been lost in his own thoughts, but he blinked and looked up, "I'll see if they still have cake."

He said it with no humor, nor hunger. It was just something to do that was, in his estimation, better than asking for a bottle of whiskey. As he left the table, Alex looked to Stephanie, and the girls sighed.

"I think I'm going to sleep tonight," the young white-coated Lady said, and Stephanie closed her eyes and shook her head.

"Don't tempt fate."

They'd see soon enough, for *George Tucker* was staggering home, and once it arrived, a different sort of chaos would begin.

THE CHAMPIONS OF 1941   PART 2
GRAND BANKS
KENNETH TAM

PROLOGUE

The giant rock was icy in places, but Lady Alex Smith was managing to keep her balance as she stood (rather dramatically) upon it. Powerful gusts coming off the Atlantic certainly would have loved to knock her from her perch, but firmly planted as she was, she wasn't going to be easy to move — she was determined to retain her excellent vantage point, so she could watch the arrival of Britain's naval might.

"See them?" the question came from Smith, Alex's father, who had accompanied her up the trail to the top of one of the headlands near Jimmystown. He was sitting atop a borrowed horse, a little ways behind the rock and partly out of the wind. The horse didn't seem terribly pleased by the cold — the gusts were positively freezing — but Smith was coping fine. His life on the new world had rarely included low temperatures, but after two decades on the island of Newfoundland, his body had adapted.

His daughter did better than simply cope; she positively thrived. Standing on the rock, her white coat fully buttoned and her hair blowing behind her, she reminded Smith of her mother. She was also every inch the angel all fathers know their daughters to be.

Now she raised a hand to shade her eyes — both against the brightness of the afternoon and the wind — then shook her head, "I think they're coming out of the fog on the horizon, but I can't tell for sure."

It seemed to Smith like she was trying to sound more excited than she was, and that was fine. Watching the arrival of these ships would have been exciting to her a month ago... and even more exciting a year ago. But now her fascination with the great pieces of machinery had been tempered.

A few weeks prior, she'd become a killer of men, and Smith

figured that would give anyone pause.

Though he hadn't been in Virginia during the attack on Fort Eustice, he'd been fully briefed. He'd seen footage of the craters, the burned-out buildings, and the murdered Champion students. He'd watched the playback captured by the wounded skycruiser *George Tucker*, which showed his daughter and her friend shooting down killers in Jeeps.

They'd done well, Smith knew... but they had killed. That meant they had questions about themselves — the sort of natural questions good people had to ask after doing such things.

And neither Stephanie nor Alex was asking those questions of anyone other than themselves.

Smith remembered what that was like. He'd been forced to kill savages on the new world from an early age, and then some supposedly civilized men too. Outlaws mainly — the sort of rogues who had gone to the Pacifica Territory to avoid the law, to prove themselves tough, to dominate other people so they could feel powerful.

But when Smith first shot one of those men, he'd wondered about himself — mainly because it had been easy. He knew men who liked killing, saw how some of them did it for no reason, and wondered if he was like them, or could be.

It hadn't been an easy question for him, and he now recognized the same worries in his daughter. She wasn't lamenting what she'd done — wasn't playing herself as some sort of victim, because she thought that'd be silly when she'd survived again.

And yet, she'd killed people without hesitation. It had been the right thing to do, and she felt no guilt... but that very lack of ambiguity made her uncomfortable. If she could kill these men, could she kill anyone?

Smith didn't doubt his daughter would find her answers. Time would pass, she'd experience more difficult days, and she'd realize that the ease with which she'd squeezed the trigger in Virginia had been tied directly to the circumstances. She was no cold-blooded killer. Others were, but not her.

She was like her mother, and Smith was proud.

Of course, all his certainty about Alex was left unspoken, because Smith was a man of few words. Sometimes he regretted that, figuring better men would have said reassuring things more regularly. But he didn't always know what to say, so on days like this he watched carefully, paid attention, and would answer a question if asked. His presence, he hoped, was a reassurance.

It was.

Alex didn't feel at all cold as she stood atop her rock. That was partly because her coat was buttoned up all the way, and partly because she was a Champion and therefore largely immune to these temperatures. Mostly, though, it was because her dad was with her.

When she'd been younger, she and her father had always come up to this headland, and this rock in particular, to watch big ships approach the Narrows. Now that the Special Service Squadron was due, repeating the routine was important.

She was still her father's daughter. That was one anchor she could always count on.

She had no idea what she'd do if she ever lost him, or her mother. Perhaps lacking such parents was the reason Emily had gone so wrong, and the reason so many other Champions could be edgy.

Alex could hardly imagine what that would be like, and certainly didn't want to think of the absolute reality that one day she'd lose her parents. That event would be... had to be... a long way in the future.

Long after she'd figured herself out, killer whitecoat that she was.

She felt very silly for being uneasy about doing what she'd done in Virginia. Killing two men in a Jeep who were trying to murder Champions-in-training and soldiers was both justified and her responsibility.

But it had been so easy. Perhaps harder in the moment than she remembered looking back, but if she could already kill with that sort of certainty, what would the future hold?

It would have been better, perhaps, if she'd been having nightmares about it... or even having her old nightmares about Emily... but instead she was sleeping soundly. It was as though her mind simply wasn't shocked by carnage any more. And that really had to make her wonder; if those sorts of days became normal, would she end up like Emily?

Deep dark questions, and as Alex realized they were preoccupying her, she shook her head. This needed to stop, but she wasn't sure how or when it would.

Surely the ships would appear soon to distract her — the

might of the Royal Navy was coming to Newfoundland for a special summit, and Alex wanted to see the great ships when they arrived off St. John's. She'd always loved big ships, because they made even her abilities seem somewhat small. She'd once been aboard HMS *Queen Elizabeth*, and that battleship had been so massive, so overtly powerful, that it had filled her with wonder.

Unlike the skycruisers, big ships from the Royal Navy were all built by men. Vessels like *George Tucker* made everything seem easy (when they were undamaged), but ships like *Queen Elizabeth* wrestled with the mighty forces of nature every day. They weren't above the storms; they drove fearlessly through them. They were awesome in every sense of the word.

And the ships due today were even grander than *Queen Elizabeth*, if that was possible. The Royal Navy's Special Service Squadron was carrying the British Prime Minister, Lord Halifax, and the fifteen-ship formation was reputed to include the mighty aircraft carrier *Ark Royal*, the battlecruiser *Rodney*, and of course, His Majesty's Ship *Hood*.

Hood happened to be, by reputation and every photo Alex had ever seen, the most beautiful warship *ever*. She was the flagship of the Royal Navy — the pride and joy — and exceedingly powerful to boot.

Alex wanted to see all these ships as they reached Newfoundland... but as was often the case, the mists of the sea were getting in the way.

"I think there's more fog rolling in," she said after a while, frowning and looking down at her father. "Maybe we should leave and see them another day?"

Ten years earlier, Smith's daughter would have refused to give up until she'd spotted what she'd come to see, or until night had made seeing it impossible. Her more reasonable stance now was probably wise, but the former-drifter didn't accede to it, "We can sit a spell longer."

"You sure?" she asked, and he could sense that she wasn't just wondering if he was cold, or bored, but whether she wanted to be there herself. It was one of those double-meaning questions that the former-drifter had become accustomed to since starting a family, and now he shifted slightly in his saddle before responding.

"I'm still here, whatever you want, and whoever you think you are," he replied. "You're always my daughter."

Alex was caught off guard by the answer to the question she technically hadn't asked. She shouldn't have been — ask a loaded question, get a loaded answer — but she was so surprised she looked away. Fortunately the wind was sharp enough that it was making her eyes water anyway.

She was glad she'd come up to the clearing with her father, even if they couldn't see a damned thing. It was an important place to her, and one that somehow proved that, while she wasn't a child anymore, she was still her father's daughter. Having such an anchor made it easier to put other things in context.

Just as she thought that, and with the sort of timing that was slightly unnerving, the sun came out from behind a bright cloud and shot a beam of (relative) warmth at both of them. Narrowing her eyes, she managed to look back at her dad, "Did you time what you said to go with the sunlight?"

Smith had noticed the strange timing of the cloud too, but he was no good at fibbing, "No."

Choosing to hear the word 'yes' instead, Alex smiled at her dad, "You're the best."

He knew better than to start an argument, so he simply shrugged his shoulders, then changed the subject, "I see ships."

The sunlight was spreading fast over the headland and the water beyond — the speed of weather changes in Newfoundland was legendary — and sure enough, as the fog lifted, a flotilla of great gray leviathans appeared in the water, still miles out to sea. Mighty ships, beautiful ships, riding the choppy waves with majestic power.

Alex smiled and then started rocking up onto the balls of her feet to wave to them. They were too far out to have a chance of seeing her, especially since her white coat caused her to blend into the snow-covered trees that backed the clearing, but...

She shouldn't have rocked up onto the balls of her feet.

Alex knew this boulder well — she'd been climbing it for years. But usually she didn't get atop it in winter, and she'd momentarily forgotten the patches of ice that had tucked into its crags.

The next thing she knew she was on her back, looking up at the sky, with an explosion of fine snow particles — blown into the air by her landing — flurrying down on her. She lay there for a second, not sure if she should be embarrassed or not, and then her father edged his horse sideways so he could lean out of the saddle and into her line of sight.

"Making a snow angel?"

That sounded like a workable excuse, so she nodded, "That's exactly what I'll tell people. Do you think anyone on the ships would have seen me fall over?"

Smith reached up and adjusted his hat, "Probably not."

"Good," she said. "But if they did…"

"Snow angel," Smith confirmed. "Intentional."

Crisis averted, and with good news for everyone: Lady Alex Smith was still at least a little awkward. Probably more than a little.

As she lay there in the snow and felt some absurd relief at that revelation, the monster that had been watching from the woods shook his head. Of course Alex was still herself — she hadn't suffered, or done, half the horrible things that could poison her.

Thinking that, the watcher turned his gaze knowingly on Smith. Neither the former-drifter, nor the whitecoat, noticed the attention.

CHAPTER I

Sitting on the very northern edge of Jimmystown, the massive metal-and-concrete hospitality warehouse was tucked out of sight, and ignored by just about all visitors to the post. Much more interesting were the Saa residences, where dragons stayed when posted to the base. Those were nearby — just through a stand of trees — and as such, were the destination that drew the attention of visitors.

That diversion was, of course, by design: no one was supposed to go into the hospitality warehouse. Stephanie Shylock didn't know exactly who had come up with said scheme — whether it had been Lord James Devlin, or Sass (the dragon liaison, and Colonel in the Special Service Regiment), or Caralynne, or even Smith. It could have been any of them.

But whoever had come up with it, they'd clearly been smart... because it worked.

"I'm really sorry, Lieutenant, but sneaking iced cream isn't going to help in any way," Champion-in-training Constance Cormack was doing her best to be polite as Stephanie led her up a narrow, snow-covered trail towards the nondescript warehouse.

"You keep saying 'Lieutenant' when you try to say Stephanie," the young American officer didn't directly answer the Champion's comment, and didn't slow down either.

"I don't see what good this is doing, though..." Constance sounded altogether too defeated for Stephanie's liking, but she supposed she was in no position to judge the girl.

The past few weeks had been difficult on many of the students rescued from the Robinson Institute; they had been given no notice, escaped with only the clothes on their backs, and many of them had left friends behind.

In Constance's case, that 'friend' happened to be one of the men at the center of the mystery about what had happened on the base — the Saa screen technician Vanier Cross, whose exact whereabouts were still unclear. Major Sheldon Travis reportedly had all the technicians hidden somewhere, but no one was sure for what specific reason, or for how long.

So while some of the American students had relished the adventure (or at the very least, change of scenery) that came with a temporary move to the Lady Emily Academy, Constance's anxieties had only grown. And since she'd proved to Alex that she was perhaps one to watch, and then kept her head as a Champion should during the attack, it seemed right to bend some of the rules to lessen her fears.

Well, 'lessen' might be the wrong word. Respect them, at least.

"You must have been a nightmare at Christmas," Stephanie looked back at the younger girl with that admonishment. "Always trying to spoil your presents."

"My mother didn't really believe in presents," Constance replied, sounding even more forlorn.

"Really?" Stephanie couldn't contain her surprise. "My godfather always gave me ammo for Christmas…"

That made Constance frown — apparently a little girl getting bullets under the tree wasn't normal — but Stephanie wasn't self-conscious about her upbringing. She just shrugged and led on, until they finally reached the warehouse's side door. It was a modest entrance, looking a bit dilapidated and worn. Interestingly, there was no sentry — no one to stop iced cream thieves.

Constance's frown deepened, "No one guards your stores?"

Stephanie just shook her head, "Hang on a minute, don't make me ruin this with exposition."

She then reached out and knocked three times on the metal door — then another three times. That done, she looked up at a hemisphere of black glass that was projecting out of the wall, and batted her eyelids shamelessly.

Constance looked up at the half-orb, then down, "I don't… what's that thing?"

"Just wait," Stephanie held up a hand, trying not to be dismissive. Surprises were tough when the surprise-ees were inquisitive.

The door let out an unexpected hiss, and then there was a popping sound as its seal broke and it opened. Stephanie took hold of the handle and swung it aside, then nodded for Constance to follow her in. Confused but not reluctant, the American Champion-in-training followed, and found herself in a narrow, short corridor with a door at the other end.

That door stayed shut... until the outer one closed behind Constance. The young American looked back at that thudding noise, then heard another hiss, and then the inside door opened more softly... just in time for a terse voice to sound.

"I cannot believe I let you talk me into this," George Devlin confronted Stephanie, and as the American Lieutenant advanced towards the son of the Viscount who was still smitten with her, she smiled irresistibly.

"Of course you can believe it."

George rolled his eyes, "Yes, I know *you* can. I don't know why I even pretend to resist anymore..."

His words trailed off as she stepped past him and he caught his first sight of Constance. He blinked just once, before becoming serious as she emerged from the airlock, "Good day, Miss Cormack. I'm George Devlin, with the Hospitality Department."

That didn't help Constance much at all; she emerged into a giant dark warehouse that seemed packed with thousands of nondescript crates, some stacked all the way up to its very high ceiling. She looked up, dragged her eyes across them all, and then looked down at George, who stood rather dapperly-dressed in a double-breasted navy blue suit, with gold buttons done up.

She supposed he sort of looked like a butler... or maybe a noir detective. Obviously the Newfoundlanders took hospitality seriously.

"I... um. Hello. I think we're here to steal provisions," she replied honestly, and as George's eyebrow climbed and he turned a disapproving stare against Stephanie, the American Champion-in-training almost smiled.

She didn't quite know why, but she did.

Stopping himself short of being too abrupt with Stephanie, the young hospitality man shook his head, "Then just follow me."

Stephanie realized that perhaps she had been pushing it, so as she fell into step alongside the frustrated Mister Devlin, and waved for Constance to follow, she explained their supposed mission: "George is smuggling us in to the coolest place on this base. It probably won't make you worry less, but it might make you feel better."

Looking around at the stacks of crates, Constance could only assume her chaperone meant they were going to the freezer — an idea that fit with their next stop: a large freight elevator built into a nearby concrete wall.

Leading the way, George opened the gate on the lift, then stood aside, "In."

He wasn't being very cordial to Stephanie, but when Constance followed, he nodded pleasantly to her. Actually, it was almost a bow, "M'Lady."

The word drew Stephanie's eyebrow upward, because it didn't make sense — Constance was still in training, and even once she picked her coat, the Americans didn't give their Champions titles. Lords and Ladies were too monarchist for the stars and stripes.

But George seemed otherwise unflapped, so as he stepped into the lift and closed the gate, cranking a rather rickety-seeming lever to start the hoist going down, she set that aside. Constance did too — she was mainly just wondering what flavor iced cream she was going to get. Because evidently she'd have to choose one to be polite...

They went down further than the American guest was expecting — the warehouse's lower level obviously had high ceilings. Once the lift stopped, and George pulled aside the gate, Constance was greeted by another nondescript corridor, which she followed the young Devlin into.

"How much trouble if we're caught?" Constance asked the question a bit more tentatively than she meant to, but George didn't answer.

Instead he opened the door at the end of the short corridor, and stepped through so he could hold it open. Stephanie slowed so that their guest could enter first, and unsure of what to expect, Miss Cormack went in...

Into a future world unlike anything she'd ever imagined.

Everything was constructed of brushed metal, but because the lighting was low and the screens glowed blue light, the room almost felt like it was under water. An undersea cavern fully the size of the warehouse above it, and on every wall, as far as she could see, were Saa screens.

George had moved to one side to allow his guests to take in the sight. He was just a few yards away from his desk — the station that allowed him to work in this futuristic marvel — and he was admittedly excited to be showing it off to an impressive newcomer... even if he had dual agendas.

"This is... some kind of hospitality," Constance wasn't quite speechless, but there was no mistaking the awe in her voice.

"My department... well, it's my mother and me... we look after hospitality for the Saa when they visit. This is their headquarters on Earth. I just get to keep the place running while they're away," George explained.

"And use its screens for the betterment of humanity," Stephanie added for him, feeling it wise to give him due credit in this particular moment.

Constance's eyebrows were at the very top of her head, though she just managed to keep her jaw from falling: "Um. Wow. Who's your mom?"

"The Lady Anne Devlin," Stephanie replied.

"Me," the Lady Anne Devlin said at the very same time, so her answer was stepped on by Stephanie — who hadn't seen her, and certainly hadn't expected her to be personally present for this moment.

She supposed it made sense, though; security was of paramount importance after the events in Virginia, and even though Constance was easily the most-trusted of the students who had come from that school — and was thus allowed to see this place — precautions were being taken.

"Oh no, we're really not supposed to be here, are we? I thought we were sneaking in for iced cream..." Constance sounded flustered, but as Anne emerged from a shadowy office beside the door, the Lady — the Viscountess of the Grasslands, who had married Lord James on a whim when he was a Lieutenant and she was a maid — smiled reassuringly.

"I'm sorry to say we don't have iced cream. But George and I have talked about your situation, and that of your Corporal Cross. Stephanie, Alex, and Caralynne all thought you'd earned the right to know more about what we're doing. So we're putting a lot of trust in you."

As Constance's jaw finally dropped, and a whole new layer of concern crossed her brow, Anne stepped right up to the young Champion student and didn't help matters: "I've heard the kids say 'no pressure'. I'm afraid this is the opposite of that. Big pressure. You *must* keep everything about this place secret, and speak of it with no one beyond us here, my husband, or Alex and Sergeant Strong. You understand?"

Constance blinked, then nodded, then shook her head, then asked: "Who's your husband?"

Anne's smile grew, "Lord Jimmy Devlin, the Viscount of the Grasslands."

"Oh," Constance answered. Fair to say she was wide-eyed. "Okay, so I *can* tell him?"

"Yes," Anne confirmed.

That led to a pause, as Constance tried to process everything, and everyone else watched. Fortunately, George had been raised a gentleman, and he approached after the silence had endured long enough, "Join me at my desk, Miss Cormack? I've been working on the problem your friend Corporal Cross detected. Hopefully we'll be able to help him and your officers with their investigation."

Constance's mind focused quickly as those words reached her. With a nod, she followed George to his desk, where a second chair had been placed for her. They both settled down, and then in a display of magical, elegant movement, a few of the screens — each of them the size of a movie theatre's feature screen — came alive with text and images.

It was incredible to watch, and Stephanie took it all in with a smile. The stuff George got to work on every single day was incredible...

"I'm so sorry," Constance said to him after a few seconds. "I... I thought you were just some kind of... butler. I mean, a handsome butler. But I didn't realize... I mean, you do a really good job keeping this place secret."

George glanced at the American Champion, "I'm just going to say 'thanks' for everything you just said."

"I appreciate your diplomacy," she smiled. "You're good with these screens... I mean, you really know how to use them..."

"When the Saa are here, we have to work cheek-by-jowl, so it's important I know what I'm about," he replied, managing to sound both modest and gallant.

Her question in reply was predictable: "Do dragons have jowls?"

Stephanie heard that, then frowned... but before she could think too much on whether the American Champion was, in fact, trying to flirt with George Devlin, Lady Anne touched her arm.

"We should wait in my office," the Viscountess said, and with only a single look back as Constance laughed delightfully at George's answer, Stephanie followed.

CHAPTER II

Jimmy Devlin was late. It was his own fault — Parsons had told him to leave early because of the snow on Major's Path, but he'd figured his Land Rover could handle it. He was right, of course — the truck had done just fine. The car in the ditch halfway to the airport, however, hadn't fared as well, so Jimmy stopped and helped tow the two-wheel-drive vehicle back onto the road. Viscount or not, he was still a Newfoundlander, and no b'y would leave someone stranded on a road in winter if he could help it.

And that made him late.

As he sped dangerously through the entrance to the military half of Torbay Airport, he could see that the DC-3 had landed, and taxied, and that a party of men in suits was waiting on the snow-covered tarmac. Fortunately, they didn't look too cold yet.

Jimmy raised a hand to wave to the new arrivals, but then he realized he was driving a bit too fast. He slammed on the Land Rover's brakes, then turned the wheel... and ended up skidding sideways towards the guests, his tires kicking up a temporary blizzard.

As he slid to a stop, the Viscount of the Grasslands smiled sheepishly and raised his hand for another wave, "Morning, Prime Minister."

Though the Canadian Prime Minister's staff had retreated at the sight of the sliding truck, and the snow shower that it kicked up, the Premier (as the British sometimes called their Prime Ministers) simply stood with folded arms, and a cool look on his face.

"Good morning, Viscount of the Grasslands."

Jimmy smiled at the sardonic tone, and satisfied that his Land Rover had stopped, he hopped out with the engine still running, "Sorry I'm late, had to pull someone out of the ditch."

The PM raised an eyebrow, "Is that because you were driving

and they swerved into the ditch to avoid you?"

"Hand to God, I found them there," the Lord raised his hand towards the sky, before lowering it and sticking it out in front so the Canadian — Quebecker, strictly speaking — could take it.

Take it he did, and with a laugh, Alain Lapointe shook his head, "You are a good liar, Jimmy."

"Says the politician," Devlin grinned.

Alain Lapointe, of course, had been the Colonel of the Voltigeur Regiment during the Hubrin War, and along with his men had joined Waller's charge into the alien capital on the new world. He'd been grazed by a lightning blast — technically, a 'pulse cannon' blast, though Jimmy still wasn't comfortable with the new vernacular — and that meant his left hand was partially immobile. But that didn't slow him down. He'd come back to Canada a war hero, and was now approaching Sir Wilfrid Laurier's record for longest-serving Prime Minister of that dominion.

"I thought Alice would be along?" Jimmy turned towards his Land Rover and Alain followed, shaking his head in answer to the question.

"Sophie is unfortunately ill. Just a cold, we think, but she thought it best to stay close."

That was the other connection: after meeting her on the new world, Alain Lapointe had married Alice Waller — Colonel Tom Waller's sister. That made him an honorary Newfoundlander in just about any book that mattered, though his French-accented-English wasn't always compatible with the Newfoundland brogue.

No matter; as Jimmy led the PM to his Land Rover, he nodded, "Well I hope it's nothing. Everyone else is well?"

"Indeed," Lapointe confirmed. "And yourself? I hope everyone is okay in these interesting times?"

"Alright as can be," Jimmy replied as he got behind the wheel.

The Prime Minister climbed in on the passenger's side — entirely unconcerned that a dominion's Premier might, in other places, expect motor transport with fancy features... like a roof. Particularly on a cold day.

Without even stopping to consider how the rest of the Prime Minister's staff would make their way from Torbay Airport, Jimmy shifted his truck into gear and they rolled off.

"So what is the latest... have we identified the attackers?"

immediately Lapointe's questions turned to business, and Jimmy frowned and shook his head.

"What, since you left Ottawa? No. Only found that their fake officer had a Luger, so some folks are screaming that it's the Germans. But that's fine, because others think it's Emily..."

Lapointe shook his head as the Land Rover accelerated onto Major's Path, "So no answers."

"Of course not," was the Viscount's response. "But I can't see this being our dear old Lady. Gunning down Champion students? Not even she would go for that. Just my guess, of course."

"Caralynne agrees?"

Shrugging, Jimmy kept his eyes on the road, "She does. But that's our guess, obviously — we don't know for sure, and we'll say as much when we get to *Hood*. I figure the best thing for us to do is treat this like an unknown threat, additional to Emily, and prepare for the worst."

That sounded wise to Lapointe — in the absence of information, extra precautions could hardly be overlooked. But something the Viscount had said was impossible, and taking a breath, the Quebecker offered that news: "Before I left I received a phone call from FDR. He insisted that the meeting include only me and Halifax. I think he is worried that you or Newfoundland's Prime Minister would attempt to sway him to keep American Champions here."

Jimmy Devlin was a good political operator, but somehow he hadn't foreseen such a request, "Well... fine, I'd rather be working anyway. He embarrassed about the attack?"

"It would be understandable," Lapointe reasoned, reaching out to hold the frame of the windshield for support as the Land Rover bounced over a rock hidden in the snow. "Of course it will make little difference. I think there is going to be a big question about whether the United States is ready to commit enough resources to protect their Champions."

Such a question seemed likely to Jimmy. The Viscount thought very highly of many Americans — Smith and Stephanie Shylock, of course, as well as men like Colonel Adams, who was still missing, and the soldiers who'd served in the 25th United States Infantry during the Hubrin War.

The problem with the Americans had nothing to do with their men and women, or even the inherent quality of their soldiers. All of their woes, at least as far as Jimmy could see, came from the constant meddling of their politicians in military affairs.

Of course, no democratic country could remove civilian oversight from the realm of the military — the German Empire had done that, and now their people were nearly in revolt. But the Americans went too far the other way. All the powerful Senators and Congressmen seemed to think only as far ahead as the next election, and how they could leverage influence with the Champions to their advantage. Sometimes that meant spending more on them, in return for advantageous appointments for their favorites. Other times it meant threatening to cut Champion funding, because the many isolationists in the United States surely did question why their government was spending so much money on a program that seemed highly Imperial, and hardly necessary to secure American domestic borders, or their holdings on the new world.

A political football for both sides, with only the Champions' establishment suffering in between. While the British Empire's Special Service Regiment benefited from consistent leadership and a very clear mandate that survived successive governments, the Americans saw new officers turning up every two years, and new training and equipment programs started and cancelled with equal frequency.

Now that legacy of political inconsistency had resulted in the destruction of vital technology (the US skycruisers), and more importantly, had cost lives (including the lives of Champions). Roosevelt had to decide if such resources could be similarly risked in future.

"My priority is that we get Champion security satisfied quickly," Lapointe continued, quite in tune with Jimmy's musing. "I hate flying by aeroplane when I'm coming here. It takes so long I have to ask if things have changed since I left."

That was the other half of the problem: until the source of the attack in Virginia was identified, all the Prime Ministers and the President were being confined to conventional transport. Two Saa-built skycruisers had been blown up on the ground, and *George Tucker* had been battered. That just left *Skipper Miller* properly active, and in the uncertain environment that persisted thanks to the attack, there was no way that ship could be allowed to take aboard unfamiliar passengers.

What if one of the Prime Minister's staff turned out to be an agent of whoever had attacked Virginia? It was very unlikely, but given the incredible value of the last fully-functioning Saa-built craft, they simply couldn't take the risk.

That was why Lapointe had arrived on a Royal Canadian Air Force transport, while Prime Minister the Lord Halifax was crossing from Britain in HMS *Hood*, and Roosevelt was sailing up from Washington in the United States Navy's own Special Service Squadron.

"Well, I've got George working on that registry breach problem Adams found before the attack," Jimmy jumped back into the conversation. "I still don't really know what those words actually mean, but I'm sure he'll figure it out. We're also putting some information in play, see if it flushes out enemy agents."

Lapointe looked at the Viscount at those words, "The nonsense you told me to load into my screen?"

"That's part of it," Jimmy nodded. "Did the same with mine. But more than that... you'll see in a minute. Suffice to say we're buttoning up."

"I believe so," Lapointe said. "And that is why I may propose that you keep the American students permanently."

It was a good thing the Prime Minister was holding onto the frame of the windshield — it kept him from falling out of the Land Rover when Jimmy slammed on the brakes and started another dramatic sideways slide. Somebody probably needed to invent straps to keep passengers fixed to the chairs of vehicles like Land Rovers — or at least for the ones Jimmy was driving.

"Excuse me?" the Viscount wasn't too creative when he was surprised. "Didn't you just say Roosevelt wanted me and my glorious Premier out of the meeting so we wouldn't suggest that?"

Alain Lapointe nodded, "Yes, so I will suggest it for you. We cannot afford to have our Champions resources spread across two locations when there is such an unknown threat. And if we have to pick one place, here seems better. Harder for strangers to blend in with your strange people."

This particular Prime Minister had earned the right to cheekily call Newfoundlanders strange — he'd volunteered to die alongside Waller's charge — but choice of words aside, he had a point: the whole of the rocky island was loyal to the Champions, and unlike the

Hampton Roads in Virginia, there wasn't that much incidental traffic through St. John's.

Much more difficult for men to sneak in...

But making sense didn't make it a good idea, for a couple of reasons. Jimmy wasn't shy about saying them, either: "So, number one, if I have American politicians visiting here, I'll be responsible for starting a war. I promise. Second, what the hell are they going to think? They can't possibly trust us to have a monopoly over their Champions."

Reasonable arguments indeed, but Lapointe shook his head, "Perhaps they cannot, but I will still ask. And Newfoundland is neutral ground, in between all our countries. It could not be London, or Toronto, or Virginia... but it can be here, I think."

Letting his head fall back, Jimmy looked up at the sky and shook himself. Then he dropped his chin and glared at the Quebecker in his passenger seat, "That's it. Get out."

"What?"

"Get out," Jimmy waved his hand to shoo away the Prime Minister. "You're walking."

"I don't even know where you are taking me," Lapointe smiled.

"You're walking to the hospitality warehouse," Jimmy sounded almost like he was pouting.

"I think I would prefer to ride with you. Which is not something most people would say, given how you drive," the Prime Minister shook his head, and Jimmy groaned.

"No, you're walking. Or you can wait for your staff to catch up and ride with them. I'm not driving you to my base just to make more trouble for me."

"Yes, you are," Lapointe's smile grew.

"Am not!" Jimmy resisted.

"Are too," the Prime Minister shot back.

"No!" the Lord pouted.

Obviously, he didn't win.

CHAPTER III

Mike Strong was sitting on the hood of his Land Rover, watching as the people of St. John's passed by. The truck was parked up beside one of the wharfs at the town's waterfront, making him a somewhat conspicuous mid-morning sight — particularly since he was a well-known figure in downtown.

"How's she goin', Mike?" one b'y passed with that call and a wave, and the Sergeant nodded back.

"Good, b'y — I'm workin'!"

"Makes a change," came the reply, and Strong waved at the man as he moved off.

That happened several times as he sat there, facing the water, and eventually his co-waiter looked back at him, "You really know *everyone*?"

Alex was pacing back and forth at the end of the wharf in front of the Land Rover, her arms folded as she tried to contain her excitement. Her illustrious Sergeant's reputation was a useful distraction in that regard, and he seemed willing to answer her question.

"More like everyone knows me. Or of me," he answered modestly.

"I'll bet," Alex smiled, then frowned. "So why is it more vengeful brothers and boyfriends haven't spotted you and come out to fistfight?"

The Colour shrugged, "I think they're scared away by the legend of whitecoat."

Of course he said that — apparently he was still trying to get the 'legend' going, but society was too tasteful to allow it any momentum. Considering how poor most of society's taste could be, that was quite an indictment of the whole gag.

"Maybe your reputation is a bit grander than reality?" Alex suggested, giving her Sergeant the eye. She still didn't believe he was actually going with Daphne, the girl he sought out whenever he had leave in town. They were together a lot, but their affection never struck Alex as convincingly 'romantic', despite their claims that it was.

Strong wasn't going to give away his secrets, so he simply shook his head, "Now you don't ask a magician to give up his tricks."

"I've never met a magician. But I'd certainly *ask*."

"Well yes, *you* would," Strong shook his head, but before he could load up another salvo of regrettable repartee, he spotted a launch coming through the Narrows. That was the boat they were waiting for — one of *Hood's* craft — and it was running in at quite a clip. "Not that I don't have a perfectly clever follow-up... but there's our boat."

That sounded like a cop-out, but as Alex glanced back towards the water, she discovered it was at least a cop-out grounded in facts. *Hood* was lying off the coast, but the mighty ship had sent one of her launches into St. John's with a very important person, to pick up other very important people.

Alex's heart rate increased slightly as soon as she saw the vessel. That was silly, of course — she hardly had reason to be star-struck anymore — but she couldn't control her irrational responses. Indeed, given recent events, she even found it reassuring to allow herself a bit of juvenile excitement.

"Don't get too swoony now," Strong needled her with a grin, and Alex glared at the Sergeant.

"You get in line, Colour. This one's all mine."

"Oh big talk," Strong hopped down from the hood and dusted off his hands before tugging at his battle dress blouse.

"Just you watch," Alex's tone remained decidedly competitive, which made him smile even more.

Watching as the launch crossed the harbor, the white-coated Champion and her Sergeant were soon joined by a few passers-by — the folks of St. John's knew the Special Service Squadron was lying just beyond their port, and were curious to see exactly who the Royal Navy was sending ashore.

Normally, they would have had to wait for the boat to actually reach the wharf to find out, but this time they got an early — and dramatic — preview.

Alex felt her breath catch a little as a purple streak launched out of the boat's open stern, while it was still 100 yards from the dock. Most ordinary people on the waterfront couldn't see much more than a blur as this figure somersaulted in the air, and then began to drop perfectly down over the wooden wharf. Thanks to her Champion vision, Alex caught every detail: the fluttering tails of the deep purple coat, the few wisps of golden hair that had dramatically escaped the stylishly-crafted updo, and the particularly startling white teeth.

As she landed on the end of the wharf, the arriving Champion wore a brilliant smile, and walked immediately towards Alex. It was a perfect walk, after a perfect landing, and she had perfect hair and perfect eyes and perfect boots with a perfect coat.

Lady. Anneke. Winter.

Alex honestly did swoon a little.

More than a little.

As did every other person with eyes on this striking arrival.

After Emily and Caralynne, Anneke Winter was the most senior Champion alive, and for so many students growing up in the Lady Emily Academy, she was the one they wanted to be. In fact, it had been Anneke's decision to choose a coat like Caralynne's that truly started the trend for all Champions that came after. She was the very definition of perfection, and the subject of many crushes.

This appeal wasn't simply superficial; Lady Winter's story was unique. She'd been rescued at a later age than most savage-born children, but somehow had still managed to find civilization. Indeed, she did far more than just *find* it. She exemplified it. Now she embodied everything that a young Champion strove to be — sophisticated, intelligent, graceful, beautiful, tall, capable, powerful, warm.

"You alright there?" Mike Strong leaned sideways towards Alex, and she swatted at him with a hand.

"You be quiet!"

Every Champion girl looked up to Anneke Winter as a role model. Every man, Champion or not, looked up to Anneke Winter as something else. And now she was stepping off the wharf, her bright eyes fixed on Alex.

"I do believe it's *Lady* Alex Smith," even her voice was perfect. Alex felt like she was a teenager seeing her first Fred Astaire dance number.

So. Perfect.

That's roughly when she realized she hadn't answered, and a huge amount of time had passed. Or what seemed a huge amount of time, but probably wasn't, because her heart was racing, "Welcome home, Lady Winter."

She actually sounded cool and collected. One of the advantages of having been in battle, she guessed, and Lady Winter approved: "I was thinking I'd need to get battle tips from you... now I can see I need style advice too. White is *perfect* on you."

Alex melted — worried she was even turning red.

That was wholly daft, of course — they had met a few times before — but this was their first time as supposed equals. And Alex realized she needed to say something in reply.

"It's not easy to keep clean," she blurted.

Anneke came to a stop right in front of the whitecoat and her Sergeant, "But worth it, clearly." She then glanced around with a smile for those who'd stopped to watch, before settling her gaze on Strong, "Here to break my heart again, Colour? I'm not a pretty crier, so can we wait until we're in private?"

Only because Mike Strong was a savant with women did he not physically melt inside his uniform. But even he couldn't possibly think of a quick response for that sort of greeting, so he just smiled and tried to nod. It mostly worked.

Seeing she'd disarmed Mike Strong himself, Anneke turned her eyes back to Alex, "So good to be back on dry land. I realize we can't risk the skycruisers now, but my God sea travel is taxing. *Especially* when it's with politicians."

Alex blinked. That was definitely an invitation for two-way conversation.

She started her mouth moving, and to her surprise, sound came out, "Was the Prime Minister unpleasant?"

Shaking her head, Anneke gestured to the Land Rover, thus prompting everyone to climb aboard. She jumped in the back as she answered, "Just the opposite, honestly. Lord Halifax is a quintessential gentleman, but he's much too concerned with affairs of state to trouble himself with a girl like me. I'm looking forward to my new assignment."

"He'll be completely different, sure enough," Strong contributed that helpful observation as he switched the truck on, then got it into gear.

"How was it at Windsor Castle?" Alex followed with her own question, and sitting back as they began to roll, Anneke smiled.

"Elizabeth will make a remarkable Queen. Might well reign longer than Victoria. But I must say, I'm glad to be in less formal company. Six months guarding the Royal Family is quite enough for this girl."

So. Charmingly. Modest.

Alright, so Alex knew she was suffering from a crush. It was undignified and juvenile and platonic, but Anneke was pretty much perfect, and that was difficult to ignore.

Lady Winter had been dispatched to London just after Emily had first appeared in New York, and was tasked — as she'd so smoothly just mentioned — with the protection of the Royal Family. Now that duty had been passed to another, and Anneke Winter had returned to Newfoundland to help guard the upcoming meetings, then take over personal security for the Canadian Prime Minister. And though the regal life must undoubtedly have been incredible, she was gracious enough to be happy to be home, in damp old Newfoundland.

"It's Lady Forsythe taking over. She'll be right at home there," Anneke continued easily, still smiling as she watched trees come up on either side of the road — they were passing out of downtown at a good clip. "She looks better in fancy hats than I do anyway."

Alex just couldn't help but smile. She looked at Strong, and found the Colour was keeping a very good grip on the Land Rover's wheel. His focus was clearly on the road, because if he let himself get distracted at all, they'd arrive at Jimmystown upside down.

Such was the power of Lady Winter.

"So how are you, Alex? I must say, we all cheered when we heard how you handled Emily. And then that business in Virginia, what amazing work. I must beg you for advice, truly!"

Too. Much.

Not really knowing what she was doing, Alex turned around in her chair and held on to the back of her seat with both hands, "Anything I can do. Because honestly, I'm completely swooning over you right now."

Oh. God.

Mike Strong had been doing a good job of staying focused, but hearing that he very nearly stood on the Land Rover's brakes. It would have been bad to get distracted and ram into a moose, but he had to take his eyes off the road for a second. So he geared down and slowed enough to be able to glance behind him.

"I thought it was just me," Anneke Winter played along gamely with the whitecoat.

At that, Strong did stand on the brakes.

"Sorry," he declared as the Land Rover jolted to a stop in front of some poor fellow's house. Then he turned back and pointed a finger at Lady Winter, "You. Quit it."

Anneke's smile grew, and she hit him with devastating eyes, "Don't be close-minded, Colour. You should *see* what goes on at some of the clubs Elspeth Cornish and I visited in London!"

"Pfft, you don't need to go to England to see that," Strong scoffed. "But this Lady here is not allowed suitors until she's thirty-five. Don't figure you can bat your eyelashes and get past me."

"Ah," Anneke let out a disappointed sigh, then she and Alex traded sad smiles. Covering one of the younger Lady Smith's hands with her own, Lady Winter lamented: "We would have been spectacular together. But it's not to be."

"Star-crossed and unrequited," Alex shook her head dreamily, then glanced at Strong. "You *satisfied*?"

The Colour narrowed his eyes and pointed at her, "Don't use that language with me, young Lady."

With that, he turned his focus back to the road, and got the Land Rover moving towards Jimmystown. His passengers made sure to stare dreamily at each other the rest of the way. It irritated him marvelously.

CHAPTER IV

Captain Percy Todd, suitably wrapped up in scarf and coat, watched through binoculars from his open bridge as *Hood's* launch emerged from the Narrows. *Inglefield* was posted on the landward side of the Special Service Squadron, part of the cordon of destroyers wrapped around the column of *Ark Royal, Rodney* and *Hood.* That put Todd nearest the harbor entrance — appropriate enough, since he had been in these waters more recently than any of his fellow Captains. Indeed, that recent cruise was the very reason he was back again.

Everyone who'd read stories of Alex's encounter with Emily knew the part *Inglefield* had played in tracking the rogue Lady. The notoriety hadn't sat well with Todd — he was still disgusted that Emily had been allowed to escape at all — but the publicity rather raised his star with the Admiralty. His ship was known now, which undoubtedly explained how a modest *I* class flotilla leader had been attached to a mission where six of the other seven destroyers were vaunted *Tribals.*

Inglefield was in heady company, and while Todd was not immune to that, his professionalism didn't suffer.

"I thought she was supposed to wait to take the Canadians off," *Inglefield's* Executive Officer, Lieutenant Commander Richard Oswin, broke Todd's train of thought with that question, and lowering his binoculars, the Captain frowned.

"Must have been a delay," he offered quietly in reply, not minding the candor.

Oswin nodded at his skipper's conclusion, then smiled, "What do you reckon... they'll send us in for the pickup?"

Todd glanced at his XO, "You sound rather too eager, Richard."

"Still haven't found better pubs than the ones on George Street," he replied, his grin growing. "Or at least none I vaguely remember so fondly."

Oswin was known for his drinking — he was something of a legend among the crew, but he was still respected. Since the booze didn't interfere with his duties, Todd allowed it, though he remained watchful and disapproving.

"We wouldn't have time for a pint anyway," he shook his head, then turned away from the high headlands of Newfoundland and looked off his ship's port beam.

The cruisers *Norfolk* and *Suffolk* were posted between *Inglefield* and the squadron's three capital ships, so they were the first vessels he sighted. Beyond them stood the majestic giants, all making ten knots as they paced along, waiting for *Hood's* boat to return.

There would be only a brief stop to take the launch aboard — after the recent attack in Virginia, there was no appetite among any of the armed services to make themselves vulnerable, even when no realistic threat was apparent.

With that thought, Todd glanced briefly at Oswin, "Check ASDIC again, will you Richard?"

"Of course," the XO nodded, then turned to the speaking pipe that led down to *Inglefield's* ASDIC room — the home of its underwater detection gear. Two operators would be on duty, since the ship was at cruising stations, and they were expected to call up to the bridge if they heard any signs of nearby submarines. Still, just in case they somehow hadn't reported an anomaly, an extra check wasn't unwise.

"ASDIC room, bridge. Any contacts on your recorder?"

There was a brief pause after Oswin's question, then one of the operators replied, "Bridge, ASDIC. No contacts, sir. But it's a bit choppy out there, and shallow. We're paying close attention, sir."

"Thank you, ASDIC," Oswin was gracious with his reply, then he straightened up from the speaking tube and turned back to his Captain. "All clear. But they're still concerned about the conditions."

Todd nodded at the report, though he didn't take his gaze from the big ships he was tasked with guarding. The Grand Banks that surrounded Newfoundland were effectively an underwater plateau — a shelf of land hundreds of square miles long, that were much shallower than the rest of the North Atlantic. With a bottom that was between fifty and 200 meters down, and a cold current running through it from Labrador, the sea here wasn't necessarily ideal for underwater detection. ASDIC's sound pulses could bounce off the sea floor and reflect back to the recorder... different water temperatures could distort the detectors... plenty of things could go wrong.

That was another reason it was good *Inglefield* had joined the Special Service Squadron for this mission: along with her usual flotilla-mate *Imogen*, she was one of the better sub-hunters in the group. All the *Tribal*-class ships had the equipment, but none of them had spent much time on the Grand Banks. And as big fleet destroyers, they might even have been forgiven for spending more time on gunnery drills than underwater detection.

So *Inglefield* was here, and though her ASDIC ratings might not enjoy the conditions of the local sea when it came to detection, Todd knew them to be among the best in the fleet at this job. He would have settled for nothing less, and neither would the men themselves. They'd make certain no visitors came from below, while *Ark Royal* kept the skies clear.

Raising his binoculars again to look quickly at the mighty carrier, and the Seafires that were lining up for takeoff from its gently-pitching deck, Todd didn't see the Yeoman of Signals arrive from the flag deck.

"Message from flag, sir," the young man declared as he came to a stop.

Todd began to turn, but Oswin was there first, hand outstretched, "Let's see what they have for us."

The Yeoman nodded and handed the paper to the XO, who read it as he moved up alongside his Captain, "I am clairvoyant, in case you were in any doubt."

"Doesn't explain why you're such a disaster at cards," Todd indulged in the dry banter as Oswin passed along the paper, then he read the orders aloud for good measure. "Enter St. John's harbor and take aboard dignitaries. Squadron will steam for rendezvous, follow once guests aboard."

Oswin nodded, obviously pleased with himself, but Todd was undistracted, "Yeoman, make to *Hood*: understood, will rejoin presently at pre-established coordinates. Also signal the St. John's harbor master, let him know we'll be coming in."

"Sir," the Yeoman nodded, then hurried off.

Glancing back towards the headlands on either side of the

Narrows, Todd found he was not so eager as his XO to enter the Newfoundland port again. He'd lost men on the street there, and then failed to capture the villain who'd slain them. But his own preferences were irrelevant, so as Oswin got on the PA to alert the crew, he ordered *Inglefield's* helm over to starboard, so his destroyer could approach the port where she'd recently done battle with Emily.

There was something particularly awkward about waiting in Anne's office. Stephanie wasn't sure why the Viscountess didn't want them to be in the central control area with her son while he essentially showed the whole world to Constance... but surely being there wouldn't have been as strange as simply sitting on either side of the austere, essentially-unused desk, making small talk about snowfall.

But snowfall is exactly what they talked about, while George made his own reading of Constance, and passed along some carefully-selected information to her as well. It was necessary work, but he did rather seem to be enjoying it. Were they... hitting it off?

Looking out towards George's desk again, Stephanie had only a few seconds to ponder the question before a new distraction arrived.

"...and she says that it is not Prime Ministerial," Alain Lapointe led the way into the control chamber, sounding a bit amused as he explained some plight.

"She's probably right. I've never known a politician who could dance in anything but a metaphorical sense," Jimmy Devlin answered as he shut the door behind him. "You should listen to your wife."

Clearly the two leaders were having a deeply relevant and important conversation, so Stephanie and Anne both hurried to their feet and emerged from the office to rescue them. Alain noticed the ladies out of the corner of his eye, and turned to them with a predictably charming smile.

"I could not ever deny that a lady is right when it comes to dancing," he said. "I, however, do not always behave."

Stephanie let Anne take the lead on that one — those two had known each other for as long as the Lieutenant had been alive, after all. The Viscountess approached the Prime Minister with a smile that was somehow cool and warm at once, then stopped so he could kiss her on each cheek.

"The world would be a dreary place if you did behave, Alain," she indulged the Quebecker, and he grinned as he pulled back.

"You see, your wife agrees with me, Jimmy," he glanced back to Lord Devlin, who folded his arms and looked particularly impressed.

"She's a sympathetic soul, Alain. She's indulging you."

Lapointe scoffed, turning back towards Anne. She shrugged innocently, "I don't know about being sympathetic…"

With a shake of his head, the Prime Minister decided to seek backup, so his eyes shifted to Stephanie, "Maybe *Lieutenant* Shylock will be more honest? Stephanie, what do you think a Prime Minister should do when there is dancing at a state dinner?"

Definitely deep and profound conversations about important matters of state. And what was worse: as Lapointe turned towards her, Stephanie could tell he actually expected some sort of response. A clever retort, at the very least.

She blurted: "What would Mike Strong do?"

That was bad, obviously — not even funny. But what made it worse was that the door had opened the moment she said it. And needles to say, the person stepping in *had* to offer a follow-on comment.

"What would I do where?"

For it was the Colour himself leading his party into the control room, and he sounded excited to hear his catch phrase.

"I do not want *his* opinion," Lapointe seemed entirely unfazed at the perfectly-timed arrival. "He *cannot* dance."

"Not like you, Colonel," Strong didn't miss a beat. "But the ladies *enjoy* my methods."

Oh God. Stephanie had said the wrong thing.

Alex and Anneke Winter slipped in behind Strong, and as the Lieutenant and the whitecoat caught each others' gazes, they communicated their mutual sentiments: *Oh no, the old folks are trying to be funny.*

They hurried to stand near each other — along with Anneke, over whom Stephanie swooned for just a second — so that they could support each other through the terrible humor to come.

Strong was advancing on Lapointe, pretending to be puffed-up: "I've just threatened Lady Winter for trying to charm Lady Alex. You going to make me punch you for charming my Lieutenant?"

"I take a hit better than your war minister," the politician replied easily.

"I know that..." Strong began to retort... but then his words ground to a halt.

Because his back was to Alex and Stephanie, neither girl could see his face — see the look that crossed his eyes. Lapointe recognized it immediately, and then it struck him too. For a brief moment both men were looking back in time...

Mike Strong knew Alain Lapointe could take a hit, because on the day when Colonel Waller had led the b'ys into the lightning at the Hubrin capital, Alain Lapointe and his Voltigeurs had been right at their side. Alain had been hit by a pulse cannon blast that day, and yet he hadn't faltered until his men dragged him off the field.

For a politician who loved to dance, and compared himself to Vernon Castle (or more recently, Fred Astaire), he was a tough soldier. And the fact that he and his Quebeckers had been on that field, on that day, and had paid the same deadly price as the b'ys of the Newfoundland Regiment... made him like a brother to Strong.

They were from different worlds, and that would never change. But they shared a dreadful moment in common, and the sameness of its pain played out on both their faces, as Mike Strong suddenly dropped his bravado — he simply couldn't keep the joke alive — and extended his hand.

"You're well? And Missus Waller?"

He was referring to Missus Lapointe, of course — the sister of Tom Waller. Alain understood, and didn't mind.

With a difficult smile, he shook Strong's hand, "We are. And you too — you are not traumatizing our two young ladies?"

The mention of Alex and Stephanie was enough to jog the Colour back to some semblance of reality, "They're traumatizing me, more like. They have terrible senses of humor."

Alain nodded intently, "I just heard. You may not want to admit it, Mike, but part of that might be your fault."

"I am a bad influence," Strong took a breath as their hands parted, and started to get his thoughts back in shape. "But then, Lady Winter thinks I'm charming."

"Unattainable," suddenly Anneke was beside the men — perfectly and graciously timed, of course — and with a smile she drew their thoughts entirely back to the present. As Mike Strong took a step back to let the Lady and the Prime Minster charm each other (it was a perfect storm, really), Alex shook her head.

"That was scary."

"I think it could have been worse," Stephanie shrugged, trying to play it down. Then she frowned and glanced sideways at her friend, "Did Strong say Lady Winter charmed you?"

"I was defenseless," Alex sighed, shaking her head. "But it was just a phase."

Stephanie sympathized. Any girl looking for a role model could look no further than Lady Winter, and her purple coat.

"So," the Lieutenant observed a little hopefully, "you're saying she's available?"

The question came at the very moment that Anneke laughed warmly at something the Prime Minister said to her. Narrowing her eyes, Alex therefore shook her head, "Sounds like you've missed your chance."

"Damned Quebeckers," Stephanie soured. "Always getting there first."

There were several different ways Alex could have run with that. She was, however, a Lady, so she just let them all go by.

"Prime Minister," George Devlin rose a moment later, and as Lapointe turned away from Lady Winter, he faced the hospitality man with a smile.

"George, you make your father look more disreputable by the day."

"Not setting the bar very high, are you?" Jimmy interjected, but despite the terrible, terrible humor, the younger Devlin seemed unflapped.

Instead of engaging, he stood aside so he could gesture to his companion: "Allow me to present Constance Cormack, a Champion-in-training from the Robinson Institute."

Realizing she'd become the center of attention, Constance slowly stood, hoping there wasn't any color rushing to her cheeks. Her mother was a very well-regarded woman in Georgia, and that meant she met politicians — mainly state officials, and some Congressmen — from time to time. But she wasn't good at it.

"Honored to meet you, sir," she defaulted to politeness, and being rather a canny politician (and dance partner), Lapointe detected her unease.

"It is my honor, of course," he replied warmly, extending his good hand so she could take it. As they released their grips, he continued thoughtfully, "From the reports... it is you who know the operator of the screen, Corporal Cross?"

Being recognized made it even more likely that Constance's cheeks would turn red — not for any particularly good reason, just because. She opened her mouth to answer but nothing came out, so George Devlin rode to the rescue.

"That's why we're here. Taking a look at the registry systems... and I'm just showing her the map of the Grand Banks, and the rendezvous point for the Special Service Squadrons," he said, waving back towards one of the big screens and locking onto Alain's eyes with his own.

The Prime Minister looked up at the glowing map, processed it for a moment, and then almost began to frown. But after meeting George's gaze again, he nodded, "Of course. That point of light on the screen is where we and the Americans will meet to discuss the future. My dear Lady Constance, I'm afraid secret matters about that meeting must now occupy us, and this chamber. Could we beg your pardon?"

Constance actually felt a wash of relief at being allowed to escape; she nodded, "Yes of course."

"We can get her back," Stephanie spoke up again, and with a nod, Jimmy agreed.

"You three go ahead, then find Caralynne and get her down to the harbor. Actually, tell her to call me first, at Headquarters. I'm off the hook, but she's still going."

"Will do," the whitecoat nodded, and then she, Stephanie and Strong moved to wait by the door, while Constance took George's hand.

"Thank you so much," she said warmly, and he replied with a gallant nod.

"Rest assured, we'll do everything we can to prove Corporal Cross' fidelity."

Talking, of course, like a total hero — and he didn't even seem aware of it.

With that, Constance nodded one last time to the PM, Lady Anne, and Jimmy. Then she crossed the room, smiled at Stephanie, and exited with her escort.

As the door shut behind them, Jimmy moved over to stand beside Anne, then began to explain, "Turns out I'm not on the boat."

"The President doesn't want too many Newfoundland repre-sentatives," Lapointe elaborated. "Too intimidating, perhaps."

Anne shrugged, "I won't complain. Though I'm sure Caralynne will be thrilled to be on her own."

Jimmy grinned, "She'll be off as soon as she can." With that he turned back to his son, "Everything go as planned?"

George stuffed his hands into his pockets, and his eyes seemed fixed on the door that had shut behind Constance and Stephanie... but he still nodded, "She had plenty of time to internalize the rendezvous coordinates."

"They are the wrong ones, unless something has changed?" Lapointe asked, turning back to the map of the Grand Banks and allowing the frown he'd suppressed a moment ago to form. The light marker on the Saa screen was certainly in the wrong place — the Special Service Squadron was bound for an entirely different piece of ocean. Such misdirection implied one thing, and as he thought of that, the PM asked: "You think Constance could be a spy?"

With a shrug, George finally shifted his gaze to the Prime Minister, "We don't believe she is, or she wouldn't have been allowed down here. Everyone vouches for her... and I certainly hope she isn't... but someone at Eustice set up that mess, and she's very close to one of their screen operators. *And* she went out of her way to make a good impression on Alex. If I were a spy—"

"You *are* a spy," Alain interrupted with a slight smile.

"We call it 'hospitality' here, Prime Minister," George corrected. "But were it me, that's the approach I'd take. So while we're fairly certain she is no threat, a little extra caution."

"We've sent different sets of wrong coordinates to various different stakeholders," Anne added for her son. "George's idea. So we can put *Skipper Miller* up, and if something strange happens at any particular set of coordinates..."

"You will know which person is sending information to our enemies," Lapointe nodded with approval. It was a simple — indeed, perhaps obvious — way to find a spy.

George went back to looking at the door, but shook his head, "We can't be certain of how the spy is communicating, so if nothing happens this time, it won't prove anything for certain. We have a ways to go before we can really trust anyone."

A prudent observation, and the Prime Minister didn't disagree.

Looking up to the point of light over the Grand Banks, he simply nodded, "Still, I hope nothing bad happens at that marker, George. Because you two make a very handsome couple."

The junior Devlin began to nod... then he blinked: "What?"

That was one of those moments where the elders in the room chuckled knowingly, even though it wasn't funny.

CHAPTER V

Smith had hoped to get back to his house before his wife and the girls, but as he stepped through the door into the kitchen, Winchester '92 in hand, he knew immediately he was too late. Checking that his rifle's hammer was in the safe position, he leaned it up in the corner and bent down to pull off his boots. As he did, he tuned into the conversation that was crossing the house, from living room to bedrooms.

"At least you'll have Anneke," his daughter was saying. As Smith's mind went to work to put that comment in context, Alex's attention turned to his arrival — thanks to her Champion hearing, she could detect his quiet return. "Hi dad!"

He didn't need to raise his voice as he replied, "Hi Alex."

Free of his boots, he took up his rifle and advanced from the kitchen into the living room, where sure enough, Alex and Stephanie were sitting on the couch, fully dressed for the day. Mike Strong was sitting in one of the chairs opposite them, so he twisted back and raised his hand in a wave, "Smith."

"Strong," the former-drifter nodded back, moving over to the rifle case in the corner and putting away his Winchester before participating in further discussion. The rifle was loaded — something that was generally considered unsafe, but which Smith figured was allowable under the circumstances, and in a house where he was probably the worst shooter.

"Where were you?" Alex asked as he turned away from the cabinet and advanced towards her a little stiffly, stretching his back, which had tightened in the cold.

"Moose tracks out there, followed them a while."

It was plausible enough, but something about the comment seemed to bother Alex. He could see her brow twitch just a little, as though she was going to frown, but she stopped herself, and turned her gaze to the cabinet, "You were going after a moose with your Winchester?"

That was a good point, and one Smith should have thought of: a .45 Colt carbine wasn't his best moose gun — the Enfield in the cabinet would have been much better if Smith had been planning to do some hunting.

"Wasn't planning on shooting it," he said. "Just habit, to keep a rifle close."

Alex stared at him for a second after he spoke, but then decided no further discussion was needed. With a nod she looked back in the direction of the bedrooms, and Stephanie instinctively picked up the narrative.

"The Americans don't want Jimmy or the Newfoundland Prime Minister in the meeting, so Caralynne's on her own for the whole thing."

That would be bad news from Caralynne's point of view, though Smith didn't necessarily mind hearing it. His wife had insisted on going aboard *Hood* for the meetings, both to brief the politicians on what she'd seen in Virginia, and to help ensure security was tight aboard *Hood*. The navies and air forces would protect the Special Service Squadron against conventional attack; the last thing anyone needed was an assassin sneaking aboard and shooting up the meeting.

Having Jimmy there would have made the trip less onerous... though it also would have given her more to worry about.

"You'll have Alain Lapointe too," Alex called out to her mother again at that point. "So you'll know lots of people."

Finally, Caralynne emerged from her room, a case in hand. Her face was set in a manner that Smith knew well; she wasn't looking forward to the duty that awaited her, but she was set on doing it. Now she looked from the girls to her husband.

"That's all fine. But when Jimmy telephoned me... well, apparently Alain is going to lobby to have all the US Champion students stay here. Permanently. So that we can combine security and look after them."

Alex hadn't heard this yet, and her eyes widened slightly at the prospect... as did Stephanie's. It was a conflicting sort of prospect: people like Constance Cormack would probably be great to have around, but some of the American students were rather full of themselves.

"Probably be good to get them all some proper training — and away from the politicians," Strong weighed in, his thoughts reflecting much of what Alex had related about her classroom experience with the now-dead students.

"Yes, of course," Caralynne nodded. "But I'm going to have to be in the room for the whole argument. Start to bloody finish. All fifty rounds of it. Because I don't think Alain will back down, and I don't imagine Roosevelt will either. This could go on for *days*."

Caralynne sighed. The summit was a good idea, and necessary to coordinate efforts against whatever this new threat was. Being trapped on a ship with a room full of egos squabbling over a piece of violence they hadn't witnessed, and possibly becoming targets themselves, was clearly not a prospect she relished.

"Well, we'll be overhead, however long it takes," Alex read her mother's consternation easily enough, and offered that reassurance as she got to her feet and hurried over to give her a squeeze from the side. "If it gets really bad, send up a signal and we'll drop a ladder for you. You can come up for a break."

Technically they could have done that — Champions like Caralynne could physically survive the climb up a swinging 300-foot rope ladder better than most — but it was an offer that simply couldn't be accepted. Caralynne was stuck on the ship until everyone went home. And hopefully — hopefully — it would be both boring and short.

Using her free arm to squeeze her daughter back, Caralynne nodded, then sighed again, "Alright, we need to go."

With that, Stephanie and Strong rose as well, and as Alex released her mom, the trio started to file out of the living room. The whitecoat stopped beside her father on the way, "We'll be back to get our bags before we go up in *Skipper Miller*. You be here?"

Smith wondered if there was some underlying meaning in his daughter's straightforward question — another inquiry as to where he'd been — but he chose to answer as if there wasn't, "I will."

"Good," she smiled and gave him a quick kiss on the cheek, then hurried after her friends. That left the former-drifter and his wife, and as Caralynne reached him and they put arms around each other, she pressed her forehead against his.

"I have an uncomfortable feeling about this," she said rather darkly. "I just... they're politicians."

Smith was never surprised by his wife's intuition, so he spoke reassuringly, "If you feel trouble coming, just take care. Keep yourself safe."

He wanted to say more — point out that, with no Jimmy to protect, she'd have less to worry about if a crisis happened — but that would have been too much.

"I will," Caralynne was unaware of her husband's troubled thoughts, and she leaned back enough to give him a kiss. Then, with one more squeeze, she slipped past him and out the door. Feeling uneasy, Smith moved to the window and watched as Strong drove their Land Rover down the lane from the house. After a moment, he decided to collect his Winchester from the cabinet again, and return to the woods.

Inglefield was keeping steam up as she waited alongside the wharf in St. John's harbor, ready to make revolutions and withdraw quickly through the Narrows upon the arrival of her passengers.

Captain Todd had returned to his bridge after receiving those he believed to be his only passengers; the Canadian Prime Minister, some of his staff, and Lady Anneke Winter had boarded without much fanfare, and were now settling in his dining room for the cruise out to the Grand Banks. But apparently, there was to be one more guest.

"So he said Lady Caralynne?" Oswin was on the bridge with his Captain, and Todd nodded.

"He did," Todd answered. He was standing at the starboard wing, hands on the sides of the armored bulkhead as he looked over it at downtown St. John's.

"Hope she doesn't take too long," the Lieutenant Commander folded his arms. He sounded rather disgruntled, and Todd sympathized. Waiting was not the problem — even if they waited an hour, this would still be a spectacularly short stop in St. John's. The point of friction was with the passenger herself. There was no rational reason to dislike Caralynne, but it was known to every man on *Inglefield* that her daughter Alex had been present when Bosun McKenna and his men were killed... and that she'd failed to apprehend Emily.

The papers had spent much time lionizing the whitecoat for that night, and had made heroes of Strong and Stephanie Shylock... but to a ship's company of fewer than 150, the loss of seven men under such circumstances was bitter.

Of course Emily was to blame for the murders — no one disputed who pulled the trigger — but when Stephanie Shylock could have shot the woman down, she had instead shot the *gun* from her hand. A foolish thing to do. Then Alex had somehow let Emily disappear over a cliff after chasing her down with the help of *Inglefield's* illumination.

Such circumstances left bitterness, and fairly or unfairly, that sentiment was bleeding from the girls to the Lady who'd sponsored them. Caralynne would not be the most welcome guest *Inglefield* had ever entertained.

But she would be a guest nonetheless.

"The men are ready to receive her properly?" Todd quietly asked his XO, and Oswin nodded.

"Of course," his reply was flat, slightly disgruntled that the question had even been raised.

"Right," Todd nodded, then sighed. His crew was good — some of the best men he'd ever served with, and that was a high bar. They'd pulled together even tighter since that night against Emily, and no matter their attitudes, the Captain knew well he could count on them.

Distaste or no, they'd treat Lady Caralynne with due courtesy.

Whenever she arrived.

Letting go of the bulkhead, Todd straightened and turned away from St. John's, just in time to note the arrival of guests on his bridge.

"Permission to join you, Captain?" Alain Lapointe stopped as he reached the threshold of the command deck, and Todd stiffened before nodding.

"Of course, Prime Minister. Honored to have you join us."

Todd knew very little of Lapointe — nothing beyond what anyone could read of the man's storied military history, and his time as Canada's Premier. He thus defaulted to formality, and that made the Quebecker smile.

"I am sorry to intrude, but whenever I can be with fighting officers, I take that over being with politicians. I am not very good in my new job, at least compared to my old one," he said easily, advancing across the bridge toward the Captain and his XO.

Oswin turned now, a little more star-struck than his Captain,

"We're pleased to have you, sir."

"This man is a good liar, Captain," Lapointe grinned, waving in the direction of the Lieutenant Commander, who smiled in surprise.

"I try not to let it show," was Oswin's answer, and Lapointe shrugged.

"There are *some* things I am better at as a politician," the Prime Minister said, then shook his head as he looked out on the town. "I assume that we are just awaiting Caralynne?"

Todd nodded, "Yes sir. I have steam up, so we'll depart as soon as she arrives."

"Good. Then please do not mind me... I will just hide in a corner here," Lapointe moved over to the opposite side of the bridge, then folded his arms and leaned against the bulkhead. His smile seemed irrepressible.

Though both Todd and Oswin did their best to comply — to ignore his presence — any candid conversation they might have continued was at an end. They remained largely silent, only exchanging the odd order with their crew, until a Land Rover drove into sight.

"Looks like she's here, sir," one of the lookouts on the starboard side called as the vehicle slowed opposite *Inglefield*.

"Good job we have such fine lookouts, Murphy. Damned if I could have seen that myself," Oswin shot back immediately, drawing a few guffaws from his men.

Todd moved over beside his XO, then narrowed his eyes at the open-topped truck. A Sergeant was driving... Mike Strong himself... and Stephanie Shylock was in the passenger seat. The white-coated Lady Alex was in the back, and climbing out was Caralynne. She hugged her daughter and they spoke to each other, but Todd obviously couldn't hear them.

He did notice the moment when Stephanie Shylock looked towards the ship... and when she met his gaze. A conveniently-timed gust from the sea reinforced the chill between them, and then Stephanie looked to her Sergeant, her lips moved, and Strong joined the glare.

Entirely unmoved by the pair's coolness, Todd simply stared back another moment, then turned to Oswin, "We best get down to receive her..."

"That won't be necessary, Captain!" a call came from the shore, and as he looked back towards the Land Rover, Todd realized Caralynne was airborne... high above his ship... and landing on the flag deck to the rear of his bridge. "Permission to come aboard?"

The Yeoman of Signals was nearest the arriving Lady, and he pulled his hat from his head in surprise, "Jesus."

"Watch that, Hobbes," Oswin called to him, crossing the bridge with Todd on his heels.

"Permission granted, M'Lady. Welcome aboard *Inglefield*," the Captain greeted her formally.

Caralynne nodded, "Thank you, Captain. I believe I'm the one who was holding you up." She seemed in no mood to waste time, and as she caught Lapointe's eye, she added, "We have an appointment aboard *Hood*."

Todd detected some displeasure in her words, but there was no point dwelling on it — the less conversation, the better. Turning towards the gyrocompass, he gave quick orders, "Let's get under weigh, XO."

"Bertie," the Lieutenant Commander immediately called out to the Pilot, who nodded. The screws began to turn a moment later.

As the bridge came to life, Caralynne shuffled carefully over to Lapointe's side, and he greeted her with a casual kiss on each cheek, "Good to see you, my finest Lady."

"I hear you're going to make me preside over quite a screaming match?" she asked softly — through a false smile.

The Prime Minister's smile was far more genuine, "I am just trying to complicate the lives of all my best friends. For the good of the Empire. And so my friends can show off their magnificent talents."

Caralynne's fake smile got faker, but at the same time it somehow warmed, "It's a good thing you're so charming."

"I know," Lapointe replied, as *Inglefield* began to move.

Standing on the opposite side of the bridge, Captain Todd spared one more look towards St. John's, and found his glare was met by Alex, Stephanie and Strong — somehow all at once. He met their gazes for just a moment, then looked away.

"We'll clear the Narrows, then make thirty knots to the rendezvous," the Captain declared. "Richard, make sure the engines are ready."

Inglefield was under weighed anchor, and soon enough, she and her passengers would be part of a summit set to decide how Britain and America could respond to the attacks against their Champions.

It was a subject on many minds.

CHAPTER VI

Though the smoke had cleared over the James River near Newport News, Virginia, the chaos from the attack on the United States Champions establishment remained profound. Many days had passed, and yet little order had been restored — rescues and searches had been the priority.

Where there should have been clarity, or at least initial progress in a search for answers, there was nothing but disorder and recriminations.

"Dammit, Travis, a *Senate Inquiry*. I've never known politicians to move so fast!"

As those words echoed down the corridors of the stockade, Corporal Vanier Cross listened with distinct displeasure. The prison structure was one of the few buildings at Fort Eustice that had not suffered damage during the explosions that had wiped out two skycruisers, and he wanted to believe its structural integrity was the reason he and the other Saa screen operators were being housed there, under guard.

But he knew better.

The man complaining to Major Travis was none other than the Commandant of the Robinson Institute for United States Champions, a General called Powell who, until the past week's events, had been expected to do little more than represent the Champions establishment at state functions. Now it sounded as though the weight of his responsibilities was crushing him.

"No sign of Adams, either — or his RSM. They were either the traitors and got away, or just bastards who were blown up with the ships," Powell continued, plenty of venom in his tone. Based on his volume, he was getting nearer the cells holding the screen operators, so Vanier looked down towards his cell mate — Captain Wendel

Fischer — and waved to get his attention.

The white officer, with whom Vanier was increasingly feeling a kinship, came to his feet and immediately joined his black compatriot at the cell's bars, though he said nothing.

"At least you have these men," Powell continued, clearly referring to the fact that Travis had kept the screen operators under constant watch since the attack. One of them was undoubtedly connected to the destruction, and presumably an investigation would find the traitor.

Or at least, *name* a traitor.

Vanier knew he could very well be accused — he was the only black man on the screen team, and would be a natural scapegoat, especially considering the number of well-connected men who now occupied the cells with him. If a rich white officer was accused, his family would undoubtedly move heaven and earth to make sure the blame was redirected.

No, Vanier's best hope was that the investigation, and the inquiry, would uncover evidence of who had truly broken into Fort Eustice's Saa screen. It was a search that he knew he should be a part of — he was one of the best, perhaps even the best they had.

But no, he was behind bars.

The bitterness of that thought was clear on Vanier's face as Powell turned the corner into the corridor of cells, Major Sheldon Travis of the Champions Regiment following him. Neither man looked impressed, though of the two, Powell was clearly the most disgusted.

His reputation was at risk, after all. The Commandant who had allowed the loss of two precious skycruisers...

"You men," he declared without hesitation. "One of you may be responsible for all of this. Major Travis has done right keeping you here until we can find out who. And rest assured, we will."

Perhaps that was meant to sound menacing, but to Vanier, it sounded desperate. He glanced at Fischer, and the Captain's eyes reflected the same assessment: the Commandant was trying to cover his own deficiencies.

"We can consider putting them in the screen room, to collect evidence," Travis suggested more quietly, seeming unaffected by Powell's menace.

The Commandant whirled, "You really think that's wise, Major?

No, no. The President is meeting with the British this very day, and he will secure outside inspectors to do that work. Then the responsibility will be theirs. None of these men will be trusted. *We* will not be accountable for any more breaches."

Of course, whether he intended it or not, the Commandant revealed himself with those words — God forbid he be responsible for his own base. Politically-appointed fool.

Powell's eyes turned on Vanier, and the man's face seemed to twist as he began to shake his head, "And you say you discovered all of this, did you, boy?"

Stiffening slightly at the unexpected assault, Vanier managed not to reply at all. Looking to the Corporal and feeling rather more forthright, Captain Fischer answered, "He detected the problem, yes sir. I reviewed the findings, and we went to Colonel Adams to report. Together."

It sounded almost like testimony, and Powell's eyes narrowed as he listened, "You may want to think again before pinning your fate to this negro, Captain Fischer. Lest your inheritance be depleted by your lawyers."

Fischer blinked, rather surprised at the hostility, "I'm confident any inquiry will discover that we're speaking the truth, sir. We want to find who did this as much as everyone else."

Powell simply shook his head, disgust written all over his expression, "You all should have been smarter than to let this happen. It will be the end of you, probably. You have been privileged to hold the positions you do, but if I find any of you were lax in your vigilance, and caused this..."

Of course that was beyond appropriate for any right-minded, rational General to say, but Powell was a political appointee with powerful friends. Unfortunately, some of the men he was admonishing had powerful friends too, and at least one of them was arrogant enough to say so.

"You watch your mouth," it was Lieutenant Shane Gallagher, a man who — despite his job — only ever demonstrated a very limited familiarity with military customs. He got to his feet and pressed his face against the bars of his cell as he spat the words. "My father will make sure you *never* command *anything* again."

Vanier frowned at the rolling insult — the fact that Gallagher was not a natural soldier was pretty evident by his choice of tone.

But, for once, the Corporal didn't mind the Lieutenant's attitude. Powell deserved to be shut up.

"I'll have you shot first, you incompetent fool," the Commandant snarled back, which only got Gallagher more worked up.

"Senate inquiry? My father will *own* that whole panel. And *you* will be shot, you disgrace!"

Right. Even if it was in the service of a good cause, Vanier could only stomach so much of Gallagher's declarations of power. Powell puffed up to shoot back, of course, but then was interrupted.

"I was under the impression that the most important thing is to find the guilty man," Major Travis interjected, then stepped between Powell and Gallagher's cell, to break the eyeline between the two men. Then he turned to the self-important Lieutenant, "If that means you, Mister Gallagher, your family will not save you. Whatever man is responsible will pay, and all the other men will be expected to do their jobs when this is over. So stop talking back to the Commandant, and wait like good soldiers. Or you will answer to me."

It was obvious that the Major had been careful to avoid implying his superior was wrong, but he certainly did manage to shut Powell down. Even Gallagher seemed unequal to the task of responding to the tall soldier from Oklahoma.

Powell took the opportunity to beat a retreat, "Exactly as the Major says." He then turned around in place, his eyes scanning every cell door and the men being accommodated behind the bars. "All of you wait for your turn. When this inquiry summons you, you'll be expected to provide all the information needed to clarify what happened, and how we were betrayed."

He paused for a moment, and Vanier felt a distinct chill as their gazes crossed again. There was little the black Corporal could do if he was to be presumed guilty... he'd just have to hope. Surely someone from the British side would be able to produce actual evidence and identify the real traitor.

Or not. Time would tell.

For now, Powell was done blustering, "Travis, you keep them safe. Only guards you trust, none of Adams' boys. You make sure all these men are fit for that inquiry. Understood?"

"Yes sir," the Major replied, his own cooler stare swinging around to consider all the men present. "You gentlemen will continue to be our guests here."

Hearing that, Powell set off, hands linked behind his back as he left the corridor of cells. Travis followed, and sensing the Major on his shoulder, the Commandant continued speaking hurriedly, "It's good you sent the students away. We can't be responsible for any further attacks on Champions, thank God..."

Eventually his words disappeared into the distance, leaving thick silence in their wake. The confined Saa screen operators gradually began to pull themselves away from the bars of their cages, and as he turned his back to the corridor, Fischer shook his head, "That bastard was probably in bed with his mistress while this place blew up, so we have to pay. Gives you faith in our country, doesn't it, Vanier?"

The Corporal had a certain kind of faith, but he decided against voicing it, "We'll just have to wait and see how it goes."

With that suitably subdued response, the black soldier returned to his cot and lay down. As his eyes fixed on the underside of the bunk mounted above his own, he allowed himself at least to think of Constance Cormack. Travis had indeed ordered all the Champion students to the safety of Newfoundland... he tried to imagine her there.

Surely the madness that had happened at Fort Eustice couldn't be repeated in that place, because the British didn't allow men like Powell near their Champions. No, Constance was away from danger, and Newfoundland would be unaccosted.

Vanier chose to believe that, because he had to. Perhaps he was too ambitious.

CHAPTER VII

Though the rendezvous between the Royal Navy's Special Service Squadron and its United States Navy counterpart was not due until evening, *Major Herbert Miller* — or more colloquially, *Skipper Miller* — took off in the afternoon to begin its orbit over the Grand Banks. Alex ventured onto the ship's command deck soon after it boosted from Torbay Airport, staying near the rear of the cockpit until the ship was at altitude and gliding out over a dimming North Atlantic.

"On our way?" she asked after everyone seemed to settle down, and turning his chair back towards his Champion passenger, the skycruiser's Captain smiled and nodded.

"We are indeed, my Lady."

Alex wasn't entirely sure why Flight Captain Cristobal Abel had a Spanish accent — he was from British Guyana, so she would have expected him to sound a bit more... English... but that really didn't matter. He was so tall he could hit his head on his skycruiser's hatch frames if he forgot to duck, and he wore glasses to help him see while flying, but he was undisputedly one of the very best pilots in the Empire.

And if anyone was concerned with his relative lack of Englishness (no one was), his second-in-command more than made up for it.

"Aha, Lady Alex, didn't hear you arrive," Flight Lieutenant Douglas Bader turned his chair as well, with a bit of swagger that was entirely in character for him.

Bader was, simply put, a hero. He'd been a pilot in the RAF when Saa technology had rapidly catapulted aircraft technology to new levels, and had dashingly volunteered to test-fly a Bristol Bulldog retrofitted with a new engine. All had gone well until he attempted some aerobatics over the field (reportedly on a dare), and touched the ground with the left wing tip. After the incident, the Flight Lieutenant had written in his personal logbook: "Crashed slow-rolling near ground. Bad show."

And it had been a bad show, costing him both legs — one amputated above the knee, the other below. Of course, that hadn't kept him down; a set of tin legs were fitted for him, and though the RAF wouldn't let him into a Spitfire, Jimmy Devlin had stolen him for his skycruiser division... once he promised not to attempt to *roll* one of the priceless Saa-built ships.

Now he clapped his hands together and pushed himself to his tin feet, "We'll keep an eye out for trouble, of course — let you know if we see anything. Will you be in the dining room?"

Alex blinked, "That is where they give us food, isn't it?"

"It certainly is," he grinned at her, then stepped forward with his unusual (but surprisingly effective) tin-legged gait. "I succeeded in slipping Thelma aboard with me, since we're overnighting so near home. Don't tell Cristobal, for he'd be most jealous — wouldn't you sir?"

Flight Captain Abel's wife had just given birth to their first child, so she was back in Jimmystown, unable to fly along for what everyone seemed to assume would be a calm cruise over the ocean. Now the Guyanese pilot raised his hand and waved dismissively at his English first officer, "I do not listen to you, Douglas."

"There, you see, jealous," Bader clapped his hands together again. "I know Thelma would be delighted if you'd dine with us later. What do you say, M'Lady?"

As ever, Bader was a force unto himself, and Alex didn't have the will to resist either him, or the promise of food.

"Eating is one of my reasons for existing, Flight Lieutenant Bader," she answered most earnestly. "So long as we are still scanning the ocean while we eat, I'll be there. With Stephanie and Strong."

"Good show," the Englishman nodded with a grin. "And rest assured, Lady Alex, every detection device the dragons have given us is now pointed at the sea. If any creature — man, whale, or fish — can see a thing down there, then *Skipper Miller* can see it too."

It was impossible to question such confidence, so Alex allowed herself a smile, "You are a whirlwind, Flight Lieutenant."

"You should have seen me on my own two feet," he answered with a grin, then patted her on the shoulder before turning back to his console.

Resuming his seat, he got a smile from the much more reserved Flight Captain Abel, and then the pair went about mapping their route around the Grand Banks. Alex stood and watched for a moment, then turned towards the moving picture screen built into one of the consoles at the rear of the flight deck. It was already showing a multi-colored display of the ocean below, presumably revealing some of the otherwise-invisible details that the Saa sensors could see.

She wasn't sure if this ship could detect quite as much as Bader thought it could, but it could definitely see a lot. Hopefully enough...

Or better yet, hopefully there would be nothing at all to see.

"Report says there's weather coming. We'll see heavier seas overnight," Lieutenant Commander Oswin approached his Captain with that report, and Percy Todd nodded.

Inglefield was cutting east across the Grand Banks at a full thirty knots, and was rapidly approaching the rendezvous point as the sun dipped low behind her. The sea was relatively calm as she cruised, making for a reasonably smooth ride and few waves breaking over the fo'c'sle... but if weather was moving in, that wouldn't hold much longer.

"Think the Prime Ministers and the President have their sea legs?" the XO followed up with a smile, and Todd shrugged.

"Someone will undoubtedly regret not holding this summit in a nice bay," the Captain replied. "But if it's going to get heavy, we best get our guests off as soon as we rendezvous, even if it's after dark. Couldn't bear the thought of them getting dunked."

Oswin chuckled and nodded, "The whaler?"

"See to it," Todd confirmed, then raised his binoculars and looked out over the bow.

He could already make out a few shapes on the horizon — the outer ring of *Tribal*-class destroyers that were circling the Special Service Squadron. That meant they were indeed close, so it was likely they'd have a bit of twilight on their side as they sent their distinguished guests across.

"Ships off to starboard, sir — green three-eight," one of the bridge lookouts called out that sighting, and the Captain turned his binoculars in the noted direction.

"Of course there are ships, Phelps," Oswin gave the man good-natured grief, and the lookout clarified.

"Should have said Yankee ships, sir. That make it more interesting?"

With that, Oswin came alongside his Captain and raised his own binoculars, "Why yes, you've redeemed yourself!"

It was all very sporting, but Todd ignored the banter as he swept the horizon... then stopped on the shape of a ship, probably a *Benson*-class destroyer, heading directly for the rendezvous point. Behind that vessel, he could see just the hints of smoke rising over the horizon — presumably from the stacks of the American squadron bringing Roosevelt to the meeting.

"Well, this should be interesting," the Captain said quietly.

Getting from *Inglefield* hadn't been too harrowing, despite the fact that, unlike her daughter, Caralynne didn't consider herself a sea creature. The destroyer's whaler — actually just a rowboat, as far as she was concerned — had crossed the growing swells smoothly enough, and while Alain and his staff climbed up a covered stairway from the waterline, the elder Lady Smith and Anneke Winter had leapt aboard on an upswell.

Then there'd been fanfare, which Caralynne never enjoyed, and now the Royal Marines and the officers of *Hood* were milling around patiently, waiting for Roosevelt to arrive.

That gave Caralynne time to become more preoccupied with her reason for attending this summit in the first place.

"I can have one of my officers give you a tour, if you're that concerned, M'Lady," in addition to being perceptive, Captain Ralph Kerr was clearly trying to be diplomatic — and to his credit, he was largely succeeding. He was a veteran Royal Navy officer, and one of the best to be made Flag Captain of *Hood*, so he had to be used to dealing with all manner of people, including guests who rather pointedly inquired about his shipboard security.

But what he was offering — to have someone take Caralynne through the ship, looking for dangers — was at once generous and useless, and the Lady admitted as much: "I don't think I'd be much good at spotting anything out of the ordinary with the operation of your ship, Captain. But I trust your crew will be keeping an eye out for signs of... well, sabotage?"

It sounded rather dramatic, but again Kerr proved himself a gentleman. Smiling cordially and nodding, he reassured her, "We carry the Prime Minister, M'Lady. I can assure you, every man on this ship is watchful for anything that might hint at danger. We need only worry about threats from without... and between two powerful squadrons and the armor on our sides, I can say we are well-positioned."

His words were not overconfident, just assured. Taking another deep breath, Caralynne nodded and then smiled politely, "Yes. Thank you for indulging my concerns, Captain."

Kerr's smile grew broader at the words, "No need to sound so cordial, M'Lady. We appreciate having someone with your experience aboard, especially under such circumstances. You come across anything that makes you wonder, just get word to me, and we'll see to it."

Caralynne appreciated that — it was a promise of cooperation she wouldn't necessarily have expected. But as Admiral Lancelot Holland moved over to the pair, and began polite conversation, just a little of the natural tension she'd been carrying since August uncoiled. Looking around, she saw that she really was standing on the deck of Britain's most formidable warship, in the midst of its most vaunted squadron, in the middle of the sea.

No place could be absolutely immune to danger, but this particular spot was pretty good. Unfortunately, though, there'd be politicians to deal with.

Prime Minister the Lord Halifax had been at sea for a week, so he had better legs than Prime Minister Alain Lapointe to cope with the swells as they grew beneath *Hood*. That simply made it easier for him to stare at his dominion counterpart as he heard the plan.

"You cannot imagine him accepting such an idea," the Briton said after Alain finished explaining himself, and the Quebecker answered with a shrug.

"He must."

The sun was nearly down now, so Halifax's expression was dramatically lit: "Keep all the Champions in Newfoundland? Students or graduates, either way... that will be perceived as an attack on their sovereignty."

Of course Lord Halifax was speaking sense. Though he was a new Prime Minister, having been made leader after the cancer death of Neville Chamberlain, he was a lifelong statesman, and past Governor of India. He was one of the best examples of Britain's political class — intelligent, cordial, mature and, Alain feared, occasionally inflexible.

He had also never met Roosevelt, which didn't make his guess at the President's reaction any less correct… it just meant that he had no choice but to involve the Canadian Prime Minister in these meetings, since Lapointe and Roosevelt were relatively well-acquainted.

Now the soldier-turned-politician shook his head at the British Lord-Premier: "When we face an enemy of unknown abilities, sovereignty concerns must be seen in the context of security matters."

Halifax didn't like the sound of that — as beneficial as it might have been to put all the Champions together in one place, safe from sabotage behind one elaborate protection scheme, it could be politically explosive.

"Sounds rather like I'm interrupting at a bad time."

Anneke Winter was abruptly beside both men, her boots keeping the deck very steadily underfoot and her smile somehow bright, even in the near-darkness.

Halifax had enjoyed his trip across the Atlantic with the exceptional Lady, and now he set aside his concerns with Lapointe to be polite to her, "Thank you, Anneke. We were getting ahead of ourselves."

He shot a glare at Lapointe with the last words, but the Canadian Prime Minister merely smiled, then looked to Anneke as well, "Do you bring us good news?"

"The President's boat is coming alongside," she said easily. "We all need to form our receiving lines, or whatever diplomats call them."

"Aha," the Canadian grinned, then looked back to Halifax. "The game begins."

That earned him another glare from the Briton, but together the trio moved off to join the officers and marines preparing an honor guard. *Hood* was beginning to pitch more in the waves, so hopefully this would be done quickly.

Though most people believed President Roosevelt to be an able-bodied man, Caralynne knew better: FDR had lost the use of his legs after contracting polio on a vacation to New Brunswick. This had hardly stopped him becoming a beloved President, but as she waited in line with the men on *Hood's* rolling deck, she had to wonder how it would affect his attempts to come aboard.

"They're hooked!"

That was the signal for immediate formality — eyes turned front, a bosun appeared with a pipe.

Standing beside Caralynne, Anneke Winter raised her eyebrows and then smiled — a silent message confirming that the party was about to begin.

The light was virtually gone by the time a figure appeared at the top of the stairs, so Caralynne wasn't able to make out who the broad-shouldered man was until the lights from *Hood's* deck glinted off the wheelchair he was carrying.

Then the next figure appeared at the top of the stair... actually, it was two figures melded together in shadow: a male Champion carrying the President. As soon as Roosevelt was in sight, the bosun's pipes twittered, and the marines and assembled crew came to attention.

Caralynne and Anneke stood somewhat formally, though neither Lady managed to keep their eyes front; instead they watched as the Champion... Joseph Rockefeller, by the look of him... deposited the President in his chair, then stepped aside.

Halifax, Holland, Kerr and Alain approached their counterpart and made the official greetings, trading all the niceties. Caralynne glanced at Anneke, and the two British Empire Champions waited in silence until they eventually caught Rockefeller's eye and exchanged nods.

The pageantry started pulling the politicians towards the entrance to Admiral Holland's dining room, which was in the aft section of *Hood's* superstructure, just before the ship's aft 15-inch turrets grew from her hull. Following the procession quietly, both Anneke and Caralynne found their eyes sweeping their surroundings more suspiciously.

Despite Kerr's assurances, their instincts insisted they both be even more vigilant now that the President had arrived.

That in mind, they waited as Rockefeller carried his leader up the stairs to the entrance to Admiral Holland's section of the ship, watching as the receiving party was dismissed and word reached the bridge for *Hood's* screws to begin turning. To reduce the swells, Holland had promised to turn south and avoid the weather, but as the battlecruiser began accelerating into the rising seas, water started washing over the ship's stern.

Neither sailors nor marines seemed worried by the sight of their mighty ship being swamped by icy water, but Caralynne wasn't prepared for the visual — it looked for a moment as though the tide was coming in *over* the rails.

Discerning the elder Lady Smith's concern, Anneke leaned close to offer the answer she'd gleaned during her week aboard.

"*Hood* is rather a wet ship," she said with a shrug. "Low freeboard on the quarterdeck... in heavy seas, that's quite normal. Some water even gets into the ventilation gaps, ends up in the messes."

Somehow that made the ship seem less mighty — Caralynne had always simply assumed that a ship so grand would, well, *float*. And strictly speaking, she was sure *Hood* did... just less elegantly than advertised.

"Glad we're sailing away from the storm," she observed dryly.

"You know how it is, *some* pretty ladies can have their issues," Anneke offered, smiling.

It took a second for Caralynne to realize the lady she meant was *Hood*, but then she nodded, "I guess I can't judge her for wanting to get wet."

Then she winced at her choice of words — which to younger minds could have been an invitation for bawdy humor — and glanced at Lady Winter.

Anneke simply nodded, "Glad you understand. That's when I'm at my very best."

She then bounced her eyebrows up jauntily, and turned to follow the dignitaries into the ship. Caralynne had always felt somewhat like a mentor to Lady Winter, but Anneke had obviously picked up a few things elsewhere. Maybe that was for the best.

Together, the two Ladies entered the Admiral's dining room, leaving *Hood's* stern awash in the dark waters of the North Atlantic.

CHAPTER VIII

Waiting until 8:00 for supper tested Alex's humanity. As she sat at a table in *Skipper Miller's* dining room, she was unconsciously wringing her hands together and wearing a painted smile, just barely listening to Douglas Bader explain how he'd convinced Thelma to marry him.

"...so I said that I supposed it would make sense for us to be married, and she agreed," the Flight Lieutenant grinned gamely, and his wife shrugged.

"He's very romantic, you can tell."

Strong and Stephanie both laughed politely at Bader's quintessentially British confidence. He was the sort who would twirl a saber over his head as he rode into a horde of savages, and then emerge hours later, having somehow taught those Hubrin-engineered beasts how to read.

"Done in fine style there, sir," Strong offered his endorsement, and Bader sat back in his chair with a tip of head.

"I take that as very high praise from a man with your reputation, Colour Strong. No better fellow to keep these young ladies out of the clutches of n'ere-do-wells!" he replied

Strong shrugged, "I figure they keep me out of more trouble."

Stephanie added an earnest nod, "It is a chore, but fortunately he's entrusted us with great wisdom. You see, Flight Lieutenant, we now know that whenever we face a crisis and know not what to do, we need only ask one question..."

That was meant as a perfectly lame setup for Alex, and as the American Lieutenant's words trailed off, she looked across the table to her white-coated friend. Alex's eyes were open and her hands were kneading each other... but she had stopped paying attention.

As the silence drew out for a second, Stephanie kicked her

friend's boot under the table. Alex jumped a little, blinked back into the conversation, and then said the wrong thing: "I'm sure I can smell mashed potatoes."

When everyone laughed at her, Alex frowned, "Wait. I answered the wrong question, didn't I?"

"I'm sorry we've kept you from dinner so long, M'Lady," Bader grinned, recognizing her obvious appetite.

"Being hungry makes me extra-specially awkward," she answered sheepishly. "I'd never be any good at dinner dates."

Stephanie couldn't let that one pass, "You'd also need to find a man who didn't mind you eating five times what he does, and still being slightly hungry afterward."

Alex pointed across the table at her friend and nodded in agreement, "You're right about that. You see, Mister Bader, how dire my circumstances are."

"Oh, I'm sure some chap out there will make the sacrifice, for the good of the Empire," Bader offered his encouragement. "I can even think of a few men you might consider."

Strong interjected immediately: "Can you write me a list, with addresses?"

"The Colour intends to kidnap or kill them," Stephanie narrated helpfully, and immediately the Sergeant agreed with a nod.

Bader laughed gamely again, and then fortunately the doors to the kitchen opened and three servers emerged.

"Excellent," the Flight Lieutenant greeted them as he sat back to make room for his meal to be delivered.

But then all three men, each carrying two plates, moved over to Alex's side of the table. She levitated slightly from her chair, stretching her neck extra far beyond the collar of her coat — again, as if she were a turtle stretching out of her shell — and then watched with an irrepressible smile as the plates were laid in front of her.

All six plates, that was.

Good thing it was a big table.

With the Lady's food arranged, the men retreated empty-handed, leaving both Bader and his wife with looks of patent surprise on their faces.

"So," Alex said as she picked up her fork and prepared to launch her attack, "how many men were on that list?"

Stephanie shook her head, Strong grinned, and Douglas Bader

raised an eyebrow, "I will admit, M'Lady, I'm going to revise it slightly in light of recent developments. But don't you worry, never was a woman made for whom some man wouldn't be a willing foil!"

He reached over to his wife and covered her hand with his own as he spoke, and she smiled. Odd though Bader was, they seemed happy. That was good — it gave Alex a warm feeling.

Or maybe... probably... that feeling came from the food.

The Admiral's dining room on *Hood* was an elaborate affair — bigger even than the formal dining rooms on the skycruisers. Unfortunately, as the great battlecruiser drove southward through the swells of the Grand Banks at high speed, the table was not nearly so stable as that aboard *Skipper Miller*.

"We're maintaining eighteen knots as a precaution," Captain Kerr was sitting beside Caralynne as they dined, and he was explaining the security dimension of the speed. "At this speed, we'll be in calmer waters by midnight, and we cannot be followed by any sort of undersea aggressor."

By no means was the elder Lady Smith feeling totally at ease, but she nodded at the Captain's explanation, "Yes, very good."

A few seats down from her, Alain Lapointe was making strained small talk with his 'friend', the American President, "I was surprised that you decided to come aboard tonight."

Roosevelt was perched in his wheelchair, but despite the rolling of the ship, he seemed entirely comfortable, "Our weather ships say this storm will follow us, Alain. Since it's such an ordeal getting me aboard a ship anyway, I thought we best do it when the going was good."

The President seemed to maintain an affable air — Caralynne had never spent any time with him, having only been introduced at formal functions on a couple of occasions since his election. Sharing a dinner table with him in these circumstances was rather different. He appeared to be living up to his genial and wise fireside-chat reputation, but there was an unmistakable undercurrent of tension.

"Your familiarity with the sea stems no doubt from your time as Secretary of the Navy?" Lord Halifax was sitting opposite Roosevelt, and as the British Prime Minister was the epitome of a good statesman, he recalled that fact from the President's past with great ease.

Now Roosevelt chuckled, "Well done avoiding talk of 'sea legs', Lord Halifax."

"Sea wheels, perhaps?" Lapointe raised his glass at that point, and there was a diplomatic laugh between the three, before silence resumed, allowing them to continue to eat.

Caralynne turned her attention back to her end of the table — she had Joseph Rockefeller opposite her, the American Champion who had indeed been raised by the famous family, and who was perpetually assigned to help the Secret Service protect their President. He was an earnest sort, but beside him Anneke Winter was doing the best she could to charm him for information. No state secrets, of course, just the minor details of working with Roosevelt... habits, personal interests, or anything else that might be of use to Halifax and Lapointe in the discussions to come.

Such intelligence was more relevant to Lord Halifax than Lapointe, whose greater familiarity with Roosevelt granted him more flexibility in conversation. Though with his next words, it sounded to Caralynne as if he'd perhaps become too candid: "I was interested when you asked me to keep the Newfoundlanders out of this summit."

Roosevelt looked up from his plate, his expression remaining carefully genial, "With the exception of Lady Smith, of course." He nodded down the table towards Caralynne, and she caught his eye and raised her glass of sherry in his direction. With that acknowledgement he pressed on: "Frankly, Alain, it is our personal friendship that leads me to even want you included. The security matters between Britain and the United States should really be decided between London and Washington."

"With Ottawa as a mere mediator," the Quebecker sat back in his chair, his tone going dry.

Halifax gauged the mood of the President's words, then played a sympathetic card: "The fact that our Empire possesses many first ministers must indeed complicate affairs like this one, President Roosevelt. But I can assure you, we all have a common purpose here."

"I don't doubt that," the President replied. "Still, when you have three or four men pulling on your side of the boat, and I'm the only one with an oar on my side, holding course can be more complicated."

It was a polite way of indicating that Roosevelt was not going to allow himself to be outgunned in any summit as important as this one — the fact that Britain, Canada and Newfoundland each had their own Prime Ministers, and the United States had only one President, was not going to lead to an imbalance at the bargaining table.

Which suggested...

"It sounds, Mister President, like you think this is going to be a negotiation," Caralynne spoke up, loud enough for the entire table to hear. "I was under the impression this meeting was simply about enhancing our shared security."

She shouldn't have spoken. She was not a politician and obviously found little joy in being trapped with them... and yet, without Jimmy or the Newfoundland Prime Minister present, Alain needed someone to set the table for him.

And for some reason, instinctively, she'd decided it had to be her.

Roosevelt seemed ready for such a statement, if a little surprised by where it originated. Still, his reply was polite: "You have our Champion students in your institute, Lady Smith. We have no skycruisers. The isolationists in Congress — including my own Vice President — are sensing an opportunity for my country to divest itself of its international obligations. I sit at this table on a British warship in a far less equitable position than would have been the case six months ago."

Halifax frowned immediately, and moved to put his counterpart at ease: "Of course, we are a close friend and ally of the United States. There is no inequality between us and our partner of the new world."

Roosevelt raised an eyebrow, then glanced at the Briton, "I appreciate that sentiment. But the fact remains that I'm going back to Washington in a few days, and soon after there will be a Senate Inquiry into the collapse of half of our Champion-related abilities, led by men who questioned the expense of possessing them in the first place. Now, as if to prove them right, I can't even get my Champions who are posted around the world home quickly unless I ask to borrow one of your skycruisers, Lord Halifax. And I'd be willing to bet that Alain, here, is going to suggest a new structure to our relationship."

The timber in Roosevelt's voice was already turning — though dinner wasn't done, it sounded like discussions (perhaps negotiations) were beginning.

Caralynne looked quickly across at Rockefeller, whose face

remained stern, and then at Anneke Winter, whose charms had been shelved as she listened carefully and analyzed the implications of the words.

Down the table, Alain Lapointe didn't look particularly miffed at being found out. Instead he leaned forward, glancing from Halifax to Roosevelt, "You appreciate the broader world situation; you know how important it is to protect our Champions. We can accomplish that, *and* remove from your worries the isolationist front, without lessening America's participation."

It was clearly not a matter Halifax wanted to raise at the dinner table, "Gentlemen, we can leave this subject for our meetings tomorrow."

Lapointe was unwavering: "The Lady Emily Academy has capacity for your students. It has Saa-built detection, and a strong garrison. It is remote and surrounded by a friendly and consistent population. What safer place for the Champions? In the Hampton Roads, there is no such control — preventing sabotage is not so easy. Finding the perpetrators is difficult with so many passing through. Has your investigation uncovered who attacked Fort Eustice, FDR?"

Roosevelt's face had grown taut, and he answered dryly, "Colonel Adams is the current suspect."

"*Seriously*?" Caralynne leaned forward with that sharp reaction, but Lapointe immediately held up a hand to stop her pursuing the question — no matter how ridiculous the suggestion might seen, this wasn't the place to begin that debate.

"We are the closest allies in the history of the human race, but the power that protects us is not invulnerable. If we work together, we can use your isolationists to everyone's advantage, and make certain our Champions are safe," the Quebecker persisted, and Roosevelt stared at him, looking tired.

Whatever battles he was fighting with his own legislature were clearly taking a toll on the man — one who, almost single-handedly, had forced the United States to retain an interest in affairs beyond the borders of its own possessions, despite the ease of simply disengaging from the world scene, and basking in the riches of the new world.

Could Alain's plan give the isolationists the illusion of a victory, while in fact making certain America could remain engaged?

It was worth discussing, but not at dinner. That being the case, the President looked to his British counterpart, "As you say, Lord

Halifax, we'll discuss this tomorrow. I will want Lady Smith's opinion as well. For now, let us eat."

As silence descended, Lapointe glanced down the table to Caralynne. Trying not to appear too visibly irritated — particularly at the implication that Adams had been responsible in Virginia — she looked back to her own plate, then up to Anneke. Lady Winter caught her gaze and then raised her eyebrows. It was going to be an interesting summit, and Caralynne wanted it done quickly.

The fireworks would begin tomorrow.

CHAPTER IX

Standing watch at midnight on the bridge of a destroyer in the North Atlantic could be a cold proposition, particularly in early February. Still, Lieutenant Commander Oswin had seen worse nights; it wasn't so cold that the spume coming off the sea was freezing on the ship's hull, but it was entirely possible that if the weather caught up with them, he'd have to order hands out with sledgehammers to start breaking a thick layer of the cold stuff off *Inglefield's* superstructure. If too much built up, the ship could get top-heavy, and be in danger of rolling.

For now, the XO focused on keeping warm. The wind cutting over his ship's open bridge was strong and damp, which meant it had the ability to cling to a man, and chill him down to the bone. A strong drink could provide the illusion of warmth against that sort of thing, but Oswin wouldn't allow himself that luxury now — when standing watch on the bridge of a ship guarding *Hood* and the Special Service Squadron, it would have been entirely irresponsible.

Instead he wrapped up in his coat, scarf and hat, and watched the lights of the ships riding the waves around him. For all the potential dangers facing the flagship on a night like this, Oswin's first concern for *Inglefield* was to make certain she didn't accidentally collide with a squadron-mate in the darkness — or worse, get in front of a heavy cruiser's bow. For sake of security, the squadron was steaming at high speed and in an irregular formation, destroyers maintaining a protective ring with their ASDIC. It was risky business, with so many British and American vessels in close proximity. Ships could be accidentally rammed, even cut in half, if they were careless.

So Oswin paid close attention, and below him in the ASDIC room, three operators worked the recorder — most of the ship was at third-degree readiness, but those particular men had effectively gone to action stations as soon as night had fallen, just in case.

Now, to keep warm as much as anything else, Oswin moved over to the voice pipe leading down to their room, and called for an update, "Bridge, anything interesting down there?"

There was the briefest of delays, then: "Nothing sir, but the recorder is looking better. We're in calmer waters now."

Oswin grinned, "I might have noticed, since I'm standing outside."

"Your career choice is your business, sir."

The Lieutenant Commander laughed, for indeed, the ASDIC rating was right.

Caralynne was uncomfortable occupying a cabin that one of *Hood's* officers had kindly vacated for her. She never seemed to be able to relax when imposing herself on someone else's space... she'd almost have preferred to forego sleeping that night, and simply tough out the next day.

But to do so would risk a migraine, and if she fell victim to a bad headache, things would simply get worse. So as the bells sounded for 0100 hours, she tried not to think about the fact that she was not sleeping, and just let her subconscious lull her into a slumber. Even a few hours would help.

Alex yawned and leaned back in one of the chairs on *Skipper Miller's* flight deck. The weather outside the ship was growing increasingly intense — they were nearly 200 miles north of the British and American squadrons, cruising through the low pressure system that those ships were running from, though the skycruiser was entirely unaffected by the atmospheric tumult.

The flight deck was quiet, the night blacking out its windows and its internal lights on so that Flight Captain Abel and the sensor operator could work through their night watches.

There was no role for Alex, but she, Stephanie and Strong had decided that one of them would be awake at all times. That meant two-hour shifts each from midnight to 6:00 in the morning, and the whitecoat was up first.

Fortunately, there wasn't much to see.

Lieutenant Commander Oswin allowed himself one yawn as he turned away from the cruiser he'd been watching — he was certain it was *Suffolk* — and looked back towards the flagship.

Just in time to watch *Hood's* stern blow open.

It happened so suddenly, and somehow so casually, that it didn't seem real. There was a bright orange flash, followed by an enormous thunder — an incredible sound unlike anything he'd heard before that chased a fireball into the sky.

The Lieutenant Commander closed his eyes for a second — just one — and then opened them, surely expecting to find he'd imagined the explosion. Instead he saw the greatest ship in the Royal Navy's order of battle covered in burning oil, as if her bunkers had erupted all over her superstructure and then been lit.

And in that sickening, flickering orange light, he could see her begin to settle by the stern, her quarterdeck being covered by more waves than was normal.

Hood... wait. *Hood* had partly blown up?

As it just barely began to register, Oswin opened his mouth — tried to get air into his chest. Finally, after agonizingly long seconds, he managed to call out, "Action stations! Sound the alarm!"

Alex wasn't sleeping — her eyes were simply participating in special night exercises designed to simulate darkness.

"Wait... contact."

The exercises ended immediately, and Alex turned her borrowed chair towards the technician who was sitting on the opposite side of the command deck from her, keeping a much better watch of his screens than she was of hers.

Cristobal Abel turned as well, "What sort, and location?"

The technician was already working on those two questions, and the answers came fast from his Saa-built equipment, "Heat signature, like an explosion... over the Special Service Squadron's base course."

Abel frowned, "Not over any of the false coordinates?"

Shaking his head, the man looked at his Flight Captain, "No sir, that's the actual course of the actual ships."

The words had to sink in for a full second before Alex got to her feet and rushed to the man's shoulder. Even as she moved, Flight Captain Abel was turning back to his board of switches and activating full lights throughout his ship. He then sounded the action stations alarm, and began charting a new course.

• • •

Caralynne didn't remember falling asleep, but the thunder was impossible to escape, even in her dreams. *Hood* bucked beneath her rack, and as she was thrown harshly to the deck, the impact forced her quite rudely awake. Confusion set in first — an explosion? Surely just a vivid dream of some sort, reminding her of what had happened back at Fort Eustice when the American skycruisers had blown up on either side of *George Tucker...*

Not this time. This was real.

An alarm began to sound, even as *Hood's* deck started to dip towards the stern. Metal groans filled the air almost immediately, and then the small electric light in the corner of the cabin winked out.

Wrapped in darkness, Caralynne forced herself to her feet with some difficulty, then scrambled to the chair where she'd thrown her clothes. It sounded as though the ship was sinking... which, she imagined, couldn't possibly be the case.

Whatever was happening, she hoped she'd have time to dress.

Percy Todd just managed to close his coat before the wind hit him. The shocking impact of the cold gusts was breathtaking, but he hardly noticed as he scrambled forward across the bridge to Oswin's side, "Report!"

"Explosion on *Hood*, she's starting to settle by the stern," the Lieutenant Commander wasted no time as he pointed to the mighty battleship that was now illuminated by the searchlights from *Inglefield, Suffolk* and *Zulu*.

Before Todd could inquire any further, the Yeoman of Signals arrived behind him, slightly out of breath, "Message from *Rodney*, sir. Squadron to increase speed and begin zigzag."

Zigzag... Todd had to shake his head once to get the order to register. *Rodney* was seemingly taking command of the squadron, and that maneuver order suggested the ship's Commodore believed there were submarines nearby — that *Hood* had been hit by a torpedo. Accelerating away from the stricken battlecruiser would potentially save the other ships in the squadron from a similar fate.

"Anything on ASDIC?" Todd's question came out more like a demand, and Oswin shook his head immediately.

"They've been watching close all night. Nothing suspicious... and the waters here are too calm for them to miss a boat within

1,000 yards…" the Lieutenant Commander answered.

Indeed, Captain Todd couldn't imagine that his excellent crew would be so incapable as to miss a submarine under such conditions. Leaving *Hood* behind and zigzagging would thus serve no purpose.

That in mind, Todd turned back to his Yeoman, "Make to *Rodney:* will stop to assist *Hood.*"

The man nodded and then hurried aft towards the flag deck, leaving Todd to give orders: "Take us in close, ten knots. Prepare all boats and get nets over the side — if she's going down, men won't last more than fifteen minutes in this water."

The corridor was inky black as Caralynne stepped into it — the electrical systems seemed to have been defeated by whatever had happened. Fortunately, a damage control party hurried by almost immediately; harried men, mostly shirtless and looking as though they'd been roused from sleep, and all of them carrying flashlights.

"Sailor," Caralynne interrupted the last man in line, "I need a torch."

The man considered her with wide eyes, failed to speak, and then simply handed her his flashlight. With that he set off after his mates, following the shafts of light that were dancing down the corridor as they ran.

"Is that you, Caralynne?" Anneke's voice came from further down the hall, and turning her flashlight in that direction, the elder Lady Smith caught sight of the younger Lady Winter. She was just buttoning up her purple coat, but she'd clearly been sleeping — hair was a mess, and she looked to be wearing pajama trousers and slippers instead of breeches and boots.

"What do you think it was?" the younger Champion asked immediately upon recognition of her mentor, and Caralynne could only shake her head.

"It came from astern. Must have been some sort of explosion, and we must be taking on water because we're settling."

She stopped alongside Anneke as she spoke, and then the two ladies simultaneously heard men scream. A faint smell of smoke entered the air, and then it began to grow stronger.

"The oil bunkers?" Anneke suggested, and Caralynne nodded.

"We better get aft… Find the politicians and get them on deck."

Either *Hood* had been victim of the most ill-timed accident in the history of modern diplomacy, or Caralynne was witnessing her second sabotage-attack of 1941.

If the latter, she might never leave the house again...

"Signal from *Arizona*, radio in the clear, sir: Admiral Kimmel is ordering someone to go alongside *Hood* to take off the President. Apparently he's having an argument on the subject with Commodore Pettigrew."

The Yeoman was still out of breath — running to and from the flag deck wasn't normally an exhausting chore, but as *Inglefield* maneuvered violently to get in close to the rapidly-settling flagship, he was getting a workout just trying to stay upright.

"You sent our intention to assist?" Todd asked, though he expected that, no matter the confusion, this man wouldn't forget such an important duty.

"Yes sir, not sure if it was received. Seems there's a lot of panic out there."

Naturally, there would be — *Hood* was burning and settling, and it was the middle of a dark night. Commodore Pettigrew had to be wary of the experiences of the French Navy in the last war against the Germans; on one occasion, three French cruisers had been sunk by the same German submarine, one after the other as successive ships stopped to take on survivors.

If there was a submarine in these waters and *Rodney* or *Ark Royal* stopped, the whole of the Special Service Squadron could go to the bottom... but Todd wasn't convinced.

"Send it again, open radio this time," the Captain decided. "Say we have clear ASDIC and are assisting *Hood*. Request other destroyers join us..."

"Sir," the Yeoman nodded, and began to turn, but Todd stopped him with a hand. "And if you get orders for us to leave *Hood,* give them a blind eye, will you? I'm not leaving unless we get an ASDIC contact, Harry."

The Yeoman locked eyes with his Captain at the firm words, then nodded, "Sir!"

That was it: *Inglefield* would remain in position to offer whatever help a flotilla leader could provide to a battlecruiser, no matter what other flag officers said. Todd's career might end for his stubbornness, but he wasn't concerned with such petty things.

He turned back to Oswin, "You didn't hear that conversation, Richard."

"The hell I didn't," the Lieutenant Commander protested, but there was no time for either man to argue over whose career to protect. Instead, the XO nodded towards the orange flames spreading angrily across *Hood*, "Permission to command the launch?"

"Save any men who go over the side," Todd agreed without delay, and then with a pat on the shoulder, he sent the XO on his way.

Turning his full attention back to the flagship, he was able to see that *Hood's* aftermost 15-inch turret was close to submerging. She wouldn't be afloat much longer, but he still couldn't see any men in the water. Of course the sailors would be doing all they could to save their ship, but without a clearer idea of what was going on, Todd had no way of knowing if that was even possible.

"Multiphone isn't bloody working... find the Chief Engineer and see if we can get power back..."

Caralynne recognized the voice of Captain Ralph Kerr as he came up behind her, so she turned and immediately caught him in the light of her torch, "Captain, what's happening?"

Kerr had pulled his jacket and hat on over his pajamas too, it seemed, and as he squinted and held up his hand against her aggressive light, he revealed his preoccupation, "Who the devil is that, get your light out of my bloody face!"

"It's Caralynne," the elder Lady Smith replied. "With Lady Winter. We're getting aft to try to find the Prime Ministers and President Roosevelt."

"Dammit, follow us then," Kerr's previous diplomacy had obviously been shattered with the explosion, which made sense. A Captain's first duty was always to his ship, and Kerr hardly seemed the kind to forget that in a crisis.

"We've been hit, or sabotage?" Anneke's voice sounded from the darkness, but as the Captain advanced past Caralynne he made no effort to answer. It was likely he didn't know any better than the rest of them — whatever was going on was too sudden and too unexpected.

As far as Caralynne was concerned, the only good news was that the whole ship hadn't blown up, as the skycruisers had in Virginia.

But as small blessings went, that one really was miniature.

•••

"Look there — overhead!"

Captain Todd heard the call from one of his bridge lookouts and redirected his gaze skyward, just in time to see a large array of pinpoint lights race into view high above *Hood*. At first he wondered if they were Seafires off *Ark Royal*, but their flight path was impossible. Were they shells, or bombs?

Such grim possibilities were erased abruptly, as *Skipper Miller's* floodlights lit up the night sky. When needed, the skycruiser could unleash millions of candles of illumination, and seeing the horror below, the ship's Captain had obviously decided to do just that.

"Thank God," *Inglefield's* skipper gasped to himself. He wasn't certain what help a skycruiser could provide under circumstances such as these, but it was reassuring to have at least some high cover — and better light for his men.

Gaze dropping back to *Hood*, the Captain realized the ship would need all the favors it could get: no longer was she just settling into the swells, she was edging backwards into them.

"God dammit," he gasped to himself, then he turned and called for the Yeoman.

The man arrived in scant seconds, and Todd pointed to the battlecruiser, "Broadcast in the clear: *Hood* is sinking and we must take off any survivors. All ships."

It was in no way Todd's place to give orders to the Special Service Squadron, but any delay now would certainly cost lives. The Yeoman understood the urgency, and offered useful news in reply, "*Imogen* and *Zulu* have both responded they're coming in, and the Americans are sending cruisers, but Commodore Pettigrew sent a couple of orders that… I didn't receive."

So that was it, the Royal Navy was concerned about more loss of life, while the Americans were recklessly sending help. Many arguments would undoubtedly be made in days ahead about who was right — Pettigrew or Kimmel — but those questions were irrelevant now. Three destroyers and some cruisers would be enough to save many lives.

Because, dear God, *Hood* was actually *sinking*.

"Thank you, Harry," Todd found his voice was more reassuring than he thought possible. "Send our message, and then keep at it. You're doing well."

The Yeoman nodded and hurried away, and the Captain turned back towards *Hood. Inglefield* was close alongside now, and he could see men beginning to realize their ship was doomed and jumping into the sea.

Salt water could be at a freezing temperature without turning to ice, and being February this water no doubt fell into that category. Those men hitting the waves now had fifteen minutes if they were fortunate.

"Away all boats!" Todd called.

Then a new sound filled the air, and looking up, the Captain saw a shaft of light shooting out from the brightly-lit skycruiser above.

CHAPTER X

Douglas Bader took his seat beside Cristobal Abel just as *Skipper Miller* came to hover over *Hood*. The Flight Lieutenant was shaking his head, "By God, how'd that happen?"

"We're picking up open radio chatter... they're arguing about submarines... *Inglefield* doesn't think there are any..." the technician at the communications panel reported.

"I don't have anything on my scopes here — no sign of a submerged power plant," the technician running the Saa detectors added immediately.

Flight Captain Abel nodded at the report, "Nick, broadcast to all ships that there are no submarines. They'll need to get boats in the water to take off survivors."

"May be too late," Bader said grimly as he activated one of his console's screens and switched it to display the feed from one of *Skipper Miller's* downward-facing cameras. "Her aft turrets are going under... she's sliding fast."

It was obvious and inevitable: a ship made of steel could not float when she was full of water. All the men watching from above could hope was that as many crew and passengers as possible got off before they were dragged down to the frigid bottom with their ship.

Standing silent and wide-eyed at the back of the command deck, Alex could think only one thing: *Mom.*

Again — a *second time*. An explosion on a ship, but this time instead of the victims being neighboring skycruisers, it was the mighty flagship of the Royal Navy. Who could be doing this?

That was a question that would bear much examination later, but for now she had to do something — had to find a way to help.

"Unless..."

A frown crossed Flight Lieutenant Bader's face, and then he

turned his chair towards Alex. He'd passed her on his way in, but now he fixated on her.

"Cristobal, drop the heavy cargo cable," Bader said immediately, and the Captain glanced at him with a frown.

"What?"

Bader's voice grew louder, and his words were directed right at Alex: "You can swim well, M'Lady, and handle the freezing water. If we drop our heavy cargo cable, you can get it fixed to *Hood's* hull somewhere... we can keep her from sinking, at least for long enough to save some of the crew. And your mother."

Somehow, the mad, double-amputee had arrived at a plan — an impossible notion...

"We can't lift 45,000 tons of battleship!" Abel interrupted, but Bader held up his hand.

"Not clear of the water, but just keep her neutrally buoyant a little longer."

Alex's mind was reeling, but as had happened in Virginia, some part or her brain seemed able to process the suggestion. A cable, fixed to *Hood*, not to pull her clear of the water but just to keep her from sinking deeper, for a little longer? That *might* work...

"Open the nearest hatch!" she demanded immediately, and Bader nodded, his eyes remaining intently fixed on her.

"Port side, two frames aft!"

With that direction, the younger Lady Smith turned and raced from the flight deck, a blur moving at Champion speed.

"Releasing heavy lift cable," Abel called out a moment later, flipping a switch.

Though she'd managed to pull on her boots, Caralynne knew the instant sea water began lapping at the bottom of her feet. It was beyond cold — the leather's insulation wasn't nearly enough. She looked back towards Anneke, and in the light cast by the torch she saw the woman in purple feel the same water hit her slippers. Her eyes jolted wide, and then she looked towards her mentor with a knowing shake of the head.

Sea water obviously wasn't a good sign — especially because the smoke was getting thicker behind them.

Was *Hood* burning at one end, and sinking at the other?

"Dammit all, we need to power the pumps," Kerr slowed slightly as he waded into the cold water, but then was stopped by the sound of splashes.

"Sir? Captain?" an anonymous voice sounded from the darkness ahead, and as flashlights converged on the speaker, a harried-looking bosun appeared. "Sir, we're down by the stern, taking on a lot of water, sir!"

"I know," the Captain's tone somehow changed immediately — whatever his frustrations, he seemed determined to project calm for his panicked men. "We must get the pumps working. Are you with a damage control party?"

"No sir... just a bunch of us trying to help," the bosun waved his hand back towards a group of men sloshing up the corridor through ankle-deep water.

Directing his own light further down the passageway, Kerr could just see in the weak light that the water was getting deeper further aft. There was no time for orders or collecting information — without pumps, *Hood* would surely go down.

"You men, with me — we'll get to engineering and restore power," he ordered, and then turning back up the corridor, he stopped as he caught Caralynne in the light of his torch. "Whatever it takes, we'll restore power. This corridor will take you down to the Admiral's quarters, you must look after the dignitaries."

Entirely focused on the task at hand, he didn't wait for a response. Though as he led his brave sailors forward, presumably to a ladder to a lower deck, Caralynne wondered whether saving the ship was possible.

After the men sloshed off through the deepening frigid water, Anneke crossed the dark corridor and stopped alongside the elder Lady Smith, "Let me check something."

They were near a hatch to one of the ship's mess decks, so Anneke grasped its handle and cranked it. As it opened, water spilled out from the space behind, soaking her pajama pants up to their knees before it dropped down to mid-calf.

It was all she needed to know, so she shut the door.

"I'm no sailor, but I think the ventilation shafts that serve this part of the ship are underwater, or close to it. We're definitely sinking."

"And on fire," Caralynne added, referring to the smell of smoke. "We better hurry."

She had no idea what they could possibly do, even if they found the Prime Ministers and the President... but there had to be something. Her mind simply wouldn't allow her to consider otherwise.

Directing her light down the corridor again, she started hurrying into the deeper, frigid water.

As soon as the outer door opened in front of Alex, a strong gust of wind hit her. She planted her hands against the hatch frame, then leaned forward out of *Skipper Miller's* hull and looked down. The skycruiser's powerful lights made the situation clear: *Hood's* forward superstructure was burning, probably due either to oil that had been spilled out of her bunkers or aviation fuel that had sprayed out of her spotting seaplane. The ship's stern was mostly underwater, and the rest was following fast.

No time to overthink what she was about to do; if something didn't stop the battlecruiser's slide, the whole ship would be underwater in a minute or two. She had to get down there.

Reaching up to her collar, she quickly undid the buttons on her coat, then shrugged it off and hung it over the edge of one of the control boxes inside the hatch's airlock. The trusted garment would only weigh her down as she tried to swim fast. She shed her boots as well — she'd need be able to kick freely if she was going to have a hope of maneuvering down there — and then returned to the edge.

It was going to be frigid. She was used to swimming in the North Atlantic, but even she knew better than to do so in February...

No choice. As *Skipper Miller* held its hover, she spotted the end of the heavy-lift cable that had dropped from the ship's bottom — a cable the skycruiser could use to lift all sorts of containers, but none quite so heavy as *Hood*. Still, Bader was right: they just had to keep the ship neutrally buoyant for a little while. She'd need to get that cable around something that could take the weight.

With a great big breath, Alex tried to visualize herself doing that. Then, as *Hood's* aft funnel began to touch the water, she planted her hands on either side of the hatch frame, and jumped.

"What the devil?" Percy Todd saw what was certainly a person dropping from the side of *Skipper Miller*. As he was a rational human being, he could not immediately imagine what would possess a person to leap from the sky into the freezing North Atlantic. Then he managed — just barely — to recognize the blurred shape. She wasn't wearing her white coat, but her slender form was clear in the bright light cast by the skycruiser. She had her arms crossed over her chest, her feet were together, and her toes — bare toes, he was certain — pointed towards the water.

She was following the skycruiser's cable into the water... but why?

Captain Todd didn't know, but he couldn't help but wonder whether it was a reckless venture that would end with his men saving Alex from the sea.

Or, *hopefully* being able to save her. He had no idea how long a Champion, particularly one as slender as the younger Lady Smith, could survive in the icy waves.

Alex had never been hit by a bus, but she could only imagine it was similar to the feeling of hitting the water. The shock would have instantly killed most ordinary humans — all the blood in her body withdrew to her core as soon as she struck the waves, the cold convincing her system that she was about to perish.

She couldn't breathe, could barely think. She didn't remember where she'd hit the waves, or even why. For a second, everything about her was focused on sheer survival — what the hell had she done?

Fortunately, her many swims around Newfoundland left her body with the natural instincts of an awkward sea creature. Her mind forced her legs to kick, so blood was shunted reluctantly away from her central organs and into her thighs, calves, and feet. Then her arms realized they had to participate, so flow was restored to them as well. She was a Champion; her body could function after such shock.

Her mind still wasn't fully-alert when she breached the surface, coughed, and gasped in the air. She had to force her eyes open, focus them in the simulated daylight cast by *Skipper Miller*, then... then...

Hood was sinking.

Her wits returned when she saw the ship's bow beginning to rise as the weight of the water in her stern pulled the battlecruiser down at a more dramatic angle. There was no time...

Ignoring the painful cold, she started to swim — raced like a motor boat towards the heavy lift cable that had pierced the water nearer the battlecruiser. As soon as she was close enough she went under, catching the end of the heavy braided steel in her hands and forcing it to move towards *Hood* with all the strength her frozen muscles could muster.

It moved easily — or perhaps that was adrenaline — and as she pushed it she pulled herself down towards its end. A massive hook was there, designed to secure the eight-inch-thick cable to itself when looped through load-bearing rings on whatever was to be carried.

She had to find something to hitch that hook too, or to run the cable around.

As *Hood* came into sight, still near enough to the surface to be barely illuminated by the lights from above, she realized she probably needed another breath before she could get the cable onto anything. Pulling herself up along the steel rope, she breached the surface again, sucked in all the air she could hold, and hoped it'd be enough.

Her eyes traveled around the ship for a second — she saw the funnels sliding down — and then she dove and kicked, swimming fast. As she got to the end of the cable, she clutched the massive hook and dragged it towards what she could see of *Hood*. The mighty ship's aft tripod was submerged, but she had no idea whether its masts could possibly take the weight. Just deeper than that, though, was the aft conning tower, or whatever it was called...

That. She'd pull the cable around the conning tower as though it were a lasso, hook it to itself, and then... hope. Kicking for all she was worth, she dove deeper, the cable trailing behind her.

The slope of the deck was getting increasingly dramatic, which Caralynne knew couldn't bode well.

"If we can't find them, what do we do?" Anneke Winter asked, barely managing to mask her anxiety at the angle of the corridor. It seemed a sure indication that *Hood* was sinking deeper into the sea, and the water was already up to their thighs.

Though neither Champion was as accomplished a swimmer as Alex, they could certainly survive the water long enough to get to the surface, if they could find a way out of the darkened maze of the ship... but they'd only find that escape if they tried.

And trying would mean abandoning the politicians.

Caralynne had no hunger to die — none at all — but... but...

"We keep looking until we can't go any further. After that..."

she let her words trail off, and Anneke took a breath before nodding.

Drowning while trapped in a sinking flagship was not the way she'd expected her new assignment to end, but she had no choice but to risk it. Her duty now was to protect the Prime Ministers... and more importantly, the woman who'd been her role model wasn't giving up. She couldn't turn back unless Caralynne said so.

The deck got steeper, and the water deeper, but they pressed on.

Strong and Stephanie emerged onto the flight deck in a hurry, both having taken only a moment from the sound of the alert to arrive. Surely nothing important could have happened in such short a time — they'd been 200 miles from *Hood*, after all.

"Make sure she has all the slack she needs..." Flight Captain Abel was saying, and Bader nodded in reply.

"Let's drop another twenty feet... by god she's really starting to go down now."

Hurrying forward to stand over the pilots' shoulders, Stephanie needed a second to realize what she was looking at: *Hood's* bow was reaching up into the night sky, and the great ship was burning and beginning to backslide into the water.

"What the hell...?" she asked, but she was cut off by one of the technicians from behind, who was watching the scene below on a screen.

"Lady Alex has surfaced again... she's giving the thumbs up!"

Stephanie wheeled quickly and opened her mouth to question the report — Alex had done what, from where? But things were moving too quickly.

"Vertical thrust, *now*," Cristobal Abel's order was instant, and Flight Lieutenant Bader wasted no time.

"No fear!"

He flipped the necessary switches, and *Skipper Miller's* engines roared louder than Stephanie ever remembered hearing before.

The roar was as loud as an entire battle squadron unleashing broadsides in unison... perhaps louder. Captain Percy Todd grabbed his hat just in time to save it from the gale that hit him, as the wind kicked out by *Skipper Miller* became positively stunning.

Slowly gaining altitude, the massive ship took the slack off the line it had dropped, then gradually began to force its way higher into the air.

And quite unbelievably, *Hood's* slide into the waves slowed... then stopped. And then, just slightly, some of her hull re-emerged from the North Atlantic, and her severe angle leveled off a bit.

"By God," Todd breathed the words — and then he heard some of his men cheer.

The Saa-built machine was pulling *Hood* free of the waves? Or just buying time?

"She's *down there*?" Stephanie sounded about as incredulous as a person could, but no one on the command deck answered — they were all concerned with the rather dangerous business at hand.

"Drives now operating at overload," Bader reported. "Ten minutes before we're in trouble. Fifteen before I'll say quit!"

Of course he was gallant even under such circumstances, but Flight Captain Abel was more concerned about another part of his ship's anatomy: "I don't know how long the cable mount will stand the weight."

"Right," Bader agreed. "Freddie, get men down there to keep an eye on it..."

As the Flight Lieutenant turned to give that order, he came face-to-face with Stephanie, and the American Lieutenant was more than slightly menacing: "She's down *there*?"

He blinked, then nodded, "Got our heavy lift cable secured to the hull, to keep *Hood* from going down until we can get people off."

"Dammit," Stephanie backed off, then looked to Strong. "What... do we do?"

Mike Strong didn't know what he could do, but fortunately Bader had an idea: "We have some inflatable rafts aboard. If you can get down to the main bay, we can open the front ramp and you can get them over the side. Ordinary men won't survive in that water without them."

Right. And though Alex could survive without a raft, Stephanie figured sending one down for her wouldn't be a bad idea either. Perhaps a fearless American Lieutenant could go down with it...

"Ordinary people have fifteen minutes in water that cold, if they're lucky. You wouldn't survive going after her," Bader seemed to read her thoughts, then shook his head. "I'm sorry."

Stephanie knew that. Of course. Just didn't like it.

But reality had to be respected, and there were times when, no matter how headstrong she was, she simply couldn't follow her friend into danger. But she'd still find a way to contribute, and the Flight Lieutenant had suggested a good one.

That in mind, she waved to Strong, "Let's get men together to drop the rafts."

It was all they could do, so they hurried from the command deck.

Below them, *Hood* had a reprieve — but for how long?

CHAPTER XI

The deck was dipping less towards the stern, and as soon as she was sure she wasn't simply imagining that, Caralynne stopped. Water was still up to her thighs, but the change in the ship's angle seemed to have stopped it going any higher.

"Are we leveling off?" Anneke asked hopefully. Then another thought occurred to her: "And if we are... does that mean the bow's underwater and we're sinking flat?"

Neither Champion had been trapped inside a sinking battleship before, so it was impossible for them to do more than guess. The sound of twisting metal was getting worse, though... whatever that meant.

"We better just assume it's good news," the elder Lady Smith said quickly, and with an uneasy nod, Anneke agreed.

"Let's keep moving."

The wind and the roar was intense as Alex surfaced. She was entirely out of breath and gasping for air, but the down-thrust from *Skipper Miller* was doing everything it could to drive the oxygen right past her. Her lungs fought back, taking in what they could as she let her legs drift up to the surface.

She floated like that for a moment, restoring oxygen to her body, and as she did she turned her head just enough to see that *Hood's* superstructure had temporarily stabilized. The cable was holding... for now.

But she had no idea how long it could possibly last. *Skipper Miller's* engines were clearly operating at the top end of their ability, the cable was only so strong, and the conning tower might not hold either.

As oxygen finally made its way back to most of her system, and the danger of suffocating resigned its position as her top-of-mind worry, she gradually let her legs drop back into the sea. They began kicking to keep her upright, and that positioned her better to watch. Hundreds of men — ordinary, frozen men — were in the water not far from her, some of them swimming, others looking as though the frigid waters had already caused their bodies to shut down.

They needed to get dry soon, and fortunately, boats were hurrying into the picture. Spinning around in the water, Alex could see one destroyer was very close, and a handful of freezing men were climbing up the nets that had been lowered over its sides. She could also see two other ships hurrying into the area, so more help was at hand.

But where was her mother? Was Caralynne among the survivors? Were any of the dignitaries?

She didn't know...

"There away! Stop engine!"

Alex didn't need Champion hearing to detect the urgent call. She turned again in the water and discovered a motor launch was hurrying up to her — had just, in fact, cut its engine so as not to race past her. Leaning over the side was a disheveled-looking British officer.

"Lady Smith, your hand!" he called as the boat drifted to a stop, but Alex instinctively shook her head.

"Have the Prime Ministers or my mother come off yet?"

It was perhaps ambitious to think any man could possess that information in the midst of such confusion, and indeed, the officer could only shake his head, "No idea, M'Lady, but you can't tolerate this water."

"Where in the ship would they be? Bow or stern?" somehow, despite the cold and the circumstances, her tone assumed the air of aristocratic authority that she'd learned from her mother, and the Lieutenant straightened up in surprise.

For a few seconds he thought about it, then shook his head, "Stern, behind the turrets. The Admiral's quarters are right under the after conning tower, usually... though I've never been in *Hood*..."

She knew where that was. She had literally been right there.

But the whole section was under water... how long could she hold her breath? What if she got in there, got trapped... drowned...

Alex resisted the brief panic that flashed through her mind — let it freeze in the water. She fancied herself a sea-going creature. She had a better chance than anyone, and she had to try.

"I'll go for a look…" she said, then turned away from the launch, directing her eyes to the hundreds of men in the water. Many of them were swimming back *towards* their ship — proud sailors, some of the Royal Navy's finest, undoubtedly hoping that the stop in their ship's slide meant they could get back aboard and save her. Even though half her superstructure was still a blazing inferno.

The ship was beyond saving, and such brave men didn't deserve to die trying.

"We don't know how long we can hold her up, but there isn't much time," she shouted, looking back to the Lieutenant. "Don't let those men back aboard. Save all you can."

The officer was open-mouthed with surprise, but before he could protest, Alex let herself sink back into the water, then turned for *Hood* with the strongest kick she could manage.

"Hello? Who is that?"

Caralynne was honestly surprised by the relief she felt at hearing Alain Lapointe's hail — she hadn't quite realized how anxious she was about his possible survival.

"It's me and Anneke," she called back, not immediately certain where the Prime Minister's voice was coming from.

He didn't make her guess: "In here!"

The words were coming from behind a half-open door, and as she shone her light in that direction and waded through the water, the elder Lady Smith was able to see that it led into a wardroom. With Anneke right behind her, she reached the door and shouldered it open, then looked into a cramped, swamped compartment holding a half-dozen men.

Turning her light in the direction of the survivors, Caralynne immediately picked out four: Lapointe, Lord Halifax, and Rockefeller were standing around the wardroom table, upon which Roosevelt sat. Two of Lapointe's staff were in the corner, too… and everyone looked exhausted.

Only the Canadian Prime Minister seemed to possess any energy — true to his character as a soldier who'd stormed the Hubrin capital of the new world alongside Colonel Waller. He waded forward through the frigid water, grasping Caralynne's shoulder as soon as he was near enough, "We had to escape from the flooding, but we cannot move the President much further."

Turning her light back towards the table, Caralynne could see FDR was barely conscious. For a man who had already survived so much in his life, there could hardly be a worse circumstance.

"We'll have to try. I don't know why we've leveled off, but we better not waste the chance. Can you carry him, Joseph?" the elder Lady Smith put that question to Rockefeller, and he nodded.

"I can, but where do we go?" he replied, and then Caralynne realized none of the men had a torch — they would have scrambled to this place in darkness, with even less idea than she and Anneke about what was going on.

"Forward... hopefully the fires that caused the smoke we've been smelling are out," she concluded.

It was all they could do, so they prepared to collect the President and make their way out of the wardroom.

All around them *Hood* groaned and struggled to hold together under the strain.

Alex surfaced for one more breath when she reached the cable, and then she dove straight down. Following the steel line to the hull, she could see the lasso was already crushing the armored conning tower — metal was buckling and would undoubtedly give way.

But she still had time.

Diving down further, she was able to see thanks to *Skipper Miller's* powerful lights: there was a hatch right off the quarterdeck, under the nameplate 'HOOD'. She swam to that hatch, cranked its handle. The water pressure inside and outside must have equalized, because it opened with ease.

She swam through... right into something heavy, but soft.

The impact shocked her; then, as the tiny amount of light let in through the room's portholes allowed her to see it was a body, she swatted it away... swam blindly into the chamber and hit a bulkhead. Just enough light was coming in for her to see it was a wall, and to detect a nearby hatch. She checked her breath — wondered how much air she had left, and then decided to try it.

She could last longer underwater than most...

So she swam to the hatch, put her hands on the handle, and forced it. Again it opened with ease — the whole damned stern of the ship had to be flooded. Surely her mother would have escaped towards the bow... unless there was damage somewhere and she was trapped...

Alex didn't know. But half her air was expended, and as she pulled herself into place at the opening of the door, she realized there was no light in the corridor beyond — it was an interior passageway without portholes. If she went in, there was no telling where it would end, or if she'd be able to get back out.

For a few seconds she wondered what to do — wondered how brave she was, to swim into a sinking ship — and then her mind decided she wasn't brave at all. She was floating down here with dead men, in a ship that was minutes from going to the bottom. The water was frigid — so cold that she wasn't sure she was even feeling it anymore, which was worrying — and she needed to escape.

She had to run away, and that was the end of it. Her mind was made up.

Her body, in the meantime, was pulling her straight into the blackness, and she was kicking for all she was worth. If there was no air at the end of this corridor, she'd need all her Champion speed to get out again before she tried breathing water.

Though Roosevelt might have been physically impeded by his paralysis, all the men in the wardroom were showing signs of hypothermia. Only Lapointe was somewhat active, perhaps because he'd previously suffered nerve damage from a Hubrin pulse cannon. He was shivering and chattering, and his body might be dying in the icy water, but it was too wounded or too stubborn to know.

Dragging Lord Halifax away from the wardroom, Caralynne could only hope she could find a dry compartment for the man soon — else his body would give out completely due to the cold. Anneke Winter moved to help Lapointe, but the Canadian swatted her away, "My men. Quickly."

They waded away from the wardroom, but the water was starting to rise again — up to their waists. Speed was essential, but impossible...

Lord Halifax tripped on something. Caralynne didn't know what, but it was irrelevant; she just managed to keep him from going face-first into the water. He actually tried to apologize as Caralynne hoisted him up as best she could. Gritting her teeth, she carried him in her arms.

The fact that lifting the relatively light man hurt her was sign of how cold her muscles had to be. She could keep functioning longer than the rest, but she was by no means immune. Still, she had to keep trying.

With difficult strides through the water, she walked for the bow, hoping beyond hope there would be a means of escape.

After years of swimming, Alex could instinctively sense when there was air above her, and as soon as she knew it was present in the black passageway, she rolled over and came to the surface, breathing in all she could. The air tasted smoky, but it was enough to keep her going; she rolled and dove again, then kept swimming. It wasn't long before the water shoaled, and she was able to put her bare feet on the deck.

As her feet touched the passageway floor, though, she realized her toes weren't sending back much sensation. She was still functioning, and she was reasonably confident that she wasn't experiencing frostbite yet, but she couldn't waste time.

Struggling forward into the darkness, she called out: "Hello? Is anyone here?"

Caralynne didn't hear anything — she was too focused on keeping Halifax out of the water — but Anneke Winter was further behind, and the men she was helping were still partly on their feet.

"I hear something," she said as she stopped abruptly, then turned back towards the darkened corridor behind them. "Hello? Who's that?"

The call echoed down the enclosed passageway, aided by the water that was lining the bottom half. Sound always traveled better over the waves, so while Alex couldn't quite gauge the distance to the shouter, she felt a moment of relief — someone alive.

"Lady Alex Smith, I have a way out here, but you must hurry! The ship is about to sink!"

"It's *Alex*," Anneke barely managed to rasp the name out in surprise, and turning with wide eyes, Caralynne struggled to say anything at all. Lady Winter continued instead: "She must have swum in. We could escape that way..."

She trailed off as she looked at the men around her — ordinary men who were already almost dead because of the water. Surely they couldn't survive being fully submerged, but to *not* try would guarantee death...

Anneke didn't know the answer. For all her many perfections, she wasn't quite ready for this.

Fortunately, President Roosevelt — cradled in Rockefeller's arms — was somehow alert enough to decide, "Yes, we must try."

Water sloshed and splashed as a party came down the corridor towards Alex. The level was rising past her waist as she waited — it had to be flooding into *Hood* from other parts of the hull. Wherever it came from, it was collapsing the air pocket available to the survivors, and making the ship heavier too.

Soon the cable would give way. Time was running out.

"Who's that?" she called out as they approached, moving so slowly they were presumably ordinary.

"Anneke's here, with Alain and the President and Lord Halifax!"

For a second, Alex didn't recognize her own mother's voice. Then relief warmed her as she forced herself forward through the water and was captured by the light of a bright hand torch.

"Mom?" she asked the obvious, because she needed to know for certain, and Caralynne called to her.

"Don't hug me, I'm carrying Lord Halifax!"

It might have sounded funny under different circumstances, but it was clearly a serious warning now. Alex stopped her advance just as Lapointe, now in command of the flashlight, reached her, "We are all having hypothermia."

His teeth were chattering and his accent thickening as he forced out the words, so Alex reached out to wrap her arms around him in a bid to at least share some warmth. When she felt nothing at their bodily contact, she realized she might not be able to help matters at all — it was a miracle of Hubrin genetic engineering that she was able to function, but she certainly had no heat to spare.

"*Skipper Miller* has a cable around the conning tower, keeping us from going down... but it's buckling. We must go now. I came in through the Admiral's quarters, I think... it's very cold but if we pair Champions with men, we can probably drag everyone out. There are boats up there to take us aboard," she began explaining the situation with surprising certainty, and Caralynne could only agree.

"It's our only chance," she replied, looking to Halifax. "Prime Minister?"

"Try," he rasped.

"Yes," Roosevelt agreed.

Whether either man was able to think rationally in the cold was impossible to know, but their determination to survive overrode everything else. And this was their only remaining chance.

"Alright," Caralynne called to her daughter, "lead us out. We'll wait until we lose the air to go under."

Stephanie gave a last heave, and the inflatable raft went over the side of the ramp. The wash from *Skipper Miller's* downward-facing thrusters caught the rubber dingy and drove it straight down to the water, and as she leaned over the edge she could see men swimming towards it, some of them dragging their shipmates with them.

"Next one!" she called, putting her hands on her safety line and using it to pull herself back into the main bay.

Strong and three of *Skipper Miller's* crew were already pulling the inflation cord on the next raft, and the Sergeant looked up as it made a ripping sound and started to take shape, "See her yet?"

It was a testament to her fortitude that Stephanie kept her answer short, "*No.*"

Alex was still alive, surely…

As the water reached her chin, the younger Lady Smith turned back to her mother and shook her head, "I think we swim from here."

Caralynne was still holding Halifax as high as she could, but the water was too deep for her to keep more than his head and neck dry. His shivering had already stopped.

"We can't waste time. Is there any light out there?"

Shaking her head, Alex took the torch from Lapointe's hand — he was just barely able to keep it from submerging — and tucked it up between some pipes overhead, to cast better light for the freezing party.

Then she recalled the route: "A corridor straight down to the dining room, and there will be some light from the portholes there. The hatch will be on our left as we're going out. Get through it and then surface fast. If you go straight kicking strong, maybe thirty seconds."

That was Champion-speed swimming, of course — ordinary people wouldn't have had a hope of covering the distance on a single held breath... certainly not in this water, anyway.

"Just..." Alex nearly said that she hoped the hatches she'd opened hadn't somehow drifted shut behind her, but that would have served no purpose. Any Champion would have the air to stop and open one if it were closed, but the delay would almost certainly kill an ordinary person.

"We have five people and four Champions," Anneke interjected with a more pressing concern. She was keeping the heads of the political aides above the water, but they were both only barely conscious. "If I don't need my hands, I can take both at once."

That was an ambitious hope, but there was no time to argue. Instead, Alex nodded, then pulled Alain Lapointe closer to her, "I'll go first, with the Prime Minister. I'll make sure nothing's in your way."

Everything felt like it was in a rush. In matters of life and death such as this, time was supposed to feel as though it was moving slower. But it wasn't. They were freezing, and couldn't afford to delay.

Looking to Alain Lapointe, she found his earlier lucidity was fast fading. He managed to meet her gaze for a second, but then his head started to loll to one side.

"Alain," she used his Christian name in a whisper, then clasped the side of his face and shook him. "Deep breath."

He blinked a couple of times, just long enough for a second of recognition, and then took a deep gulp of air. Without even looking back to her mother, the younger Lady Smith collected her own breath and dove into blackness.

It was terrifying.

She trusted her sense of direction, but as she clutched Lapointe close to her body and kicked hard, she found herself travelling through a tunnel of blackness, with no light at its end. She could only hope, pray, believe that she hadn't lost her mind — that the escape she promised existed, that she hadn't just killed herself, her mother, Lady Winter, Lapointe, and everyone else.

Inside her own mind, she panicked. Hey body kept working — a skill it had obviously gotten better at since August — but in her mind, all the monsters and terrors were floating near her. And seconds ticked by.

She desperately held onto Lapointe. She kicked.

And then the Prime Minister's arms suddenly tightened around her — she feared that meant he was out of air. Kicking harder, she wondered when the light would come — how much farther?

Quite abruptly, it was around her — faint but real. The dining room she'd entered through, dead men floating within, and its hatch still open. She didn't wait, just freed one hand from Lapointe to change directions, then kicked straight out the portal.

Suddenly she was free — in the open, frigid ocean, with the light growing around her as she neared the surface. She breached with a gasp and a cry of relief, then used both arms and all her determination to lift Lapointe as far from the waves as she could.

"Help!" she called as loudly as she could manage. "Please help us!"

She tried to turn — to see who was nearest, if anyone — and then she nearly bumped into the motor launch that had come to her before.

"Get him aboard, hurry there," the same officer was leaning over the side, and suddenly his hands were on Lapointe. The Prime Minister was pulled from her grasp. Freed of that responsibility, Alex didn't wait: she filled her lungs and dove down again.

Anneke was the next out of the ship, and like the heroine she was, she had one man under each arm. Alex swam to them and got hold of one of the aides. Together the two young Ladies breached again, then held up their men to the waiting hands of the boat's crew.

"We must help the others," Anneke gasped as soon as they were clear, and without any delay, she and Alex both dove again.

Caralynne was already coming up. The daughter felt the warmth of relief at seeing her mother, but the elder Lady Smith was waving frantically, and pointing down. Rockefeller and Roosevelt had not yet emerged, and understanding the message, Alex and Lady Winter dove deeper.

As they drew nearer *Hood*, it became clear that time was short: the heavy-lift cable was sliding off the conning tower, tearing away some of the armor as its grip slipped. Alex tugged on Anneke's coat and pointed to that as warning, and then they both swam for the open hatch.

Into the dining room they went, pushing aside the body of one man with much braid on his sleeve — Anneke recognized him as Admiral Holland — before heading for the entrance to the passageway. There was no sign of either Rockefeller or Roosevelt, and no light by which to see them.

The two younger Champions looked to each other, then with wordless and mindless determination, they swum back into the blackness.

"Get him inboard, I must go help with the President!" Caralynne was calling orders as she helped hoist the limp form of Lord Halifax into the motor launch.

As soon as he was clear, she turned back towards *Hood*, seeing for the first time the fires spreading across the ship's superstructure.

Then there was a new sound.

"Dammit!" Douglas Bader just managed to grasp the sides of his console as *Skipper Miller* rocketed skyward at great speed, the heavy-lift cable shooting out of the water below. Like a massive whip it slashed through the air, narrowly missing *Inglefield's* superstructure before it was violently pulled to a much higher altitude.

Stephanie was thrown off her feet by the sudden acceleration, and as the wind rushed past the ramp she realized with no minor terror that she was sliding down towards the opening. She had a line on — surely it could take her weight if she violently dropped out of the ship...

"No you don't!" Mike Strong landed on his stomach with a grunt, and got a hand around hers before she could go further.

Behind him, one of *Skipper Miller's* crew hit the emergency close, and the ramp shut at maximum speed.

Lying on it as it came up, Stephanie realized she was out of breath, "God. Thanks."

Strong managed a smile as he picked himself up off the deck. He'd done quite a leap to get to her before she fell out of the ship, and he wasn't even wearing a safety line.

But before he could say something gallant, he was struck by a revelation. Locking eyes with Stephanie, he said: "*Hood's* going down."

• • •

It was easy to lose one's orientation while underwater, and it was even worse in a dark, enclosed space. As such, Anneke Winter didn't notice the difference in the passageway she was gliding through — she had no special instinct for the sea.

But Alex knew something was wrong.

The sound of shearing metal was one warning — it was sharper than before — and as soon as she heard it, the younger Lady Smith felt something shift around her. Urgently, she reached out and caught hold of her companion's purple coat. Thank God Anneke was still wearing it, otherwise Alex might have missed grasping her in the darkness.

Pulling hard, she convinced Lady Winter to change directions — to retreat down the corridor they'd been blindly following in search of the President. Anneke didn't resist; together they kicked hard back the way they'd come.

By the time they reached the dining room, it was barely lit at all — the ship was clearly going down — so they scrambled for the exterior hatch.

And, of course, it was shut.

They both saw that at the same time, both raced up to it with all the speed they could manage. Anneke got her hand on it first, and then cranked its handle with formidable strength... too much strength. It came off.

As the light dimmed, the Lady in purple looked at her younger counterpart, eyes wide. Alex panicked again — it was impossible not to — but found herself swimming towards one of the nearby portholes. It was by no means big, but neither were the two trapped Champions. Wrenching it open, Alex waved to her fellow and then pulled herself through, balling up her shoulders to fit. As soon as she was clear, she turned herself around in the water, then caught hold of the porthole frame.

She was very clearly being pulled down. She didn't know how deep, but as Anneke started through she took the Lady's hand and pulled. Despite her wider frame, the elder Champion was able to get her shoulders clear...

Then she got stuck.

Alex's eyes were fully wide now. The light was nearly gone — only her Champion senses were allowing her to make out details.

She pulled, and Anneke struggled but didn't budge. Time seemed to speed up and slow down at once. The Lady in purple then looked to her younger counterpart and waved with her free hand — an order to the Lady usually in white to make her escape. No sense them both dying.

But before Alex could react, Lady Winter quite abruptly came free.

As soon as she did, both Champions let go of *Hood*, then watched the mighty ship sink into oblivion. It went down so fast...

With Joseph Rockefeller visible through the porthole. He waved once before vanishing.

Alex suddenly felt cold — colder than she ever had. Positively frozen. The darkness of the water seemed even more oppressive, but she knew which way was up, so wrapping one arm around Lady Winter, she began to kick for the surface.

The air came faster than she'd expected — the darkness wasn't a sign of depth, but of the absence of *Skipper Miller*. As the younger Lady Smith breeched, a new wash of light hit her: a beam from the searchlight of a nearby ship. The air was quieter without the skycruiser overhead — Alex could only assume it had been knocked out of position when the lasso slipped off — so she could hear splashing, coughing, cries for help...

And shouts of reassurance. There were boats everywhere she looked, and as Anneke caught her breath and kept a close hold of her, Alex turned towards the nearest rubber raft.

"Hello there," she tried to call, but realized her voice didn't work. A man on that raft still somehow noticed her, and looked over the side.

"Come on, lads," he revealed a Scottish accent as he spoke, then pulled an oar from inboard and started dragging his octagonal craft towards her.

Anneke helped as Alex kicked for it, and then both Ladies took hold of the raft's ropes. With the helpful hands of the three men aboard, both were pulled out of the water and into the cold night air.

Alex and Anneke began to shiver. The officer and two sailors were no dryer or warmer, but they quickly helped the pair out of the bottom of the raft, where some water had pooled, and up onto the rubber sides. It felt no warmer, but was probably better.

Alex honestly tried to smile at the men — to thank them for their help — but her voice was gone. Anneke was barely better-equipped, but as she forced her heavy, frozen purple coat off her shoulders, she managed to say, "Thank you."

"Of course, M'Lady," the Midshipman among them took it from her. "I'm sorry we have no blankets, these rafts were dropped from your skycruiser."

Lady Winter shook her head, then only managed to answer faintly, "I'm just happy to be here... Midshipman..."

"Dundas, M'Lady," the Scot answered, then gestured to the men sitting opposite him. "This is Tilburn, and Briggs."

Sprawled as she was in the relative safety of the raft, Alex felt she had to try again to express her gratitude, and this time she was able to force something out of her voice, "You men... thanks..."

It was all she managed to say before *Skipper Miller* roared back into position overhead. Having wound up its dangling cable, the skycruiser flooded the sea with daylight once again. At least the down-thrust was less oppressive, since the ship was no longer trying to lift a battlecruiser.

Seeing the familiar vessel, Alex took a deep breath, then held up her hand and waved. It probably looked awfully strange to the men in the boat with her.

"She's waving. Proper heroine, that one," Douglas Bader grinned as he watched the exhausted, drenched, shivering girl on his screen.

Standing behind the Flight Lieutenant, Stephanie Shylock folded her arms. She was half intent on blurting out some sentiment like 'I'm going to kill her', but she realized there was literally no reason to.

"Well thank God," Strong's words reflected his relief. "Hope everyone else is okay."

Of course, everyone else wasn't okay, but as they watched a boat come alongside Alex's raft to take the Ladies and crewmen off, the Second Lieutenant and her Sergeant were satisfied with the survivors they were aware of.

Hood was gone. More than a few had made it off the ship alive... but unfortunately not everyone.

CHAPTER XII

Most of Alex's wits, such as they were, had returned by the time she reached the deck of the nearest destroyer. The ship was a mess of activity, and everything was complicated by the fact that the seas were swelling heavier — the weather the Special Service Squadrons had been avoiding was already beginning to catch up.

Dozens of men... perhaps even hundreds... were hurrying across the deck. Men from the ship were wrapping blankets over the shoulders of men plucked from the water, or putting them on stretchers, or trying to get them below — anything they could do to help. Such was the code of the sea; those in distress were to be helped at all costs. It was a doctrine any Newfoundlander understood, and Alex actually felt a little warmer for seeing it in action.

The Royal Navy looked after its own.

But there was still chaos. Boats were putting men aboard and then turning back to look for more, and other ships — she could see three other destroyers in the nearby waters, two of them British and one clearly American — were doing the same. The race was on to get men out of the water before the cold killed them.

It was that thought which smacked Alex's mind rather indelicately: where was her mother? Where were Alain Lapointe and Lord Halifax?

Could the President and Champion Rockefeller have somehow escaped?

Anneke was beside Alex as the madness on deck routed its way around them, and she too was still collecting her thoughts. As she became more lucid, the younger Lady reached out and tugged on her pajama sleeve — her purple coat had been lost somewhere — before saying her name, "Anneke?"

The exemplar Champion turned to Alex, then wrapped her cold

arms around the shorter girl. Not what the younger Lady Smith had expected, obviously, but it was the sort of urgent hug that no one could ignore.

For just a second, Alex allowed her eyes to shut, and she hugged Anneke back. Together they had managed to survive.

"Where did you even come from?" Lady Winter asked in a whisper. "God, I was afraid."

Well, at least there wasn't going to be any pretense between them, so Alex nodded, "Jumped from *Skipper Miller*. We need to find my mom, and the Prime Ministers."

Anneke didn't answer for a second, but then Alex could feel her taking a deep breath and nodding, "Yes. I hope... we were in time... because I don't think Joseph..."

She stopped. She didn't want to finish that sentence because it seemed too soon to draw conclusions — even based on the evidence of their own eyes. Alex simply nodded, then they parted and began to look around.

Both their eyes settled on the figure of an officer standing stoically on the deck, staring at them. He appeared to be wearing pajamas with his blue coat over them, and his hat was pulled down tight on his head. His quintessentially professional expression, however, overrode his haphazard appearance.

Alex wasn't sure what he was thinking — whether he might praise her courage, or berate her impetuousness — but she had no time for sentiment: "Captain Todd, has the boat with my mother come in yet? And has there been any sign of President Roosevelt? We fear... we think he might not have escaped."

Todd's eyes turned from Anneke to Alex and back, then he held up his arm, directing them towards a hatch, "With me, please."

Caralynne had stripped off her clothes behind a curtain, and dried quickly before donning borrowed pants and a shirt. The new attire was much too baggy for her, but the warmth and dryness was welcome as she wrapped a fresh blanket around herself. Now that she was free of the water her shivering had stopped, but inside she could feel her organs quaking. She probably wouldn't be able to feel warm for weeks.

As she finished wrapping up, she stepped out from behind the curtain and was confronted by the hectic wardroom. *Inglefield's* surgeon was hard at work on Lord Halifax, but the man was blue and he didn't seem to be breathing. He'd been that way since before the ship's navigator had convinced her to change out of her wet clothes, and she feared it was irreversible: the Prime Minister of Britain was dead.

She was too numb, both physically and psychologically, to quite process that.

Alain Lapointe was sitting on the deck in the corner, stripped to the waist and coughing out sea water as men tried to get him warmed up. His teeth were chattering fiercely, but as he looked up and caught Caralynne's eyes, she could see thoughts behind them — his brain might have been temporarily slowed by the cold, but Alex had gotten him out in time.

Before she turned back and went for Roosevelt. Thankfully, Lieutenant Commander Oswin had assured Caralynne that both her daughter and Anneke had escaped the sinking ship, and were being brought in by *Inglefield's* whaler — she hadn't been forced to live with any anxiety about her child's fate. This time.

Oswin had also explained that Alex had leapt from the sky and apparently tied a cable around *Hood*, keeping the ship afloat just long enough to save some of the crew. It was hard to describe what Caralynne felt about that as just 'pride'. Perhaps, after everything that had already happened, the elder Lady Smith was getting accustomed to her daughter's ability to achieve such feats.

And so she was proud.

Terrified, and worried also. But proud.

"Mom!" Alex hurtled through the door and had her arms around her mother before any ordinary eyes could see her. She was saturated with water, which partly negated all Caralynne's efforts to dry herself, but it took little imagination to realize the elder Lady Smith didn't care. She hugged back, eyes shut and an honest smile on her face.

"We have to stop doing this. Seriously," she said to her daughter.

Alex's answering laugh was almost pleading, "Not allowed to be in the same country when anything important happens. Okay?"

"We'll try that," Caralynne agreed, and then they were silent for a moment.

Anneke entered with less urgency, taking in the sights of the wardroom as the surgeon finally gave up his desperate attempts to revive Halifax.

"I'm sorry, sir," he said, looking up to the navigator who was presiding over the room.

Captain Todd had followed the Ladies in, and he immediately asked for clarification, "That's the Prime Minister, Michael?"

The surgeon turned towards the door, shaking his head in frustration, "Was just too damned cold, sir. I thought we might get him back, but no."

"You did your best," Todd offered reassurance that might have sounded disingenuous to an outsider, but which seemed to truly assuage some of the doctor's pain. There were other frozen men on the ship, though, so with a quick look to confirm the other survivors in the room were past danger, he begged his leave and hurried off. One of his orderlies covered Lord Halifax with a blanket.

Alex and Caralynne pried themselves apart as the doctor left, and both turned to that grim sight.

"Dammit," the elder whispered.

Struggling to his feet despite his prodigious shakes, Alain Lapointe staggered towards the three Champions. Sitting in the opposite corner of the room, his two aides watched him wearily, but didn't try to rise.

"The President?" Lapointe's question was weak but sharp, and Alex bit her bottom lip as she caught his gaze.

"We tried to go back for Rockefeller. But the line went while we were in the corridor," her voice was heavier than she expected, as it hit her that she had indeed failed to save one of the most important men in the world.

"I think... I got stuck getting out of the dining room porthole after we turned back. I couldn't feel my feet, but I think Joseph pushed me out. But he could... I mean, we went out a porthole. He couldn't have fit," Anneke sounded unusually uneven. She then sniffed, closed her eyes for a second, and shook her head to right her thoughts. "If it was him, he was trapped and went down. And... well, by the time we got down there, I doubt the President could still have been holding his breath."

Those words demanded silence — a heavy and reverent moment of quiet to acknowledge the unjust loss of a man who, whatever his particular political agenda for the summit, was among the great Presidents in the history of a great nation. He had died because he put himself at risk — had chosen, despite his personal afflictions, to meet at sea to discuss the safety of his people.

And had drowned after the destruction of the Royal Navy's flagship.

How could there be two tragedies in such quick succession? And as Alex asked herself that question, she felt others creeping into the back of her mind. She was the strongest swimmer, should she not have taken the President, or at least Halifax? Lapointe was clearly more robust than either of them, he might have been able to survive with one of the less aquatic Champions.

It was the sort of question she could ask herself in silence, but the quiet didn't last: Lapointe began to cough harshly, as more seawater agitated his lungs. He tried to wave away the two men from *Inglefield* who came to his assistance, but his cold legs buckled and he had to let them sit him down.

He wasn't dying, though — he held up his hand strongly as if to prove that fact. His hacking coughs simply... perhaps mercifully... shattered any contemplation, and left Alex, Anneke and Caralynne standing numbly.

Eventually, Captain Todd turned to them. The Briton's face was not so stoic now, and as his eyes settled on Alex's, it seemed his own thoughts were heavy. He said nothing — simply shook his head and then turned for the hatch. He had a ship to run, and more men to save from the water.

That last part triggered Alex's memory — something she'd overheard on *Skipper Miller's* flight deck came back to her.

"Captain," she said abruptly, stepping away from her mother and following him to the door.

He stopped as he heard her, then seemed to square his shoulders before turning back, "Lady Smith."

He sounded resigned, as though expecting some sort of assault. Perhaps that was unfair to her, or perhaps it was prudent. She remembered not liking Todd — knew how harsh he'd been about Water Street, when Emily had killed his men.

But... this was different.

"You had orders to sail away," she said to him. "You were right not to. I hope no one says different... but if they do, I'll speak for you. Whatever that's worth."

Percy Todd stared at the small, soaked girl standing in front of him, and found her eyes were weighted by more insight than he'd given her credit for. How she knew what orders his Yeoman had ignored, he didn't know — she must have overheard them from her skycruiser, before she jumped out of it to save the Canadian Prime Minister from the sea.

He let his eyes fall, and as his gaze dropped he realized she'd extended her hand towards him. Immediately he took it — was shocked by how cold it was as he shook it. Then he let go, reached up and touched his hat in salute before turning away.

As he disappeared into the passageway, Alex turned back towards her mother, and found she felt colder than she'd realized.

"Fresh clothes?" she asked, and Caralynne nodded, then pointed to the makeshift changing room behind the curtain, with stacks of dry pants, shirts, and blankets. Anneke was already back there, and as she painfully started to shed her pajamas, the perfect Champion shook her head.

Catching the elder Lady Smith's eye, she said: "Turns out I'm not at my best when I'm all wet."

Alex heard that, but didn't understand. The statement was sad, though — as if it had been a joke, and now was almost a lament. Caralynne's chin dipped as her daughter came alongside her: "Seems none of us are... except maybe you."

The last words were directed at the whitecoat who'd left her coat behind, and not really understanding what was being said, Alex shrugged, "I pretended to date a manatee for a while, to make a gull jealous. Guess it paid off."

Why she grasped at humor in a room where the dead Prime Minister of Britain lay, she didn't know. The other Champions present didn't know either, but somehow they both laughed briefly — desperately — at a joke that wouldn't have been funny at any other time, and wasn't funny now. They just needed that release. The elder Lady Smith hugged her daughter tight again, as all around them, *Inglefield* continued to take aboard survivors, under the watchful eye of *Major Herbert Miller* and the slowly-reforming British and American Special Service Squadrons.

EPILOGUE

The stove was burning hot, and filling the Smith house with one of life's better smells — that of a wood-fueled fire. Together with a cup of warm milk, some absurdly fluffy pink socks, and a roll of blankets that were wrapped around her shoulders, Alex found that the warm flames were starting to drag up her body temperature.

In point of fact, she figured her body temperature wasn't significantly lower than usual — she had all feeling back, and her mind was operating at its usual pace — but the latent memory of the cold was still shaking her deep inside.

She'd never had such a chill, which made sense since she had always avoided swimming during the coldest months.

It helped that it was midday; lunchtime never felt quite so cold as the middle of the night, no matter what the actual temperature. Daylight also kept her from being reminded of the dark corridor through which she'd blindly swam… and the shadowy face of Joseph Rockefeller, if it had been him in that porthole… and the feeble voices of Lord Halifax and President Roosevelt…

Perhaps Alex had earned herself new nightmares — unique ones, so that she and Stephanie didn't have to overlap all the time. But she'd managed to come back from Virginia without the terrors, so maybe she was cured of bad dreams now.

She was a killer, she was a rescue swimmer… it had been a busy couple of months for the whitecoat, and she had no idea what was coming next. So she drank her milk, and then felt her stomach grumble.

"Is that your stomach?" Stephanie was sitting on the other side of the kitchen table from her friend, trying to keep a stern frown off her face.

It was painfully obvious that the American was irritated that she hadn't been able to dive into the ocean with her friend the night before. Her arms were folded and her body language might have only appeared more closed-off if she'd been wearing a 'closed' sign on a string around her neck.

Of course they'd both known there would be times when they simply couldn't stick together, but *Hood* had been the first real case where Stephanie had been forced to sit and watch. Even on Signal Hill she'd driven to the rescue. Not possible on the Grand Banks.

So she was frustrated, but she realized too that there was no one to be frustrated with. It wasn't as though Alex could have brought her friend along on the jump, obviously, so this was just irrational irritation, and she bottled it up in an entirely unhealthy fashion as they sat together.

Getting back to her question, Alex shrugged a little sheepishly, "I did swim a lot last night. And I think swimming in the cold burns food faster."

"Probably," Stephanie nodded. "Well, we can go to the club for a big lunch, if you like?"

Alex smiled at her friend's dogged determination to be civil, and then shrugged, "In a little while. I'll warm up a bit more, and we'll miss the rush."

There wasn't really a rush to miss — there were very few graduated Champions in Jimmystown at the moment, which meant little competition for the food at the club. It was just a thing to say — the sort of awkward thing Alex could produce when she was enjoying a terribly uncomfortable silence with her friend.

Deciding she wanted to be smarter than the tension, Alex shook her head, "If it helps, I'm sorry about... that."

Stephanie looked at her, frown deepening, "Don't do that."

"What? We both know you're frustrated, and that you know you shouldn't be, and you're doing a great job not actually saying you want to smack me because there wasn't anything else we could have done..." she tried to lay it all out, and as she did, one of Stephanie's eyebrows went up. That prompted Alex to taper off, wondering if she'd read it wrong: "Right?"

"Yes," Stephanie replied with a bit of a pout. "So if we both know it, let's just let it be. It'll burn off like fog in sunshine, just... just let it. If we talk about it I'll get even more irritable *because* I'm frustrated."

Alex nodded slowly, because she knew her friend well enough to realize she seriously disliked her own occasional moods.

"You're very self-critical," the young Champion offered easily.

"Thanks," the Second Lieutenant answered. "I am American, after all."

"Delusional!" Alex began to recall the previous joke, but before she could take it anywhere, the side door of the house opened and Caralynne stepped in.

Though she'd been no warmer than her daughter, the elder Lady Smith had headed to Jimmy's headquarters right upon landing in St. John's, and now her expression revealed it had been a delightful visit.

Raising her cup of milk towards her mom, Alex offered a rather laconic greeting: "It's gone all wrong?"

Closing the door and beginning to kick off her boots — an older pair that weren't as warm, since her good ones had been ruined in the swim — Caralynne nodded: "The Americans are criticizing the British for not sending help sooner, because they don't realize it would have made no difference. That'll blow over pretty quickly, I think... and I'm not sure what happens next. Could be war."

"Right," Stephanie sounded unimpressed. "War."

"Maybe," Caralynne nodded. "Or maybe the opposite. I imagine the Americans will want retribution, but something Roosevelt was saying at dinner aboard *Hood*..."

The mention of the President's name made Alex shiver, but as her mother tapered off she parked the discomfort and frowned, "The man taking over more in favor of peace?"

Caralynne's own brow was creased in thought, and it took her a second to process her daughter's words before shaking her head, "He's from Texas. John Nance Garner. So he might want to fight..."

"But he's known as an isolationist," Stephanie put in quietly, before sipping her milk again. "Roosevelt brought him in as Vice President to keep the southern democrats on side, and he's been against excessive spending since the start."

Alex looked to her friend at those words, not immediately following. Realizing she needed to supply extra context drawn from her years in the classroom at Memorial, and her regular listening to the radio news, the American Lieutenant sighed, "Do you know how much it costs to run the American Champions program? From the institute to the regiment? Some politicians love it for the glory...

many in Congress have been quietly wondering what they gain from it. They don't need to spend all that money to maintain access to the riches of the new world."

For a few seconds, Alex said nothing. Then she looked from her friend to her mother and back, "Money? They might let this go unanswered because it's expensive?"

"The American people won't stand for that," Stephanie shook her head. "But when the dust settles, you can bet some politicians down there will be trying to use this as an excuse to reduce their commitment. And Garner might be one of them."

That just sounded alien to Alex — how any nation with Champions could give them less than full support was baffling... but not a problem for this day, or this table.

"The King has asked Churchill to become Prime Minister," Caralynne dropped that bombshell next, and both Alex and Stephanie looked to her with surprise.

"What?"

"Him?"

Their responses were simultaneous, which would have been funny in another context.

"If anyone can stiffen our resolve against an unknown foe, and convince a man like Garner not to completely withdraw the US from the world stage, it's Winston," the elder Lady Smith recited grimly. "We don't have to like it."

"Good," Alex scoffed. "He's such a malcontent."

"And a drunk," Stephanie added.

So that was it; the British Empire's Premier was now a jingoist supposed-war hero, and the American President was a possible isolationist. The special friendship between the Anglo powers was undoubtedly about to change — and change in the face of some unknown adversary. Who was doing this, and to what end?

That was the question that drew a sigh from Alex, and as she looked down at her warm milk she asked: "I presume someone's actually searching for those responsible for *Hood*, even with all the change afoot?"

Caralynne nodded a little more firmly, "MI5 and MI6 are investigating in Britain... and just to be certain, Jimmy's put Elspeth Cornish on the job."

With Anneke Winter now staying very close to Alain Lapointe, the deployment of her best friend, Lady Cornish, to head the investigation seemed wise. Glancing at Stephanie, the younger Lady Smith therefore shrugged, "I guess we're not going."

"For now," Stephanie replied, sounding both reserved and slightly determined.

The Lieutenant did want to get back out there, and given a bit more time and warmth, Alex knew she would too. Too many questions were lurking, and somehow, despite everything they'd already endured, neither she nor her friend could imagine *not* participating in the search for answers.

Alex, her mother, and her best friend all fell silent with those thoughts. Standing outside the kitchen window as quiet ensued, Smith turned and started walking into the woods. He had his Winchester '92 in hand.

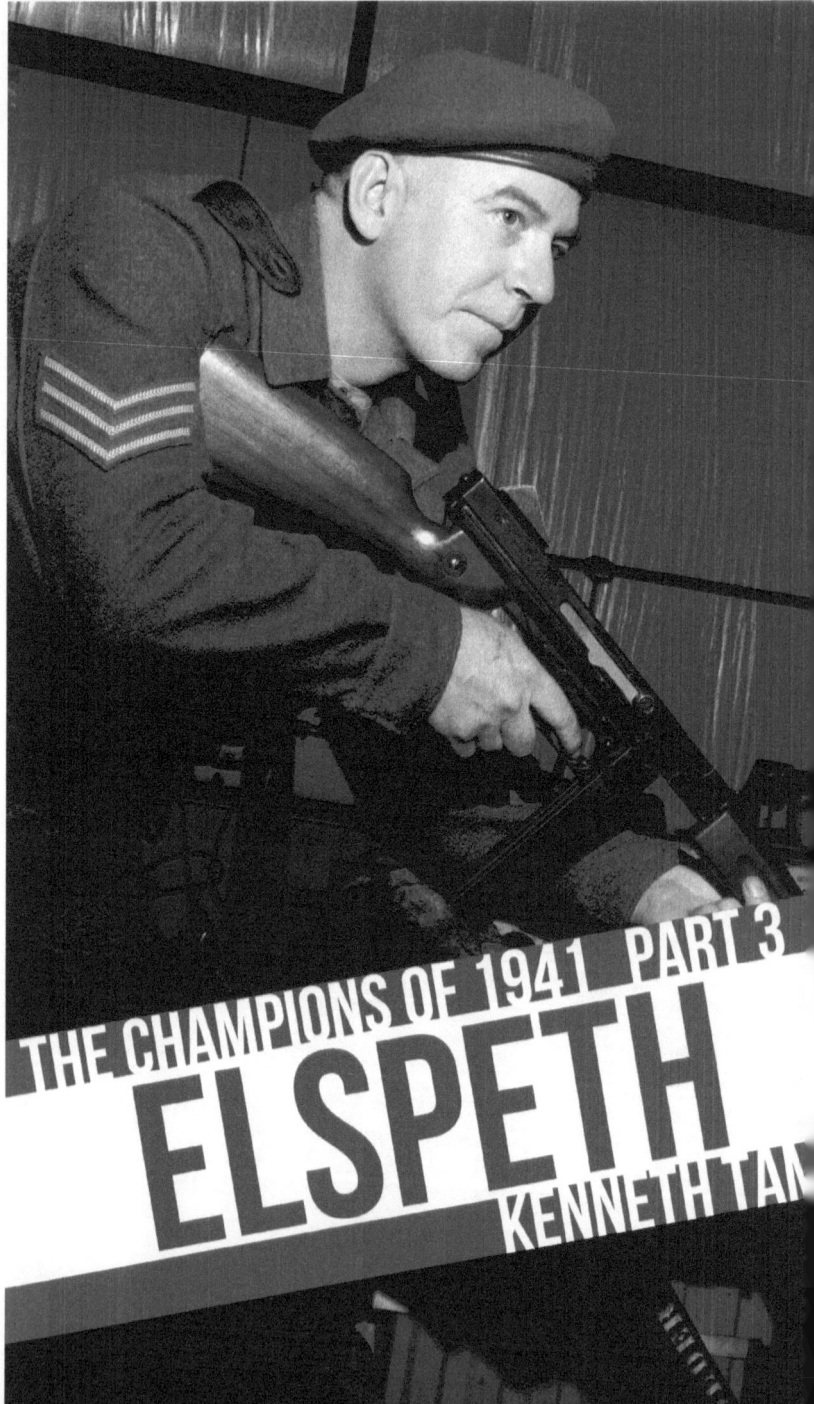

THE CHAMPIONS OF 1941 PART 3
ELSPETH
KENNETH TAM

PROLOGUE

The trail should have been cold. Three weeks after the destruction of *Hood*, the person who'd planted explosives on that ship should have been long gone from Rosyth. The culprit should have known the investigation into the sabotage would lead to the Dockyard, and his trail would be followed.

He should have been long gone. This didn't make sense.

As Lady Elspeth Cornish, one of the toughest Champions ever posted to London society, staggered down the steep slope through Castleandhill Woods, she couldn't understand...

Actually, there was a lot she couldn't comprehend. Like why her legs were barely carrying her, and why her head was spinning. She'd dropped her pistol somewhere, and her coat was undone and the collar of her shirt pulled roughly open so it wouldn't restrict her breathing. A terrible blizzard was covering Scotland with three feet of blowing snow, but she was so hot she was sweating, and her stomach was starting to rebel.

What was her name again?

Elspeth Cornish. She remembered that.

Most people thought Cornish was too common a name for a Champion, and maybe it was, but her working-class parents had won the chance to raise her... won her in a lottery, in actual fact. They'd always called her the most wonderful prize, a gift to a mum and dad who could never have babies of their own, but who got the chance to raise a Champion.

Her toe caught a tree root and she toppled head first into the snow that had fallen through the canopy overhead. She didn't even bring her arms up to protect herself as she fell. It was good that there was so much snow — not as much in the woods as in the meadows beyond, but enough to cushion her collapse.

Her name was... Elspeth...

Where was she?

Rolling onto her back, she looked up at the stars but found they were green and looked like trees. That was confusing... and the movement made her retch. Her body began to revolt against her, but as she struggled onto her hands and knees to lose the dinners she'd eaten at the local pub, she had a single moment of clarity: *poison gas*.

Her body buckled soon after that thought, and falling sideways into the snow, she began to shake.

What was her name?

Colour Sergeant Bob Freeman was a veteran of the Hubrin War. He'd served with the Calgary Rifles in that conflict, and had then gone on to join Lord Jimmy's Own Champions. Since she'd picked a coat three years prior, he'd led Elspeth Cornish's lance, first on her posting to London, in Ontario, and then to the rather larger London, in England. Together they'd walked the streets of that city, helping the police with crime, and MI5 with some domestic spying. They'd all become friends with the much posher Lady Winter; Anneke protected politicians, then Royals, while Elspeth guarded the shopkeepers.

In her brown coat and with her lower-class accent, Elspeth seemed grittier than most of her kind. But she was a sweetheart with a kind soul, raised right by parents who'd wanted only the best for her. They'd done well.

Bob Freeman secretly loved Lady Cornish as if she was his third daughter, and often told his wife he hoped their girls would take after the Lady in brown. He was sworn to protect her, and he'd do all he could.

Now his belly dragged along the snowy ground as he pulled himself up a miserable road, towards the lights of what he had to believe was a house. The building seemed to be getting farther away with every effort he made, but he knew that was just an illusion caused by the blizzard, the wind he was trying to pull himself through, and the amount of blood he was losing.

At least two bullets had passed through his guts, and he knew the wounds were mortal.

But all his men were dead — poisoned by gas, as far as he could figure — and Elspeth had run off into the woods, looking ill as well.

There was no chance Bob Freeman would see his wife or children again, none at all, but at least he could get help for his Champion.

Or literally die trying.

If only there wasn't a blizzard. He hadn't thought Great Britain could get weather like this — a storm almost as bad as any in Canada or Newfoundland. They should have waited until it had broken to check that house, but they'd underestimated the weather, and never suspected a trap. And even if they had expected danger — even if the trail hadn't seemed cold — they would have gone anyway. Who would have been able to threaten Elspeth? She was a Lady who fearlessly took the initiative. Freeman liked that about her.

And now he was dying because of it

At least the light was getting closer.

As he continued to pull himself along the snowy road, a streak of red trailing behind him, Bob Freeman felt colder and colder… but then, as he reached the light, he felt warm again. He rolled onto his back to let the wonderful feeling wash over him, and as he did he slid off the road. Lying face-up in a ditch, he watched as the brilliant, powerful snow covered his eyes in white light.

In that way, he died.

A shape loomed over Elspeth, and then she felt a hand cupping her cheek. For a few seconds she willed herself to believe it was someone dear to her — her Sergeant Freeman, who was as close to a father as she had, since her own dad had passed.

But the hand was rough; it wasn't Bob. It wasn't any of her lance… any of that special family of hers. They were dead. If she hadn't already felt so sick, she would have become ill at that thought.

"Found you," the stranger said softly, his English marked by a continental accent.

Then his hand traveled down from her face, and was accompanied by the other. How he handled her next wasn't right — any man from her lance would have beaten him dead for his groping, had she somehow not done it first.

But they weren't here now — there was no help at hand.

"Stop that," she insisted, but instead of sounding angry the words slurred out with a giggle. That wasn't what she intended… why was her body not conforming to her thoughts?

"I wish it would be my pleasure," the man said, his wording

awkward. "But you will be very useful to our cause."

Even though the words chilled her, and she could feel tears freezing on her cheeks, she began to laugh. It wasn't right — wasn't what she was supposed to be doing.

What gas had they used? How had it done this to her?

She tried to sit up — succeeded, in fact — and then the shadowy figure took shape, crouching in front of her. He appeared to be a nondescript man, but he was carrying a Mauser rifle. That seemed stupid; if he was a spy trying to blend in, why not have a British Enfield?

"You're caught," she said to him, realizing she sounded nonsensical, but unable to stop. "I caught you."

It was like a nightmare. She *wanted* it to be a nightmare, because then her boys — Bob, her Lieutenant, the seven men she'd watched choke to death — might still be alive.

She saw them all suddenly... remembered laughing with them at the pub... remembered how polite they were when she sometimes tried to cook for them, and it was terrible. They were... had been... like brothers. They made sure she never felt alone, or unsafe, and did so without ever making her feel any less for enjoying their reassuring company.

And in this nightmare, they were dead.

It was almost a mercy when she giggled again, and the man with the accent crossed her temple with the butt of his rifle. Unconscious, she couldn't remember — could forget it had been real.

After she went face-first into the snow, the man checked her pulse. Satisfied with his work, he slung his weapon and began the chore of dragging her away through the storm.

The compound was working: an ordinary man had killed a lance, and captured a Champion.

CHAPTER I

Mike Strong's eyes opened when he realized the bangs he was hearing were knocks at the door, not the thunder of 18-pounder field guns. In the grips of a dream one could easily be mistaken for the other... but there had been no artillery left to fire during the battle he'd been reliving in his sleep. The New Brunswick batteries had been destroyed by lightning from the Hubrin capital, forcing Strong, Waller and the b'ys of the Newfoundland Regiment to attack without cover.

Almost all of them had died, but Mike Strong had survived.

Sitting up, the Colour took a breath to remind himself that he wasn't in the midst of that battle — that two decades had passed and his life now was full of different responsibilities. After so many years of waking from such nightmares, he'd learned to accept reality with a relative swiftness, which was good.

He'd still sweated right through his nightclothes, blanket and bedroll, though. He'd have to get them into the wash — he hated leaving sweaty sheets for Daphne to do, even though she never seemed to mind — and he'd probably want a quick bath too, before he got a start on the day.

It was dark outside the window of Daphne's room, which suggested it was early enough to get that bath in... though since it was just March in St. John's, he supposed days were short and the sun rose late. He might not have as much time as he wanted.

The banging resumed, and it finally registered that someone really was knocking at the door. Strong shook himself into some semblance of consciousness, then looked down. Soaked-through with sweat, he wasn't really fit to answer, but he didn't want Daphne to wake—

"Is that someone at the door?" his young guardian sounded tired as she sat up, and he craned his neck so he could look up over the foot of her bed.

"I can get it."

The bed squeaked as she swung her feet out and stood, "No, I will."

In the darkness of the room, he could just make out her shape as she moved over to the closet and pulled out her housecoat, then found the switch for the single bulb in the ceiling. It clicked, and he squinted at the soft yellow light before offering another half-hearted protest, "No, I'll get it..."

"In your state?" she wasn't having any of it, and she crossed her small room in a hurry, reaching the door before he could do anything but pull his blanket up to shield whoever it was from his horrible visage.

He couldn't see the clock from his position on the floor, but it still seemed like a strange hour for the landlady, or anyone else, to come calling.

"Yes?" Daphne swung the door open before Strong could speculate further.

Then things got awful.

Lady Alex Smith — fully dressed and looking completely awake — and Second Lieutenant Stephanie Shylock — also fully dressed and with an almost conspiratorial air — were standing there, and Daphne simply wasn't large enough to block the whole doorway. They could see around the girl, and that meant Strong had nowhere to hide... except behind his blanket, which he pulled up to shield his face.

Unsurprisingly, that was insufficient concealment, and its glaring failure to camouflage him put his well-crafted reputation in dire danger.

"Is that..." Alex started to ask, then stopped and turned her eyes to Daphne with a smile. "He sleeps on the *floor*."

"Knew it," Stephanie folded her arms and smiled a bit smugly.

Daphne was really just waking up, so she looked back over her shoulder, then blinked a couple of times before sort of answering, "You're looking for Mike, of course..."

"Yes they are," Strong stayed rather absurdly behind his blanket. "Send them away so I can hide my shame."

Alex wasn't buying it, "Your feet are sticking out the bottom of your blanket. I can see you're wearing long johns."

Stephanie was no more sympathetic, "Admit it: your shame cannot be hidden, and you sleep on the *floor*."

Those were the words that led sleepy Daphne to realize the conclusion the two women in Strong's life had reached — and that she was letting down her side by not resisting.

"Actually, we were just having... um... doing it on the floor..." she tried to intervene, but unfortunately the words couldn't get out without her beginning to blush.

Stephanie's eyebrow climbed, "If you turn red saying *it*, you clearly weren't doing *it*."

Daphne wasn't ready for that, but of course Mike Strong tried to have an answer for everything.

"That's not fair, lots of people do things they would be embarrassed to say," he called defensively from behind his blanket. "I don't tell anybody that I hang out with the two of you."

Ouch — Alex dropped her jaw in genuine mock offense, "That remark wounds me."

Before Stephanie could get in on that act, Daphne tried again: "I don't know about that. I'm simply embarrassed because you caught us in a compromising situation."

"The compromising position of him sleeping chastely on the floor," the American Lieutenant replied. "Also, that remark wounded me too."

This was going poorly. Strong considered conceding some part of what his girls were claiming, but Daphne remained determined. Collecting herself, she went for it — all in.

"In the compromising position of me being naked," she declared.

It was definitely too early for her to be sparring on this subject, because she should have thought through her words a bit better. Stephanie looked her up and down, and then Alex did the same.

It was the Lady in white who broke the bad news: "You're covered from head to toe. Literally."

That was true; Daphne's housecoat was pooling on the floor around her feet, and her pajama blouse was buttoned so high that it looked both positively uncomfortable and entirely virtuous.

Not one to accept defeat, Daphne surged with another, wonderful answer: "Yes. But *under* these clothes, I'm completely naked."

Alex stopped, and Stephanie did too, because that revelation was *incredible* — so incredible that neither the Champion nor her officer could quite figure out how to respond. They looked at each other, far too excited by the lob and desperately trying to figure out how to most cleverly send it back. Their mouths both struggled to form words, but nothing was adequate.

Strong recognized the silent sound of his girls over-enthusiastically preparing a woefully unclever retort, and he sighed before intervening.

"That's really nice of you to say, Daphne," he lowered his blanket just enough so he could peer over the top. "What do you two need, exactly?"

Neither Alex nor Stephanie wanted to give up on the banter — they had to say *something* to recognize the wonderfulness of Daphne's remark, but they were at a loss. Too much trying to be clever, so they ended up saying nothing before reluctantly looking back towards their Sergeant on the floor.

Sounding a little defeated at her failure to convert, Alex answered the question with very little abuse, "Dad woke us early and told us to come get you. Something perilous, probably. We need our heroic Sergeant."

She didn't even manage to sound sarcastic when she said 'heroic'. The wheels had totally come off her repartee, and Stephanie was equally deflated. Daphne had somehow beaten them. This time.

Strong figured that was fine, but not wanting either girl to rally and renew the assault, he stayed with the more important subject, "Fine. But I'm not getting up with you two watching."

That was probably in everyone's best interest, so Alex looked at Stephanie, and Stephanie returned the gaze before nodding. Time to beat a hasty retreat — to think of amazing comebacks and kick themselves for failing to unleash them in the moment.

"I'll wait in the Land Rover," the Lady in white said.

"I will also do that," the Lieutenant agreed.

"Good," Daphne said jauntily, and then she closed the door right in their surprised faces. She was awake now.

With that done, the Newfoundland girl shook her head, shrugged off her housecoat and tossed it to her bed. Strong groaned as she crouched down beside him.

"Why does everyone think I'm too innocent to seduce you?" she asked, giving him a kiss on the forehead.

The Colour shrugged, then allowed himself a smile, "They've led sheltered lives."

"Pity," Daphne took hold of his sweaty blanket and shook her head. "Well whatever they need, it can wait until you have a bath. I'm not sending you out into the world in this state — my reputation would be in tatters."

A bath seemed an unnecessary waste of time to Strong. Something perilous was happening, after all, and stopping it likely trumped smelling okay... but Daphne gave him one of the looks he wasn't particularly allowed to argue with.

"Wouldn't want that," he surrendered, and with a satisfied nod, she stood up and retreated to her private bathroom — her flat's most luxurious feature.

Watching her go, Strong just managed to stop himself sighing again. Daphne in a repartee fight against Alex and Stephanie was about as bad as things could possibly get... it could only be worse if all three of them turned their wit against him at once.

God, life was complicated. He needed more male friends.

The sky was starting to brighten by the time Sergeant Mike Strong emerged from the boarding house, and descended its steps to the road where the Land Rover was parked. Stephanie was behind the wheel and Alex was sitting in the passenger seat, her boots up on the dash as she tapped her fingers impatiently on her knees.

Detecting the sound of his approach, the white-coated Lady turned her head, caught sight of him, then looked away a bit disinterestedly, "I'm not going to speculate why you took so long, because I know you'll just lie about it."

"He was probably having a bath," Stephanie sounded equally petulant. "He looks too respectable to have been spending his time in any disreputable way."

Grinning as he climbed up into the back of the Land Rover, Strong told the truth, "Of course I had a bath. But you can do disreputable things in the bath."

Mmhmm. He was caught but he didn't want to admit it, so with a flick of her hand Stephanie obliged her friend to get her boots off the dash, then started the engine. As Strong settled onto one of the side-facing bench seats in the back, the vehicle rolled off down the lane.

"You two are just jealous," he decided to go on the offensive. "But rest assured, there are men out there who are nearly as perfect as me, and they'll come for you."

That was almost sweet, and as Alex raised an eyebrow she glanced at her friend, "The words of a romantic optimist?"

Strong interjected before Stephanie could reply, "And when they come, I will kill them. All of them."

"Shakespearian romantic, apparently," Stephanie suggested.

"That means he's scholarishly tormented — and, therefore, attractive," Alex pointed out, sounding slightly swoony. Clearly she couldn't wait for other men; she had to fight for the Sergeant she had, so she looked back over her shoulder at Strong, then lowered her voice, "Now Colour, I don't know if you realize it... but under all these clothes... *I'm naked.*"

Stephanie blinked, then looked to her friend in shock. If there was to be a competition for Mike Strong, she surely couldn't be left out.

"I am also completely naked under all my clothes," she added almost defensively, managing to look back for a few seconds to reinforce her point. "Even *under* my underwear."

Alex dropped her jaw and glared at her friend, "How dare you try to one-up me!"

Stephanie shook her head dramatically — looking totally genuinely falsely exasperated, "No *trying* about it, I completely just one-upped you..."

Strong had expected this teasing. There were numerous tacks he could take — plenty of ways to call out both girls, or to defend Daphne, or steer the conversation in another direction... but he figured the best approach was more proactive.

Leaning forward and putting one hand on the back of each girl's seat, he said: "Ladies, ladies, I know. Under these clothes, *I'm naked too.*"

And then he smiled. And then — *then* — he winked.

That was not right.

"Oh *God*," Alex instantly screwed up her face. "Oh no, when he says that, it's... ew."

"He makes it sound so creepy," Stephanie looked as though she'd smelled something rotten. "That's not okay."

"You took it too far," Alex glared back at her Colour. "You are *never* allowed to say that. Ever."

"Or wink. I saw you in the mirror. That's... like... that's not okay."

"Completely wrong," Alex agreed. "That's... just no."

"Yeah. Stop that."

"It makes me very not comfortable."

"And I take no responsibility whatsoever for causing it, because I believe in double standards," Stephanie added that last part, just to make sure Strong understood how inherently incorrect he had been.

"Exactly," Alex confirmed. "Double standards. Make a note of that, so you know why you're always wrong. You should feel terrible."

Strong did, of course. With a grin, he sat back on his bench, then held on as Stephanie turned a sharp corner onto the main drag leading out of St. John's, towards Jimmystown. Whatever had gotten him off Daphne's floor at such an early hour was undoubtedly serious, but it was hard to imagine that it could be worse than the humor in the Land Rover.

Unfortunately, of course, it was.

CHAPTER II

Perhaps Vanier Cross was a pessimist, but he didn't hold out much hope for a positive outcome when he was hauled out of his cell before sunrise. The black Corporal who remained one of the United States' best Saa screen operators had been asleep on his bunk when white soldiers from the Champions Regiment had arrived.

Over protests from his cell-mate — Captain Wendel Fischer, with whom he'd discovered the security breach nearly two months earlier — Vanier had been escorted through the stockade's darkened corridor, then out of the building and across the frozen remains of Fort Eustice.

The barest hint of order had been restored to the base — six weeks of work by the Army Corps of Engineers had undone a little of the damage the January assault had wrought — but it seemed too quiet to Vanier. The hours before sunrise were never particularly busy, but the destruction seemed to make the grim silence even more intense. He elected to dwell on that, as it was better to be preoccupied by his surroundings than by the reasons for this removal from his cell.

It was unlikely that soldiers would be dragging him out to be shot without trial, but it was possible. Vanier's uncle had been lynched back in Georgia, for suspicion of a crime without any evidence whatsoever. As a youngster, the Corporal had thus learned never to take his safety for granted, no matter what company he was in. The past weeks of constant confinement had done nothing to reduce his suspicions. After nearly two months under guard in the stockade, his patience was reaching its limit. Some of his colleagues, who were far less accustomed to such treatment, had already cracked... but none were freed, no matter their state of mind, or the influence wielded by their families.

All the screen operators who had been present during the attack remained confined. Evidently the death of the President, along with the British Prime Minister and the warship *Hood*, had given the United States Senate all the moral authority it needed to override the cries of both wealthy industrialists and some of its own politicians. No one who *might* have been connected to the Fort Eustice security breach would be freed. The culprit would not be allowed to slip away.

Vanier endured the situation because he had to. It wasn't the first injustice he'd experienced, and this time he wasn't alone... though he knew his fate would still probably be different than his white counterparts. Equality of assumed guilt only went so far. There was no point being bitter about it; it simply *was*, and he'd have to make do.

Crossing the cold pre-dawn through the darkened Fort, the Corporal wondered if this unexpected release would be the first step along one of those separate paths. The soldiers escorting him seemed unwilling to provide any insight — from their dour expressions, they truly could be his executioners. But as they approached the headquarters building, Vanier began to get the sense that he'd been summoned for questioning. That would surely be unpleasant, but it likely wouldn't be fatal...

Deciding he should stop speculating about how the outing would end, he put it out of his mind and climbed the steps to the door, then was guided inside. He'd almost expected the building to be bustling with activity — day or night, the United States Army surely needed to maintain constant vigilance in these dangerous times. But no: Vanier's boots, and those of his escorts, were the only sounds echoing through the corridors as he was led to the stairs.

Descending to the basement, the Corporal realized he was likely being returned to the scene of the crime — the screen room — where investigators might want to walk him through what he'd discovered. If that was the case, he'd of course cooperate... and more importantly, he'd get to see the screen again.

Because for all this chaos, he had desperately missed working with that dragon-built marvel. And this might be one of his last chances.

As he was led into the basement corridor that ended with the door to the screen room, Vanier noted that all the sentries on duty were white — men of the United States Champions Regiment, instead of the 25th United States Infantry. Undoubtedly the black soldiers had been pulled away from any duties considered important — the regiment would be an easy scapegoat for the attack...

No matter. The Sergeant leading Vanier's escort entered the screen room first, and as the Corporal followed it became immediately apparent that the screen was already in use... and that only one operator was present.

"Corporal Cross, as ordered," the Sergeant declared as he came to a stop, and halting behind the big guard, Vanier looked from the screen — glowing as magnificently as he remembered — to the man sitting at one of the control desks.

That fellow cut something of a melodramatic figure: he had his back to the door, was clad in a long rain coat, and wore a fedora atop his head.

"Thank you, that'll be all Sergeant," he said without turning around. "Leave no men inside this room, or in the corridor, while I speak with him."

It sounded more than a little cryptic, and Vanier frowned while the Sergeant struggled with the suggestion, "Sir? Orders are to keep him under guard."

"I have him under guard, Sergeant," the man's voice remained calm. "You can consult with Major Travis if you like, but rest assured."

There was authority in the man's words — a natural command that the Sergeant involuntarily responded to, "Yes, sir. I'll leave men at the end of the corridor."

"Thank you," was the reply, and then the stranger sat still while the Sergeant and his soldiers gave Vanier a last look and departed.

When the wood-and-glass door shut behind the men, silence returned to the screen room. Unsure what was expected of him, Vanier simply stood motionless, hands at his sides as he studied both the lone figure, and what had been pulled up on the screen.

"You seem to have been quite thorough, Mister Cross," the newcomer said, finally turning to face his guest. Vanier was surprised by the man's youth — he couldn't even be twenty, and yet his tone and his eyes suggested much more authority than most boys of that age. "Your reputation is deserved."

Vanier wasn't sure how to interpret the words, so he elected to say nothing.

Taking the lack of reaction as an answer, the stranger rose and took a few steps in the Corporal's direction, "You don't know me, but my name is George Devlin. A couple of weeks ago, I assured a certain Champion-in-training that I'd do everything I could to validate your innocence."

Eyes starting to widen in realization, Vanier took a couple of steps forward, "Constance? She's doing okay?"

George was enjoying being a bit dramatic, but it would hardly be proper to torture the man about a girl he clearly cared for, "Proving to be a leading light among her class... and from what I understand, she may be graduating from the Academy instead of coming back here."

"What?" it probably would have been more politic to be discreet about his interest, but two months of confinement without any news had worn down the Corporal's discipline.

"There's talk of moving all Champion education to Jimmystown, for better security, though my father doesn't much like the idea," George explained. "We'll see what your new President decides. For now, I can tell you that Constance is thinking about you. And she has vouched for you."

That sounded like good news to Vanier — mostly the part about her being okay. Her endorsement of him probably wouldn't make much of a difference.

"That's good," he replied. "She's... special."

"I gathered as much," George reached up and pulled his hat from his head, then began absently adjusting its band. "Must be difficult, being in love in an environment with such built-in prejudices."

Vanier considered his answer carefully, "You can't choose your family, right?"

Not quite the reply George had expected, and he looked up, "You can choose your lovers, though."

The comment didn't bear the type of innuendo Vanier was accustomed to hearing. It actually sounded more like a leading statement... from an interrogation.

"She's as close as I have to a sister," Vanier answered, a hint of defensiveness in his tone. "And my family doesn't go in for that sort of thing."

"Wise not to," George narrowed his eyes, falling silent as he studied the black soldier in front of him. Vanier began to feel nervous — something about the young man's stare was more piercing and intelligent than he was used to.

Then George took a breath, and shook his head, "I have to be careful here, Corporal Cross. I have my father's prejudices. I assume that you, being a black soldier in the United States Army, are as good as the men he fought alongside at Promised Town, and on the Badlands. But it would be naïve and perhaps even racist for me to assume that, just because you happen to be black, you couldn't possibly be evil. So I'm trying to decide if you might, in fact, be responsible for this."

Vanier blinked, then realized his mouth had fallen slightly open, "What?"

Obviously that wasn't the sort of racism he was used to.

But the young white man wasn't done: "I also like Constance — she seems both sweet and accomplished — and I choose to believe that she would associate only with men of good character. But again, I have to watch my personal biases in situations like these, because on paper there are plenty of rational reasons why you could be a traitor. Or she could be."

"Not her!" Vanier blurted it immediately — almost angrily — and George paused. It looked as though that was a sentiment he shared... or wanted to... but it was premature.

"Perhaps not her. But there's rational reason why it could be you, Corporal. Isolated and excluded, perhaps even abused by the white people here. You'd be a logical person for foreign agents to target. Or for Emily to empathize with."

The young man tapered off, his eyes narrowing once more as he watched Vanier relax slightly after his defense of Constance, and process everything he was hearing. Being accused of treachery, however politely, could have incensed the black man... but there was no point being defensive. Better to fall back on what his momma had taught him — to always take a bigger view, and understand a problem on its merits.

That in mind, the Corporal said: "So you still don't know who's responsible for the breach. And when *Hood* was blown up, that complicated things even more... because all your suspects were in custody."

"I think they're being polite and saying you're in *protective* custody," a smile twitched at the corners of George's lips. "And the attack on *Hood* clearly originated in Britain. We've just sent people over there to continue the investigation."

Vanier turned his head slightly, his analysis continuing: "So whoever attacked us here has agents in a lot of places, which means it's tougher for you to track them down. You're hoping to pick up a trail — or to find someone here who might have had contacts in Britain?"

It was quite a bit of supposition for someone who'd been living in a stockade for two months, but Vanier Cross was no average soldier. Obviously his assignment to the room in which he now stood evidenced his abilities, and his capacity for analytical thinking was not lost on his guest.

Smile growing, George shook his head, "Actually, I'm here for orientation so I can testify before a Senate Inquiry. But what you say probably makes sense too. I just hope I'm not giving you the benefit of the doubt because you're black and I have some notion of how difficult that has made your life here."

"I can pretend to be white, if it helps," Vanier surprised himself with those words — not the sort he'd normally utter in front of white company… let alone *to* a white man.

George winced at the sentiment, "I expected you to be funnier."

Somehow the pushback didn't trouble the Corporal: "It's black humor, so you wouldn't understand."

"Right," George agreed immediately. "I'm entirely unequipped for it. Don't even have a black friend."

Vanier shook his head, "Don't worry, that's not about to change."

"Optimist," was George's answer, and then the two men remained silent for a moment, digesting their banter. It seemed obvious that Vanier's conclusion was incorrect, but neither of them saw any point in commenting on the fact.

Instead, George waved towards the screen, "I've done a quick look, but maybe you want to take me through?"

That was it; an invitation to work on the Saa screen was more than enough to prompt Vanier into motion. Turning to his long-abandoned desk, he couldn't help but feel some enthusiasm. For all that was wrong in his world at the moment, he would have at least one more chance to use the greatest machine in the world.

It was consolation enough as he settled in and started explaining to his new white non-friend about the registry breach.

CHAPTER III

When Lord Jimmy had explained that they were bound for Scotland to consult on an investigation, Alex's naturally positive outlook led her to imagine that they'd be bound for Scotland *Yard*, to be consulting *detectives* on a *criminal* investigation. Unfortunately, the mission that was causing her flight across the Atlantic in *Skipper Miller* was not going to require her best impersonation of Sherlock Holmes. A shame — she might have liked the hat.

But there would be no such humor on this trip.

Sitting in one of *Skipper Miller's* lounges and watching the ocean blur past below the window, the younger Lady Smith found her pre-dawn good spirits tempered by several important facts.

Chief among them: the world was on the verge of going entirely awry. It was a slow unraveling, but she couldn't help but think that every headline from Britain and the United States represented another thread being tugged. Things couldn't hold together much longer with half the American public demanding revenge for Roosevelt, and the other half insisting that if their country hadn't been tied up in international affairs, he would still be alive and well.

Some people held *both* opinions — isolationists who wanted to declare war on someone so that revenge could be secured. It was confusing, and no one quite knew where old John Nance Garner would fall. He'd bought himself time by pledging to wait for the Senate Inquiry report before taking any executive decisions, but by the summer, it seemed likely that the United States would either be at war with someone, or cutting its ties with almost *everyone*.

Churchill, at least, didn't seem too hotheaded. He was an aging, drunk, jingo... but he seemed to possess the common sense to wait for answers before sending the forces of Earth's most powerful Empire against any of the suspected culprits.

Answers were essential, so the special intelligence branches had been rallied to investigate. Each of them — MI5, MI6, the FBI, the CIG, the RCMP and the DSI — had their agents out listening for signs of treachery, but as far as Alex knew, they hadn't found much yet. Evidence of who was responsible would have to be uncovered soon.

Whether that villain was a state — Germany was the prime suspect — or a rogue Champion, or some combination of both, remained to be discovered. Anyone who had any real insight into Emily found it difficult to believe she could be part of any plot that led to the killing of Champion students, as had happened in Virginia. But the developments that were flying the whitecoat to Scotland seemed more like the work of the rogue Lady than anything else.

Just hours earlier, a dead Sergeant had been found: Bob Freeman, from the now-missing lance of Lady Elspeth Cornish. A plow driver clearing roads near Firth and Forth had discovered him in a ditch, and questions had arisen as soon as he'd been identified.

Elspeth had been sent to Rosyth Dockyard to investigate *Hood's* destruction, but she and her lance had gone missing shortly after arriving. Such a disappearance would normally have been cause for immediate concern, but the whole of Britain had been hit by one of the worst blizzards in recent memory right at the moment of her vanishing. Entire towns had been snowed in for the past week, and some en route trains had been buried on the tracks, with people still aboard.

With that kind of snow everywhere, Jimmy had simply assumed Elspeth and her lance had gone to ground, waiting until the storm settled. The alternative possibility — that they could have found trouble — seemed largely unlikely. What danger could she really find in Scotland? Anyone who'd been involved in putting the bomb aboard *Hood* would surely have made an escape as soon as the ship was destroyed. Lady Cornish and her men had been looking for clues, not battle.

But obviously battle found at least one of them, and the rest were still missing.

Since the only adversary to ever defeat a lance was Emily, the rogue Lady had again become a suspect, meaning Champions had to be sent to investigate, instead of intelligence services. The Edinburgh Champion would have already arrived in Rosyth to begin the search, and Alex, Stephanie and Strong were expected to reinforce him.

"Elspeth was London's Champion, right?"

The question was neither abrupt nor particularly unexpected, but it still jolted Alex from her expository thoughts. With a blink, she looked back into the lounge, where Stephanie Shylock was sitting on a much-too-comfortable couch, checking to make sure her Browning was ready if needed.

Nodding once, Alex looked back down to the water, "She was Champion for the more common parts of town. Not the Royals or the Government."

"One of the lottery Champions?" Stephanie was frowning, and since she was so comfortable with her sidearm — goddaughter of a gunfighter, and all — the expression was tied to the subject as opposed to the pistol.

"Raised by commoners, yep," Strong confirmed from further back in the room, sitting in a chair and similarly checking out his Thompson.

"Right," Stephanie replied, satisfied with the answer.

Alex didn't add anything further, because her Sergeant was correct. When Champion children had first been rescued in 1920, there had been numerous well-off families willing to adopt them... but with the rise of so many socialist movements in Europe after the Franco-German War, Sir Julian Byng had feared the outcome if *only* aristocrats and the wealthy were allowed to foster the savage-born. Middle and lower class Britons had to be represented among parents of British-raised Champions, so a lottery was instituted, and families allowed to apply to win the right (and state-sponsored means) to raise a Champion.

Elspeth was perhaps the best known of those lottery Champions. She proudly spoke like a common shopgirl, which made her a bit of a novelty in London society, but her talents were beyond question and she had a reputation for being fearless.

Now she was missing.

"Well," the younger Lady Smith said rather rhetorically, "today we'll try to find her."

"God willing she's alive," Mike Strong agreed.

The landing field for the Rosyth Dockyard was a few miles away from the heavily built-up industrial complex, so after *Skipper Miller* touched down there, a Land Rover picked them up. As they drove in, Alex, Stephanie and Strong silently stared at the industrial wonder of the place; it was like a village of huge workshops and warehouses lying across a field of tarmac. This was by no means a beautiful use of coastal land, but it was productive. Some of Britain's most powerful warships — including *Hood* — were built, maintained, repaired, and equipped here.

The vehicle rolled between huge structures and eventually halted before an administrative building. Alex considered her surroundings carefully; not too many people apparent nearby, but at least the pavements were mostly plowed. As the young whitecoat opened her door and hopped out, then waited for Stephanie and Strong to join her, she wondered how long the grounds had been cleared — getting people back to work at the yard was undoubtedly quite important, but most workers were probably still snowed in. Indeed, there wasn't even anyone to greet the new arrivals...

The door to the yard's administrative headquarters abruptly swung open, and just as Strong and Stephanie came to a stop beside their Lady, a new Lord appeared. His coat was gunmetal gray, and his expression was sour.

His introductory announcement backed up his visage: "Expected you sooner."

He sounded properly Scottish, which normally might have tweaked Alex's interest, but his choice of words and tone seemed far less collegial than was proper. She just managed to fight off a frown as she turned to consider him.

Stephanie was less successful concealing her first impression: "You expected us to cross the Atlantic Ocean on no notice *faster*?"

The Champion stopped in surprise at the back-talk, his eyes hardening as they locked onto the American.

"Where's the rest of your lance, Lieutenant?"

So he was rude and ignorant; this promised to end well.

Seeing Stephanie begin to bristle, Alex took a step forward to interdict, "This is my whole lance. Just the three of us."

The Scottish Champion continued to glare at Stephanie for a moment, but eventually pried himself free to look at Alex. Grudgingly, he stepped nearer to her and extended his hand, "I'm Lord Duncan, of Edinburgh."

"Alex Smith," she took his hand, and found his grip coarse.

"You're lucky you don't have to put up with so many camp followers," the Scot lowered his voice slightly with that observation — as if that would somehow prevent Strong and Stephanie from hearing, even though he was right in front of them. "I've asked many times to be relieved of mine, but General Kennedy refuses. Perhaps you'll be proof of how much more we can accomplish *unencumbered.*"

Perhaps 'rude' wasn't really strong enough a word. Alex just managed to keep her jaw from dropping, and Stephanie Shylock's fists began to clench.

But Mike Strong, fortunately, had a clearer head around the arrogant Scotsman: "You've begun an investigation?"

Releasing Alex's hand, Duncan nodded, "Come this way. Smartly."

With that, he wheeled and hurried back into the building, leaving Alex, Stephanie and Strong surprised in his wake. They looked at each other, and after a few seconds Strong said what they'd all immediately thought: "Shucks, I was planning to do it *dumbly.*"

"I was going for *middlingly intelligently,*" Alex offered.

Stephanie shook her head, "I was thinking *smartly but not applying myself, and therefore disappointing my teachers.*"

That one took a lot of effort to say, so the Lieutenant won the repartee competition.

"That's pretty good," Strong nodded, and then with sighs all around, they followed Duncan into the administration building.

It seemed mostly empty — even with her sharp Champion hearing, Alex couldn't make out too many sounds suggesting other occupants. As she'd suspected, the storm must have confined most of the yard's personnel to their homes, or required them to take part in rescue missions. A half-dozen trains full of cold — perhaps frozen — civilians needed digging out after all.

But helping the recovery efforts wasn't the purpose of the trio from Jimmystown; as they followed the sound of Duncan's boots, they consoled themselves with the fact that such storms were common in Newfoundland, and the aftermath there was usually cleared away by a much smaller population.

It was for them to find the missing Lady, and as they rounded another corner and found an impatient Duncan standing beside an open door with his arms folded, they knew they'd reached the beginning of that particular venture.

"We got started as soon as we arrived... found the room where Elspeth and her lance had set up," the Scot explained as they joined him, and then followed him through into a short corridor. "Looks as though they'd been working out of there a couple of days, if not longer. But they kept no notes that we've found, suggesting where they would have gone. Or why."

As they proceeded down a short hallway, Alex digested those words with a frown. It seemed silly for a Champion of Lady Cornish's experience to work so long without a record of her intentions. The disruption of the storm could logically have prevented her from telling others of her plans and suspicions, but to not even leave a note...

"Was anyone looking through the room before you arrived, Lord Duncan?" Strong asked thoughtfully.

The Scotsman turned back to him with a scowl before replying, "We've been here only two hours, Sergeant. How are we to know?"

It was pointed, but fortunately Stephanie had grown more conciliatory, "Sorry, Lord Duncan. We thought you'd have been here longer."

Actually, that probably wasn't any more diplomatic, and it earned her quite a glare. She was sufficiently chastened to smile sweetly, but no more words were exchanged before they arrived in a larger planning room.

A room *full* of paper.

A half dozen long tables were deployed throughout, and blackboards and bulletin boards on wheeled frames stood around the perimeter. Everything was covered by files, photographs, books, logs...

"Jesus," Strong breathed as he came to a stop just inside the door. "It's like someone filleted a library."

"Have you found anything yet?" Duncan ignored the Colour, and instead directed that demand at the men of his lance, who were gathered around tables and boards as they tried to make some sense of the work that Elspeth's searchers had been doing.

A few of those soldiers now looked up despondently, but most avoided eye contact with their Champion. The love in the room was obvious to everyone, and as they came to a stop, the whitecoat, the American and the Sergeant traded more surprised glances. Evidently, and unfortunately, not all Champions had good chemistry with their infantry guardians.

Waiting for a moment as Duncan raised his voice and demanded progress, Alex let her eyes drift across the room. There was a huge amount of data — so much as to be slightly intimidating — but as she looked to her friend, she realized Stephanie was beginning to brighten.

Of course she was going to love having so much raw data handy…

"Have a look here," Duncan finished his scoldings and waved to Alex, summoning her like a child. Whether they were supposed to or not, Strong and Stephanie followed as their Lady moved after the local Champion, eventually joining him at a map pinned to one of the boards at the front of the room

He looked to the whitecoat as she arrived, then spotted the ordinary people with her and scowled again before electing to ignore them and planting his finger on the map, "Where they found Freeman, see."

Alex frowned. Freeman had been discovered miles from anywhere.

"Which way was he going?" Strong asked.

Duncan's scowl didn't waver, but he forced himself to reply — a Champion's life might be at stake, after all: "Coming back this way, but with quite a distance to go as you can see. I haven't gone out to check his trail yet, as I was needed to supervise here. And we could not send ordinary men on such a mission."

More ire directed at his own men. Either the Champion from Edinburgh was having a particularly bad day, or he was an utter bastard. Or, perhaps, both.

Either way, Alex had enjoyed quite enough of his company — she feared that sharing the air with him much longer might be poor for her health.

Folding her arms, she flooded her tone with the sort of aristocratic authority her mother had taught her, "Then we'll go for a look."

"Of course you will, because you don't have a lance to contribute to our shuffling of papers here," Duncan's retort was somehow both insolent and dismissive.

Such a charmer.

"Oh, let's not leave him hanging, Alex. I'll stay and help."

It went down really well when Stephanie turned to her best friend and said that — not just because Duncan seemed to have a deep and profound affection for the headstrong American, but because she used her Champion's first name. Scandal.

"You sure?" Alex appreciated that her American friend liked to pick fights on principle, and she wasn't even opposed to it this time, but it seemed more like masochism than anything else.

With a smile, Stephanie nodded, "Oh yes. With all this information in one place, shouldn't take long for me to figure everything out."

Another comment Duncan didn't appreciate, but it made Alex smile too, "I'll hold you to that." Then she looked back to the Scotsman, "My Colour and I will go look at the place where Freeman was found, and follow the trail from there. You and your men catch up once my Lieutenant finds the answer for you. Good?"

Perhaps Stephanie was rubbing off on her a bit, but the whitecoat didn't mind. Strictly speaking, Duncan was senior — this was his country, so technically he was in charge.

But Alex was asserting some kind of intangible authority.

As if to resist the momentum, which had clearly turned against him, the gray-coated Lord scowled, "I do not believe your Sergeant is a *Colour* Sergeant."

Because that was relevant.

Smiling with greater delight at her counterpart's obvious displeasure, Alex replied: "It's definitely a good thing Stephanie's staying to help you sort through all this. You certainly do miss the obvious sometimes, my dear Lord Duncan."

Without giving the Scotsman a chance to fume too much, the young Champion winked at her friend, nudged her Sergeant gently with her elbow, and headed for the door.

As they left, Stephanie laced her fingers together and cracked her knuckles before drawing Duncan's glare again. As he glowered at her, she smiled: "Don't worry, M'Lord, we're just getting warmed up. Let's find our missing Lady."

Elspeth was conscious, and she supposed she was even awake, but for some reason her command of her body was nonexistent. It felt like it had been this way for only a few minutes, but she suspected it was actually much longer.

Forcing herself to sit up, she recognized that she was inside a small room. There were no windows, and the ceiling was low, so as she rolled free of her cot and got her boots onto the ground, she had to crouch. She wasn't steady, though, and as she fell immediately to one side, her hand found the wall to try to keep her upright.

She failed, dropping down to her knees, then falling onto her backside. But her hand didn't leave the wall, and as she processed the cold smoothness of that surface, she realized it was made of metal. She was in some sort of metal cage, probably because it would hold her. If it was wood she could simply have broken out.

If she'd been able to stand. If she'd been able to remember how to spell her name.

For a moment she thought to call for her lance — they were never far away, because she never strayed too far from them. They were her friends, after all. Why would she ever go anywhere without her gang of heroes?

Because, of course, they couldn't always survive where she went.

And this time, they had all died.

Elspeth knew that had happened — and she knew it would be nearly impossible to cope with when it truly sank in. But inside the metal box, with her equilibrium destroyed and her mind twirling, it all still seemed like a terrible dream.

That was a mercy.

Suddenly, a shaft of light hit her, and she tried to hold up a hand to shield herself from the brightness. She missed — somehow held her hand in the wrong direction — meaning she could watch as a figure filled what had to be an open door at the end of the room, then advanced toward her.

"You're moving around," he stated the obvious, but the words were muffled, as though he was speaking through a gas mask. Sure enough, his face was eclipsed by one...

"Obviously," Elspeth replied, seeming to speak without much conscious control of what she said. "I got lost, though. It's very dark."

Why couldn't she ask what was going on, or think to run away? She was a Champion, but as he put his hands under her arms, lifted her lean-but-sturdy form off the floor, and placed her back on her cot, she could do nothing but *giggle*.

And she kept giggling as he slid her hands and boots through restraining loops.

"Are you restraining me?"

He didn't respond to that — maybe he hadn't heard her, because he was wearing a gas mask. It also made him look like an elephant.

"You look like an elephant," she spoke again without meaning to. He still didn't respond as he finished securing the cuffs that held her down, then pulled a new leather strap across her waist and buckled that too.

"Nothing is torn," he shook his head, his accent again noticeable, even through the mask. "How do you keep getting out?"

She blinked a few times, then declared: "I'm flexible!"

What was she even saying? And what was going on — had she just been caught attempting escape? She didn't... didn't remember trying to escape. And where were the men from her lance?

"I'll increase the concentration," the man sounded frustrated. "We're close to a lethal dose, so you better calm down."

"I'm calm," she protested, and then she let her head fall back to the uncomfortable cot. The man disappeared, and the shaft of light vanished after him. She was alone again in the dark, inhaling thick, tasteless air as she wondered where her men were.

CHAPTER IV

The grave atmosphere around Fort Eustice was no great surprise to Lady Caralynne Smith — the place had been devastated, and then the President of the United States had been killed, so a certain somberness was inevitable. More unexpected, though, was the slow pace of rehabilitation.

Like George Devlin, Caralynne had arrived before sunrise for the day-long layover on the way to Washington, where they would give testimony in the Senate Inquiry into the attack on the United States Champions base. She and the Viscount's son had traveled together to Eustice ahead of their scheduled appearances. But while George had a screen to examine, the elder Lady Smith elected to tour the base after the sun came up. She'd started at the headquarters building and made her way towards the craters on the skycruiser landing field — a place she remembered with uneasy vividness, considering she and *George Tucker* had been between its two craters when they'd been formed.

Around the landing field, she looked at half-repaired buildings, scattered among many ruins that would warrant full reconstruction if they were to serve again. Between the structures she found craters filled with pools of water, presumably left over from fire-fighting efforts and now half-frozen in the cold. She even ventured to the road leading to the training fields — the road on which twenty Champion students had been killed.

The bodies had been cleared, of course... but Caralynne had no difficulty remembering precisely how gruesome the scene had been. She hadn't seen so many dead people together in decades, and she rather hoped she'd never see it again.

But someone had attacked the Champions of the United States, and that had to be answered. The problem, near as the elder Lady

Smith could figure, was that the American government wasn't fully committed to doing what was necessary. If the new President was bent on facing this new threat actively, he surely would have made every effort to restore Fort Eustice in short order, or at least have allocated more reconstruction parties to the base.

Instead, Caralynne was alone as she paced around the grounds. Occasionally a few white soldiers would appear in the distance, but never did they look to be on reconstruction business. Perhaps, as Roosevelt had feared aloud during his last dinner aboard *Hood*, the isolationists were going to take control now — let a place like Eustice, and the Champions establishment it once commanded, quietly fade away as they paid only lip service to finding the culprits.

As she entertained that unwelcome thought, Caralynne spotted another white soldier. This one wasn't passing in the distance; he was coming directly for her.

And she wasn't particularly glad of the approach.

"I understand they're broadening the Senate Inquiry to include what happened on the Grand Banks," Major Sheldon Travis was a very tall man, and he spoke directly with a sort of country accent Caralynne couldn't quite place.

Even though he'd been the one to convince her to take the American students to safety back in Jimmystown, she still didn't understand this man, and there was something about him that felt distant, verging on unwelcome. Under the circumstances, he seemed a convenient target for her anxieties about the United States situation.

"Good morning, Major," was her answer to his greeting — if the opening statement could be called that — and he nodded to her, then tugged on the brim of his hat.

"Hope this trip is less eventful," he offered simply.

Without intending to, she reacted poorly to the tone, "Than what, the last time we were here, or on the Grand Banks when your President drowned?"

The words failed to change Travis' expression, "Either. Or both. I'd rather not have anybody dead."

"So you'll keep them locked away, safe and sound until their time before the inquisition?" she asked sharply — too harshly, she realized, but was unable to stop herself.

Travis eyed her, then nodded once, "Yes."

Well at least the straight-talking was consistent. Caralynne took a breath, then shifted subjects by directing her gaze past the Major, towards the burned-out Fort, "Not much effort going into reconstruction?"

"The Inquiry plans to tour the damage, and the Corps of Engineers wants to investigate further. So we wait in this wreck," the Major replied.

Caralynne's eyebrow climbed at the thin excuse, and in the spirit of being direct she answered pointedly, "Or perhaps isolationists are in control now that Roosevelt is gone, and they're using the Inquiry as an excuse to let this place rot."

Again Travis seemed unaffected — as though his temper was invulnerable — and he answered plainly once more: "Could be that too."

His tone was flat and unimpressed, but his unpretentious candor was disarming. Caralynne looked away, eyes crossing the husks of destroyed buildings as she wondered if he was friend, foe, or something else.

There were too many questions in Fort Eustice, and Senate Inquiry or no, the elder Lady Smith got the distinct impression that few answers would be readily forthcoming.

Perhaps her daughter would find them in Scotland.

"I never even knew this was here," Vanier Cross was standing right in front of the screen, eyes wide as he watched the data scrolling across the mighty display.

Sitting at the Corporal's desk behind him, George Devlin simply smiled, "It helps to learn the systems directly from the Saa."

"I'll bet."

Shaking his head, the black screen operator fell silent after that, his eyes traversing the data that the Newfoundland hospitality man had scrounged up. Every *single* entry ever made under Vanier's code had been logged and stored, separate from the main registry... but beyond just a list, the screens that had been displayed in each action could be recalled, shown again... nothing was forgotten.

"Incredible," Vanier shook his head once more, turning away from the wall of light. "You think whoever did this might have failed to erase this log?"

It was a possibility, though George wasn't nearly as hopeful as Vanier might have liked: "This screen pulls registry data from the same central database. Everything should corroborate what you already found... I'm just hoping..."

His words fell off as the punch of a key revealed Vanier's entries for the eve of the attack on Fort Eustice. Those entries, and the ones from the period immediately before, were identical.

"See, the same duplication right here," George nodded to the screen. "Whoever did the overwrite copied the data at the central source. So this is just a different way of looking at the same problem."

Vanier let some of his enthusiasm slip as he exhaled. Folding his arms, he advanced towards the screen again and shook his head, "We're not going to find an answer, are we?"

George probably should have resisted that sentiment — should have suggested that the answer would turn up — but he wasn't sure he disagreed. Whoever was behind the attack on Eustice, and on *Hood*, clearly wasn't leaving loose ends. Things had gone wrong with each operation... the men Alex and Stephanie had killed in their Jeeps probably had been meant to escape, while Alain Lapointe was undoubtedly supposed to have died... but everything else had worked. Unless a trail was picked up in Scotland, it was entirely possible that the perpetrators would get away.

And while they ran, George would be testifying before a bunch of American politicians about why their rather haphazard security had allowed the lapses of recent months.

"What's their big picture? That's the question my momma would want me to ask... maybe it's the one we should be trying to answer."

Vanier's words caught George by surprise — he'd been preparing for a lengthy period of expository musing — but instead he frowned and looked up. The black soldier was pacing back and forth in front of the screen, arms folded as he tried to extend his mind around the girth of the problems they were facing.

"If everything they tried worked, what did they achieve? They blew up our Saa machines... they drove our Champions to you in Newfoundland..."

It was a worthy line of thought — one that many had pursued already, of course, but George wasn't opposed to revisiting it.

"The trick is not to assume that everything we've done is what they wanted us to do," the hospitality man replied. "They might have *thought* we'd receive your students, but if they have any sense, they'd know it wasn't a sure thing."

"But... but they'd know it was a much *better* chance that we'd restrict use of your two Saa machines after ours got blown," Vanier stopped his pacing. "And they'd know there had to be some kind of meeting between leaders... could they have known that attacking this base would lead to a meeting aboard *Hood*?"

George shrugged, "They might have thought it possible... and obviously they were in position to take advantage when it did."

That wasn't really an answer to the question, and both men knew it. Had Eustice been attacked specifically to get the Special Service Squadrons from both fleets to meet on the Grand Banks? Had the villains planned from the outset to assassinate the Prime Ministers and the President? If so, attacking Eustice seemed a very long-shot way to set the conditions for the murder. Getting explosives aboard *Hood* would have had to take a great deal of special effort... effort spent with no guarantee that the ship would host any politicians.

"I can't imagine that anyone smart enough to break into the screen would build a plan with so many variables," Vanier was following the same path of reasoning. "Killing our leaders was obviously something they were happy to do, but what if it wasn't their point? What if... what if they just wanted to blow up *Hood*?"

Frowning, George joined in, "Destroy the Royal Navy's flagship, after attacking the American Champions, and you're going to heighten tensions — drive both our nations onto war footing. Perhaps even spark a conflagration."

"And if the opportunity arises, you also kill the leaders from both countries, and it's 1914 all over again," Vanier took over again. "If you're *trying* to start a war, there's no better way."

It sounded all too plausible, and George sighed as he leaned back in his borrowed chair and folded his arms. Vanier Cross was definitely a sharp man — well deserving of his post in this screen room. While everyone had become so focused on the assignations, assuming they must have been the primary agenda of whatever culprit was behind all this, it was entirely possible that they were unintentional... or at the very least, an unexpected 'bonus' of plans already in place.

But who could have wanted to draw the wrath of the two most powerful empires in human history, and to what end? Was this, after all, Emily trying to get ordinary people to fight each other?

"Actually," Vanier interrupted George's thoughts again, and the Viscount's son looked up. "Maybe they *thought* killing the politicians would make war more likely. But look what it's actually done."

For a second, George didn't follow... then he recalled the sights of destruction still evident throughout Eustice, and realized the point his not-friend was making.

"They got isolationists instead of war mongers," the younger Devlin answered.

Vanier nodded firmly, "So if they wanted a war, they're getting the opposite."

"For now."

The black soldier conceded that, "Yeah, for now. But... but if they wanted it to happen fast, maybe they'll do something else to stir tensions."

That was an unwelcome thought, but a reasonable one. With another sigh, George Devlin nodded at his counterpart's wise insight before looking down for a moment. They desperately needed to know what had gone on inside this Saa screen. Help was needed soon, but there was no telling when the next Saa envoy would arrive.

With nothing but their own wits, then, they'd have to locate the villains. And one of the sharpest people for that job was spending his days locked in a cell.

CHAPTER V

As she hopped out of the Land Rover, Alex had a tough time imagining anything deadly could have ever happened in her placid surroundings. Though the road they'd taken was plowed, the vast pastures and fields it cut through were blanketed by serene snow, and were glowing brightly in the midday sun. To the south, the Forth was glistening too — icy water not unlike the kind she'd barely survived on the Grand Banks... but somehow still peaceful.

Nothing about this place seemed to invoke death — at least not to Alex. And she supposed after recent events, she knew better than some what death was like. Had Sergeant Freeman really died here?

"Over here," Mike Strong had hopped out of the Land Rover too, his Thompson in hand.

Alex turned north and caught sight of him standing on the road's shoulder, his shoulders weighted by the sight as he looked down. Rounding the vehicle quickly, the young Champion slowed at the first splashes of red in the snow. There was a great deal visible — scarlet jumping out of the pure whiteness — and she felt a genuine chill as she examined the gore.

"He got this far, in the driving snow. Dragging himself on his belly," Strong was ostensibly speaking to his Lady, but perhaps the words were also for himself. Alex remained silent — there was nothing clever to say. Instead, she let Strong take a step forward, then shake his head and look west, back towards the yards.

About a mile down the road towards Rosyth was a line of houses — cottages for the workers, by the look of them. Immediately the Colour knew those buildings had been Freeman's destination: "The snow probably wasn't too deep when he was dragging himself... so through the blowing snow, every now and then, he could see the lights from those cottages."

The heaviness filling Strong's words was unmistakable, and Alex felt herself growing colder as her Sergeant relived the dead man's final moments.

"He was thinking he had to make it. He was figuring it was his only chance to save his Champion," the Sergeant had no trouble imagining Freeman's motives. "He was a soldier... he knew he wasn't going to see his wife or his girls again, but he figured he could save Elspeth. Or die trying."

Even to Alex it seemed an awfully long way to crawl, but she trusted that her Sergeant, of all men, would know what someone like Freeman would have been capable of, right to the end.

"They found him on his back, didn't they?" Strong turned towards her with that question, and her response was a simple nod. Information confirmed, he pressed on: "Bob didn't want to die with his face in the snow. He wanted to see the sky. And he probably knew when he died, there was no one left to help his Lady. Maybe... hopefully... he forgot that in the last moments..."

The Sergeant's words trailed off, and his eyes turned back to the red snow as silence settled over the cold, bright roadway. Alex probably should have followed his gaze back to the red, but she elected to give herself a few seconds to think instead. Beneath the snow, there might have been a blood trail they could follow... but it wasn't obvious. Perhaps it had been plowed away, or perhaps it cut across the field to the north, and was thus completely covered.

They'd find where he'd come from eventually, but first... first Alex took a step towards her Sergeant, reached out and looped her arm around his, then pressed up against his shoulder, "I didn't know Sergeant Freeman. But it sounds like he did exactly what you'd do."

"I don't know if I'd have gotten this far," Strong replied darkly, and though she refused to discount her Colour's own heroism, she knew it was not the right occasion to argue with him.

A brave man had died in this place, and that required respect.

After a moment of silence, Alex released Strong and began pacing down the road, heading east, "You think he came from this way?"

Following his white-coated charge with his eyes, Strong took a single breath to clear his thoughts, then nodded, "It would probably be the easiest way for him to go."

That sounded sensible to Alex as well, so she narrowed her eyes. A mile on, the road disappeared into a thick stand of trees... more like a small forest... that stretched north from the road and up a hill. Recalling the aerial photograph, Alex tried to place all its features.

"Isn't there a house somewhere in those woods?" she waved towards the trees further north.

Strong finally advanced past the bloody patch in the snow, swinging the Thompson upwards so he could cradle it in a single arm, "I think I saw that. Probably be a couple of miles at least."

That was quite a distance — an impossible distance for a man to cover while wounded as Freeman had been. Still, it was probably the closest building in that direction, so Alex rocked up onto the balls of her feet and puffed out her cheeks thoughtfully, "Good place to start? Maybe... maybe we just drive up to the woods and park, then see if we can pick our way through the trees. There might be clues in there."

It seemed a worthy idea, so Strong shrugged, "Alright, let's do that."

A simple decision, and with it they returned to their Land Rover, so they could leave behind the blood of Bob Freeman.

Stephanie was in her element. A copious amount of information to sort, and something to prove to a rather arrogant fellow who was unkind to others? She'd spent three years at Memorial College of Newfoundland training for precisely these sorts of moments.

Suitably motivated, the American Lieutenant was quickly working her way through a pile of transfer bills that had been collected on one of the tables — slips of paper that told the shipyard's personnel to collect certain supplies and bring them aboard *Hood*. Since there was a good chance explosives had been brought aboard that ship with the express purpose of sinking her, the bills were a good place to begin, and evidently Elspeth, or one of her men, had thought the same. The slips had all been collected together into a single stack, which was what first drew Stephanie's attention.

She had a feeling that these bills held an important clue, but as someone who'd spent more than her share of hours digging through piles of documents for research purposes, she knew that a feeling didn't count for much. Many times during her career as a student, she'd sought a quote that she was certain she'd read somewhere... which she'd in fact based an entire argument on... but which seemed impossible to find when she needed it.

Nevertheless, Lieutenant Shylock kept at it — with practiced discipline, she carefully went through every bill. The one Elspeth's people had left on top of the pile was for a load of 5-inch shells (for *Hood's* secondary armament), and reading through it carefully she had been able to determine that it was likely the last shipment *Hood* took aboard before she sailed. Whether that was unusual or not, she had no idea — Stephanie knew nothing about naval supply operations.

Her best bet, then, was to compare the details of the top bill to the dozens of others bundled with it. What warehouse or arsenal did the supplies come from? Who signed and who countersigned? What time of day? Any detail might be important.

Or none of them could be.

"I realize she was in the moment, but damned if some better notes wouldn't have come in handy," Duncan's officer — a Lieutenant called Turnbull — erupted with that commentary from across the room, and some of his men grunted in agreement. Whether the words were spurred by frustration at doing a paper search, or were actually targeted somehow at Champions in general, Stephanie couldn't tell... but the mood in the room wasn't getting any better.

"That sounded as though you were speaking ill of a Champion, Lieutenant," Duncan's answer was almost belligerent, and with a glance up, Stephanie saw the thundercloud cross Turnbull's face.

"Wouldn't dream of it, M'Lord," he muttered his reply, then went back to sifting.

Such a warm working environment. Stephanie wasn't sure who was to be blame for the atmosphere — whether the men of the lance were suffering with a consistently awful Champion, or if Lord Duncan had been soured by bad soldiers. Either way, the result was not in keeping with the high expectations she had for the Special Service Regiment.

She said nothing, though, and instead maintained a close focus on the stack of bills. The effort was beginning to pay off... something here was wrong.

Strong insisted he lead the way into the woods — the circumstances almost inevitably made him feel even more protective than usual. Of course, being a few yards in front of Alex as they advanced between the trees would do little to actually protect her from danger. Indeed, her Champion senses would probably detect danger before his eyes and ears anyway. But it was a matter of principle.

Thompson up, he stepped across the snow-filled ditch that ran along the northern shoulder of the road from the yard, then strode into the trees. The snow beneath his feet was soft but wet, so every step was marked by a muffled crunching sound. Sneaking around in such conditions wouldn't be easy — and because this was a civilized stand of Scottish trees (not a Newfoundland forest), it wasn't even thick enough to offer much underbrush for cover.

As she stepped lightly under the canopy of trees behind her Colour, Alex drew her Browning from the holster on her hip, but let it hang down at her side. Nothing about the woods here felt menacing — it was still a pretty winter day after snowfall.

But she was not naïve. Thumbing off her pistol's safety, she made sure to keep her finger away from the trigger as they advanced.

"We'll go up the hill until we find something," though phrased like a command, Strong's words were in fact a suggestion, and Alex nodded.

"Sounds good to me."

Good might have been the wrong word, but it didn't matter: with the Sergeant slightly in the lead, the duo left the road behind, moving deeper into the woods that might have been the site of Elspeth's trouble. If there were signs of a fight, they'd detect them.

"Wait."

It was the sort of quiet-but-significant word that could stop a room, and as Stephanie looked between pieces of paper held in each hand, it became clear to all the men of Duncan's lance that the newcomer had something.

She set the two pieces of paper side-by-side on the table: the first 5-inch shell bill, and then a bill for a similar shipments of shells, but from a week earlier. That done, she looked up and declared, "Found it."

People put down what they were reading, or brought it with them as they advanced to surround her table. Duncan came darkly around to stand beside her shoulder, and as soon as she had everyone's attention, Stephanie pointed to the first bill.

"The last load of 5-inch shells that *Hood* took aboard was routed from the 'Amstalden Engineering Workshop'. The rest of them came from the arsenal," she explained. "Why would the ship take aboard shells from a workshop? It makes no sense, and Elspeth must have noticed that too — she had these bills bundled together with the Amstalden one on top."

Duncan was frowning, but silent. For a few seconds he glowered at the two pieces of paper, his displeasure at having been beaten to the clue rather impossible to miss. But he wasn't out yet, so he issued a demand to his men: "Get me *Hood's* sailing time!"

One of the private soldiers with the Scottish Champion's lance swallowed before replying, "Sailing out? She left port at 0937 on the morning of January 19th, sir."

Didn't get much more precise than that, so everyone did their best to lean closer and check the delivery time on the bill.

"You missed that this last load of shells was delivered and signed for five hours after *Hood* put to sea," Duncan turned to Stephanie. "That is the more important clue."

Perhaps it was, but the reason the American Lieutenant began to smile had nothing to do with the facts of the case, and everything to do with her intentions for the next few minutes of polite conversation.

Turnbull seemed to detect what was about to happen, and he threw his words between the two in a bid to head it off, "How does that make sense? If they forged a waybill to get a load of explosives aboard, what use is it if the delivery time was *after* she sailed?"

That was a good question — good enough to force its way to the front of Stephanie's mind, and drag her eyes back down to the papers. Duncan could be dealt with later.

The bill could have been some curious kind of clerical error... a misprint or a mis-delivery... but again, the fact that Elspeth and her lance had put that bill on top suggested the working-class Lady had given the question some attention. Had she gone to the Amstalden Workshop to investigate further? That building would have to be somewhere in the Dockyard — well away from where Freeman had been found — but perhaps the next clue in the trail to Elspeth would be there...

Or perhaps there was a shortcut.

Realizing there was yet another clue to be found, Stephanie quickly leaned down and shuffled the bills again. The Amstalden Engineering Workshop wasn't just an unusual-sounding place for a load of shells to be stored, it was the only *specific* place mentioned on any of the bills. Why?

"None of these other bills actually spell out the warehouses or the workshops. This one gives us a full name. Couple that with the impossible delivery time, and perhaps this bill was created to get the attention of investigators. To draw attention to the place mentioned."

It was starting to become clear to Stephanie: someone had baited a trap for Elspeth.

This was the point where either Alex or Strong would have jumped in to confirm that notion, but as Stephanie trailed off she realized that no one present — not even Duncan — was keeping up now.

She tried again: "What if someone forged this?"

The Lord blinked, then shook his head, "Obviously, to get the bomb aboard, a false waybill..."

"*No,*" Stephanie turned a sharp glare against the Champion. "No, this bill wouldn't have gotten anything aboard *Hood*. But it would have been the sort of clue that Elspeth and her investigators would have followed up."

Duncan's brow sunk deeper into a scowl, and realizing she was still on her own, Stephanie looked around at the rest of the men.

"If you knew a Champion was coming out here to investigate *Hood's* destruction, and you wanted to set a trap for her, this sort of thing could *make her come to you.*"

There it was — she couldn't put it any more clearly. She held her breath, wondering if any of these browbeaten men would follow her reasoning. Thank God, Turnbull did.

"Whoever blew up *Hood* waited until he knew a Champion was coming, then planted a document that would lead her investigation to him?" the Lieutenant asked, then shifted his gaze to Duncan before backpedaling a little. "That man would be condemning himself to certain death."

It was evident that this lance had been schooled never to question the prowess of Champions, which was just foolish... but there was no time for Stephanie to correct such deep-seeded problems.

"Bob Freeman probably wouldn't agree," was her sharp reply. "So if Elspeth was their target, then the question is simply what they wanted with her. And where this led her."

By now Duncan had managed to get his mind around the concept — alien though it had to be to his understanding of the hierarchy among ordinary men and Champions — and he unleashed another frustrated question on his men, "Anyone know where this workshop is?"

"Sergeant, find us a map," Turnbull ordered immediately, and his Colour Sergeant hurried off quickly, then returned with a large paper.

"In the middle of bloody everything, M'Lord," was his quick answer, as men gave him room to step up to the table and spread out the map.

Stephanie's frown deepened again — it was obvious that, even in the middle of a blizzard, Elspeth's lance couldn't have been in a firefight in the Dockyard without drawing attention. And even if this had been the site of the trouble, how would Freeman have gotten so far away, and why would he have been dragging himself back towards Rosyth?

"We're missing one piece," Stephanie pushed them forward again. "Everyone... start looking for other references to this Amstalden place. People who work there, for instance."

Though she was the room's junior officer, she was giving the orders — and, admittedly, enjoying it. The men of Duncan's lance scattered in search of more evidence. Now that they had proper guidance, it didn't take long.

"On top over here!" one man called almost immediately, and Turnbull hurried to his side before taking over the narration.

"There's a Swiss engineer called Saager, who's the head of the Amstalden Workshop. And he lives near here."

The Lieutenant held up the file he was referring to — one that Elspeth's people had clearly singled out too — and Duncan hurried across the room to seize it.

"Castleandhill House," the Champion read Saager's address.

"Right up the road from where we found Freeman," Turnbull added, looking across the room at Stephanie. She wasn't sure what message his eyes were trying to convey — thanks or scorn — but it seemed irrelevant.

They had a possible location, and it definitely needed to be checked out.

Duncan seemed fully convinced.

Lowering the file, he turned to his Lieutenant, "We have them now. We will go there, perhaps see if Lady Smith is somewhere on the way — though we *do not* need her."

Apparently, he just wanted to make that clear. Stephanie smiled again at the arrogance, then shrugged, "That's fine. I'll ride with you guys. No wait, better: I'll drive."

Duncan whirled on her, thunderclouds almost forming over his head... but her viciously pretty smile was pure ice. He clearly didn't like her, but at the same time, she'd needed only a handful of minutes to piece together a very compelling possible case. Better than his own men, by his estimation... so he would tolerate her.

"Very well," he said sharply. "We move, *now*."

"That's good, I was worried we might not move 'til later," she answered sweetly, and then clapped her hands together. "Smartly!"

Stephanie Shylock then turned and headed out of the room. She sure was popular.

CHAPTER VI

Being long-accustomed to Newfoundland forests, which were often virtually impassible, Alex and Strong had expected a slow-going slog up a snowy slope.

Instead, the dense canopy of trees overhead had kept too much of the snow from getting to ground inside the woods, and the lack of deadfall and underbrush made the climb altogether pleasant.

Still, neither Strong nor Alex took for granted the ease of the passage... and they remained cautious of their surroundings. There was lots of daylight left as they made their way, so visibility wasn't a challenge, but as Alex's father had taught her, the woods could always hide a person — sometimes even in plain sight.

Following the techniques of her former-drifter dad, the young Lady in white kept her eyes moving at all times, sweeping back and forth across the trees ahead, then behind. Never did she let her gaze linger on any one place, because as her dad would put it, a brain could get too accustomed to a single scene if it stared for too long. Better to keep the picture changing, because every time one's mind reacquired an image, and did a new assessment of its content, the chances of discovering something out of place improved.

So Alex let her eyes drift as she followed Mike Strong up the increasingly steep climb. For his part, the Colour simply trusted his hard-earned instincts. He moved in a crouch that, combined with the cold, would probably do his back no good by that evening... but future discomfort was secondary to present security. And his eyes moved too.

Strong had fought savages on the new world. He'd never done a lot of shooting inside the new world forests, but he'd passed through some of them on the way to battle — notably at Promised Town — and that was enough experience to make sure he knew the basics of fighting in trees.

If there was danger close, he'd do his best to see it first...

At the very same moment that he was assuring himself of that fact, Strong jerked to a stop. His eyes landed on a lump in the snowy blanket at the base of a very steep section of slope.

"There," he breathed the word — barely more than a whisper — and Alex blinked and hurried forward.

Training his Thompson in the direction of the lump, the Colour dipped his head to the side, suggesting his Lady space herself out a little further. Realizing he didn't want them too closely grouped in case of trouble, she nodded, then side-stepped and found a position partially covered by a big tree.

As she reached that point and lifted her Browning partway, she nodded to Strong, and the veteran Sergeant nodded back. He then crept slowly forward, still crouching with his Thompson primed and pointed.

The lump in the snow could have just been a rock, he supposed, but its top surface and sides looked too flat. More like a case, he decided as he got closer... and positioned as it was, it looked as though it could have fallen down the very steep slope it sat beside.

Raising his Thompson to sweep that high crest, Strong looked around for threats, but there was still no sign of immediate danger. Alex saw the point of his interest, and she raised her Browning too — swept the heights carefully, to give the Colour all the cover she could.

But her ears were sharp, and they detected nothing. It seemed as though they were the only people in the woods. Maybe they were.

As he reached the lump in the snow, Strong did one more sweep — first above, then turning back the way he'd come to make sure nothing had appeared to the rear while he'd been distracted. Alex spotted him do this, and did the same herself. Between the two of them they looked in every conceivable direction, even examining the canopy of trees.

Finally satisfied it was clear, Strong turned back to the lump and put one knee down beside it. Keeping his right hand on the pistol grip of his gun, he used his left to reach out and brush aside the snow.

Sure enough, it was a canvas case.

Two things about it warranted notice: the first was that it was a standard-issue army gas mask case, which based on its shape was still holding a mask.

The second was that it was covered in frozen blood.

As soon as the red registered, Strong looked up again — it wasn't quite a moment of terror, but the blood was a sure sign of nearby trouble, and he had to check again that no danger had come upon them during the few seconds he'd been looking away.

It hadn't, so he pushed around the snow with his left hand until he found the case's strap, then lifted it up and held it out to the side so Alex could see it.

Though she was a dozen yards behind, it was clear enough to the young Lady. Its significance didn't need to be explained.

Rising from his kneeling position and resuming his crouch, Strong turned away from the steep slope and hurried back to his Champion, carrying the case with him. As soon as they were near enough to each other for a whisper to carry, Alex nodded to the steep ground ahead, "Think they were up at the top, and it came down in the fight?"

Her assessment seemed reasonable, and Strong nodded, "That or Bob had it on him and it came off while he was crawling. Or falling."

Either way, whatever was atop the steep slope was undoubtedly quite important — was perhaps even the site of Elspeth's final battle. Were there bodies up there? Alex didn't relish that thought, but obviously they had to find out.

"Let's go see," she whispered, and stepped away from the tree.

Mike Strong was no Champion, but somehow his powerful hand was on her shoulder before she could see it, "Oh no you don't."

Alex blinked, honestly (perhaps even naively) confused at her Sergeant's reaction. But as he tugged on her shoulder enough to get her to turn and face him, his message was clear: "You're not going up there."

She frowned, "We can both go, quick and quiet. We can't come all this way and turn back."

"We can go back and bring more men," Strong countered, but Alex shook her head.

"The snow is being cleared. We can't risk letting something that was trapped here get out before we return. Let's just take a quick look," even as she was speaking, the young whitecoat started to wonder whether she was sounding impetuous. After the death of Freeman, wasn't prudence warranted? Hadn't she learned that in Virginia?

Certainly. But diving into the waters of the Grand Banks, she'd also learned that seconds could count. And all she wanted to do here was have a look...

Strong knew she was probably right — that if it weren't Alex (or Stephanie for that matter) he'd probably have agreed automatically. But now he was holding a gas mask case covered in frozen blood... no, actually, he'd dropped it to grab her. Realizing that, he let her go, then quickly brushed some red snow off her beloved white cloth, before it melted and threatened to stain.

He was being too protective and he knew it. They needed to look.

But carefully — just a peek.

With a compromise in mind, he spoke up, "I'll go, you listen for me and if there's trouble, get me out."

Alex didn't like the sound of that, and she did a bad job keeping her feelings from her face, "Now just a minute—"

He gave her a formidable look — raised eyebrow and all — that shut her down.

She pouted: "This is what Mike Strong would do?"

"*Will* do," he corrected gently. "Listen close... come if you hear shooting. If you don't hear anything, though, just stay put unless I call you. Alright?"

Sticking out her bottom lip extra-far, Alex looked away. Then she thought up her counter-argument, "What if someone's actually down here, and they attack me as soon as you're not here to protect me?"

Strong scoffed, "You really think I'm protecting *you*?"

"Certainly," Alex replied, then shrugged before adding, "From myself, if nothing else."

The candidness of her words made Strong smile, and he shook his head, "Just come if I need rescuing, okay?"

"Obviously," was her answer, and then she looked back up the slope. "Maybe even if you don't."

That was good enough for the Colour, so he nodded. Then, adjusting his Thompson so it would be held safely as he started to scramble up the steep, snowy slope, he left his young Lady behind.

"Think there's anyone else we can round up to join us?" Turnbull was asking that question of Lord Duncan as the two men and their lance emerged from the administration building.

"Only ordinary men of no use to us," was the predictably arrogant answer.

Stephanie had trailed the Scottish Champion and his soldiers, so she listened carefully to his conversation with his officer as they emerged into the sunlight, her smile growing ever-bigger as they swiped at each other.

She'd concluded that Duncan was the problem with this team — that Turnbull and his men, given the chance, were probably alright. But certain in his superiority, Edinburgh's Lord was not about to tolerate anyone he believed inferior.

Certainly, he was not the finest graduate of the Lady Emily Academy — he possessed as much hubris as some of the American students Alex had run across at the Robinson Institute... but he was already in the field, a part of the real world, so he had no excuse for his foolishness.

That was fine. In her own little way, Stephanie decided she would continue to needle him, at least demonstrating to the rude Champion that not all ordinary people could be cowed. More importantly, she'd also stay close enough to hopefully make certain that, if Elspeth was somewhere needing rescue, the man in the gunmetal gray coat didn't somehow miss the plot entirely, and leave her in distress.

Given his single-mindedness about Champion superiority, that might have seemed unlikely... but how such a man as Duncan would respond under stress, she didn't know.

Time would tell; for now, Stephanie strode past both Duncan and Turnbull, and neared one of the two Land Rovers that had been secured to take them to Castleandhill House.

At least she was driving.

The cold was making Mike Strong's joints start to ache, but it was the sort of pain he was still able to ignore when circumstances warranted. Scrambling up the snowy slope was not easy — particularly since he meant to do it silently — so focusing on every step and handhold was enough to keep his attention elsewhere.

As he neared the crest and slowed, carefully planting his feet on what felt like the partly-exposed root of a tree, the Colour pointedly ignored a flash of discomfort, and focused on what was beyond. Though he was hearing nothing, he still had to be cautious; what if there were machine guns up there, or lightning rays... any number of unexpected dangers that could have defeated Elspeth's lance? It was unlikely — bordering on impossible — but he was still wary as he checked his footing, shouldered his Thompson so he could look down the sights, and then straightened up. His head — and the muzzle of the gun — emerged over the crest.

Anyone lying in wait to kill intruders would see him then — a head-and-shoulders silhouette that could easily be picked off with a good shot.

But the pounding of his heart was the loudest thing he heard as he eyed the level ground beyond. The woods there were silent and still — frozen, almost — but not empty. A gray stone building stood in a clearing, and it was reasonably grand. Had they approached from the other direction, the place might have appeared to be only one storey, but standing on the downhill side, Strong could see it had a basement level with a walkout.

A door to that lower level was facing him as he looked at the structure... but there was no light coming from under it, or from any of the windows he could see on the south-facing side. No smoke rose from the building's chimney, either. The place seemed entirely static... but that was just a first impression. Turning slowly, Strong panned across the house and the grounds that surrounded it, waiting for any sign of trouble.

But there was none. He went from left to right, then right to left, then back, and found no suggestion of a threat. Indeed, had it not been for the knowledge of what had happened to Freeman, he probably wouldn't have considered the place any sort of danger.

But Freeman *had* died. Prudence was required.

Deciding there was nothing more to learn from his partially-concealed position, Strong straightened up further, then climbed the rest of the slope and stepped into the clearing. He was on the left side of the house as he faced it, so he could see up that side of the building — the ground sloped upward around the house, and there was no door on that side. No sign of activity, either.

Maintaining his crouch, the Colour therefore side-stepped to his right, keeping his Thompson fixed on the basement door as he moved. Beneath his feet, the wet snow continued to crunch softly, and he cursed that betrayal... but there still seemed to be no danger.

There was, however, a shed.

Strong stopped in place as the edge of the wooden outbuilding began to creep out from behind the right side of the house. The structure was notable because it looked as though some yellow light was flickering inside. Perhaps someone was here after all — someone potentially dangerous.

Again, Strong's heart became the loudest thing in the woods. He quickly considered his options: continue to move along the rim of the slope he'd just climbed, thus being nearer to escape... or advance to the corner of the house, so he could use its stone for protection as he leaned around for a better look at the shed.

Advancing would put him at greater risk if someone emerged from the house... but instinctively, it was the thing the Colour decided to do. Indeed, his feet were carrying him forward by the time he consciously made his choice — his Thompson up and shielding him as best it could.

He was halfway between the crest of the slope and the house when he heard accented words call out, "Who are you?"

Strong froze in place, his eyes sweeping back and forth quickly in search of the speaker. He started to dash left, for the shelter of the house, but as he turned that way, he saw a man leaning around the opposite corner, a rifle shouldered and aligned with his chest.

As Smith might have said in his drifting days, the shooter had Strong dead to rights.

"I asked who you are!" the man called, and the only answer that came to the Colour's mind was simple, and uncreative.

"A man needing rescue," he replied.

Fortunately, he'd come with an avenging angel.

CHAPTER VII

"Is this the road where they found Freeman?"

The Land Rover's wheel was rebelling against Stephanie's grip, and as she wrestled with it to maintain direction up a track that could only generously be called 'plowed', her question drew a head-shake from Duncan in the passenger seat.

"He was on a road south, down there…" he pointed down the hill towards the Forth. Had Stephanie been comfortable enough with the road conditions to divert her attention, she might have looked that way, and seen a much clearer-looking road cutting through serene snowy pastures. But as the wheel jumped out of her hand again, she decided it was better just to believe the Champion's assertion.

"Are you capable of handling these road conditions?" the Scotsman asked flatly, then glanced her. "You are an ordinary girl, after all."

That made Stephanie's smile broaden, and sharpen, "If you're offering, of course you can take over, M'Lord."

She took a gamble there, and won.

Duncan scowled, "I do not *drive*."

Of course he didn't — not even Alex had learned, because her time was better spent practicing her Champion-speed running.

"You're welcome to walk, then," Stephanie's answer was so very polite, and Duncan grumbled and looked out his window.

Enjoying her victory for just a second, Stephanie then returned her attention to the road. It wasn't easy going, which was probably just as well: a track barely passable by a Land Rover could have been enough to snow in whoever had attacked Elspeth. Maybe they would find a villain at the end of the bumpy ride…

That was perhaps optimistic, but Stephanie didn't mind hoping — and, she figured, Alex and Strong might be ahead of them already.

The trail from the other road had probably been easy enough to follow; she and Duncan's men just had to catch up.

The Land Rover started to side-skid towards the shoulder of the road. Narrowing her eyes, she shook her head, "Now don't do that to me..."

Of course she was already in her lowest gear, so she just eased off the accelerator and turned gently in the direction of the skid. She watched the ditch approach slowly, pumping the brakes, then after a second, one of the tires grabbed better snow, and she counter-turned into the traction. With a bit of a wiggle, the truck pulled itself back on track, and she shook her head.

"Sure you don't want to walk?" she asked.

Duncan stopped himself swearing at her, so perhaps he wasn't entirely rude.

Mike Strong wasn't in a hopeless position; he was a good shot with his Thompson, and though the submachine gun lacked the precision of a rifle, it was still accurate *enough*. But the man with the rifle had the corner of the stone house for cover, and he was already lined up. For Strong to win the contest, he'd have to dive one way or another, to try to avoid being hit before cutting loose with his weapon.

It would be risky... survival would undoubtedly depend on how good a shot this fellow was. And that was impossible to know.

Bearing the dangers in mind, Strong decided to remain still, keeping his sights on the man while he silently counted down in his head. Five... four... three...

"Now let's not be hasty."

Alex was officially two counts early, but as she appeared behind the shooter and politely pressed the muzzle of her Browning against the back of his head, Strong decided that wasn't so bad.

The man with the rifle stiffened at the feeling of metal against his skull, and though he was far away, the Colour could read his thoughts on his face. Who had the gun to his head? What kind of gun? Could he do anything about it? In his time, Strong had seen skilled fighters disarm gunmen right up close — a gun pressed against someone's head wasn't necessarily decisive, because it put the wielder within reach of the threatened man.

But there was no ordinary man fast enough, or strong enough, to disarm Alex. And in case he didn't realize who he was up against, the Lady in white decided to introduce herself.

"My name is Alex," she said politely. "I'm a Champion, so please make your next decisions carefully."

That seemed enough; the man took one hand off his rifle, then used the other to lower it towards the snow, and toss it away.

Strong didn't mean to let out a sigh of relief, but he did anyway — and immediately he advanced, keeping the man carefully in his sights. Sure he'd dropped his rifle, but there could always be more danger.

Alex was smiling as he arrived beside their captive, and taking a step back she shrugged, "You called for a rescue."

"Could get used to this," he grinned.

His Lady shrugged bashfully, but stopped herself short of more delightful banter — they had someone to interrogate, after all.

That man had turned so his back was against the stone wall of the house, and his hands were up as panic crossed his face. Strong straightened up from his crouch once it was clear the fellow's hands were visible, though the Thompson remained ready.

"Who are you?" the Colour's question was flat, and the man blinked a few times, then shook his head.

"Are you here to... to help? Did someone send for you to help? None of the soldiers survived, but the Champion Lady was wounded... she is alive..."

His English was good, though tinged with a continental accent. That was no barrier to comprehension, though, and Alex and Strong simultaneously felt their eyes go a little wider.

"Take a breath and explain carefully," Strong waved the Thompson very slightly to emphasize his instructions, and the man swallowed, took a deep breath, then nodded again.

"I am Henrich Saager. I am an engineer for Amstalden Workshop in the Rosyth Yard. This is my house. One week ago, I was here when a shooting started in the woods. It was a blizzard, I could not see... but a Champion woman came for shelter, wounded. She said men pretending to be her own soldiers had attacked them in the snow. One of her men went for help. We have been in hiding since."

He was taking deep breaths to apparently maintain calm through the story, but his meaning... the implications... were obvious. Alex couldn't help but start making associations: men in uniform attacking a Champion party? She'd been on the receiving end of that in Virginia — though not in a blizzard. Freeman going for help... a wounded Elspeth hiding out in this house, with an immigrant engineer...

It was altogether plausible; it could also be a lie. She looked quickly to Strong for his thoughts, and found her Sergeant's expression reflected certain suspicion.

"You're saying Elspeth is inside?" he asked severely, and Saager started nodding in rapid fashion.

"She is wounded," he said. "I was able to bring in the bodies of the other men as well. All hiding in the basement, where it is most secure..."

"Elspeth is inside this house?" Alex didn't want him rambling off, so she returned to the most important point.

The engineer's eyes switched to fix on hers, and he nodded, "Please, come with me."

Alex looked to Strong, and Strong looked right back. It was the perfect invitation for a trap — the sort of promise that couldn't be ignored. If Elspeth was really inside, they couldn't delay... but if not...

How much risk could these two face on their own?

Stephanie Shylock had only been driving for a few months... less than half a year. Surely that made her a novice, and it would have been a fair excuse for putting her Land Rover into the ditch on the treacherous, half-cleared, icy roads leading to the top of Castleandhill Woods.

As it happened, it also left her bewildered as she stopped her truck, hopped out, and looked back at the following Land Rover. It was in the ditch, with Turnbull trying desperately to climb out through its driver's side window.

"Help, please!" he called to her. "We've rolled!"

Though she didn't know Turnbull, she supposed he had to have been driving longer than she had, which meant he really should have been able to handle the track. Perhaps he hadn't learned to drive in Newfoundland — he'd have trained there of course, but maybe he never drove winter roads on the rock. Or maybe Stephanie's years of horse-handling skills had made her a better driver.

Alternatively, he might in fact be incompetent, which would

conflict with her earlier conclusion that all the problems with this lance were Duncan's fault.

Either way, the Scottish Lord's reaction was predictable, "You fool!"

The Champion leapt from Stephanie's truck, then surged back towards the waylaid vehicle with a couple of slips — even his boots were finding the road difficult to handle. Without much decorum, he then grabbed Turnbull by the collar of his battle dress and lifted him out onto the road.

"Everyone out, I must pull this damned thing out of the ditch," the Edinburgh Champion snarled, and the half of his lance that had been in the back of the waylaid Land Rover started scrambling from the rear, as best they could.

Stephanie simply watched with folded arms for a moment, then shook her head and looked back towards the woods. They weren't far now, and presumably once they got into the trees, they'd find a lane that ran to the house.

Hopefully both Land Rovers could make it... because surely it was only her impetuous side making her think she might be better off checking the place on her own.

Inside the stone house seemed about as cold as outside, and as Alex led the way in — Strong keeping the muzzle of his Thompson in the small of Saager's back as he guided the man in behind her — she was reasonably certain she could see her breath.

Saager seemed aware of the conspicuous chill, "I have been worried that someone would come to take the Lady, so I have kept the house dark."

"And yet you left the light on in the shed?" Strong wasn't feeling too charitable towards the man.

"I was hoping to get a truck running, to take her for help now that the storm has passed," the man replied somberly.

Still plausible, Alex supposed, but as she looked around the kitchen — the room into which their chosen upper-floor door led — she was having a hard time being convinced. There were only a few scattered signs of food being prepared, and if someone was really nursing a Champion who'd been wounded, wouldn't food and water be important to the process?

The house also sounded entirely abandoned. Even if she was

injured and perhaps unconscious, Alex would have expected to hear Elspeth breathing. Perhaps there was a hidden room that muffled noise very well, but the whitecoat knew her ears.

"You'll understand if we don't believe a word you say, won't you Mister Saager?" she asked rather bluntly as she turned back to face the man.

Strong had grabbed the foreigner by his collar from behind, to make sure he couldn't try any sort of escape, but the fellow didn't look particularly resistant. What was his game? He'd come at them with a rifle but now was so passive...

"She is in the basement. It was the safest place," Saager was sticking to his story, and Alex frowned, then shifted her gaze to Strong.

"I'm thinking we should go get more men," she suggested, and the Sergeant nodded.

Those words seemed to agitate the supposed engineer, "But we must get her to help. Could you help me carry her to the truck in the barn? Then we could drive her to the hospital."

He was earning points for consistency and persistence, at least, but Alex remained skeptical. Her gaze settled rather coolly on the foreigner, and then she folded her arms (carefully keeping her Browning in hand and very visible as it rested on her sleeve).

"If she's actually here, sir, why hasn't she called out for us? Her hearing is good enough for her to realize who we are."

Saager started to respond, but Strong cut him off, "Why, she's unconscious, right? That's what you were about to say, right Mister?"

The man turned his head to look back at the Colour, some displeasure finally starting to appear on his face... but Strong gave his collar a jerk to convince him not to move.

"No sir, you're going to sit down and put your hands on the table in front of you," the Sergeant said, then pushed the foreigner towards the dark and miserable-looking kitchen table. Carefully, then, Strong let go the man's collar and pulled out one of the chairs.

Saager settled into it, his hands laid flat on the surface before him.

His glare was getting more intense, and as Strong rounded the table and stood alongside his white-coated Champion, Saager's eyes traveled between them, "I know I do not sound trustworthy. I am Swiss, and you have no reason to believe a foreign man. But I am thinking of her best interests. Please, you must just look."

Oh that sounded like *such* a trap. Alex looked at Strong, and she could see from his expression that he thought the same... but still, there was a tiny nagging possibility that this was simply a man who was having trouble communicating his true intentions because English was his second language.

If Elspeth was in the basement, gravely wounded and in need of care, they really would need to get her out.

"You know the movies where the girl goes alone into the basement of the spooky house, and finds, like, a Dracula?" the whitecoat sighed and glanced at Strong. "I always make fun of them."

"Strictly speaking, you should just say 'find *Dracula*', not 'find *a* Dracula'," Strong corrected immediately, and Alex blinked and looked at him.

"That's your feedback?"

The Colour shrugged slightly, "Well if Dracula's down there, why don't you see how he feels about it? And if he's not, how about you be very careful, so I don't have to fill this man with lead and come after you?"

So that was it; even protective Mike Strong believed they had to check.

"Or I could go," he offered, but Alex shook her head with a sigh.

"No, I can sense traps and avoid them better than you."

She didn't sound eager. Her white coat wasn't (just) a fashion statement; it was a cloak of responsibility.

"Maybe it'll be a mummy. They're not as scary," she tried to maintain the humor as she backed towards the kitchen door.

"If it's snakes, you're on your own. I hate snakes," Strong didn't take his eyes off Saager as he contributed his own groaner. Then his tone grew more serious, "You so much as peep, I'm killing him and coming for you."

There was no mistaking his earnestness, and though she was volunteering to go down into a probably-booby-trapped basement, that somehow made her feel better.

With a last look at the scene in the kitchen, Alex turned and moved carefully into the house.

"Elspeth?" she called ahead of her, then tried a different name, "Nosferatu?"

Neither answered, shockingly.

• • •

The lane leading to Castleandhill House was not very wide, and it certainly had not been plowed. As Stephanie carefully stopped her Land Rover short of the entrance, she tried to gauge the depth of the snow based on the trunks of surrounding trees, but it was not particularly helpful.

"We could be grounded if we try to drive in there," she concluded, and that earned her yet another glare from Lord Duncan.

Surely he had to be tired of looking insulted by now. Or perhaps the wind had changed, and his face was stuck that way...

"I will lead on foot, to defeat any ambushes," the Lord declared bitterly, and Stephanie just managed to stop herself from rolling her eyes... or, more precisely, delayed doing so until he opened his door and climbed out.

That man had probably never seen a gunfight, and Stephanie definitely hoped his first was not upon them. Without Alex or Strong around, she wasn't sure how things would turn out.

"Hello?" Alex stopped naming names and went for a more general greeting as she reached tentatively for the knob to the basement door, then stood to one side as she grasped it and turned. The door wasn't locked, so it opened easily, and as she stepped around it she aimed her Browning down into the darkness.

It was *very* dark. She hadn't noticed from the outside, but there must have been blackout curtains covering the windows down there. She stared into the intense gloom for a moment, letting her eyes adjust as much as they could, but then shook her head. It was *not* sensible for her to wander into a darkened basement.

"Light switch?" she called back towards the kitchen, and this time Saager was more immediately forthcoming.

"Inside the door on left," he said — and for some reason, Strong didn't criticize him for missing the second 'the' in his sentence.

Reaching carefully through the doorframe, Alex found the switch and hit it. The stairs were suddenly bathed in dim yellow light, and at their bottom, a stone floor was similarly illuminated. It didn't look particularly ominous, but still...

She had to go look. Carefully.

"I'm going down," she called back. "If a Dracula is drinking Elspeth's blood, I'll start shooting."

Obviously it wasn't the right time to persist with such a silly gag, but the bad humor helped fortify the whitecoat as she cautiously advanced. One boot crossed the threshold, then dropped onto the top step. Nothing exploded.

Swinging forward her other boot, she took the next step down, and it similarly didn't lead to Armageddon. The silence seemed a little more intense, but nothing was jumping out—

Then Alex's left boot hooked on something she couldn't see, and she went head first down the stairs.

The yelp and the thud were neither dignified nor elegant — not the sorts of sounds Strong was used to hearing from his Champion. Immediately his eyes went wide, and he shouldered his Thompson and looked straight down its sights at Saager.

But the foreigner looked concerned — as if he didn't know what had happened and was actually worried for Alex. Strong had a pretty good sense for people, but this one was unfathomable... was he genuinely on their side?

He didn't have long to decide, and he called towards the basement without looking away from his target: "Alex?"

There was no answer for a long time... though based on the speed to which Strong's heart rate had climbed, that long time might have been measured in fractions of a second. Still, too long. He'd have to go help her, and there was no way he was leaving a suspicious Swiss supposed do-gooder to cause trouble.

"If you're innocent, I'm sorry about this," Strong said sharply, then lowered his sights to the man's knee—

Alex coughed. Even though he didn't have the hearing of a Champion, Strong was able to detect the sound — perhaps because it was so loud, perhaps because it was his responsibility to hear anything that suggested she was in danger.

Then she coughed again... and again. It was the hacking sort of sound that suggested something terrible was being expelled. And it was getting worse.

Whatever it was, he had to go help.

And then he remembered the gas mask case he'd left outside in the snow. Men from a lance wouldn't typically carry one with them when storming a house — weapons and ammo only. What if... had they...

Mike Strong cursed himself immediately for not having recognized the obvious, and as his eyes widened he got ready to squeeze off a crippling burst of Thompson fire.

But Saager noticed the distraction caused by the Sergeant's thoughts, and he was fast. Suddenly, the supposed Swiss engineer was moving, and all the Colour saw was the kitchen table flipping up in front of him.

As his view of the prisoner was eclipsed, Strong hit the trigger of the Thompson... but that was by instinct, and he should have thought better of unleashing a half-dozen rounds in a house made of stone. The sound was painful, and the ricochets made it worse. He backed off from the table as it toppled back to the floor, then turned his body just enough to make sure he was covering Saager's possible line of attack.

But by the time the table finished dropping, the outside door had been flung open and the foreigner was gone.

Bastard. Strong's obvious instinct was to give chase... but even though he couldn't hear Alex coughing any longer — firing a Thompson indoors was bad for one's hearing — he knew she needed him.

There was a stabbing in his right leg as he turned from the kitchen and hurried down the hall that had taken his Lady to the basement door, but there was no time to wonder what the pain meant. The door was still open as he reached it, his Thompson in one hand and the other against the door frame to keep him upright.

He still couldn't hear Alex hacking — his ears were ringing — but as he looked down the stairs into the dim yellow light, he could see her white coat glowing at the bottom. She looked as though she was trying to crawl up the stairs, but her back and shoulders were jerking hard with every cough.

It was gas, and she had to be brought out of it.

Leaving Bob Freeman's gas mask back in the snow had been foolish, but there was no time to go fetch it. Without another thought, the Colour set aside his Thompson and started down the stairs. His boots weren't moving as deftly as he'd have liked — his right leg was dragging, so he kept his hands on the stairwell walls to keep him upright.

Good thing, because on the third step down, his left boot caught something — maybe an invisible wire. Moving slowly as he was, and with his hands bracing him, he was able to struggle over it... but that must have been what tripped her.

No time to ponder; Strong continued to hobble his way towards the bottom of the stairs. Alex didn't seem to be able to lift her head as he got to the bottom, but he reached out to her with one hand as soon as he was close enough, put his palm against her back so she'd know he was there.

"It's me," he said immediately.

Sliding down one more step, so his boots were just above her head, he positioned himself to reach below his feet with both hands and pull her up.

Then something hit his lungs. He'd done the natural thing — breathed in to fortify himself to pull her up — but the air he'd taken in hadn't been pure. There was no taste to it, but somehow his body knew it was wrong, and he coughed hard.

It was gas for sure. It would probably act faster on an ordinary man than on a Champion, so he couldn't waste time — he *had* to shift her. Unceremoniously, he got his hands under her arms and pulled. She wasn't unconscious — she tried to help — but he was already going weak.

Looking back up the stairs, Mike Strong discovered he had a mountain to climb, and with every second the light at the top seemed farther and farther away.

He had to hurry... but the light was starting to dim, and blood was dripping out of his trouser leg.

The sound of Thompson fire was unmistakable, and as Stephanie followed Duncan through the snow towards the house, she immediately knew her friends were ahead of her. That was good... potentially. But firing meant trouble, and as she drew her Browning from its holster and started scanning the lane ahead, then the trees to either side, she wondered whether the situation was in hand, or not.

"How much further?" the Champion of Edinburgh turned back to her with that question, and she blinked and frowned at him.

"You're asking the girl who's been here less than a day?" she somehow sounded even less sympathetic, and the Scottish Lord considered her with disgust. Since she was feeling diplomatic, Stephanie then decided to make a suggestion, "How about you get out of my way, so we can find out?"

Without waiting for an answer, she surged forward, breaking through the knee-deep snow with sheer determination. She moved past him quickly, and though she knew he could easily outrun her if he wanted, Duncan simply stood back and watched her go, letting his men pool around him as he did.

Fair enough, the American Lieutenant would do this on her own...

She heard an engine start. It wasn't too far away, but getting an exact bearing and distance was impossible with the trees eclipsing either side of the lane. There was a bend ahead, so perhaps the house was near.

A good bet, because a Land Rover bounced around that bend seconds after the engine sounded. The vehicle looked as though it came from the Rosyth motor pool, and it was speeding forward, plowing through the drifts as it headed for the main road.

At first Stephanie assumed — perhaps, hoped — that it was Alex and Strong. But her eyes were good and the distance wasn't too great. Just one person was behind the wheel, and his bearing was not that of either of her friends.

That became especially clear when the Land Rover turned slightly, looking as though it was aiming straight for her — and accelerating. The snow seemed to be slowing it not at all.

Well fine.

Leaning forward into a good shooting crouch, Stephanie raised her pistol and aligned the sights with the windshield. The truck was seventy yards out, which too far for a realistic hit — even for her — but it was closing fast, so she needed to be ready. Experience against Jeeps in Virginia had proven to her that firing fast was important.

Lord Duncan literally dropped into her path. The Champion in his gray coat must have leapt straight over her while she wasn't watching, and as he landed heavily in the show ahead he kicked up a thin cloud of white crystals. He was halfway between Stephanie and the Land Rover, and then he was running straight at the truck, as if he meant to ram it.

Alex had half-tipped a Jeep at Fort Eustice, but that had been by charging from the *side*, not the front. What Duncan was attempting looked to Stephanie like a sure way for a Champion to die.

She started forward again, doing her best to keep her crouch as her boots dragged in the snow. Even if she didn't like Duncan, it was her job to keep him alive.

Of course, he moved too fast for her support to matter. He was supremely confident, and perhaps he had reason to be; his gloved hands hit the grill of the Land Rover, and as his boots dug into the ground beneath the snow, he was able to slow the already-laboring truck, then stop it. Evidently he'd read of Alex's encounter with a Newfoundland moose, and as the truck roared and groaned, he got his hands onto one of its fenders and started to lift it onto its side.

Started to, because the driver hadn't given up on the gas, and as soon as the wheel cleared the ground it became a massive, spinning weapon. A pile of snow spewed out from under the wheel arch, much of it slamming into Duncan without ceremony. He coughed, spat, and lost his focus.

Then the wheel dropped back into the snow, and he lost his footing, and the Land Rover started to drive him back. He scrambled and began to panic, realizing he was now pinned against the front of a truck, and was in genuine danger of going under it. He cried out for help.

But Stephanie didn't have a shot, because no matter how good her aim might be, the risk of hitting the Champion of Edinburgh was too great...

Duncan lost his footing completely, and dropped to the ground before the Land Rover. It was the sort of thing a person simply wasn't supposed to see; he disappeared down into the snow, and then the truck bounced up on one side as its wheels rolled over him. And then, because Saager hadn't spared the throttle, the Land Rover jumped forward at high speed, heading right for Stephanie.

No longer worried about hitting Duncan, she started firing immediately — but conscious of what she'd just seen, she wasn't staying put. With whatever speed she could manage, she pushed herself sideways through the snow, squeezing the trigger with every step.

But she couldn't aim properly, or even point-shoot the way she'd have liked. For the second time in a few months, she was diving out of the way of a raging vehicle.

Duncan's infantry were less experienced... and less active, too. Again, Stephanie's belief that the Champion was the problem with this lance was challenged, because they simply stood and *watched*.

How many lances were this bad — made lazy by comfortable posts and mild police work?

It was a strange thing to be wondering as she made her final dive to get out of the Land Rover's way. Regardless, as soon as the truck hurtled past, bouncing over the snowy track, she rolled up to a kneeling position and started shooting again — blazing away until her magazine ran dry. Still no shots from the lance, and the Land Rover was almost on top of them.

"Fire!" she bellowed angrily, and finally — *finally* — Turnbull was prompted to action.

Thunder started as Thompsons and Garands turned against the speeding truck, but it was past them in a blur and a cloud of snow… then showed no signs of slowing down. Perhaps that was one mark in favor of a closed-top Land Rover over a Jeep; in Virginia, the drivers of those machine-gun carriers had been easy targets, but concealed behind the aluminum body of the truck from the Rosyth motor pool, this man managed to escape.

And there was no way they could give chase, especially if their Champion was wounded…

"Lord Duncan! Lord Duncan!" Turnbull bounded forward through the snow, his men following him in a panic. Suddenly they all cared about the Scotsman?

Their sudden speed was impressive, if poorly timed and inexplicable. They were all standing over Duncan by the time Stephanie was able to get back to the site of the Champion's fall, and they thus found the unpleasant sight of a Champion gurgling and writhing as he tried to breathe.

"Go get a Land Rover!" Turnbull looked up to Stephanie with that plea.

She was reloading her Browning, and she caught his gaze icily, "Get it yourself. I'm going to find out who did the shooting at the house."

These poor souls could look after themselves; she had to find her friends. Hopefully they were in better condition.

CHAPTER VIII

The door to the stone house was open as Stephanie approached. Thanks to tracks in the snow, she could see clearly that Saager had emerged from the place, but it also appeared that two other people had gone inside: Alex and Strong. There was no mistaking the whitecoat's bootprints in particular... even if Stephanie hadn't recognized the track automatically, not too many young women would be traipsing through the snow with big-booted Sergeants.

"Hello?" the American Lieutenant called as she advanced, hoping to get an answer. She didn't — but her hearing wasn't nearly as good as Alex's.

Slowing just short of the door, Stephanie kept her Browning trained on the entrance, then listened for signs of danger. Nothing jumped out, and her impatience wouldn't allow her to wait too long. Assuming a careful Fairbairn-Sykes style shooting crouch, then, she stepped inside.

The kitchen was a mess — a table was flipped over and there was a small puddle of blood on the stone floor. Stephanie swept the room carefully down the sights of her Browning, then stood beside the blood and looked for a trail. Sure enough, there were drops leading out of the kitchen and down one of the halls.

Who had been shot, and how badly?

She was careful as she moved forward. Her posture was straight out of the pages of *Shooting to Live*, with her pistol held in close to make it tougher to grab if someone came out of nowhere to try to disarm her. There were still no sounds... nothing but...

A cough, and then a groan — sounded like Alex.

Stephanie's immediate desire was to hurry, but she forced herself to be more deliberate. She didn't move slowly, but she couldn't afford to get into more trouble in here — not with only the remains of Duncan's lance supposedly in support. Relying on the instincts that her godfather had long ago impressed upon her, she advanced deeper into the house, following the blood.

When the basement door appeared around a corner, she stopped abruptly. Lying in the opening was Alex, face down... basically sprawled across Mike Strong.

Quickly Stephanie checked the other directions — made sure no one was nearby to jump her — and then she hurried to her friend's side, crouched and used her free hand to rub her back, "You okay?"

"What?" the question almost sounded slurred, and Stephanie frowned. Alex had never been drunk — her powerful body burned off alcohol much too fast — but it sure sounded as though she was inebriated.

"It's Stephanie... you okay?" the American Lieutenant tried again, and Alex giggled.

"Why am I on the floor? Who am I lying on?"

With the question, she pushed herself sideways, rolling partway off Mike Strong. Looking down towards her boots she realized it was the Colour under her legs, and her eyes became comically wide, "Oh no, don't tell Daphne!"

Clearly there was some agent at work in the whitecoat's mind, so Stephanie put her free hand under her friend's arm and pulled her off Strong. As she slid across the stone floor, then stopped with her back against the wall facing the basement door, Alex giggled again.

Satisfied that her friend was, at least, conscious, Stephanie moved back to Strong's side. He was mostly sprawled on the stairs down to the basement — just his head and shoulders had made it out onto the stone floor. It was difficult to tell if he was breathing, so the American put her hand in front of his face, hoping for a sign of exhalation.

She got it.

"Thank God," she blurt to herself, then tried to pull him from the stairs.

Unfortunately, he was slightly heavier than Alex — like, twice her weight.

Looking back at her giggling friend, Stephanie pointed to Strong, "Come on, I need your help."

"Help?" Alex blinked a couple of times, speaking now with almost childlike enthusiasm. "I can help!"

Pushing herself to her feet, she looked as though she'd gone dizzy for a second... then she giggled yet again and hurried to Strong's side. Stephanie backed off as her friend put her hands under the Sergeant's arms, then hoisted him up and turned so she could carry him across her back and shoulders.

"Where to?" she asked, and Stephanie pointed back towards the door. The American then hung back as Alex escaped down the hall and out through the kitchen... swaying and staggering like a drunk with every step.

Something had clearly happened, but before she could start to wonder what, the Lieutenant needed to make sure her friends were alright. She looked back at the basement once, then shook her head and followed.

She got out the door just in time to watch Alex lay Strong down in a snow bank. The Lady in white turned back to her friend, gave a great big thumbs up... and then coughed. The coughing got worse very quickly, and hearing the harshness Stephanie holstered her pistol and hurried to Alex's side.

By the time she got her hands on her friend, Alex was already doubling over and beginning to wretch. Taking her friend's hair in hand, the American held it out of the way as the young Lady began to vomit violently into the snow.

Clearly, it wasn't pleasant for anyone.

A rock under the snow woke Mike Strong. It was a bit bone-jarring as the Land Rover tire hit it, and he distantly heard Stephanie Shylock apologize... and Alex groan... but it didn't make a great deal of sense to him.

In point of fact, nothing did. He'd been on the stairs... had tried to lift Alex over him and push her up the stairs, away from the gas.

Now he was lying in the back bed of a truck, his right leg lassoed and held to the canvas canopy's frame, a bandage around his calf. And they were moving. Because his feet were pointing towards the rear, Strong couldn't see anything, but he tried to roll sideways so he could twist for a look...

The pain in his leg convinced him that was a bad idea.

"I've been shot?" he blurted the question, and somehow only then realized his head was pounding.

Alex was slumped forward in the passenger seat, elbows on her knees and her head hanging over the front edge of her seat, in case she had to vomit again. Stephanie, however, was able to look back over her shoulder, "You're awake!"

She sounded relieved, and then she looked at Alex, "He's awake."

Strong wasn't able to see, but the whitecoat tried to nod, "Thank God."

Perhaps she didn't sound too enthusiastic, but the fact that she made an effort to respond was telling enough. She'd been concerned about Strong, just as Stephanie had been, but now they could stop worrying for their Colour. Mostly.

Not wanting to prod her ailing friend any more, Stephanie looked back over her shoulder towards Strong, "Think you caught a ricochet. It doesn't look deep... it's stuck just under the skin. We're going to the hospital now, so someone can get it out and patch you up."

Turning his gaze back to his leg, Strong nodded, "Right."

He felt like hell... but unlike Alex, who could never be drunk because of her Champion metabolism, he recognized the discomfort that was pressing down on him. On occasion, perhaps, he might have experienced such feelings before. Though to be fair, he'd never been drunk and shot by his own bullet — not even a ricochet — at the same time.

It hurt.

Letting his head drop back to the bumping and swaying bed of the rover, he swallowed and focused on taking deep breaths. He had no intention of throwing up if he could avoid it... and even if he allowed himself to do so, what good could it do? Expelling the contents of a stomach couldn't clear a gas from the lungs, surely?

That was a question to which he had no answer... but it spurred another question: what had happened to Saager, and the basement of that house?

"What did I miss?" he called out, and again Stephanie looked back quickly, before returning her eyes to the road as she answered.

"Our intelligent host Champion got himself run over," her response was sharp. "Saager got away. He had Land Rovers in his shed... probably the trucks Elspeth used to get to the house a week ago. He escaped in one — and ran over Duncan in the process. He got away. So we're driving the other one."

The situation sounded somewhat bleak to the Colour, so he

steeled himself for more bad news with his next question: "Any sign of Elspeth?"

Stephanie shook her head — not that he could see the gesture — and replied, "When Alex stopped throwing up—"

"Stopped throwing up *the first time*," the Lady in white interjected with a groan.

"Yeah, that... I checked the shed, found this truck, got a gas mask, and went into the basement for a look."

Of course she did. Many people might have balked at the idea of descending into a gas-filled cellar, even if the right equipment was at hand. Not Lieutenant Shylock, though — Mike Strong never failed to be impressed by her straightforward manner when it came to getting unpleasant things done.

"All the rest of Elspeth's lance was down there, dead. The place was icy... I guess Saager was keeping the house cool so they'd stay frozen," she clearly didn't like the taste of the words, but she continued anyway. "No Elspeth, though. I figure when he took off, he was heading for wherever she's being kept."

Strong felt as though he might have missed a couple of steps in that logic, so he stayed quiet until his throbbing brain could piece everything together. Saager hadn't killed Elspeth... had told the intruders at the house that the missing Champion was alive. Perhaps she was... and perhaps the same gas that had knocked Alex off her feet had made Elspeth easy to capture.

Capturing a live Champion for study would undoubtedly be *very* useful to many enemies of the Empire.

"We need to go find him," Strong called towards the front seats as he reached his conclusion, and Stephanie shook her head.

"Duncan might be dead, and I'm not going looking for him without the two of you. Once you're both patched up, we'll look."

Considering the pain in his leg, Mike Strong decided he wasn't going to grumble too much about that. He'd be no use to anyone if he bled to death while driving around, looking for a needle in a haystack.

But if he wasn't to begin searching immediately, at least he could start wondering, and the logical first question centered on the gas.

If it had indeed made Elspeth weak enough to capture, that was one thing... but even with a dose like the one Alex must have gotten, the London Champion couldn't have been off her feet for too long.

How could an ordinary man keep a powerful Lady captive for a week after that? He couldn't simply handcuff her to a chair, or even lock her in a cellar... unless, of course, she was dead and he'd just taken her away for dissection.

Hopefully that wasn't how it had happened. And as he let his head rest again on the bouncing bed of the rolling Land Rover, Mike Strong let himself wonder what agenda had been at work at Rosyth, and how it might still be disrupted.

CHAPTER IX

Though the Saa Screen room at Fort Eustice was underground, and therefore offered no windows to suggest the position of the sun, George Devlin had a pretty good idea that it was time for lunch. His usual office in Jimmystown's hospitality warehouse was similarly window-less, so over the past couple of years his body clock had become quite precise, and his stomach was equally intelligent.

All that being the case, he sounded confident when he sat back in his chair and declared, "We need to eat."

Vanier Cross didn't seem to hear the words at first — the black soldier was entirely entranced by the screen in front of him, in a manner that seemed a bit foreign to George... but then, the young hospitality man had built up a certain immunity to the magic of screens, because he was so often surrounded by them.

He waited a few seconds to see if Vanier shook himself free of the thrall, and when he didn't, he reached out and gave him a tap on the shoulder, "You alright there?"

Jumping a little, the Corporal blinked and looked at his counterpart, "What? Yeah."

"Good, so it's lunchtime."

"Is it?" Vanier raised his hand and looked at his watch, then nodded. "Right. So. What?"

George's eyebrow climbed, and he stated the obvious: "Where I come from, we tend to mark the occasion by consuming foodstuffs."

Obviously. Vanier frowned at the tone, "No kidding. Am I going back to my cell to eat?"

"I hope not. I need someone to lead me to the cafeteria," the hospitality man answered, and the black soldier began to smile... then stopped. It had literally been weeks since he'd been anywhere away from the stockade, and he could only imagine he'd be an unwelcome sight in the base's fancy headquarters dining room.

But George was already rising from his chair, "Come on, I get cranky when I don't eat."

"You mean you're not cranky now?" Vanier's counter-shot was effortless, and George shrugged.

"My personality right now is shining. Not my fault if you can't appreciate it."

Right. They went for food, summoning guards back to the door of the screen room as they left.

Sitting in the headquarters dining room, Caralynne was glad to have food on the way — she was hungry, but wasn't having the easiest time maintaining her appetite.

"It's quite obvious that the conspiracy lies with the blacks, I think," Commandant Powell was sitting opposite her, and he was talking.

Still talking.

She'd agreed to have lunch with the man because she was on his base, and because given recent events and the inquiry to come, she thought it wise to get a preview of the narrative he was pushing to explain the events of the past couple of weeks.

His efforts at scapegoating were impressive.

"Colonel Adams... I always thought of him as a good boy, but he wasn't really cut out for this, you understand. I realize he was a hero from the war on the new world, but that's really just because he survived, isn't it? When your Newfoundlanders were fighting on the Badlands, he ran away and his white officers didn't, so he survived... and then the sacrifice of the negroes was romanticized, so the papers basically got him his rank," Powell shook his head, disappointment pouring from his words. "Too simple, he was. Then someone came and confused him, and made him turn on us."

Caralynne just stared at Powell as he kept talking — kept repeating the same basic points about Robert Adams, as if he was trying to convince himself of his theory. Perhaps deep down, even he didn't believe it... but he was sticking to the story, because blaming treacherous negroes for the disaster of Fort Eustice, and by extension the death of the President, might save his career... *if* the Senate Inquiry bought the excuse.

Caralynne simply didn't know what the politicians would choose to believe.

But with Adams missing — at this point presumed dead — there seemed to be no one to give evidence against the charges, so Powell's line might well be adopted. And if it was, a new round of racial violence might break out in the United States, as history elected to condemn a good man as a traitor.

No, Caralynne definitely didn't have an appetite anymore.

Powell eventually let silence return, and as he did he looked up at the Lady sitting opposite him, quite ignorantly assuming her face would reflect agreement — or at least, would not show disdain. His expectations were ambitious; the ice in her glare smacked him, and he actually recoiled back into his seat.

"We must get to the bottom of this, so it will never again happen," he said defensively, as if the words somehow made his previous declarations less reprehensible.

Caralynne's head tilted, and then she asked: "I'm sorry, were you expecting me to agree with you?"

Powell blinked a few times — he did appear almost manic — and then shook his head, "You can't... I mean, you have no evidence to contradict the theory."

That literally didn't make sense, and as Caralynne laced her fingers together and laid her hands on the table, she replied rather unkindly: "How the hell do you know what evidence I have? I honestly cannot understand what's in your head, Commandant. Not just this theory, which is disgusting, but the fact that you're so inept as to actually tell me about it, and expect me to be on side."

Powell was horrified — Lady Caralynne herself was calling him out, and challenging the narrative he had so carefully been constructing to protect his career.

"I don't know the new President. I certainly hope he's smarter than you, though, because if he isn't I expect our Empire's special relationship with your country will not last very long. And all the Champions, Commandant, will be with us, not you."

Alright, so she was getting a little carried away with her rebuff of the man — but understandably so, given his words. She couldn't set British foreign policy, but damned if she'd just tell the Senate Inquiry what it wanted to hear.

Powell's mouth was opening and closing — working to try to form words, but not having much success until a few sounds finally escaped, "If... but you are trying to steal our Champions. I will tell my friends and they will make sure the Senators view your testimony in that light."

He was fighting back. Amazing.

"They can listen to my testimony in whatever light they please. I'm going to tell them the truth... and in particular, I'm going to let them know that Adams was a good officer — one of the best, in fact. And that the reason I was on your base the day this all happened was because he asked for *our* help to make your men better soldiers. And — *and* — if you think it was wrong for a Captain to be promoted to Colonel for surviving one of the biggest battles of the Hubrin War, you are impugning Lord Devlin's own promotion from Captain to Colonel after the assault on the capital. What *is* an indictment of your backward system is that Adams never got beyond Colonel, and that he had to fight for scraps to help his men train. I'll say all of that, and... and—"

"What's all this?"

It was probably a good thing that George Devlin abruptly cut off Caralynne's words, because she was obviously agitated. Indeed, the elder Lady Smith was often glad that her daughter took after her husband when it came to tempers, because Caralynne had been known to go off without fully thinking things through from time to time. Indeed, an impetuous instinct during a bloody encounter at Farfield City had led to her death in 1919.

So, as much as her passions demanded that she rightly tell off Powell, diplomacy required a more measured approach, and George Devlin was well-established as a diplomat — at the ripe old age of eighteen. He continued his interruption, "Did I hear my father's name?"

"I did not raise it," Powell sounded huffy, but offered no more context before his eyes settled on the black soldier who was alongside the hospitality man. "What is he doing here? Soldier, you are under arrest."

Vanier Cross was beginning to wonder if he was actually asleep, and having a nightmare. Struggling with anxiety, he basically stood at attention and swallowed, "Sir, I'm..."

"I was under the impression he was in protective custody," George answered immediately — smoothly, as he'd learned to do. "And he's here for lunch with me. We've been working all morning to find more evidence in the screen, but without much luck so far. We'll try again this afternoon."

There was nothing aggressive in George's tone, but the words themselves were a challenge to Powell — he would of course have been informed that work was being conducted on the screen, and even that one of the 'prisoners' would be participating, but clearly he was preoccupied.

He had to decide whether to argue the point (since he was clearly doing well with arguments today) or simply to retreat.

Being a good political sycophant, his course was clear: "Good day."

Literally, that was it. He got to his feet, dramatically throwing the napkin that had been across his lap onto the table to show he was serious. Then he stormed out, leaving Caralynne at the table with a sour expression, and George and Vanier standing by. The Corporal let out a breath that he'd very consciously been holding, and the hospitality man looked down at the table. It had four chairs, even though only two had been occupied.

"We'll join you," he decided, and then nodded towards Vanier, suggesting the soldier sit down where the Commandant had been.

That seemed like a really bad idea to the black soldier, but George was insistent, nodding very exaggeratedly towards the chair until he reluctantly complied. Then the hospitality man pulled out one of the other chairs and settled into it, catching Caralynne's gaze as he did.

"I really must know what started his tirade," George said.

"I asked him if he had any advice about the Senate Inquiry," she replied, clearly trying to cool herself down.

"Shame. I'd hoped you'd just asked him to pass the bread, and that had set him off," George smiled. "Would have been more amusing."

Of course there was nothing funny about Powell's words... but George, being skilled at this sort of thing, was already diffusing Caralynne's tension.

She took a few deep breaths to help the process, then looked to Vanier — sitting *very* awkwardly across the table — and nodded, "Sorry. I'm Caralynne Smith. You're Cross, right? Constance's beau?"

"Um. I'm Cross, yes ma'am," he answered with yet more unease (the entire situation really was quite uncomfortable). "Constance is my friend."

He really wondered what Constance was getting up to in Newfoundland, since both George Devlin and Lady Caralynne seemed to speak for her. His young Champion had obviously made an impression, though in case she'd had to tell some white lies, he wasn't going to volunteer too much information about what they were to each other. Silence was never a bad option — at least not in the kind of circumstances a black soldier sometimes found himself in.

"Sorry about that scene," Caralynne seemed not to notice any of the analysis that was happening behind the Corporal's eyes. "I don't think I get too emotional, but sometimes I get carried away. Got me killed once, but it's a hard lesson to learn."

Vanier blinked at the elder Lady Smith's words — it was never natural to hear someone talk quite that way — but he didn't reply. Instead, George answered, his tone coming across as annoyingly wise.

"You say that as though it's a bad thing."

"Getting killed? Usually falls into the 'bad' category."

He shook his head, "You know what I mean. Speaking as the fellow who dragged Stephanie Shylock out of a pub so she wouldn't beat a Hitler-apostle to a bloody pulp, I do think there's value in being so passionate about something that you must speak your mind."

Of course he was being a gentleman. Caralynne narrowed her eyes at her friend's son, then turned her gaze across to Vanier, "Don't you find him annoying?"

The Corporal blinked, "Um. What?"

Waving dismissively at the hospitality man, Caralynne shook her head, "All that time with Stephanie has made you much too tolerant. But I appreciate you letting me beat myself up instead of doing it yourself."

Vanier was quite confused, and before George could say anything, he blurted out the word again: "What?"

Caralynne looked back to him, as did the young Mister Devlin. Immediately he got self-conscious for having dared to question — it was a bad idea to try to make sense of the weird talk of white people like these...

"Lady Caralynne is criticizing herself for starting to tell off your Commandant for being ignorant, because telling people off isn't necessarily diplomatic. I'm telling her that sometimes telling people off is important, even if it's not very diplomatic, and that she shouldn't beat herself up for having done it. But because she's convinced she should be beating herself up, she's complaining that my association with Stephanie Shylock, who I don't think you've met, has made me more accepting of people getting headstrong about things they believe. And underlying all of that, she's a bit put off by the fact that me, an eighteen-year-old precocious brat, is giving her a talking to as if I was her grandpa."

By the time George finished that explanation, Vanier Cross really didn't know what to say. Which was entirely understandable.

Meantime, Caralynne frowned, "I wasn't thinking 'brat'. I was going for 'kid'."

"You were thinking 'brat'," George shook his head.

Caralynne looked down, and found herself conceding rather absurdly, "I was actually thinking 'brat'."

Vanier looked from George to Caralynne and back, then shook his head and asked again, "What?"

It really was a bit much. People didn't talk to each other this way — at least not in his world — so he was digesting. Fortunately, a distraction quickly arrived: a server came out of the door from the kitchen with two plates, only to stop beside the table in surprise as he realized one of them was for a Commandant who had transformed into a black soldier.

Before that poor waiter could manage to ask anything, George offered him a smile, "I'll have some sort of fish and mashed potatoes, if you have them."

"Um. Yes, sir," the man replied, and then went back to eying Vanier.

"Well serve them and hop to it," George persisted, just to make sure no questions were asked... and deciding his job was not to think too hard, the server nodded, laid down the plates, and disappeared.

"Hopefully the Commandant has better taste in food than in lies," Caralynne gestured to the meal that had landed before Vanier — the one that the Corporal's gaze was completely fixed on. The aroma alone was almost intoxicating.

"I've been eating stockade food since January, ma'am," was his simple answer, and then he looked up as he reached for the fork on the table. "I'll get seconds."

George nodded approvingly, "Damned right you will."

Both the soldier and the Lady dug into their lunch, while George waited for his. That was fine; sitting in silent thought, the young Devlin began to reflect on what he'd overheard — Powell's scapegoating plan. It was perhaps fair to wonder whether any evidence they managed to find would actually change the Senate's verdict on the crisis.

Too much American blood had been spilled... and too many politicians had face to save. There might not be enough room left for the truth, no matter now much the American people — the real American people, that was — deserved it.

Time would tell.

CHAPTER X

"Take two Aspirin and keep your weight off it."

The Scottish doctor was giving good advice, but as he finished wrapping a bandage around Mike Strong's shin, the look on the Sergeant's face must have given him away.

"And you're not going to do that, now are you?" the silver-haired man with whiskers gave the Colour a glare. "Well don't come back here whining if you hurt yourself."

Strong appreciated the bedside manner, "I didn't want to come here in the first place."

"First bloody sign that you've got some sense," the doctor maintained his disapproving air as he finished with the bandage, then stepped back. The fact that he had applied the dressing himself was sign enough of the sort of day he was having — the nurses were all out dealing with blizzard-related cases, it seemed, so this gray-hair had been called back to the trenches to deal with wounded soldiers.

"What about Duncan?" Strong asked the man, not sure if any news would be forthcoming.

With a shake of his head, the veteran doctor turned for the door and muttered, "I don't care who you bloody are, you don't try to stop a truck with your bare bloody hands."

"Will he live?"

"They think so. But getting his bones back on the right headings before they set, that'll be the challenge. Don't let your girl... Smith, isn't it... don't let her do that stupidity."

Strong didn't need to be told — nor, he imagined, did Alex. Stopping a moose was one thing, a Land Rover was quite another. But then, perhaps Duncan had possessed good reasons for his action... there was no point speculating.

"She's smarter than that," Strong decided just to go with the doctor's interpretation, and the Scot looked back with one nod before opening the door.

"Thank God for that, since she's stuck with you."

Then the silver-hair smiled once, wryly, and left the room. Strong could hear him speaking to the girls outside — a much softer and gentler tone, so it was impossible to make out the words. After a few moments, Stephanie led them both inside, Alex hanging her head slightly as she came through.

"How are *you* doing?" Strong immediately asked his Champion, and Alex shook her head.

"You said this is what it's like to be drunk?"

"Hung over, by the look of you," he clarified.

"Dear God," Alex groaned. "How can people drink if this is how it ends?"

It was a fair question, but it was both meant and received as rhetorical. As Alex detected a chair in the corner of the room and plopped herself into it, Stephanie advanced to her Sergeant's side, "The doctor said you were very brave."

"He lied," Strong replied instantly. "He had to give me time to collect myself before you came in, because I was weeping."

"I heard you through the door. You weren't crying even a little," Alex had her elbows on her knees again, and was hanging her head as she spoke. Then she paused and looked up: "Sorry, I just killed your joke."

"Put it out of its misery, more like," the Sergeant shook his head wryly, then decided to pivot right to the serious stuff. "The doctor said Duncan will live. Was it really his fault?"

Stephanie couldn't quite stop herself from rolling her eyes, "He leapt right into my sights, and right in front of a speeding Land Rover. So yes, it was his damned fault. And then his men did *nothing* when Saager ran him over. I was shooting and they were just standing there."

Strong could only shrug, "Hate to say it, but seeing as how they all got along so well, they may not have wanted to try extra hard."

"Yes, but they were trained in Newfoundland. They're *ours*," Stephanie folded her arms, a bit indignant. "I'm the amateur who wasn't afraid to give him grief, and I still tried to save him. They're the professionals."

She was agitated, and there was much more to it than simply not liking the way the engagement had gone; she was starting to realize that she was more than just someone pretending to be a soldier so she could stay beside her friend. When it struck her that she was proving to be as natural an officer as youngsters like Jimmy Devlin before her, she'd have to decide how she felt about it.

But Strong wasn't going to force that question right now, "That'll be for someone else to decide. What about my Lady in white — you finished throwing up your guts?"

Though her chin had dipped again, Alex took one hand off her face and gave a lame thumbs up, "Mostly."

"Good," Strong nodded. "So we can more or less go looking for Saager. So I can kill him."

"Or otherwise harm him," Stephanie sounded severe — it'd take a moment for her mood about Duncan's men to pass. She then looked to her best friend, "I'm guessing you don't want to wait?"

"The longer he has, the further he gets," Alex confirmed from her seat. "And if he did this drunk-gas thing to Elspeth, she's going to need someone to hold her hair."

It was a joke, sort of, but it did the job of pivoting conversation to the missing Lady.

"So," Stephanie took up the question. "We think she's alive?"

Alex looked up once more, her eyes shifting from her friend to her Sergeant and back, "Might as well?"

"At least for now," Strong agreed. "If we assume otherwise without proof, we might let him steal her away."

Maybe it was hopeless — the idea that Elspeth could have been held captive for a whole week was rather spectacular, but Saager had obviously succeeded in doing much harm already, so underestimating him seemed unwise. And if he had killed her, little would be lost by trying to find her alive anyway.

"So if he's got her captive somewhere, the question is... *where*?" Stephanie sort of mangled that question, and Alex scrunched up her nose at the repetition of 'where'. But that was fine, everyone was tired and stressed and it was getting late in the day.

"I don't think this drunk gas is a coincidence," the younger Lady Smith observed. "If that whole lance was in the basement, and none of them were shot..."

Stephanie shook her head, "No wounds I could see."

It didn't sound as though she'd enjoyed looking.

"Well then they all went into that house in a blizzard, and somehow they got gassed. Freeman realized what was happening and went for a gas mask, and Saager shot him... but if Elspeth was in as poor a state as me, he could have taken her anywhere."

Alex's assessment was sound, and Strong actually felt a little pride at her clear reasoning. Of course he had no business feeling that — she was her own young Lady, and no one had ever thought her unwise, but it was good to see her overcoming the misery of the gas.

Stephanie took a deep breath, then nodded, "The bill I found that led us up to the house looked like it was planted. Like it was bait for a trap. So maybe Saager's plan was to catch whatever Champion came up here to investigate *Hood*..."

"He had the gas waiting for her, and his plan was to capture her," Alex followed her friend's reasoning, drawing another nod from the American.

So whoever was behind the destruction of *Hood* also wanted to have a live Champion.

"And then because of the weather, he wasn't able to make good his escape... because I can't imagine he stayed around his house just expecting to catch another Champion," Stephanie continued, more or less thinking aloud.

Strong picked up on that thread, "If he was planning to transport her somewhere, alive, he'd either have to keep dosing her with gas, so she'd be cooperative, or he'd need her in very strong confinement. Either way, it'd be a big setup."

A big setup indeed — either a cage with restraints, or a box filled with gas, that could be moved conveniently out of Rosyth... probably out of Scotland altogether... without drawing too much notice.

"Shipping container?" Alex easily followed the line of thought.

"Shipping container," Stephanie agreed, her eyes narrowing thoughtfully.

"Shipping container," Strong repeated it, and both Alex and Stephanie looked at him abruptly.

"Repeating it once was okay, but two times was a bit much," Alex scolded him gently.

It was good that they were ready to give him a little grief, but for all his pride in his charges, he was hardly unequipped to counter: "Daphne never complains about a second repeat."

Stephanie's riposte was immediate and unforgiving: "So why do you sleep on the floor?"

"She complains about repeats five and six," he tried gamely, but neither girl was buying it. He paused for a moment, wondering whether he should try any harder to sell his story... then elected to do his job instead. Swinging his legs off the table he'd been set upon, he winced at a stab of pain, then put his feet on the floor. "Hell with it, let's try to go save Elspeth Cornish."

"Finally," Alex stood up quickly. Then she blinked a couple of times, and sat back down until Mike Strong finished putting on his boots.

After that, they went looking for a shipping container.

The dark world in which she was living seemed to rock, and bounce, but Elspeth couldn't figure out why. Then it stopped moving — settled again — and she decided it must have been just a dream. Everything was a dream now, and as she contorted against the ties that were making her lie down, she giggled at the feeling.

When she'd been a girl, some boys had once tied her to a chair. It had been a game, because they wanted to see if a Champion could break the twine... but back then she'd been too young, and so she'd been stuck to that chair in the woods near their house for a whole day, and a whole night, until her daddy had found her and freed her.

She laughed about it afterwards, because it had been silly — the sort of childish abuse she'd take from bullies until her strengths manifested, and she broke the nose of one of them. He'd been very mean to her, and he tried again when she was eleven... taunted her and pushed her down in the mud, because she thought she was special when she and her mum and dad were just common folks.

He'd made fun of her family, so she'd stood right up and swung a punch at him. She didn't even know how to make a fist, then — she'd put her thumb inside her fingers, and nearly dislocated it in the process — but his nose had never been the same.

After that, the teasing had stopped, and she'd gone to Newfoundland to train. There she'd met Anneke Winter, who she was ever so close with, and after that the men from her lance — her second family — had found her.

She'd never had to worry again about being teased — her only fear, which she'd never really given much credence, was that something could happen to those men who traveled the world with her, who pretended to like her cooking.

And who, in the end, had died for her.

She pictured them now, still giggling as she struggled and tugged and fought.

Then the box moved again.

Maybe she was going somewhere. Maybe, if she went far enough away, she would never remember Bob Freeman and the rest of her fellows. Maybe this dark box was taking her somewhere to forget everything.

That idea terrified her, so she giggled more, and struggled harder. She needed to get out. Somewhere, there had to be help.

Strong was letting his right leg dangle out through the Land Rover's open door as it sat in front of the Rosyth administration building. He'd taken off his webbing so he could breathe a little easier, though his Thompson was still conveniently positioned beside his feet.

Sitting on the passenger side rear bench behind him, Alex leaned her head back against the canvas, her eyes closed.

"What the hell was in that stuff?" she asked again, because even though the nausea had mostly passed, her head was pounding.

The gas — whatever it was — would of course be analyzed, as soon as men could be sent up to Castleandhill House to collect samples... but that wouldn't happen for a while, since there was no sign of reinforcements. As the sun was settling low in the west, all of the soldiers near enough to Rosyth to be of any help were still assisting with blizzard recovery operations, and Duncan's lance had entirely disappeared. Presumably they were at the hospital with their Champion, but under the circumstances it might have been better for them to actually *help*...

Alex knew she couldn't — or at least shouldn't — dwell on those men, and their apparent failings. It would probably be wise for Lord Jimmy to start assessing the lances that had been posted away from Newfoundland for any length of time — to see if they were still as effective as they should have been — but focusing on Duncan's issues now would not help Elspeth.

"We'll get some back to Jimmystown for study," Strong quietly answered her question about the gas, doing his best to keep his physical discomfort out of his voice.

Aspirin was a wonderful pill, but damned if it could mask the pain of being shot *and* gassed. No drug short of morphine was probably equal to that task, and there was no way he'd allow himself to be dosed with such a narcotic.

So like his young Lady, he just sat and nursed his suffering, while Stephanie did the work inside.

"Thanks for coming into the basement for me," Alex opened her eyes abruptly — realizing that she hadn't yet voiced her gratitude.

Strong looked back over his shoulder at her, "Thanks for going down there in the first place."

Alex frowned, "Well, it's my job. Draculas and stuff."

"And pulling you out is my job," Strong shrugged. "Trust me, it's not personal. I don't even like you."

"Oh thank God, I was afraid the feeling wasn't mutual," she actually managed to smile.

As she spoke, she reached over the seat with one hand, then planted it on his shoulder. He covered it with his own, gave it a quick squeeze, and she let him go. Of course they didn't like each other — what was there to like about either of them?

"Sounds like Stephanie is really bothered about Duncan and his men…" the Lady in white sat back and closed her eyes again, and Strong nodded slowly, turning his eyes back to the front door of the building.

"She's a good soldier, just like you're a good Champion."

"Aww," Alex smiled, thinking her Sergeant was trying to be sweet.

But Strong was actually growing serious, "No I mean it. She might think she's just in uniform so she can play around with her best friend… but she's good. She reminds me of Jimmy Devlin, when he was young. Like you remind me of your mom."

Alex opened her eyes again, the somber words sinking in as she looked at the back of Strong's head over the seat. He meant that, and it actually made her feel better.

But she didn't feel like she should let on, "Lord Jimmy didn't play nice with others?"

Strong raised an eyebrow, and looked back again, "What do you mean, 'didn't'?"

Alex met his smile, and then they had a sweet moment just smiling at each other. It was entirely too much, and after a second of feeling warm about her Colour, Alex shook her head once more, "Being gassed together has made us way too chummy. I'm starting to feel nauseated again."

"Glad it's not just me," Strong replied with a chuckle, and then a wince — chuckling didn't help his head.

Fortunately, Stephanie emerged from the administration building just a moment later, looking more at ease than any time since they'd left her with Duncan's lance. She passed in front of the Land Rover and then hopped up into the driver's seat, turning to her friends before making any moves to switch on.

"Jimmy was out, but I got Brigadier Kennedy. He's going to send Captain Ghale over with 'K' Company to help us. Should be here in three hours."

Her words were most welcome — now that there was a clearly-defined threat, not just a cold detective case to follow, 200 men could be allocated to assist with the search for Saager, and Elspeth.

"I also checked with the yard people... there are a ton of shipping containers here, but none of them can move for a few days — nothing's coming in by sea or rail. So there's lots of time to search, and physically no way for anyone to get anything in or out without being obvious," the Lieutenant continued.

Alex's eyes were open again, and she frowned, "So we wait for Captain Ghale?"

"Well, you've been gassed and he's shot himself *and* been gassed, so I think we could be forgiven for not trying to climb through a freight yard full of containers without help," Stephanie shrugged.

That was entirely sensible, but somehow it left all three of them feeling slightly odd. The failure of Duncan's men to take the initiative had been a disaster, so could these three really afford to stop trying?

"Maybe we just drive around, see if we can find the Land Rover he took?" Strong suggested, and Alex glanced at him, then shrugged.

"That's better than nothing."

"I'll try not to hit the bumps too hard," Stephanie actually sounded a little relieved at the prospect of action, so she pulled her door shut and switched on. With a groan, Strong pulled his leg into the vehicle and closed up his side too.

As the sun began to set behind them, the trio drove east in search of Saager.

CHAPTER XI

"There any torches in the seat boxes back there? It's going to be dark soon," Stephanie looked back over her shoulder as she guided their Land Rover along a narrow, snowy track that appeared to have been traversed by at least one vehicle — another Land Rover based on its width — already that day.

Much like the lane leading to Castleandhill House, this one was cutting through the trees, but it was well south of that building — closer to the shoreline and the railway that ran from Rosyth to the Forth Bridge.

It was a long shot, but perhaps Saager was making his way south and had followed this route after his escape. Worth a look, as long as there was light.

Sliding off the bench and crouching in the back bed of the truck, Alex lifted her seat and started rooting around in the storage box beneath it. There were some gas mask cases, which she decided to pull out just in case, and then two flashlights. She laid them out on the bench facing hers as the Land Rover continued to roll along, then folded her seat down and slid back onto it.

"Have them," she replied, and Stephanie nodded.

The American Lieutenant was keeping her eyes on the lane, of course, because getting stuck out in the middle of nowhere just before dark would have done no one any good. Granted, the 'middle of nowhere' was a relative term in this part of Scotland — so near the Forth, nothing was quite as remote as they were used to in Newfoundland, where there could be hundreds of square miles occupied by just a handful of people (and a larger number of moose).

Still, best not to get stuck, and it helped that whoever had come down this way before had blazed a reasonably safe and sure-footed trail.

It had been Strong who spotted the southbound track as they cruised slowly along one of the roads that paralleled the rail line, and now he leaned forward in his seat, Thompson close at hand as he watched the dimming snow gleam yellow under the truck's headlights.

"Where was this guy going?" he muttered ostensibly to himself, but Stephanie opted to weigh in.

"Somewhere quiet."

That was likely, but the question was whether this was the track made by an innocent man going to visit his parents in a little cottage in the woods, or a nefarious killer seeking escape…

"That's no house."

Alex was looking over Strong's shoulder when a large structure came into view ahead. It stood tall in the center of a large clearing, but detail was hard to make out in the failing light — only the straight lines of the sides and the angle of the roof gave it away at all.

Then the Land Rover jumped violently once, then again, as it hit something hard under the snow — something that felt suspiciously like a pair of steel rails.

Stephanie hit the breaks immediately, then looked back on her side of the vehicle, as Strong did the same though his passenger side window. There was nothing visible under the deep blanket of white, but based on the interval between the bumps…

"Those could be tracks. A spur off the rail line, leading in there," the Sergeant was first to vocalize what they were all thinking.

Stephanie nodded immediately, "A railway shed of some kind. If you were hiding a container meant to go by rail to some port for shipping…"

"This is as good a place as any. And also, it checks the 'spooky' box, which is important, especially at dusk," Alex added, sounding a bit more like herself. "I've been in one creepy basement today, and that went fine, so why not an ominous railway shed in the middle of the woods?"

With that, she tugged her Browning out from under her coat and racked back its slide far enough to be sure there was a round in the chamber.

"Bringing the gas masks this time," Strong set his condition, and Alex nodded.

"Definitely."

That settled it; the place warranted close inspection. Stephanie switched off the engine and everyone hopped — or fell — out of the truck, collecting weapons, gas masks and lights as they went. Assembling behind the Land Rover, they waited until they were all set, then looked to each other.

It was too dark for them to communicate much through their knowing stares, so finally Stephanie asked aloud: "Well you two have done this already today. How?"

"Badly," Alex answered with a shrug.

Strong smiled, but was more productive, "If he were in there, he could have heard us pull up already. So someone could jump onto the roof, someone could sneak through the woods and go around behind, and someone could go straight in for a look."

That sounded somewhat sensible, so Alex shrugged, "Okay. I'll volunteer for the roof."

"Good thing, otherwise we'd be here all night," Strong replied. "I'll go straight in."

Stephanie frowned, "Not sure about that…"

"With a gimpy leg, you want me tramping around in the woods?" he countered, then added extra emphasis: "Besides, if any of us is going to get gassed twice, better it be the guy who knows something about being drunk, and hung over."

"I know something about being drunk," his Lieutenant protested, but Strong shook his head.

"Not like this. Tipsy doesn't count."

"He doubts my drinking ability," Stephanie looked to Alex for support, but the Lady in white simply raised an eyebrow.

"Maybe this isn't the time to prove him wrong."

No doubt that was true, so Stephanie shrugged, "Fine. Let's go."

There was no more time to waste on decisions; the two girls moved off carefully through the snow. Mike Strong stood still for a moment, considered whether he'd pull on his gas mask, and then decided just to carry it along until he got a closer look at the shed. Rounding the Land Rover, he started hobbling through the darkness.

It took no time at all for Alex to reach the roof — going airborne was faster than tramping through the snow, and as she landed carefully and planted her feet on the building's roof, she held her breath for a second.

She was light, but she was no bird — no matter what certain seagulls in her past might have thought. It was entirely possible that anyone inside the shed could have heard her land, and roofs weren't usually bulletproof.

Silently, then, she waited — listening carefully to see if her hearing could detect anything. At first there was nothing but peaceful silence, but as she tuned in more carefully she began to pick up something mechanical, rhythmic... like a motor, or perhaps a pump.

There was some activity inside, and as she looked quickly around the darkened roof, she spotted the hood for what appeared to be a small vent. Trying to move silently on the balls of her feet, she went for that outlet, and every step brought her nearer to recognizable sounds.

Unfortunately, all her hard work to gain some weight seemed to have paid off — and the first clue she got that she was making noise was the sudden explosion in front of her feet. It was the sort of cloud that could only be kicked up by a burst of submachine gun fire pounding through the roof and out into the night sky, and it had been *close*.

Alex let out a yelp as the roof shook under her feet, and then she instinctively leapt up and backward... but too far. She wasn't going to land anywhere on top of the building. As she fell towards the ground, the roof where she'd stood continued to explode. Someone was giving it a whole magazine.

Strong looked up, saw the snow bursting off the roof and starting to flurry down, then detected the blur of Alex as she withdrew. There was no time to wonder if she'd been hit; he was the ground-level straight-assault man, so he had to stop the shooter.

Hobbling quickly to the shed, he spotted the shadow of a door and put his hand on it, then found the handle. Without delay he gave it a heave, and it swung open. For a second he stood aside, in case whoever was shooting noticed and changed his aim... but the racket continued, and it was directed above. Moving fast, Strong raised his Thompson and swung into the doorway. His eye was locked down his sights as he stepped into the gloomy shed...

It was no mere shed.

As roughshod and modest as it might have appeared on the outside, the building within appeared to be framed in steel, and its interior walls were covered in some kind of plastic sheeting — as if designed to keep gas in. Recognizing the possible implications of the cladding, Strong sucked in a big breath and held it — there was no time to get the mask on now.

The rails ran straight through the big plastic-lined structure, entering and exiting through large doors — both closed — that sat in opposite walls. And atop those tracks was a railway container car. Elspeth could be in that container. They just needed to take care of the shooter so they could get to her...

The shooting at the roof stopped, and Strong realized that was probably due to a reload. But the Sergeant couldn't see Saager. The bastard was probably on the far side of the container car, so ignoring the pain in his leg, Strong assumed a roughly-proper combat crouch and began advancing obliquely from the door, his gun ready.

Distantly, he noticed there was a word painted on the metal side of that container: *Trevanyon*. He didn't know what it meant, nor did he intend to dwell upon it. He'd been caught looking the wrong way at the house when they'd first encountered the foreigner; not this time. Just a few more feet...

It was almost anticlimactic when the shape of a gun-wielding man appeared around the side of the container. Thankfully, that man wasn't wearing a gas mask — it was safe to breathe, which was important.

Curiously, though, the man struggling with the weapon wasn't Saager.

Strong had been focused on finding that man, though it probably made a certain kind of sense that there would be more than one culprit. Why would anyone trying to kidnap a Champion be working alone?

It was a good question, but not one Strong would have a chance to dwell on; the shooter looked up, spotted the Sergeant, and threw himself sideways. The move seemed neither controlled nor deliberate — not the carefully-honed maneuver of an experienced fighter like Saager — but it got the job done. Strong couldn't shoot, he had to give chase around the car.

"Give it up!" he bellowed, not really expecting a response but figuring he might as well try.

Still denying the pain in his leg, he continued to edge around the box car, his finger laid across the trigger of his Thompson so he could fire with minimal notice…

Then he got his answer. Unfortunately, it came in the form of a hand grenade.

He wasn't looking up as the potato masher arced over the shipping container, but he heard it clatter to the concrete floor a dozen yards behind him. Turning with a wince, he spotted the explosive as it rolled away from him — thank God it had been overthrown — and then stopped at the bottom of a set of shelves against the far wall.

Within a split second he realized the danger, and his body was already reacting; he dropped to the ground and got one arm around his head to cover up.

The blast wasn't as loud as he expected, and certainly lacked the power and the shrapnel to harm the Sergeant from fifteen yards away, but it upended the contents of the shelf, some of which were flammable…

Sure enough, as Strong looked up and tried to assess his hearing damage, he began to see the beginnings of a fire, which immediately leapt upon some flammable liquid and became much more than just the *beginnings*. There was a tearing sound, audible even after the blast, as the flames abruptly swept along the entire far wall of the shed.

That would be a problem.

Struggling to get his free hand under him, Strong pushed himself upwards — he had to get to his feet, get the shooter, then see if Elspeth was…

As his head came up, he found himself staring down the muzzle of a German submachine gun. Behind the weapon was a skinny-looking fellow, sweat dripping from his brow and chest heaving as he glared down at the man he'd tried to bomb.

Strong's Thompson was basically on the ground, and though the Sergeant's hand was around the grip, he had no hope of raising it in time. Dead to rights all over again — but this time he lacked the support of his white-coated angel of death.

Defiantly, then, he locked his eyes on those of his soon-to-be killer, "Guess you have me."

The fellow didn't seem talkative, but as Strong's heart began pounding harder and his concern over everything else around him — rapidly-spreading fire included — began to wane, he became aware of the man's every move. Even the muscles in his right hand, which would ultimately depress the submachine gun's trigger, were abruptly very obvious to the Sergeant.

He would be fully aware of his own death — possessing a sort of clarity that he'd first experienced on the new world, as he and his b'ys charged into fatal lightning.

Now, he would join the rest of the Newfoundland Regiment.

Except, *obviously*, he wouldn't.

Their close friendship notwithstanding, the fact that both Stephanie Shylock and Alex Smith seemed to fire into this shooter at the same time was remarkable.

Watching as closely as he was, Strong was confronted by the man's look of surprise as one bullet slammed into his shoulder from the side, and another then passed right through his skull. It was devastatingly effective shooting, and the shooter probably hadn't even had the chance to realize death was upon him.

He pitched sideways, but just in case his muscles spasmed on the way, Strong quickly reached up and shoved the barrel of the gun aside. It was hot from the previous firing, but he obviously didn't care.

For a second he looked at the fallen man, trying to drive down his heart rate, and then he pushed himself to his feet.

Stephanie entered his vision first — though he heard Alex saying, "I'll try the container door!"

The Lieutenant was frowning at him as she approached, keeping her pistol on the fallen man just in case. There was no mistaking her concern, "You alright?"

He nodded instinctively, then blinked once as his mind regained its grasp of the situation. The air was getting *very* hot — the fire that had started on the far side was climbing up the plastic-sheeted wall. Strong hadn't even known that was possible.

"We better get out of here fast," he replied quickly.

"No argument here," Stephanie agreed, then reached out and patted his shoulder. "Thanks for keeping him busy."

"Is that what I did?" was his immediate reply, before catching himself.

Perhaps she could have seized upon that remark for a joke, but Lieutenant Shylock didn't. In fact, she did the opposite: gave him a firm nod and then waved towards the container, where Alex was holstering her pistol and starting to work on a latch.

"You did your job," Stephanie confirmed steadily, then added:

"Come on, need you."

Those were the words of an officer — a real officer, not someone pretending to be one — and they injected precisely what any soldier would have needed under the circumstances: urgency and structure amidst chaos. As Mike Strong followed his Lieutenant around the box car, he couldn't help but feel some pride in the way she was growing into her battle dress. That was a sentiment for another time though, because as the pair reached the front of the shipping container, Alex had her hands on the crank and was waiting for them.

"Are we trying to burn down this place?" she asked.

"He overthrew a grenade," Strong replied, his tone already settled down. "Frankly, I prefer him starting the fire to blowing me up."

"Not very selfless of you," Stephanie shook her head with a gallant smile as she holstered her pistol, then swung her gas mask case around. "If she's in there, I'll drag her out."

There was no time to argue about who would do what; as Stephanie started to unfold the mask, Alex cranked on the lever, and Strong swung his Thompson up to his shoulder, just in case.

The trio literally held their collective breath as the door swung open with a groan. The dim light from the shed's lamps spilled into the container, and Strong narrowed his eyes to try to see if anyone was inside…

Then he heard a cough.

"Hello?" it was a strangled call, and from the working-class British accent it was unmistakably Elspeth. "Is that you, Bob?"

It wasn't Bob Freeman, for that man was dead, but as the Lady of London staggered towards the light, clearly disheveled but still wearing her brown coat, at least the fallen Sergeant's soul could be at peace.

Elspeth had been rescued.

CHAPTER XII

The sun was about to set over Fort Eustice, and as George, Caralynne and Vanier Cross emerged from the front door of the headquarters building, they came face to face with a party of armed guards from the Champions Regiment.

"I think that's for me," Vanier nodded to the squad of infantry, then looked to the pair who'd joined him for an afternoon of fruitless screen-searching.

Despite their new examination techniques, they'd found no trail to the person who'd broken into the screens. It was another inconclusive search, and one that would do nothing to help Vanier's cause in the coming trial. Still, the black Corporal couldn't help but feel that it had been a good day — that, whatever the result of the search, he'd benefited from the presence of two people from a world quite different than his own.

Whether working with Caralynne and George would actually change his fate, he couldn't say. It seemed unlikely. But it was still a good day, and he chose to leave in that state of mind.

"Good luck," George extended his hand toward the soldier, and Vanier shook it with a nod.

"Thanks. You too."

"I expect we won't need it as much," Caralynne's saddened tone reflected her own somber awareness of the danger Vanier faced.

With as game a smile as he could manage, Vanier shrugged, "You're probably right."

Such was the nature of his optimism, and with nothing more to say, he descended the steps from headquarters, and nodded to the escort sent to take him back to his cell. They moved off without ceremony, leaving Caralynne and George together on the stairs.

"So?" the elder Lady Smith's question was flat, and stuffing his hands in his pockets, young Mister Devlin shook his head.

"I don't think we're off about him. Neither he nor Constance strike me as the type... but then, I suppose that could just mean they're exceptionally good spies."

"Right," Caralynne agreed.

Attempts to flush out the spy simply weren't working — but part of the lack of success undoubtedly had to do with the haphazard approach they were forced to pursue. Spreading misinformation about the Grand Banks rendezvous point had been a good idea, but since *Hood's* demise had been due to sabotage, it had been fruitless. This stop at Fort Eustice seemed only to confirm that Vanier Cross, the likely scapegoat, was probably as innocent as Constance Cormack.

If not those two, then who?

Literally anyone else in Fort Eustice, no doubt.

"I was really hoping whoever broke into this screen was clumsy," George shook his head. "But they really weren't. I checked it all... Sass herself might be able to get a little more out of the logs, but there's nothing more for me to see."

Caralynne glanced at him, "You're suggesting whoever did this was as good as you?"

"At least," George confirmed. "We're going to need Saa help for this one. I'll ask my dad to check in with them, see if we can get the next envoy here soon."

That seemed the only solution now — the next dragon envoy wasn't expected on Earth until at least 1942, but perhaps a call for urgent assistance could get them here sooner. Because without Sass or someone else from her government working on the machines they'd built for the humans of Britain and the United States, it seemed unlikely there would be any real answers.

And an absence of real answers could cost a man like Vanier Cross his very life.

Caralynne nodded slowly as she listened to George's words, and reached the same conclusions. Then she took a breath and wondered after her daughter, and whether any new answers were being found in Scotland. Perhaps the villains in Rosyth had left some information that could make up for the screen's refusal to reveal the traitor.

If not, the message the elder Lady Smith and the younger Mister Devlin would provide to the Senate Inquiry would be both cryptic and bleak. Somewhere out there, a mysterious force was plotting against the British-American alliance. Whoever it was had the resources to attack bases, and blow up the flagship of the Royal Navy — all without leaving a hint as to who they were.

"I get the sense we're going to be very popular in Washington," Caralynne said eventually.

With a nod, George Devlin turned back towards the headquarters building, "Inevitably. And on that note, we better get our kit ready. Night train."

Their visit to Fort Eustice was indeed over, and they were leaving with no more answers than they'd had when they arrived.

As the cell clunked shut behind Vanier, he felt the optimism of his relatively good day deflating with great speed. The pitiful stockade lighting did little to push back the darkness that spilled through his window, and after a whole day of remembering what it was like to be a functioning, contributing human, the cell seemed even smaller.

Captain Wendel Fischer had been lying on his cot and trying to read, but he sat up immediately, "You alright?"

Vanier nodded as he sat down on the edge of his own bunk and took a breath, "A team from Newfoundland was here to go through the screen. Guess they wanted me because I was the one who initially found the breach."

He didn't want to mention anything about Constance, even to Fischer — the fact that she'd seemingly vouched for him remained a source of comfort, but it wasn't one he wanted to lose by sharing.

Fischer frowned, "They find anything?"

"Nothing," Vanier shook his head. "They looked places I didn't know existed... their man George Devlin is the best I've ever seen. But there was nothing. Whoever scrubbed it out did a hell of a job."

Fischer's frown relaxed for a moment, but then it deepened again as he shook his head, "So we're all back to where we started. They'll try us and either find a traitor... or a scapegoat."

The words clearly tasted bitter to the Captain, and he shook his head as he looked out through the bars to the corridor beyond. Little hope seemed to remain for the operators of the United States Saa screen... their fates were in the hands of their Army, and their politicians.

With that cheery thought, Vanier let out a sigh, then lifted his feet up onto his cot and lay back. Now there would be more waiting, and after that, undoubtedly something worse.

It had taken an hour for Elspeth to stop most of her coughing and retching. As they took turns holding her hair, and rubbing her back to try to alleviate some of the discomfort, Alex, Stephanie and Strong had simply sat in the snow a safe distance from the burning shed, and watched as orange flames gutted the structure.

It didn't seem as though the fire was hot enough to melt the building's steel frame, but the conflagration was more than dramatic enough to serve as a beacon for the reinforcements from Newfoundland, when they arrived shortly thereafter.

Captain Ghale and 'K' Company had the structure surrounded before midnight, and with the unit's medic assisting, Alex, Stephanie and Strong guided a shaken and hugely-disoriented Lady Cornish towards a stretcher.

"My men are dead, aren't they?" the Champion of London asked again, the timber in her tone positively heartbreaking.

While Duncan might not have thought anything at all of the soldiers who protected him, this Lady clearly cared deeply for her men, and as her wits returned in the clear night air, the revelation of their loss was hitting her very hard indeed.

"It's going to be okay," Alex had nothing better to offer by way of comfort, but as soon as she said it, Elspeth's boot struck something in the snow and she started to topple. Quickly the whitecoat got her arm around the browncoat, and held her fast.

"It can't be okay," the elder Lady's answer was honest, and anguished. "My men have been killed…"

To those words, Alex had no answer. She looked sideways at Stephanie, but the American Lieutenant had no notion of what to say either.

Fortunately, Mike Strong was on the other side, and he carefully extended an arm around Elspeth to balance Alex's effort to keep her on her feet. As he then guided the stricken Lady's arm around his shoulder, she blinked a few times and looked at him, then looked away sharply — as though she didn't want to see him.

As though he reminded her of…

"Tell you a secret, M'Lady," Strong summoned her eyes back with his soft words. "They would have given anything to make sure you made it away. And you did. They gave up their lives so that you could escape. And you didn't let them down."

Alex heard her Sergeant's words distantly at first, but when they processed she realized she had to blink. An image of the venerable Colour standing between her and Stephanie, and all the evil of the worlds, slashed through her mind. It stung her eyes for just a second.

Fortunately, Mike Strong had more to say: "And you won't start letting them down now, right?"

Elspeth was looking right at him as spoke, and with a blink of her own, she started to nod... before beginning to cough again. She had a lot of that damned gas to get out of her lungs, so conversation halted and they focused on getting her to the back of a Land Rover.

Once she was safely inside, the trio stepped away and let the professionals take over. Lady Cornish would get the care she needed for her body... though what could be done for her emotional pain was a separate question entirely. At least she was alive, and safe.

"Well," Alex swallowed against any further thoughts of an emotional nature, "I'm glad we didn't just sit and wait for help."

"It turned out," Strong agreed with a nod.

Stephanie was about to contribute, but a newcomer preempted her.

"Lady Alex, Lieutenant Shylock, Sergeant Strong," Captain Ghale was abruptly before the three of them, nodding firmly to each in turn.

The Nepalese officer had come to the Special Service Regiment from the King's Own Gurkhas — the regiment that, during the Battle of the Badlands, had fought savages with just Kukri knives. Gurkha infantry had been legends before that day, but the fact that they'd used knives alone to defeat beasts that were effectively cannibalistic Champions, made them seem supernatural.

"Captain," Alex answered Ghale for all of them, and he nodded politely to her.

"*Skipper Miller* is collecting water into tanks, to be dropped onto the structure. We will attempt to douse the blaze, so we can collect evidence."

Straight to the point... and what he was describing sounded awfully grand. Could a skycruiser carry enough water to put out such a fire? Strong didn't know, but he figured they'd soon see. It certainly would be preferable to get more evidence out of this mess — more than a simple name. Which, he remembered, he should make sure was shared…

"There was a word painted on the container she was in," the Sergeant said.

"*Trevanyon*," Alex nodded. "Saw that. Think it's a name?"

Strong had never heard a name quite like it, but then ships could be called all sorts of things, "Maybe the freighter meant to carry her away."

It was plausible, if thin. Hopefully more information could be spared from the flames.

But Ghale's dark expression suggested there was more than just missing information to be concerned about

Stephanie reacted to this first: "What else, Captain?"

Ghale looked to her, then shifted his gaze to Alex and replied, "Whoever sought to take Lady Cornish appears to have possessed an alternate plan. To secure a Champion."

At first, the whitecoat wasn't quite sure what the Captain was implying — a backup plan to take someone else? Who else was Saager after?

With a frown, she asked: "Was there some sort of trap for us in there — something we dodged by luck?"

Ghale looked up to her and slowly shook his head, "Not that we have found. But you are not the missing Champion."

Obviously she wasn't missing, so with a confused glance, the young whitecoat looked first to Stephanie, then to Strong. It was the latter man who followed the Captain's line of thought.

"When's the last time any of us saw Duncan?"

Stephanie blinked, and then she and Alex exchanged slightly wide-eyed stares. Of course they hadn't seen him since his lance had spirited him off to hospital… and then they'd tried to put him and his ineffectual men out of their minds. They were of no use in helping find Elspeth.

"I sent a platoon to collect Lord Duncan from the hospital. All inside were dead, including Lieutenant Turnbull, his men, the patients and the staff. And Lord Duncan is missing."

No wonder they hadn't found Saager at this building. Either he'd known they were coming, and had made his escape… or, more likely, he'd gotten greedy — assumed his lair would go undetected, and hoped to add one more Champion to his railway car. A matched pair for study.

"They cannot have taken him far, and if this was their apparatus for transporting Champions..." Ghale waved towards the structure, but Stephanie blinked and shook her head.

"He'd been run over by a truck, Captain. He was... supposed to live. But he probably couldn't fight his way out of simple restraints. At least not immediately. They could probably have moved him in the back of a car."

As she said it, her shoulders grew heavy, and she began to mentally review all her encounters with the Scottish Lord that day. If she'd been less gleeful about putting him in his place, could she somehow have prevented this?

Battling similar thoughts, Alex leaned forward again, taking deep breaths to stave off the sense of nausea that was beginning to return. The butcher's bill for the day was much too high.

"We will send you back and continue our search. I will request at least one more company to join the effort... but remember, please, that without you three, these men would have *two* Champions. You have saved Lady Elspeth."

When none of them replied to that positive reinforcement, Captain Ghale decided to leave them in peace. As he stepped off, Strong shook his head, "All those doctors, and patients."

For a moment he recalled the old Scotsman who'd patched him up — had he gotten out before the attack? Given the events of the day, and all the success with which these schemers had operated in Rosyth so far, it somehow seemed unlikely.

"Who the hell are these people?" Alex straightened up slowly.

"Whoever they are, they're either good at thinking on their feet, or they're really good at predicting what we'll do," Stephanie reasoned quietly.

The big question was too much for Strong, so he shifted his weight with a slight hop, taking the pressure off his wounded leg, and then let out a louder sigh than he meant to, "Well they didn't get Elspeth. Whoever they are, we screwed up one of their plans today. So let's be happy about that."

It was a helpful dose of perspective. There would be much to wonder about in the days ahead, but at least the villains hadn't been given a total victory. Surely that counted for something.

EPILOGUE

Daphne was waiting on the steps of her boarding house when the Land Rover pulled up. The sun was beginning to rise, making it just about twenty-four hours since the vehicle had last been at this curb. As the truck stopped, Mike Strong nearly fell out with his exhaustion — though of course he had enough pride to make it a graceful near-fall.

Sitting in the front, Alex was trying to work up the energy to say something witty to either the Colour or his girl, but she wasn't having much luck. She'd eaten on the trip back across the Atlantic, but not slept.

Behind the wheel, Stephanie was able to do only a little better, "Look after him, Daphne. He shot himself and got drunk on gas."

She probably wasn't supposed to be so candid about what had happened, but she hadn't slept either. And though any sensible girl might have been appalled at the list of misdeeds, Strong's chaperone simply shook her head, then got an arm around him as his boots touched ground.

"Sounds like you crammed a whole weekend into one day," she said.

Well, that was one interpretation, and Alex and Stephanie looked at each other before waving to their Sergeant and his young Lady. They stayed beside the curb, ready to help as Daphne and Strong carefully took each step up to the door. Evidently, both the Aspirin and the adrenaline had worn off, so each stair was a bit difficult for the Colour... but with his girl's assistance, he made it.

"How bad?" Daphne asked after she was satisfied they were far enough up the stairs not to be overheard.

Being more familiar with Alex's hearing abilities, Strong wheezed out a bit of a gallant deflection, "You know, not as bad for me as a bunch of the poor fellows we left there."

He then hissed as weight was placed on his right calf, and Daphne gave him a particular frown, "You're not supposed to put weight on it, I bet."

"No," he agreed, turning a bit red from the exertion. It wasn't that bad, comparatively speaking... but he'd abused himself plenty over the past twenty-four hours, and it'd take a while for him to recover.

Daphne reached out and opened the door, letting Strong in ahead of her. As he stepped in, she added: "You definitely need a bath, and to relax."

"I'll see to myself," the Sergeant replied quickly.

Shaking her head as he stepped inside ahead of her, his companion shook her head, "Nope, six hands are better than two."

Those were the last words Alex heard before the door shut, and they made her frown.

Despite their finely-honed friendship instincts, Stephanie didn't notice that frown at first, "Home?"

When Alex didn't answer, the American checked her friend's expression, "Now what?"

Blinking, Alex looked towards the boarding house's door, then out through the windshield towards the glowing harbor, then back towards her friend, "Daphne just said *six* hands are better than two. When it comes to him being bathed."

Stephanie's brow creased into a frown, "Six hands? But... if she helps him bathe... which, no... but if she helped, that's *four* hands."

"I know," Alex nodded earnestly. "That's why I'm frowning. It's a confusion frown."

"Right," Stephanie nodded. "I am also frowning because I'm confused. And tired."

"Six hands?" the whitecoat tried to make sense of it.

"Maybe... maybe under all her clothes, she's not just naked. She has two extra arms," the Lieutenant tried — terribly.

"Maybe, under all her clothes, she's two small people, one standing on the shoulders of the other?" Alex's attempt was worse — which was, in a way, impressive.

Silence fell for a second, and they both wore sour expressions at the images their struggles at reason were conjuring up. Then Alex sighed, "After a day like this, why do we say things that make such unsettling mental pictures?"

"I don't think I even want a bath now," Stephanie sympathized.

"I just want to go to sleep," Alex concurred. "Home?"

"Immediately."

So with that, the two friends elected to leave the mystery of Mike Strong and his lady... or ladies... unsolved. They'd get to the bottom of it one day... but not this day. They were home and safe, which given recent events, was a privilege not to be discounted.

The Land Rover rolled off for Jimmystown moments later.

THE CHAMPIONS OF 1941 PART 4
MANDARINS
KENNETH TAM

PROLOGUE

Lord Reginald Bates frowned as he approached the dark ship. Tied up at the wharf with only a few lamps illuminating its upper decks, the freighter seemed altogether ominous — an unusually quiet visitor to a harbor that he'd always found to be alive at night.

Glancing sideways at the Lieutenant commanding his lance, Patrick Wynne, the Champion nodded towards their destination, "Seem a bit too quiet to you?"

"More than a bit," the officer responded evenly, and to emphasize the point he drew his Browning Hi-Power from its holster, then held it ready down by his side.

Bates agreed, drawing his own pistol from beneath his brown coat and turning his gaze back towards the ship. Being summoned from their quarters in the middle of the night for a discreet inspection of a merchantman was hardly a normal occurrence, and while Bates and Wynne both trusted the policeman who'd come to call on them, they had reason to be wary of a trap.

It was June of 1941, and just a few months earlier some unknown force had made a serious attempt to capture Lady Elspeth Cornish, before succeeding in taking Lord Duncan, the Champion of Edinburgh, from his hospital bed.

Though there'd been no activity since — and no sign of Duncan, despite months of thorough searching — threats clearly existed, which could endanger both Champions and their men. Bates hardly thought himself or his lance immune to such concerns, and he had adopted a policy of caution when it came to his duties... but when the police called, it was his duty to attend.

Now the ship was their destination.

With a nod back to the rest of the soldiers in the lance, Wynne began edging his way forward. Bates kept in step with his officer, though he didn't move far out into the lead. Given the risks, they'd adopted the practice of staying near to each other — soldiers and Champion would always be close enough to offer mutual support.

As a cluster of nine men, they approached the dark ship. A single police officer in khaki stood at the gangway leading aboard, and he quickly came to attention at the arrival of the Lord in brown.

"Please go aboard, sir," the man said in perfect English. "You're expected on the bridge."

Bates considered the officer for a moment, then narrowed his eyes, "Yes, but expected by who?"

The constable's response was a blank stare, followed by honest words: "I don't know, sir."

That inspired no confidence at all, so Bates turned back to Wynne, "Wait here, with half the men?"

For all the benefits of moving as a single formation, now seemed like a wise moment to leave some men in reserve. Wynne's brow creased with a frown, and he turned his gaze back to the ship — called *Xinjiang* — and studied it for a moment before conceding a nod.

"You so much as speak loudly, we'll be in with guns blazing," the Lieutenant agreed, and Bates nodded sharply.

"Good man."

With a look back to the lance, then, the Champion waved for half his soldiers to follow him aboard. There seemed to be no one in sight, and leading the way cautiously, Bates stopped as soon as his boots touched the deck. For a second, he scanned his surroundings, looking around for signs of a trap.

Nothing much… only a few faint sounds from the bridge, which suggested people might indeed be there. With a wave to his men, Bates headed for the nearest stair and began to climb.

A single lamp cast yellow light over the tramp steamer's bridge, and as Bates arrived he narrowed his eyes to get a good look at the men inside the cramped compartment. There were three: two police, and one older man with round glasses, wearing a gray suit.

That man was the first to look up, and as he spotted the arrival of the local Champion he turned partway towards him, "Lord Bates?"

The Champion eyed the man carefully, and then one — only one — of the soldiers of his lance followed him onto the bridge, ready to cover the policemen with his Thompson in case they somehow turned out to be imposters.

"My name is Eric Schwabe," the man wearing glasses spoke genially, then laced his fingers together and held his hands in front of him in a non-threatening manner.

"Good evening to you, sir," Bates was polite, but no less suspicious; the name was familiar, though difficult to place. "What was that name again?"

The Briton smiled at the question, "Eric Schwabe, M'Lord. I am an estate agent."

An estate agent...

Bates blinked as his mind seized upon the man's identity. He'd read the name before, in a few different kinds of reports — one of which had mentioned that his 'other' work was indeed as an estate agent. When not selling properties, however, Schwabe was known for other reasons.

Taking a step forward, Bates voiced his recognition: "You are the Captain of the special civilian sniper unit, attached to the police force in Shanghai."

A small smile appeared on the man's face, and he nodded, "I serve where I can."

"You also work for MI6," Bates added directly, and Schwabe's smile grew.

"I have many interests in this area," was his reply.

Bates considered the man for a moment — a man whose reputation as a marksman was known in this part of the world, but whose unassuming appearance betrayed no suggestion of his martial abilities. Provided he actually *was* Eric Schwabe, of course... but it seemed unlikely anyone would dare pretend to be that man. Bates decided to place some trust in him.

"What brings you to our port, Mister Schwabe?" the Champion asked the pertinent question, and the supposed-estate agent turned back towards the bridge.

"I was here on business, Lord Bates," he remarked easily. "But it so happens that a nefarious band of fellows from Shanghai were here at the same time. So as a civilian member of my police force, I decided to keep an eye on them, best that I could. One of them led me here."

Sounded about as mysterious as any MI6 operative would normally be, and Bates' frown reflected his impatience with the spy-novel vagaries, "What sort of band, and what were they about in your fair city?"

"A bunch of Chinese, all of them speaking a gruff dialect of Mandarin. Stepped on rather a lot of toes in Shanghai, I might tell you. Were acquiring a lot of medical machinery, and killing some of the people who helped them. All very messy."

Bates was the sort of fellow who concerned himself with law and order — as a Champion, he was much less intrigued by the idea of diplomacy, or politics, or spending time with fanciful people. His priority was enforcing civilization, so he did take some interest in the criminal activity Schwabe described. He did not, however, have any idea how it could possibly warrant summoning a Champion to an abandoned freighter in the middle of the night.

"When I came aboard for a look this evening, I found this," the spy fortunately continued to explain himself, and as he did he advanced towards a shelf at the back of the bridge. From that shelf he collected a ledger — nothing unusual for a vessel of this kind, which would presumably track its cargo in some fashion. "Please, come and see."

By now Bates was sufficiently satisfied that this was no trap, so he holstered his pistol and joined Schwabe beside the book. The MI6 estate agent had opened it, and as he looked closely in the dim light, the Champion could see the remnants of a number of pages that had been ripped out.

"Torn out?" Bates observed thoughtfully. "I expect that means they've been doing something illegal."

"Undoubtedly," Schwabe agreed, "but for a ship in this condition, that's no great surprise. I did find this interesting, though."

With that, he leafed his way deeper into the book, then stopped at one of the pages towards the back. There was a note about the ship's registration. One name had been printed in, then crossed out an replaced by *Xinjiang*.

The name that had been crossed out was *Trevanyon*.

Bates blinked, then looked up at Schwabe. Immediately his heart began to beat faster — the *SS Trevanyon* had been the apparent destination for the storage container that had trapped Elspeth. For months the vessel had been sought by the Royal Navy, the United States Navy, and agents of both nations around the globe. It had not been found.

"I looked around, and there's a life preserver on the next deck down with *Trevanyon* still painted on it. They weren't quite as thorough as they thought they were when renaming her."

Schwabe's words drew Bates' gaze for just a moment, and then the Champion looked back towards his soldier, "We must lock down the city, immediately."

If this was indeed the ship that had eluded them for months — the ship that might have carried Lord Duncan away from Britain — then they needed to start a full investigation.

But as Bates began to turn for the door, Schwabe's hand closed on his shoulder. The spy moved quickly and very quietly, and Bates was surprised by the firmness of his grip — very sturdy for any ordinary person, let alone an older gentleman.

"Lord Bates, there's a very good chance whoever hired this ship doesn't know we're aboard right now. And I found the log: this ship has been here since April. Just enough time for the direct passage from Britain. Combine that with the fact that the men I've been after are probably hired enforcers, and they were acquiring medical equipment..."

Those were very disparate threads, but Bates was no slouch: the implication was that Lord Duncan had been brought here, and was still in the city — perhaps still healing after the wounds that had put him in hospital.

And if he and his captors had been here unnoticed since April, they could have grown complacent. Investigators might be able to surprise them, if they were able to concentrate strength quickly and quietly.

Turning back, Bates concurred, "Quite right."

"Then we leave quietly, M'Lord," the MI6 man continued. "And you summon help from your base, not anyone here locally. Better that some of your Special Service types come to us out of the sky, with no warning."

Bates nodded, "Yes. Join me, Mister Schwabe. It seems we have a common case to solve."

It was a welcome invitation, though the estate agent from Shanghai doubted theirs would be an easy task, no matter who was sent from Jimmystown. Stepping out the bridge hatch and onto the exterior bridge wing, both Bates and Schwabe took a moment to look out on the lights of the city that might be concealing Lord Duncan and his captors.

Even at night, Hong Kong was a thriving, active, bright town — a free port where the world could come to trade under the benevolent rule of the British Empire.

Perhaps the enemies of that Empire were hiding in plain sight. Unfortunately for them, they would soon be pursued by some of the most formidable agents either world had ever seen.

CHAPTER I

It was what some would call a 'girly' sort of day in the Smith house.

Second Lieutenant Stephanie Shylock was sitting at the dining room table, listening to the radio while she painted her nails. She was coming to the end of another bottle of the green polish she'd adopted the previous August, but that was fine — the Bowring Brothers store in downtown St. John's had promised to keep bringing it in for her as long as she needed it.

Stephanie figured that would probably be a while — some years, at least. She'd gotten accustomed to having short green nails, and though they were a nuisance to maintain, it seemed right that she made the effort.

The same determination kept her using a special Japanese moisturizing cream, also being imported by the Bowring Brothers. It was expensive and made of things she couldn't hope to pronounce, but applying it regularly had become a part of her hand maintenance.

Of course, the care could only do so much; constant exposure to gun oils and cordite, and constant use of soap to wash off the same, tended to give her hands the texture of sand... and working a Browning Hi-Power chipped away at her nails incessantly. The callus that ran between the first and second knuckle on the middle finger of her right hand wasn't going to disappear — not that she'd want it to — and at the end of the day, she'd never possess the dainty digits of the average young woman who graduated from a college like Memorial.

Fortunately, that wasn't her intent. She just figured she should do the best she could to look after her hands, since they were the final interface between her mind and her pistol. They'd work fine whether they were hard or soft, but she wanted to give them the same level of care she reserved for her guns.

So just like most other girls her age, she was sitting at the table, listening to the radio and painting her nails. It could have been a scene from any home in fashionable St. John's...

"Your nail polish smells like gun oil," Alex was passing the dining table, and she dropped that remark as she headed to the kitchen for a snack. It had been nearly an hour since lunch, so she was overdue.

"No, my gun oil smells like gun oil," Stephanie corrected helpfully, nodding towards the Hi-Power that was sitting on the table just beyond the nail polish.

It had already been stripped, cleaned, oiled and reassembled, because as much as she wanted her hands to get equal favor, Stephanie always put the needs of her pistol first. Her nail polish wouldn't have stood a chance if she reversed the order, anyway.

Alex was already coming back out of the kitchen — Champions were fast to food — when she offered her next retort, "You going to stick with the green, even though it's such a pain?"

"I think so," Stephanie carefully put down the brush, then held her hands out in front of her to inspect her work. "It's so stylish."

Pulling out the chair beside her friend, Alex settled down with a leftover breast of chicken, then set about attacking it with knife and fork, "It doesn't even match your uniform."

"It would have matched your coat, if you hadn't picked white," Stephanie bounced that one back, and Alex narrowed her eyes while she chewed.

"Mmhmfmhmhm," was the younger Lady Smith's answer — mouth shut and eating, so Stephanie glanced at her and smiled.

"Well when you put it that way."

Alex just gave her a glare, and then quickly wolfed down the rest of the chicken. By the time she was done, the brush was put away and the cap of the nail polish was screwed back on. With her hands laid on the table to let the varnish dry, Stephanie was condemned to simply wait beside her friend for the next jab... and to listen to the radio.

"God, he likes the sound of his own voice," Alex said as soon as she could, referencing what they were hearing from the set in the corner.

"He's a politician," Stephanie shrugged, which Alex figured was a good answer.

Perhaps it would have been more appropriate if Stephanie had been listening to music as she beautified herself, but instead she was listening to a live broadcast of the Senate Inquiry into the destruction at Fort Eustice, which after a few months was finally winding down. It wasn't pleasant; a Senator called Pollock had basically been driving the whole thing, turning it into the worst sort of witch hunt.

"The fact remains, though, Commandant: your base wasn't prepared for a fight, was it? You can't make excuses over that," Pollock's voice crackled from the speakers, and only after the Senator finished repeating that same thought a few different ways did Commandant Powell — a man who Caralynne had told both girls was not particularly credible — answer uneasily.

"Defense of the base was in the hands of Colonel Adams and his men. They failed most directly, and it is they who are responsible for all of this, Senator."

"Of course," Alex muttered to herself, pushing her plate aside and looking more closely at her friend's hands on the table.

With a frown, she started to prod Stephanie's right hand — at the callus on her middle finger. Stephanie watched this probing with a frown of her own, "Um?"

Like a scientist discovering a new species, Alex poked at the side of her friend's right middle finger, then held her own hand up and ran her thumb over the equivalent spot before shaking her head.

"Why don't I have that?" she asked, sounding rather saddened by the perfectly soft state of her own hands.

"You haven't been shooting long enough, or as much," Stephanie's answer was more matter of fact. "And you probably can't even get calluses. Your skin's too perfect."

She didn't sound jealous, just a little envious. Shooting as much as she did, Stephanie had quite a collection of calluses and scars on her big paws. Japanese moisture cream would never get them all.

Alex's slightly smaller hands would always look as though they belonged to a delicate young Lady, with no aspirations towards war... even though, strictly speaking, Alex's hands were even more dangerous than Stephanie's.

"This is one of those times when if I complain that no one will ever take me seriously because of my delicate hands, you'll glare at me?" Alex checked to make sure her interpretation of Stephanie's mood was correct. Her assessment was confirmed with a nod from the Lieutenant.

They both fell silent, though Alex continued to look enviously at her friend's powerful hands... while Stephanie eyed her friend's perfect ones. Champions enjoyed plenty of advantages in life, and a lesser person might have been more than just envious...

Fortunately, Stephanie wasn't lesser than anybody.

"I think the situation is clear," Senator Pollock came over the radio again, sounding authoritative. "This is the case of army bureaucratic nonsense that I have long advocated against. Ours is *not* a professional army — not like the British Army, anyway. We have spent too long sending the sons of politicians to positions of power... nothing based on military merit, and everything based on the powerful influence of a select few. These bureaucrats... these *mandarins*... are the reason our Fort could not withstand the attack of whoever did this."

Both Stephanie and Alex looked up from their hands at those words. They weren't paying close attention to the Inquiry — in its earlier days, they'd tuned in to listen to Caralynne and George testify, but after a while it had become monotonous... clear that no new information would be revealed, and that the whole affair was really about politicians competing to see who could seem the most exasperated and offended, without fainting or cursing.

Pollock had been the front runner for ages, but this tactic sounded new — and on-target, for once. Was he finally recognizing that he and his kind were creating the problem, by politicizing their own armed forces?

"Clearly, any good military commanders not motivated by politics wouldn't have left negroes to look after our most prized possessions. To be so blinded by supposed *progress* as to endanger national security is damned near a crime in itself, and were it just me on this panel, I'd have a United States Attorney in here already, filing charges along those lines. But in the interests of good government, I think it's time the social progressives are thrust aside, and we point our blame at the real culprits here: the negroes. Maybe they were just negligent... in my state, we know their intellectual limitations. This incident seems to be the proof that should bar them from important service, at least until they're taught to be real soldiers."

Well. So much for that.

Stephanie was staring at the radio, but she flopped back in the dining chair. Alex simply looked at the ceiling and groaned, "So close, and then off he goes."

"I'm totally surprised," Stephanie's sarcasm wasn't especially clever, but it seemed appropriate. The American politicians were willing to blame anyone but themselves for the mess of their Champions establishment... and unfortunately, those in the line of fire were the black men of the 25th United States Infantry.

Certainly, Stephanie knew that not all the soldiers in that regiment were as professional as they needed to be... but there was a difference between needing the training and being traitors. Especially when the lack of training was also the fault of politicians.

It was a great relief when the special telephone rang, interrupting both girls in the midst of their acts of exasperation. Because that phone was connected only to Lord Jimmy's office at headquarters, its ringing usually meant something important was about to happen, so Alex looked to her friend with hopeful eyes.

"Mom's at the Academy, so they must be calling for us!"

Though it took immense mental strain, Stephanie had also reached that completely obvious conclusion. She therefore offered an exaggerated nod, "So, like, you better answer the telephone."

"Like?" Alex frowned, "Why'd you say 'like' in there?"

Her friend shrugged, "Isn't that what the girls say? I'm sure I've said it before."

"Not that I've heard," the young whitecoat answered, getting to her feet. "Maybe it'll catch on."

Stephanie raised an eyebrow, "As if that's likely."

Alex got to the phone by the third ring, and then lifted its receiver a bit excitedly, "Hello, Smith residence, Lady Alex speaking."

She sounded quite silly — she was clearly trying much too hard to come across as serious. Stephanie failed to resist a smile at her friend's irrepressibility, but as Alex's expression sobered, the American girl with the painted nails felt a more responsible air settle back over the room.

"Okay, we'll be there in half an hour," the younger Lady Smith said, then hung up.

As soon as the receiver was down, Stephanie's raised eyebrow asked the wordless question.

"They found *Trevanyon* in Hong Kong. We're flying out there on *Skipper Miller* in an hour, Strong will meet us at the ship."

Stephanie blinked, then nodded. They hadn't had any luck searching for Duncan since returning to Newfoundland from Edinburgh, but the events in Scotland had quietly hung over them both. Perhaps now was the time for some closure.

With a last look at her nails, and a quick blow to make sure they were dry, Stephanie Shylock pushed herself to her feet, collected her recently-pampered pistol, switched off the radio, and headed for her room to change.

CHAPTER II

Mike Strong certainly didn't mind that it had warmed up in Newfoundland. After so much action in the cold — first in Virginia, then over the Grand Banks, and finally in the aftermath of a Scottish blizzard — the Sergeant was happy for the relatively mild temperatures.

The fact that warmer temperatures in Newfoundland often brought drizzle was immaterial; he didn't mind being a bit damp, now and then, so long as it wasn't too cold. And by his reckoning, the temperature as he stood at the bottom of *Skipper Miller's* ramp was just fine.

With his Thompson slung over his shoulder, Strong was pacing back and forth easily, giving his recently-recovered leg a bit of time to stretch out. He'd long ago finished the exercises that had been necessary to help him heal after his ricochet wound — no more hobbling, and just about all his strength was back. Still, his calf ached when he flew anywhere... but so many other things on the Colour ached that he took it in stride.

Considering everything they'd discovered in Scotland, an extra ache wasn't a bad outcome. Scientists were still trying to understand the makeup of the gas that killed ordinary people and intoxicated Champions... but whatever the chemicals involved, its effects had become pretty clear. Anyone who breathed it in would start coughing almost instantly, but once it saturated a human body the coughing would stop.

Difference was, in ordinary humans the coughing would stop because they'd be dead; in Champions, they'd effectively be inebriated. That's how Lady Elspeth had been captured, and why Lord Duncan had been taken, while his men — and everyone else in the hospital who had been looking after him — died helplessly.

None of that had happened to Strong or his two charges; they'd dodged the gas, barely, and also managed to save Elspeth.

Well, they'd saved her from the villains. Her own personal torment might never let her go. With that thought, Strong turned back towards the brown-coated Lady, formerly of London, who was also standing at the bottom of *Skipper Miller's* ramp. Her arms were folded tight across herself, as if she were cold, and her gaze was fixed on something far away.

Since she'd returned to Jimmystown and regained her wits, the hard-nosed Lady from London had been a shadow of herself. She'd refused to take on a new lance, and Caralynne and Jimmy had decided it best to just let her have time alone — to be a more free-floating Champion attached to the base, like Alex and Lord Grey. Perhaps that helped, but Strong figured the time was probably coming when Lady Cornish would need to reconnect with other humans.

And since he was standing there in the drizzle, he figured he might as well start the ball rolling.

"How's yourself this morning, Lady Elspeth?" he asked a little jauntily, but quietly enough that no one around could have heard... had there been anyone else nearby, standing out in the drizzle.

Elspeth blinked and looked towards Strong, then just barely stopped frowning long enough to smile at him politely, "Thank you, Colour Strong. I'm well."

It was the most obvious sort of lie — and one she'd been using successfully since she'd gotten out of hospital. No one believed her, but everyone was too polite to say so.

"So we're going out to find the men responsible for gassing you, and your lance," Strong approached her as he spoke. He watched the smile melt from her face and be replaced with the distant stare from before. "How are you feeling about that?"

Of course he had a good idea how she was feeling; he'd been in a similar state after the battle for the Martian capital, back in 1920. He'd watched hundreds of his friends die, and he'd survived... and though Elspeth likely felt more responsible for the death of Sergeant Freeman and her men than Strong had for the loss of the Newfoundland Regiment, it was similar enough.

"Nothing I could remember helped find the villains," Elspeth answered sharply. "So I'm pretty glad that a lucky chance made up for *me*."

Despite hours in interviews, and countless attempts to remember, nothing Lady Cornish had seen during her captivity had been useful in finding Duncan's captors. She'd tried for more than a month before everyone collectively decided she needed to be given a chance to step away from it.

More reasons for her to be angry at herself.

"I understand," Strong nodded, then found himself looking down at his boots. For a moment he allowed his mind to wander back to the old days again — just a brief visit to the Martian capital... to that afternoon after the slaughter, as he and the survivors sat in mourning under the shadow of a Saa dragon, and a collapsed spire...

Elspeth didn't notice the look of reflection: "*Do* you?"

She blurted it out more quickly than she should have, and when he looked up and she caught sight of his eyes, she realized her mistake. Of course everyone knew where Mike Strong had come from — whatever his reputation had become since, it had always been set in the important context of his time soldiering with the RNR on the new world. He was one of the survivors... that's why his zeal for life (and women) was so well-accepted.

But when a Lady was too preoccupied with her own dead friends... her *family*, in many senses... it was easy to lose perspective, and lash out.

"I'm sorry, Colour," Elspeth looked away as she shook her head. "I just need to get out and do something about this."

"Do something about the fact that eight men died trying to save your life, and that eight more died at the hands of the bastard who nabbed you?" Strong didn't mince his words, because he knew that a Champion as tough as Elspeth didn't need to be coddled.

"And the fact that Duncan was taken, too."

Strong nodded, "Action might help with all that. If you feel like you're undoing some of the damage... catching the bastards... that might help. But be ready for this: you're never going to stop remembering those b'ys you were close with, and who died. Bob and the rest. They were your family. You'll never forget them."

Elspeth's face seemed to freeze at the promise, and Mike Strong knew why. The thought of being haunted forever was frightening; he knew such hauntings had driven some of the other survivors of Waller's charge to end their own lives.

"Don't worry, though. Some day you're going to be glad they're all with you. Think of that: those men will always be with you, wherever you go. And one day, when you need them most, maybe they'll make the difference somehow," he said softly, and then he blinked a couple of times because he was feeling the slightest burning in his eyes. He shook it off, "You just don't let them down. Live extra for them. Drink lots of drink, laugh often, love lots of women…"

He trailed off and winced slightly, as though he hadn't thought through his last few words. Elspeth's eyebrow went up, and her tone shifted, "You slipped that in there pretty quickly, Colour."

"Funny, you're not the first woman to say that to me," he replied, missing not a beat.

She considered him for a moment, eyes narrowing, and then the slightest hint of a smile touched the corners of her mouth, "When I talked to Anneke on the telephone, when I was getting ready to go up to Rosyth, she said you broke her heart."

Strong frowned thoughtfully, "Anneke… is she the redhead? Or the brunette…?"

He was playing smooth, of course, and they both knew it. His words were gentle, and for a moment he could see they'd done their job. Elspeth was one of the good ones — she'd had good parents who'd raised her well, good friends in people like Anneke Winter, and good soldiers around her. Until recently.

She was the sort of hero who would be forever changed by the loss of her men… but would emerge more powerful from it. Mike Strong liked her, and hoped that if Alex was ever to suffer the same way, she'd cope so well.

But better that he never make Alex find out.

For now, the Sergeant heard the approach of a Land Rover in the distance. Quickly he closed the gap with Elspeth, then reached out and put a hand on her shoulder, "You ever need to talk, find someone smarter than me. But if you can't, then just buy me a drink."

The hint of the smile became just a tad bigger, and Elspeth shrugged off his hand, "I'm sorry Colour, you'll be buying *me* the drink."

Strong could live with that. He and Elspeth considered each other for another moment, and then the Land Rover arrived. Alex hopped out of the passenger seat, Stephanie switched off and got out from behind the wheel. They both hurried over to Strong's side, then exchanged greetings with Elspeth and boarded.

•••

Skipper Miller was fully loaded as it crossed the Atlantic, hopped the Mediterranean, and made its way out over the Pacific. In the ship's hold, 'K' Company was preparing for action — more than 200 men and their vehicles, who would help scour Hong Kong and turn up any clues they could about Duncan's whereabouts, and Elspeth's kidnappers.

Commanding the Company was Major Tokutaro Mitsui, the officer Jimmy had stolen from Japan on a more permanent basis than his temporary exchange would normally have allowed. Now the Major was standing around a table in *Skipper Miller's* dining room with Alex, Stephanie, Strong, Elspeth, Lord Grey, and the officer of Grey's lance, Lieutenant Kendrick. Unfortunately the table bore no food — just maps of Hong Kong.

"The ship has been in Hong Kong since April, so hopefully they've gone a bit complacent," Grey was saying — as the man who'd been Champion of Hong Kong until the previous year, he was obviously the correct expert to translate Bates' report. "Apparently there was an investigator on the trail of some Mandarin-speakers who'd been through Shanghai picking up medical equipment. They turned up in Hong Kong, and led him to the ship."

An interesting connection, and as Stephanie heard it, the detective-aspect of her mind which had been awakened in Rosyth started to pull together the threads: "So we're hoping whoever took Lord Duncan is hiding in Hong Kong until he's well enough to be moved elsewhere?"

"Yes," Grey confirmed. "Of course he may be long gone, but at the very least there might be a trail in the city that we can pick up. God knows there's been nothing anywhere else."

This was indeed the first warm lead — if it could be so generously labeled — anyone had found since Scotland. Correctly investigating it would be important, which was why there was an assault company aboard.

"We'll hopefully have surprise on *our* side, this time," Elspeth offered the last two words slightly bitterly, then looked across the table to Major Mitsui. "How are you planning to deploy, Toku?"

The Major's arms were folded, and his bearing was impressive — he always came across like a Samurai, though he was quite friendly when serious work was not at hand. Now he made no attempts at geniality, his finger instead stabbing the map, "I will work with the local authorities to search comprehensively the city, and control points of escape. Lord Grey, can you assist us in finding areas where these Mandarins might be hiding?"

Nodding in answer, Grey took a deep breath, "They'll undoubtedly have made some ripples in the city. Everyone there speaks Cantonese. Be rather like having some French move into Jimmystown, hoping we wouldn't notice... but Hong Kong is a free port, lots of coming and going, so they'll have gotten away without too many questions from local police."

"Probably why they went to a different city to get equipment," Stephanie added dryly, folding her arms. As a frown settled over her brow, she looked from the map to Grey, "You and the Major sweep the town... perhaps we could work with that investigator, follow up other angles. Perhaps look for a trail based on the medical supplies?"

That sounded sensible, and Alex began to nod, "We did okay sniffing around last time."

"We stay in constant contact, of course. But if you and the Major are making a big impression by looking for the Mandarins, we might slip by unnoticed," Stephanie continued her case, and Grey listened silently.

Being both senior and well-acquainted with the city, the elder Lord had authority over this mission. It was his decision... and he made it without much difficulty.

"Wise plan," he nodded, then his eyes turned to Elspeth. "Would you go with them? Your... experience... might be of more use to that sort of search, than to a bunch of canvassing."

With a glance to Strong — which surprised the Sergeant — Lady Cornish nodded firmly, "Done."

It was settled; *Skipper Miller* would be over Hong Kong soon, and when they arrived, everyone would know their jobs. Hopefully Duncan could be found.

CHAPTER III

"Coming in to land," Flight Lieutenant Douglas Bader's voice sounded over *Skipper Miller's* intercom as the skycruiser arrived above Hong Kong. Waiting beside the forward embarkation ramp, Stephanie took the words as the cue to give her Browning one last look. It remained to be seen whether the people responsible for Scotland, and the Grand Banks, and Fort Eustice, were actually in Hong Kong, but each of those events had taught her well not to take anything for granted.

After a last scan of her pistol, and a quick draw back on the slide to make sure a round had been chambered, she confirmed the safety was on and then secured it again in the holster on her belt. Beside her, Alex mirrored the process — checked her gun, then slid it into the holster that sat on her hip, concealed beneath the tail of her coat.

She then twisted her torso around, making sure the lining didn't snag on the hammer... something it was occasionally prone to doing. Stephanie watched in silence, knowing the full-sized pistol was a bit inconvenient for her smaller friend to carry, but saying nothing. Alex had never complained about the sidearm, and even if she did, there wasn't much she could do — the Browning was standard issue for good reason. She could always move the holster from her hip to the small of her back to make it more comfortable, but that would make it much less accessible.

While Alex reset herself, Mike Strong gave his Thompson a silent once-over as well. His confidence and comfort with the weapon were clear enough to Stephanie — she could see his familiarity with the submachine gun in the way he held it, checked it, turned it, and then slung it back over his shoulder with ease.

There were many cues that could reveal how familiar a person was with his or her guns, and though Stephanie rarely spoke of them, she recognized them all. Her godfather — the slightly notorious gunfighter Cameron Kard — had made sure she could always size up a gun-handler, friend or foe.

What struck the young American Lieutenant as interesting, though, was the way neither Lord Grey nor Lady Cornish paid close attention to their own sidearms. Some Champions never seemed to think of their pistols until they were needed, which Stephanie knew could be a dangerous habit. Guns — particularly semi-automatic pistols — tended to be temperamental if not looked after... and sometimes even when they were cared for, they would act up.

Nothing was as reliable as a revolver... but that was another point Stephanie wouldn't voice. As a younger girl, she'd learned that most people didn't want to hear what she had to say about guns, and particularly the gun habits of others. She knew more than most, but even if people knew better than to underestimate her, they rarely took kindly to advice from a young (and apparently pretty) girl.

So if Elspeth and Grey wanted to rely on their fists and their leaps, that was fine; Alex and Strong were ready to shoot, and looking back towards Major Mitsui and the men she could see from the assault company, she knew all those b'ys were ready too. There was no way men stationed permanently at Jimmystown would lose their edge, the way Duncan's lance had.

"Touching down... now," Bader's voice sounded through the speakers again. "Opening ramps."

Because a whole assault company was stepping off, all *Skipper Miller's* ramps would be dropping to facilitate a fast disembarkation. The skycruiser would then launch again, bound for home, since it was the only fully-operational Saa-built craft left in British or American service. *George Tucker* had been patched up sufficiently for short hops, but no one wanted to risk flying that valuable ship too far — particularly over the water, where even a controlled emergency landing would likely see it lost forever.

Stephanie turned back towards the ramp as it opened, wondering what light conditions would greet her. They'd left Newfoundland just after lunch, local time, had been in the air for hours, and now...

Apparently it was daytime — probably morning — because sun was spilling through as the ramp dropped.

Noticing a glance from Alex, Stephanie gave a nod, and together with Strong the two girls started walking down the still-descending ramp. As usual, they timed their strides so that as soon as the metal lip touched ground, they stepped gallantly off — a properly heroic visual, which might have drawn applause in certain company.

But once again, there wasn't much of an audience.

Skipper Miller had come down on the air strip from which Hong Kong's RAF squadron operated, and only two men had come out to meet them, neither in uniform. One was the Champion Lord Bates, the other was a past-middle-age man wearing a gray suit, and round glasses.

Stephanie sized up Bates quickly — from his bearing, he instantly seemed much more agreeable than Duncan had upon first encounter — then turned her attention to the other man...

He was unexpected. Something about his bearing commanded her attention, and instantly she could see he was sizing her up too — but not in the way some older men did, when they spotted a young woman fitting neatly into battle dress. It was as though he...

"Lady Alex, Lord Grey, Lady Cornish..." Bates interrupted Stephanie's musing with his greeting... and strangely, his words didn't attempt to extend the greeting to any of the ordinary soldiers accompanying the Champions.

"Bates," Grey replied with a nod, sticking out his hand as he moved swiftly around Stephanie. "How have things been here?"

Perhaps that was a silly question, but it was asked politely enough that the current Champion of Hong Kong elected to indulge his predecessor, "Quiet, until recently. Thanks for coming with such haste."

"Of course," was Grey's reply, and then he and Bates moved off to begin speaking in low tones.

Stephanie managed to overhear a little of it — talk of Mitsui and deployment — but not being able to make out much, she glanced at Alex. Her friend in white had raised her eyebrow without realizing it, and was listening to the pair as they discussed options. Realizing she'd have to wait for Alex to pass on the update, Stephanie turned her attention back towards the man in glasses, and she subtly continued her assessment of him.

Outwardly there didn't seem to be anything dramatic about his appearance... he was a typical-seeming British expat. But it was almost as though he *wanted* to seem unimpressive...

"My name is Eric Schwabe," he was the first one to break their silent examinations, stepping towards her with his hand extended. Stephanie matched his polite smile, and she took his hand.

Their grips were all too similar — strong, coarse, and callused in the right places. This man knew something about gunplay.

"Second Lieutenant Stephanie Shylock," she introduced herself cautiously.

Schwabe's smile grew slightly as he recognized her name, "I'd hoped we'd meet."

"Sounds like it," her reply probably sounded a little suspicious, and then their hands parted.

"Alex Smith," the whitecoat was suddenly beside her friend, and as she shook Schwabe's hand she threw a quick glance in her direction. The young Champion had noticed that her Lieutenant had marked this man in glasses.

"You'll have heard of me, I'm Mike Strong," the Sergeant arrived next, with his usual modesty.

Schwabe frowned at him, "Actually, I can't say that I have…"

Those words sounded earnestly regretful, and Strong met them with a slight look of concern before deciding they were humorous, "Funny man, Mister Schwabe, pretending not to have heard of me. That's alright. But who are you, precisely?"

Though a man wearing a suit and glasses was likely to be a local bureaucrat, or perhaps a translator, both the Sergeant and the Champion were sufficiently attuned to Stephanie's suspicion to think there was more to the fellow's story.

And thanks to his own aptitude — essential to his interests — Schwabe elected not to play too coy: "I'm an estate agent, and a volunteer sniper with the Shanghai Police. I followed men here, and they led me to *Trevanyon*."

"You're the investigator," Alex didn't really sound surprised, though somehow she'd pictured the man who'd followed the Mandarin-speakers from Shanghai to be younger… less unassuming.

Stephanie had pictured the same — but like her friend, knew better than to be trapped by such assumptions. Now she narrowed her eyes a little at Schwabe, placing what he'd said in the context of what she'd gathered from her scan of him.

It still felt like there was more to shed light on, so she persisted: "Civilian snipers in Shanghai use the 1911?"

Schwabe's hands didn't quite seem right for a rifleman — the calluses were in the wrong places for a man who *only* shot longarms.

He looked straight at Stephanie, then shrugged, "Some have asked me if I work for MI6, on occasion."

Stephanie's eyebrow climbed, just as her friend's had, "And how do you answer when they ask?"

Schwabe's answer came with a smile: "I don't, of course."

All four of them knew immediately that he was saying 'yes', but before Stephanie, Alex or Strong could say anything further to pin down the spy, Grey summoned their attention, as well as Elspeth's.

"You four best be getting along with Mister Schwabe there. We'll deploy with Major Mitsui. You can meet us at the Police Headquarters if you detect anything."

With that, their mission was set to begin; Lady Cornish drifted towards them, and Stephanie returned her attention to Schwabe, "We're supposed to go with you, snoop around quietly while they look for the Mandarin men you followed here. Any thoughts on where we might begin?"

Schwabe looked from Grey to the American Lieutenant without revealing his surprise, "Well it's not my city, I must confess... but if they're after the men I followed, perhaps we should look into the things those men were trying to acquire when they were in Shanghai. Medical supplies, drugs... anything to nurse your Lord Duncan."

"Sounds like a plan," Alex was the first to seize upon it — good that the MI6 man was following the same line of thought they'd discussed in *Skipper Miller's* dining room.

"Then we should acquire a Land Rover," Schwabe nodded, and with a last look at Stephanie, he waved in the direction of the airstrip's car park. As he led them away, 200 men from 'K' Company unloaded their vehicles.

Any enemies of the Empire in Hong Kong who happened to be paying the slightest bit of attention would have to know danger was at hand... but whether they could do anything about it was a separate question.

Though everyone referred to it as *Hong Kong*, the city through which Schwabe was driving Alex, Stephanie, Strong and Elspeth was officially called *Victoria* — it was simply the only settlement situated on the island of Hong Kong.

Situated, or perhaps *perched*, because as Stephanie looked out from the open-topped Land Rover, she could see buildings climbing up the lower slopes of the island's mountain in a rather precarious fashion.

"Like home, isn't it?" Strong nodded towards the same buildings, directing his words to Alex — the only other native Newfoundlander in the vehicle.

The Lady in white was busy unbuttoning the collar of her jacket — she had to be careful not to get too warm, or she'd start sweating — but she managed to nod anyway, "It is. Buildings here look a bit grander, though."

That was true. Most of the structures that lined the harshly-sloping streets of St. John's were fairly modest. There were courthouses, warehouses, and other practical buildings... but Hong Kong's slopes seemed dominated with construction that was intentionally grand — the sort of things built by proud Imperialists, to prove to the locals how powerful they were.

Such demonstrations of grandeur didn't leave a good taste in Alex's mouth — she hadn't been raised to think too much of showing off — and they were received no better by Stephanie.

"Very imposing, aren't they?" the American Lieutenant glanced at Schwabe with that observation, and the MI6 man smiled easily.

"There are a million Chinese on this island, and only 20,000 Europeans. Sometimes people feel the need to... compensate," he replied, then added: "But British rule has been good for this place. Law and order for all — it's a rather new concept for some of these orientals, but we take it seriously."

Schwabe's tone seemed a bit too self-assured — again, Stephanie felt her American values struggling with such notions of racial paternalism. Perhaps deciding his words weren't striking the right tone, the sniper-spy diverted himself to slightly more pertinent matters: "When it comes to those Mandarins I followed here, we don't know precisely what they took, because they killed the men they acquired it from. But if they were looking for that in my city, I expect they might have need of medical supplies from here as well."

Stephanie concurred with that assessment in a single, slow nod, "That's what we concluded."

"Hopefully that narrows down the search? Looks as though there's a lot to sift through, otherwise," Elspeth weighed in at that point, the same investigative instincts that had led her to Rosyth grasping the difficulty of the present circumstances.

The deeper they got into the city, the more homes and structures they saw, and the more people were on the street. Thousands of people, in fact — even Elspeth, who had spent so much of her life in busy London, found herself beginning to feel overwhelmed.

"We'll do our best," Schwabe seemed immune to the bustling city through which he was navigating. As rickshaws and sedan chairs started complicating the streets, he also slowed down.

"Look at these people, walking right out in the middle of the street," Strong rose off his bench in the back of the Land Rover, then braced himself on one of the uprights that would have carried the canvas roof, had it been set up.

Schwabe smiled and glanced up at the Colour's agitation, "Driving here is rather more fluid than you're used to, Sergeant. Human obstacles, instead of natural ones."

That was clear enough. As the truck got in amongst some properly tall buildings near the waterfront, its pace slowed to a scant crawl.

"We'll be a few minutes," Schwabe continued, patiently riding the truck's heavy clutch as he shifted down. "To your point, Lady Cornish, we can try to find places where the Mandarins, or their employers, would have sought drugs, or other disposable supplies. That would mean dispensaries, or a medical warehouse."

Stephanie glanced again at the spy as he spoke, "And you have a man in town who happens to know the likeliest ones to check?"

As his smile broadened, Schwabe geared up to jump into an opening between rickshaws, then continued down the street towards the harbor.

"I know men with certain interests in this city, yes," he said, sounding just a little too coy.

"Good thing such advantages don't make you sound too pleased with yourself," the American answered dryly. "That wouldn't be gentlemanly at all."

Alex had been listening distantly — paying more attention to the city which, despite its familiar sort of layout, had a population literally twenty times greater than St. John's. There were *so many* people...

But Stephanie's jab at Schwabe caught her attention, and she shot a look at her friend. She was prodding the spy an awful lot...

was it suspicion?

The MI6 man simply grinned, "My dear Lieutenant Shylock, if you don't think smug self-satisfaction is a native characteristic of the English gentleman, you mustn't spend enough time with us."

Well volleyed, and Stephanie found herself impressed, "I think I've already had my fill. But duty calls."

Schwabe was a paternalistic English agent of Empire, and few sorts of people would be more alien to the kind of men with whom she'd grown up. And yet his hands, his bearing, and his candor were all quite familiar. Stephanie was beginning to feel as though she knew him from somewhere, but as she turned her eyes back towards the buildings and busy streets of Hong Kong, she couldn't quite figure out where.

In the meantime, of course, there was a city to search.

CHAPTER IV

Even though *Major George Tucker* had made its appearance over Washington, D.C. after sunset, it was too loud to make a secret arrival at the White House. The wounded skycruiser was still functioning despite being down one engine, but without absolute certainty of the reliability of the repairs carried out by human hands, Lord James Devlin had restricted the ship to short hops — like one down the eastern seaboard of the United States.

It had been slower going than the Viscount of the Grasslands was used to, but as Flight Captain Levi Bogoraz put the ailing ship down on the White House lawn, the Newfoundlander patted the Russian expat on the shoulder.

"Thanks, Levi."

"Sir," the severe pilot nodded back, and Devlin turned and made his way off the flight deck.

As he moved silently through the darkened ship, Jimmy had little else to do but wonder at the summons he'd received from the United States President. He didn't know John Nance Garner at all — just that he was a Texan, reputed to be an isolationist, and despite everyone's expectations after the death of FDR, he hadn't immediately hurried out to start a war with anybody.

So much for being a gunslinger.

Why the President wanted to speak in person with Devlin wasn't clear... but Jimmy wasn't going to ignore a call from the White House. To do so would be impolitic, especially considering the Viscount was currently the guardian of all the United States Champion students.

That, in all likelihood, would come up in the conversation.

Reaching the stair that would take him down to the embarkation ramp on the lower deck, Jimmy elected not to think too far ahead about that subject — to wonder if he was about to get into an argument with the leader of the United States. The descent to the embarkation deck, and the ramp, took very little time, and once he arrived one of the technicians standing post nodded before calling up to inform the flight deck.

With a ring to warn the crew, the ramp began to lower.

Warm air started to spill in as soon as the ramp's seal was broken — Jimmy had been to Washington enough times to know that June could be both warm and a bit foggy, and it seemed this evening lived up to the expectation. The night outside sounded quiet, though — not too much noise from passing vehicles, which the Viscount supposed was a sign of the late hour.

George Tucker had put down on the south lawn, and probably had ruined some of the gardening in the process, but that's what Garner had wanted — not to have to drive out to Camp Springs Air Force Base for the meeting.

As the ramp touched the turf of the lawn, Jimmy waited a moment to see if anyone would appear. When no one did, he started down carefully, not sure why he felt the need to be cautious, but feeling that way all the same.

Once his boots touched grass, he stopped to look around. Night had obviously obscured most of the details of his surroundings, but the White House was clearly lit up in the distance, and a few shadowy shapes appeared to be working their way towards him from that vector.

Deciding it best to wait for those shapes under the illumination of *George Tucker's* running lights, Jimmy stayed put for a few more moments and watched as four people strode into closer view.

Two were clearly secret service men — the sorts of agents always wearing suits, and trying to seem unobtrusive while, in fact, being very intrusive. One was a Champion whose coat appeared to be a bluish gray. The last was President John Nance Garner.

Heavily built and white-haired, the Texan had the weathered look of a cattle baron — or something to that effect. As he fell under *George Tucker's* lights, Jimmy noticed his eyes were slits and his face was set in an expression approaching a scowl.

"You're Lord Devlin," he stated as he extended his hand, clearly having recognized the Viscount from photographs.

"Mister President," Jimmy took Garner's hand.

The handshake took a long second, as the Newfoundland Lord

studied the Texas President, and vice versa. Garner was not a young man, and he looked as though he were made of leather, but his firm grip suggested his ambitions were to live much longer.

His purpose in requesting this visit still remained unclear; only one way to find out.

"Come aboard, sir?"

"You boys wait for me," was the President's manner of agreeing, and with that instruction passed back to his escorts — including the Champion, who Jimmy didn't recognize — he put his boots on the ramp.

Garner nodded to the technician at the top as he climbed aboard, then stopped in the massive embarkation chamber as he arrived within. Like a rancher looking over a plot of land, he examined the big space with narrow eyes. Eventually he grunted.

"Never got onto one of ours before they blew," he observed before shaking his head. "How much do these things cost?"

It was perhaps the last question Jimmy Devlin had been expecting, so he scrambled for a second before coming to the answer, "Nothing, sir. They're kindly provided by the Saa, like all our other non-human-built equipment."

Garner grunted again at the answer, "Always wondered what they're getting out of us, for all this generosity."

Perhaps it was a fair question, and Jimmy imagined a diplomatic answer might be appropriate... but somehow, he got the sense the Texan required a firmer hand, "The same thing the Pathan tribes give us when we buy them off: peace and quiet. Maybe allies, if they ever need us."

The President looked from the embarkation bay back to the Viscount, eyes narrower, "So the dragons figure we're a bunch of nasty primitives?"

It was harsh, and Devlin felt his back getting up slightly... but then Garner shook his head and looked away, "Don't bother being offended, Lord Devlin. I'm a common man, you're an aristocrat. If we allow ourselves to get offended at each other, nothing will get done."

His words were gruff, and perhaps demonstrated why he'd long been successful on Capitol Hill. However, they weren't entirely informed.

"My parents were fish merchants, Mister President. My wife was a maid and I was a soldier destined to be killed in wars of Empire. You're more of an aristocrat than I am."

Jimmy didn't mean to sound aggressive, but he was pretty certain he did — his sheer lack of nobility was one of his few points of pride, and the fact that someone as important as the U.S. President didn't know about it was displeasing.

Glancing back to the bay, Garner shook his head, seeming not to be interested in correcting himself, "So we both like fishing. Good. You know why I asked you here?"

"Obviously I don't, because you didn't tell me what you wanted," Jimmy's counter was sharp, and Garner grinned.

"Guess we're getting along," the President answered, then took a couple of steps into the huge bay, looked up and around thoughtfully, and turned back. "You've got our Champion students, and we have nothing. And I'm trying to decide what to do about that."

So he did indeed want to discuss the most obvious subject. Jimmy could handle that.

"They're yours. Just tell us when you want them back," the Viscount answered easily, but Garner shook his head.

"I know that. You're not going to start a war with us just to keep our headache. FDR left some memos on the matter — figured that was going to come up at your little sea summit. He didn't want to give up our hold of all this magical machinery... figured it kept us great."

The President waved at the silver walls around him to emphasize his point, but Jimmy didn't react.

Garner didn't seem to notice the failure to respond: "I never really liked Roosevelt. He was my party, and I'm loyal to my party. He beat me in the nomination, and then asked me on. Having me gave him credibility. Made people think he wouldn't overspend. And then he went in and increased spending on anything to do with your Saa friends, and your Champions, and these machines. Millions of dollars into all of this."

That sounded about right — and as far as Jimmy was concerned, the investment was entirely sensible. While the Saa machines had been given to Britain and the United States for free, using the knowledge provided by the dragons to create home-built weapons, like the upcoming Snapdragon, cost money. Maintaining a strong Champions establishment — with all its supplies and Special Service regiments — was no less expensive.

But taken together, the new machines and the Champions were what set the English-speaking powers apart from the rest of the world. Few investments could be more valuable.

But Garner's logic was different, and he said so: "I'm standing here wondering why we bother."

Jimmy stared at the President. Why *bother?* Of course the Viscount had tried to prepare himself for the possibility that Garner was a true isolationist. But this just seemed too blatant — almost as though it was a test of some kind. He couldn't let it go unexamined.

"So you're an isolationist, just like everyone says," the Newfoundlander put it to the Texan directly. "You're here looking for an ally who will help convince you to back out of the Champions system?"

Garner shook his head immediately, "Not back out. Just turn the bills over to you. The treaty won't change, but I can undo a bunch of the Executive Orders. Your government runs the Champions, keeps them all secure, and you send us our share upon demand."

Share. Upon demand.

"The United States doesn't need to be dragged into whatever foreign wars your Champions are starting. We don't have overseas interests, you do. So you worry about your Empire, and we leave you to it, until we need them."

Just like that. Normally, Jimmy would have assumed such a blatant statement of purpose, coming so early in a discussion of this sort, was misdirection... but everything about Garner's bearing suggested he was actually being direct.

Was he truly trying to get his government out of the Champion business? How *could* he?

Not willing to believe the case, Jimmy tossed back a pointed question: "What will your army think of that?"

"They can go to hell. They're so damned infested with bureaucrats and glory-seekers that I can't trust them. Give them any budget and they'll overspend it, just because they think they're important enough. America doesn't need them... so I'll let you boys deal with the temptation."

Temptation? Trying to maintain an orderly presence in the world, and make the most of the technology provided by the Saa? Even though he should have been focusing on the President's game, those words started to get Jimmy's back up again — the implication that somehow his life's work was just succumbing to *temptation*…

"You don't know me, Devlin," the President took a few steps toward the Newfoundlander, breaking Jimmy out of his thoughts. "I've been in Washington since the turn of the century. I will make the Senate Inquiry say what needs saying, and both Houses will back whatever moves we need. That's why Roosevelt kept me around — because all the men that matter come to my house for a drink and a cigar. That's how business is done. These Champions are an expense we don't need. I'm cutting them out before they get any more Americans killed on home soil… but I want access to them. That's the deal you and me are going to come up with tonight, and that you're going to sell to your governments tomorrow. You understand?"

Jimmy's stare was cool, and he didn't reply. There seemed to be too much wrong with the President's thought process. Apparently, though, silence was all the answer Garner needed. He was a political dealer, perhaps a political *bully*, and for all his abilities and experience, Jimmy Devlin was neither.

"Glad you agree. And hell, maybe I'll come up to visit when they're settled. You and me can go fishing," the President smirked, then he turned back to the embarkation chamber, shaking his head at the size of the compartment.

Staring at the Texan's back, Jimmy Devlin found his mind churning. When Alain Lapointe had first suggested that all the Champions be permanently situated in Newfoundland, Jimmy had been most reluctant. Months later, as the American students settled in and some even prepared to graduate, his discomfort with their presence had waned.

And perhaps, if Garner was the ultimate decision maker who would dictate what those young Champions were to do with their lives, they would be better off outside his hands. If — if — the whole scheme could be arranged without setting up the preconditions for some sort of war between Britain and the United States… because whether the President wanted to admit it or not, the children of the savages were his nation's biggest strategic asset.

Putting them under the control of another state was foolhardy and could end in total disaster. Didn't he realize that?

Of course he must have, and yet he didn't seem to care. And at some point, the Viscount of the Grasslands had to stop thinking in terms of what his opposite *should* do... and explore the options if he decided to carry forward with his mad plan.

Folding his arms at that thought, Jimmy Devlin addressed the President, "If you want the deal, we're going to have to work out some very delicate details. I'll have terms."

Garner wheeled immediately, a grin on his face, "Well if you didn't, you'd have been the wrong man to call. Let's find a place to sit down and drink."

CHAPTER V

Stephanie wasn't certain if they'd crossed into the seedier side of Hong Kong, or if she was just misinterpreting the number of suspicious looks she was getting. As Schwabe stopped the Land Rover in front of a tall building that loomed over the narrow, people-packed street, everyone nearby — all of them Chinese — seemed to be staring.

For his part, Schwabe was unaffected by the attention, and as he opened his door and hopped out, he reinforced his easy demeanor with words: "A few people should stay with the vehicle. No one around here would try to steal it, of course, but keep an eye for lookouts. If we're noticed, we should know about it."

Seemed somewhat prudent, but glancing at Alex, Stephanie wasn't sure she wanted the job. Her friend seemed entirely in tune with her thoughts: "You keep an eye on him. Elspeth, the Colour and I will stay here."

"Yes, I prefer to remain seated," Strong added helpfully, drawing him a look from Elspeth, which ended in a very slight smile.

Nodding simply, Stephanie then hopped out of the truck, calling after the spy: "Wait up."

Schwabe was stepping off the street and over to a small, unmarked door. He didn't look back at the words, just replied, "Should be no trouble here, but I'll be most obliged if you watch my back."

He sounded a little pleased at the company, and Stephanie supposed she could understand why — no matter how good any one person might be with a pistol, he or she would invariably be better off when help was close at hand.

That in mind, Stephanie reached down to the holster on her belt and made certain the flap wasn't tied down. British Imperial Army holsters were by no means designed for quick-draw — not at all like the ones her godfather wore to great effect on the new world — but she could fish out her Browning swiftly enough if necessary.

Perhaps Schwabe would be right, and there'd be no need for shooting here. Wherever here was…

Coming up behind the gray-suited man, the American kept her eyes mostly on the street, and the Chinese people passing by. Their gazes continued to be suspicious, but she figured she could draw no conclusions from that. She was a white girl in the middle of a very not-white part of town… and worse, she was clearly in uniform. People similarly dressed probably tended to bring trouble when they ventured into such areas, so wary glances seemed entirely fair.

Hearing Schwabe's knock, Stephanie glanced towards him, then saw the door open a crack. She looked back to the street as the MI6 man exchanged some pleasantries with whoever stood behind it, and then he summoned her, "Lieutenant, join me?"

With the invitation, Stephanie turned a final time and followed Schwabe through the narrow door into a badly-lit small room. Quickly scanning the space, she looked for doors and windows, as well as any areas that might have concealed dangers. This was all instinctive, of course — another legacy of her upbringing — but as a small Chinese lady led them deeper inside, she realized there wasn't much to see.

It was just a large room with a few folding chairs opened up around a card table, and precious little else in terms of furniture. The air smelled of pipe smoke, and there was a single door leading further back into the building… but as she glanced through it, Stephanie didn't get the sense that there was much more back there.

"This is just a place for chaps like me to sit about between our endeavors," Schwabe turned back to her with that explanation. "Here to see a man with certain interests in this town."

Spies — especially British ones — surely did delight in finding ways of explaining their work without actually saying anything concrete. Stephanie had always found George Devlin's insistence that he worked in 'hospitality' a little charming, but these guys took it to another level.

"It's an *interesting* place," she offered a mildly clever reply, and Schwabe nodded.

"We like to think so."

As he said it, a man in a cream-colored linen suit emerged from the deeper room. He was larger — about the same age as Schwabe, but puffier and with a mustache and beard that were a bit too dramatic for modern fashion.

"Schwabe, dear fellow, back so soon?" the man in linen asked that of his colleague, but his eyes had locked onto Stephanie almost immediately. She got the sense he was choosing his words because of her presence.

"It's alright, Grovner, she's Lieutenant Shylock."

"I bloody recognized her, wasn't sure if she had you here under duress," the man replied immediately. "I suppose you're looking for some local insights about that ship?"

Schwabe nodded, and pressed straight on, "You said it arrived in April."

"And did a good job of being uninteresting. No one would have imagined it was *Trevanyon*," the linen man — who Stephanie gathered was called Grovner — replied. "I figured it for criminal, but not so interesting as all that. Good job you went aboard for a look."

"Yes," Schwabe replied, then tilted his head. "So if they did transport Lord Duncan here in that ship, and the men I followed from Shanghai were connected to it, and the men I was following were indeed trafficking in medical machinery…"

He let the words taper off right in the middle of his apparent point, but Grovner didn't need any help to follow the line of thought, "I looked into the local medical equipment and machinery situation. There's been nothing unusual at the hospitals, but one of the warehouses has been sending special deliveries of morphia and laudanum up to the peak. Nothing so grand as to warrant police attention… but knowing what we do now, rather doubt it's some poor man nursing an old war wound, or a filthy habit."

Stephanie's brow began to crease as she listened to Grovner's information, and as Schwabe nodded, she took a step forward with a slightly-pointed question, "You just happened to be looking into this?"

Grovner's eyes shifted back to the American Lieutenant, and he looked rather amused, "I did just happen to be, Lieutenant. Convenient, wouldn't you say?"

"I came to town after criminals trading in medical equipment, so of course I asked Grovner here what that was about," Schwabe added helpfully, as he turned partway back towards Stephanie.

Narrowing her eyes, the American folded her arms, "I see. How silly of me."

"No need to be rough on yourself," Grovner's reply came with a smile that stuck her as being just short of condescending. He was lucky it didn't cross the line, but he didn't pay any heed to the danger he'd nearly put himself in as he pressed on: "It's a house owned by a German count, who supposedly came here to spend his final years. They've put up a good story around it, of course — he's presented as a man who did business here a few decades ago... long enough that none of the people he'd have known would be left to visit him. And they've spread a whiff of scandal around him. Some have even suggested he might be secretly a Jew."

With those words, the linen-clad spy turned for the doorway that led deeper into the building and waved for Schwabe and Stephanie to follow.

"Has anyone actually seen him?" the gray-suited spy asked as they moved.

"None that I've spoken to, but I haven't had enough time to be able to say for certain. I do know the house, though. And the woman living across the street — a very delightful French spinster, with some questionable morals to which I may have, on occasion, been subjected — tells me there are nurses in and out of there every day."

Grovner fell silent after those words, leading his guests to another card table surrounded by folding chairs — but this one wasn't empty. A few photographs, a sketched map, and a couple of pages of notes lay there, which Schwabe began to consider carefully.

"Nurses, indeed?" the Shanghai sniper asked, and Grovner nodded.

"Mostly white women, seeming to trade shifts fairly regularly. My dear French lady never saw the same one more than a handful of times," Grovner confirmed. "I interrogated her thoroughly, to be sure."

Schwabe looked up at the cheeky remark, then glanced back at Stephanie — as if concerned that she was too delicate for such implications.

Recognizing the kind paternalism, she set out to correct him, "Don't worry, I'm not jealous. I can seduce Grovner any time I want to."

The advantage of being red-faced by nature was that Grovner

couldn't blush — or at least not visibly in the bad lighting of the room. With a grin, Schwabe looked back to the table, "Dear me."

"Quite," the linen-clad man concurred.

Stephanie stepped up to the table while the two spies displayed their stereotypical Englishness, her eyes falling on the map in particular. It appeared to mark each of the houses on 'the peak' — apparently the neighborhood that stood highest on the slopes of the mountain around which Hong Kong was built.

"The wealthy Europeans live up there," Grovner offered some contextual narration. "There are fewer than 100 homes, so it's hardly a good place to keep a low profile."

"Hence the cover about the German count, who might secretly be a Jew," Schwabe nodded, glancing at the American Lieutenant. "Good excuse for no one to visit, and for nurses, and for him never to be seen…"

"What, because he's a Jew?" Stephanie asked pointedly, her eyes not leaving the map as she tried to get her bearings.

With a smile, Schwabe glanced back to Grovner, "She tried to punch out a Nazi when he came to St. John's last August. Apparently it was a sight to see."

For a second, the American Lieutenant didn't process that comment; she was trying to make sense of the peak, which seemed a very overtly imperialist part of the city. When the words sank in, though, her frown deepened and she straightened up, turning her sharp eyes on Schwabe, "Repeat the thing you just said, explaining each part."

The spy from Shanghai raised an eyebrow, "The Nazi boy, speaking in the pub. You dragged poor Mister Devlin along, and nearly started a fistfight."

Stephanie remembered, of course — it had happened just before she'd gotten her commission, and Emily had appeared. But how did Schwabe know — was it by some connection that she should have recognized? Was it why she felt he was familiar?

She folded her arms and confronted his knowing smile, "Stop looking pleased with yourself and explain how you know about that."

There was no mistaking the authority of her demand, and Grovner chortled happily, "Dear me, the women of the new generation are going to be a handful."

Schwabe ignored his counterpart as he considered his answer,

"Of course your hospitality man reported it. We've been keeping an eye on the Nazis for some time."

"Nazi?" Stephanie wasn't sure she'd heard the word, which was forgivable.

"The latest name for Drexler's crowd... well, now it's Hitler's. Stands for National Socialists," Schwabe added helpfully.

Fair enough. It was probably a good thing that MI6 was keeping some tabs on the racists who were doing their best to undermine the German Empire, but whether it was right for George to have reported on her near-altercation with that particular boy... well, she supposed that was fair enough, too. Just the sort of thing that could make her rather grumpy — like Alex jumping out of a skycruiser into the North Atlantic without mentioning it first.

"How much else do you know about me?" she put the question to Schwabe directly, and the spy shrugged.

"Enough to be glad you'll be here if I find trouble. And don't worry, my dear: you know as much about me. You just don't realize it yet."

That was altogether too clever, so she narrowed her eyes even further, "Well if that's the case, I suspect I'll wish I didn't."

Smile growing, Schwabe nodded towards her, "How can you see when your eyes are so narrow?"

"Practice," her answer was immediate, and flat. She left it there, and sounding as unimpressed as she did, both Schwabe and Grovner caught a chill from her words.

"I daresay you best stop teasing the child, Schwabe. She's libel to shoot you," the linen-suited agent suggested after a moment. "At the very least don't let's have that happen here."

Schwabe tilted his head and then nodded at the suggestion, "Perhaps a trip to the peak, then. Lieutenant Shylock?"

As much as she'd have liked to continue her efforts to scold the older gentleman, the more pressing matter of Lord Duncan denied her the chance. Letting her hands fall to her sides and turning back to the card table, she let out a sigh.

"We'll revisit this discussion," she promised, then questioned: "Should we go direct, or summon help?"

Grovner had the answer to that: "I'll get word to your headquarters, but I'd suggest you go direct. Were it me, my dear, I'd have started clearing my operation the minute I heard a skycruiser over the city. You still might be in time to catch them... but only just."

Stephanie looked up at the man, then glanced back to Schwabe. The Shanghai Briton agreed with a nod, "Let's be about it."

He said it with the sort of assuredness that reflected confidence in difficult situations... a confidence Stephanie herself was starting to possess, by simple virtue of near-death-experiences. Hopefully it wasn't unfounded.

They'd find out soon.

CHAPTER VI

"How old is this thing?"

Alex settled down into one of the tram's padded seats as she asked the question, and as she lowered herself into a matching chair across the aisle from her friend, Stephanie frowned and shook her head, "I don't know."

"I think at least fifty years," Schwabe was sitting in the seat in front of the Lieutenant, and he provided that information helpfully.

It was terribly comforting.

Taking the seat in front of Alex, Mike Strong had slung his Thompson and was fiddling with a pamphlet, "Says here she opened back in '88. Thing's older than me... and will take us almost a mile up the side of the mountain... elevation of over 1,000 feet... in *eight* minutes."

He actually sounded impressed. Looking across the aisle at each other, neither Stephanie nor Alex felt quite the same. Surely the tram seemed to be well built, and the upholstery on the seats and the fresh coat of gray-blue paint were fine... but the mountain was steep, and this geriatric piece of kit was supposed to fly up it?

"I'm sure it's safe," Elspeth offered her own assessment as she moved over to the seat directly beside Strong and settled down. "Just hope we don't have to get out and push."

"Right," Alex agreed, then decided to put one boot up against the opposite seat, just for an extra point of contact in case the tram started to tumble.

It didn't. Instead, after a moment of waiting, the operator moved into his control cabin and activated the electrically-powered car. With a call of warning, he set off... and suddenly they were all moving fiercely upward.

"Very steep here, if you're not ready for it," Schwabe called out the gentle warning, but Alex shot him a look.

"From *Newfoundland*, remember."

Schwabe had never been to the island, so he shrugged, "This steep?"

"This steep and covered in ice," Strong didn't lift his eyes from his pamphlet as he rallied to the defense of his homeland.

Because, as a Newfoundlander, he considered announcing the occasional treacherousness of his home to be equivalent with defending it...

"Fair enough. Just enjoy the view," Schwabe nodded towards the windows, and almost as soon as he spoke, the tram climbed far enough up the slope to clear the trees. Bathed in the light of a sinking sun, and with its mighty harbor glistening, Hong Kong appeared before everyone's eyes. It was more than a little breathtaking.

Schwabe smiled as even Strong looked up, then put a fair question to the newcomers: "Have you ever seen a view this magnificent?"

He should have known better than to ask the silly question.

"Signal Hill," Strong's response was immediate.

"And it's cooler up there," Alex added.

Stephanie's breath actually was a little caught — Hong Kong was amazing, and though her years at school in Newfoundland had done much to familiarize her with the sea, the Pacific and its glistening bright waters were a bit mesmerizing for a girl from the landlocked Pacifica Territory.

"Don't mind them," she said after a moment. "It's pretty."

"High praise," Schwabe smiled approvingly, and then fell silent — it had been ages since he'd seen the city himself, so there was no harm in taking it in.

Grudgingly, Alex did the same... until she detected something out of the corner of her eye. Head sharply turning to the left, she looked out one of the tram's windows and almost saw a blur... but didn't. She blinked a couple of times, then planted her hands on either side of the seat so she could twist around and check other directions...

There was nothing.

A frown descended over her brow, and Stephanie matched the expression as soon as she noticed her friend's sudden distraction. Shooting a glance across the aisle, she wordlessly asked the question: *problem?*

For a second Alex didn't respond; then she shook her head very slightly, as if casting off the feeling. Something unusual... but she didn't know what. Instinctively, then, she reached down and began unbuttoning her coat, to improve access to her holster.

Recognizing the significance of that movement, Stephanie checked to ensure her own Browning was accessible too. It seemed too beautiful a place for danger, but beauty obviously couldn't preclude lethality — in places or in people. If it could, Stephanie Shylock couldn't have existed to begin with.

As clues went, the German count's house came with a good one: it looked like it had been ransacked.

Schwabe knocked first, then tried the knob. When the door swung immediately open he stood back, Stephanie and Alex ready just behind him in case he needed support. But all was quiet, and after ducking his head quickly inside to see whether he'd be interrupting some German aristocrat's tea — or some Jew's escape from persecution — he quickly found signs that neither man existed.

With a nod towards the door, he produced a pistol — a Colt 1911 — from under his suit jacket, and pushed inside. No fear from the British spy, which Stephanie supposed made a certain kind of sense... though had he experienced gas in Scotland he'd probably have been more cautious.

The American Lieutenant drew her own pistol, then glanced back to her Champion friend and they conferred wordlessly. Alex was fishing out her Browning too, and then with a frown she nodded — her silent way of saying there was nothing else for them to do but follow. She turned to Strong and Elspeth, a few yards back on the lawn of the house, and waved for them to join them.

Fair enough; everyone in to search the ransacked house. Without further delay, Stephanie led her friends inside, to follow the spy on his investigation.

The American held her Browning close to her body — a shooting technique found in books like *Shooting To Live*, which was almost identical to the common-sense gunhandling Cameron Kard had taught her. Quite simply, by holding a pistol close she could make it more difficult for some unseen foe to disarm her as she moved into close quarters. Though the house seemed abandoned, she wasn't about to risk such an altercation.

After the brightness of the Hong Kong afternoon, the darkness of the foyer was tough to adjust to. Visibility improved as she led the way into a living room with large windows. The chaos that had been wrought inside was obvious — furniture turned over, all manner of discarded items covering the floor. Ransacked indeed.

"Looks like someone left in a hurry," Alex observed in a whisper.

Strong and Elspeth entered just as she spoke, the Colour looking down the sights of his Thompson as he cautiously crossed the living room. With just a quick glance back, Stephanie could see his primary concern was gas; he was holding his breath.

But there was no gas — at least none that she could detect. The air tasted bad, and there were some unsettling smells, but there was no coughing. And given the state of the place, it seemed unlikely anyone would have had time to set a gas trap.

Seeming to reach that same conclusion, the Sergeant moved further inside, Elspeth coming on his heels, and together the quartet scanned the mess in the living room. It wasn't clear whether someone had been searching for something, or just seeking to create havoc, but as they took in the signs of chaos, both Alex and Stephanie noticed that Schwabe had disappeared deeper into the house. Though he was no Champion — and indeed, no youngster — he still moved spryly and silently.

The house was just one floor; grandly decorated and posh, but not so big as to make it impossible to figure out where he'd gone. Catching Stephanie's gaze, Alex nodded towards a hallway that branched off from the living room, then took steps in that direction.

Looking back to Strong before she followed, the American Lieutenant waved to indicate he should go through a separate doorway on the far side of the living room. Though he didn't necessarily like the idea of being in a different wing of the house from his girls, he nodded. Silently, he and Elspeth set off that way, while Stephanie followed her best friend.

Alex had waited silently at the beginning of the hallway, and as the American arrived beside her, the whitecoat nodded ahead. The hall was a dozen yards long and littered with more overturned pieces of furniture... perhaps shelves that had stood along the walls. Schwabe was already at the far end, advancing towards a partly-open door that was letting in a great deal of light. The house backed onto the view of Hong Kong harbor, and whatever room the MI6 man was approaching appeared to be positioned to enjoy that grand vista.

Glancing back to see where his support was, Schwabe seemed glad that Alex and Stephanie were at the end of the corridor. He nodded to them once, then leaned back against the corridor wall and reached out with his free hand to push open the door. His pistol was perfectly-poised as he did this, and Stephanie noticed again his textbook technique. She supposed it made sense for a spy to know how to handle a pistol in tight confines, but it looked as though Schwabe came from the same pedigree as her own godfather. Perhaps he'd just read the Fairbairn-Sykes book — *Shooting To Live*, which she kept recalling — and taken it to heart.

But that was obviously irrelevant. No one but Stephanie was interested in the details of shooting, so she forced her mind to focus on more immediate concerns as the spy from Shanghai stepped through the doorway in a shooting crouch.

She watched him sweep one way, then the other... then straighten up and shake his head.

"Dammit," he said, looking back out the door to the waiting young ladies. "Best you have a look for yourselves."

His tone was flat, and none too encouraging, but without hesitation both Stephanie and Alex moved down the corridor, pistols at their sides as they watched their footing to avoid the mess. It was the Lady in white who reached the door first and went through. Her immediate reaction gave Stephanie some forewarning.

"Yikes."

It was perhaps too light a word for the sight, but Stephanie couldn't improve on the reaction. They found themselves in a large bedroom with grand windows overlooking Hong Kong. Like the rest of the house it had been trashed, but what remained was telling: a large bed with a metal frame, from which handcuffs and ankle shackles dangled. The sheets were a stained mess, and scattered across the floor were bandages with spots of blood on them, amongst other wrappers, vials, and assorted papers.

"We'll have to get a team up here to sift through all this, but I suspect we can all interpret the purpose of this place," Schwabe remarked dryly.

Alex was already assessing the sight, "Those cuffs wouldn't be enough to hold him if he struggled, unless he was still very badly injured... or unless he was gassed."

"Maybe they had a mask on him," Stephanie suggested in agreement. "Keep the mask with the gas flowing, so he doesn't struggle... then keep him here while he recovers."

It was a grim picture for both girls, and as Strong and Elspeth emerged into the room with nothing to report from the other sections of the house, they both were taken aback by the sight.

"Jesus," the Colour muttered. "Wholesome sort of place."

"Suppose this was what they had in mind for me," Elspeth's follow-up remark sounded much more dire, though it actually took a second for her — and everyone — to fully comprehend the implications of her words. Had she been chained to this bed, and rendered indefensible by gas... as soon as those pictures flowed into the browncoat's mind, she swallowed uncomfortably. "I'm going to wait out... somewhere."

She turned from the room and its gruesome implications, then departed in a blur. It was understandable, and Stephanie sighed deeply — a mistake, because the air had a musky scent that was none too enjoyable — and shook her head.

"That probably wasn't the most sensitive way for her to see this," the American observed.

"No," Alex agreed, then glanced at Strong. "Maybe go see that she's alright? We'll... look around. Which won't be at all creepy."

Strong looked out the door, then back to his girls, "Yell if you need me."

He departed slowly, watching his step as he slung his Thompson over his shoulder. Alex and Stephanie watched him leave, then turned their gazes back towards the bed, as Schwabe picked his way nearer to it.

"I fear Lady Cornish's instincts mightn't be wrong," the spy said. "I daresay a woman caught in a place like this... well, it would have been terrible for her."

The implication was clearly that she would have been raped, and unfortunately it was probably quite correct. Duncan had been fortunate in that sense... though that made the visuals no less unpleasant. With another glance at each other, Alex and Stephanie decided not to get too absorbed by their disgust, and instead began looking for clues.

Where had Duncan been taken, and how long ago had he been carried away?

CHAPTER VII

The sun was beginning to set as Major Mitsui and two sections from the assault company combed the abandoned house. Their efforts were just one element in a rapidly escalating search.

Because there was no longer any doubt that Duncan had been held on the island, and that the investigators searching for him had been detected, stealth was of no benefit to anyone. Hong Kong's Governor had thus ordered the port shut for twenty-four hours, and put his entire police force at Lord Grey's disposal — hopefully enough resources to track down the lost Champion, or his captors, or even just their Mandarin-speaking allies.

While the city was put under scrutiny, investigations on the peak had to move quickly. To that end, Schwabe and Stephanie were canvassing the local residences for any witnesses, while Alex liaised with Mitsui. Only Strong was left on the lawn of the abandoned house, and standing not far from him was Lady Cornish.

The former Champion of London was silently staring at the façade of the building that would have been her prison, and either consciously or not she'd folded her arms tight against herself — again looking as if she was cold, even though it was much warmer at the peak than it had been on the drizzly tarmac at Torbay Airport.

Strong recognized the expression she wore well enough; she was visualizing where she'd been, and how much worse it might have been had she, instead of Duncan, been taken to this house. There was no avoiding such thoughts — at least not in Strong's experience. It was natural for a person who'd been close to disaster to wonder how things might have gone, had luck flowed in a different direction. After their battle with Emily, both Alex and Stephanie had been haunted by such questions; now it was Elspeth's turn.

And it wasn't pretty. The prospect of being chained to a bed, drugged, treated like a science experiment... at best... there was no dignity in such an end. At least being shot down doing one's duty bore a certain kind of nobility.

Strong thought it was noble, anyway, because he had to believe the 700 men who'd died all around him one day in 1920 had done so with dignity. He needed to hold to that, no matter what.

Kidnapped, trapped, chained... no. So as far as the Colour was concerned, Elspeth had ample reason to be preoccupied, even haunted. The question was how long such anxious thoughts would grip her. There was only one way to find out, so he adjusted his grip on his Thompson and advanced silently towards the Lady in the unassuming brown coat.

She heard him coming, and he detected a slight sideways glance as he stopped alongside her, "How's Lady Cornish this fine evening?"

He didn't see the very unexpected hint of a smile turn up the corners of her mouth — just for a second — but her answer surprised him anyway, "Well I'm better now that you're not ignoring me, Colour."

It probably wasn't her best-ever attempt at a pretend-flirt, but it was still pretty good. Taking the invitation to don his trusted charming persona, Strong grinned, "Waiting for sunset. If you ever want to charm someone, wait 'til sunset."

"As if you need the sun on your side," she glanced at him more directly, and he noticed her smile... saw that it was fighting against a heaviness in her eyes.

She then looked back to the house, and spoke more candidly than he was ready for: "By now they'd have raped me enough times that I'd have to be pregnant. After that, they could have spirited me off somewhere."

Mike Strong was obviously a man of the world, but there were certain things he didn't expect to hear. Now his humor faded and he hedged badly, "Who says they'd do that?"

"Chains on a bed, Colour? I'm not as worldly as I pretend to be, but I'm not naïve either."

There was literally nothing Strong could offer by way of argument; there were few visuals quite so striking as the chains on a bed. In Duncan's case, they'd clearly been meant to restrain a wounded Champion while he recovered, but for a Lady savage-born, it would have been different.

"That's not what really upsets me, though," Elspeth interrupted his thoughts abruptly, and he looked at her again as she blinked a couple of times. "You know, I still can't get over the fact that I'm here with you, and not my men. These people killed all my men to take me, and get me here so they could do... whatever they wanted with me. But Bob got away far enough to get help, and then you and Stephanie and Alex found me..."

Guilt. Gratitude. It was difficult for good people to comprehend why they'd been spared, particularly if those they cared about had suffered to give them the chance. Strong knew well how persistent those feelings could be.

"You're worth all that," he offered quietly, but firmly, and Elspeth smiled and blinked a couple of times more, unfolding her arms so she could stop a tear from sliding down her cheek.

"I don't know about that. Getting overwrought about *surviving* is a bit stupid."

"You're bawling like a spoiled school girl," Strong agreed somberly. "I didn't really want to say it, but you should be ashamed."

He looked at her as he spoke and she met his glance with a smile full of sadness, "Don't worry, Colour, I'm just as ashamed as you are."

Strong stared at her for a minute; though no Champion other than Alex knew her birthday, Lady Cornish couldn't be a day over twenty-six. She just seemed so much older. He hadn't known her before Scotland — didn't know if her more common upbringing had given her a deeper maturity than many of her fellows — but she seemed to have an understanding of her own pain... and perhaps his too.

Whether she was conscious of that or not, it was impressive.

"You know how you're going to get past all this?" the Colour's next question was serious.

Elspeth stared at him distantly for a second, her smile draining away and her eyes going a little wider, as if she was remembering each of the men she'd led to their deaths in Scotland. Then she blinked, and her sad smile resumed.

"I'm reliably informed that I just need to test my decisions by one question, Colour," she refocused on Strong.

Then she fell silent, waiting expectantly... but he said nothing — kept staring at her. It didn't take long for that to get awkward, so she prodded him again.

"One question," she repeated more firmly — her common London accent sharpening.

He kept staring at her. No answer.

"Oh Colour, you don't usually leave a girl wanting," she tried flirting again, then reached out and put a hand on his shoulder to give him a shake. *What would Mike Strong do?*"

"What?" he asked, then blinked as his poor brain put it all together. She'd said she'd be governed by one question... and because she was being playful, she picked his catchphrase. Which wasn't the right question at all, if he was serious — because perhaps he didn't know quite as much about putting past losses behind him as he liked to pretend...

But that wasn't something to say to Lady Cornish, so with a quick blink and a rush of thoughts, he recovered: "I just wanted to hear you say it. Say it *slower* next time."

Smile growing just a little, Elspeth let him off the hook, then looked away from the house, "I will. Now let's go find the spy. I want to know what they did to Duncan."

Having been educated from a young age in the practices of survival, Stephanie Shylock knew better than to get between a predator and her prey. With her canvassing done, she was standing a dozen yards away from the front door of the house opposite the one Duncan had been held in... and that was as close as she was going to get.

A predatory cat was standing on the step, smiling toothily at Mister Schwabe... and there was no chance the American Lieutenant would try to get between that French woman and her meal.

"Oh God, she's like a cougar ready to pounce."

Alex arrived in a blur with that whispered observation, and Stephanie blinked, then looked at her friend, "Cougars go after the young. Keep your voice down so she doesn't notice us."

"As long as I can run faster than the person I'm with, I'm safe," the whitecoat replied, folding her arms.

That earned her a glare, and then Stephanie nodded back towards the abandoned house, "How is it in there?"

The gentle humor ended, and Alex shook her head, "The fireplace is full of warm ashes. Mitsui and Grey are hopeful they failed to burn something, as they did on *Trevanyon*, but it'll take days to find it. We're better off looking for the Mandarin-speakers."

Stephanie let out a quick sigh at that prospect, but then nodded, "I suppose with the whole police force helping..."

"There are a million people here. It's still a needle in a haystack," Alex didn't sound optimistic, and with a tip of her head, the American decided to be equally realistic.

"Well hopefully the cougar knows something useful."

As both girls turned their attention back towards the front door of the French woman's house, they found that Schwabe had managed a half-step back. He seemed to be holding his own, but even from a dozen yards away, the smell of perfume was obvious to the younger Lady Smith... and the longer the door stayed open, the more detectable it became to Stephanie as well. Having grown up in the clean airs of the new world, she found her eyes becoming agitated, so she looked away. That didn't help much, but at least it gave her the chance to look out at Hong Kong harbor. The port was dramatically lit by the setting sun, making all the tiny ships seem extra impressive and the warships easy to pick out.

"Looks like the Royal Navy's on the job," she pointed out towards the vista, and with a quick frown Alex followed the gesture.

"That's *Exeter*," the whitecoat observed immediately, referring to the large, elegant cruiser that was steaming across the harbor.

A frown settled on Stephanie's brow, "You can read the name from here?"

Champion sight was good, but there were limits. Making an 'of course not' face, Alex therefore shook her head, "No, it's just *obvious*. Only two 8-inch cruisers in the Royal Navy with three turrets, and *York* has different funnels. Come on."

"Let's not even try to pretend you're the normal one in this part of the conversation," Stephanie wasn't too charitable — unlike the Lady in white, the American Lieutenant found no special romance in the warships of the Royal Navy. She certainly wouldn't climb up on an icy rock to watch them approach Newfoundland...

"What's really impressive is that I can tell you those two destroyers..." Alex pointed to two smaller ships that were working at opposite sides of the harbor "...are *Encounter* and *Electra*."

She sounded impressed with herself — one of the small sorts of victories that could distract her even in the midst of all this mess —

and Stephanie's eyes narrowed before she replied: "Just to be clear, I'm not going to ask how you know."

Alex raised an eyebrow, "That's fine."

Stephanie nodded, "Good."

"Excellent."

A quiet standoff ensued, as they both watched the three warships that had been lying in Hong Kong's port do their best to prevent vessels leaving unexamined. With the number of small Chinese craft that frequented the port, it was impossible for *Exeter's* Captain Beckett to stop everything that floated... but any vessel that looked like it *might* be capable of smuggling away Duncan would be checked out.

"It isn't impenetrable, but hopefully they weren't ready to run a blockade," Stephanie observed eventually.

Alex began to nod... then her Champion ears picked up something that made her wince.

As ever, Stephanie seemed to instinctively know when her friend heard such unpleasantness, and she prodded for particulars, "The conversation just got very... *French?*"

"She seems to think all the different nurses who were going into that house *weren't* nurses. Or at least they weren't limited to nursing duties."

Stephanie frowned, trying for a few seconds to figure why that would make her friend wince... it was pretty obvious, but sometimes the American could be blissfully naïve.

Alex didn't let the confusion persist, "She says the way they walked out was... well, she's implying that Mister Schwabe might... well, she knows what causes that kind of walk..."

It took Stephanie another second, but then her reaction was instant — like she'd bitten into something awful, "Oh God, she's talking about intimate relations. She's too old to talk about that. Stop it."

"I'm not the one saying it to begin with," Alex held up her hands defensively... then she heard something else and her face screwed up too. "That's not okay. Why is everyone so... *worldly?* It's offensive."

Stephanie considered herself rather worldly in many ways — not quite so well-behaved as her dear friend — but there were limits to who should speak of certain things. Geriatric French ladies needed to give it a rest. Please.

"What's causing the faces?" Elspeth appeared beside them abruptly, Strong trailing behind at a more ordinary pace.

Turning away from the house and the view, Alex waved in the direction of the French woman's door, and the predator looming over Schwabe, "Madame there thinks the nurses visiting the house weren't *just* nurses. You know."

The implication wasn't immediately clear to Elspeth either, but after a few seconds of tuning in with her own Champion hearing, she caught on. The French lady had a very colorful vocabulary, probably built on experience. Lady Cornish had done enough time in London to not find such pastimes among her elders quite so unthinkable... but given the visuals of chains on the bed, she couldn't help but respond with a grimace of her own.

"Feels like the sort of place where... things like that could happen," she observed darkly, doing her best not to picture nurses being subjected to the bed and its chains. Unfortunately, the mental images were too pungent for her to ignore, and her gaze grew distant as she grappled with them.

Strong arrived in time to pass a glance to Alex and then Stephanie — one suggesting they just give the browncoat a chance to clear her own head, just as they'd grant the Colour space if he was possessed by a mood. The whitecoat and the Lieutenant silently agreed to his proposal, and remained quiet until Elspeth took a few extra breaths and got her mind back on course.

"Hard to see those chains on the bed, you know," she tried to dismiss her discomfort with a wave of her hand. "They might have been for me. You three came to save me after my friends died. Otherwise I might have been in there, getting raped."

The last word was harsh to Alex and Stephanie both — as it should have been. All joking about an amorous French woman aside, there could have been true injustice committed in that house, had Duncan not been fortunate in his gender.

After all, wouldn't any force capable of capturing a Champion want the opportunity to raise one all their own? Elspeth might have become the captive dam for a group of children who, within twenty years, could become the first genuine threat to the established Champions of the British Empire and United States. It seemed highly unlikely that the men who had taken her would have passed up such a chance.

With a heavy sigh, Stephanie looked back towards the harbor, and was glad at least that Duncan's chromosomes made him immune to such... mistreatment...

Her mind stopped that line of thinking as soon as she realized how incorrect it was. She felt her eyes going wider, and she looked immediately to Alex. The whitecoat's eyes had gone wide too, and they looked at each other for a second, before turning back towards Elspeth and Strong.

The Sergeant's expression revealed his thoughts were similar; only Lady Cornish was too distracted to have made the same leap of reasoning.

"But..." Alex began, and Strong nodded.

"They could have done the same to him."

Elspeth didn't tune in immediately, but Stephanie's eyes shifted to the French woman again, and she elaborated, "Different nurses, every day..."

"With a male Champion, they could... God, *sire* dozens of children at once," Strong concluded. "Just get ordinary women to volunteer to carry them, and... oh God."

Women, of course, were not alone in their ability to be exploited for their sex.

Elspeth blinked a few times as she pulled herself back into the conversation, and as the words of her three rescuers processed she felt her face going taut.

"But if... if he was drugged he might not have realized. And he could be father of dozens..."

"There could be dozens of mothers who are too early to be showing," Alex was already moving on to the more immediate problem, and she looked to Stephanie as she thought out loud. "We're busy trying to stop them from getting Duncan out of the city, but what about the... the *nurses*?"

Stephanie felt her stomach drop as she turned back towards the harbor, and the warships gliding elegantly through its waters. They'd never be able to stop every young woman seeking to leave the island... some would already have to be gone.

This was a new crisis — a bigger, entirely more dangerous one, and as Stephanie's mind reeled Alex turned to the harbor as well, then shook her head, "He was chained to that bed, and made the father of a whole brood of Champions who we may not see... until they're coming after us."

Perhaps they were assuming too much, but it all made such dreadful sense that Stephanie couldn't deny it. The villains behind this were merciless, and had to be found. But how?

CHAPTER VIII

Staying up from dusk to dawn was something Jimmy Devlin had become accustomed to during his years commanding soldiers and Champions, but this particular long night was made more trying than most largely because of the company — and the subject. Clutching another cup of coffee, he stood on the opposite side of one of *George Tucker's* dining room tables from the President of the United States.

"One regiment for garrison, one for operations," the American repeated as he puffed again on a foul-smelling cigar. "We'll pay to install the base and deliver the equipment. We pay the salaries. You pay *all* operational costs."

It still felt wrong to the Viscount of the Grasslands to be haggling with a politician over that man's *own* Champion establishment... but such was the surreal nature of the night.

How little could the United States spend, while still being seen as a full partner and participant in the hunt for culprits after the destruction at Eustice, and the sinking of *Hood*? Presently, they were down to a single regiment of infantry guarding a United States military base somewhere around St. John's, and one to supply lances to work with their Champions. In return for that modest investment, the American Champions would be able to operate from Newfoundland, and their students would be educated at the Lady Emily Academy; all the costs of upkeep, maintenance and training would be shouldered by the British Empire.

Shaking his head at the thought, Jimmy turned away from the table and noted that the sky was starting to brighten beyond *George Tucker's* dining room windows.

"I still don't... how could *anyone* want to abandon direct control over their own Champions?" the Viscount repeated the question again, hoping that this time the Texan would have a better answer for him.

Instead, John Nance Garner laughed, "Devlin, we're not all Imperialists."

"Neither bloody am I," the Newfoundlander couldn't stop the retort. "But they're not just weapons, they're what's next for all of us. How can you abrogate your responsibility for them?"

"We'll still have them in every major city," the President said around puffs of his cigar. "The only difference as far as we're concerned is where they'll check in for new assignments. No one will mind, and my friends in the Senate will be happy to rid themselves of a hefty budget item."

He sounded so sure of himself — and was almost amused that he was justifying himself to the man who'd be benefiting from the arrangement. On that front, he added, "If you think having Champions in hand is so important, seems funny to me that you're resisting getting all of ours on your island, Devlin."

Still staring out the window at the White House, Jimmy found himself shaking his head, then releasing a sigh. It probably was ridiculous to resist — certainly there would be complications to bringing in the Americans on a permanent basis, but the opportunity to get those Champions out from the political yolk that had stifled them in Virginia could do a world of good... and keeping them all close to Jimmystown, and its familiar garrison, *and* its Saa-enhanced abilities, could seriously improve their safety.

But the most important question remained: what bitterness would follow later?

Future generations might rue the day this deal was struck, but it seemed as though Garner would not take no for an answer. Jimmy knew that he'd have to resign himself to that reality, and simply make sure the terms were to the greatest advantage of all the savage-born children.

With that in mind, he took a breath and turned back towards the President.

"One regiment, and a garrisoned base at St. John's. We'll continue to protect by air and sea as normal. No visits allowed by your politicians, either. They want to see a Champion, they call down for one to visit," the Viscount's tone was flat, and Garner's eyes narrowed as he detected the final concession from the Newfoundlander.

As ever, the Texan was going to get his way.

"That'll be unpopular," the President's reply sounded thoughtful, but he nodded anyway. "I'll see to it."

He spoke with more confidence about what he could achieve than Devlin thought was necessarily correct for a President... but no matter. There had to be more conditions: "None of your personnel will have access to our Saa technology, unless I personally clear them. I set the secrecy and security arrangements."

"Whatever pleases you, Lordship," Garner pulled his cigar from his mouth and waved it towards Devlin. "You run the island however you figure is best. You keep our boys and girls safe, and you send them when we call for them."

Jimmy stared at Garner again, shocked by the seeming lack of foresight in that final declaration: "Yes, but what if you call and we don't send them? You're trusting us to be honest?"

Garner's eyes narrowed slightly, and he puffed on his cigar before replying, "You saying I can't trust you, Lord Devlin?"

Blinking, the Viscount shook his head, "You damned well know better."

"I do," Garner finally shifted from his seat, pushing himself up to his feet and rounding the dining table to stand right in front of the Newfoundlander. "You know, I survived forty years of Washington by being loyal to my party, and by figuring out how to find and keep loyal friends. When you find those men, you take them at their word. You're one of those men. Take it as a compliment that I trust you."

Well that was lovely — it was the sort of noble sentiment that truly could resonate with the Viscount of the Grasslands — but he'd been around too many politicians to buy it at face value.

Garner seemed to understand that, and he reached out and clasped Devlin's shoulder a bit roughly, "Besides, you decide to ignore us, I'll have two regiments right in your belly, and Champions on your base. And both of us know better than to ever find out how that would go, if we got into a friendly dust-up."

That was actually a threat of some kind — one that instantly rung hollow to Devlin, because he had a difficult time believing any Champions, no matter their flag, would turn on each other at some politician's whim. Naturally, the Viscount's instinct was to respond in those terms... but he held back. If this was the sort of leadership the Champions were to expect with Roosevelt gone, they really would be better off in Newfoundland.

And he'd best stop fighting that.

"You pay to install, we pay for operations. I command," Devlin's tone was low as he replied, and Garner patted him twice on the shoulder before turning away.

"Good man. I'll take it over to the Capitol and have Pollock write the recommendation into the report from the Inquiry," he said with a grin.

Frown deepening, Devlin shook his head, "You're awfully confident you can convince them to do what you want."

"Roosevelt couldn't make them," Garner crushed the end of his cigar in an ashtray on the table he'd been sitting at, then looked up. "I've been making deals in this city since you were born, Devlin. That's why he wanted me. Most VPs are mascots, not worth a boot full of piss. But I like to pull my weight."

He repeated his qualifications with a distasteful swagger. Taking a sip of his almost-forgotten coffee, the Viscount's reply was sharp, "Sorry, have you mentioned that already tonight? I don't think I've heard how good you are at politicking."

"I do my job," Garner didn't seem put off by Devlin's dry jab. "You might be my scapegoat with some of the Senators whose boys are losing jobs with the Saa screen, but that shouldn't smart you too much."

"I'll brace myself, just in case," the Newfoundlander's reply was more than a little sardonic, drawing a bigger smile to the President's face... but before he could respond, another question on the same subject occurred to Jimmy. "What about your screen operators, then? Keeping them under lock and key until we can get a Saa to figure out who broke into your screen?"

The question seemed less interesting to Garner, "When's the next Saa due?"

"Don't know yet."

"Couldn't hold them like that," the President shook his head. "Not without better evidence. We'll let them out, keep an eye on some, promote others. Except for one — we'll hang him."

Jimmy had begun sipping his coffee again, but as he heard the answer, he found himself frozen with his cup up to his lips. As he glared over the ceramic mug, the President noticed how popular his words had been, and grinned again: "The people need someone to blame."

"I suppose that's Corporal Cross," Devlin lowered his cup with the reply, and Garner's eyes narrowed.

"The negro," he said, then he turned the question back at Jimmy, speaking with the sort of quiet menace that had undoubtedly won many Capitol Hill battles: "Problem, Viscount of the Grasslands?"

His attempt to sound intimidating was unsuccessful, though after a long night of arguing over particulars and settling on the obvious outcome, the prospect of opening a whole new round of combat was not welcome for either man.

Softly, then, Jimmy raised the question: "You'll let everyone else go, even though they're all suspects. Then you'll kill the man who discovered the breach because he happens to be black, and therefore has no allies?"

Garner seemed as though he'd been ready for the question: "There's no evidence that the boy is innocent. You want us to let him go back into the world, and disappear into some slum? All the others are from noted families, we can watch them."

"Unless one of those noted families is *complicit* in all this," Devlin advanced a step, setting his cup down on his table as he did.

"The FBI is going to put watches on all of them, we'll see if there's trouble. But there's only one way you get our Champions: if our people believe they have the culprit. And if he's a negro, that's how we get public opinion on side for moving our Champions to Newfoundland. Because you don't have any coloreds to worry about up there, now do you?"

Jimmy blinked, and then blinked again. So this was the game: scapegoat the black men of the United States Army, and use America's racial problems as one of the justifications for delivering the Champions safely to a rock in the middle of the sea. Apparently no one would mind that most Newfoundlanders were Irish Catholics?

Looking away for a second, the Viscount of the Grasslands tried to picture the headlines... the arguments... the white hoods... and then for some reason he felt a smile slip onto his face. With a quick nod to himself, he turned back to the President.

"You won't know this, but once I was in a place called Promised Town, with the negro troops of the 25th. We'd just shot down a bunch of outlaws, and had wounded men, so we had to take over the local hotel. But the woman who ran the place didn't like that we had colored troops with us, so she tried to make trouble about it with

Major Waller."

Garner frowned at the unexpected story, but as Jimmy took one step closer to him, the President detected menace. He was no wilting politician — the Texan had been born in a log cabin, and he wasn't about to be intimidated by some dandy aristocrat.

But Devlin locked onto him with a fierce stare, "The Major drew out his Webley revolver, and pushed it into her face, and said he: *my mission, my men, my rules*. Which, funny enough, is almost the same thing you said to me just now."

Getting very close to the President, Jimmy stuck his nose into the man's personal space, "Those men are now *my* men, John. One garrison regiment in Newfoundland, and it will be the 25th. All those negroes… they'll be in Newfoundland. You'll have to cope."

Garner's eyes were already slits, so they could narrow no further, but he took a step forward — so close Jimmy almost had to back off, "You can have whoever you like. I need a pound of flesh. And there's no way it's going to be a white man, whether they deserve it or not."

"You should rethink your prejudice."

"You should realize it isn't *my* opinion that matters about those boys," Garner wasn't backing off. "My country still lynches black men, *despite* the laws we passed making lynching a special crime. Sure there's lots like you, who don't care about the coloreds being different… but too many *do* blame them. So if you take them, it'll be sold as the British knowing how to control native troops better. And Colonel Adams is going to be held responsible, and that boy Cross is going to be their live culprit."

He wasn't backing down. Jimmy didn't quite understand — maybe he needed to produce his own revolver and stick it in the President's face? How could Garner remain so chained to his prejudices, when evidence didn't support a death sentence? Of course Cross *could* be guilty, but when the rest were walking free, the man who had tried to stop the attack, and who George thought well of after their time together working the Fort Eustice screen, was to shoulder the blame alone?

"He can't be executed," Devlin's counter was sharp, and Garner stared at him for a few more seconds before smiling.

"That's better," the President said. "The court marital sentences him to death… then I commute it to life in prison. I'll take some heat for being soft on negroes, but he doesn't die."

That sounded not at all appealing... but at least it left more options than a noose.

"If we prove him innocent after the Saa arrive, you'll release him," Jimmy added the condition, and with a shrug, Garner nodded.

"Fair."

It wasn't fair — not at all — but better than the absolute alternative.

"I suppose the black boy does have some powerful friends after all," the President backed off a few steps, looking pleased at the deal that had been struck.

Jimmy didn't share the mood: "Apparently believing in equal justice makes me his friend."

Garner's smile split back into a grin, "You Newfoundlanders such good fishermen because you can walk on water? Or you just *think* you walk on water?"

That was enough. Striding forward, Lord James Devlin raised his finger and just about drove it into the President's face, but before he could unleash any harsh words in reply, the Texan simply chuckled and turned away, "I'll have a copy of the Inquiry findings sent to you... when I finish writing them. Nice dealing with you, Viscount."

With that, the President headed for the door... and Jimmy just let him go. Standing in the dining room on *George Tucker*, and wrinkling his nose at the stink of the smoke, the Viscount of the Grasslands found himself unsure how much good he'd managed to do in that negotiation. Hopefully enough.

CHAPTER IX

"*Skipper Miller* should be back in four hours."

Looking at his wristwatch as he returned to the table in the midst of the darkened command post, Lord Grey offered those words bitterly. Though the Hong Kong night was a relatively long one, it had yielded no results in the search for Duncan's captors — or the women who might have seen him.

The revelation about the 'nurses' had obliged Duncan to summon reinforcements from Newfoundland — General Kennedy had committed two more assault companies without hesitation — but even at top speed, it would take a skycruiser hours to deliver them. In the meantime, Hong Kong at night had proved too big and chaotic for the searchers to do much more than fill the streets with constables, picket the likeliest routes of escape, and hope for luck.

"Damn them," Grey shook his head as he peered down at the map of Hong Kong island that he and Mitsui had spread across the room's central table.

Opposite the Lord, the Major was silently studying the map too, trying to find any clues that might direct their efforts. Certain points were circled in red pencil; the airport, various sections of the harborfront, and roads that led out of the city and around to the back side of the island were all being monitored by men from the assault company. At the same time, all the constables from the Hong Kong police had been deployed to the streets, looking for the Mandarin-speakers.

But the night had yielded nothing.

The villains might have found an unexpected way to slip from the city under the cover of darkness... or perhaps some unforeseen problem had contained them. That was the only hope now — that daybreak would somehow bring with it a renewed opportunity to find Lord Duncan in the city.

Both Grey and Mitsui found themselves silent at that thought, and standing a little ways down the table from them, Stephanie folded her arms, then glanced sideways at her friend. Alex's hands were resting on the tabletop, her fingers strumming it softly as she frowned at the map. Elspeth was standing opposite the whitecoat, Strong next to her, and both looked severe as well.

All of them had been eager to continue the search into darkness — it would hardly be their first time carrying out a dangerous duty by moonlight — but Grey had denied them. Citing his experience in Hong Kong, he said it would be foolhardy to try. Standing around in the command post and hoping was clearly a much better use of resources...

Stephanie cut off that thought. She was getting irritable, which was mostly due to her frustration at confinement, and partly due to the fact she hadn't slept. Of course, like the rest of the team from Jimmystown, she was on Newfoundland time, so she wasn't even sure when she was supposed to attempt sleep. But there was no doubt she was running low on the sort of mental energy that normally curbed her tongue.

"With the sun coming up, should we get patrols out there... since we didn't have them out last night?"

At least she stopped herself from saying, 'since you wouldn't let us go looking last night'.

Looking up, Grey seemed as though he'd been preparing to defend his choice in tactics, "Searching the city blindly at night would have served no purpose, Lieutenant. Better that what few men we have are guarding the likeliest ways to escape the city on short notice. Aided by daylight, and more men, we can be more decisive."

Yeah sure. Stephanie felt herself bristling, though she bit back any attempt at an immediate retort. Her job was action — she and Alex were supposed to go out and work. Waiting for others to do the job was more trying than she liked, and when those others were just passively watching for a clever foe, it seemed especially hopeless. But she wasn't just going to blurt that out. Grey was wrong, but at least it was well-intentioned — not ignorant or bigoted foolishness.

His patience, however, was not shared.

"This is an occasion when waiting is sensible, unfortunately," Major Mitsui inserted himself very politely into the conversation, and then he looked back across the table at Grey. "But soon we will begin decisive action."

Recognizing the balance of opinions in the room, Grey conceded with a nod, "As soon as *Skipper Miller* arrives."

That was a different way of saying it would take four hours for patrols to be launched into the city again. Stephanie understood not wanting to be spread too thin — the assault company was probably too divided already, due to all the patrols — but it still felt wrong. Her hands balled up into fists, and she started to rock forward onto the balls of her feet, unconsciously preparing for a verbal sparring match...

"I think I'm going to get some air. You too, Stephanie."

Alex's interruption was abrupt, and it drew the young American's gaze. The lady in white had raised one of her eyebrows, and then nodded slightly for the door — basically saying that there would be no arguments allowed in the command post. At least, none yet.

Realizing it was wise to allow herself to be reined in, Stephanie sighed and then nodded, "That's probably the best idea. It's a bit thick in here."

By 'thick' she meant the stifling air, of course — not the apparently thick head of the Champion in command. Because that would have been improper to comment upon.

Emerging onto the street outside the police station, Stephanie had hoped she'd get a lungful of cool air, and some peace and quiet to go with it.

Unfortunately, she was in Hong Kong.

The sky was already brightening, so the street was alive with people and vehicles — all of them exhaling warmth — while the tall buildings on all sides prevented any cool air from flowing through... if there was any cool air to begin with. For a girl who'd grown up beneath the mountains of the new world, and their perpetually-perfect cool breezes, it was slightly stifling.

"I was expecting a bit more... fresh," the American sounded slightly dour, and Alex didn't improve the mood.

Unbuttoning her coat and flapping it by its hem, she agreed, "Way too warm."

If it was *slightly* stifling for a girl from the new world, it was positively ridiculous for a Newfoundlander. Letting go of her coat, the younger Lady Smith took a breath as she looked out over the busy street, and all the Chinese residents who were coming and going.

"I don't think I could survive long in a city this busy."

Stephanie nodded immediately, and tried not to notice that the air tasted as though it had been exhaled a hundred times just before it reached her.

"Makes me miss home," she replied. "I don't know if there are even a million people on the whole of the new world. I guess there probably are, but you'd never see them all in one place."

"Same in Newfoundland," Alex nodded. "I guess that makes the two of us antisocial."

Eyebrow climbing, the American looked at her friend, "You're only *guessing* that now?"

A small smile turned up the corners of the young Champion's mouth, "Educated guess?"

"Better," Stephanie was slightly appeased... but that victory was hardly enough to offset her general malaise. "Feels weird just standing here."

"I know," Alex nodded. "Think Schwabe is up to anything useful?"

The MI6 man had disappeared as soon as they'd returned to the command post — off in search of intelligence from other gentlemen with interests in China, no doubt. But he hadn't been heard from all night, so hopefully that meant he was discovering something useful.

"Lucky him if he is," Stephanie folded her arms, then shook her head and looked to her friend. "So I was too pointed with Grey?"

A smile crossed Alex's face, though the Lady in white didn't meet her gaze, "I was kinda let down, really. You were way more passive than aggressive."

Stephanie shrugged, then sounded a little disappointed with herself: "Really? I am now slightly disappointed in myself. *Slightly*."

"It's been a long night," her friend tried to sound reassuring. "You just need some food and a bit of sleep."

"Who *doesn't* need more food and sleep?" Stephanie batted back the question.

Alex's eyebrow climbed, and naturally the young Lady interpreted those words generously: "Yes, I *do* think we should sneak out and find some place to have our first breakfast of the morning. Thank you for suggesting it, and offering to pay."

As she watched her friend start to levitate very slightly from the step, Stephanie rolled her eyes, "I'm glad you picked up on the subtext. I was afraid I was being too subtle."

"Nope," Alex shook her head. "What do you think Chinese food is like? I wonder if they have cookies... maybe cookies with pieces of paper in them, which tell your fortune..."

Stephanie blinked, "That literally doesn't make sense. Why would they have such things? That doesn't sound like something that they'd invent... maybe something *we'd* invent, and attribute to them."

Alex shrugged, "I don't know. But I bet they'd become very popular. Could see Chinese restaurants spread all across the world."

"Maybe you actually do need sleep, and food," the American replied. "You're talking crazy."

Chuckling, the younger Lady Smith looked back to the street, "If sleep or food could stop me from doing that, we wouldn't be friends anymore."

"True."

On that undeniable truth they let their words taper off, returning their gazes to the street beyond the station. The Chinese people hurrying back and forth seemed not at all interested in either of them, which Stephanie figured was just as well. Nothing would stop her feeling out of place in Hong Kong — feeling like a rude guest who'd overstayed her welcome. It was better when the hosts didn't notice she was there.

But what about the other rude guests... the ones who were also kidnappers?

"What do you think the chances are that we're actually going to find these guys?" Alex asked eventually, her tone sobering.

With another sigh, Stephanie began to shake her head... but someone else was first to answer.

"Not terribly good, I must say. But don't discount the old methods. Though they're not so active as you or I would like, there's true utility in having a police presence on every street."

Alex hadn't heard Schwabe step out onto the stairs behind them, but there was no mistaking his voice.

"Back already?" Stephanie glanced over her shoulder at his arrival, and a certain coolness had worked its way into her tone.

With a shake of his head, the spy stuffed his hands into his pockets and advanced to stand at the top of the stairs, between the two youngsters, "Nothing."

Of course. In a city as densely-packed as Hong Kong, there were simply too many currents of human activity for all of them to be successfully penetrated by the tendrils of British Intelligence. It was proving a wise place for the captors to hide — a crossroads where all manner of people could come and go without attracting suspicion, but still orderly enough to allow for intricate plans to be carried out.

And escape would be easy.

"We're basically waiting for them to make a mistake, or someone to get lucky," Alex didn't sound impressed. "Comforting."

Schwabe nodded briefly, though his response was rather philosophical, "Might surprise you how much of the work we do comes down to luck, Lady Alex. When we look back on operations we often try to make sense of things — make it seem as though everything happened to some plan — but the truth is that chance is sometimes our best friend."

"Or our worst enemy," Stephanie offered the opposite position, and Schwabe nodded before replying easily.

"Either. But I must say, I find it liberating to know we're not in control of everything."

Perhaps spies were prone to sounding extra-philosophical in the early hours, but Alex's mood wasn't quite so accommodating — she really did need her first breakfast.

"Of course we're not in control of *everything*," she said sharply. "But there's plenty we can influence. Our job is to make the most out of what we can do."

That summed up one of Stephanie's core beliefs quite eloquently, but not wanting to get too lost in fine rhetoric — or worse, to encourage the same from the older Briton — she quickly maneuvered the conversation: "Exactly. For instance, we could get breakfast."

Schwabe had indeed been filling his lungs to offer some soliloquy, but he paused and considered Stephanie.

Alex's head had whipped around at the renewed promise of food, so she was the next to speak: "Yes, Mister Schwabe, you must take us somewhere for food. I'd love something Chinese. I think they should have cookies with slips of paper in them!"

That stupid joke again? Stephanie winced, then tried to draw attention in a different direction: "Yes. And you can explain why I feel like I know you, Mister Schwabe."

The direct return to her earlier preoccupation would have done Stephanie's parents, and especially Alex's dad, quite proud. Smiling immediately, the spy looked back out to the street, "Oh that's simple, Lieutenant Shylock: I wager you've read my book."

Stephanie looked sideways at the man, then back to the street before beginning to recall the many books she'd read. That was no simple task, as her mother had always encouraged reading — had said gunplay was only a skill, but knowledge was power. After three years at Memorial College in Newfoundland, the Lieutenant must have been through hundreds of volumes...

None by a 'Schwabe', though.

Certain of that, she looked up with narrowing eyes. She wasn't in the mood for much more sparring, so she'd continue her direct assault on Schwabe's coyness just as soon as Alex retorted...

Nothing.

Stephanie stopped. She knew that Alex should have quipped something after Schwabe's last words — probably lamented that, by answering the question on the step, he wasn't going to buy breakfast. That was the sort of joke she'd go for... but she'd been silent.

And now she was moving slowly down the steps, and her hand was pushing back the tail of her white coat — clearing the way towards her holster.

Without so much as thinking, Stephanie followed her friend, reaching for her own pistol as she went. She had no idea what the whitecoat was responding to, but whatever it was, they would confront it together.

"Is he...?" Alex began a question very quietly, and the words helped Stephanie know what to look for.

Following the general direction of the whitecoat's gaze, and seeking a 'he', she quickly discovered what had caught the young Champion's attention: a Hong Kong policeman was hurrying towards the station, one hand pressed on his scalp and blood spilling down his face as he pushed his way through the crowd.

He was yelling something in Chinese, and as he heard it, Schwabe descended the steps past Alex and Stephanie to intercept him. The pair remained where they were, eyes tracking the crowd for signs of pursuit until the spy managed to get the wounded man back to them.

"Luck," the MI6 man declared as he helped the officer up the steps to the station door. "He's saying he found the men we're looking for."

Blinking, Stephanie looked across at her friend, and found Alex frowning. Perhaps they didn't have to do everything themselves, all the time...

They'd soon find out.

CHAPTER X

There hadn't been time to grab much as everyone raced from the command post, but Stephanie had managed to secure a handful of extra magazines for her Browning from a box beside the door. As the Land Rover driven by Schwabe honked its way through Hong Kong's brightening streets, she busied herself with sliding the extra ammunition into her trousers' patch pockets.

"Could I have one of those extra clips?" Grey was sitting on the bench opposite the Lieutenant, and he leaned forward with the surprising question.

She blinked, then looked towards Alex — sitting next to the young Lord — who raised her eyebrow and shrugged. It didn't seem worth correcting Grey's conspicuously incorrect word choice, so she simply nodded and extended one towards him.

"Extra *magazine* for you," was all she said.

That done, and her pockets loaded, she directed her gaze over the front seats: Schwabe was behind the wheel and Strong was in the passenger's seat with his Thompson pointing forward, in case someone had to be shot on sight.

The wounded policeman had directed the team to a warehouse nearly a mile from the command post, lost in one of Hong Kong's lower-rent districts — an area that, kidnappers aside, could be dangerous for numerous reasons. Gangs of knife fighters weren't uncommon in certain parts of the city, but few of them spoke Mandarin. The men who'd jumped the constable and his patrol partner had indeed spoken that language.

It was evidence enough to warrant strong reconnaissance, so Bates had raced ahead to scope the place white Mitsui summoned a platoon from the waterfront and was leading them to encircle the area. The rest of the Champions, along with Strong, Stephanie, and

Schwabe, were going direct.

Of course, it could be the wrong place — a case of police stumbling upon a criminal enterprise unconnected with Duncan. But it was the closest thing they'd had to a lead all night, and was definitely worth investigating.

"Remember, the average Chinese will mostly defer to us because we're white... but they may look at you suspiciously. That is natural — don't assume it's a sign that they are connected with our enemies," Grey offered those reminders firmly, and though Stephanie disliked the imperialistic paternalism that underpinned them, she had to nod.

The fact that the Chinese people of Hong Kong glared at the white faces among them was not necessarily a sign that they were enemies... not in this specific context, anyway. If they someday decided to throw the Europeans out of their lands, Stephanie mightn't blame them. But that was a subject for a different day.

"We have gas masks under the seat?" Elspeth was sitting beside the American Lieutenant, and she asked that question as she patted the bench on which they were both sitting — a bench that doubled as the lid to one of the Land Rover's cargo boxes.

"You do," Strong answered immediately from the front. "I checked before we got going."

How he'd found time to look before their rapid departure, Stephanie didn't know, but it was irrelevant. They wouldn't don the masks immediately, because in such a densely-populated city gas would probably have been noticed. Still, it was good to know they were nearby if needed.

"Okay," Elspeth's tone was cool and a bit strained, but as she spoke she nodded to herself. Whatever was to come next, she seemed as prepared as anyone could reasonably be, particularly given her recent experiences.

The Land Rover continued to push its way along the steep streets of Hong Kong, out of the shadows cast by the newer, posher buildings and into a grimmer, denser part of town. As the roads narrowed, the numbers of people, rickshaws and sedan chairs seemed only to increase, and watching over the top of the front seats, Stephanie found her eyes darting back and forth quite quickly.

So many faces...

"Close," Grey was watching over the seat too, and he reached out and patted Schwabe's shoulder, then pointed to a brick building standing on the corner of a narrow intersection ahead. No electric lights were shining through its grimy windows, and since the sun was only barely above the horizon it seemed entirely likely that no one would be at work there.

But it was clearly the place the policeman had mentioned; Stephanie spotted Lord Bates leaning against the column of a nearby building, keeping himself partly concealed.

"There's Bates," Grey pointed him out, then added: "Pull up."

Perhaps Schwabe didn't like the back-seat driving, but he kept his own counsel if that was the case. Negotiating the pedestrians, he pulled the truck up alongside the curb, then switched off.

"Out quietly, stay out of view," Grey's commands were insistent, and Stephanie followed them. With a glance towards Alex she climbed out, dropping onto the street behind the Land Rover.

Bates was immediately beside them, "I've spread my lance to cover the three corners we can see, but there are apartments flush up against that place on all sides. I'm guessing alleys back there, so we need some people on the streets above and behind to patrol."

Grey nodded, but didn't speak to that point before looking to Alex and Elspeth, "We have four Champions..." He leaned forward slightly so he could look around the side of the Land Rover. After studying the building for a second he made his decisions: "We four Champions will go in together, from the roof. Major Mitsui will be here soon to cordon off the whole area, but Lieutenant Shylock and Sergeant Strong, take Mister Schwabe around the rear. We'll drive them out, and if they try to escape with Duncan on a stretcher, you must stop them."

He spoke rather definitively... but Stephanie's mouth fell open despite that evident confidence, "What?"

"Should we send all Champions inside, if we mean to drive them out?" Alex's question was more specific, and Strong reinforced it with a nod.

"It might take all of us to overcome the defenses and get Duncan," Grey replied. "Speed will be essential."

That sounded... plausible... but something in Stephanie's stomach began to knot. Sending four Champions inside without protection struck her as unwise, so she looked to the Lord, "You *sure* you don't want someone at least going in on the ground floor while you come from above?"

Grey shook his head, "Could be a death trap down there. Better that we drive them out and you capture them. That's it, let's go."

He ended the discussion with those abrupt words, before turning back to Bates and drawing his pistol. After quick glances to Strong and Stephanie, Elspeth moved over to join those two Lords, leaving Alex standing with her friends at the back of the Land Rover.

Drawing her pistol from under her coat, the younger Lady Smith frowned, then swallowed, "Okay. So if... um. You guys catch them."

She did not sound comfortable, for reasons that were obvious. Of course four Champions represented a formidable combat unit... but as someone who'd received fire, and fired in anger herself, Alex would much rather have been storming a gloomy Hong Kong warehouse with friends she knew well and trusted.

"Be careful," Stephanie's quiet reply reflected her identical concern, and the whitecoat locked eyes with her friend for a second before nodding and moving off.

Stephanie was inclined to watch her go for a second, but the spy from MI6 started moving immediately: "We better get into position."

He headed back for the driver's side of the Land Rover.

Looking from Alex to Stephanie, Strong allowed a moment of quiet before clearing his throat, "We have to let her go do that. You set?"

"Of course," Stephanie said it literally without thinking — because her body was ready for a fight. She just got a bad feeling about the entire scenario... perhaps too many people around, perhaps too many unknowns.

Either way, she had a role to play, and Grey wasn't wasting any time. If Lord Duncan was being held in that warehouse, they had to move before he could be dragged out and stashed elsewhere.

"Remember, look for documents that might lead us to the mothers," Stephanie just managed to hear Grey say those words to his party of coat-wearers before Strong gave her a gentle nudge to the shoulder.

"Come on, you," the Colour said, and though his choice of words was mildly playful, his tone was dark. She complied thoughtlessly; climbed up into the back of the Land Rover while Strong resumed the passenger's seat.

As soon as they were in, Schwabe switched on and started rolling forward again, maneuvering to try to get into the street behind the warehouse. Hopefully they weren't going to be left waiting, with nothing to do.

Alex tightened her grip on her pistol as she advanced up one of the streets opposite the warehouse. Grey's plan was fine, she supposed; he and Bates would leap to the roof from the opposite corner, while Elspeth and Alex each took one flank. Basically they were deploying in the shape of an 'L', to try to hem in as much of the building as they could... and to spread themselves out, in case anyone was watching with a machine gun.

How wise it was to leap, Alex wasn't certain. The rooftop attack would have the advantage of catching a gang of knife-wielding Mandarins off guard, but what about the sort of men who'd attacked Fort Eustice? They'd known too well how to deploy a firebox.

She worried about that, but as was becoming her habit, Alex set her concerns aside and let her body work. As she came to a point on the opposite sidewalk that was parallel with the corner of the warehouse, she stopped and looked back towards Grey.

His eyes were wider than usual — he was anxious, even though this was his town, and he'd undoubtedly fought his share of crime here. Alex supposed he hadn't experienced the sort of combat she had.

He nodded.

And then, from the street, all four Champions crouched low, leapt high, and landed on the roof. It sloped gently and was made of corrugated metal, so even her soft landing made a bit of a racket. Nothing she could do to avoid that — and perhaps not a bad thing, if their job was to herd people out of the building.

Still felt odd. It shouldn't have, but it did.

Quickly scanning from left to right, she spotted Bates and Grey, along with the shape of Elspeth in the distance. Outlined as she was against the rising sun, she looked burlier, and her coat longer and darker... but there was no time to dwell on optical illusions. Almost immediately, the whitecoat heard glass breaking — perhaps a skylight somewhere — and she blurred towards it.

The Lady from London had dropped into the building before Alex even arrived, driven on by some sort of fearless determination that Alex probably would have better understood had she been the victim in Scotland. But motivation was secondary to duty, so the whitecoat dropped straight through the skylight after her compatriot.

That blind leap was the most reckless thing she'd done in some time, she realized as she landed — especially because Stephanie wasn't right behind her. The corridor she dropped into was empty and lacked windows, making it dark after the dawn sun. As her eyes adjusted and she made out the shape of Elspeth crouching nearby, covering one end of the corridor, Alex did her part and covered the opposite direction. The pair would wait until Bates and Grey arrived so they could sweep the place.

As the Land Rover turned down the street behind the warehouse, Stephanie peeked out the canvas flap at its back. Some apartments stood between the brick building and the street, and as Schwabe guided the truck along she could see there were narrow alleys between them — lanes too narrow for a vehicle, or perhaps even a horse, but wide enough for a person. Each would need to be watched, in case men fleeing the warehouse attempted to escape through them.

"There's a lot of places for people to get out and disappear," Strong was getting the same impression as he peered out through the windshield.

"Indeed," Schwabe agreed, his eyes narrow as he leaned over the steering wheel. "Best that we're on foot."

"Yeah," Strong didn't sound too enthusiastic at that prospect — not because he minded being on his feet, but because the crowds on the road would make it dangerous. "Sound good?"

He looked back over his shoulder with that question, and Stephanie nodded, "We'll need to find a place to keep our backs to the wall. I don't want anyone behind me in crowds this big."

"Right," Strong concurred — though having one's back to the wall might sound bad, it was a basic tactic for surviving in potentially hostile crowds.

Schwabe smiled, "I wish I could take credit for that idea, but I suppose you will have learned it long before me."

That remark seemed to make no sense at all, but under the circumstances there was no time to question him. Instead, Stephanie waited as the spy pulled over and switched off, then dropped out the back of the Land Rover and onto the street.

All around her Chinese people were coming and going — no white faces at all. Some passersby were giving her glares, and as she met those gazes coolly, she kept her Browning in hand, but held slightly behind her thigh so as not to be too obvious.

Strong was around the truck and beside her almost immediately, but though there was no hiding his Thompson from the crowd, the stares did not become fearful. Whites clearly were not expected — or perhaps welcomed — in this part of town, but the locals were not easily intimidated.

"This way," Schwabe came around the other side of the truck, keeping his Colt pistol out of sight as he gestured towards the front of the vehicle. "There's another warehouse, solid brick wall to put at our backs."

Stephanie nodded, though she didn't turn her gaze back towards the spy. Too many people in the street — so much to take in. As her godfather had long ago taught her, she needed to do a quick assessment of the place, figure out what was normal and what would be out of place. If shooting started, these people would probably scatter, but amongst the chaos adversaries could hide.

"Come on," Strong's tone stayed low as he prompted her to move, and she nodded, backing away with her Sergeant.

She still didn't turn her back as she moved… which meant that she was facing the general direction of the warehouse when the shooting began.

Someone was cutting loose with a submachine gun, and none of the Champions carried those.

CHAPTER XI

Alex halted at the sound of gunfire, then sunk lower into a crouch and began to extend her pistol towards the door at the end of the corridor they'd dropped into.

The shooting was muffled — clearly coming from beyond that door, and possibly from a lower level of the tall building. It was nowhere close to her and the Champions... what had triggered it?

Grey was behind her in the corridor, but he surged forward at the sound, his posture far less in keeping with the combat techniques laid out in the *Shooting To Live* book. Alex supposed Stephanie might have disapproved of his casual bearing... just like she seemed to disapprove of most of the rest of the characteristics he'd exhibited in recent hours... but now certainly wasn't the time to criticize.

"Could some of our men have moved in prematurely?" Bates asked from behind, sounding as though he didn't believe that was possible. Alex was of similar mind; it was unlikely Stephanie and Strong would have assaulted early, unless there was a very good reason...

The shooting abruptly stopped.

Silence fell quickly, causing the whitecoat to glance back towards Elspeth, then forward again. What had that all been—

The firing resumed, but this time multiple pistols... and a rifle... and then another submachine gun. And another...

Once more the shots ended abruptly, as if those doing the shooting were being killed, or were on the move — perhaps covering each other as they withdrew?

"If the cordon is off, we need to get down there quickly," Grey declared as he interpreted the same sounds, then raised his hand and waved for his colleagues to follow him to the door.

Alex wasn't necessarily as eager as the elder Lord, but she knew he was right about one thing: they'd gain no knowledge by standing around and listening. Moving low and smooth, the younger Lady Smith thus followed Grey to the door, and stood on the opposite side from him as he reached for the knob. Elspeth came to stand alongside her, while Bates joined Grey. With everyone suitably stacked up, the senior Champion nodded, raised his pistol, and turned the knob.

The door opened without difficulty — no need even for Champion strength — and then Grey leaned sideways and peeked around the frame.

Alex was just filling her lungs to ask what he was seeing when he flung himself back, and the air where the door had been received a vicious, breathtaking mauling.

It was a machine gun. Unlike the rest of these Champions, Alex had been on the receiving end of one before — Fort Eustice, where it had played a part in a firebox trap — and she wasn't about to forget the lessons.

Rolling away from the doorframe just in time to avoid lead that started battering it to pieces, she grabbed Elspeth by the arm and dragged them both down to the floor. Opposite them, Bates was already diving, though Grey was both dropping and turning — trying to get his Browning aligned to fire back.

Had she a chance to think, Alex would have questioned the wisdom of that move — no matter what the range, a pistol was never going to be a reasonable match for a machine gun, and having not looked beyond the door herself, the Lady in white had no idea how near or far away the weapon might be.

She therefore stayed low, and as she felt the .30 caliber machine gun rounds continue to churn the air over her head, she caught Elspeth's eye.

"We need to get out of this corridor!"

The London Champion was wide-eyed, but nodded immediately. They were trapped in a corridor of fire — unless someone could get to the gunner.

The morning crowds began to flee at the sound of intense gunfire, and Stephanie found herself trying to keep eyes on everyone as they moved. This was impossible at first, but as the street rapidly cleared, there were fewer faces to keep track of... and no sign of any who looked like they were trying to spirit away Duncan.

Moving laterally with her Browning held downward at a forty-five degree angle, Stephanie advanced into the street and kept her eyes moving. The entrances to the alleys were all before her... if any people attempted to get out this way, she'd see them.

And yet, there was no sign of anyone.

Mike Strong moved into the street alongside her, his Thompson up and ready. She spared him a glance for just a second, and he met her eyes with his eyebrow up, implying that he didn't like the situation.

They both looked back to the alleys, but still nothing — no sign of anyone taking flight.

If felt as though minutes had passed since the beginning of the gunfire, but it couldn't have been more than seconds. Stephanie didn't bother to check her watch, just waited.

The shots from the warehouse were continuing sporadically, including the reports of all sorts of weapons. At least one was a machine gun — not a submachine gun, but a proper mounted weapon. By going in, the Champions had clearly triggered a powerful response... Stephanie had to believe they were handling it okay.

But if the gunfire continued much longer, what was she to do? Grey's hastily-crafted plan had been based entirely on the premise that whoever was holding the warehouse — the Mandarins and their masters, presumably people like Saager — would flee at the first incursion.

If they instead stood and fought with obviously-superior firepower, four Champions could be defeated. And Stephanie Shylock wasn't about to stand on the street and wait for that to happen.

"We should get in there," she glanced back to Strong again, and though the Sergeant wasn't wild about the idea of moving into close quarters against so much firepower, he didn't shake his head.

His conclusions were the same as his Lieutenant's: no matter how powerful four Champions might be, they were profoundly outgunned. If Alex was pinned down, it didn't matter if the bastards had lightning cannon like the Hubrin of the new world... he had to go in and get her.

Still, there was the question of what would happen if they went down one alley, and people — including, perhaps, the men carrying Duncan — simultaneously made a run up another. To let the broken Champion slip away now would be a waste of all their effort.

Fortunately, there were only three alleys, and they had three guns.

"Dangerous, but if we each go down one alley, we can still cover our side," Schwabe was suddenly beside them, and looking at the American girl. "It's a risk, but I agree with you: it was folly to post us out here."

The MI6 was clearly not impetuous, but he knew when action was necessary. Both Lieutenant Shylock and Sergeant Strong nodded immediately, and wasting no more time they advanced towards the entrances to the alleys, splitting up as they went.

Surely it was dangerous — arguably quite unwise — but taking no action would have been worse... Stephanie just *knew* it.

Crouching directly below the skylight, Alex waited until the machine gunner shifted his fire so she could jump. She was far enough back from the doorway that the weapon's master couldn't, she hoped, see enough to lay a trap for her, but it was obviously still dangerous. There was no other option, though; she had to get out of the confines of the corridor and find another way into the building, to flank the gun.

Elspeth was right behind her, ready to follow her younger colleague up as soon as it was clear, while both Bates and Grey sprawled on the floor nearer the door, firing blindly out the opening. They didn't think they could hit anything, but it was for them to create the impression that the entire assault party was pinned down.

Looking back towards the two Ladies, Grey nodded as he reloaded coolly, despite the splinters continuing to rain from above his head, "We'll try to get him when he reloads, or swaps barrels! You must find another way in!"

Had she not possessed Champion hearing, she wouldn't have heard his words over the thunder... but she did, and she nodded. Whatever the faults of his plan, the elder Champion was keeping his wits while under fire.

Staying low as lead swept overhead, Alex gritted her teeth, looked up, took a breath, and finally sensed her opportunity. As the shots raked to her left, she leapt upward through the skylight, and into the rising sun of the Hong Kong morning.

When her feet dropped onto the roof, she crouched once more, pistol extended as she looked for any sign of aggressors. None were present, and as soon as Elspeth cleared the skylight, the pair hurried across the roof in search of another access point. There had to be some other way in.

The alley was predictably narrow, and the sides seemed incredibly tall. If shots were exchanged in such narrow confines, Stephanie knew it would be very difficult to avoid being hit — she'd simply have to fire first. That in mind, she was advancing with her Browning extended in front of her, finger poised to cover the trigger if a threat appeared.

None did. The alley wasn't particularly long, and even with her heart pounding in her ears, time hadn't slowed sufficiently to make the run seem excessive. As she neared the end, she slid to a stop and shifted position to lean against the wall to the right, then ducked her head out of the alley to look one way, then the other.

The alley fed into a slightly wider lane that ran alongside the warehouse. It was entirely possible that some of the men from the building would be watching this side for further incursions... But no, again there were none.

Satisfied that the way was clear, Stephanie edged out into the lane, looking quickly in each direction before turning her attention to the warehouse itself. Sounds of gunfire were still sporadically sounding from inside... joined by screams, in fact... and those spurred her to advance more quickly, a frown covering her face as she looked for a door.   ·

Emerging from his own alley a dozen yards from his American Lieutenant, Mike Strong swept both directions quickly before hurrying to join her. She didn't wait as he arrived — simply gestured towards the warehouse and nodded.

With the fighting still going on inside, they needed to move quickly. If they could just find a door...

A quiet hiss from behind — like a muted whistle — was clear enough to draw the attention of both Lieutenant and Sergeant, and looking back they spotted Schwabe as he emerged from his alley. He was waving with his free hand towards the wall of the warehouse directly opposite him. With a quick nod to Strong, Stephanie turned and moved that way, and the spy crossed the lane so that he could wait beside the brick wall of the warehouse for her arrival.

Though the sun was climbing, the angle and the height of the buildings that loomed on either side of the lane denied much light. Stephanie squinted against the gloom as she joined the MI6 man, then advanced a couple of paces past him to get a look at the section of the wall he'd indicated.

A door, indeed. It was fairly nondescript, appeared to be made of painted metal... and there was a dark pool oozing out from beneath it.

Blood, obviously, and Stephanie looked back to Schwabe and Strong before nodding, then waving them forward. It was the Colour who moved first, and as he spotted both the door and the ominous welcome mat, he scowled.

"You open it, I'll be ready to fire," he said quietly to his Lieutenant, leaving her no room for interpretation.

Perhaps she might have been headstrong enough to fling open the door and simply jump inside, no matter the implications of a pool of blood... but he'd have none of it. If there was something worth shooting on the other side of this entrance, his Thompson would get first crack.

Stephanie nodded firmly, then stepped nearer the entrance and extended her free hand to the knob as she planted one boot in the sticky blood. Schwabe stepped away from the wall so that he was obliquely beside Strong, and then the Sergeant bobbed his head.

With a solid jerk, Stephanie pulled the door open, then sidestepped so that she'd stay out of Strong's line of fire. But the Sergeant didn't shoot, and as she got a look around the door, the young American was greeted by the sight of a Chinese man lying on the floor just inside the warehouse... his head *almost* separated from his body.

It was undeniably gruesome, but she was too focused on her task to fully process the visual. With a glance to Strong, she ordered the incursion. The Colour would lead the way — he wouldn't allow anyone else to go first in a situation as apparently dangerous as this.

Stephanie followed closely, and Schwabe brought up the rear. Once through, he paused just long enough to close the door behind him — just in case.

The screams and shots sounded much louder inside.

CHAPTER XII

Alex was still on her feet, watchful for any threats as Elspeth lay on her stomach and leaned over the edge of the roof, looking for other points of entry. There had been no other conveniently-placed skylights — it had to be quite dark inside — so now they were left to look for other ways to gain access.

"There's a row of small windows along this entire side, right along the top of the wall," the Champion from London reported.

"Can we swing through them?" Alex asked more impatiently than she meant to — the continued gunfire inside was making her worry for Stephanie and Strong.

Pulling back from the edge and getting to her feet, Elspeth nodded, "Think so. We swing around and go through them... I bet it's a drop all the way down to the ground floor, though. You know how some warehouses have windows high up, to let in the natural light?"

Alex vaguely knew what her counterpart was referring to, and that was enough, "Be ready for a long drop before landing?"

"Exactly," the elder Champion confirmed, then pushed aside her coat tail and slid her pistol into its holster. "We'll need both hands."

That sounded sensible, if a bit worrying. As Alex did the same — reached beneath her coat and slid her Browning into the holster on her hip — she knew it wouldn't be particularly easy to access. Still, better to have it safely stowed than to accidentally drop it during the breach... and besides, even a relatively slow pistol-draw for her would be fast by ordinary standards.

"Let's go," the Lady in white said, hurrying to the edge of the roof.

Elspeth was right behind her, and then having spotted the jump already, the Lady in brown took one breath, stepped forward, and dropped right off the warehouse roof. She let her arm trail behind her, and it caught the edge as she fell, giving her an anchor point to use as she redirected her momentum and drove her boots through one of the windows she'd identified.

Any sounds of discomfort were muffled by the sharp noise of shattering glass; Alex simply had to trust that the Lady from London had made it safely, then replicate the move. With a deep breath of her own, she extended one arm towards the roof, then took a step into midair.

Walking off a building was a distinctly odd feeling, but she did it — dropped for a split second before her hand caught the roof, and her eyes fixed on the row of filthy-looking windows. She swung her boots towards one of those panes of glass, then looked away as she released her grip and allowed momentum to swing her through. When the glass shattered around her, mercifully little of it seemed to catch her — it exploded inward, so that she seemed to be falling just fractionally behind it.

And falling she was. The warehouse was a tall building — three storeys high, and as Elspeth had supposed, the side with the street-facing windows had no upper floors. Opening her eyes, Alex spotted a dirty-looking concrete floor below, and squared her boots for landing.

All around there were stacks of crates, not dissimilar to the stacks one would see in the Saa warehouses in Jimmystown… but much dustier. And though the sounds of gunfire were louder, there was no sign of shooters or victims nearby.

As her boots touched ground and her knees bent to absorb the shock of landing, Alex's hand was already dashing under her coat and collecting her Browning. A few yards away, Elspeth had her pistol out, but her free hand was wiping her brow; blood was oozing from her scalp.

"I'm fine," the Londoner was already insisting, sounding frustrated with herself. "Got nicked, let's just move."

There was no wound evident as Alex approached, but Elspeth quickly clarified: "Glass scratch somewhere on my head. It'll ooze into my hair. I can still see."

That was most important — cuts to the scalp could bleed terribly and disrupt vision, but if the blood was dammed by hair, it hopefully wouldn't cause trouble until the warehouse could be cleared.

Pivoting in place, Alex looked for a way deeper into the building.

None was immediately visible, so with a nod to Elspeth she advanced into a maze of stacked crates — hurrying towards the sound of the guns.

The corridors seemed to be littered with dead Chinese men. As she stepped carefully around them, Stephanie saw that many had either been armed with pistols or knives — two very effective weapons for fighting in the warehouse's dark corridors.

Most of them, however, appeared not to have had a chance to use their weapons. Instead, they were either full of bullet holes, or their bodies were broken in dramatic ways.

"Your Champions are on their game," Schwabe observed as they passed another clump of dead men, and Strong answered without humor.

"Looks like they should have come in with help."

That was true enough; no matter how well Grey, Bates, Elspeth and Alex were performing in combat, there were far too many armed men in the warehouse — and it would take only one lucky shot for a Champion to go down.

The machine gun that had been roaring abruptly fell silent, relieving some of the nearly-deafening thunder that had filled the building... then another scream echoed down the corridor.

"Stairs up here," Strong reported, ignoring the horrible sounds. "On the right."

He advanced with a bit more haste as he identified the stairs, and then stopped just short of the door to the stairwell itself. Stephanie advanced behind her Sergeant, but with his eyes to the rear, Schwabe lingered for a moment.

Standing in the middle of the corridor, crouched low with his pistol tucked close under him, he looked like quite a target, and as she glanced back at the spy, Stephanie filled her lungs to whisper a summons to him...

She didn't get a chance to use the air.

When the Chinese man with the knife hurtled around the corner behind the spy, she simply started to raise her Browning... but Schwabe's Colt snapped first. Inside the tight confines of the corridor, the shot was particularly deafening, and Stephanie's ears instantly numbed. The next three shots from Schwabe's gun were thus less painful, and the two other Chinese knifemen who'd followed the first dropped into a pile in the corridor.

It was quite evident the MI6 agent knew how to shoot.

As he quickly moved to reload — not wanting to be down half a magazine in such tight quarters, he looked back towards Stephanie, "I hope they were villains, not just confused."

It seemed a strange sentiment to voice in the heat of the moment, but Stephanie began to nod nonetheless.

Then Strong backed into her. She wasn't facing the stairwell, so she didn't know why, but it was no accident; he was backing away and roaring something as he pushed her behind him.

When he clamped down on the trigger of his Thompson, the resulting thunder denied her any chance to make sense of his words, or ask any questions about his purpose. She simply trusted he was right, and moved behind him...

Until the grenade went off.

The dark corridor vibrated with the concussion of a small explosion, then two more. Alex halted immediately, and following close behind, Elspeth stopped too, then turned around to cover the rear.

There were dead men strewn across the floors all around them, most shot and a few knifed, but until now neither Champion had heard any explosions. The fight was escalating?

Alex didn't know. The amount of carnage was already confusing, because unless a full platoon had attacked the warehouse with bayonets fixed, the damage seemed excessive. Perhaps the Chinese were fighting amongst themselves... Mandarins in a gang fight against the locals? And one side had explosives?

"This is so grim," Elspeth's observation was sharp, and Alex could only nod.

"Let's hurry."

Together, they pressed deeper into the warehouse's corridors. Surely there couldn't be too many to clear...

Stephanie had fallen into a seated position against the corridor wall, and her backside felt warm and wet. At first she wondered what that sensation could mean; then she came to the gruesome realization that she'd dropped into a sticky pool of someone's blood.

Pushing herself upward against the wall, she tried to blink away the fog in front of her eyes… then discovered it wasn't fog, but putrid smoke mixed with dust kicked up by at least two grenades, perhaps more.

She couldn't hear anything but ringing, and as she tried to stagger from the wall, it was only instinct that dropped her into a shooting crouch, and tucked her pistol close into her body.

Thank God for her years of training.

The first Chinese knifeman who came out of the smoke was barely five yards from her, and he was in full gallop. His eyes were wide with terror, but Stephanie had no chance to wonder why. Two squeezes of her pistol's trigger knocked him down to the ground — he fell beside Mike Strong, who was peeling himself unsteadily off the floor.

Stephanie wanted to stop to help her Sergeant, but two more Chinese came forward, similarly fierce. Four presses on the trigger, and they fell as well.

It was all instinct — all textbook.

She sidestepped unevenly across the corridor, lowering her crouch as she traversed, then steadied herself against the far wall. More Chinese came out of the smoke, and again she squeezed her trigger quickly, accurately. Six shots, and they fell — two rounds in the chest of each.

Strong was up onto one knee by then, and shakily searching the gruesome floor for his weapon. The Thompson had to be somewhere — he'd dropped it as he'd tackled Stephanie so they could avoid the grenades in the stairwell. It couldn't be far…

Another knifeman came from the smoke. The putrid fog was beginning to thin, so Strong saw the man charging… but Stephanie put one bullet into him while he was still well short of the Colour.

When she tried to press her trigger to deliver the textbook follow-up shot, though, her Browning's hammer fell on an empty chamber. She hadn't reloaded — she needed to switch to a fresh magazine.

This was not a difficult task for one who'd been shooting for as long as Stephanie Shylock, and she began the process with dazed efficiency. Her thumb pressed the mag release on the grip of her pistol, and the expended metal sleeve began to slide down the handle, though it didn't drop free. Unlike the magazines on Colts, Browning magazines never dropped clear of the pistols, probably because of the magazine safety.

But that was fine; as Stephanie's free hand dove to her pocket for a new magazine, she held the pistol right up in front of her face, so she could watch the reload without losing sight of the corridor.

Her heart was pounding, she could hear nothing, and she might have been concussed by the blast... but she needed to do this quickly.

Unfortunately, she wasn't as fast as the Chinese knifemen who raced again from the smoke. Four more, and Strong wasn't even on his feet, or armed, as they hurled themselves toward him. The men looked almost feral in their desperation — as if the Sergeant was standing between them and escape from a monster.

Shaking the empty magazine free, Stephanie pushed herself from the wall with a stagger, then raised her charged mag to jam it into her Browning. She was shaking on her feet, and as her boot toe caught on a dead man in the corridor, she stumbled, but didn't lose control of the pistol...

Too slow.

That was the first thought that managed to surface clearly in her mind, and it came with a flash of terror. She watched as Mike Strong threw himself forward, tackling the first Chinese man. Fortunately — mercifully — the Colour's abrupt bar-fighting attack caught that man off guard, and knocked the blade from his hand.

That gave Strong a chance, if Stephanie could just start shooting again...

Seven more men with knives. The smoke had cleared just enough between the stairwell and her position for Stephanie to see men emerging from the stairs, and the tide seemed endless. How many could there be in the building, all armed and willing to fight in close quarters?

Were they defending the stairwell, so that someone could use it to escape?

She didn't know, but as she finally slid her magazine home and raised her Browning, she knew her bullets would be spoken for...

Then her pistol was gone from her hand.

She must have screamed in surprise as the gun was seized from her, but she couldn't even hear herself. Mike Strong was too busy giving his attacker a hell of a beating to see the trouble, and given his proximity to the grenades his hearing was probably no better.

He couldn't see as Stephanie was shoved powerfully aside, or watch as she hit the wall with so much force that the wind was knocked from her. She wasn't even able to raise her hands to protect herself; her head collided harshly with brick.

If she'd been dazed before, it only became worse. And she was helpless as a new figure emerged from the smoke, raised a Colt 1911 pistol, and fired.

Alex rounded another corner, but found only dead men to greet her. They'd encountered at least forty so far — how many had been inside the warehouse to begin with, and who was doing such a thorough job butchering them?

"This is madness," Elspeth breathed as she came up close behind the whitecoat, then stopped, again watching the rear.

There was definitely truth to the browncoat's statement, but Alex knew there was no time to speculate. With another centering breath, she prepared to step out into the carnage of another hallway.

Elspeth's hand closed around her shoulder, and Alex looked back sharply. The Lady from London was already pointing her Browning to the rear, and recognizing the silent warning, the whitecoat pivoted away from the corner and lined up her pistol that way too. Whatever Elspeth had heard was worth being suspicious of...

One of the doors far behind them suddenly burst off its hinges — thrown with such power that it slammed into the wall on the opposite side of the hall. Both Ladies prepared to empty their pistols into whoever emerged...

And then Grey leapt out, his pistol extended in their direction.

By the time Bates followed him into the corridor, the Champion in command was already lowering his pistol and rising from his crouch, and Alex and Elspeth were letting go the breaths they'd held.

The two Lords then hurried down the corridor to join their counterparts, Grey greeting them with a nod, "Good job getting the machine gun. But... how many have you killed?"

His eyes darted to the many bodies on the floor around them, and Alex's eyebrow went up before she looked to Elspeth.

"We haven't killed any," Lady Cornish reported firmly. "We didn't get the machine gun."

Grey's frown deepened, and Bates asked the obvious question for all of them: "Then who?"

•••

Stephanie could feel virtually nothing. She struggled to keep her eyes open, but though the smoke and dust were clearing from the hallway, her vision was bitterly distorted. She heard the shots of a .45 caliber pistol. She heard screams and felt a spray of hot blood across her face. Nothing quite made sense.

Mike Strong wasn't in her field of vision. There was a figure in the corridor, and there were Chinese men with knives attacking that shape...

One of them fell, his own knife protruding from his skull.

There was more shooting... this time, it was Stephanie's own Browning. Her hearing was numb — seemed to be almost gone — but she could recognize the pistol's report anywhere. It was firing... firing... *firing*.

She tried to plant her hands on the floor, to push herself up, but her palms landed in a pool of warm, sticky blood. It was pooling all around her, she realized. Somehow she disassociated herself from that — from the nightmare of such a dark, smoky, gruesome corridor — and tried again to struggle to her feet.

Her godfather had always told her to keep her feet under her during a fight. She'd always thought it a silly piece of advice — obviously no one would ever *sit* during a gunfight — but now she understood why. Being immobile... helpless...

A hot, heavy piece of metal abruptly landed in her lap, and she stopped struggling for just long enough to recognize it: her pistol, its slide locked back to prove it was empty. But how — who?

And then, of course, the answer — the inevitable answer.

A face appeared before Stephanie, and even through her distorted vision, the young American recognized the woman with round tinted glasses.

"Sit back, child. And do not try to follow me."

The words were simultaneously harsh and maternal, and leaving them behind, Emily straightened up out of Stephanie's field of vision, then disappeared into the stairwell.

The young American Lieutenant couldn't hope to follow... or do much at all. Mixing force of will and instinct, she managed to retrieve a fresh magazine from her pocket, and slam it into her Browning. That done, she looked left and right for danger... then lost consciousness.

CHAPTER XIII

Stephanie heard voices before she was able to see anything. Her head was throbbing and there was a hand fumbling around on her neck, as if checking for a pulse, so with her eyes shut she furrowed her brow and groaned.

"Thank God," it was Alex's voice. "You shot or stabbed? There's so much blood I can't tell."

That sounded ominous, and with great effort Lieutenant Shylock started to force her eyes to open. Fortunately, the corridor was no brighter than it had been — the light wasn't too painful to take in. She blinked a few times, her eyes feeling gritty, but her vision was almost immediately clear enough to recognize her best friend's face right in front of her.

"Where...?" she started the question, but then shook her head slightly, and Alex seemed to recognize her concern.

"Mike's over here, groaning and moaning but okay. Schwabe's cut up but he says..."

"I'll be okay," the MI6 spy was suddenly crouching beside Alex, his suit jacket off and a white bandage wrapped around his upper arm. "Getting slow in my advanced years. One of the knifemen got me in the smoke."

The pounding in Stephanie's head actually began to ease, which surprised her — she'd have expected it to get worse as she started to move around, and her hearing to be entirely gone. She spared a second to feel lucky, then countered the spy's modesty, "You did fine."

Schwabe smiled easily — very easily for a man who looked to be losing a lot of blood into a bandage — and shook his head, "I've been telling Fairbairn we should adopt the Browning. He's been suspicious of the stopping power of the 9mm, but when I explain how I ran dry, and you were still shooting, I expect he'll listen."

Fairbairn. Stephanie knew the name — knew it was important — but her mind was already moving in different directions. She turned her head from side to side, both to check to see whether her neck was stiff, and to get a better look at the carnage all around. The hallway was literally full of bodies, some of them two-deep. A massacre had been carried out behind all the smoke from the grenades in the stairwell...

How had that gone again?

She knew she was forgetting something vital, and she tried to focus on that just as Bates emerged from the stairs, his pistol at his side and his face dire, "There's a room with a cot upstairs. Looks like where they had Duncan."

His announcement was abrupt and grim, drawing the eyes of everyone conscious in the corridor — Alex, Schwabe, Strong, Elspeth, a couple of other soldiers who must have come in from the street, and Stephanie too.

Grey appeared behind Bates, but he was looking down the stairs that must have headed into the cellar, "There are four dead Europeans up there, and another dozen Chinese. Lots of rounds fired, but no guns lying about. Perhaps the whites got into some sort of disagreement with their Mandarin accomplices."

He didn't sound convinced, but Stephanie could entirely sympathize. The whole situation was greatly confused.

"Must have gotten out, though... they used grenades to clear the stairs, so my bet is there are tunnels out of the cellar. Bates, we should go for a look. They can't be that far ahead."

The Champion of Hong Kong nodded to his predecessor, and they began to turn for the stairs — to go after Duncan, and presumably Emily...

Stephanie blinked, then blurted, "Did anyone else see Emily?"

She managed to say it loud enough for all to hear, and her words succeeded in stopping all movement. Alex turned back to her friend with wide eyes, "What?"

The rest of the American's mind seemed to be clearing, and with a quick breath she nodded, "It was her. I was disoriented after the explosions, and we were shooting... I was reloading too slowly, but she took my gun and finished off the corridor."

Even as she said it, Stephanie was surprised by her own words.

Emily, here?

Helping?

It was fantastic, and difficult to grasp. Perhaps she'd hallucinated it?

"You saying Emily was in command of this warehouse?" Grey wasn't following the train of thought, and again Stephanie was sympathetic — because it would be natural to assume the rogue Lady was their enemy in a situation like this.

"No," her answer sounded more like a croak.

"You sure?" Alex's question came from much closer, and as the friends locked eyes, Stephanie's certainty was clear.

"I couldn't have done all this. I'm no... not capable of stopping all these," the Lieutenant waved her hand around, to indicate the carnage. Her voice almost sounded hopeful — perhaps determined to believe she couldn't have killed so many men, no matter what their purpose.

But she was also sure of what she'd seen.

"Someone got me from behind, threw me into the wall," Schwabe spoke up with a frown. "I assumed it was one of the Chinese, and that Stephanie shot him down before he could finish me."

That sounded like corroboration, and then just to make it certain, Mike Strong sat up with Elspeth's help, wheezed and added: "It was Emily. She pulled the bastard off me, then punched me out. Gently."

The Colour ruefully rubbed his forehead as he spoke, and Elspeth looked up to Alex and Stephanie as she helped support him, "Why would she be here?"

"Why would she be saving our people?" Bates questioned immediately after.

But Grey wasn't in the mood to speculate: "She will have followed them. Bates, shall we try catching her up?"

"Gladly."

The two Lords suddenly sounded quite confident, and as they turned to go down the stairs Alex called after them, "She could jump you down there..."

"We'll be fine," Grey dismissed her, his prudence seeming to have evaporated at the promise of finding the rogue Champion. "Check the building for documents — we must know who these people are, and their purpose!"

Stephanie's sympathy for the Lord evaporated again at his seeming recklessness, but she couldn't raise her voice in time; he and Bates blurred off at top speed, and fortunately neither of them triggered any sounds of gunfire.

As they departed, Schwabe was the first to stand up and shake his head. The spy then rolled his shoulders slightly, as if trying to improve the comfort of his bandage, and nodded towards the stairs, "I'll go up for a look, along with some of these men. See if we can't find some evidence."

He sounded positively fine, though the patch of red soaking his bandage did seem to be growing.

"You sure you're alright to?" Elspeth was the one to ask, and the spy nodded.

"Certainly."

With that confident statement he departed, waving for the soldiers who'd come into the corridor to follow. That left just Alex, Stephanie, Strong, and Elspeth in the dim, bloody mess. It was the whitecoat who spoke next.

"Ready to try to stand?" she asked her friend, and Stephanie nodded.

Extending a hand which the Lieutenant took, Alex stepped back and helped pull her up, while Elspeth did the same for Strong. With all four on their feet, there was another moment of quiet, and Stephanie turned around slowly in place, trying to count all the dead.

"It was like... they had an army of Chinese."

"We saw even more in other parts of the building. Maybe a hundred, possibly more," Elspeth reported. "And... you think Emily did all of this by herself?"

Stephanie blinked at the question, and had to admit it seemed unlikely. No matter how powerful she was, could the original savage-born have killed so many ordinary men in close quarters? Perhaps given the advantage of surprise, and enough ammunition...

"Whether she had help or not, she was definitely here," Alex's mind was drifting in a different direction. "I'm more worried about why."

A smart question, and as the Lieutenant managed to look down at herself — and saw all the dark fluid matting her battle dress, her hands, her boots... and felt the stickiness on her skin...

Stephanie lost her train of thought as her fingers reached up to her blood-spattered face, and reality abruptly started to settle in. Again her eyes traversed the hallway — the butchered dead men with lifeless faces and wide eyes. Her heart rate climbed and she found her breathing was sharper.

She was in the middle of pure carnage. She was covered in gore.

Not at all how she'd expected the day to end... or start, she supposed. It was morning, at least in Hong Kong.

"Emily came for Duncan. She must have heard a Champion was being held captive, and either found her own way here, or followed us..." Alex was understandably thinking more clearly, and her words caught enough of Stephanie's attention to help the Lieutenant blink her mind clear.

Temporarily, at least. She needed fresh air — not that Hong Kong seemed to offer much of that.

"If she came for Duncan... they tried to stop her and she did all this. Then they decided to run for it, and in the confusion assumed we were with her..." Elspeth was thinking out loud, drawing slow nods from her whitecoated counterpart.

Strong pitched in too, "She wouldn't have had our intelligence resources... so she followed us here, knowing her only chance to get Duncan would be ahead of us, in the confusion."

"Yes, but what could she want with him? Obviously she can't have the same agenda as these people," Elspeth was frowning as she looked to the Sergeant, and he began to nod in recognition of her point.

"Must be something important, for her to risk us catching her... though she was pretty confident about getting away from us before..." Alex added next, and she looked to her best friend for thoughts on that point.

Then she stopped.

There was so much blood smeared across Stephanie's face that it was tough to actually see her going pale, but Alex knew she was. The American needed some air. Having this terribly interesting conversation about motives was fine, but better not to do it in a corridor full of butchered men.

"Let's step outside," the Lady in white immediately changed gears, authority abruptly filling her voice.

Strong instantly looked to Stephanie, then reached out and put his hand on her shoulder. She returned his gaze quickly, nodded, then looked around, "Fastest way out?"

Elspeth had an answer to that, and carefully watching her step — for she was not covered in gore, and didn't want to be — she led the way down the corridor. Slowly, Alex, Strong and Stephanie followed.

Whatever Emily's purpose had been in coming to this place, the evidence of her destruction was dramatic. Fortunately, they could leave it behind. None of her other victims, right or wrong in their agendas, had the same opportunity.

CHAPTER XIV

"Jesus Christ wept."

Jimmy Devlin's blasphemy was warranted, at least as far as he was concerned. Sitting behind his desk in his absurdly large office, and facing both Caralynne and Smith, he found himself confronted by literally no good news.

"We're all guessing at her motives," Alex's mother was unflapped by the Viscount's oath, and continued reporting what she'd learned from her daughter's message. "But when Grey and Bates caught up to the stretcher they think was carrying Duncan, all they found were dead Chinese men, and two decapitated Europeans."

Wincing at the mental pictures, Devlin shook his head, "She kidnapped Duncan. And we don't know why."

It was a succinct summary of what Emily had managed to do in Hong Kong, and it left a profoundly bitter taste in his mouth. What the hell was the rogue Lady playing at — helping to rescue a Champion in peril, but then spiriting him away? Perhaps it was impossible to know… though for all the mystery, she had at least cleared up a few questions of allegiance.

"So the kidnappers, who we presume blew up *Hood*, and attacked Eustice, are not aligned with her," the Viscount thought aloud after a moment. "Or if they were, she just lost faith with them."

"Indeed," Caralynne nodded. "Either way, she has Duncan, and given her skill at disappearing, I don't expect either of them will be found in Hong Kong."

That seemed inevitable. The whole operation at the free port had turned into a shambles because of that savage-born woman. Grey and Alex had found the villains, but had been prevented at the last moment from capturing them.

And from finding any clues as to their organization.

"Nothing more about those women — the nurses?" Jimmy pushed the questions forward, and Caralynne shook her head.

"Mitsui's men are still sifting through the warehouse, but it doesn't look promising. If they were smart, they kept no written records on site. The police and MI6 will take over the investigation, see if they can identify any of the women based on witness accounts… but there's no easy answer."

Of course there wasn't. It would have been terribly helpful of these people to leave a pamphlet explaining themselves, but for some reason they hadn't. And by hiring Mandarin enforcers who were not from Hong Kong, the villains had managed to confuse even the local investigators.

No one could say who they were, or where they'd come from, or where the women they'd potentially impregnated had gone. *Nothing* was known.

"We're fairly certain Saager is *not* among the dead, by the way," Caralynne added.

More helpful news, and Jimmy Devlin sat back in his chair and sighed. As he did, a cool breeze mercifully blew through his office — he'd left the balcony doors open because it was an uncommonly sunny June day in Newfoundland, and he needed the air. As his brow cooled, it felt as though the land and sea of his home rock were trying to calm his nerves. That was a kindness… though it was no magic potion.

Steepling his fingers in front of him, the Viscount forced himself to sum up: "So we found Duncan but he was carried off by Emily. Didn't find out the identities of the whites who kidnapped him, or the Chinese they hired. Did figure out that they've probably been using Duncan, in a drugged state, to father children with ordinary women, thus giving whoever they are a long-term source of Champions. But we don't know who the mothers are, or where to find them. And we need to do that within six months, before the children are born."

"Nine months," Caralynne corrected gently, and Jimmy blinked before nodding.

"Right, the mothers aren't Champions themselves. So nine months."

After that, Lord Devlin fell silent, and let his eyes drop to his desk. It was covered in papers, not least among them the findings of the Senate Inquiry. Somehow Garner had managed to get a copy of the dense, 200-page document to Jimmystown just hours after *George Tucker* returned.

Obviously they'd been pre-written, and then just tweaked based on the 'negotiations'... and if the pre-written drafts needed so little editing, it suggested the President had gotten from Devlin exactly what he wanted. Sending the findings so quickly was probably a sneaky way for the politician to prove he'd won.

That made Jimmy Devlin feel so wonderful he was tempted to vomit. Obviously he refrained, and instead said: "The past two days have been very special."

Caralynne's eyebrow climbed, and it was her turn to sigh anxiously and fold her arms, "The Inquiry?"

Leaning forward, Devlin hoisted the document from his desk and tossed it in her direction. She plucked it out of the air and flipped it open, though she made no attempt to read — eyes fixed instead on Jimmy.

"We're getting their Champions regiment, a garrison, and an American base somewhere around St. John's. They want to pay a pittance, while we cover all the operational costs... and we're in charge of security. Which isn't necessarily a bad thing. But I just know it's going to be overcomplicated, and potentially dangerous."

Caralynne nodded, "We'll be in their political crosshairs. And if there's a division between Washington and London, we'll be the fulcrum."

"Did I mention my abiding love for politicians?" Jimmy asked grimly, and the elder Lady Smith managed a sardonic smile.

"No one needs a reminder of that," she replied... then her smile faded. "What about blame for Virginia?"

God, Jimmy had even managed not to think about that for a few moments. Now he let his head fall back against his chair and closed his eyes, hoping for another breeze.

"Guess."

That was answer enough; Caralynne figured the blame was going to Colonel Adams, and probably to Constance Cormack's black friend.

"Will he be executed?" she asked more quietly, because it seemed somehow appropriate to lower her tone for the question.

When Devlin opened his eyes to answer, she could see in them that it wasn't *all* bad news, and he confirmed as much: "Life in prison. Unless we can find evidence exonerating him. The rest of the screen operators are being freed, but they won't come here. Though — *though* — we are getting the 25th United States Infantry for the garrison. Once they find a new officer willing to command a regiment of colored men."

So there were some positive things to take away from the negotiations, and under the circumstances Caralynne would gladly accept them. After her daughter's grim report from Hong Kong, any good news had to be seized upon.

As they tried to clutch at the positive, the elder Lady Smith and the Viscount both fell silent — as though they'd tired themselves out. It was as this silence settled that Smith spoke for the first time in the meeting: "No indication of who truly gave the enemy information for the attacks?"

The security breaches were definitely still a question, and as both Smith's wife and his Lord-friend looked to him, their expressions darkened further.

"None," Jimmy said it first, and then sighed.

"After all this, we still don't have a clue how they're getting information on us... even how Emily knew we were going to Hong Kong," Caralynne let her deep frustration slip into her tone, and Smith nodded.

Then another breeze crossed through the room, and the drifter looked towards the balcony. Thoughts were playing through his head, but as ever he was economical with words. That was fine; both Caralynne and Jimmy knew him well enough to figure he was worrying about how to find the breach. If he came to any good ideas, he'd raise them... there was no point prodding.

Indeed, after the furious activity of recent days, perhaps it would be wise to resume a more passive stance... see if the MI6 investigation in Hong Kong yielded anything, or if one of the freed American screen operators led the FBI to evidence of treachery.

Sometimes doing nothing was, in loose terms, actually equivalent to doing *something*...

But it was surely a desperate stance to take.

With a sigh, then, Jimmy Devlin looked to Caralynne and began to shake his head, "I think I need to sleep on this. Maybe an answer will present itself in time..."

Or, immediately.

There were few things that could make the Saa screen in Jimmy's office bing... but bing it abruptly did. The sound was soft and pleasant, but in the context of the conversation it was so unexpected it actually made the Viscount jump slightly in his chair.

Then, without any instruction from the humans in the room, the screen brightened and a new display frame glowed to life. Inside that frame, a moving picture showed a wind-blown desert on some other world in the far-flung cosmos... and into that moving image stepped a whale-sized lizard.

As soon as she was in the frame, the familiar dragon began to hiss.

"Jimmy, it's Sass," a pleasant female voice followed immediately — words being produced by a narrow metal band worn like a necklace (or, less politely, a collar) around the dragon's neck. "I got your message. Very sorry to hear about Emily, and these attacks. I've been able to bump up our next envoy, so I'll be arriving in August, your calendar time. Because of the rush, I'll be coming by way of the new world."

Staring at the screen — knowing the message was pre-recorded, and probably had been sent days earlier — Jimmy Devlin felt words fall immediately from his mouth, "Oh my dear beauty big dragon, thank God."

As the weight lifted from his shoulders, the Viscount felt a smile coming to his face. August was months away... but was still sooner than he'd dared hope. And with Sass back, they'd have far more help in keeping the worlds from going wrong.

Caralynne was similarly buoyed by the abrupt announcement — so well-timed as to be nigh-unbelievable. She smiled at Jimmy, then looked to her husband. Smith seemed studied at the news, as if it bothered him. A frown at her husband's reaction began to form, but before the Champion could inquire, Sass added something that seemed to explain the former-drifter's instinctive concern.

"Unfortunately, I have news for you: our Empire has been attacked by another. We are in a state of war, and your new world is near enough to contested space that we have some concerns for its safety. I'll brief you fully when I arrive."

Sass's synthetic voice had been designed to sound rich, warm, and perhaps a little matronly to humans, so that particular announcement sounded absurdly pleasant — as if she was announcing that cookies were coming fresh from the oven.

But Jimmy wasn't fooled, and after all the other ridiculous news he'd been forced to absorb during this dense meeting, he could have but one answer to it all: "*Fer fuck's sake.*"

Really, there was nothing more to say.

"I'll see you all soon. Give my best to everyone... tell Alex I look forward to seeing her in white, and Stephanie that I look forward to seeing her in green."

With that, Sass's head bobbed from side to side — the Saa gesture for happy sentiments, or laughter. The giant dragon was a starship engineer and ambassador, but perhaps more importantly she was a mother who'd known both girls from the time they were smaller than her eyeballs.

Which admittedly sounded weird, but was also endearing.

As the message ended, and Sass disappeared from the screen, Jimmy Devlin settled deeper into his chair — perhaps wondering whether he could actually melt into the leather, and hide from the mess that the world... apparently the *cosmos*... was becoming embroiled in.

"Can I quit?" he asked half-heartedly.

With a shrug, Caralynne replied, "No?"

That was truly the size of it, so Devlin fell silent, and the elder Lady Smith did too.

Meanwhile, the former-drifter in their midst stared out the balcony window, lost in thought. He had much to prepare.

EPILOGUE

Stephanie emerged from her stateroom's bathroom in a fluffy white robe, and breathed a sigh of relief. *Skipper Miller* was taking her, Alex, Strong and Elspeth back to Newfoundland to report, while Grey and Mitsui carried out an expanded search that everyone expected would be futile. The American Lieutenant was fine with leaving them to it; after getting a once-over from a local doctor, who seemed to think she was mostly alright, she'd been sent away to rest.

That suited her.

Now her uniform was in a laundry bag on the floor at the foot of her bed, and whether the cleaners could save it from all the gore she'd rolled around in was a fair question. It had taken a solid hour in the shower to scrub the gruesome feeling from her skin, and she figured she'd probably feel pretty raw for a while.

But now she could breathe easier, and get some sleep. Outside the stateroom windows, the sky was presently dark — whatever time zone the skycruiser was passing through, it was night. Her own body clock sort of agreed with that... though mainly she was just exhausted. If she counted back to the morning in Newfoundland, she must have gone for nearly thirty hours without sleep.

Sitting down on the side of her bed, she decided to do something about that... though she paused for a moment as she held her hands out in front of her. As usual, her green nail polish was mostly chipped away, and the backs of her hands were puffy and red. They'd gleefully sucked up the moisture from her hot shower, but she'd have to use some Japanese-made moisturizing cream on them when she got home. Perhaps it wasn't just the gunpowder that was drying them out, though — the amount of scrubbing with soap probably contributed just as much to their bleak condition.

Ah well, raw hands were better than dead ones...

And with that lovely thought, the American girl let out a sigh, then let her head sag forward. She had no idea if there would be new nightmares, but it seemed entirely reasonable to expect them. That corridor had been horrifying, and there was no way the relatively sedate reaction she'd had so far could be the extent of the psychological consequences.

Time would tell, but for now she just wanted sleep. Since she hadn't packed pajamas, she simply knotted her robe tight, shifted to get under the covers of the stateroom's bed, and prepared to drift off into whatever miserable nightmares might lay ahead.

She was stopped by a knock at the door.

At first she wondered if she imagined it... but then it repeated, and she lifted her head from her pillow and looked in its direction.

"It's me!" Alex somehow knew that was the moment to identify herself, and Stephanie frowned.

"I want to sleep!" she called back, and there was a pause before the whitecoat answered.

"No you don't."

Well that was a plainly false statement, but the fact that Alex — of all people — was willing to interrupt something as sacred as sleep suggested her matter must be important.

Stephanie reluctantly acceded, "Make it quick."

The door shot open, spilling extra light into the stateroom before closing again, "You okay?"

Alex was coatless as she sauntered over to the side of the bed, and she wore an expression of genuine concern with the question. Stephanie appreciated the sentiment, but her natural reaction was still to grumpily fold her arms under the blankets, "I no longer look like a victim in a horror movie."

Alex raised her eyebrow, "I don't think you looked like the *victim* in a horror movie."

Perhaps she'd chosen the wrong word, but Stephanie wasn't in the mood for semantics, "Right. Well my battle dress is probably ruined. Did you keep your coat clean?"

Alex took that particular question quite seriously, "Just spent an hour inspecting it. There was a spot, but I defeated it."

"Good," Stephanie nodded firmly, and then noticed that the young Lady was holding something beside her leg — trying to conceal the fact that she was carrying it, perhaps. With a bob of her head, the

Lieutenant asked, "That's something?"

"It's a book," Alex raised it immediately, and Stephanie could see it was indeed a hardback with a dust cover. It looked familiar, and the Lady confirmed it was well-known to them both, "*Shooting To Live.*"

Of course, the authoritative volume on combat shooting — a book that taught young gunpeople how to survive in gruesome corridors full of death and chaos. Stephanie wasn't sure she was actually happy to see it; she'd long appreciated the book for reinforcing the lessons taught to her by Cameron Kard, but perhaps a break from thoughts of gunplay would be appropriate, given recent events.

Apparently she had no choice.

"Before we lifted off, a messenger brought it over. It's from Schwabe, and it's addressed to you," Alex explained, then extended the hardback to her friend.

A frown immediately settled on Stephanie's brow, and she shimmied up in bed, so she could sit against the pillows as she accepted the book and began to turn it over in her hands.

"There's a note inside," Alex added helpfully, then quickly preempted any accusation, "which I didn't read. The messenger said so."

Eyebrow up, the young American looked from her friend to the book and back, "You don't think... like... he didn't seem creepy."

"Well, he *is* male, and you're... you..." the Lady-usually-in-white shrugged back. "But even someone that eccentric would probably send flowers, instead of a book you don't need."

Stephanie nodded slowly, turning her eyes back to the cover. It looked brand new and unread, and as she slowly opened it, the spine gave a satisfying new-book sound. She loved books dearly, though that aspect of her character was often overlooked by people who knew her as a shooter. Now she inhaled the smell of printer's ink, and felt a little relief.

Carefully, she flipped to the title page, and there she found more ink than she was expecting: the book was signed by both William Fairbairn and Eric Sykes, the two authors.

"Aw, it's a signed edition," she probably sounded slightly swoony — she couldn't help but love a signed edition, and this was a particularly important book. Overcome by that simple book-joy, she then flipped ahead until she found Schwabe's note.

Pulling it free, she laid the book on the bed beside her, then looked again to her friend. Alex was waiting eagerly, and there was no point delaying.

It was a simple piece of paper folded in half, so Stephanie opened it, and read aloud for her friend's benefit: "The publisher worried my last name would sound too German. Fairbairn suggested 'Sykes'. Do you think that sounds more in keeping with my Englishness? Sincerely, Eric Schwabe."

Lowering the note slightly, Stephanie frowned and met Alex's gaze. The younger Lady Smith's brow creased too, and then she looked at the cover of the book — re-read the names of authors William Fairbairn and Eric *Sykes*. The MI6 man was Eric *Schwabe*. And the note suggested...

"I know! Sykes is his pen name!" Alex declared triumphantly — a bit too triumphantly, though that was possibly a deliberate attempt to be funny.

"Yes," Stephanie sounded terribly impressed with the overplayed attempt at humor. "That's literally what the note says."

Not to be dissuaded, Alex clapped her hands together and hopped to her feet, "Wait until I tell mom who we met! That was Eric Sykes!"

It didn't really seem *that* exciting... but it did explain why Stephanie had felt as though she'd known the man, and how he'd survived. His experience and habits had been familiar because they were like Cameron Kard's... like hers. Not many people knew how to wield a pistol so well, and when such people found each other, she supposed that meant they felt a certain kinship.

But there were limits.

What she didn't read to Alex was the note's postscript, which said: *By my count you killed nine. Well fought. Thank you for saving me.*

Stephanie Shylock wasn't sure she could be proud of gunning down so many men so easily. It was her responsibility, and she had probably saved lives in the process. She didn't regret that. But she still had to question herself — wonder if the ease with which she was pulling the trigger was, or could become, corrosive to her identity.

Who was she now, and who might she turn into?

She'd figure it out. For now, she closed the note and tucked it back into the book, then Alex sat down on the end of the bed so they could start piecing together all the clues Schwabe had dropped while they were in Hong Kong.

That was fine; perhaps sleep was overrated.

Skipper Miller sped on through the night, and back into daylight, as it cruised for Newfoundland.

THE CHAMPIONS OF 1941   PART 5

DRAGONS

KENNETH TAM

PROLOGUE

"A whole other planet…"

Alex couldn't help but sound excited as she sat beside the train car's window, watching the yellow electric lights that lined the new world tunnel pass by. She was bouncing a little in her chair, rocking from side to side too — as if she was listening to music, but there was none.

She was eager, because she still thought it was a novelty to be able to take a train from a town in the foothills of Alberta to a whole other planet — a world that might have looked and smelled like Earth, but which was in fact far across the cosmos.

Unfortunately for the younger Lady Smith, none of her friends and family were quite so wowed by the trip, and since they were sitting all around her in the car, her enthusiasm was greeted by indifference.

"Just going home," said Stephanie Shylock, who was across from her friend. She sounded anxious — she'd been born on the new world and would shortly be seeing her parents.

"How many times have we been back and forth, do you think?" Caralynne was across the aisle with her husband beside her, and Smith simply shook his head.

"Plenty."

Plenty was right. For reasons that no one had ever been able to divine, the Hubrin had geo-engineered the new world to be not just a training ground for the humans they genetically modified into 'savages', but also to be rich in resources. Precious metals, fuels, lumber… it was all available in excess, and with the savages no longer roaming the lands (and eating settlers), the planet was even more lucrative in 1941 than it had been in 1919.

Every day and every night, trains full of riches passed through the same tunnel that Alex was now eagerly traversing. It was expected and understood that the goods would always successfully make the trip — that an ordinary-seeming rail line through a mountain would somehow cross the vastness of space, and fill the Exchequer's treasury.

And still no one could figure out how it worked. The Saa had been studying the tunnel on and off for twenty years. They'd used all manner of incomprehensible sciences to unlock its secret, and still, all they could call it was an 'unknown singularity'. Clearly, someone had put the gateways in the Rocky Mountains, but how and why remained unclear.

All that was certain was that the technology was beyond the Hubrin. Those blue men had certainly taken advantage of it, but while they had been skilled genetic and planetary engineers, they had no capability to create something so inexplicable. Had they possessed such means, the Saa surely wouldn't have been able to defeat them.

So the tunnel remained a mystery — but a mystery that could be ignored, since its frequent use had turned it into a mundane and expected asset for both Britain and the United States.

Still, Alex thought it was special. She didn't often get to the new world, and for her this was going to be an important visit. For others, it would be a nostalgic one.

"I remember when we came through here the first time," Mike Strong was sitting beside Stephanie, and the Sergeant's eyes were fixed on the tunnel walls beyond the windows. "Sure didn't know what we were in for then."

His words were a bit reverent — reflective of all the trials he and Waller's Royal Newfoundland Regiment had been through on the grasslands, the frontier, and in the badlands beyond. Reprisals, expeditions and a duel of empires had played out before those hearty b'ys, and most of them had died. Mike Strong had lived, and now he was coming back to the new world with different comrades at his side — people he had to protect.

But as Alex leaned to the side and pressed her face against the window, watching the light appear far ahead of the train, her enthusiasm partially reflected their purpose. It was the 23rd of August, 1941, and the following day, a Saa cruiser was to arrive over the planet to deliver Colonel Sass, a whale-sized lizard Alex and Stephanie had known for as long as they could remember.

The dragons were coming back, and considering all the inexplicable chaos of the past year, that was very good news indeed.

"Almost there," the whitecoat observed as the light grew towards the end of the tunnel. She gradually moved her face away from the glass when the Champion who was sitting beside her leaned forward for a better view out the window.

Lady Elspeth Cornish had remained in Jimmystown since June, and had refused politely to take on a new lance. She'd thus attached herself to Alex, Stephanie and Strong for a handful of fruitless missions in search of Lord Duncan, and the pregnant mothers of his possible children.

Those endeavors had been endlessly frustrating, but the browncoat now hoped the trials were at an end. Like Alex, she was excited to visit the new world, and eager for the return of the Saa. Deep down, both Champions admired the dragons; they were grander and stronger than any Lord or Lady who had ever picked a coat, and somehow that was comforting.

Stephanie was numb to such doses of perspective. It was probably symbolic that she'd chosen a seat that put her back towards the new world, but she elected not to read too much into her subconscious choices. She just wasn't sure she wanted to be home to see her parents. Since she'd left for school in Newfoundland, she had been back for only two visits, and in the past four years she'd changed a great deal.

She'd killed nine people, for instance.

Since Hong Kong, new nightmares had proved that her skill with a gun was beginning to weigh upon her — she could see the terrified eyes of Chinese knifemen in her sleep. That was reassuring… reduced her fears that she was one for whom death was too convenient a tool.

But she was also distinctly aware that the nightmares had been thinning, that she was thinking less of those she'd killed, and that she remained dedicated to her training. She was neither remorseful nor trying to change, and part of her had to wonder whether this meant she was foregoing some humanity. Alex and Strong saw no sign of it. Alex's parents, who were Stephanie's surrogate family, gave no indication…

But they were all watching the changes as they happened.

When Stephanie Shylock saw her parents again, would they recognize her? Would she have changed too much — become a killer, or the nascent form of one? So many stories had been told of the violent old days on the Pacifica frontier... of Murdo Gang bandits who raped and pillaged with no care for the death they were causing.

Was she at the beginning of that? Had she begun the journey which would turn her into a cold, callous murdering sort of villain?

Fingers were snapping in front of Stephanie's face, and with a blink she realized her eyes had lost focus. Light was spilling in through the train windows, and sure enough, the new world was all around them. It was a bright and sunny afternoon...

"Hey," Alex said gently, as if she could read her friend's thoughts. "You're home."

As awareness returned to Stephanie's face, she began to nod. Alex sat back in her seat with a smile — impossible to contain, given her excitement — and looked out at the train station. It was a massive structure built of steel and glass — not at all the rough-hewn timber terminal that had once welcomed Waller's b'ys to the new world.

"By God, they keep building this place up," Mike Strong whistled.

"Progress and civilization," Elspeth responded with a wry smile. "Look what you b'ys caused, Colour."

Strong shrugged, "I didn't really want to be the guy who takes all the credit... but we do deserve all the credit."

Alex and Stephanie both ignored the gentle repartee between the browncoat and the Sergeant. The American Lieutenant peered through the glass and felt her heart rate spike at the thought that her family was near. Looking up at the blue sky, and the mountain that stood behind the station, Lady Alex Smith felt a little bit as though she was levitating in her seat.

She was back in the magical place that had brought her parents together — even after her mother's death — thus making her entire life possible. The new world always seemed a catalyst that sparked change, so she rather optimistically believed that things would be better by the time she took the train back to Alberta.

Perhaps that was too dangerous a thought.

CHAPTER I

The air was warm and humid over Fort Leavenworth, Kansas. Home to one of the United States Army's finest staff colleges, the base was also the site of the United States military's Maximum Security Prison, and as he sat in an isolated cell in the latter facility, Vanier Cross found it possible to believe that the former part could even exist. Why put a staff college, or a staging base, so near criminals and traitors?

Perhaps because not all the men in the prison were the villains they appeared to be?

That was a fanciful thought, and no matter how much he wished to, Vanier couldn't let himself hope that others were innocent. Sometimes he even began to wonder whether he was; in the months since his transfer to the prison, he'd been beaten within inches of his life three times for being a traitor, and survived now only in solitary confinement. After so much punishment, even his sharp mind could begin warping memories... trying to divine whether he'd done something to earn his mistreatment.

And, of course, he had: he'd been born black. How inconsiderate of him.

He wasn't sure why his captors didn't simply let him die... surely they all saw him as the man responsible for the attack on Fort Eustice, and the death of President Roosevelt.

And yet they kept him breathing.

Lying back on his cot, staring up at the cold ceiling of his cell, Vanier had little else to do but wonder at his fate. The powerful mind that had served him well for so many years — that had led him to work on the Saa screen, despite being black — was now so underused that it *had* to fixate on something.

So he wondered, and hoped, and despaired — all silently — over and over again.

He feared the day when his brain simply gave up and accepted that he was done for. That would be the end of him, or at least the end of his soul.

But that day was still a ways off, and as if to push it just a little further, the sharp claps of footfalls sounded from the corridor beyond his cage. The guards were coming, and whether that was good or bad for him, it was at least a diversion.

Constance Cormack was soon to be named a Champion, but for the moment she remained just a graduate of the Robinson Institute senior class — a class that had finished its schooling at the Lady Emily Academy. Her convocation was of little importance to her; she was not nearly as preoccupied with choosing her coat as she once had been, because her dear friend — her brother, in all ways except biology — had been taken to Leavenworth as a convicted traitor.

Now, as the young American strode uneasily through the corridors of the military prison, she found herself wishing for a coat — for anything she could wrap tightly around herself to keep out a chill that was more psychological than physical.

"It'll be good to see him, won't it Miss Cormack?"

That question came from Major Wendel Fischer, the man who'd been detained with Vanier Cross for many months in Virginia. After being set free, he had been promoted in anticipation of a new assignment and had been on leave with his family. Now he'd been summoned by the War Department to join the delegation greeting the Saa on the new world... a duty which allowed him to connect with Constance, and to join her as she traveled to Leavenworth.

Her survival in Virginia, and her performance as a leader among the graduates, had earned her a place as a VIP with the same American delegation. Because so many of the lofty army officers who were part of that group were leaving from Leavenworth, Constance had insisted she travel via the Fort, not direct from Newfoundland. Officially, she made that decision for patriotic reasons — so she could arrive on the new world alongside fellow Americans. Really, it was so she could see Vanier.

Now Fischer was striding ahead of her, his mood clearly not so darkened by the prison surroundings as hers was. Perhaps his time in detention had numbed him to the grimness of the concrete walls, the dampness, and the hollow echoes that sounded with every step. He was enthusiastic — happy to be seeing Vanier — while Constance was at war with her own anxious stomach.

But she shook herself. Even though she wasn't yet a coated Champion, she was expected to conduct herself with dignity and authority, and Vanier would need to see she was alright. With that thought in mind, she squared her shoulders, then followed as Fischer turned a corner ahead before stopping at a door.

A sentry there nodded to the Major, then reached out and turned the knob, allowing both the officer and the graduate access to a small room. The space was mostly eclipsed from Constance's view as Fischer stepped through, but she followed without delay and found herself in what resembled an interrogation chamber.

It was bleak... but it contained Vanier Cross.

He was sitting in a chair on the far side of the room with his ankles and wrists shackled and two guards looming over him.

"No crossing to this side of—"

One of the burly guards beside Vanier's chair started giving instructions, but clearly he wasn't accustomed to dealing with Champions; no sooner did he begin to speak, than did he discover Constance's arms around the prisoner. He hadn't even seen her move, but his reaction was instinctive: he began to raise his billy club.

Fischer stayed his hand, "Hold fast, man. She's a Champion."

The guard blinked and looked up at the Major, then shook his head, "That's not allowed."

Of course it wasn't, but Constance didn't care, and Fischer seemed willing to defend her: "If she meant to help him escape, you'd both be dead. Let her hug her man."

Had she not been so distracted, Constance would have been displeased by the Major's choice of words — why did everyone seem to assume that Vanier was her lover, not her brother? In the eyes of the racists, one was probably as bad as the next, but it was no matter what other people thought.

She just wished he could hug her back... and Vanier wished that too.

Because for the first time since January, the condemned black Corporal was able to feel the familiar embrace of the small young lady he'd looked after growing up. Her arms around him were firm but careful, and as he was fully encompassed by her embrace, he breathed in the fresh, warm air that she always seemed to carry with her.

"It's okay, CeeCee," he said without thinking — trying to comfort both her and himself at the same time. "I'm okay here."

"You shouldn't *be* here," her answer was immediate, but he wasn't going to waste precious moments on that futile subject.

"That doesn't matter. You okay?"

Gradually, Constance let her grip loosen, then leaned back far enough to meet Vanier's gaze, "I'm graduated, just have to pick a coat. We're going to the new world because the Saa delegation is arriving. They'll get into the screens... they'll prove you're innocent."

As she made that pledge, she detected a shift in the posture of the guard standing behind Vanier, and her eyes darted up to him. He was scowling — clearly skeptical.

"He *is* innocent," she snapped at that man, and he avoided eye contact, but maintained an expression that was both snide and dismissive.

Constance began to fume. It came on quickly, but naturally — for these brutish men to think the worst of her brother, simply because of his color... to impugn his dignity by holding him in this dank place... how could she let it stand?

As she straightened up, Vanier detected the fire that was starting to burn in her belly, and tried to interdict, "Don't worry about it, CeeCee. That's good news."

"Yes, and when the Saa prove you're innocent, I'm coming back *here*," she was beginning to sound slightly pointed, and Vanier tried to shift forward in his seat to calm her.

His chains didn't allow that... but fortunately, his longtime cellmate was at hand, "Miss Cormack will have to get in line behind me for that, Vanier."

As the Major advanced towards Constance, he used his most commanding tone to draw the attention of the two soldiers. Even though the young girl before them was a Champion, they were more inclined to listen to the authoritative words of a Major, and they both took Fischer's firmness as reason enough not to engage in any back-chatter.

Carefully extending a hand around Constance, Fischer set eyes on his black compatriot, "Not to worry, Vanier. I'll make sure she doesn't get into too much trouble before we get you out of here. And then she'll be your problem again."

Perhaps it was a cheeky line — maybe Constance should have glared at the Major, who did have a wooing reputation — but instead she was fixed again on Vanier. The black man was similarly distracted, though he still managed to answer Fischer's words with a nod.

"Thank you, sir."

"Don't mention it," the Major nodded immediately, waiting for a second until Vanier dragged his eyes from Constance's so the two men could exchange gazes. Then Fischer added: "I know that the Saa's arrival will change all this. Just hold on a bit longer."

It sounded hopelessly optimistic to Vanier. Certainly, it was plausible that the dragons could detect the culprit behind the attacks of the preceding months, but deep down he couldn't bring himself to believe it. Still, Fischer was right: it was a chance. Even if it came to nothing, holding onto hope was important, both for Vanier himself, and for Constance.

"I'll see you again soon, then," the black man nodded to his former officer, and Fischer mirrored the gesture before stepping back.

"We should go, Miss Cormack."

Only moments had passed since their arrival, and those minutes felt as short as heartbeats. Constance didn't want to leave — of course she didn't — but their visit was irregular. There were Generals, or Brigadiers, or Colonels waiting somewhere in Fort Leavenworth for a DC-3 flight to the Rocky Mountains, and delaying their departure would do no one any good.

So as Constance flung herself forward for one more forbidden hug — and the guards wisely stood back, determined to punish Vanier later for his good negro luck — she steeled herself. With a ragged breath that she'd rather have had under control, the young graduate squeezed her brother one last time, kissed him on the forehead, and backed away from him.

"I *promise*," she said, and as he met her intense gaze, he nodded, then smiled.

"You take care. You take care and I'll see you soon."

It all sounded like lies — probably was lies — but it was how they had to part.

Gradually, and under the gentle prompting of Major Fischer, Constance withdrew from the room. As the white officer backed out, he and Vanier exchanged one last knowing glance — one that said *look after her* — and then the door was shut.

Constance shed tears as they walked from Leavenworth. She did her best to let no one see them — to walk tall and with purpose — but she shed them. Vanier returned to his cell, and tripped a few times on the way, bruising himself and busting his lip.

Black boy getting love from a white Champion girl? If he wasn't such a known prisoner, he'd probably have been lynched.

Such was his fate, for daring to achieve. Perhaps respite would find him… or perhaps not. Time, and the arrival of the Saa, would tell the tale.

CHAPTER II

The room was full of important people, which made Alex feel terribly out of place. The new world was magical and she loved the thought of exploring it, but right off the train there had been stately cars, a processional drive to Government House, and all manner of indoor niceties to satisfy... not at all what she had in mind.

Now she was trapped in a posh reception meant to welcome the Jimmystown delegation to New World City, and with all the natural social graces of her mother, the Lady in white was hovering safely near the door, managing to look only mildly uncomfortable.

"There's a lot of smoke in this room," Stephanie was beside her friend, arms folded as she scowled rather unsociably at anyone who dared make eye contact with her.

Mike Strong was with them too, and though as a Sergeant he was the least welcome in such a lofty room, he seemed most at ease as he explained: "The cigar smoke is how you know they're important."

"Cigars? I thought the smoke was because too many dense brains were straining to make polite conversation," Stephanie's quip came without delay... but unfortunately wasn't quite as clear as she meant it to be.

"Huh?" Alex frowned.

Stephanie shot a glance at her friend, "*Huh* what?"

"That didn't make sense," the whitecoat didn't back off.

"I'm saying I thought the smoke was coming out of their ears because they were thinking too hard," the Second Lieutenant clarified.

"Right," Alex caught on, sort of, and then shook her head. "That didn't work out so well for you."

"I'm getting that sense," Stephanie didn't sound too impressed, though whether that was because she'd been called out, or because she was too anxious to be joking in the first place, she wasn't sure.

The failure of the joke was no great concern, though, particularly in a room full of people who were trying not to stare too pointedly at the two girls and the Sergeant standing near the door. Over the past eight months the papers had reported on many of their missions, so apart from being the sorts of young women who older cigar-chomping dignitaries enjoyed looking at, these two were naturally notable. The long stares were impossible to miss.

Fortunately, neither of them looked too approachable, and Mike Strong was looming nearby for good measure. So far there'd been no attempts whatsoever to talk to (or charm) them, and that was just fine.

"I shouldn't be hugging you in public, but I can't help myself."

Suddenly there were arms around Alex — arms clad in purple.

Stephanie lurched sideways in surprise as the purple shape basically hit her friend, and Mike Strong took a step forward... but both of them stopped when they recognized Lady Anneke Winter.

Alex just managed to contain her look of surprise before hugging back gently, "That's okay. I'm an awkward magnet."

As she released Alex and stepped back with a smile, Anneke shook her head, "You still calling yourself awkward?"

"Yes," the whitecoat's answer was instinctive.

"I don't think you're awkward, but then I'm biased because you did save my life," Anneke was a bit on the nose with that observation, and Alex actually winced. For some reason, she found it extra-awkward to hear such things.

Stephanie set aside her preoccupation and rallied to her friend's defense: "Saying things like that just makes it more awkward."

That was too true, but well said. With a winning — perfect — smile, Anneke therefore turned towards the American Lieutenant to offer an unnecessary hug, but she was interrupted by the blurred arrival of another coat-wearer. Elspeth Cornish and Anneke Winter were dear friends, and hadn't seen each other in months — since Anneke had been sunk in *Hood*, and Elspeth had been gassed and kidnapped in Scotland.

It was immediately evident that they were both glad to see each other alive.

"Sorry," Elspeth offered distracted apologies to her adopted friends as she latched onto the Lady in purple. "We need to catch up."

Anneke nodded in agreement and then they disappeared into

the reception, presumably looking for some place quiet so they could speak to each other uninterrupted. Watching them go, Stephanie actually breathed a sigh of relief — no hug required.

"Well they're happy to see each other," Alex observed after a moment, then frowned and looked at her friend. "Why aren't we ever that happy to see each other?"

Stephanie grumbled: "Because you don't understand my jokes."

Alex pouted: "Look, smoke's coming out of everyone's ears!"

"It's too late," Stephanie folded her arms and shook her head as the duo returned to scanning the room.

Anneke's presence had been no coincidence; Alain Lapointe had arrived, and now the Canadian Prime Minister was alongside Jimmy Devlin and Lady Anne, speaking with Selkirk Mandate Governor Arthur Currie — the man who'd commanded their brigade during the last battle of the Hubrin War. The nostalgia was evident even from across the room — a strong bond existed between the people who'd been part of those battles in 1919 and 1920. One day, Alex imagined she might understand the depth of that bond, but for the time being there were nearer distractions.

Indeed, one such diversion was arriving with Caralynne: some man was accompanying Alex's mother as she headed towards the whitecoat at the edge of the room, and it was clear the elder Lady Smith planned to present him.

He was at least fifty, wore a gray suit as though it were an old-style army tunic, and walked with a stiff gait that suggested he'd done his body some damage over years of action. His face was hard, but his eyes seemed warm as Alex accidentally locked onto them. She didn't know this man, but somehow it seemed as though he knew her...

"Is that Captain Quinn?"

Suddenly Mike Strong was pushing his way — gently, of course — between his two charges, and as Alex and Stephanie sidestepped in surprise, the man with Caralynne blinked a few times, his expression changing.

"I am Quinn," was his answer, but his eyes were already narrowing as he tried to place the Colour. It took only a second: "You're Mike Strong."

"I am that man, sir," the Sergeant grinned as he stopped right before Quinn, then nodded in lieu of a salute.

Shaking his head, the suited man glanced briefly at Caralynne before explaining himself, "Glad to meet you again. I suppose we'd seen each other in the old days?"

"A few times, sir. I was just a boy back then," Strong answered.

"We all were," Quinn concurred distantly, before shaking himself back into the moment. "Good to meet you properly now. So few of us left who saw those days."

Such dark words inevitably clouded Strong's good humor, but not enough to halt his response, "Yes sir. You've come to see the dragons in?"

Quinn nodded, "It's a rare chance. When I heard Sass was landing here instead of on Earth, I knew I'd be a fool to miss it."

That was impossible to argue with, so Strong bowed his head in a slow nod before stepping aside and making way for Quinn to approach his girls, "Well sir, you'd be a fool to miss these two as well. They're much wiser than we were at their ages."

Alex and Stephanie had been listening, of course — piecing together enough to know that Quinn was yet another veteran of the adventures on His Majesty's new world, though not one either of them could place.

Strong therefore made the introductions, "This is Captain Quinn, of the Canadian Rifles. He survived Farfield City when it was overrun in 1919."

Alex felt her polite smile tighten as she listened. She *had* heard Quinn's name before; he'd been one of the men to survive by hiding in a burned out town after savages had come through and eaten every living soul. He'd been found by Alex's parents when they arrived in aero planes with Air Marshall Carstairs... meaning he'd been with Alex's father after Caralynne had been killed.

Focused on that reality, Alex's voice began to tighten as she offered her greeting, "How do you do, Captain Quinn."

Recognizing the natural tension, Stephanie's own greeting was rather somber as well: "Mister Quinn."

His eyes seemed almost glassy as he looked them both over — the familiar nostalgic gaze of many veterans from his era. It was as though Alex and Stephanie's existence confirmed to him that past sacrifices had been worth it.

"Delighted to meet you both," Quinn said. "Your mother tells me of great deeds, Alex. I don't get the papers out in my headquarters, so

I'm afraid I haven't followed your exploits to date."

"Exploits would be too generous a word," Alex's deflection was immediate, and terribly polite, but Quinn waved his hand.

"I suspect you are being too modest."

That's where the conversation stalled for a moment — Quinn looking from Lady to Lieutenant and back. For her part, Caralynne was no good at nudging the exchange along; her general lack of social graces was compounded by the fact that this man still reminded her of the day she'd died.

The awkward silence had one enemy, though, in Mike Strong: "Your headquarters, sir? What's your business in these fine times?"

Quinn blinked, then cast a glance at the Sergeant, "My company rescues the next generation of Champion children from savage parents... so they have a chance to grow to be like Lady Alex here."

Though Quinn clearly knew how to position his work in a favorable manner, the words still came as a surprise to Strong. He blinked and glanced towards Alex; she was unconsciously beginning to raise her eyebrows, while Stephanie's brow was creasing.

The American commented first, "I didn't realize there were still companies for that."

Quinn was ready for the comment — seemed likely he heard it often, "We are not the bounty hunters of old, Lieutenant. There is no great profit in it, as there was in the past. But we find one or two dozen children a year still on the other continent of this planet, and bring them from savagery to civilization."

Stephanie's frown didn't ease, but she did offer a gentle nod of understanding. The new world had two main continents: a massive central landmass, and a smaller one sitting across wide oceans on the other side of the planet. That latter territory was largely wild and untamed — the infrastructure of sea travel on the new world was still being developed, so its links to the rest of civilization were tenuous.

And there, evidently, hordes of savages still roamed — bearing children who, once rescued, could join the ranks of the Champions.

"Even after all this time?" Alex was as surprised as Stephanie at the revelation, and Quinn nodded.

"Until that continent is settled, I expect there will always be some children. And my company will make sure they are not forced to grow up savage."

That was a noble sentiment, anyway; in decades past, as the

last of the savages were exterminated on the Selkirk continent, bounty hunters had made fortunes by gathering as many savage-born children as possible, and delivering them to British and American authorities for rewards. With the dwindling number of wild savages, children were only found occasionally by accident in remote corners of Selkirk and Pacifica — the mercenaries had long since moved on.

But evidently, there were still some children to save elsewhere, and Quinn was doing it — making sure that Britain did not stop gaining Champions, before those like Elspeth, Anneke, and one day even Alex began bearing the next generation.

"No better man for such work," Strong remained diplomatic. "After all they did to you, good job that you're saving children from a savage fate, Captain Quinn."

The veteran nodded his thanks, though his smile remained sad, "It's brutal work, Sergeant. But my men are all veterans like us... better that we who already have the nightmares simply acquire more, than to subject new generations to them. And though I know young Lady Smith here was born to her greatness, never rescued... I must say she is..." he paused and looked right at Alex, "...you *are* a great example for all of us. You give us hope that those we save will make our terrors worthwhile."

That sounded both sweet, and a little tragic. Alex barely nodded before stopping herself, and simply saying: "I look forward to the day your company is no longer required, Captain Quinn. Until then, thank you for saving the children."

It seemed the right thing to say, though somehow it still made Alex feel quite uncomfortable. As she glanced back to Stephanie, and saw equal unease on her friend's face, the whitecoat knew she felt awkward... though this time, she wasn't sure it was her fault.

Such was the nature of conversation at these parties, it seemed. What she wouldn't give to simply get outside, and go exploring. After all, her father had managed to make his escape...

CHAPTER III

Smith had managed to both avoid the fancy reception, and to borrow a horse. With some anonymity, he rode the streets of New World City... though they were very different streets than those he'd become familiar with in 1919 and 1920. Dirt roads had been paved over, and horses largely replaced by automobiles.

Much of the traffic would be suspended for security purposes around the Saa arrival, but for now there were still Land Rovers, Jeeps, and all manner of cars rolling around as Smith eased his borrowed gelding towards the older part of town — a side of the settlement with buildings he still recognized.

Occasionally he was spotted — someone would call out his name, and he would wave in silent passing — but for the most part he was left to himself. Eventually, he came upon a grand hotel. The building was all wood, like the old-west style inns he'd seen across the new world in his years drifting... but it was well-painted, bright, and cared for. The Shylock family owned this hotel, so when Vonn and Miranda came to town, it was where they stayed.

Riding up to the hotel's front porch, Smith saw that a hitching post still stood out front, defying the cars that passed it by. Guiding his borrowed mount up to that wooden crossbar, the former-drifter dismounted and looped his reins around before advancing towards the steps up to the porch.

As he climbed the stairs, a couple emerged — finely-dressed people, but by their gait, frontier types. Probably wealthy locals, come to town for the arrival ceremonies, but electing to stay in the sort of hotel they were familiar with instead of the more modern city-style hotels that had sprung up in the newer parts.

Smith touched the brim of his hat to the couple, and the lady smiled, then nodded as her husband touched his hat in reply. They went on and Smith advanced towards the door.

It opened before he could reach it, and a great big dark figure loomed there, waiting for him.

"Knew you'd come this way," the man's voice was as burly as he was, and Smith stopped on the porch at the greeting.

"Figured you'd prefer the quiet," he answered immediately, and the man took a step out the door, then squared off facing him.

"Figured right, Smith."

Bo Shylock was not what anyone would consider smart, but he was no fool either, and his heart was proportionally larger than most. He let his mock standoff with his great old friend last for a second, then he stuck out his good hand and advanced one more step so Smith could take it.

"I'll shake your hand," he announced as their grips met, and Smith nodded to him immediately.

"How you been, Bo?"

"Persisting," he answered. "Learning new words too. Found me a lady with some learnin', and she is making me acquire new vocabulary."

Bo Shylock was in his fifties, just like Smith, but the man seemed as youthful as ever. It was good to hear he was well… still finding new ways to make his life interesting.

Behind the big Shylock, another figure emerged from the hotel. Smaller, lean, and still moving like a predator cat, Cameron Kard smiled, "He figured you'd come over. Been waiting by the door most of the day."

The gunfighter who had taught Stephanie her trade moved up beside the bigger Shylock brother, and Smith shook his hand firmly, "Kard. Keeping well?"

Kard snorted a bit of a laugh, "Not as well as our girl. Arthritis getting into my hands, would you believe? One day I might have to hang up my guns."

Smith was surprised to hear that — he wasn't naïve about aging, but somehow he'd figured a man who used his hands as deftly as Kard would be among the last to get arthritis. Poor health played no favorites.

"My brother and his wife are upstairs," Bo offered that bit of extra information before Kard's plight could become the subject of any discussion. "Miranda needed to lie down a spell before Stephanie arrived."

Those words drew a frown to Smith's face, and he looked back to the big Shylock, "She not well?"

Bo's warm expression seemed to cool, and he looked towards Kard before the gunman answered diplomatically, "She gets tired travelling. Just needs some rest."

It was as poor an excuse as Smith had heard, but it was not for him to question. Instead, he nodded towards the door, "Go in?"

"Sure thing," Bo replied. "It'll do them good to see you."

"We all want to know how Stephanie is... so we're ready when we see her," Kard added, and though he was speaking kindly, there was a seriousness underlying his words.

Stephanie hadn't been home in a long time, and she'd become a soldier and a shooter since then. She'd killed men, and her combined Shylock-Kard family wanted to be ready if she'd been changed greatly by her experiences.

Smith sympathized. He'd been able to watch Alex grow from right up close. Had he left just before August of 1940, and only returned now — a year later — the changes in his daughter might have struck him as dramatic.

Stephanie, too, was a different woman, but Smith knew the Shylocks didn't need to worry. Good sense, given by good parents, was helping the young Second Lieutenant stay on the right track. With that positive thought, Smith followed Bo and Kard into the hotel, and headed for the stairs up to the Shylocks' suite.

George Devlin had also managed to escape the Government House reception, though as he stood in Currie's office two floors above, he supposed the man in charge of security for the Saa delegation arrival probably wished he hadn't.

"We have *four* separate platoons tasked with that, Mister Devlin. They examine the tunnel in random order, on an hourly basis," Colonel Neville Grier had his arms folded as he stood on the opposite side of Currie's meeting table from the hospitality man. His glower was, no doubt, quite intimidating — but George took no notice.

"Four separate platoons, walking the tunnel back to the old world on an hourly basis?" the young Devlin asked for confirmation, his eyes not leaving the map of New World City that was unrolled before them.

"Yes," Grier confirmed immediately. "We know what we're

about, Mister Devlin. We know the risks."

It was fair to say that Grier did know the dangers the city faced. Given the events of the past months, it was difficult to imagine that the culprits behind the attacks in Virginia, on the Grand Banks, in Scotland, and ultimately in Hong Kong would fail to try *something* to disrupt the arrival of the Saa delegation.

And though Hong Kong had made it apparent that Emily was an enemy of these people, it was possible she could still cause some kind of trouble as well. That being the case, New World City had to become a fortress — the landing field where the Saa transport would put down was two miles from the tunnel, so every step along the route between them had to be double-checked for explosives, or any other type of destructive tool.

At least the Saa dragons were big enough to be largely invulnerable to bullets, but anything that could possibly pose them a danger had to be checked.

"I have 2,500 men in the city, I have men checking to make sure your train back to the old world won't be blown up. I've enlisted the local constabulary... by God, Mister Devlin, we've even enlisted known local citizens... good men, who've been here for decades, to watch out for unfamiliar things. Every responsible citizen in this town will be an armed deputy in case of crisis," Grier clearly had thought of virtually everything, and he was frustrated at being questioned by a boy who was not yet twenty years old.

George sympathized, but still didn't look up, "The landing field perimeter?"

Grier sighed rather conspicuously before answering, "A regiment will be picketing it on all sides. Brigadier Webb chose the men himself. We will also have a squadron of Spitfires overhead, so if any trouble comes from the woods, we'll throw purple smoke and the RAF will strafe that area immediately."

Sounded thorough. George's eyes traveled back and forth across the map as he pictured the various arrangements, and tried to imagine any attack that could be mounted. For the past month, access to the new world had been carefully monitored — because there were only two tunnels to and from Earth, it was possible for Britain and the United States to control the flow of both people and supplies. Anything that appeared even remotely dangerous had been impounded or turned back, and anyone seeming slightly suspicious had been similarly denied entry.

But obviously, the naval yard in Rosyth had been carefully guarded, and attackers had still managed to get their bombs aboard *Hood*. No matter how tight security had been, George could not take the safety of the Saa — or the many dignitaries who had assembled to greet them — for granted.

It would have been ideal, of course, to have Sass and her party delivered directly to Jimmystown, but that space trip would have been impractical for her; the new world was closer to Saa trade routes, and George's father had rightly asked her to return early. She had to land here, and the resulting spectacle — with all its risks — was inevitable. It would undoubtedly have been safer without a parade, but there was literally no other way for a creature the size of Sass to travel. She'd have to walk the two miles from the landing field to the railway station no matter what, so denying good citizens the chance to line the streets and see her would be petty.

At least the landing field on the Alberta side of the tunnel was near the exit — there would be no matching tour in Gateway Town. *Skipper Miller* would be waiting there for the delegation, and would take off for Jimmystown as soon as they were aboard.

As long as they got to *Skipper Miller*…

"Look, Mister Devlin, I realize your father wants you involved in all this, but we haven't been ignoring the headlines these last few months. We're ready for whatever those bastards will try to throw at us," Grier's tone pitched just slightly towards the conciliatory. "We'll get the job done."

Still staring at the map, George Devlin let out a sigh of his own, then shook his head.

"I hope you're right about that, Colonel," he replied. "Perhaps the villains have simply been fortunate so far."

"They certainly have been," Grier took the younger man's words as a concession, which he graciously tried to parlay into candor. "It's been luck for them. But luck can't beat our preparations."

Perhaps that wasn't an unreasonable thing to say, but it nevertheless struck George the wrong way. Looking up, the young man locked his stare on the Colonel and raised an eyebrow, "Until we know for certain that they are not being informed by some very deeply-rooted spy, Colonel Grier, I don't think it's wise to speak in declaratives."

It was a measured scolding, and as the cool words hit the soldier his expression hardened again. Fortunately, he elected not to pursue a debate. Tomorrow they'd have their answers; when nothing went wrong, he would have the satisfaction of being right.

And in that case, George would have the satisfaction of getting his dragons home safe.

Smith was standing back from the suite door with Bo and Kard, but as it opened, the former-drifter advanced one step with hand extended. Vonn Shylock took that hand immediately, but said nothing — his expression asked for quiet. Smith obliged as Stephanie's father stepped out into the hotel corridor and shut the door behind him.

As the latch clicked he nodded to his friend, "Smith. Sorry, Miranda's sleeping. Needs the rest."

Vonn didn't try to explain, simply looked to his brother and Kard, "We'll go talk upstairs. Stay with her?"

Bo nodded firmly, and Kard smiled with a short dip of his chin to confirm.

That done, Vonn gestured in the direction of the stairs, and together with Smith he headed for the roof.

There was a terrace atop the building — nothing overcomplicated, just a decked area on the flat roof, with some chairs and tables. Stephanie's father walked past those, then stood on the edge of the deck and looked out across the town and the trees beyond.

Smith had never actually seen New World City from such a vantage point — one hadn't existed before he moved away — but as he joined his friend, he found himself looking out over the foothills through which he'd so often ridden... the place he'd called home before finding his family, and setting down roots in Newfoundland.

Memories swirled around him at the sight... sensations revived in his chest. Life had been pure in the old days — uncomplicated by politics, and by family. Though Smith loved his wife and child more than anything, and would sacrifice everything for Caralynne and Alex, he still felt nostalgia for his time on this planet. For the simpler decisions, the unknown trails, the clear morality...

But recent complexities were necessary ones. All feelings had their time, and Smith's simple life as a drifter was long in the past. Vonn Shylock's years on the trail were over too; this hotel, and a half-dozen others like it around the new world, belonged to him. He had gotten his start from money Smith had given him — pay from the British that Smith hadn't wanted — and now he'd made a great success of himself.

Unfortunately, money could buy only so much. Smith knew this, and with a breath to clear his mind, he asked: "Is she dying?"

Though they saw each other only every few years, Vonn and Smith had the sort of friendship that never fallowed. Without taking his eyes off the trees beyond the town, Stephanie's father shook his head, "The doctors can't say. Every year it gets a little harder for her."

Smith remembered Vonn's wife Miranda very well — she'd been young and alone when she'd met then-drifter Shylock. She'd survived when her family had been wiped out by tuberculosis, and with Vonn she'd had one daughter. In many ways, Miranda epitomized this world: strong, practical, caring, realistic. She'd been a voice of calm for Smith after Caralynne's death, and a dear friend after Caralynne's resurrection. She'd raised her daughter right.

She wasn't the sort who needed to lie down in the middle of the day, particularly when it was the first day in years she'd see Stephanie.

"How's my girl? If her mother is dying, will that hurt her?" Vonn turned away from the vista at last, and his question was direct — if not entirely redundant.

Both Smith and Vonn had left their families at such young ages that they barely remembered their parents — theirs had been a different life. But Stephanie and Alex had come up in a world where mother and father were the opposite of faint memories, and both girls possessed their fathers' hearts in ways that only fathers could understand.

Now Vonn was worried for Stephanie, and Smith understood that too well.

"It will hurt," was his answer. "She's strong, but it'll hurt."

Vonn swallowed, then looked away again, "That makes two of us. Can't figure what I'm supposed to do anymore, Smith. There are days she's good... but some days she just can't get herself up and around. She feels so sorry about it, as if there's something she should be doing different... but there's nothing. Her body's just letting her down."

Miranda couldn't yet be fifty, so those symptoms did indeed sound grave to Smith. And having watched the woman he loved die once, he understood the pain in his friend's voice.

"Nothing easy about it," he said slowly. "When the Saa get here, I'll ask if there's something they can do."

Though it would have been typical of Vonn to resist an offer for unsolicited help, he didn't this time, "Okay. But my girl... she's well?"

Smith nodded, then felt a rare smile form on his face, "She and Alex... you can never get daylight between them. Both our girls are smarter than we were."

A smile came to Vonn's face too. It was good that daughters did better than their fathers; that gave a man his purpose for living. And sick though his wife was, Vonn knew Miranda would appreciate it too.

"Can't wait to see her," the elder Shylock said, and Smith nodded.

"She'll be nervous, because she's different, but she wants to see you too."

Vonn frowned a little, "Different?"

Smith tipped his head slightly, "Like we were, after the Rory Ranch."

Of course, Vonn understood. Killing — even rightly — made a person question. That was natural, and he'd make sure his daughter knew it. With a nod, Vonn turned back towards the town and watched the trees beyond shiver in the fresh wind coming off the mountain.

The Shylocks were all dealing with a new reality, but at least they had their friends the Smiths to help them through. Some things never changed.

And some things did.

CHAPTER IV

Gateway Town was by no means the largest city Constance Cormack had seen, but nestled as it was at the base of a mighty mountain, it was breathtaking in its own right. Or perhaps that was just the altitude.

Emerging from the DC-3 that had flown her up to Alberta from Kansas, she looked up at rock on all sides — powerful gray-and-white peaks that stood sharply in the cool air. They stared back at her with a thin air of disinterest, as though they were titans who could barely be bothered with the comings and goings of humanity.

Such rocks could make even a Champion feel small, and Constance didn't mind at all. Descending from the aircraft, she found herself enjoying the feeling of being lost within a mountain range — Gateway Town was very much in the midst of the Canadian Rockies — and that wonder pushed some of the anxiety about Vanier from her mind. She could only imagine what the mountains were like in the Selkirk Mandate... how they'd feel so distantly magical...

"Hello, beautiful."

Fischer's voice interrupted Constance's thoughts, and she stopped beside the bottom of the DC-3's ladder to glance back at him with a frown. The Major was just planting his boots on the grass of the field, and as he stepped aside to let more lofty VIPs pass, she saw that his gaze was directed not at the peaks (or fortunately at her) but at a different sight.

"Must be *Major Herbert Miller*," he raised his hand towards a shining silver shape across the field, and Constance's gaze followed the gesture as he added: "No scars from the blast in Eustice, see?"

The young graduate nodded; she'd been aboard *George Tucker* the day it had been damaged in the Fort Eustice attack. Her lunch with Alex, Stephanie and Strong had probably played no small part in building the confidence that had led her to the top of her class, and resulted in her being invited to join the American delegation for the Saa arrival.

Since that attack, she hadn't been too near any skycruisers — even though she'd been in Newfoundland for the balance of her final year, the ships had been carefully guarded at Torbay Airport. Perhaps now that she had graduated, she could get more time aboard one… but until then, only a select few were lucky enough to get the chance.

And despite his previous experience with Saa technology… or perhaps because of his proximity to it… Fischer was not one of the few.

"Were you ever aboard our skycruisers, before we lost them?" Constance asked as the rest of the dignitaries from the plane left them behind on the field.

The Major smiled sadly, "Not once, if you can believe it."

Constance frowned, actually finding that surprising. The United States Army had certainly instituted some strange policies in past years — not limited, obviously, to restrictions placed upon black troops. That one of the experts on Saa technology wouldn't be sent aboard a Saa-built ship for training seemed silly.

"Well with the Saa back, perhaps you'll have a new opportunity," the young Champion from Georgia offered that conciliatory hope, but Fischer shook his head.

"Not likely. Security is paramount, my dear, and don't mistake my being invited to join this delegation for confidence in me having been restored. I'm sure someone must still have me on a list of suspects after Virginia."

Well, at least he wasn't deluding himself. With a delicate smile that would have done her mother proud, Constance nodded, then shrugged, "Well one day, then. Once we have the villains in hand, and the world is a safer place."

Fischer's smile brightened, and he considered Constance warmly, "Spoken like a true Champion. But I fear I still doubt that day will see me aboard a skycruiser."

So much for being polite and positive; with another shrug, Constance waved toward the town, and the train parked at the railway station near the mountain, "They'll let you on the train, though."

"I certainly hope so!"

With that, the pair left the DC-3, paying no attention as the men unloading luggage from the aircraft paused to smoke cigarettes.

Anne Devlin hadn't been back to the new world for a few years, and after briefly stealing away from the lofty reception, she drifted towards one of the hall's grand windows. She wanted to get a look at the place that had changed her life.

Coming to the new world as a maid in 1919 had been an adventure, and an escape. Through some creative references she'd been able to secure a post with two mysterious women intent on leaving the old world behind, which had suited her purposes perfectly... but she'd never foreseen her adventure leading where it had.

Then again, no one could possibly have predicted everything that had happened.

The charming young Lieutenant who had accompanied Colonel Waller to meet Emily and Caralynne that day in New World City had proposed to her under the two moons of the grasslands, not long before his first battle with the blue men. Annie had let herself be swept up in the courtship, which had been so much finer than anything she'd previously experienced, but somehow she'd never thought it could last. Then they'd been wed, and he'd survived every battle — even the one that was surest to kill him. After that came promotion, and peerage. In the space of a year on this planet, Anne Devlin had gone from maid to Baroness. Now she was returning as a Viscountess, and yet she couldn't help but feel the butterflies in her stomach once more.

Important things seemed to happen in this place — new beginnings, and bitter endings too. Which one would Sass's return bring: life or death? Such were the heavy thoughts weighing on Lady Anne's mind when she was interrupted by a welcome voice.

"If anyone asks, we're talking about the old days."

Caralynne arrived at the window beside her long-ago maid, and as the elder Lady Smith let out a long sigh, it was impossible for Lady Devlin to keep from smiling.

"Enjoying yourself thoroughly, of course," she observed.

"Are you implying that I don't love these soirees?"

Anne's eyebrow climbed at the question, "Have you offered to show anyone your scars yet?"

Caralynne folded her arms at the question, and as her expression changed Anne was reminded again where Alex had gained her ability to look amusing as she pretended to pout, "*Maybe.*"

"Good for you," Anne's smile remained as she turned her gaze back to the town beyond the glass.

Silence settled for a few moments, neither of the Ladies doing much to convince any onlookers that they were talking about anything at all. Finally, though, Anne shook her head, "If we'd known all this was going to happen when we came here first, what would we have done?"

It was a particularly reflective question, but Caralynne was in similar spirits, and she shrugged, "Probably everything the same."

Perhaps it was a cliché to say that she'd change nothing about her past, but how could either woman — both proud mothers — suggest they would have altered anything that had occurred in the old days.

"I'd even die again," Caralynne's words were somber as she acknowledged that point in her history. "If I hadn't, Alex wouldn't be... well."

Anne knew what Caralynne was saying: "She'd still be Alex, but she wouldn't be the whitecoat."

"Yes," Caralynne agreed immediately. "I don't think I've known anyone else who fits a coat better. I'm biased, I know... but what we did in the old days made that possible for her. I couldn't change it."

"Nor I," Anne agreed. Sometimes sacrifice from parents — even before their children came to be — was more important than comfort, ease, or *not* dying. But then perhaps Caralynne was particularly biased, since her death was uniquely not permanent.

Fairly uniquely.

Anne frowned for a second as that thought appeared in her mind, then shook her head and elected to lighten the tone of the conversation: "I might have packed better boots for marching."

"So many blisters," Caralynne agreed immediately. "Hard to be dainty and fashionable when you're all chafed up."

"Hard to be dainty or fashionable when you're a maid and a frontierswoman," Anne pointed out in reply, and Caralynne was compelled to nod.

"Glad some things haven't changed," she said, but that was a bridge too far for the Viscountess of the Grasslands.

"Speak for yourself. I'm the height of fashion now."

Caralynne smiled, "Yes. You keep telling yourself that."

It was rare that Caralynne and Anne Devlin got to chatter and joke anymore, but such was the magic of the new world. They'd enjoy it while it lasted.

Seeing two moons rise was something Constance Cormack hadn't really prepared herself for. As she waited on the platform at New World City's train station for Fischer to find out their billeting arrangements, the young Champion had been staring up at the mountain that loomed over the British town.

As she'd hoped, it was magical — a whole new world.

Only when she was sufficiently full of awe at the mighty peak standing against the dark blue sky did she turn, and discover the twin orbs beginning their nightly climb over the city. Honestly, that just stirred up more awe. It was getting excessive.

She wondered what it must have been like for the man who'd first discovered the tunnels to the new world — a railway surveyor called Rogers — when he stumbled out of the mountain, looked up and saw them. Had he realized how much his discovery would re-shape the world he'd left behind, the one he'd return to? Could he possibly have known how—

"Hello?"

Suddenly a hand was waving in front of Constance's face, and she blinked before realizing that Fischer had returned, and perhaps had even been trying to talk to her while she was lost in thought.

Sheepishly she apologized, "Sorry. Was miles away."

"Looked like more than miles," the Major's answer was dry — a little harsh, actually, which brought a frown to Constance's face, but he continued. "Turns out, the British didn't plan any accommodations for us. They say the War Department was supposed to, but obviously our brass didn't. So we're supposed to find a hotel on our own, and pay our own money for it."

That would explain the harshness. Constance blinked.

"I know," Fischer shook his head with no attempt to conceal his frustration. "I'm going to look up a girl I knew once. She might slap me, but then she'll see to me. Meet you at landing field in the morning?"

Constance stared at him, then nodded. She shouldn't have done that — it was just reflex — but she did anyway. She wasn't bound to Fischer in any particular way, aside for their mutual friend, so it was entirely his business if he wanted to spend the night with a random woman from his past.

But though she was an adult at eighteen, and a graduate, Constance Cormack was new to this world — obviously — and had no idea where to go.

She should have stopped Fischer to ask for suggestions, but foolishly she let him walk off the platform, and disappear into the darkness.

Where would she spend the night?

CHAPTER V

As the moons rose and the electric lights lining New World City's streets switched on, a yellow glow was cast over the three-storey hotel owned by Stephanie's parents. The resulting visual was slightly ominous — the building itself was neither menacing nor unwelcoming, but the young Lieutenant found herself stopping in the street to stare.

Beside her was her best friend in white, and they stood shoulder-to-shoulder for a couple of moments, gazing up at the light spilling out of the building's top-floor windows. Those rooms were surely accommodating the Shylock family — the rest of the hotel would have been booked by people coming to town to see Sass's arrival (and by the Smith family, who wouldn't stay anywhere else)... but the top floor would be for the owners.

And like square yellow eyes, with lids caused by half-pulled-down shades, those windows were leering down at the prodigal Shylock daughter.

Stephanie was really apprehensive as she met that metaphorical stare; her posture was uncommonly taut and her hand was starting to tap her thigh as if she was working up her courage. Considering all she'd been through, it might have seemed silly... but Alex had sympathy for her friend.

Leaning sideways a little, she expressed that sentiment, "It *does* look creepy and haunted."

At first Stephanie didn't seem to hear the words, but as they processed she scowled, "What? No it *doesn't*."

She was definitely wound-up, and it was doing nothing for her already suspect sense of humor. Alex wasn't about to back off from the joke, either: "Then why are we standing outside staring, like two girls getting ready to go into a haunted house in a film?"

"Because… reasons," Stephanie glowered and looked back to the building, knowing her friend was trying to lighten the mood, but not wanting to accommodate.

"Reasons like there's a *Dracula* inside, I bet," Alex folded her arms, and Stephanie contained a groan.

"I am behind you!"

The fact that Mike Strong's horrid Transylvanian accent actually got them both to jump made the Sergeant much too happy. Coming to a stop behind his girls, he put his hands on his hips and looked up at the hotel too.

"I remember climbing out that fire escape, to avoid being shot by a particular unruly husband," he said warmly, rocking up onto the balls of his feet. "Ah, memories."

Stephanie really wasn't playing along with the attempts to improve her mood, "He was offended by you sleeping on the floor?"

Naturally, Strong had an answer, "He was offended by who was on the floor with me."

Apparently the Colour was on a roll, but Alex wasn't giving up on her own lame joke, "Was it a Dracula?"

Strong grinned at her, "I'm the only one he lets call him 'a' Dracula. It's our term of endearment."

Then he winked, just in case he wasn't being sufficiently creepy, and Alex rolled her eyes, "Well this is going badly. Can we go inside yet?"

If nothing else, the horrific attempts at humor were doing a good job of pushing Stephanie off the street. Whatever her anxiety about seeing her family again, she could only cope with so much of Alex and Strong trying to make her laugh.

Which was entirely their plan.

"Okay," was the Second Lieutenant's defeated answer, and then she advanced slowly towards the hotel.

Lingering behind a moment, Alex glanced at her Colour and extended her hand to him, "Well fought, sir."

Mike grinned and shook her hand, but as he let go a pantomime look of fear covered his face: "Now do me. I'm nervous I'm going to run into a Dracula in there."

Alex's smile melted, "You have two feet and a heartbeat, Sergeant. Move yourself."

"Yessir," he grinned, and together they scuttled after their officer.

• • •

As she entered the hotel, Stephanie immediately recognized the lady behind the counter; Eve had been working for her parents for nearly a decade, and she smiled at the sight of the American Lieutenant's return. Unfortunately — or perhaps fortunately, given Stephanie's mood — the veteran landlady was also busy with a man in a suit, who seemed to be handling a group booking.

Leaving her greeting at a simple nod, Stephanie thus headed straight for the stairs. Having played in this hotel as a girl, she knew where her family would be, and now that she was inside she figured she best not delay her fate, whatever that was. Two flights of stairs took her no time at all... they seemed less steep now than they had when she was young. Perhaps she really was in the best physical condition of her life.

Would her parents notice? Of course they'd notice, that was a silly question. They'd see everything about her — who she was now, as opposed to the headstrong, overconfident girl who'd left them for school years prior. And if she was becoming the sort of killer her father, her uncle, and Cameron Kard had stared down time after time in the old days, they'd see that too.

She'd killed nine Chinese — men with knives, fleeing Emily in panicked desperation — without any difficulty. What did that *mean* for her homecoming? Would the smiles that greeted her be truly warm, or anxious? Would there be whispers... recollections of more innocent times, before she'd forced herself into a uniform and gone off to kill, to let Duncan be captured, to shoot a pistol out of Emily's hand?

They'd know everything she'd done wrong, and she'd be able to see in their eyes if they thought less of her as a result.

"Stephanie?"

That voice stopped Second Lieutenant Shylock dead in her tracks, halfway up the stairs to the third floor of the hotel. She wasn't looking up — couldn't actually see who had spoken — but it was said that children learned to recognize their mother's voice before all others.

And apparently the recognition caused Stephanie to burst into tears. She was completely unprepared for that reaction — she'd hoped to keep herself under control somehow. But after working herself up into something of a state, fearfully wondering about things that were beyond reason, it was almost inevitable.

Fortunately, her mother's arms immediately wrapped around her, and though the squeeze they gave seemed less firm than she remembered, the peace they provided was beyond compare.

"Welcome home," Miranda Shylock said gently, and Stephanie sniffled in a way that might have horribly embarrassed her, had she been with any other person in the two worlds.

But this was her mom, and that made things okay.

"I think I hear her crying on the stairs," Alex was standing in line for the check-in counter with Strong, and she whispered that to him with a bit of concern. "Think she's... okay?"

The Sergeant nodded, though it appeared he was more interested in looking through the doorway that led into the bar, "She'll be good."

Alex wasn't entirely satisfied with the answer, "Nothing to worry about?"

Strong leaned partway out of line, doing a very obvious job of seeing if there were any ladies present for him to charm, before turning back to his whitecoat, "She's just been saving up her tears for her mom. Because your mom is always close, you don't have to store them all up like that. And you know as well as I do: there are always tears."

"Of course there are," Alex agreed — though she knew hers usually came in the middle of the night, along with her nightmares. Those had been less frequent, at least.

"Nice thing for you girls is you aren't all hung up about the tears. You know me, I have to run and hide every time I bawl. Reputation to protect," Strong went on, still pretending to pay more attention to candidates for his affection.

Alex considered nodding at his words, though she somehow felt as though they were for her benefit. Because when Strong's moods came over him, tears never seemed to be involved — not because he was a big strong man with a reputation, but because when he remembered all his friends who'd died on this very world, what awoke inside him seemed so profoundly grave that even tears were not enough for his pain.

In those moments, he just seemed as though life left him. He probably would have been happier to have a good manly cry, but he lacked the ability.

Stephanie could still cry — was still fully human, whatever her anxieties about her lethal actions of recent months. Hopefully her mother would put her fears to rest, as Alex's parents always did for her.

Either way, the whitecoat would check in to their shared room — the one that Stephanie probably figured would give her refuge if her parents somehow hated her...

"Here they are!"

Anneke Winter's voice interrupted Alex's musing, which made no sense, since she was guarding the Prime Minister. Alain Lapointe would surely be staying in one of the government residences in town...

Nope. Obviously.

As Alex turned towards the hotel door, she was confronted by an onslaught of faces from the reception: Anneke and Elspeth, Alain Lapointe, Jimmy Devlin, Anne Devlin, and her own parents.

Suddenly, the suited man who'd been absorbing a lot of time at the check-in counter was brushing past Alex and hurrying to the Canadian Prime Minister, reporting that the government party was all checked in. Naturally, the Lady in white was confused; she'd expected her parents, but everyone else?

Recognizing the expression on Alex's face, Alain Lapointe advanced past his aide and caught her eye with a smile, "When I come to New World City, I must stay in the hotel owned by a man who assaulted the Hubrin capital with us, Lady Alex. It is the only right place I could stay."

Of course; the Shylocks had been part of the fighting that day when the Royal Newfoundland Regiment, and Lapointe's Voltigeurs, had been cut apart by lightning. Such a bond was impossible for a man of the Prime Minister's quality to overlook — and the same kinship led him to turn next to Mike Strong, "Jimmy and I will be in the bar for drinks about old days here on this world. You will join us, of course."

"I hear Quebeckers are good with the ladies, Colonel. You can be my wingman," the Colour bowed grandly to the Prime Minister, and Lapointe scoffed.

"You are fortunate that I am happy in my marriage, Sergeant Strong, or you would have not a hope," the counter-shot was effortless, and Strong grinned.

"I was counting on the fact that you'd never abandon your Newfoundlander wife," he answered, and for some reason that inspired Lapointe to extend his hand. Strong took it, and then seemingly uncaring of the need to check in, both veterans wandered off to the bar.

After giving his wife a quick kiss, Jimmy Devlin joined them — three men who had watched too much death on this world were to relive the good days with the help of some drink. Alex watched them go, then looked to Anneke, Elspeth, Anne and her parents with one exaggerated shrug, "So... I guess we booked up the whole hotel?"

Helpfully, the woman behind the desk confirmed, "We're all full up tonight, so I hope your name is on my list here."

Unable to stop herself, Alex decided to be funny in her response: "Well then, I hope I don't have to sleep on the floor with *a Dracula*!"

That was one of those jokes that sounded better in her head... though to be fair, even in her head, it didn't sound all that good. No one took pity with a laugh, so she just checked in quietly, and fled the lobby as quickly as she could.

Stephanie was between good cries. Sitting at the top of the stairs to the third floor of the hotel, she could hear activity from all the way down in the lobby, and wondered if someone would come up the steps and discover her red-faced as she sat entangled with her mom.

But of course she didn't care.

A daughter was supposed to be able to take comfort in her mother's presence. If anyone had a problem with Stephanie getting her share, well... people would have better sense than to give her any grief about it. So she rested her head on her mother's shoulder and enjoyed the feeling of not having to be the responsible adult for just a few moments.

Miranda Shylock sat silently for much of this time, too. Naturally she was glad to have her daughter back — to see her at least one more time while she still had strength to comfort her — but she was also aware of the state Stephanie had worked herself up into.

When someone had a mind as sharp as Stephanie's, and possessed a strong sense of right and wrong, the ambiguous and often brutal realities of life could be difficult to absorb. Miranda knew her daughter was not naïve, and was intellectually comfortable in her new role as an officer of the Special Service Regiment.

But at some point, killing and seeing others kill caught up with most people. Not everyone — Miranda had known a few for whom it never seemed to matter — but with most good people, it raised questions. Such questions could only be answered in time, by living through them... but the process could be tough.

And even though the Smiths were among the best people Miranda knew, and Alex seemed the sort of friend that a mother could normally only *wish* her daughter might have, there were still certain reassurances that could only come from family.

Stephanie needed those now, because in just the past few months, she'd shot and killed more than ten men.

"How's pa?" when Stephanie found her voice, that was the question that emerged — not at all on topic with Miranda's musing.

Smiling and squeezing her daughter a little tighter, Miranda answered, "Well. He and your uncle and your godfather are all proud of you."

It was Stephanie's turn to squeeze tighter, "You know I'm anxious about that."

Miranda nodded and pressed her cheek against the top of her daughter's head, "You did burst into tears the moment you saw me." "The moment I heard you, actually," Stephanie sniffled again. "I'm an officer of the British Army now. I'm not supposed to do that."

"Everyone is entitled to cry with their mother. I thought it was fine," Miranda answered earnestly, but Stephanie remained reluctant. "Maybe."

She was deeply conflicted, and as Miranda assessed her daughter's words, she could sense the consternation was about far more than just the shooting work she'd done. Perhaps that was just the visible reason for her torment — the thing she was consciously concerned about.

So her mother made an observation: "You're worried that being an officer makes you a grown-up, and that you're leaving us all behind."

Miranda had never been shy about sharing her thoughts, and as she spoke her daughter felt a flash of heat hit her cheeks, and she started crying again — which in her own mind made no sense. She tried to blink away the tears, and make sense of them... and...

Her mother was right, of course.

Killing people was not a good thing to do. She was right for having done it — for fighting to stay alive, just like Kard had taught her. Her parents, her uncle, and Smith and Caralynne had always made it clear that, so long as she was doing it out of necessity, and for noble reasons, she was choosing the lesser evil.

But Miranda was correct: being the officer who made the decisions to shoot, and who felt as though she was no longer entitled to cry before her mother... that was what distressed her most.

She was growing up — turning into an adult, just as Alex was, not simply in age or station, but in mind. She took her responsibilities seriously, believed in what she did, and was ready to risk her own life for others. She wasn't just worried about Kard looking at her and seeing the beginnings of a stony-eyed killer... she was worried about her whole family looking at her and seeing a strange adult woman who they no longer could love, for she was part of a different world.

A soldier, educated with a Bachelor's degree, who'd been across the old world alongside a Champion... sure they would be proud, but... but did she belong with them anymore?

Swallowing against the thought, Stephanie closed her eyes and let her mother's reassurance warm her. She supposed it didn't matter, in a way: she was growing no matter what, and if that meant losing where she'd come from, she'd simply have to cope.

She just hoped... wished...

"You know that wherever your journey takes you, we're always with you inside. And proud. Remember that when you worry. Remember that you're the best of all of us, and that your achievements are a gift that we hold dear. Never fear that we'll be disappointed. We read of you and Alex, and feel only awe."

Well Miranda still knew how to say the things that were so honest they could make anyone cry. Once she had forced Smith to confront the death of Caralynne — something he'd never had to do before, or since. Now she held her daughter tighter as she cried, and they remained silent for more long minutes, as they listened to people hurrying to their rooms on the floors below.

Fortunately, the third floor remained their private preserve, so Stephanie was given time to let the feelings spill out for a while. It was good and therapeutic — she needed to let go some tears.

Eventually, though, she felt the burning ebb, and as she sniffled herself into some semblance of order, she raised her head from her mom's shoulder, "It's good to be home, ma. We should go see pa."

She was starting to sound more like herself, though as she sat up straighter Miranda considered her with a frown, "Not until you've cleaned yourself up. If your father realizes you've been crying, he'll start crying. And then he'll be surly for the rest of the week."

Stephanie smiled and laughed the way one does when coming out of a good spell of tearful catharsis. She nodded and tried to wipe her eyes before shaking her head, "We better get me to a mirror."

Standing up first, she then extended her hand down to her mother, and helped Miranda rise. It took every bit of determination the mother possessed not to reveal the agony that move caused. Her body was failing her, but for now it would be simpler if Stephanie had only one life change to worry about.

Together they went in search of a mirror, so the young officer could tidy herself up.

CHAPTER VI

After finding her travel case among the bags that had been delivered from the train to the hotel, Alex checked into the room she and Stephanie would share for the night (and in the absence of competition, took her choice of the beds). After unpacking her nightclothes and washing her face, the whitecoat sat down on her bed and breathed in the chilly air that came through the open window.

She'd always liked the fresh air of the new world. Her father had spoken of it often — the way it was different than the wind of Newfoundland, or the atmosphere anywhere else on Earth. Not completely alien — obviously it was breathable — but it had a distinct quality that was impossible to properly articulate.

Scientists could probably quantify what made it unique... the blend of inert gases, or whatever... but Alex didn't want to overthink it. She just enjoyed the chill as it filled her lungs, and settled in the room around her.

For a full half hour, she simply sat still and breathed, but finally her lungs were sufficiently soothed, and she found herself wondering how Stephanie was getting on. The Shylocks were good people — all of them — so the young Champion expected her friend was doing quite well. But that left Alex on her own, with nothing to do but sit and wait until it was late enough for bed.

Even the new world air wasn't tranquil enough to keep her stationary for *that* long.

Tapping her hands on her knees for a moment, she tried to decide what would be the best use of her time. She hadn't had a chance to do any exploring after the reception, so a run around the city might be good — with the town lit up by all its electric lights, such a jaunt could yield some dramatic sights.

Or she could go downstairs and make sure Mike Strong wasn't

trying too hard to convince everyone that he was a Lothario. That might be even more fun than a run... and it *was* partly her responsibility to make sure he didn't hurt himself, trying to keep up his pretense... so yes, she'd do that.

Decision made, the whitecoat clapped her hands together and rose from her bed, then headed for the bar.

Standing on a roof across the street, a man wearing a long gray raincoat — which he insisted was called a 'trench coat' — breathed a sigh of relief. He sure as hell wouldn't have been able to keep up with her on a run.

The hotel bar was lined with heroes of the Hubrin War. None of them would have used such a grand term to describe themselves — except, of course, for Mike Strong. But to him the word 'hero' was employed most ironically.

"Remember how many girls the b'ys found at that damned hotel in Promised Town?" Jimmy Devlin waved a pint of beer as he smiled at the memory.

Strong pointed at the Viscount and laughed, "My God *yes*. Remember Conway and that lady of his... where did she end up after?"

"Bay Roberts, I hear, with his family," Brigadier Kennedy — also in town for Sass's arrival — had joined the group.

Lady Anne was beside her husband, and though she tried to look appropriately disapproving, her sentiments couldn't quite be shielded, "I remember them dancing at our wedding. Don't you remember? He was in the corner and he kept stepping on her feet. She was jumping awfully."

Mike Strong did remember Jimmy and Annie's wedding — two full companies of the old RNR had been there. And indeed, Mike Conway's girl had been hopping around as if her toes had been crushed.

However, knowing Lieutenant Conway — the Regiment's informal surgeon — Strong had another theory, "I'm afraid, Lady Anne, that the good Lieutenant was not stepping on her feet. He was pinching her bottom."

Only Mike Strong could say such a thing to a Viscountess and not be slapped; instead Anne turned on him with a glare, "Not fair slandering a man when he can't defend himself, Mike."

That was a gentle scolding, and as everyone at the bar recognized the firm, maternal tone, they quieted.

For his part, the Colour frowned in confusion, "His defense is timeless!"

He then braced for a laugh — looked quickly around for the first person who would indulge him with one — but then realized he must have worded it badly.

Seated at a table across the room, Alex helpfully played chorus: "He means that Conway didn't need to defend himself, because according to his persona, pinching bottoms is perfectly appropriate. You're all supposed to laugh."

The unexpected narration dragged all eyes to the table where Alex, Elspeth and Anneke were enjoying tall glasses of milk, and a plate overflowing with cakes and cookies.

Realizing she was suddenly the focus of attention, Alex waved her hand dismissively, "That is all. Proceed with your reminiscing."

As if to emphasize her point, she shoveled a cookie into her mouth, puffing out her cheeks as she began to chew. For another second, everyone continued to watch her, until Prime Minister Alain Lapointe jumped in to rescue Strong from his poor joke.

"I do remember one of the first impressions your b'ys made on my men, when we were at Fort Martian..." he looked mischievously past Devlin at Kennedy. "You remember that night... before the planes flew away?"

The Brigadier began to frown, trying to recall any sort of embarrassing humor that could have come from that evening. It didn't take much effort: "Oh God, the Colonel was mortified when he realized we heard *everything*."

"Oh yes," Strong nodded, grinning and waving his mug of beer towards the Prime Minister. "It was mostly Lady Emily we all heard. God, she was enthusiastic."

"My men gave the credit to Colonel Waller," Lapointe chuckled, shaking his head.

"She was always after him... remember when she was concussed, and kissed him right out in public? We all saw!" Kennedy nudged Devlin with that recollection. "On the *Florizel*, coming back from Promised Town."

The Viscount chuckled and shook his head, "Savage-born girls, I tell you... they're determined in their passions."

It was a joke about romancing — about the way Emily had, during her courtship with Colonel Tom Waller, been largely inconsiderate of the social expectations of the era. Public kissing, and being an enthusiastic lover while sleeping in a canvas tent in the middle of a camp filled with gossiping soldiers... it was one way to be noticed.

But unlike many, Emily had never done such things to try to gain attention. For her and Waller, it had been a genuine love... one that probably got them both into trouble, and which was likely still getting Emily into difficulty.

But this was not a night to dwell on the darker sides of the stories — at least, not yet. Everyone around the bar — Anne, Jimmy, Kennedy, Strong and Lapointe — knew how their reminiscing would end: the stories that were funny (perhaps a bit racy, considering Anne's presence) would spiral closer and closer to the day when all the men they were speaking of were obliterated.

Stares would grow more distant, eyes would glass over, and eventually one among them would speak of that hateful afternoon — the moment when all those misbehaving b'ys, who married frontier girls and pinched their bums at weddings, charged into an enfilade of lightning. Telling funny stories was just a matter of delaying the inevitable, and everyone knew it.

But by God if they wouldn't delay it a little longer.

"Well, I don't think any of that was as brazen as the time my faithful Viscount here took a ride on Sass, while she was naked," Anne got things going again — proving that being the matriarch of the Royal Newfoundland Regiment required a worldly sense of humor.

Jimmy Devlin put his drink-free hand to his heart immediately, and looked to his wife, "Bride, I cannot tell a lie: that ride took me to a whole other world."

The groans after that particularly bad joke were appropriately loud, but laughter followed. Good memories of the new world would circulate for a little longer yet.

When Caralynne and Smith reached the Shylocks' room, Alex's mother had to spend ten minutes giving hugs. These were long hugs, offered with as much strength as ordinary bodies could tolerate, because the Shylock clan meant more to Caralynne than any other family, bar her own.

On the day Smith had flown into the Hubrin capital to search for his beloved — a woman he had seen killed, but somehow believed was alive — the men who'd gone with him to probable death were Vonn Shylock, Bo Shylock, and Cameron Kard. It had been Miranda, too, who insisted her husband join the mission. Such was the character of good people who drifted on the trails of the new world, back in those days. Granted, there had been villains and bandits aplenty, but for two brothers and a gunfighter to have such a strong kinship with Smith was remarkable, and it formed the foundation of a relationship between the Smiths, the Shylocks, and Kard that was at least as strong as blood.

A bond realized in living brilliance by Alex and Stephanie.

It was also a relationship that respected hugs, and so there wasn't much speaking until Caralynne freed herself from Cameron Kard and stepped back with a deep breath, "There. Okay. What's new?"

With a chuckle, Kard shrugged, "Stephanie was just here. She's come along so much... I don't believe I ever want to get into a gunfight against my girl."

"You definitely don't," Caralynne agreed warmly. "Or a scholarly debate. Or a fistfight. Or an exchange of witticisms. She's absolutely blossomed."

"Just like Alex," Bo sounded pleased.

With a proud nod of her own, Caralynne turned to the big Shylock, "Thank you. You're right there too."

She glanced at Vonn as she spoke, but found his expression dimmer than the others. It wasn't hard to guess why — though there hadn't been much time before they'd come up, Smith had managed to fill her in on the particulars.

"We're definitely going to ask the Saa about care for Miranda, Vonn."

Blinking a couple of times, Stephanie's father nodded, "Thanks for that. She's just gone to lie down again... but she didn't tell Stephanie she's poorly. She asks that you don't let on about it either."

Caralynne's expression tightened at those insistent words, and Smith could see his wife was not easy with the request for secrecy. For his part, the former-drifter wasn't either; he'd never in his life been a skilled liar, but he knew also that certain circumstances required a man to make compromises — sometimes profound ones.

The welfare of a daughter was one of the few matters that could compel him to act outside his normal way, and with a quiet tone, he conveyed that, "I trust Miranda to decide when she should be told."

"I can't tell her differently if she asks me directly..." the elder Lady Smith replied, but her husband's eyes struck her somberly as she spoke. "I don't like lying to them."

"I think it's one of those times when it's best to keep things quiet, until circumstances are right," Kard suggested. "She'll be able to handle it, but let's let Miranda choose the time."

Caralynne still felt uncomfortable, but as her husband nodded gravely, she decided to relent. Smith was often her barometer for questions of morals and ethics; he was a man raised on the trail, where honesty and directness were staples of life. If he thought it fair, she could cope with it.

Hopefully Stephanie would understand.

An empty plate of cookies was being replaced on the Champions' table when Second Lieutenant Shylock arrived in the saloon's doorway. All the laughter (and groaning) from the bar was enough to mask her arrival from most of the occupants, and with one more quick sniff, the American checked that she was all back together — ready to be seen by outsiders.

There was little doubt Alex would know she'd been crying, and Strong probably would figure it out too, but that was okay — those two were allowed to know. She just didn't want the others to realize that she had needed a cathartic mother moment.

Advancing into the room, Stephanie approached Alex's table from behind, and saw that her friend had saved her a seat — and a glass of milk. Champions never drank booze at a bar; there was no point to it, since their metabolisms forbade them becoming so much as tipsy. Instead, they drew their satisfaction from sweets, and though Stephanie had lifted her share of drinks in her life (surprisingly *fewer* since moving to Newfoundland), tonight she was an honorary Champion too.

Cookies, cakes and milk. Excellent.

Silently she strode over to the free chair, and though Alex, Elspeth and Anneke were all pointed towards the bar while they started on the next stack of baked goods, the whitecoat held her right hand out to the side as Stephanie arrived.

Of course she knew.

Taking it, Stephanie gave her friend's hand a squeeze, and Alex squeezed back gently before letting go. It was all either of them needed to say.

It also freed the younger Lady Smith to greet her friend in a normal manner: "I find it disconcerting how many of their old stories have to do with people, um, romancing each other." "A *lot* of sex," Anneke was less diplomatic with her words, and she shot a glance at Elspeth. "But you don't mind, do you Lady Cornish?"

Elspeth had been staring mindlessly at the veterans assembled at the bar — one in particular, perhaps — but the words shook her free of her daze, and she blushed immediately, "What?"

With a grin, Anneke looked away, "Excuse me while I dip another cookie into my milk."

She did precisely what she said — cookies tasted better when they were dipped in milk — but somehow it still sounded like a double entendre. Elspeth looked down and proceeded to do the same, but she was flushed, as if Anneke had struck a nerve.

Neither Alex nor Stephanie elected to join in; clearly the girls who had garrisoned London together had a close connection, and their humor was a little more forthright than the whitecoat and the Second Lieutenant normally went in for.

At least the subject of the conversation wasn't Stephanie's absence, and as the American leaned silently forward and collected a cookie (which seemed the size of a pancake, probably because it had been prepared for Champions), she was glad no one was asking how her visit with her parents had gone.

"I suppose one day we could be that irreverent with each other," Anneke decided not to needle Elspeth any further, instead looking over the plate at Alex. "We could become wily veterans at a pub, telling stories of the trouble we got into when we were together…"

Quite unexpectedly, the always-perfect Lady Winter found her good spirits beginning to darken. Of course she was right: the four women at the table might, in twenty years, look back over drinks and laugh at all they'd seen. But would a couple of decades be long enough to allow them to laugh about these times… or would the cold terror on the Grand Banks, the death of men like FDR, and the effective rape of Duncan cast too bleak a pall?

Worse: would all four of them even survive two decades?

Anneke returned her focus to the cookies — such a wholesome-seeming distraction — and tried to push those questions from her mind.

Stephanie set them aside, too, and glanced at Alex after the silence had endured for a moment. The whitecoat was adeptly shoveling two cookies into her mouth at once, and yet somehow appearing quite dignified in the process.

That made Lieutenant Shylock smile, and noticing that she'd been noticed, Alex shrugged. She didn't need to say a thing; she gulped milk instead, and then assaulted the plate once more. At peace in each other's company, the friends continued to stuff themselves with sweets until the Shylocks and the Smiths descended to the saloon, and the reunion was renewed.

CHAPTER VII

George Devlin was in the mood for neither cookies nor spirits. Standing on the porch of the Shylocks' hotel, he stared at the moons looming over New World City, and listened to the sounds of the town at night. Though he'd been to the new world plenty of times before, it was rare for him to be outside on his own after sunset.

As a Viscount's son with the penchants of a scholar, he filled his time with responsible pursuits and was usually in bed early. Perhaps that meant he'd missed out on excitement — the night life in New World City did have something of a magical reputation, as young people seeking adventure gathered at the gateway joining two worlds. He could hear no signs of it this night, but he knew there were clubs about where one could dance closely — out of frame, with bodies touching — and drink to excess.

Those sorts of activities had never interested him. It was not that he judged them to be evil — he was no puritan — they simply never seemed interesting enough to distract him from the much more important responsibilities he possessed.

This night was no different; though he was not in charge of overall security, this would be the first Saa arrival in which he would play a leading role. Sass's last mission to Earth had begun before his hospitality appointment, so he'd been nothing more than a spectator during her arrival. On that occasion, she'd also landed directly in Newfoundland during a time when there was no particular threat to the British Empire. Now things were obviously different — there were many more risks to manage and George was determined not to let anything slip past him.

That was his reason for standing out in the pleasantly cool night air, and listening to the sounds of another planet. Even though the Saa had explained how this world's similarities to Earth were by design (the Hubrin had 'terraformed' the planet to serve as an ideal training ground for their savages) he still found its familiarity remarkable.

Of course the air tasted a little different, and George was certain he felt just a little bit lighter in its gravity, but all the things that mattered about the place were so like Earth. He marveled at that, even as he scanned the landscape for dangers.

Somewhere in this familiar place, was there a familiar threat? Would the villains have found a way through the tunnels... found a way to launch an attack on the dragons who could probably reveal them?

It would be incredibly difficult, and yet George expected it. He just hoped it didn't cost anyone's life when it came. He was quite conscious of the good fortune his friends and colleagues had enjoyed throughout the year so far — few had died, and only Duncan had been captured. If an attack was to be mounted against the Saa, he had to assume it would be stronger and better coordinated than any before, and that would put all the people around Sass at even greater risk.

Some might die. *He* might die, though better that it was him than someone he was responsible for, or who had so much more to do than he did. Hospitality was important service, but any apt young man or woman could be trained to work a screen. People like Alex and Stephanie were, as far as he was concerned, far less replaceable.

And, if he was honest, they were ladies. Neither of them needed his protection — perhaps he needed theirs — but that didn't stop his chivalry from bubbling up every so often. If it were between him and them, he'd naturally sacrifice himself. Such were the expectations of any real gentleman.

Hopefully, though, it wouldn't come to that. Better if tomorrow, no one was forced to make a sacrifice... if Sass simply arrived, was ferried to the old world, and was flown safely to Newfoundland. Deciding that thought was as close as he'd get to optimism, George suspended his musing about the dangers of the next day, and resumed his study of the night sky. He knew his parents had met and romanced on this world, and he could imagine some of the eager excitement that fueled their quick courtship. There truly was an air of magic about the planet — enough to encourage young lovers to be bold and adventurous.

Naturally, that's what young Mister Devlin was thinking when he spotted a girl walking down the street, arms folded as she frowned up at the tall buildings.

Why Constance Cormack was walking alone and so slowly, George didn't know... but he didn't mind. Perhaps she was looking for her hotel?

Holding up his hand, the Viscount's son waved to the Champion graduate, and she noticed him after a few seconds. Her frown evaporated, her arms dropped from their closed-off fold, then she looked both ways before crossing the street to arrive at his side.

"George!" she was genuinely excited to see him, and he met her enthusiasm with a shallow nod, and a polite smile.

"Constance."

That was all he said, which was probably insufficient... but Constance didn't mind.

"The War Department didn't set us up with any accommodations," she reported, rolling her eyes and reaching up to play with her hair. Then she realized what she was doing — that fiddling with her hair probably looked flirtatious — and she dropped her hands again, instead rocking up and down on the balls of her feet.

George's brow creased, "Really? That's unusual, even for them. Just you they overlooked?"

Constance shook her head, "I came in with Major Fischer, the man who's trying to exonerate Vanier. He doesn't have a room either, but he knows a girl in town who he can sleep with. I don't have that."

"You don't know any girls in town?" George's immediate counter-question was deadpan, and for a second Constance wasn't sure if it was supposed to be a joke.

After quick consideration of his humorless — but still warm — expression, she shook her head, "Only people I know came from Jimmystown. I need to find a place to stay tonight. And I guess they didn't send ahead my luggage either, so I have nothing to wear."

Constance felt some color rushing to her cheeks as the words slipped from her mouth. Her mother had raised her as a good southern girl, which stereotypically meant very... proper. But southern women knew their own minds, and were fiercely practical. And she liked George Devlin very much. They hadn't seen nearly enough of each other since she'd been posted to Jimmystown — the base wasn't so huge that running into each other was impossible, but because he was constantly at work on the screens, he rarely crossed paths with in-training Champions.

She hoped that her graduation would mean she got to see him more often — perhaps even work with him — but in the interim, she only knew a few fundamental things: he was smart, handsome, charming, and had quickly befriended Vanier. All of that was enough to make her glad to see him on a dark night on the new world.

In the electric atmosphere of New World City, she even wondered if she should, well... well she was graduated now, and by all measures a woman. If the Champions since Emily had proved nothing else, it was that she could do whatever she liked — whether or not her mother, or society, approved. It was a whole new world, after all, and George was the sort of gentleman that she genuinely fancied...

If, of course, he was interested. At the moment, his deepening frown suggested he was simply in problem-solving mode.

"I'm afraid that could be a challenge," he said severely, then looked back towards the hotel. "Everyone in town for the arrival... I know this place is booked solid, and I'm sure there are no beds to spare anywhere else. Even the barracks are full up... most of the soldiers deployed here are bivouacked in their own tents. We could try to secure a tent, but it wouldn't be proper for you to sleep in one of those..."

His words trailed off, and he turned fully away from Constance, looking back out over the city. For a second he thought he saw the shape of a man standing atop one of the roofs opposite the hotel, but when he focused his eyes he saw nothing but night. It was just a distraction; more important that he find a solution for the stranded Champion.

Not really sure where she was getting her courage, Constance moved over to stand very close to George, looking out at the city, "I don't want to impose... but do you have a room?"

Young Mister Devlin blinked, "Of course, I should have thought of that. My apologies, I'll find a place to bed down... perhaps on a train car..."

That was his response, and glancing sideways at him, Constance again wondered if his aloofness was genuine. By all appearances it was, and that made her smile.

"I'm sure we can both fit," she suggested, and his frown deepened as he glanced at her.

"The chair did look reasonably comfortable," he thought aloud, and both Constance's eyebrows went up.

Really? This was a lot of effort.

"George," she turned slightly in his direction.

He looked down at her — she was shorter than many Champions — before answering, "Yes?"

As she met his gaze, Constance found herself questioning her impetuous feelings. She really wasn't even sure why she was suddenly so brave — so certain of what she wanted, and so willing to go after it. The magical atmosphere of the new world, she guessed... it was a place where young people took great risks, just as Jimmy and Annie Devlin had in 1919.

In that tradition, then, Constance Cormack summoned up all her foolish courage, and her savage speed, and kissed George Devlin on the lips.

He really wasn't ready for it — not that he could have stopped her if he tried. She was a Champion, just waiting to choose a coat. There was no slowing her down, let alone stopping her...

Until she stopped herself, and leaned back from him. She knew she was beet red, though whether her flushed face was obvious in the yellow light streaming through the windows of the hotel, she didn't know.

Instead of worrying about how she looked, she stared at George. He appeared properly confused and started frowning again as his mind worked through everything that she'd said. Taken in a different context.

Right.

George Devlin began to nod slowly, and then he looked back out at the night sky for just a second.

"I see your point," he said, and then with speed that was pretty good for an ordinary person, he turned and kissed her back.

Apparently the adventurous air of the new world was affecting everyone.

Most of the people assembled in the Shylock hotel had made it an early night, owing to their duties on the following day. Alex and Stephanie hadn't lingered too long — as soon as the American was filled up on cookies, they'd both elected to retreat to bed.

When Alain Lapointe lost his second wind and headed to his room, Anneke did the same — the Prime Minister was her responsibility, so when he was put to bed she had to be on the same floor, just in case. Jimmy Devlin looked fruitlessly for his son — not realizing he had already gone up — before turning in with Anne, and the Shylocks and Smiths departed.

Only one Sergeant remained seated at the bar, and though he knew he had important work to do the following day, he dove deeper into drink as the clock struck 1:00 a.m. The bartender didn't seem to mind; he was a young man, and had been listening to the stories told by the veterans of the Hubrin War. As a survivor of Waller's charge, the mighty Sergeant at his bar was entitled to stay up as long as he wanted.

And Mike Strong would last a bit longer.

Being on the new world was never easy for him. Back on Earth, it was less difficult to ignore the memories of his dead friends. Under the two moons of the new world, there was no fighting off the images of the past — and not just the joyful memories.

More than 700 of his countrymen, with whom he'd left Newfoundland, seen Egypt, warred in Afghanistan, and discovered the Hubrin... they'd all died, and he had not. They were all buried in the dirt of this world, all gone in a storm of light when most of them were barely Alex's age.

But of course, being buried didn't mean those b'ys weren't with Mike Strong in the bar — far from it. He could hear Sergeant Whealan raging away on the fiddle, Captain Sesk telling stories of a fight won, and Major Miller offering words of wisdom. There were laughs at the best kinds of bad jokes, claps with old shanties, and a few fights for good measure, because it was late enough for card games to have gone on one or two hands too long.

The empty hotel bar was full of soldiers from the Newfoundland Regiment — Strong could nearly see them.

And if not for the drink, he feared he actually *would* see them. Talk to them.

So with a nod and a sad smile to the barkeep, the Sergeant summoned another drink. It was delivered with speed, and as soon as he had it Strong raised his glass, clinked it up against Major Tucker's, and grinned, "Here's to being too old, and too round."

"Cheers to that, Strong," the long-dead Major replied with a grin, and drank his own.

He downed the fierce drink, then laid the glass on the counter. The bartender watched him do that, but didn't respond to the words — not knowing who they were meant for.

Strong considered another... though he knew he was getting too close to his limit. Years of soldiering had taught him how much he could handle on a late night, and still function the next day; while many men couldn't stop themselves, the Colour certainly could.

Especially when his ability to do his job might mean the difference between Alex and Stephanie living or dying.

When that grave thought slashed through his head, Strong straightened up, then shook himself, "Alright, it's time for water. Lots of it, my good man."

Some men thought coffee broke drunkenness, but Strong had always found water to be the best way to prevent a hangover. At his age, it also meant getting up a few extra times in the night... but that was a fair trade.

Hopefully, though, the booze would continue to stay in his brain long enough to keep him from seeing apparitions before his head hit the pillow. Just *knowing* the b'ys were with him was enough.

When one hopped onto the stool beside him, he actually groaned, "Dammit, I thought I'd had enough."

Elspeth looked right at him, her eyebrow up, "It sure looked like you did."

Strong hadn't expected a woman's voice — let alone Lady Cornish's common London accent — so he looked to her quickly, then laughed at himself, "Apparently I did. I thought you might be George Tucker."

"I hear I need to get older, and rounder," her answer was pitch perfect, and Strong's laugh grew louder.

Water was deposited in front of him, so he drank it before continuing, "I'm sorry, my dear Lady, but I am drunk. When I come to this planet, in the nights, sometimes I need to be drunk. It's the only way to stay sane."

Studying the Colour, Elspeth began to nod. She could see the puffiness around his eyes, and hear in his voice a sort of tension that wasn't his custom. It didn't take too much imagining for her to realize what it was all about — to realize that the haunted feeling she sometimes got when remembering her men who'd died in Scotland probably couldn't compare to the scale of his torment.

After all, she'd lost only eight men. He'd watched hundreds of his fellows be slaughtered in front of him.

"You'll not turn out like me, Lady Elspeth," Strong seemed to be invading the London Champion's thoughts, and she turned a frown against him as he spoke.

"My loss wasn't nearly as bad."

Strong scoffed, and emptied the glass of water into his throat before insisting on another, "Don't say something so foolish. No one can measure the pain of losing people you love like brothers... believe me. But you, you're like my girls. You were raised right. You're not too proud. Sometimes we b'ys who survived got too proud... tried to pretend we weren't all bloody hurting for what we saw. And the ones who were best at that... lied the best to themselves... where are they? They rejoined the regiment, you see — shot themselves, jumped off cliffs... whatever way seemed most sensible."

More water arrived before him, and it was enough to stay his speech before the emotion beneath it started to spill over. Elspeth stared at the side of his face as he gulped from his glass, and recalled all she knew about the survivors of Waller's charge. Many had taken their own lives because of the guilt... but not Mike Strong. He lived large enough for every man who'd died — drank, ate and loved enough for 700 of his fallen fellows.

That was how he justified surviving, she supposed. But some nights he was obviously no better at coping with the reality of his life than she was when she woke up calling out for Bob Freeman... or checking to make certain her wrists and ankles weren't shackled.

Swallowing at those difficult thoughts, Elspeth took a breath, "You're getting by."

Strong nodded emphatically, "That is exactly what I'm doing. You know what's helped? I have two beautiful daughters, all of a sudden. You've seen my girls... you see how wonderful they are, bless them. You know how much I've learned from them? Having them... that's why I lived, you see. The b'ys knew one day, one of us would have to look after them, and they chose me. So that helps, to know I lived for a reason."

The drink was making the Colour far more candid than he would normally have wanted to be, and it didn't take much intuition for Elspeth to realize he was saying things that she could never repeat...

but which were true.

"If I have to die for those girls, I will. That's what I've been left here to do... the last mission of my regiment. And it's me. Hope to God I'm good enough."

With that confession, Strong gulped down the last of his water, then fished into his pocket for some bills. As he slammed them onto the counter — a week's pay, and far more than he owed — he looked to the young barman, "You sir, are a master of your trade. I am honored to say I've been drunk in front of you."

Understandably, the bartender didn't quite know how to respond. Strong didn't mind; with the gallant words said, he slid off the stool, put his boots onto the floor... and started to keel over.

"Ohhhkay," it was a good thing Elspeth was a Champion, because her speed allowed her to get one arm around him before he fell. "Time for bed."

"I appreciate the help," Strong chuckled. "God, I think I'm right on my limit."

For some reason that assessment made Elspeth smile, "I suppose you'd know best."

"Rarely!" Strong laughed, and together they stumbled out of the saloon, and onto the stairs. "I was only a little less drunk than this when I broke the face of a politician. Did you hear about that?"

Though the Sergeant was a robust man, Elspeth's strength meant she had little difficulty moving him, and had plenty of capacity to focus on his words.

She quickly recalled his dalliance with the wife of Newfoundland's Minister of War: "Everyone knows that story."

"Bastard was beating her, right there on the lawn. I swear, I couldn't believe that. His neighbors should have put a stop to it — for God's sakes we could hear her crying from up the street. But I guess a man like that... he's untouchable, so they say. But I gave him a right touch, or ten, with my fists."

Strong jolted to a stop when Elspeth did, though his drunkenness precluded him wondering why she'd halted halfway up the stairs. It had been surprise that stopped her cold: she clearly *hadn't* heard the story about the Minister of War... or, at least, not the real one.

"Sorry, now, I think you're right: the last time I gave him a touch, it was with my boot. I'll tell a secret: I don't figure I'm strong enough to break a man's jaw with just my fist."

Elspeth wanted to ask questions, but this obviously wasn't the time. Slowly — perhaps grudgingly — she continued up the stairs with him, and then let him direct her to his room. Had she been more familiar with intoxication, she would probably have been impressed by his comparative lucidness; Strong was a skillful drunk, and a kind one.

As she sat him down on his cot, and crouched to start undoing his boots, he stopped her with a hand cupping her cheek. She froze at the touch, then looked up slowly. His eyes were still glassy and puffy when she met them, and his smile was sad.

"Look at you, Lady Cornish. You're an angel and you don't even know it. There's a reason for you being here, don't you doubt it. Just don't you wait as long as me to find it. Be happy, and be loved. You're more fit for it that I ever was."

When he let her go, he flopped sideways onto the cot, then instantly started snoring. It was an impressive feat, though his half-twisted position would undoubtedly not do him any good in the morning. Mindful of that, the Champion from London carefully pulled off the Sergeant's boots, swung his legs up onto the cot, and repositioned him so his head could rest on the pillows.

After that she moved to the door and paused there for just a second before shutting it. Everyone in the world knew what Mike Strong *would* do... but it seemed to her, few knew what Mike Strong actually did. To her, at least, the distinction seemed important. She decided to sleep on it.

Anne Devlin was trying to sleep, but her husband was fidgeting.

The window in their hotel room was open, and the cool air was breezing in to relax them both... but the Viscount's mind was rolling along at too great a pace for sleep to come easily.

Finally, the Viscountess had to call him on it: "What?"

Jimmy had been waiting for the question, "First of all, do we know where George went? I mean, I'm sure he's fine... I just... it's *dangerous* for him to just vanish without saying anything..."

"He and Constance Cormack are in his room right now," Anne answered matter-of-factly.

Jimmy had been preparing to continue on to his next concern, but those words stopped him: "Wha?"

"Saw them sneaking in. Didn't want to say anything when you

asked in mixed company," Anne smiled with a bit of satisfaction. There was a reason she was the head of hospitality; few things escaped her notice.

The Viscount of the Grasslands was, perhaps, less prepared: "Oh." He then fell silent, and after a moment Anne could feel him sigh heavily before saying, "Well. I had figured on a different American for a daughter-in-law, but this... works."

The Viscountess tried to sooth him: "It's just a night together. We had a few."

"Yes, and we ended up married. And do you really think our son is going to take a night together any *less* seriously than you or me?"

Her husband was making a good point, and Anne nodded.

"We'll worry about it tomorrow, dear. Once we're sure no one dies."

Jimmy sighed, then nodded too, "I guess. But now I'll never get to sleep."

Smiling, Anne Devlin decided to let her husband stew a little longer. Eventually, they both drifted off.

Watching the hotel from the opposite rooftop, the observer in the gray coat sighed.

"Well," he muttered, "that was a process."

CHAPTER VIII

The early morning hours on the new world were Stephanie Shylock's favorite. Growing up in Terminus, the town that sat on the border between the planet's British and American territories, she'd often been up in time to see the sun rise. It was something that never got old.

New World City was 200 miles east of her hometown, and it sat at the foot of a massive mountain, but that just made sunrise more dramatic; there was no way she was going to miss it.

After a more peaceful sleep than she'd enjoyed in months, Stephanie rose early — and quietly, to let her friend continue to slumber in the next bed over — before the sky even began to brighten. She dressed in complete darkness, then grabbed her boots and gun belt and slipped out of the room in stocking feet. The welcome smell of eggs, sausage and bacon greeted her as she emerged into the hallway — with a hotel full of Champions and soldiers, the cooks had started early.

Sitting herself down on the stairs, she stuck her feet into her boots and did them up one at a time, then wrapped her belt around her waist and tightened it with a frown. It pulled tighter than she liked; perhaps she needed to take after Alex for a while, and eat more. It was tough to keep weight on when she worked and trained as much as she did, so she'd have to make a concerted effort to gain some back.

Standing up from the steps, she adjusted her holster so that her Browning would sit conveniently over her hip, then reached up and checked that her hair was still largely in place — she'd tied it back for sleep, realizing she'd want to rise early. She could neaten it up later; for now, she had a few minutes before the sun would make its appearance. Time to get into position.

Descending the stairs carefully, the young American tried to step as lightly as her boots would allow. The hotel was silent but for the growing sounds of activity in the kitchen, and that was fine — Stephanie preferred to have sunrise to herself.

As she reached the lobby, she nodded to the tired-looking young man behind the counter. He perked up and smiled at her, but then deflated as she waved to him and pressed on to the bar, which was also the breakfast room.

Only one table had been occupied, though it was now abandoned — just an empty plate with a discarded napkin strewn across it. That had probably been the cook getting breakfast before anyone else rose, so Stephanie turned away with a smile; sunrise would be all hers.

Crossing the lobby again, she took a deep breath of the fresh air that was breezing in through the windows on either side of the door. So fresh, so *home*. Though she had very much adopted Newfoundland, the new world would never be replaced. Just as Alex got wonderful shivers breathing in the air from the North Atlantic, Stephanie got them here.

And she could just *taste* the coming dawn.

There was no keeping the contented smile off her face as she opened the door and stepped out onto the porch.

It was a beautiful morning — the skies were working their way through wonderful shades of blue, and the stillness of the city was peaceful. Everything was absolutely perfect... except for the fact that sunrise wasn't all hers. Obviously.

Stopping in the doorway, Stephanie didn't do a very good job of hiding her surprise, "Are you levitating?"

Alex was standing at the top of the porch stairs, her face in profile against the glowing sky as she looked east towards the mountain with one of her typical happy-with-everything-because-life-is-amazing poses. She was also fully dressed — boots to coat, with her hair done — and appeared as though she'd been awake for hours.

At the question, the whitecoat simply shrugged, "I don't *think* I'm levitating. But the gravity on this planet is fractionally less, so... maybe?"

Not only was she up and dressed, she was well fed. Stephanie could hear that in her voice, which probably meant they spent way too much time together.

"How many?" the American asked, sounding unimpressed.

Alex couldn't keep herself from smiling — though at least she tried to appear sheepish, "Three?" Stephanie folded her arms, but remained silent. After too many seconds of silence, the young Champion felt the weight of her conscience, and confessed, "Five."

That was five breakfasts she'd had — before sunrise. Such was the discipline Stephanie would need if she was to gain back some weight.

Turning away from the mountain with an apologetic shrug, the Lady in white tried to make excuses, "The cook offered... I just couldn't help it."

Stephanie held up her hand, "Let's just not talk about it."

"Okay!" Alex bounced up and down on the balls of her feet... and she was sort of adorable, like a puppy getting off with a glare after eating a Christmas turkey. "Sunrise is soon. After all the times you talked about it, I wanted to see one."

"I thought you were asleep — I got dressed without turning on the lights," Stephanie replied, crossing the porch to stand next to her friend.

"I can tell," Alex's answer was immediate and sweet-sounding, but then she glanced at her friend with a smile. "*Sorry*, it's early and I'm giddy because I had a lot to eat. And it's exciting!"

There was something contagious about the young Champion's joy, and Stephanie let go a sigh before nodding, "Yes it is. You're going to love this next part."

Alex took a deep breath at that promise, and then she proceeded to say nothing. Stephanie was equally quiet. They just stood there on the porch as New World City sleepily began to wake from its slumber... and the skies overhead rose through shades of blue.

The silence was so very peaceful, and so proper. Sunrise was not a thing to be accompanied with conversation, no matter how good (or horribly un-funny) that chatter might be. Anyone who knew a place, was bonded to a land, understood that sometimes human words simply weren't equal to articulating its majesty.

Where the sun in St. John's rose over the sea, the sun of the new world shimmered behind the mountains, casting a halo around the mighty peak, and leaving shadows in its wake. The town was in that wake — was last to see the sunrise, because it had to wait for the moment the star crested the highest reaches of rock, and smiled over.

It took minutes... maybe an hour. Stephanie didn't care, and neither did Alex. They were both distantly aware of the beginnings of movement in the street, and of sounds of activity from inside the hotel, but they paid no real attention. Neither sat; both leaned against the railings of the porch, shoulders pressed together and arms alternately folded or in their pockets as the mountain cast its last shadows... and the sun appeared.

When it did, it smiled at them — *good morning, ladies* — and Alex and Stephanie smiled back. Warm light beating down on their faces beneath a clear, cool sky... a sunrise that seemed for them alone, even though many others around town, and across the new world, were probably seeing the same sun, at the same moment, and feeling as though it were smiling at only them.

Such was the power of a sunrise: it could smile at everyone.

After that, it began climbing higher — getting itself ready for a busy day — and the spell of its rise gradually released Alex and Stephanie.

Finally, it was the Champion who looked at her friend, "Breakfast time?"

Stephanie blinked and tried not to smile. That effort failed, because there was simply no way such a good start to the day could allow her the pretense of being stern. She had seen her first new world sunrise in years... and she'd seen it with the friend who was, in every way that mattered, her sister.

"You are single-handedly going to put my family out of business," the American Lieutenant replied.

A concerned frown crossed Alex's face, "But... aren't you going to help?"

Dammit. Stephanie's smile got bigger. Shaking her head, she turned for the door and tried not to give her Champion the satisfaction. Unfortunately, the whitecoat could basically read her best friend's thoughts.

"I know, right?" Alex asked. "I'm even funnier and more adorable after five breakfasts!"

As the server came to take away the plate from breakfast seven, Alex felt herself starting to... settle. Sitting back in her seat, she nodded in a slow and deliberate manner, then looked thoughtfully at the table before delivering her verdict.

"I have had sufficient."

Stephanie was almost done her one breakfast, and looking sideways at her friend, she asked, "Is that a sentence?"

"Of a kind," Alex replied.

"Impressive," the American smiled, then went back to her eggs. "Took seven breakfasts to stuff you."

Alex shrugged, "If I had to, I could eat more. But all things in moderation."

Stephanie's eyebrow darted up, but she didn't get a chance to comment any further. Instead, it was Mike Strong who appeared in the breakfast room, his head hanging as he walked steadily to their table, pulled out a chair and sat down.

Waving to the server, Alex pointed to Strong, "Bring him one plate of what I had, and a pot of coffee?"

The young man who'd been watching Alex completely demolish plate after plate of food could only nod wide-eyed in reply — as if he was taking orders from some sort of a food goddess.

While Alex summoned the breakfast, Stephanie leaned forward and sympathetically patted her Sergeant's arm, "It's alright, we have food and black coffee coming."

"What did Mike Strong do?" Alex asked with equal empathy, and with a groan, the Colour answered.

"Drank enough water not to need to be mothered by you two."

"Someone's grumpy," Stephanie sounded less sympathetic that time, and Alex shrugged.

"He's probably achy. Was the bed too comfortable, or did you sleep on the floor?"

Looking up slowly, Mike Strong wore an uncommonly curmudgeonly frown — not charming at all — but he didn't engage directly with the question, "I've been getting over hangovers longer than you two have been living. This one's gentle."

"Aw," Stephanie went back to her food. "Well you're first up among everyone else, so that's actually pretty impressive."

Strong looked to her, then made a point of straightening up and looking around the breakfast-bar. It was indeed empty, which surprised him — the sun had been over the mountain for at least twenty minutes. He'd have expected a hotel full of soldiers and Champions to be bustling at such an hour, but perhaps he was just being too ambitious.

"Not even Elspeth?" he asked that question as he was looking around, and then he realized it was probably the wrong way to carry forward the conversation.

Alex was still letting her food settle, but the satisfied feeling of sufficient feeding didn't dull her wits. Glancing to Stephanie with eyebrows climbing, she tried to find out what spurred Strong's interest in the browncoat: "Why, did she turn in early?"

Recognizing the mistake, Strong went for a smokescreen, which was probably ill-advised, "Well, she knocked me back pretty good and stormed off. But don't tell Daphne."

Alex and Stephanie locked eyes at the excuse, and then the American frowned, "Hang on. He's pretending he made a pass at her... and saying she knocked him back."

"We know he doesn't actually make passes at girls, because he *sleeps on the floor*," Alex concurred.

"So does the fact that he's saying he did it mean he's hiding something they really did?" the American's eyes narrowed thoughtfully.

"Or felt?" the whitecoat frowned. "Wow."

Strong hadn't handled this right, and up against his two very-awake girls he had no hope of maneuvering or charming his way clear. Shaking his head, he rubbed his brow and sat back in his chair, "She put me to bed, and I probably said a few things to her that I shouldn't have."

Anyone familiar with Mike Strong's well-crafted reputation would naturally assume the things he'd said were lustful, but knowing the man, both Alex and Stephanie suspected it was something quite different. Those expectations turned teasing frowns into more genuine ones: why would Mike Strong admit things to a relative newcomer that he couldn't say to either of them?

Alex was working herself up to ask, but Strong predicted the question and raised his hand to stop it, "No. And don't pressure her to say anything, either. I'll talk to her..."

He sounded pretty serious. Alex and Stephanie looked at each other again, trying to imagine what sorts of things he could actually be ashamed to have said... or perhaps what things he didn't want them to hear. Did he really think that, put together, the whitecoat and the Lieutenant couldn't figure it out?

"Sometimes it's a bad idea to try to read people too closely," the Colour seemed to be predicting their thoughts. "Might not like what you see."

That sounded way too self-pitying, so Stephanie shrugged, "I've yet to encounter one of those times."

Now that was a perfectly good thing to say — it was important to make the point that Mike didn't need to hide anything from the girls (except for the fact that he intended to die for them — neither of them would have liked to hear that bit). But Stephanie's phrasing and timing worked against her, because as soon as the words fell from her mouth, they all heard a giggle.

Then George Devlin walked into the breakfast room, looking very dashing... extra dashing because Constance Cormack was holding right onto him, and they were walking in perfect stride towards one of the free tables.

Briefly they turned and waved to Alex, Stephanie and Strong, none of whom managed to react. Well, Stephanie's jaw dropped, and Mike Strong's eyebrows rose to the top of his head, and Alex blinked. But none *responded*.

Apparently that didn't matter to George and Constance. They parted just long enough for the hospitality man to pull out a chair for the Champion graduate, and then he settled down beside her and they proceeded to chatter in low tones. Anyone with eyes could see the girl from Georgia was glowing, and the Viscount's son was... extra gallant.

"In my defense, I didn't plan this as proof of my last point," Mike Strong sounded honestly stunned.

"Well. That escalated quickly," Alex was equally unprepared for the sight.

"I didn't even realize she was coming for the ceremony," Strong added.

Alex shrugged before speculating: "I guess she came with George."

Right. Poor word choice there should have earned the younger Lady Smith a glare from Stephanie, but the American Lieutenant was still sitting with her jaw dropped, staring rather conspicuously at the other table.

After that dragged on for a moment, Alex subtly kicked her friend's boot under the table. It took two of those bumps for Stephanie to finally shake herself out of catatonia, and look to her friend, "I... guess I always knew he had it in him."

Knowing it was the best way to get minds at the table working again, Strong went for the raunchy joke: "Strictly speaking, it wasn't in *him*..."

He said it slowly enough for Alex and Stephanie both to hear it, and process it, and stop him with matching glares. Smiling at his success he sat back, and silence returned to the table.

Stephanie Shylock knew she had absolutely no reason to feel anything approaching jealousy — she may have teased George over the years, but that had always just been innocent fun. Naturally she'd known he'd find someone in due course, and she'd be entirely unaffected when that happened.

That in mind, she forced herself to focus on what a good morning it had been, starting with the beautiful sunrise.

The sunrise George and Constance probably hadn't noticed from *bed*.

And with that thought, Stephanie stuck up her hand and called for another breakfast. Alex had another one too — purely as a show of solidarity. It helped.

CHAPTER IX

No technology made by humans had the ability to detect the Saa heavy cruiser exit FTL in the 'new world' system. However, recognizing that her human friends would need a precise arrival time, Sass had sent ahead a very specific transit schedule, and as the vessel reached planetary orbit, she was glad to see it was on time.

Waiting in the ship's massive landing bay, the Saa engineer-turned-ambassador watched the orb of the human-controlled world grow on one of the flight technicians' monitors, and she felt apprehension growing within her.

Based on Jimmy's message, the humans were finding themselves increasingly at odds — something she could sympathize with on one level, but which seemed terribly wasteful on another. As far as recorded history showed, the Saa had never gone through a period of internal warring; their civilization had only grown to the point where resources were scarce at the same time they gained space travel, and the ability to find more. Combat had always been individual, not between collectives, and war had been something they learned when they encountered species from other worlds — the Hubrin being the most recent aggressors.

But humans were obviously following a different path, and though it was a foreign concept for them to be fighting internally, the Saa leadership remained committed to a formal relationship with the species, in particular through Britain and the United States. For centuries, the Hubrin had used attackers to devastate Saa bases, so none of Sass's people would underestimate the possible value in having the same creatures (more or less) as possible allies in the future.

And, to be fair, it counted for something that Waller and his Newfoundlanders had rescued Sass and her comrades. Few life forms the Saa had encountered in the cosmos had attempted to be friendly with the giant lizard race; considering the small commitment it took to maintain friendship with the humans, it seemed completely logical to do so.

All of that suited Sass just fine — she'd grown quite accustomed to her life in Newfoundland, and now that the human language could be translated by her collar, she had built an even stronger kinship with people like Jimmy Devlin, his wife Annie, Smith, Caralynne, and their families.

She was glad to be returning, but still anxious because another alien foe had found its way to the borders of Saa space.

And these ones — the armies of the Scourge Queen — were something very different.

The planet Sass watched on the screen before her was not far from those very warriors, and though she did not underestimate the abilities of the humans one fraction, she knew well that no species, including the Hubrin, had stopped the Scourge so far in their march across the cosmos. It was the Saa's turn to try. Perhaps one day, the humans could even help.

That was not the sort of warm and relaxing scenario to which Sass had wished to return, but she'd make the best of it. The first step was simple: get herself and her party down to the new world, and back to Newfoundland. She assumed that would be a relatively standard operation, but given Jimmy's reports it was possible trouble could begin.

She'd be ready, and soon — at last — she'd be back.

"I'm fine. Don't be silly."

Alex was standing beside Stephanie, saying absolutely nothing as they both waited in the VIP line at the side of the New World City airfield. Of course, between two friends as close as these, silence was a conversation all its own, so naturally the American had perceived the Champion's general concern.

"Seriously, I'm fine and we're not talking about it," the Lieutenant persisted, then shook her head. "Really."

"Okay, we actually were *not* talking about it until you started talking about it. But let's not start pointing any fingers," Alex used logic against her friend's denial, and Stephanie made a face and sighed.

"We're here to receive Sass. Let's do that and not worry about what some guy — who is completely free to do whatever he wants — actually did with some girl who he's only met a handful of times. Or the fact that they're now acting like they're all in love."

It was a good thing George wasn't part of the VIP line — he was waiting on the opposite side of the field, behind a wind shield, so that he could be one of the first to greet Sass when she stepped off her ship. Constance had joined Major Fischer with the line of American dignitaries a long way to the left, so she couldn't overhear either.

Indeed, the only people listening were much nearer: Mike Strong, and someone a bit more helpful.

"I'm afraid the new world can bring that sort of thing out of people," Lady Anne Devlin leaned towards Stephanie from the opposite side. "I speak from experience — it happened to me and Jimmy."

Stephanie raised an eyebrow and then looked sideways at the Viscountess, who was conveniently next in line.

"I was born and raised here. It didn't happen to me," she protested, then paused and thought back to a few particularly eventful months before she'd left for Memorial College. How many boys had she been dating at the same time? Not wanting to count, she simply amended her statement: "It didn't happen to me *much*."

Alex smiled at the concession, "I'm surprised none of your exes have come here to try to win you back today."

"They know I'd kill any who tried," Mike Strong inserted himself into the conversation at that propitious moment, then backed out again having done his duty.

"I'm sorry, Stephanie," Anne's apology was genuine, but hardly morose. "My son doesn't go in for flings, so I'm afraid this really might be it — circumstances allowing. But really, you have plenty more options."

Stephanie rolled her eyes, then sighed. Pausing for a moment, she chose her words carefully: "This is absolutely what we should be talking about on the eve of Sass arriving. This is completely the best time to be talking about it. There could be no better time to engage in this discussion."

A good point, so Alex deflated slightly — obviously feeling chastened at her silly distraction. She then conceded: "You're right. We should wait until Sass is here, so she can weigh in too."

That was enough; Stephanie elbowed her best friend, drawing a smile, and then they both fell silent. It would have been a good time for the awkwardness of the day to end… but then Elspeth arrived. The Lady from London seemed entirely herself — not at all out of sorts — as she hurried up the line of VIPs, smiling and nodding to people she knew as she passed them.

When she finally found her spot — which was very unfortunately on the other side of Strong from Alex — she quickly nodded to Stephanie, then apologized to Alex, "Was with Anneke and the Prime Minister. Lost track of time."

With that, she nodded towards the wind shield that stood out on the landing field — the shelter where George was waiting. Alain Lapointe, Currie, Jimmy, Smith and Caralynne were there too — all people who'd been in the Hubrin War alongside the great dragon Lady. Anneke was with them, because security still warranted having a Champion alongside a dominion premier, but she and George were the only two non-veterans.

So Elspeth had come back, and that was probably very awkward for Mike Strong…

"Morning, Lady Cornish," he sounded altogether charming as he smiled at her, and Alex immediately frowned and looked sideways at him.

Elspeth noticed the glance of confusion, and then did some calculations in her own mind about what might have been said between the Colour and his girls. Undoubtedly Strong had been too candid the night before — by his own standards, at least — so perhaps he'd been self-conscious. Now he was masking it with charm, and she could easily help his cause.

"Good morning, Sergeant," she smiled very warmly. "Thanks again."

"No, *thank you*," he replied, doing a professional job of shielding his relief at the browncoat's discretion.

That was all they said, and with a sigh, Alex shook her head just a little. She had a best friend in denial about feeling some regret over the good young man she'd passed up, a Sergeant trying to pretend he was romancing a Champion who was nearly twenty years his junior, and that Champion playing along to cover something he wished he hadn't revealed.

By contrast, she wasn't even *pretending* to date a manatee

anymore, or being hit on by a seagull. Had she dedicated her life to romantic adventures, she'd have been an abject failure. Fortunately, her pursuits were of a different kind, and the noise that she began to hear from high in the sky was the sign that she was soon to be rewarded with the return of a friend.

"Is that them?" Elspeth asked, leaning forward and glancing around Strong towards Alex.

With a quick nod, the whitecoat looked up towards the clear blue sky, "They're probably not coming in right overhead... they only drop straight down on us if they're doing an assault landing. They'll angle their way into the atmosphere and circle us to land, sort of like a plane."

"Neat," the Lady from London smiled — whatever else was occurring, she was excited for the moments ahead.

Indeed, everyone around the field was eager, and as Alex twisted quickly in place to get a look at the crowd that had surrounded the airstrip, she had to guess that number was in the thousands. There would be even more lining the streets between the field and the tunnel... tens of thousands of people here to see Sass's return.

And among them, hopefully, no villains.

Looking back to the field, Alex wasn't sure if that thought counted as tempting fate, but it almost certainly was.

"There it is, coming in from the west," Caralynne was the first to spot the approaching landing ship, and all the dignitaries behind the wind shield followed her finger as she pointed to the dark shape in the sky.

Though the elder Lady Smith was the first to see the approaching vessel with her Champion-enhanced eyes, the radar tower that stood alongside the airstrip had long ago marked its arrival. By the time it was in sight, the Spitfires that had been circling high above were already cruising through the blue yonder to meet it.

Any notion that those planes were present to protect the Saa craft would have been fanciful; indeed, if they weren't careful, and got themselves caught in the thrust wash of one of the landing ship's engines, the planes might be thrown out of control into the ground.

But it was a respectful gesture, and the Saa welcomed it. As the halo of Spits arrived over the growing vessel, it carried out an approximation of a wing-waggle — the old maneuver that the dragons had learned from then-Flight Captain Alistair Carstairs, the pilot who was the first human to meet a Saa.

The Spitfires waggled their wings back, then took post above the ship as it dropped closer and closer to the ground. It was very near indeed, and with a look at his gathered friends, Jimmy Devlin grinned, "Hold onto your hats."

He said it slightly prematurely, but it was still good advice; the Saa ship came down to landing altitude out over the trees to the north of the field, and as it did the roar escaping its engines became enormous. The trees — old-growth pines that bent before no wind — rustled violently under the gale kicked out by the thrusters as the craft glided over their tops towards the field.

Pulling in close behind the wind shelter, the gathered veterans held onto whatever hats they might have been wearing, and then the thruster wash hit them. It was just warm air — not hot flames — but it would easily have bowled them over if they weren't prepared. The wind got more powerful as the massive vessel lowered its landing feet, then tentatively eased itself onto the grass. Thanks to its counter-grav technology — a type of machinery that Jimmy Devlin simply did not understand — it was rendered light enough not to sink into the turf (or to need harsh flames to land), so when the wind finally died down, the Viscount was able to peek around the wind shield and see a glistening bronze-colored vessel sitting powerfully before him.

The craft was larger than a skycruiser, which just made the dragons seem even grander — they had a fleet of spacefaring warships big enough to carry dozens of such 'small' craft? The Saa were mighty indeed. And they were friends.

Applause from the massive crowd surrounding the field began while the veterans emerged from behind their shelter. As a lady who had fought the Hubrin and helped save the new world, Sass was an adopted daughter of the Selkirk Mandate — everyone was glad to see her.

Well, hopefully everyone.

"Here we are," Alain Lapointe was smiling broadly as he waved towards the ship... and as if at his command, the large disembarkation door on the front began to open. The applause and cheering grew louder — enough to mute the roar of Spitfires circling overhead — and the veterans roughly lined themselves up to wait for Sass to emerge.

It didn't take long.

Though Sass was a dragon the size of a whale, the way her head emerged from the shadows cast by her ship reminded Jimmy Devlin of a gopher sticking its head up out of a hole. And then, rather surprisingly, another head stuck out of the shadows to her right, and yet another did the same to her left.

All three dragons were scanning the field with their big eyes, and Jimmy could see precisely the moment when Sass spotted him. Raising his hand quickly, he waved to her in an exaggerated fashion, and she strode forward on all fours, nodding back to him.

On either side of her, the other two dragons followed, and as they all padded down their ship's ramp and struck out under the bright blue sky, it became immediately clear that Sass's companions were both only half her size.

Having never seen a dragon of such dimensions, the Viscount found his eyebrows rising in surprise. He didn't have long to wait for an explanation, as the massive, silent strides of the three Saa brought them right up to the group of receiving veterans in no time at all.

Stopping before her alien friends, Sass immediately rose up onto her back legs, turning herself into an imposing tower for all the distant audience to see. Beside her, the smaller dragons did the same. It was undeniably impressive, and the crowds literally went wild.

Sass found that interesting, but before she could comment the official welcome began.

As the man in charge of Saa hospitality, it was George Devlin who advanced, stopping at a point just far enough from her to still be visible without her having to dip her chin too much. He then held up his hand and waved. Sass held up her hand and waved back.

Like waggling wings between aircraft, the wave traded between Saa and human had special meaning, as it had been the first gesture a captive dragon engineer had exchanged with a Newfoundland Colonel, after the latter man rescued her from a horde.

"We're really glad to see you back," the son of the Viscount announced as he lowered his hand. "Pleasant journey?"

"It was," Sass agreed immediately, her hisses being converted to English by the narrow metal band strapped to her neck. "Allow me to present my delegation."

When the Saa linguists had built the translation matrix for the collars worn by Sass and her fellows, they'd worked with British counterparts who had insisted that proper grammar be observed. Though Sass's resulting accent paradoxically sounded more Canadian than British, she certainly could come across as though she were a polite socialite. Fortunately, the band was smart enough to change her tone when circumstances warranted.

"These are two children from my recent hatching," Sass announced as she extended her arms to either side, and the proudly-standing smaller dragons both raised their hands to wave at the tiny humans before them.

"Hi," the one on the left said, and to the credit of the translator, the mechanical voice that emerged conveyed some sheepishness to match her body language.

"Hiya," the one on the right added, and his translator had a male-sounding voice that came across as a bit more eager.

"My daughter has chosen the human name Imogen, my son has chosen the name Ciaran," Sass added.

The kids kept waving, and George Devlin politely waved back, before nodding to each in turn.

Jimmy Devlin wasn't about to hang back after those introductions, "You didn't tell us you were bringing your kids!"

"I didn't bring them all," Sass sounded amused. "You wouldn't have room. But they both wanted to come, so I thought it might be a good experience. You and I are getting older, Jimmy. Your next generation is already in the field, and mine should be too."

As the Viscount stopped beside his son, he smiled at that reasoning, "I didn't think either of us were that old."

"She's not," George interceded immediately. "You, on the other hand."

Sass bobbed her head from side to side, and then watched as Smith and Caralynne approached with Alain Lapointe half a step behind.

"Hello Smith, Caralynne," Sass's greeting to them was simple and warm.

The former drifter touched the brim of his hat in reply, leaving the speaking to his bride, "Good of you to bring the family."

"We're really excited," Ciaran took that as an opportunity to insert himself into the conversation, and the eager weaving of his long tail reinforced his translated words. "We spent the whole trip picking our human names — they're *Irish* — and learning about your planet, *and* doing mechanical training!"

Imogen didn't add anything to her brother's enthusiastic announcement, but Sass bobbed her head from side to side before adding, "It'll be a great experience for them."

"And us, no doubt," Alain spoke for the first time, and Sass gave him a special head bob.

"Still Prime Minister, Alain?"

"Would not want to disappoint you," he replied. "Come, we must introduce you and your family to the worlds!"

Indeed, there would be much time for talking later — for now, it was important they begin the long process of getting through the adoring public, and safely back to Newfoundland.

CHAPTER X

Alex Smith had never been part of a parade before, and she really hoped another wouldn't be in her near future. The procession that was making the slow walk from the airstrip to the train station was not particularly well-organized — participants were making their way in whatever order suited them — but the route had been very carefully mapped out and infantrymen were standing to, like fence posts on either side of the street, keeping the assembled onlookers back from the Saa.

Those onlookers were numerous, and loud. With the streets lined with well-wishers, the noise was vast enough to be particularly unpleasant for the ears of a Champion, and everything felt a bit claustrophobic. For someone who hadn't enjoyed the crowded streets of Hong Kong, this was particularly delightful...

But at least they didn't have far to walk, and the company certainly was interesting.

Sass was leading the way with Alain Lapointe, Jimmy, Annie, Smith, and Caralynne. Anneke was naturally keeping pace.

The two younger Saa were trailing behind their mother. Ciaran seemed to be basking in the attention, stopping for waves and photographs, and generally pleasing the crowd. Stephanie, Strong, and Elspeth were staying close to him, making sure he didn't get into any trouble.

Right at the back was Sass's daughter, and she appeared to be liking the parade even less than Alex. Given her natural affinity for anyone awkward, it seemed only proper for the whitecoat to drop back and saunter along with young Imogen.

"Hey there," she said as she came alongside Sass's daughter, then looked at the dragon to make sure she knew she was being addressed — with all the surrounding noise, it could have been easy to mishear.

But Imogen was decidedly aware of who was walking near her feet, and she returned the gaze, "Hi."

Alex found the Saa translation collar's ability to convey moods to be quite remarkable — how the machine knew to make its wearer sound nervous was beyond the young Champion. But in concert with Imogen's wary eyes and her uncomfortable four-footed gait, the words entirely confirmed the impression that this wasn't her preferred environment.

With her usual tact, Alex was sure she'd be able to make that unpleasant feeling even worse: "I'm Alex. I'm very awkward."

Imogen's head rotated slightly as she heard that, then her eyes narrowed a little — an expression humans and Saa shared for thoughtfulness, "My mom doesn't think you're awkward."

"Moms never think their kids are awkward. But sometimes we are," Alex shrugged.

That sounded fair to Imogen, so she started to turn her palm up in mid-step... but stopped as she remembered that the human gesture for agreement was an up-and-down nod of the head. She did that instead, before saying, "I'm Imogen."

"You picked a nice name for yourself," Alex seized onto that point for some small talk, and Sass's daughter tilted her head again.

"I like the sound of it," the young dragon replied. "My name in my language would be unpronounceable for you."

"Some names in my own language are unpronounceable for me," the whitecoat replied. "Like I said, I'm awkward."

Imogen was young, and certainly ill-at-ease while being made a spectacle of, but she was absolutely her mother's daughter — a very intelligent and capable young dragon. Most of her skills were in the engineering trade, and she hoped to follow her mother's path in that direction, but she was also very astute when it came to reading her fellow Saa.

And just as her mother had promised, the ability to interpret nonverbal cues from one species seemed to somehow translate to the other. Had Sass and Waller not been able to communicate without language in 1920, the history of both races would have been quite different; now, the ability allowed Imogen to see right through Alex's words.

"Are you lying?" the young dragon asked innocently, and Alex's eyebrows went up.

"What?"

Imogen's head tilted further — she was clearly puzzled, so Alex didn't think the words represented an accusation.

"You said twice that you are awkward, but you are clearly quite confident," Imogen explained. "You are walking very upright, and you don't appear flustered. You are also being creative and having pleasant conversation with a stranger of another species. Do I not understand the word 'awkward'?"

Ouch. A frown fell onto Alex's brow as she listened to the entirely logical assessment, and she found her eyes dropping from Imogen to the road ahead. It looked as though Stephanie, Strong and Elspeth were having a good conversation with Ciaran, and beyond them, the much larger shape of Sass was sauntering along easily, her legs pushing more side-to-side than straight back as she moved like one of the grand monitor lizards from Komodo.

Those sights were a pleasant distraction from Imogen's question, because the innocent young dragon had pretty much directly challenged Alex's comfortable identity. Was she actually awkward? Or had the past year made her more confident in her own boots?

The Lady in white hedged, "Well, I don't *think* I'm lying. But maybe I'm just more comfortable with Saa than humans? You are much larger, after all."

"Oh," Imogen answered, then nodded again. "I don't understand, but that's okay. I'm here to learn."

"And to make friends," Alex suggested, relieved at the apparent success of her deflection. "You just made one. See, it's easy."

Imogen turned her head back towards Alex, and for a moment the two young females shared a long look. Then, entirely honestly, the dragon asked: "What friend did I make?"

Alex was pretty sure the need for that question was proof that she was still awkward. That made her feel better somehow, and she was about to say so.

She didn't get the chance.

Making small talk with a young dragon as enthusiastic as Ciaran was interesting. Stephanie wasn't sure exactly how old Sass's son was, but he seemed to possess a lot of irrepressible enthusiasm. She found it quite delightful.

Also, Sass had obviously told him a bunch of stories from her time on the new world, and Earth.

"So when you first met my mother, how small were you?" the Saa directed his question to the American Lieutenant, and his eagerness was clearly telegraphed by his translation collar.

Considering her answer, Stephanie crouched down slightly and then held her hand flat over the ground as they walked. Watching her movement, Ciaran tilted his head briefly before hissing a follow-up for translation.

"You'd just hatched?"

For some reason it was very cute that he said 'hatched', and though Stephanie could have tried to explain the actual mechanics of being born, she figured that was too much for a first conversation.

Instead, she shook her head, "I was three years old, or so."

Ciaran's head tilted even more, and then his tail began to swing thoughtfully behind him as they padded along the roaring street.

After doing some calculations in his head, the dragon hissed again, "How old are you now?"

Stephanie raised her eyebrow, and glanced at Mike Strong. The Colour had been silent for much of the conversation, but at this point he felt it his duty to weigh in, "Listen, Ciaran... word of advice. You never ask a woman how old she is, or how much she weighs. That's just asking for grief."

"Wise advice," Elspeth agreed, and poor Ciaran's head basically rotated through ninety degrees before leveling off again.

"Mom didn't mention that. Thanks for the warning," the young Saa said. "I'm just asking, though, because I'm... hang on."

He started doing sums in his head again, which led him to narrow his eyes in an adorably obvious bid to speed the calculations. Strong waited patiently, and cast a glance at Stephanie, who shrugged. They strode along a little longer, and then Ciaran began to nod to himself — he'd picked up that mannerism quickly.

"Yes, that's it. I'm *two*."

There was a smile painted on Stephanie's face, which was convenient when she heard the number. She looked to Strong, and the Sergeant was similarly unsure of the pronouncement.

"Two... what?" the Colour asked, and Ciaran bobbed his head.

"Years old. Based on Earth years. Sorry, I had to do that math in my head, and I'm bad at that. Imogen is much smarter than I am. I'm more good at knocking things over."

Many two-year-olds were good at knocking things over. Most of them lacked the ability to accidentally knock over buildings. Or do sums in their head.

"Sorry, just to clarify: two *years* old? You didn't forget to carry a ten or something?" Strong persisted with his question, looking back at the size of Sass's son.

Sure he was smaller than an adult dragon, but the Colour would have figured him for a teenager at least.

"Nope... I got it right. I hatched in... 1939, I think?"

He was getting the hang of those numbers. Not bad for...

"Two?" Stephanie knew she shouldn't be surprised. The Saa were obviously not human, and a dog at two was pretty mature... so perhaps this made sense... but really, no, it didn't.

"I guess I'm big-boned?" Ciaran asked innocently, and Stephanie, Strong and Elspeth all looked at him.

It was the browncoat who asked, "Where exactly did you learn that expression?"

Bobbing his head side-to-side in his version of laughter (which the collar didn't translate) the young dragon decided to be cryptic, "I have my sources."

No doubt he did. Perhaps George had sent through a package of human colloquialisms for the Saa to program into their collars... or something. But however he was doing it, young Ciaran was proving himself rather astute for a two-year-old.

Charming, even, and Stephanie found her smile growing more genuine. Having the new kids around would be a good thing, she decided, and with that thought she looked to Strong.

The Sergeant was scowling at her.

"What?" she asked immediately.

His reply was predictable: "He's too young. Don't get any ideas just because you've been scorned."

Of course he had to play his part — it was as inevitable as it was groan-worthy. But as Stephanie rolled her eyes, she realized poor Ciaran would have literally no idea what her Sergeant was on about. Explaining would be a bit of a chore, but the dragon deserved to be warned as early as possible...

"I'm not opposed to older women, Sergeant. I tend to think age is just a number," Ciaran replied before Stephanie could open her mouth. "A twenty year age difference between mates? What would

Mike Strong do?"

The crowd lining either side of the street was loud, so there was no way anyone could hear a pin drop... but if not for the cheers, the silence that suddenly radiated from Stephanie, Elspeth, and the heroic Sergeant Strong would have been sufficient to hear a pin land softly.

For the second time in one morning, Stephanie's jaw dropped, and her eyes were wide. Elspeth's look of surprise was more mixed with delight, and Mike Strong's expression turned from surprise, to shock, to joy, to excitement.

The three humans stopped in the street, and Ciaran stopped with them, his head tilting as he wondered whether he'd deployed his Mike Strong joke too soon.

He hadn't.

Raising his hand towards the young dragon, Mike Strong grinned, "I knew my saying would go cosmic!"

Then he stood still, hand up with its palm facing Ciaran. The dragon's head tilted further before he decided he was supposed to mimic the gesture, and raised his hand from the street to match. As soon as it was in the air, Strong hurried forward and then hopped up, slapping his tiny fleshy palm against the Saa's scale-covered pad.

"This guy's alright," the Colour grinned as he turned back to Stephanie, clenching his fist and shaking it in victory. "Handsome too. A lot like me."

Ciaran literally didn't miss a beat, "I still need to develop your modesty, though, Sergeant. My mom expects me to learn a lot from you."

"Your mom is a smart lady," Strong nodded and gave the youngster a thumbs up, before turning back to Stephanie and Elspeth with a grin.

Naturally, he was pleased with himself: though it was a joke, Ciaran had not only heard of the Sergeant, he knew the catchphrase. That meant the name Mike Strong was resonating across the stars, striking fear into evil-doers and charming ladies under the light of a thousand suns.

Or, something like that. Strong was going to be optimistic, but as he set eyes on both Stephanie and Elspeth he could see his confidence wasn't quite shared. Being less acquainted with the horror of tolerating his bad humor for prolonged periods, the browncoat appeared amused, but knowing there'd be no living with him for months after the revelation of his interstellar fame, Stephanie Shylock shook her head.

Neither one of them saw the man in the gray raincoat hurrying up to one of the soldiers standing post at the side of the road ahead, screaming that there was a bomb.

Neither was facing the general store when its facade exploded.

CHAPTER XI

Neither Constance Cormack nor Wendel Fischer were important enough to join the dragon parade back to the train station. They'd stood in line with the American delegation on the side of the airfield when the Saa had landed, but after little more than an inspection and the trading of a few words, Sass and her two companions left the VIPs behind, proceeding quickly out onto the streets.

Constance had been a little disappointed, but she understood nonetheless; she'd been surprised to have been asked to attend in the first place. Simply being present for the arrival was honor enough — she'd try to meet the dragons later, in Newfoundland.

As the crowds began to clear, she'd been satisfied with that thought. Major Fischer had seemed equally at peace, though something was distracting him: trucks with flat beds on their back ends had driven onto the airfield, rolled up to the Saa landing craft, and now the dragon crew from that ship were loading them with massive crates.

"I suppose a delegation coming to stay for a few years can't travel light," he observed, pointing to the heavy luggage.

Looking back towards the ship, Constance frowned for a second before realizing what he was referring to and nodding.

"Wish the War Department had been so considerate about getting our bags here. Do we even know where they are?"

Fischer smiled, then shook his head, "Probably back at the office at the train station, or even back on Earth somewhere. Along with our hotel reservation. I trust you found suitable accommodations last night?"

He asked that last question with a hint of a smile — it was the first time he'd referenced his disappearance the night before, and the fact that the young Champion had been obliged to find her own bed.

Or someone else's.

Perhaps his instincts had told him she had been romantically occupied; perhaps the fact that she'd deliberately said nothing of her sleeping arrangements gave her away. In either case, Constance didn't really want to speak about it with Fischer — he was something of a friend to Vanier, but still not the sort she'd gladly confide in. As such, she opened her mouth to offer words of deflection.

And then the ground shook beneath her feet.

It was just a tremor, but when a roar followed she realized what it meant. The same sound had come during the blasts at the Robinson Institute, but this time it was much, much closer. Turning in a blur, she looked back at the row of buildings that bordered the airfield, and saw smoke beginning to rise over the nearest roofs. Somewhere on the parade route...

She blinked, looked to Fischer, and saw the paleness of his face. He swallowed, but did nothing.

"Come on," she blurted the words without thinking, and then drawing her pistol from the holster on her hip, she began to walk quickly towards the rising smoke.

It took the Major a moment to regain his wits, find his own sidearm, and follow.

The street was filled with dust and smoke. As she peeled herself off the tarmac, Alex couldn't help but cough — though that only slowed her slightly as she swept aside the tail of her coat and drew her pistol from its holster. There was no telling whether the blast was just one part of an elaborate attack. She wouldn't meet whatever came next unarmed.

But what would come next?

She had no concept of what to expect — wasn't quite able to grasp what had just happened. An explosion from the side of the street... an explosion that had cut right through a crowd of innocent people who'd been standing and waving, eagerly watching the Saa march past.

It was another attack, like Eustice and *Hood*, and it had come in spite of all the security.

How much damage had it done? There was no way to see — so much smoke crowded her like a putrid fog that she couldn't even make out the shape of Imogen. Was the dragon okay? Saa hides were tough — indeed, they were bulletproof — but the dragons were also large targets, almost certain to be struck by debris.

Alex turned to search for Sass's daughter, and after two quick steps, she walked straight into the youngster's leg.

There was a sharp yelp of surprise as the dragon felt the impact, "Hello?"

"It's me," Alex answered. "We have to hurry forward, find your mother and your brother."

That was simply instinct talking — perhaps it would have been more logical to keep the dragons apart, especially if someone was attacking them with explosives, but Alex wasn't able to stop and think so clearly. She wanted to find Stephanie and Strong, and her parents, and then get the dragons together into safety. So she would.

"Okay," Imogen was not about to argue, though she sounded more anxious now than before. "Straight ahead?"

"Slow and steady... watch your footing, there might be people down on the road after the blast," Alex replied.

They pushed forward into the dust cloud.

As they emerged onto the parade route, all Constance and Fischer could hear were screams and yells. The dust cloud was vast and billowing towards them — it seemed impossibly large for the modest size of the blast — and within it might be the villains behind the attack.

"I guess this pretty much clears Vanier," Fischer said abruptly, sounding rather bitter.

It was a welcome thought, but Constance couldn't spare time for it, "We should get in there, see if anyone needs help."

Fischer had been a screen operator, never a combat officer, so his words were predictably reluctant, "I don't know about that... there are lots of soldiers around..."

He was correct; men in British battle dress were hurrying to and fro, apparently leaderless as they tried to do whatever they thought constituted their duty. Some were readying their Enfield rifles and hurrying towards the explosion, others were running the opposite way, presumably looking for their officers, and more still were trying to direct civilians away from the blasted area.

It was pandemonium — people everywhere — and in the midst of the confusion, Constance could easily imagine some culprit slipping away.

"We have to try," she shook her head, and then for the first time she wondered if George Devlin had been near the explosion.

When that thought struck her, it was accompanied by a whole different feeling in the pit of her stomach — an anxiety unlike any other she could recall. It set her moving toward the fog of dust and smoke, her pistol leading the way, though angled down just enough that she wouldn't accidentally point it at anyone who was innocently seeking to escape. She didn't know if Fischer was following her — didn't really care — she just wanted to get forward, locate George, and find anyone else who was trying to take control of the situation. Though she'd yet to choose a coat, it was still her responsibility to help.

What confused her was the moment her face hit the pavement.

The sound of the gunshot didn't catch up to her until after she dropped, and she felt nothing at all. Her legs had stopped working so suddenly that her arms somehow didn't know to break her fall. She was most aware of the fact that her pistol was knocked from her hand as she dropped — it skidded across the tarmac out of reach.

Distantly, she heard other shots being fired — a .45 caliber pistol thudding, getting closer.

She felt Fischer's hand on her back before the pain began to throb in her leg. She was aware of the warm, wet feeling of what had to be blood beginning to soak into the breeches around her thighs.

Had she been shot? Who was shooting?

There were more screams from the street — a new urgency to the chaos as men, women and children tried to find safety from the confusion, and soldiers looked for some enemy to fire upon.

"Jesus," Fischer was beyond flustered. "Are you okay? They're heading towards the airstrip!" Constance was face-down on the street; she couldn't look up at him, but she knew the moment he saw her wound by his words: "Oh my God. Oh my *God*!"

The panic seemed a bit overdone, but Constance wasn't about to criticize. She started to shake her head, which was beginning to feel lighter, then made a good suggestion: "Can you get me to help, please?"

"Yes of course!" the non-combat officer's harried reply was immediate, and soon Constance was being carried deeper into the cloud.

• • •

The scattered sound of gunshots obliged Alex to turn and look back in the direction of the airstrip... but the dust was too thick. Were shooters taking advantage of the carnage as they had at Eustice... or were soldiers in a panic starting to fire improperly?

There wasn't enough consistent fire for her to tell, and she wasn't about to break off to investigate on her own.

Imogen seemed equally concerned with the noise, "That's the firing of your small arms?"

"Yep," Alex confirmed, but resumed her course. "Let's keep moving."

"That you?" a call came from close by, and it was Stephanie's voice.

Just hearing her was a relief, and Alex replied, "Me and Imogen. Where are you?"

Neither the younger Lady Smith nor Sass's daughter stopped advancing, and quickly they were upon Stephanie, Strong and Elspeth, with Ciaran looming over them. The two dragons touched the sides of their heads together, which very much seemed to ease Imogen's anxiety, but there was no time for more than that.

"You hearing shots?" Stephanie asked her friend as they got close to each other, and the whitecoat nodded.

"Might be gunmen out here. We need to get up to Sass, make sure everyone's okay and then figure out what to do."

Stephanie met those firm words with a nod, "Exactly what I was thinking."

In some situations, the fact that they shared the same ideas might have seemed sweet. In this context, the similar thoughts were simply a blessing for efficiency, and as Strong nodded to confirm his agreement, they all started forward again — everyone with pistol (or Thompson) ready to fire.

More shots sounded in the distance, and panicked people hurried to and fro, appearing and then vanishing again into the putrid smoke and choking dust.

The absurd thought that came to Caralynne's mind as she sat up was that hopefully explosions only came in threes. If so, she'd had hers — Virginia, *Hood*, and now this? She forced herself to her feet, consciously checking that all her limbs seemed to be working, and then as the ringing in her ears began to dim, she turned in place to see who might be nearby.

Screams were sounding from all around… cries for help… officers bellowing for their soldiers to find them… in the midst of the dust and smoke, it was utter chaos. She couldn't even see Sass — was the giant dragon alright?

The one thing she was certain of, as always, was her husband. When Smith appeared and put his hand on her shoulder — both so he could feel that she was well, and to confirm his presence for her — she didn't need to say anything.

Then she heard Alain Lapointe call for help. He was close, so it took only a moment to find him and realize he was kneeling over someone.

Caralynne sunk into a crouch, "Who is it?"

"Anneke," he answered. "She covered me against the explosion."

He sounded shocked, though clearly his mind was working. Of course there was no questioning the layers of experience possessed by the Prime Minister — from his survival of the Hubrin War to *Hood*, he had seen much, and his wits could not be doubted.

Any more than the wounds in Anneke Winter's back could be overlooked. Her purple coat — new, since the Atlantic had destroyed her previous one — was flayed to tatters, as was the blouse beneath it. Her back was thus partially bare, and it looked as though she'd been flogged raw. A pool of blood was oozing out beneath her.

"Is she…" Caralynne began to ask, but then saw the perfect Champion's back quiver.

Lady Winter then struggled for enough breath to say: "Get him out of here."

After that, she deflated with a wheeze, and forced herself not to cry out in agony as she lay face-down on the street.

"We need to get her out of here," Lapointe had never been good at allowing himself to be withdrawn from a battlefield, particularly when he was unwounded. His protector, however, needed to be taken away from harm.

Caralynne began to nod, then stopped when she sensed a shadow looming over her. Twisting, she looked up and was relieved to see Sass's head was just in view in the fog.

"You alright?" the Saa lady asked her friends, and Caralynne was candid.

"One badly wounded here. We need to get her, and Alain… everybody important out of the street. Including you," the elder Lady Smith answered.

"I'm hearing gunfire," Sass replied. "Not much, but some. Are your troops positioned to respond?"

Caralynne began to nod, rising from her crouch as she did. Before she could add anything, though, Jimmy Devlin hobbled into view, his arm around his wife's shoulder as she helped him along.

"Dammit," his greeting was honest and pained, and as proximity allowed him to see everyone through the smoke, his eyes fell on Anneke. "We best get her out of here now."

"All of you out of here," a new voice joined the conversation — it was George Devlin, coming around Sass. "This much chaos is too dangerous. You're all too important. We need to get you to Earth and airborne immediately."

So much clarity filled his orders that his elders were surprised, but George Devlin wasn't to be delayed. His duty was to be hospitable to the Saa, and that made his first priority their safety… and the safety of the rest of the important people with them.

"We need to get control of this situation," Jimmy countered his son's assertion, then took his arm off Annie's shoulder and applied weight to his left ankle. After a grimace, he shook his head, "I'm fine. I can stay and coordinate…"

The sheer number of glares the Viscount got as he started to make that case shut him up. He was both too important and injured. And if reinforcement of George's point was required, new shapes emerged from the mist: two smaller dragons, and four more people.

"Is everyone alright?" Alex was leading the way, so hers was the first question.

As Caralynne turned to her daughter, the relief she yet again felt was set aside, "Anneke's wounded. We need to get her out of here… and Alain, and Jimmy, and Annie."

"And the Saa," George added immediately.

Even as they were speaking, Elspeth was rushing forward in a blur, then dropping to her friend's side with calming words. As she scanned the savage wounds on Lady Winter's back, she looked up, "We need to get her moving."

She sounded calm, but there was no doubting the high tension. Confusion was beginning to give way to action, and as Stephanie came up beside Alex, the Lieutenant offered her own thoughts: "There's shooting, so we should stay to check it out. But George is right: we need to get the VIPs out of here, and Lady Winter."

"We can look after things here," Alex picked up the thread, as though she and her best friend were simply splitting passages of the same script. "You get everyone to Newfoundland, and send reinforcements back."

Such were the orders from the whitecoat and the American. Together they were delivered with the sort of quiet authority that Caralynne had always employed herself... and they were difficult to resist.

"Done," George agreed, then looked up to Sass. "I know you could probably help here, but let's not give them any more opportunities to go after you or your kids."

Sass herself was an engineer, not a warrior, so she had no specific hunger to stay and fight — at least none beyond her loyalty to her friends. But the daughters of those friends were proving themselves very clear in their command of the situation, and she would trust their judgment.

With a nod, she therefore hissed back to her offspring, "Let's get ready to run."

"Perhaps we could get a lift from you?" under other circumstances, that request from Jimmy to Sass would have been fodder for humor — the Viscount asking the lady for another ride.

No one laughed, or even tried to.

"Of course," she agreed. "Everyone on... we'll avoid your train, run straight through the tunnel ourselves."

Just that quickly, the plan was struck — three dragons would race from one world to the other, carrying the VIPs to the safety of their skycruiser. And Alex, Stephanie and Strong would remain behind.

"Can I go... carry Anneke?" Elspeth stood up with the question, but from her tone Alex knew it was more a demand than a request.

"Of course, and look after them if there's an ambush further along," Stephanie answered.

With a nod, Elspeth crouched again, and whispered to her friend about what was to come next — it would undoubtedly be painful, if hopefully not too traumatizing. Lady Winter's wounds didn't appear mortal, but sometimes...

"Help us!"

If calm had begun to set in because of Alex and Stephanie's certainty, it was shaken again as a harried-looking American hurried into sight, carrying a crumpled girl who was dripping blood.

"Jesus," George Devlin recognized Constance Cormack immediately, and he was beside her as soon as Fischer stopped and dropped to one knee. The American was exhausted, but he attempted to be lucid.

"There are men heading for the airfield... I think they're after the dragons' luggage. I shot at them, but they got her from behind."

George was listening, somewhat, as he got his arms around Constance again. She was in a daze as she looked up at him, blood running down her face from what appeared to be a broken nose, and his attempts at remaining calm were shaken.

But that was for him to deal with; Alex looked to Stephanie, and the American nodded, "We'll go."

Turning back to Fischer, Alex nodded towards Constance, "Make sure she gets on the flight with the dragons, Major."

That was it; those fleeing would have their own challenges, but keeping Anneke and now Constance alive was a battle for surgeons. Both the whitecoat and her Lieutenant remained numb to the possibility of friends dying... it was time for them to act.

Without another word, they both hurried away from the dragon party. Mike Strong went with them, his expression set and his Thompson ready.

Silence remained in their wake, until Alain Lapointe called for action, "We must make haste."

Sass started explaining to her children how to carry humans, George and Fischer hurried to get Constance onto Ciaran's back and to hold her there, while Elspeth draped Anneke across her shoulders.

As Jimmy and Annie made their way onto Sass's tail, Caralynne turned to her husband, "I shouldn't go."

The former drifter considered his wife with a long stare, and as if foreseeing something grave in the near future, he concurred, "I'll get everyone back to Newfoundland. See to our girls."

His words were heavy, but they still provided calm. With a nod and a very quick kiss, Caralynne left her husband, following Alex, Stephanie and Strong into the putrid fog.

This time, the villains would not get away.

CHAPTER XII

As chaos raged through New World City, Colonel Neville Grier raced towards the Saa landing craft on the airfield. The madness could not be allowed to endanger the alliance with the dragons, and no villains could be permitted access to the crates of luggage that Sass had brought with her — most were undoubtedly mechanical in nature.

Riding in the passenger seat of a Land Rover, Grier was able to see that baggage through the windshield; the dozen trucks that had been brought in to ferry it to the train were all lined up, ready to drive out onto the roads behind the parade. Thank God the convoy hadn't already departed; while they were on the airfield they were largely secure, thanks to the soldiers who continued to protect its perimeter.

A platoon was also in place directly beside the Saa craft, its men warily watching all directions for any sign of assault. Spitfires were continuing to circle overhead, clearly ready to strafe any enemy that tried to breach the perimeter. Sounds of gunfire had just begun to taper off — the shots coming from the street had been intermittent and unorganized, suggesting they could have as easily been caused by confusion as by a genuine threat. But Grier would take no chances; the Saa on the field were as secure as could be. Once that was beyond any doubt, he would worry about the parade route.

The dust thinned as Alex, Stephanie and Strong cut between two large corrugated-metal warehouses, and hurried towards the airstrip. The whitecoat led the way, listening for more shots as she moved. It seemed as though they had died down now — perhaps the attackers had been defeated. Or they'd gone to ground, which might make them even more dangerous.

Slowing as she reached the edge of the nearest metal structure, Alex waved for Stephanie and Strong to drift to the right — closer to one of the walls — while she cut left at Champion speed. They'd spread out as they advanced, and because she was faster she'd run the longer route without cover.

Such decisions were instinctive; forgotten were the uncertainties of just a year before, when chasing Emily up Signal Hill had required such careful concentration. Alex raced to the left, watching the perimeter of the airfield and the sturdy-looking soldiers in battle dress who picketed it at close intervals. None appeared to have been under attack, so she wondered if she'd arrived too soon, or if the assault might come from a less obvious direction.

As she considered that, Stephanie and Strong emerged carefully from the cover of the warehouse. Perhaps they should have stayed concealed, but there seemed to be no immediate danger — the only eyes that fell on them belonged to the men standing guard.

"Where are they?" Stephanie whispered to her Sergeant, and glancing back at her, he answered honestly.

"I don't know."

Flight Lieutenant Douglas Bader had expected a dull morning of sorting baggage. Such were the duties of the second-in-command of a skycruiser like *Skipper Miller* — when Champions or VIPs were flying between destinations, and did not want to be encumbered by their travel bags while doing heroic things, the luggage was usually sent ahead. It was his duty to make certain the bags were distributed to the correct staterooms.

Of course, the process was seldom seamless; paperwork was often lost, bags mis-tagged, and so forth... but dealing with such frustrations was a minor price to pay for the opportunity to fly a Saa-built machine. Bader therefore tolerated it... but he was not at all heartbroken when the energy around Gateway Town abruptly shifted.

He was standing near the embarkation ramp when *Skipper Miller's* general alarm sounded, and Captain Santiago Abel came over the intercom: "All hands prepare for emergency departure. There has been an attack on the Saa delegation."

Bader actually smiled, "Damn them."

Tossing his clipboard cavalierly aside, the tin-legged pilot hurried towards the embarkation ramp control panel with all the speed he could muster, while calling for a couple of his men to clear away the baggage.

As soon as he reached the console, he flipped the necessary switches, and the great ramp began to descend. Moving towards it, he sauntered carefully down to stand on its end as it lowered itself to the dirt. Before him was the tunnel to the new world... and almost as soon as he set eyes on that impressive, five-track opening, a dragon burst from it at great speed.

Always impressive, the Saa; Bader thought very highly of them, and not just because they built wonderful flying machines. Raising his hand in a wave, the Flight Lieutenant called out in the direction of the tunnel, "This way! Come along here, dear lady!"

The distance was likely too great for him to be heard, but Sass had no trouble spotting *Skipper Miller*, and surging in its direction. Behind her, two smaller dragons followed...

And then before they arrived, someone appeared at Bader's side, "I need the sick bay, *now*."

Turning sharply — an impressive feat when it came to keeping his balance — Bader found himself face-to-face with the common-raised Champion, Elspeth Cornish. She was carrying the exemplary Champion, Anneke Winter, who looked to be going limp.

"Of course, Lady Cornish," Bader was not one easily fazed, and he turned back to the technicians who were in the bay with him. "Simon, get this Lady to our infirmary at once, and call for the doctor!"

Elspeth nodded her thanks, but clearly had no time to say more. Bader watched as she hurried off, and caught a glimpse of Anneke's flayed back. It was gruesome, and taken together with that Lady's limpness, the Flight Lieutenant feared her condition was serious. He looked back out into the daylight and found that Sass was near — they could leave presently, and since *Skipper Miller's* 'doctor' was, in fact, just a technician trained in advanced field triage, reaching a hospital quickly might be essential to the survival of the Champion.

Mindful of that, Bader collected his thoughts and hit the intercom, making certain to sound calm — even a little jaunty — to help reduce the tension of the situation: "Hello flight deck, this is Bader at the ramp."

There was a pause before Spanish Captain Abel responded to the

Englishman, albeit without any niceties: "Report situation."

"Delegation coming aboard. We have one seriously wounded Champion, Lady Winter. Suggest we'll need to get her to a hospital without delay. High speed."

"Understood," Abel was quicker to respond the second time.

Bader withheld further comment until Sass reached the ramp and lumbered up it in silence. The fact that such a massive creature could move with so little evidence of her presence was genuinely impressive, though even Bader's occasional eccentricity didn't allow him to dwell on that detail.

More interesting was the fact that Jimmy Devlin, Anne Devlin, and the Canadian Prime Minister had been hanging onto Sass's tail — and were falling off just as the two other dragons hurried up into the hold.

"We have to get airborne, Douglas," Jimmy Devlin recognized *Skipper Miller's* co-pilot instantly. "Two seriously wounded Champions need to go to hospital, and we have to get Sass and her children to safety."

That was a lot to process, but Bader employed his usual sharpness in maneuvering around the extraneous information, and landing on the most salient point: "Back to St. John's, or a nearer hospital?"

He asked the question as George Devlin appeared, cradling a crumpled Champion student in his arms. She was very bloody, and though the young hospitality man was by no means heavily-built, he appeared to have no thought of letting someone else carry her.

"Infirmary," he insisted — one low, desperate word — and Bader waved another of his technicians to come forward.

"I'll go with him, see if I can help," Anne Devlin said as her son passed her, and then with a quick kiss to Jimmy's cheek, she added. "Get off your feet while you make the calls for reinforcements."

Perhaps it was unnecessary doting, but Jimmy nodded anyway, then hobbled toward Bader. Smith was sliding off the tail of one of the smaller dragons, so he and Lapointe joined them.

The conversation was life or death.

"Your surgeon aboard..." the Viscount began to ask quietly, even though his son was almost out of earshot.

Bader shook his head, "Merely a medic, M'Lord. We could be at Calgary Hospital in but moments — Captain Abel has the engines warming now."

Devlin heard those words, then looked to Sass as he tried to digest them. She was busy checking on her son and her daughter — making sure neither had been harmed by the blast, or by the shooting that followed. Now that they were on Earth, and *Skipper Miller's* ramp was rising, the Saa were mostly safe.

But stopping at a nearby hospital might be risking too much.

"All hands, stand by for liftoff," Captain Abel's voice cut across the bay — he'd clearly taken the rising of the ramp as sign that it was time for his ship to get into the air.

What was their destination?

Looking from Bader to Lapointe, Jimmy Devlin found his thoughts running out. Two Ladies might die if denied immediate care — including Constance, the girl his son had apparently fallen for. But any delay before returning to the safety of Jimmystown would put the Saa, and *Skipper Miller*, at risk. Slight risk, to be sure... but could they take any chances now?

Lapointe's answer was clear in his eyes, "I think we can make the stop brief, and then be—"

"Newfoundland."

Smith's single word was low and steady. As both the Prime Minister and the Viscount of the Grasslands looked to the former drifter, his face revealed his stoic unhappiness... but his perspective was clear. No one would accuse him — Alex's father — of being callous, but he was the sort of man who understood the bigger picture, and had instincts that could save lives. He knew that Jimmystown was the only place on Earth where the Saa could be absolutely safe, and he trusted that the wounded Champions could hold on long enough to get there.

His clarity now would be trusted.

"How fast can you get us home, Bader?" there was no uncertainty in the question as Jimmy looked back to the Flight Lieutenant.

A sporting grin crossed the Briton's face: "The book says forty minutes, sir. Naturally, we'll do it for you in less."

Such swagger might normally have struck Jimmy Devlin poorly, but this time he wanted to believe it. At some point it would sink in that he might have just condemned one or two Champions to die, but for now he simply nodded, and with Lapointe's help, headed for the hatch. With a sprained ankle, it would take him longer than usual to get up to the flight deck.

Bader didn't follow; turning back to the console, he piped up to his Captain once again, "Hello flight deck, this is Bader. We're for Newfoundland, at full maximum thrust. Orders to be there in forty minutes or less, sir, so we'll need to push up to 4,000 knots."

He sounded positively eager at the prospect; Abel was more subdued in his reply, "Understood. Setting course. Please come up immediately."

A skycruiser was built to cruise at speeds that were simply impossible by human standards — indeed, even the new snapdragon fighters would not be able to match their top velocities. But flying at six times the speed of sound was no mean feat, so Captain Abel would need his trusty co-pilot alongside.

That in mind, Bader nodded to Smith — the only remaining VIP in the hold — and offered an unnecessary, jaunty salute, "You'll excuse me, sir?"

The former drifter stood aside with a nod, then watched the man with tin legs hurry off with surprising agility. There was no particular sensation in the bay as *Skipper Miller* rocketed up into the sky, but as Smith turned back to face Sass and her kids, he took a deep breath and pulled his hat from his head.

He didn't like the situation — it felt wrong to him. But he had to trust that his daughter, her friend, her Sergeant, and his wife would be safer this way.

CHAPTER XIII

From her vantage point at the edge of the airfield, Alex could see the dragons from Sass's small craft finish unloading the last of the baggage, then wave towards the men around their ship. It looked as though none of the Saa crew were wearing translation collars, so they had to rely on hand gestures for communication, but they weren't leaving much room for interpretation.

As she narrowed her eyes against the sunlight, she was able to see one dragon make a broad sweeping gesture directed across the field, essentially suggesting the humans get clear. He then pointed to the craft, and skyward. The landing ship was obviously departing, since by now it was clear that Sass and her children wouldn't be returning.

Alex wasn't sure whether she'd have been as willing to leave as the small craft's crew, but clearly the dragons had their own protocols for situations such as these, and she wouldn't second guess. More important: all the humans in the field had to get clear — including those driving trucks loaded with Saa baggage that would have to be secured until it could be transported back to Newfoundland.

That was probably the prize. The attack on the street might have been intended to kill... and almost certainly, it would have succeeded in murdering some of the spectators. However, the past year's events suggested it might have also been a distraction — misdirection from the real objective. And stealing even one truckload of Saa equipment could be world-shifting for an enemy of the British Empire.

With a glance down the perimeter towards Stephanie, Alex saw that her friend and her Sergeant were ready, watching all directions for signs of an ambush, or any other villainy. There were hundreds of soldiers nearby, which naturally made that seem less likely... but anything could happen.

Looking back toward the field, Alex saw an officer standing up in the front seat of a Land Rover, and her Champion hearing could just pick out his calls to the platoon on the ground, "Withdraw to a safe distance! Move the trucks!"

The engines of those vehicles started, and as Alex looked on they began rolling in the direction of the town — almost straight at Stephanie and Strong, in fact.

"If you were going to steal one of those trucks, how would you do it?"

When that question came from behind Alex, she very nearly jumped. Only the fact that it was her mother's voice prevented total fright, and with an abrupt glance back, the younger Lady Smith questioned her elder, "You're supposed to be with dad."

"He can take care of them. I think it's time you and me actually get to be together for the entirety of one of these fights."

Strangely, that warmed Alex. Since Emily's return, and the chaos that had followed, mother and daughter had never really been together for a single action. They'd swum out of *Hood*, but that wasn't the same... they'd been apart in Virginia, Scotland, and Hong Kong. Now, though, the Ladies Smith could confront the villains behind this year of infamy together.

And to that point, Alex answered her mother's original question: "If I wanted to steal one out from under the noses of everyone here... I'd just swap the driver."

"Get past the checkpoint and then run for it, to a safer location, with ambushes along the way," Caralynne was proud that she and her daughter were thinking along the same lines, and as she tightened her grip around her Browning's handle, the whitecoat nodded.

"So we follow them to whatever depot they're bound for, and see who tries to make a run for it," Alex concluded. "Sounds good to me."

For once they had a plan — now they just needed to make sure Stephanie and Strong were in on it.

Standing in front of the metal warehouse at the edge of the airfield, the Lieutenant and her Colour watched as people scattered before the humming of the Saa craft's engines. The vessel was powering up for launch, and with a glance at each other, the two soldiers decided to move closer together.

Even at long range, a crash launch could kick out a hurricane of winds, and while the sensible way to avoid falling over would have been to take shelter, neither Stephanie nor Strong wanted to risk losing sight of the Saa baggage.

Alex and her mother appeared alongside them almost as soon as they drifted towards each other.

"I thought we sent you packing," Mike Strong addressed Caralynne with a small smile.

"You'd discard me just like that, Mike?" she answered dryly. "I guess it was inevitable, but I still want to be able to say I fought with you just once."

His smile grew a tad, but not much — humor really didn't have a place in a city under fire, and so he nodded his head in the direction of the trucks, "Think someone's going to try to drive one away?"

"Literally," Alex confirmed. "We'll tail the convoy on foot... you guys get a Land Rover and do the same?"

That made sense, so Stephanie nodded, "As soon as we watch liftoff. We'll be right behind you."

With a single nod of agreement, Alex and her mother both leapt skyward. In seconds they were safely atop a nearby building — far enough away from the airstrip not to be obvious, but with a clear view of the roads leading away from the gate.

Stephanie and Strong braced themselves against each other; the Colour crouched, facing the airfield with his Thompson ready and his eyes squinted both against the sun and the promise of wind, while the Lieutenant turned obliquely to one side and held her pistol ready, using him for support.

They were prepared for the wind... and that was good, for it came in a rush.

Everyone in the vicinity of the airfield had to get low or brace themselves as the Saa ship shot into the sky.

Though she wasn't well, Miranda Shylock had insisted that she watch the arrival of the Saa craft from the bench on the front porch of the family hotel. She had thus remained there with her husband, Kard and Bo as the drama unfolded. The men had been tempted to ride out and help, but thought better of it, and so they were all still together for the departure of the Saa ship.

As the dragon vehicle climbed high into the sky, escaping the supposed protection of the Spitfires circling overhead, Stephanie's mother watched through squinted eyes. With the Saa gone, would calm be restored?

"I think we should go for a look now," Bo Shylock said to his brother, anxious at all the sounds of chaos.

Vonn was sitting beside his bride on the bench, and though he was certainly older than he'd been last time he'd ridden towards the sounds of trouble, he couldn't help but agree with his brother. Casting a glance at Miranda, he posed the question wordlessly.

Still looking up, watching as the Saa flying machine shrunk so small that her aging vision couldn't distinguish it from the bright blue sky, Stephanie's mother considered the question. She did not fear for her daughter — somehow, she just knew her young Lieutenant was safe — but still, there was no harm in Vonn, Bo and Kard going for a look.

"Take it easy out there. Many nervous people," she replied, and with that her husband nodded. His expression seemed slightly pained, though, so she scolded him: "Don't have that face, now. It's not as though you're going forever."

A smile crossed Stephanie's father's face, and he kissed his wife gently on her lips. It was a feeling Miranda didn't mind at all, no matter how poorly she was.

With that, the Shylock brothers and Kard headed inside the hotel to collect their guns and then exit through the back, so they could get their horses from the stable. Miranda remained on the bench, watching the sky over the rooftops.

When horses trotted out from around the back of the hotel, she lowered her gaze and waved to her three men as they rode out into the street. Being the sort of people who couldn't sit still when danger was afoot, they were eager to see what was occurring. That was why Miranda loved Vonn — why she'd had to let him join Smith's mission to find Caralynne. He had to be true to his nature, then and now...

As they rode out of sight, a man stepped up onto the porch. He was shorter than most people of his era, but fit, and he wore a long gray raincoat that looked almost like a duster.

Touching the brim of his hat, he asked, "Miranda Shylock?"

She frowned up at the stranger, "I am. Are we acquainted?"

Pulling off his hat and smiling, the man shook his head, "Not directly."

His bearing was friendly and his tone warm, but his words were cryptic. Miranda was not naïve, so she felt a certain discomfort from his presence. She made to push herself to her feet — to face the man standing — but he crossed the porch and stood before her, shaking his head, "Better if you stay seated."

He still sounded friendly, but Miranda's concern was growing, "What's your purpose with me, Mister?"

"It's awkward, but I'm here..." he paused, and his smile faded, "...regarding your death."

With the Saa craft gone, the way was clear. Knowing Alex and Caralynne had the airfield under close watch, Stephanie and Strong hurried away from the perimeter in search of a Land Rover — a vehicle that was surprisingly difficult to locate.

As they hurried from street to street, looking for an officer's truck to appropriate, they found roads that were alternately abandoned, or full of panicked-looking people. No cars of any sort were in sight.

"I expected this part to be easier," Mike Strong lamented after a few moments, and Stephanie nodded.

"Where the hell did they put them all?"

For minutes they continued their search, and still found nothing. Fearing the luggage trucks would begin moving, the Lieutenant and her Sergeant then hurried back towards the field, hoping that a vehicle had driven in behind them...

"Stephanie!"

The young American was striding down the side of one road when she heard a familiar voice call her name, and looked back. Her father was riding towards her, and behind him Bo and Kard were turning their horses and following. A smile suddenly leapt to her face — it was not at all in keeping with the serious situation, but somehow the world became brighter when she realized three of the men she'd grown up trusting were arriving to help.

As Vonn Shylock slowed, he looked down at his daughter both with relief and questions, "What's going on?"

She waited just a second to answer — long enough for Kard and Bo to get within earshot. Then she explained the blast, the escape, and the overall chaos... as well as the likelihood that it had been a diversion, and the trap they were setting for whichever driver tried to steal the Saa baggage.

Vonn listened silently to his little girl — both to what she was saying and the certainty with which she spoke. There was no doubting she was a woman now, or that she was a natural officer. The way Strong looked to her proved that; the Newfoundland Sergeant was a known man, with a reputation for soldiering and for women, and yet when his eyes fell on Stephanie they held real pride.

Vonn shared that pride, and was further buoyed by what she said next: "You came at the perfect moment. Can you help?"

"Us?" Bo sounded genuinely surprised. "You got lots of soldiers who's younger."

"Yes, but we trust you," Mike Strong piped up. "We were both in the Hubrin capital that day, after all."

It was true. These villains had proved their ability to infiltrate just about anything, so having absolutely trusted men was important. No one who'd been in the Hubrin capital that day could be a traitor now — except for Emily, but that was different — so these three men were the only ones Strong and Stephanie could be sure of.

"Happy to," Cameron Kard touched the brim of his hat, and then started opening and closing his right hand, trying to fight off the arthritis in case he needed to shoot again.

Together, the three riders and the two soldiers headed back towards the field.

"What's he doing?" Alex frowned as she watched Colonel Grier.

Standing beside her daughter, Caralynne was puzzling too; the Army intelligence officer was waving his arms as though he were giving flag signals to a warship... but it appeared as though he was herding the trucks with the Saa baggage back *onto* the field.

Why would he be doing that?

Alex didn't know, but not wanting to reveal her presence, she decided to simply wait. Perhaps they were forming up in column to drive out, which would mean they were departing any time now. Would Stephanie and Strong be ready?

That thought drew the whitecoat's glance towards the road, and she was rewarded with a new arrival: Stephanie and Strong on foot, with three horsemen behind them.

"Looks like we have trustworthy reinforcements," Alex said, and her mother glanced back and spotted the Shylocks and Kard — the men who'd helped Smith save her. She couldn't help but feel some relief; logically, they were getting a bit old for a fight against an enemy agent, but she would never underestimate them…

Or perhaps, they wouldn't have a chance to find out.

All of the trucks carrying Saa luggage switched off in the middle of the field, and the drivers hopped out and hurried away to rejoin their regiment. That left all the precious cargo sitting in the open, and as Caralynne watched, the same platoon that been guarding the dragon small craft hurried into position to protect it.

Colonel Grier's vehicle was the only one moving — his Land Rover bounced across the field at high speed, then hit the lane that led out to the street. That meant he was driving straight for Stephanie and Strong. Could he be the villain?

Nudging Alex, then nodding at Grier's approach, Caralynne figured they'd better find out. The whitecoat agreed.

Stephanie and Strong watched more than a little suspiciously as Grier's truck slowed before them. The Colonel was staring at them with even less goodwill, and as his Land Rover finally stopped, he called out, "What's your purpose here? This is a secure area!"

Surely he recognized Lieutenant Shylock and Sergeant Strong — everyone did. But… perhaps he was being extra protective?

Advancing a few paces towards the Colonel's vehicle, with Strong keeping pace and Kard riding not far behind, Stephanie called back: "We got reports that men were coming for Sass's baggage. We're here to make sure it's safe."

"I have that under control," Grier's tone shifted slightly — no longer did he sound suspicious, but he did come across as… uncompromising. "You and your… men… should depart, Lieutenant. Until these trucks can be moved out under proper guard, and directly to one of your skycruisers, I will keep them in the middle of this field, under constant guard by a full regiment."

That was a lot of guards. Before Stephanie could counter, Caralynne and Alex both blurred into the picture to join the conversation.

"Have you had any sign of attack, Colonel?" the elder Lady Smith asked, and Grier masked surprise at her abrupt appearance.

"None yet, but as you can see we are prepared. I don't know what they could possess that would defeat all of us without also damaging the baggage, and if they try to come through our lines, it'll make such a racket the whole town will be upon them."

Alex was inclined to be skeptical of that assessment. Too often during the past year, claims of certain security had been proven entirely unfounded... but this time the Colonel wasn't exactly speaking out of turn. The airfield *was* surrounded, and unless every soldier in the city was in on some plan to steal Saa technology, there was no way to get at the baggage trucks without drawing attention.

That in mind, the young whitecoat frowned, first at her mother and then at Stephanie. The American Lieutenant frowned too. Together, the two friends turned away from Grier's Land Rover, their eyes scanning all the buildings nearby — looking for signs of men with guns, bombs, pulse cannons... *anything.* Surely the attack on the parade hadn't simply been an attempt to strike terror in the hearts of civilians, or to kill one of the Saa. Nothing this year had been so simple... why would the villains start now?

"I guess security here has been pretty tight... maybe one explosion was all they could manage?" Alex asked quietly, intending the question for Stephanie alone.

With a long sigh, the American girl shook her head, "I know... but it's just too simple. They had to want to use that confusion to some advantage. What are we missing?"

It was an honest question, and though her mind was grappling with it, Stephanie couldn't quite figure out the weak point. Alex couldn't either — again, the situation was just too uncertain, and there was too little information.

"We better start canvassing the town. Whoever planted that bomb *must* be here, and if they're not after the luggage, there must be something important that we're missing," Alex's tone had gone dark, but her words were correct.

Her friend agreed with a nod, and with that, the pair turned to their Sergeant and their parents to discuss ways to sweep New World City.

Where else could the villain be?

CHAPTER XIV

It took Imogen a few minutes to find the auxiliary control screen in *Skipper Miller's* cargo bay. Designed only for use by Saa operators in case of emergency, the interface was protected beneath a blank section of bulkhead, and its presence had been masked by the luggage that Bader's men had stacked against it. After asking some of the crew to kindly take away those bags (her claws were not small enough for her to do so without destroying them), the young dragon slid aside the bulkhead, and activated the panel.

Smith stood beside Sass and watched the process, and when the screen came to life he glanced up at the mighty dragon lady, "Your daughter is gifted."

Sass answered with a reminder: "So is yours."

That was true, and Smith nodded back his appreciation.

"Imogen's really good with all sorts of equipment. Much better than me," Ciaran was sitting on his mother's far side, but he'd heard the former-drifter's words, and swelled with pride in praising his fellow hatchling.

Sass's son's enthusiasm had been dulled by the chaos, but not quashed; for Imogen, though, getting access to something familiar — even a simple control screen that was frankly rudimentary compared to what she usually played with at home — helped restore calm.

"Do we need to do anything to assist flight control, mother?" she asked.

A quick downturned palm accompanied Sass's response: "No need. The humans have controls up on a smaller bridge deck, and they are very good at flying. You can observe, though."

Imogen turned her palm upward, and then did exactly as her mother said: she watched all the telemetry readings crossing her screen, and got her first look at the planet Earth through the downward-facing cameras and sensors built into *Skipper Miller's* hull. Far below the skycruiser, prairies were giving way to coarser terrain — rocky ground, covered in lakes and trees. It was different than any world the young Saa had seen, though at the age of two she could hardly profess to be an experienced traveler.

Eventually, she tired of looking at the ground scan; the detail available in the images was limited because the ship was traveling at such a high altitude to maximize speed on its nearly-sub-orbital-hop to Newfoundland.

Turning instead to the skycruiser itself, Imogen called up a systems summary, and began acquainting herself with the particulars of *Major Herbert Miller*. It was interesting to see what technologies the Saa had decided to incorporate into a vessel that was constructed for, and exclusively controlled by, a race of freed attackers. There were numerous pieces of equipment within the hull that truly were at the cutting edge of Saa science, many which Imogen suspected the humans had yet to learn how to unlock.

But there were some issues, too. The humans likely didn't understand the details of maintaining reactors, or certain aspects of the counter-gravity technology that allowed a ship of such mass to move so quickly, without doing harm to the surface of the planet.

And...

Imogen paused as she came across a malfunction that seemed entirely within the ability of human engineers to recognize.

"Mother," she said, and Sass detected concern in her daughter's hiss — concern that was also translated by her collar.

Smith and Sass thus advanced towards Imogen's position together, with the mother asking, "Something the matter?"

"Environmental controls are overridden..." she observed, and then her head rotated to the right and her eyes narrowed. "Correction. They are currently being overridden. From the control center... tail end of the ship, on the upper level."

"Being overridden?" Sass's head rotated to match her daughter's, and her large eyes swept the same screen carefully to confirm the findings.

There was no mistaking it; someone was adjusting the ventilation controls aboard *Skipper Miller*. Unsure whether that was normal procedure, Sass looked down to Smith, only to be greeted by a frown and a head-shake.

"Can't say for certain, but that sounds off," the former-drifter said.

That was reason enough to be concerned, so Sass nodded to her daughter, "Call up to the flight deck."

Imogen turned her palm upward, then pressed the intercom key. Sass then gave her an encouraging nod, and having listened to Bader's communications earlier, the young dragon began to imitate his protocol: "Hello flight deck... this is Imogen in the embarkation bay."

Jimmy and Alain were on the flight deck, the former sitting in an extra seat and the latter standing behind him as *Skipper Miller* cruised at altitudes so high they were beginning to see the blackness of space beyond the windows. When the intercom kicked in, and the synthesized voice sounded, the Viscount and the Prime Minister both perked up.

With a glance back, Captain Abel questioned the identity of the speaker, "Is she one of yours?"

"She's one of our Saa," Alain answered immediately. "Sass's daughter."

A serious frown had been on Abel's face since liftoff — taking *Skipper Miller* to the edge of space was not something he did every day, so ample focus was necessary. Distractions were not welcomed, but when a Saa called it was usually wise to listen.

Bader took on that duty, keying the intercom, "Hello Imogen, Bader here on the flight deck. What can we do for you?"

There was a pause, and then the dragon replied, "Hello, Bader. I was consulting the auxiliary control screen, and noticed that someone in your environmental control center is overriding ventilation controls. Is that standard procedure?"

With a frown, Bader looked to Abel, and the Captain shook his head, "We could be having malfunctions because of the altitude. We do not climb this high often."

"Equalizing pressure manually, because of the atmospheric density?" Bader asked — and the question was beyond both Jimmy and Lapointe as they listened in.

"Possible," Abel posited, but his frown deepened. "It should have been reported, though."

Indeed, any system override needed to be handled cautiously, particularly at such altitude. A check-in would be required, so Bader returned his attention to Imogen, "Hello, Imogen. That is not our procedure. We'll look into it right away. Thank you."

"Hello Bader. You are welcome. Thank you."

Then the line cut, and for just a second Bader smiled, "She's very good on the intercom."

But that was all the warmth he could spare; even as he said it he was sitting back, beginning to recall the crash launch. Had he overlooked any standard protocols on the way up?

Nothing came to mind, so with a glance at Abel, he leaned forward to the intercom once again, and flipped the necessary switches to connect to the environmental control center.

"Hello ECC, this is Bader on the flight deck."

He waited a moment for a response to that hail... and waited a moment more. With every second of silence, tension began to mount, and Jimmy Devlin forced himself up from his borrowed chair.

"Can we confirm she's right?" the Viscount asked, and one of the engineers sitting behind Able nodded.

"Yes sir, I'm looking at it now. Not sure what's happening, but I think someone back there is doing it on purpose..."

It obviously didn't take much effort to understand the implications of that statement. Abel looked to Bader, and the two began working hurriedly on their panels.

"I'm sorry, sir, but we're going to have to reduce speed and decrease our altitude," the tin-legged Lieutenant said, glancing just briefly back at Devlin. "And we need to get someone down there to find out what's going on."

Abel was already acting on that, keying his intercom to another compartment, "Warrant Officer Harvey, take two men to the arms locker for pistols. We think there is a saboteur in the ECC."

Lapointe advanced to stand beside Devlin, "What damage could he do?"

Bader continued working his board as he answered, "The environmental controls aren't wired to our main alarm boards. If someone started overriding propulsion or gravity, we'd get instant warnings. Not so in the ECC..."

"But it's serious?" Jimmy appreciated the context, but was more concerned with the bottom line.

Pausing, the Lieutenant looked back at the Viscount once more, "At 80,000 feet, if our pressurization failed, we'd all die quite brutally — either by suffocation, or freezing, or when this ship dropped from the sky."

"Christ," Devlin looked to Lapointe, and the Quebecker appeared no less pale than the Newfoundlander felt.

Both were interrupted again by the bridge comm, "Harvey here, sir. We're on our way."

A security detail was en route... hopefully Imogen's precocious observations had come in time to save them. But somehow Jimmy doubted it would be so simple. As the sky became bluer outside the windows — a function, he supposed, of declining altitude — he thought quickly of who'd come aboard with them.

His son and a Champion were available to help secure the ship, and though both were undoubtedly preoccupied by the wounded Ladies they'd brought aboard, their involvement might be necessary.

"Patch me in to the infirmary," the Viscount nodded towards the intercom switch, and after tapping a few more controls related to whatever important operation he was conducting for the ship, Bader obliged.

"Fortunately, sir, it's not the artery. Damned close, but if it was the artery she'd have died before she got here."

Skipper Miller's medic looked as though he'd done dishes in a basin full of blood, but at least he was giving George Devlin good news as he wiped his hands on a gruesome towel. Neither Anneke Winter nor Constance Cormack were likely to die in the half hour it would take for the skycruiser to get home. After that, well...

"They're both out of danger?" Anne Devlin was standing beside her son, and she asked that question carefully — in such a way as to make certain the medic would agree with her, even though it was a lie.

As that man — named Crane — looked to the Viscountess, he opened his mouth to correct her, but then stopped as their eyes met. He began to nod instead, realizing that keeping calm in the room was probably more important than acknowledging the real chance that both fallen Champions had lost too much blood to ultimately recover.

"Out of danger," he replied.

George wasn't impressed by the assurance: "I saw that, mother."

Anne paused, then glanced at her son. Perhaps trying to soften the blow was wholly foolish, so she shook her head instead, "Well there's nothing more we can do here."

"That's correct," the medic agreed. "I've got them both on plasma... that'll hopefully keep them going, and we'll have them to hospital within an hour."

Elspeth was standing beside Anneke's bed, and her expression darkened at the uncertainty. But she too understood there was nothing more that anyone could do, other than getting home quickly.

"Flight deck to infirmary... Anne, you there?"

The room abruptly filled with Jimmy Devlin's voice, and looking up to the speakers in the ceiling, the Viscountess frowned. When she looked back down to the medic, he gestured to the intercom control; because Crane was too bloody to work it, Anne went to the panel herself, then flipped the switch.

"We're here. Both our patients are unconscious, but as well as can be. If we get home quickly, they both have a chance."

Naturally she assumed her husband was calling for that update, but she was quickly proven incorrect.

"There might be a saboteur aboard. Don't know how, but we're sending armed men to the environmental control lab. Is Elspeth there?"

The Lady from London looked up at the mention of her name, "Here."

"Can you get back to environmental control, make sure those men are looked after?"

It sounded simple, but no one in the infirmary was blind to the potential danger.

"I could go," George offered from across the room, but immediately his father declined.

"If it's a saboteur meaning to fight it out, Elspeth is better equipped," he replied, and despite her reluctance to leave Anneke, the common-raised Lady nodded in agreement.

"On my way."

"Thanks. Stay in touch with us on the flight deck."

That was it; the comm cut and Elspeth took a few seconds to breathe, exchange glances with Anne and George, and then look once more at her unconscious friend. After that she drew her Browning and exited the infirmary, heading aft.

●●●

"They should be in the ECC by now," Abel had one eye on the clock, even as he and Bader drove *Skipper Miller* further down into Earth's sky. Outside the flight deck windows, bright white clouds drifted on all sides… from touching the heavens, they were now back on a more manageable — and slower — flight plane.

But their team had not reported from the environmental control center, which boded not at all well.

Leaning forward to the intercom, Bader punched up the compartment again, "Hello ECC, this is Bader on the flight deck. Hello ECC?"

He didn't call directly for Harvey — if there was a villain in the compartment, better he not know the name of one of the men coming to capture him. But there was no answer, and glancing at Abel, Bader shook his head.

"Sir, the vents in all compartments are now locking open," the engineer who'd been monitoring the environmental system reported at that point, and the news obliged Bader to shake his head.

"We need to reduce altitude. We're at 45,000… if he opens the ventilation gaps we'll lose all our atmosphere in less than a minute," the Flight Lieutenant explained, mainly for the benefit of the Prime Minister and Viscount standing behind him.

Abel agreed, but then he looked back to Jimmy with the question, "We can reduce altitude to a point where depressurization cannot harm us, but we would have to slow down… perhaps be an hour away from Newfoundland."

In other words, the girls struggling to stay alive in the infirmary would have to wait at least twice as long for help. Weighing their possible deaths against the loss of the ship, Devlin knew there was really only one option.

"Try to balance it as best you can, but if anything goes wrong we have to make sure the Saa are protected."

With a nod, Abel tapped on more controls. *Skipper Miller* continued to fall through the clouds, to an altitude where the air was more breathable.

Though she was a few corridors away, Elspeth's Champion hearing allowed her to detect Bader's call to the environmental control centre. There were no signs of crew as she made her way through the narrow passages in the utility section of the craft — no indication that the security detail was nearby — but perhaps she was ahead of them, or they were coming from a different direction. Surely they couldn't all have been silenced without her hearing anything of the struggle...

Or perhaps they had.

Turning the last corner to the ECC, Elspeth halted at the sight of one boot sticking out of the chamber's hatch. Based on the angle, it looked as though its wearer had fallen face-first into the compartment, and there were no signs of movement. Looking around quickly, the browncoat found that she was still alone, so she raised her Browning and advanced to the hatch frame. Her breath caught and her heart started pounding. Though most of her confidence in her own combat abilities had been rejuvenated after Hong Kong, she still felt both alone and somewhat claustrophobic in the narrow utility passages. If it came to shooting, she'd have little room to maneuver, so focus was essential.

Centering herself with a deep breath, she prepared for the possibility of gunplay, steeled her resolve, and swung around the hatch frame into the compartment.

Several things struck her all at once: first, the ECC was long, narrow and dark. Second, there was a man at the very end, laboring over a cylinder that had a flexible rubber hose sticking out of it. Third, the three men who'd been sent ahead were all piled in front of her, with no wounds on their lifeless bodies. Fourth, the man laboring over the cylinder wore a gas mask.

Fifth: she coughed.

No.

No, not again.

She took a step forward, but already she could feel her head beginning to swim. She raised her pistol and squeezed the trigger without clear aim — just point shooting, because her vision was blurring and she couldn't line up her sights. At the same time, she tried to race into the compartment — tried to use her Champion speed — but as her lungs instinctively filled themselves, the nightmare closed in all around her.

Gas.

Time was short — she had to stop the saboteur before his gas stopped her, but the toe of her left boot got caught in one of the bodies she was trying to race over. She fell on top of that dead man, and giggled.

She hated herself for giggling. It was happening again... why had no one realized it was the gas? In the enclosed environment of a skycruiser, gas could immobilize or kill the whole crew, leaving the ship to be flown anywhere by the one man wearing the mask. *Skipper Miller* would be uncatchable — the ultimate prize.

Elspeth pushed herself up blindly, raised her pistol again and squeezed, squeezed, squeezed the trigger. Thunder clapped in the tight quarters, and then she heard the man swear. There was also a hissing — she didn't know what it meant.

She giggled, and laughed, and then suddenly the man was in front of her. He was wearing a uniform, but she didn't recognize him because of his gas mask.

"You're an elephant," she said instead, and apparently he didn't think that was very funny. With a snarl she could hear through his elephantine mask, he pointed a pistol at her chest and fired.

She giggled again, but blood came out this time... and for some reason, he didn't spend another bullet on her. That was probably fine... she was pretty sure the wound she'd already received was mortal, and that made her laugh.

Then the man in the elephantine gas mask vanished, and she was left alone — bleeding and coughing. Dying. Beyond saving. Well, probably. She couldn't tell... but she was...

She was so angry inside...

As her body was bombarded by the familiar toxin that had nearly led her to ruin in Rosyth, her mind fought back. If she was dying, and this was to be her last effort, she was going to make it her best. Bob Freeman would expect no less. She sat up, and then she stood up. It felt as though blood was running from her like a river, but she stood right up, turned to the intercom, and pressed it.

She didn't realize she was coughing until she tried to talk, but she managed to say: "Gas... Champion Gas..."

Then she fell.

On the flight deck, those few words took a moment to process, then Douglas Bader blinked. As he looked back to Jimmy Devlin, the Viscount's mind was filling in the blanks too... and his eyes went wide.

He started to ask what could be done — the ventilation system was locked open, and if gas was flowing through the ship's ducts it could potentially incapacitate every Champion, and kill every ordinary man and woman aboard *Skipper Miller* so that the ship could be seized by a gas-masked saboteur.

Recognizing the same grim reality, Captain Abel looked to his engineer with the urgent question: "Can you close the vents?"

The man was already laboring over his console, "Working on it, sir..."

But 'working on it' was no certain answer, and if he didn't succeed, the only warning any of them might receive was a quick and brutal death.

"I'll set the automatic pilot, so we don't fall from the sky if we are incapacitated..." Abel looked back to his controls, but before his hands could move, Bader's were flying.

In one motion, he activated the ship-wide intercom, "Gas-gas-gas! Get onto alternate breathers, and move away from all exterior hatches and ventilation gaps. Someone with a gas mask get to the ECC, and look out for a saboteur!"

There was no polite 'hello' that time, nor did the pilot with tin legs waste a moment explaining what he had in mind. Instead, with single-minded haste, he pushed *Skipper Miller* down to 20,000 feet, then he called out: "Stand by for depressurization!"

"What?" Abel's eyes went wide, but before he could so much as move to intervene, Bader had turned to a console that was just beyond his normal reach.

Then he began flipping switches.

The medic Crane was hurrying to draw oxygen masks from his medical cupboard when both George and Anne felt their stomachs drop.

"We're descending *fast*," the younger man observed as Crane held a small oxygen canister in his direction. He took it and handed it to his mother, then grabbed the mask the medic offered.

With a surprising amount of calm dexterity, the hospitality man attached the mask's tube to the cylinder and helped his mother put it on.

"They are not gas-proof, but they are pure oxygen," Crane explained the limits of the breathing apparatuses as he handed

George the next cylinder.

"Good enough," the young spy nodded. "I'll get back there to check on Elspeth."

His declaration was firm, though his mother didn't like the sound of it. Putting one hand on his shoulder as he began to assemble his own breathing kit, she shook her head, "You shouldn't risk it..."

"I have to try," George replied evenly, with a determination that reminded her of his father.

Realizing it was futile to argue, she pulled him close into a hurried hug, "Be careful."

He nodded sharply before hastily pulling on his mask and racing from the compartment. As he drew his small .38 revolver from its holster under his suit jacket, he didn't trouble himself at all with the shortness of that farewell — with things he should have said before going to possible death.

Hopefully he wouldn't regret that.

"Outer doors are opening — hold on!" one of the technicians in the embarkation bay roared that warning just before jumping through the hatch that led to *Skipper Miller's* upper deck. For a moment, Smith wasn't sure what the man meant, but then the ramps on either end of the massive bay began to open.

As the atmosphere from inside the skycruiser was torn out into the much lower-pressure, high-altitude air, the breath was literally sucked from the former-drifter's lungs. Almost immediately he was pulled from his feet, and then he began to slide towards the bow ramp. He struggled to find something to hold onto... saw the bright blue sky grow before him, ready to pull him clear of *Skipper Miller* and into certain death...

A massive tail suddenly eclipsed the rectangle of bright blue, and then the not-quite-as-massive head of Ciaran was looming over him, the young dragon's eyes narrowed against the wind.

Smith couldn't even breathe a sigh of relief as the Saa encircled him; his lungs wouldn't fill. Realizing that, he fought back the urges of a drowning man and managed to hope that this wasn't an error by the men on the bridge. He couldn't hear Sass hissing to her daughter, or see Imogen standing ready to take over flight controls.

•••

The air on the flight deck became too thin to breathe, and Jimmy Devlin held desperately onto the back of Captain Abel's chair as he watched Douglas Bader's hands fly over the console. Presumably the Briton was noticing the lack of air, but he wasn't letting it slow him down...

Then, as *Skipper Miller* hurtled lower into the atmosphere and the air became thicker, breathing became more manageable. Marginally.

Jimmy felt his lungs inflate just a little, and it was agony — so much so it nearly took him off his feet. Unimaginable burning... but it got a little easier... and then...

"Below... 10,000..." Bader gasped out the words, revealing his own discomfort, but not slowing his efforts. Perhaps a man who had recovered from a double amputation knew something about working through such difficulty. "That should have sucked any gas out of the system, I hope. We'll leave every airlock and ventilation gap open — keep fresh air blowing through."

That explained the madness, Jimmy supposed, but as the tin-legged Flight Lieutenant sat back with a grin, his next words were still slightly incomprehensible, "By God, always wondered what would happen if we tried that. No fear!"

No question, Bader was as mad as another pilot Devlin knew: Alistair Carstairs. But that was not a relevant observation for the moment, so looking to Lapointe, the Viscount spoke quickly, even as he caught his breath, "We should go help."

A Viscount and a Prime Minister had no business going near gas, or a saboteur... but no one on the flight deck possessed the will or the authority to stop them. With a single pat to Bader's shoulder, Lord Devlin turned away to go in search of an arms box.

The airlocks that lined *Skipper Miller's* upper deck were all open as George hurried past them. Alex had leapt from one of those ports over the Grand Banks... now they were presumably being kept open to make sure the gas couldn't concentrate — perhaps even to suck it out of the ship, along with the rest of the stored air, to protect the crew.

If that was the reasoning it was sensible indeed, but without certain knowledge that the air was safe, George kept his mask on. Fresh oxygen would hopefully give him enough time to undo whatever the saboteur had done.

He staggered into the utility section of the ship, giving the open airlock hatches a wide berth. Attempts to lead with his pistol were largely unsuccessful — the winds whistling through the corridors buffeted him mercilessly, and because he had both revolver and oxygen cylinder in hand, keeping his balance was difficult.

Fortunately, by the time he reached the hatch to the ECC, there was no villain present.

Hitting the door frame unsteadily, the young hospitality man swept the compartment with his .38 revolver… and then he breathed anxiously. He didn't cough, which either meant the mask was sufficient, or that the gas had been expended. Taking a step inside, he found three fallen men… and Elspeth.

She was coughing, though as he pocketed his pistol and dropped to his knees beside her, George was reasonably certain that had nothing to do with gas. There was bright red blood foaming from her mouth as she sat with her back against the wall, and her gaze was glassy and distant.

George was a smart young man, but no medic. He needed Crane, but couldn't summon him unless the compartment was safe. Rising quickly, he looked deeper into the long chamber, and quickly detected the cylinder which must have contained the gas.

Two neat bullet holes had been punched right through it.

That meant it *had* to be empty, especially after the depressurization of the ship. The poison would have been sucked out the airlocks, along with the rest of the skycruiser's atmosphere. Whoever had done the flying would certainly deserve a pat on the back… but that was for later: Elspeth's wound was urgent.

Turning back to the Lady, George found she'd in fact slid down the wall beneath the intercom, so he hurried to that console and keyed it, before pulling down his mask, "Elspeth shot the cylinder of gas… it must have emptied itself when we decompressed the ship. All clear but no saboteur here, and I need Crane immediately. She's been shot and I think it's the lung."

As those words came over the intercom, Crane looked up to the ceiling speakers, then down at Constance, then Anneke. Both Champions were still unconscious… there was little point to staying by their side when another was gravely wounded.

"Go quickly, I'll watch them," Anne urged him on, and within seconds he'd collected his kit and hurried out of the infirmary.

Only as Anne Devlin watched him rush out into the corridor did it fully strike her that she had no experience in keeping wounded people alive. She just hoped neither Constance nor Anneke needed saving before Crane's return. Would decompression affect either of their wounds?

Jimmy Devlin listened to his son's voice over the intercom while pulling a Browning pistol out of an arms box, and handing it to Alain Lapointe. The Newfoundlander and the Quebecker were still near the bridge, drawing weapons and ammunition from one of the smaller caches that could be found throughout *Skipper Miller*.

Neither of them liked what they were hearing.

"If she punctured the tank, but was shot, she's stopped his plan... but the saboteur will be trapped aboard," Lapointe said as he quickly checked the pistol, then slid a magazine into its grip before racking the slide.

Closing the arms box, the Viscount drew his own sidearm from its holster — true to tradition, Devlin was still carrying the very same Webley .455 revolver that he'd fought with on the new world, twenty years prior. It functioned just as well as Smith's old guns did, and he trusted no other pistol — especially in moments like this.

"Shall we guard the flight deck, or go hunting?" Jimmy asked in reply. The Viscount was of two minds: protecting the command deck was important... but what if the saboteur went into hiding, as he'd obviously done to get aboard in the first place? Or worse, what if he had some way to get off the skycruiser? Would they simply give him the time he needed to escape?

"I say we look," Lapointe gave his vote firmly, and his was the more impetuous option.

Coincidentally, it was the option Jimmy Devlin himself favored. Though there were many corridors on a ship as big as *Skipper Miller*, and it was possible to miss the villain, or be ambushed, both veterans had stood by long enough. If they were to be killed, it would be *doing* something. Others — Elspeth, Anneke, and Constance — had already put their lives in peril, so it was time for these two men to emerge from safety, and do what they'd built their reputations on.

With Alain leading, and Jimmy doing his best not to hobble on his sprained ankle, the pair set off into the ship.

• • •

George put his hand over the wound in Elspeth's chest, and as she exhaled he was sure he felt as though his palm was being sucked tight against the hole. She was barely conscious, her head shaking as foamy blood bubbled from her mouth.

"I'm going to see Bob," she managed to say — almost sounding coherent.

George had been party to none of her conversations with Mike Strong, but he knew that Bob Freeman was the Sergeant who had died trying to bring her help in Scotland. It would do her no good to dream of seeing him now, so with his free hand, the young Devlin reached up and clutched her rather firmly by the jaw, "No, you're going to stay here with me. Damn you, Lady Cornish, enough fine women have been harmed today. If any are to die, you will not be among them."

The force of his grip, and of his words, seemed to cut through just a little of the fog that was closing in around the browncoat.

She tried to answer, "I... shouldn't... be..."

"Enough of that. Look at me. *Look* at me, Elspeth. You survived for a reason. Saving us from this gas was not it. You have not lived long enough to make good the sacrifice of your men. You *will not* die here."

George was not himself fully aware of where his passion was coming from — not conscious of the fact that his forceful demands for Elspeth's life were, perhaps, fueled by his fear for another woman — one much closer to him. So possessed was he by determination that he did not see Crane arrive, or hear the medic's orders. Instead, he only moved aside when nudged, and then he watched wide-eyed as an attempt was made to save Elspeth from a collapsing lung, and a sucking chest wound.

It was desperate work, and not being acquainted with the science, George Devlin couldn't guess if it would succeed. Deep in his bones, though, he knew that at least one Lady on the skycruiser was about to die.

He was right.

When Constance Cormack woke, she began coughing violently. Anne had been standing near the door, watching for Crane's return or sign of the saboteur, but she hurried to the young American's side and laid her hands on the girl's shoulders, to try to keep her still.

Constance's eyes were wide. She was disoriented and could tell she should be in agony, but that she'd been numbed to it somehow. Morphine, probably. But masking the pain didn't make it better... she was wounded, she understood, and if it was mortal she had to know...

"Help," the young American gasped, trying to reach up but missing the Viscountess' shoulder. "Am I..."

Anne Devlin had been mother to the survivors of the Newfoundland Regiment; she knew torment when she saw it, though never had she witnessed it on the face of someone so wounded as Constance. Shaking her head, she leaned down, "You're okay."

Constance didn't believe the words. Her mind was so clear, seemed so focused, that she tried again to rise. The fact that an ordinary woman like Anne could keep her pinned down was proof enough that something was very wrong.

The revelation must have been clear on her face, because Anne shook her head again, and tried to bring calm.

"Listen to me, Constance Cormack. You are going to be taking care of my son for me. You are going to be the woman who stays with him for the rest of his life — keeps him safe. You do not die here, in my hands. You understand that? You must look after George for me."

Anne didn't know why that was the plea she made — why she'd dare burden a wounded young girl with such a responsibility. The words simply fell from her mouth, and as they did, Constance's clear head grasped them in surprise.

George... the very thought of him seemed right. He was a good reason to hold on to life — one reason among many — and the thought of him forced Constance to remember others. Going home to Georgia, seeing her mother, saving Vanier, finding these villains... could she give up now, with all those things left to do?

She had to fight. For herself and for others, Constance Cormack decided to be defiant. She would not give way to death... but she felt death entering the room with her. It was cold, and dark — she could envision it like the pictures of the reaper she'd seen, coming and standing over her, just behind Anne.

"No..." she gasped that word, as her mind's clarity started to break down.

Pain abruptly slashed through her — whatever had been keeping it at bay seemed to disappear. Constance screwed her eyes shut, and didn't want to see what happened next. She couldn't watch death do its bitter work.

As Constance's eyes closed, Anne felt her own heart pound faster. Shaking the wounded American quickly, the Viscountess of the Grasslands realized she'd have to do something — either summon Crane, or find someone else to save her.

Letting go of the unconscious young girl, she hurried around the treatment table and made for the hatch, wondering if anyone else aboard might have medical abilities. Then an idea occurred to her: Sass was back, and the Saa, though not doctors in the human sense, might have some idea. The dragons weren't magic, but they were so very advanced...

Deciding she'd hurry down to the embarkation bay, Anne stepped out into the corridor, and turned left.

She then stopped abruptly, as she came face to face with Major Wendel Fischer.

His arrival — the promise of help — should have been a relief. But a parachute was hanging over his shoulder, and dangling from one hand was a pistol, from the other a gas mask.

Because, of course, he was the saboteur.

There could have been other explanations for what he carried... but Anne's long-honed instincts were better than to be wrong now. At first George had suspected this man, who'd been with Vanier Cross when the breach at Fort Eustice was discovered — indeed, who'd been on duty immediately before Vanier walked in and found the anomaly. But after Fischer had spent months locked up in the same cell as the black screen operator, it had seemed less likely he was the culprit, so no one had watched him too carefully.

And today, he'd earned passage aboard *Skipper Miller* by helping bring Constance aboard, after she was wounded. Perhaps he'd wounded her himself, because clearly he'd had business on the skycruiser.

How had he gotten the gas onto the ship? Who was he working for? What would he have done, had the ship's crew been killed by gas? Could he have flown the skycruiser to the lair of his masters?

So many questions filled Anne Devlin's mind, but as Fischer's dark eyes fell on her, and his pistol began to rise, she realized there would be no time to ask them. Her heart felt as though it stopped beating, and she pictured her son with his new Lady. Then she saw her home, her past, all the b'ys she'd mothered from the Newfoundland Regiment...

She knew it was the last time she'd remember any of them. She knew George and Jimmy would have to go on without her, and unravel this villainy alone.

Now, she would die.

Lady Anne Devlin, the Viscountess of the Grasslands, didn't hear any of the shots. After the first one she was on her back, growing cold. The rest struck her while she was lying down — why Fischer felt she deserved more than one bullet, she didn't know.

Another answer she'd never get.

The breeze that was flowing through the corridor chilled her; the air was fresh, and she wondered where *Skipper Miller* was. It was, in the end, an adventure to fly so high, to grand places for great purposes. Excitement filled her as she wondered where she'd go when she left the ship, and then as white light started to surround her, she smiled.

Her final memory was one she treasured: young Lieutenant James Devlin sitting beside her on a log in the camp of the Royal Newfoundland Regiment, a fire before them and two moons overhead as he asked her to marry him.

She'd said yes, and never regretted it. She smiled.

CHAPTER XV

"By God she's strong," Crane was working quickly on Elspeth, while George sat to one side and stared. His guts were churning — as though the bottom of the world had given way, and everything that mattered in his soul was falling into an abyss.

He didn't know why, but all he could think about was his mother. He thought it was for sake of comfort — thought it was because she always brought him peace.

Not because she'd found hers.

The sound of gunfire drew Jimmy and Alain into the corridor that ran past the infirmary, with the Prime Minister in the lead. Advancing cautiously, the Quebecker was the first to see that a person was lying bloodied on the deck, and he held up his free hand to slow the Viscount behind him.

Because airlocks were open throughout the ship, fresh air had blown away any scent of cordite or blood, and the fallen person seemed somehow out of place. But who was it? Lapointe was too far away to see, so looking down the sights of his borrowed pistol, he crept forward, closer and closer...

And stopped.

Down to one knee he fell — not for any reason to do with tactics, or cover, but because he felt as though his stomach had been punched. He realized he had to turn and stop his friend from walking up onto the sight, but it was too late.

Jimmy Devlin was hobbling forward, driven by his determination to find the bastards who had wrought so much chaos. Then he was still.

So very, very still.

His head became light, his grip weak. Somehow, he decided it was necessary to place his Webley back in its holster, and to carefully close the flap over the pistol. Inexplicably, his legs carried him forward across the deck at an even pace.

He did not run to her. He did not fall. He sat beside her, silent and numb, entirely not understanding what he was seeing. And yet knowing completely.

One, two, three holes in her body. A peaceful smile on her face.

She was still warm. Her blood was pooling around him as he sat cross-legged beside her. He stared — took in the sight of her eyes, that had always been beautiful and joyous, but now were empty. After one last long look, he gently closed them, and then put his hand on her chest. No rise, no fall.

Anne was dead.

Of course he knew that. As Alain Lapointe struggled to his feet, and stood over them both, Jimmy Devlin *knew* his wife was gone. He touched his bride's face, and tried to remember the wisest things that had ever slipped from her lips. Those things that had made him a better man, and made her a better woman.

Nothing was real in such a moment... but by the time Alain Lapointe crouched beside him, and laid a hand on his shoulder, the Viscount of the Grasslands began to sob. His guts churned like a storm surge, and everything in his body reacted violently.

He had left her alone. He had brought her with him in the first place. He had put her in harm's way.

And she had been killed.

George didn't know what was happening to him. Crane was trying to say something — to point out that, had Elspeth been ordinary, she would have died from the wound she'd received. But her Champion strength had somehow saved her... so who had died?

Again the young hospitality man saw his mother's face in his mind. He saw her smile, felt her hand on his cheek and her kiss on his forehead, and then she turned away, vanishing into bright fog.

The image made him tear up — he couldn't stop his eyes burning.

To avoid tears being seen, he pushed himself to his feet, turned and staggered deeper into the environmental control center. The punctured gas cylinder was rolling back and forth in the compartment's corner, so he advanced towards it, hoping that it would have some marking upon it.

He was rather surprised to see that it did.

Why would the German Army paint its Iron Cross onto a canister full of Champion gas? Why would they write on it in German? Would that not be a giveaway to whoever got hold of the cylinder, once the plot was foiled? Or had the Reich become arrogant after a year of successes, and simply assumed that this attempt would succeed — that they could be so brazen as to brand their work?

The Germans. This entire time, it *had* been the Germans?

What damage had they done?

"Help me get her back to the infirmary," Crane was suddenly standing, and George blinked back his tears, then turned and hurried to help the medic.

He dreaded every step as they carried Elspeth from the compartment. He just didn't know why.

Wendel Fischer was just containing his panic. The plan had come so close to succeeding — every necessary element had fallen into place, and all the intelligence provided by the mysterious supporters of the Party had been correct. Even the luggage had been successfully smuggled aboard. He'd been certain the cylinder would have been caught — that he would arrive on *Skipper Miller* and discover the gas had not boarded… that perhaps there were even agents lying in wait for him.

But no, the Party supporters had done as promised. The bag Fischer had planted the night prior — after lying about lost accommodations so he could escape Constance — had been waiting for him in *Skipper Miller's* embarkation bay. Everything had been ready for him to complete his final mission.

And yet, after all that, it had gone wrong.

He didn't know how. All that was clear was that months of patience, built upon years of cautious work, had collapsed within the space of ten minutes. His only hope now was escape — to leap from an airlock wearing a parachute and try to disappear into the wilds of Canada until he could be extracted by his colleagues.

It was a slim chance, but his only one — for with the canister sucked dry, he was just one man against an entire ship.

So he hurried from the infirmary door, where he'd shot the Viscountess for no good reason, and looked for the next open airlock. There was one on every frame — he'd studied the schematics for these craft for months on the Fort Eustice screen, thus enabling him to direct the bomb teams in Virginia on how best to blow them up.

He just needed to get to the next airlock, secure his parachute, and pick his moment to leap from whatever altitude they were now holding — something low enough to allow breathing.

Discarding his gas mask, the Major began slipping his left arm through the straps of the parachute, making sure to keep his right hand free so that his gun was available. They'd be coming for him soon — he had to be ready.

As he tightened the straps, a fresh breeze caught him, and he started to hear the choppy sound of an open doorway being buffeted by the wind. Hurrying forward, he caught sight of the light pouring onto the deck from that airlock, and he advanced at a jog, using his free hand to perform final checks on the chute.

He was looking down just briefly when a man stepped into the passageway ahead of him, tall and square. When he looked up, the American traitor's heart pounded.

Though Smith was over fifty, he was still formidable. The former-drifter's Colt New Service revolver was in his hand, and though his chin had dipped, his eyes were fixed on his target.

There had been no announcement, and he had seen no one else, but Alex's father knew that Anne Devlin had died. He knew the price this ship had paid — knew that the scheme against *Skipper Miller* had been foiled, as it had to be, but that the cost was great. He hated that truth, and Fischer was the man who would pay for it.

For deep down, the anger that only rarely escaped Smith was ready to come out again.

But Fischer was not unarmed, nor was he weak. To wound Constance, even in the back so that he could board with her... then to survive Elspeth and kill Anne... this was not the most dangerous man Smith had ever faced, but he could not be underestimated.

Smith watched the American Major square himself, and focus his eyes. Having been on the receiving end of gunfire many times in his life, Alex's father recognized this posture change — it represented someone preparing to fight.

Unfortunately for Fischer, Smith needed no time to prepare.

The American Major looked surprised when blood started dribbling down the bridge of his nose. His pistol was still down by his side, and he saw and heard nothing before Smith's bullet punched through the skull between his eyes.

Smith saw nothing either; as happened to him sometimes in moments of great anger, he'd fired on pure instinct, and his shot had been true. When Fischer fell, it was with a heavy thud, and no life at all. His face was smashed by the deck as they connected. That was fine.

Lowering his revolver, Smith advanced slowly towards the villain, then crouched and rolled his lifeless body over. As dead eyes stared up at him, the former-drifter opened the flap of Fischer's shirt pocket, and produced a fold of paper written in German, with a German Army iron cross upon it.

Unable to read the text, Smith simply dropped the paper onto Fischer's chest. Then he thought better of leaving it unsecured with all the wind blowing through, so he tucked it into the Major's pocket until someone better-equipped could decipher it.

As he rose slowly to his feet, Alex's father took a deep breath, then closed his eyes. What had happened was a disaster. The grief would be immense. All he could hope was that, in the end, the greater good would truly be served. With that thought, he stepped over Fischer's body and made his way towards the infirmary — towards the inevitable.

CHAPTER XVI

A swarm of vehicles was waiting for *Skipper Miller* when it touched down at the Torbay Airport, and as the ramps lowered, volunteers from the skycruiser's crew helped Crane carry off the three wounded Champions.

Watching the commotion from the embarkation bay, Sass found herself unprepared for the chaos. At no time since the end of the Hubrin War had she been involved in combat; the last losses she'd witnessed were those of the Newfoundland Regiment at the Hubrin capital. Now, her first hours after returning to the human domain were marred by carnage and death. It was obviously not what she had hoped for.

"Will they survive, mother?" Imogen approached Sass's side with that question about the Champions, and Ciaran also eagerly awaited the answer.

"If I have been overhearing correctly, then yes," the great dragon lady confirmed. "Those three are freed attackers — they are very strong by human standards, and they each have received good care."

"Are all their best warriors female?" Ciaran asked next, and Sass tilted her head briefly before turning her palm down.

"Many, but not all," she replied, and as if to emphasize the point that warriors came in countless configurations, Smith appeared beside her feet moments after.

"I reckon they'll recover," he said darkly, and Sass was surprised by the graveness of his tone. He seemed to predict her reaction, and he looked up at her, "You heard Anne was killed?"

Sass had not heard — in the midst of the all the confusion, no one had announced that fact over the intercom. The dragon's eyes grew wider at the revelation, and she felt both her children grow more tense. Before she could ask how it had happened, two more stretchers came past her feet... both covered by sheets.

Jimmy and George Devlin followed behind the second one. There was no mistaking the graveness of their postures, the heaviness of their strides. Neither acknowledged the Saa at all; they were well beyond speaking.

"It was the Germans," a new voice arrived with that revelation, and Sass looked down again in time to see Alain Lapointe. "Major Fischer was their agent. He carried documents, and the canister of the gas was marked in German. This whole time, it has been Germans."

The Prime Minister was no fool — not gullible or quick to condemn anyone on evidence too circumstantial. But after such a galling assault, and the death of none other than the Viscountess of the Grasslands, he would ask no more questions.

Of course it was the Reich; envious of British power, and doing everything possible to destabilize Britannia without triggering open war. Destroying the American skycruisers, attempting to capture and breed Champions, and hoping to steal *Skipper Miller* and the Saa delegation... the Kaiser was desperate, and soon he would pay.

"I will call Winston from Jimmy's office," the Canadian Prime Minister said quietly. "I expect it will be war — a world war unlike anything we have ever seen."

Smith swallowed, then nodded somberly. He was not a man who hungered for death, but this was indeed what must occur now. Too much had happened — too many were dead, both on *Skipper Miller*, and presumably among the civilians back in New World City.

"I come from a war, and bring war with me," Sass's observation was somber, and she shook her head in a human fashion before curling her tail to the side, to wrap partway around her two children. "I'm very sorry."

Those words were unnecessary — perhaps even wrong — so Smith shook his head.

"Not your fault," he assured her.

He was right.

The search was growing more frustrating. Together as an elite group, Alex, Stephanie, Strong, Caralynne, the Shylocks and Kard had been sweeping the parade route from street to rooftop, looking for any indication of who had set off the explosions.

Soldiers and officers from the regiments in town had offered to assist, but no help was accepted — too many suspicions still existed about who could be trusted. It was always possible that the next part of the plan was to surround someone like Caralynne with fighting men who were supposedly loyal, but were in fact agents of the enemy.

But that just seemed too much. What were the villains up to this time?

Finally, that question dragged Alex's boots to a stop in the street. She was a few hundred yards past the point where the explosion had killed at least ten people, and wounded dozens more, and her brow was creased so deeply it was beginning to ache.

Alongside her, Stephanie halted too, then began shaking her head, "We're missing something."

"What else could they have gone after? Where are they?" Alex nodded as she put the questions to her friend.

Mike Strong joined them in time to voice his own confusion, "All the dragon kit is on that field. Is there anything else here worth going after? Maybe we paid too much attention to the Saa... what if they were after something else?"

Those were very good questions, and Alex and Stephanie exchanged long glances as their minds started to pivot — to grasp for other objectives that might have seemed worthwhile. By the time Stephanie's family rode up, and Caralynne returned, they were deep in thought.

"What are you contemplating?" Alex's mother asked after a few dozen seconds of silence, and the whitecoat opened her mouth to explain... but as her gaze shifted towards Caralynne, she saw something else that made her stop.

Detecting her best friend's sudden interest, Stephanie turned as well, then almost immediately blurted out: "Mom?"

Miranda Shylock was hurrying up the street, her shoulders square and head high, but her bearing and expression suggesting she carried urgent news. As she approached, Vonn turned in his saddle and eyed his beloved with surprise, but with Stephanie before him, he couldn't ask how she felt. Surely, she looked fitter than she'd seemed in years, though perhaps that was just because whatever news she carried was extremely important.

"Miranda?" Caralynne added her own question as the lady slowed to a stop.

And then, with a shake of the head and a sigh, Stephanie's

mother made any questions about her apparent wellness seem entirely unimportant: "There was a call to the hotel, from Headquarters. They were looking for you all. There has been an attempt to sabotage the skycruiser carrying the dragons to Newfoundland — a man called Fischer tried to use gas to kill the crew and take over."

This time, the street was quiet enough to hear the pin drop. Alex's stomach seemed to fall with it, and as her eyes widened she could sense Stephanie begin to spiral just a little as well. Gas on *Skipper Miller*?

Mike Strong managed to keep air in his lungs, though he was barely able to make his voice work, "*Attempt*, you said?"

Miranda nodded, "It failed, but Lady Elspeth was shot. She is alive... but Lady Anne Devlin was killed. Smith shot down Fischer. He is dead as well."

Miranda left it there, knowing those few words would be more than enough to cast a dark cloud over the street.

Alex began to blink, and she looked first to Stephanie, who matched her gaze and began shaking her head. Caralynne's jaw had fallen open, and she did her best to understand what had been said... but she wasn't sure she succeeded.

It was Mike Strong who understood it all, from the first — Mike Strong who said what came straight to his mind: "Not Lady Annie. Not... no..."

His eyes dropped to the street, and everything inside him churned. Anne Devlin was younger than him, but she was the only mother he'd known for twenty years... the mother of the Newfoundland Regiment. She couldn't die — couldn't be murdered. Not... no...

Lady Anne Devlin. But...

"Fischer," Alex found enough breath to say his name. "But... how...?"

She didn't know. No one knew. Of all those who might have died at the hands of a traitor, why was it the one who least belonged in the line of fire? Such questions were impossible to answer, and as they stymied everyone in the street, Caralynne finally found her daughter, and hugged her.

Miranda's arms were quickly around Stephanie, who was still in shock, and then as Mike Strong's legs succumbed to reality, and he sat down in the middle of the street to grieve for his treasured Viscountess, Alex and Stephanie wrapped their arms around him, so that he'd know all wasn't lost.

    Even though, in that moment, it truly felt as though it was.

    Such was the way of 1941.

CHAPTER XVII

James Devlin, the Viscount of the Grasslands, leaned on his office's balcony railing and looked out over Fort Waller. The sun was beginning to descend behind him as he looked east towards the sea, and a fresh breeze was stirring the air. Under most circumstances, the evening would have been perfect.

Today, it clearly was not.

Anne Devlin had been buried that afternoon. Most of the people of St. John's had attended the service in the Basilica — the mighty cathedral that overlooked the town's harbor, and whose dual steeples were used by ships to chart their course through the Narrows. The crowds had been enormous, the respect evident. People assured him it was a beautiful service, and that from heaven his bride was smiling down on him, wrapping him and his son in a warm embrace.

Maybe she was, but in a way he hoped that she was busying herself with other things in the greater beyond, for she would not be proud of the thoughts that now consumed him. Staring out at the Fort and the Academy beyond, the Viscount took a deep breath and shook his head.

"Go back there and find out who helped him. He certainly didn't do it alone," harsh rational thoughts were fully in control of Jimmy's mind, and as he delivered those cold instructions, he looked to his left with a dark glare. "See what you can find."

Standing further back on his office's balcony was Caralynne, and just behind her was George. The elder Lady Smith was still wearing black from the ceremony, but she'd agreed to come back to Headquarters with the Devlins when they'd asked at the cemetery. Now her expression was appropriately grave, and a frown creased her brow as she heard Jimmy's orders.

"I can stay with you both for a while, if that would be better," she suggested gently, but the Viscount shook his head.

"It wouldn't be better, and it wouldn't help. *Someone* worked with Fischer, and the trail might be left out there. Go and look. Maybe it'll lead us to his organization... even help us find where the mothers of Duncan's children are being kept."

His determination was stone, and Caralynne took a deep breath before nodding, "Fair enough."

She knew she couldn't ease the grief Jimmy was experiencing, and his reasoning was sound. Five days had passed since the attack, and New World City was still being restored after the carnage. Local investigators had been piecing things together, but with Lady Anne buried it seemed time to send more senior eyes. It was vital they assemble whatever information they could, as quickly as possible.

Britain was to declare war on Germany within a week, and Canada soon thereafter; any further evidence that could condemn the Kaiser's Second Reich — or exonerate it — would need to be found quickly. Not that the latter outcome was likely. Too much circumstantial evidence had been pooled, and even though the elder Lady Smith remained skeptical, she knew great wars had been started for far less.

More important would be the search for Fischer's network, and any other surprises that might be thrown at the Champions during wartime. And, of course, the mothers of Duncan's children.

With all that in mind, Caralynne nodded once more, "I'll leave tonight."

"Good," Devlin didn't leave room for further discussion. "Safe journey."

There was little doubting that invitation to leave, so with a quick look back to George — who simply nodded — Caralynne departed. Jimmy waited until he was certain he heard his office's heavy door shut behind her, then nodded for his son to join him at the railing. Together they looked over Jimmystown for a few moments, neither of them showing any indication that they possessed emotions.

Neither could afford to just yet.

Then Jimmy took a breath, "She won't find anything."

"She might," George countered dryly, but his father was adamant.

"She won't. You're the only one who can."

George didn't react to those words, but as his father straightened up from the railing and turned towards him, the motherless son listened carefully.

"You are in charge of hospitality, now, and your job is to find out who's betrayed us. It has to be someone close — someone we absolutely think we can trust. Very close. You have to find that person. And then we'll have him. Or her."

The menace that underpinned the Viscount's tone was new; never had Jimmy Devlin been especially vengeful, though at times in his life he'd come close. Once he'd nearly shot a Hubrin prisoner... though he had stopped short then. Such restraint would probably not resurface this time.

And George understood — perhaps shared the feeling. With a frown, he answered carefully, "I'll need to assemble a small team. We know we can trust Sass and her children, but I'll need humans."

"Anyone you totally trust," Jimmy agreed. "But don't take anyone for granted. I wouldn't even tell Caralynne about this, yet."

George nodded slowly, then replied, "When Constance has recovered, I'll take her. She came too close to dying for her injury to have been intentional, just to get Fischer aboard."

Jimmy could have questioned that assessment — wondered aloud if George's confidence in the girl was governed by his passions. But even in this state, the Viscount knew better. George was as smart as his mother, which meant he was easily the most intelligent man on the balcony. That was why Jimmy trusted him, and why he had to lead the true investigation.

But who else could he trust? Alex and Stephanie, perhaps... but Jimmy didn't expect he'd want them in the picture. Too visible. No, someone else entirely...

"There's one other person I can trust, but I'll need your help getting him," George straightened from the railing too, and turned to face his father.

"Anyone," Jimmy agreed.

One more person would have to join the team.

Elspeth Cornish was the last of the three wounded Champions in Jimmystown's hospital, due to the unfortunate placement of the gunshot that had pierced her chest. While heavy doses of antibiotics combined with Champion strength had allowed both Constance and Anneke to leave after five days for lengthy and careful recoveries at home, the sucking chest wound suffered by the London Champion warranted much closer monitoring.

Unfortunately, penicillin had no effect whatsoever on emotions, so Lady Cornish's building frustration was reaching high levels; she wanted to be out of the hospital, and perhaps be doing something useful, if she was still able.

With that thought in mind, she lay back in her bed and stared at the ceiling, wondering how the investigation into the attack was going... if war had been declared... *anything* that wasn't as old as the last newspaper read to her by an irritable nurse.

Fortunately, relief was at hand.

"So it's war."

The words were unexpected, and Mike Strong led with them before he knocked on Elspeth's open door, then leaned in with a smile that didn't quite match the news.

War with Germany was obviously serious business... but at the sight of the Colour, Elspeth's interest was diverted from world events, "Took you long enough to come visit."

The Sergeant shrugged as he strode into the room, "I tried before, but the doctors insisted I stay away until you got your strength back."

Lying back in a hospital bed, bandages wrapped around her chest and her skin a little ashen, the Lady from London had to take exception with his observation: "Does it look like I have my strength back?"

"I was impatient," was Strong's answer, and battered as she was, Elspeth didn't have a retort ready for him. She instead rolled her eyes, looked towards the ceiling... and was glad of the company.

Just having Mike Strong walk into the room seemed to lighten her up a bit — she felt genuinely better than she had in days, and when she realized that, she found it both interesting and a little conflicting.

But good — quite good.

As Strong continued his friendly gossip with the wounded browncoat, Elspeth Cornish began to feel human again, and Mike Strong felt a different sort of rapport than he was used to with his own girls.

It was as though he was at the beginning of something, but he didn't know what. He wished the Viscountess was around to explain it to him... but perhaps it was telling that, even as he thought of

Anne Devlin, his sadness was curbed by the laugh of a common-raised Champion who had not left him to join her fallen Sergeant.

Elspeth was still here, and that was good indeed.

The exoneration of Vanier Cross had been a singularly quiet affair. He'd literally been receiving a beating from the guards at Fort Leavenworth when the phone had rung. Within an hour of that call — apparently from the President — the young black Corporal had been spirited from the prison, loaded onto a plane, and flown to Washington, D.C.

He'd half-expected to meet the President — why else would he be taken on such a flight? — but instead, he'd been led before a General who'd made him sign dishonorable discharge papers. After that he was put up in a hotel for a night, and sent a suit that was a bit big for him. A night's sleep in a decent bed, a shower, a shave and a suit... then he'd been piled into a DC-3 transport plane headed north.

Now that plane was circling over a rough-looking piece of ground that he didn't recognize — rocky and covered in ponds and scraggly trees, with a dramatic coast that was doing defiant battle with the ocean. He had never seen a place like it before... but he chose to believe it was Newfoundland.

Of course, he knew better than to hope for that — in his dreams he could wish that his inexplicable acquittal was the result of George Devlin, or even the Saa dragons, and that he was being summoned to work with more screens... but those were just warm fantasies that could comfort him on a chilly flight.

As the plane came low for a landing, buffeted by some dramatic turbulence on the way down, Vanier simply held on and closed his eyes. The wheels eventually bounced onto an airstrip, and then the plane taxied for just a few moments before coming to a stop.

Vanier waited until the pilot came back to fetch him, and then did as that red-faced man instructed: "Get off."

Emerging into the late afternoon, Vanier found the sky was gray and a cold, damp wind was blowing. His flannel suit was just right to keep out a chill, but the fact that the place lacked warmth, despite it being early September, was probably a clue.

He decided not to speculate; instead, he watched a driver in British Army uniform hurry over to him, "You must be Cross?"

Since he was the only black man in sight, that was probably a safe guess for the soldier, and Vanier confirmed with a nod, "I am."

"That's grand, your plane's late. Come on, b'y, they're waiting for you."

Cross frowned as the driver turned away, heading for a British-built Land Rover. Pausing for just a second to take in his surroundings, the discharged soldier wondered whether the place actually could be Newfoundland... or if, perhaps, he was just in Canada.

Either way, it was vastly better than his cell.

Constance Cormack was not terribly comfortable in a wheelchair, but she was absolutely not permitted to put weight on her wounded leg for two more weeks, and the chair was the only way she was allowed out of the hospital — a place she simply *had* to leave. Fortunately, the Saa control center was wheelchair accessible, thanks to its lift, so she could at least spend the rest of her uncomfortable convalescence in a massive subterranean chamber, gaping at magical screens and chattering with three different dragons.

As well as George Devlin...

Constance hated that she hadn't been able to attend Anne Devlin's funeral. The Viscountess' last words to her were *vivid*, and though they represented an endorsement of the feelings that had come on so strongly in New World City, they were also a great weight — thoroughly intimidating.

Take care of George? He was not the sort who seemed to need much protection, though perhaps those who appeared to require it least, in fact needed it the most.

Time would tell. For now, Constance was simply flattered — and relieved — to know that the hospitality man had insisted she join his unit. After her eventful introduction to life as a graduated Champion, she couldn't have tolerated a normal lance, or a post garrisoning some town.

No, the world was in the beginning stages of a war, and there were still countless questions to be answered about who had been assisting that vile creature Fischer. Now she'd have her chance to contribute — especially once she was back on her feet. And the fact that she was doing all that with George... well, she wasn't going to complain.

Of the people in her life who mattered most, only two were not with her: her mother... and her brother. Young Mister Devlin had been terribly cagey about Vanier's fate. Being so adept with screens, Imogen had almost immediately found evidence exonerating the Corporal of any guilt, and the President had been forced to release him, but beyond that George had said nothing more. It had been conspicuous...

Had been.

Constance heard the door to the Saa control centre open behind her — she had Champion hearing, after all. She also heard a gasp of surprise, and then the sort of silence that spoke volumes.

She smiled, and then tried to turn to face Vanier...

But her chair wouldn't budge. Totally ruined the moment.

"What... but..." she heard his disbelieving words, and really wanted to see his face. She knew how he loved the one screen he'd been working on, so a whole room full of them? And three dragons as well? His face had to be perfect.

She wrestled with her chair but the wheel seemed jammed. Fine, she'd un-jam it. Adjusting her grip on the wheel itself, she gave it a sharp jerk. Unwise. The wheel came off, slipped from her hand, and clattered across the room. With no support on one side, she went sideways, landing in a spectacular pile of Champion and twisted metal. This left her mostly facing the floor as people gathered over her to help, and since she couldn't see them, she had to identify them by their sounds. She could hear George's shoes, and Vanier's boots, but not the three dragons. They were silent.

"You brought me here?" she heard Vanier ask, presumably to George.

"Her idea, of course. I don't even like you," George's reply was dry, but the comment was funnier than anything he'd said in days.

"Good. I was afraid you'd want to be friends," Vanier countered immediately.

Their banter was starting off pretty good, considering the circumstances — Constance found that exciting, and warming. Her just-about-brother and her... well... *lover* were getting along. Things were looking up.

Though, strictly speaking, she was still looking at the floor.

"I want to be friends! I'm Ciaran," the dragon introduced himself, and again Constance could just imagine Vanier's expression as the enthusiastic young Saa inserted his giant head into the conversation, irrepressible as an eager puppy.

"That's an offer I'll accept. Is it too much to hope that we're going to be working together?" Vanier replied easily, and the dragon didn't miss a beat.

"They don't let me touch anything important. But if you need things knocked over, we'll definitely work together."

Ciaran sure knew where he fit in the big picture. Constance found both him and Imogen to be fine friends indeed, and Sass was just a great mother... but none of that was evident given her current position, so she finally cleared her throat.

"Nobody's going to ask if I'm okay?"

She expected someone to offer a dry or otherwise funny reply to her question, but instead she suddenly felt hands taking hold and lifting her up out of her self-made wreck. George was strong, but the way the lift was done, she knew it wasn't him. Instead, it felt for a brilliant second as though she was being twirled through the air during a swing dance at the Domino, and at the end of that arc, she somehow found herself with her arms wrapped around Vanier Cross.

"Told you we'd get you out," she said.

"I'm glad you did," he replied.

They hugged for a long time — it had been too many months since they'd been torn apart — and then George wheeled over a desk chair so she could sit down, minding her leg.

Leaving his hand on her shoulder as he helped her settle — intentionally demonstrating to Vanier the nature of their affection — the young Devlin then looked to the newcomer.

"Mister Cross, I'm afraid your freedom was conditional on you coming to work with us in this lair. I hope you don't mind?"

Obviously Vanier had figured that out already, but it seemed important that it was actually said. With a frown and then a shrug, the discharged soldier let his eyes travel up and around the amazing command center — a place full of dragons, screens, and bright blue light. He smiled at Sass and Imogen, who hadn't yet been officially introduced, then nodded to Ciaran. When he looked back to George, he saw that Constance had reached up and covered his hand with her own. She looked happy, and more grown up than he'd ever seen.

All things being equal, it seemed a bit too good to be true, and he said so: "If not for your wheelchair stunt, I'd think this was a dream."

George scoffed, "Stuck in a cave with three dragons, an eccentric girl, and the son of an aristocrat? Sounds more like a nightmare. I'm just asking you to work hospitality."

Vanier Cross smiled, "I'm pretty good with a serving tray, if it comes to that. How about you show me around?"

That was as good a start as any, and as the three humans and three dragons made their way deeper into the control center, the possibilities of the future seemed to open wide before them. Much work had to be done, and villains found, but at least they had the right team for it.

Right team... minus one Lady, who had died needlessly in the sky.

EPILOGUE

In her nightmares, Alex was swimming. It was dark all around her — blackness like she'd seen aboard *Hood* as the ship sank — but an inexplicable ghostly light still made sure she could see the horrors.

Dead Champion students from Virginia floated past her. She was accosted by the lifeless eyes of the British Prime Minister, and the American President, and Champion Rockefeller. Duncan and his fallen soldiers screamed their terror. And all the dead men she'd seen in Hong Kong chased her like a school of fish — too distant to touch her, but always near enough that she couldn't help but flee.

She swam fast, short of breath as she tried to escape the endless corridors of a sinking battleship. Finally her air ran out and she rolled onto her back, found a pocket of air and breached the surface of the water...

Found herself in a dark hallway, at the end of which stood Lady Anne Devlin. The Viscountess was backlit in red, her head tilted sharply to the side. Suddenly she charged forward as though she was a savage, hissing and reaching and clutching.

Alex had a pistol in her hand, so she shot down the Viscountess, who writhed and spit and snarled as she hit the deck. Again the whitecoat found herself in tears — why Lady Anne, of all people?

She turned away and raced out of the corridor, leaping through a hatchway that led right out into a night atop Signal Hill. As she arrived, Alex watched from afar as Emily put a pistol to her head — watched it as though she was having an out-of-body experience — and then saw the rogue Lady shoot her in the leg, and run for the edge of the hill.

That part was an old nightmare... bleeding and broken, alone because she'd left her friends behind... a nightmare that barely qualified anymore, after everything she'd seen in 1941.

With that realization, she was pulled back into *Hood*'s passageway, and dragged down into the dark water. She struggled and kicked — fighting with all her strength — but with every effort she sank lower, and her air was running out.

The ship would take her to the bottom of the sea, and all the people she'd watched die... or she'd killed... would feast upon her. Unholy terror started to reach out from inside her skin, its tendrils like spiders' legs stabbing out of every pore, and dragging her deeper. Her new nightmares were horrifying. She screamed against them — tried to wake herself up...

And then, as she reached up to escape the water, she saw her father standing there, beyond the glassy surface. He stared at her for a long moment; could he just crouch down, reach in, save her?

No. He turned and walked away. He left his daughter to die alone in the darkness with her terrors.

And die she—

There was no stifling the scream as Alex shot upright in her bed. Both her hands pressed against her chest as she tried to suck in real air — to catch her breath and prove to herself that she wasn't drowning, that her skin was not crawling. For all their vividness, her new nightmares were just nightmares. She had to acknowledge them, and then learn to move past their terror.

Eventually.

For now, she had soaked her nightclothes and her sheets in cold sweat. It was not a good feeling, so she collected two more breaths, then swung her legs out of bed, stood, and started peeling off the soggy cotton. Drawing a towel from her closet, she dried her body, then dug fresh clothes from her dresser. She would not feel clean for the rest of the night, but she couldn't draw a bath — the clock on her night table said it was just after 2:00 in the morning.

The next best thing was fresh air, so she moved over to her bedroom window and opened it all the way. An avalanche of coolness fell into her room, and that helped immensely... though as she looked out into the night, she could see very little. A moon was overhead, but low down in the trees that surrounded her house, a thick fog was blowing through.

It was strange; the moon was clear overhead, but the mists were thick below — indeed, glowing slightly blue-green because of the moonbeams. It was more than a little creepy, though Alex realized the shiver she felt at the sight had more to do with her dream, or the temperature, than the glowing fog.

Turning away, she focused her mind on more pertinent matters: whether she'd need to change her bed as well as her clothes, or if she could just lay a towel down to soak up the damp...

Then she heard her father's voice.

Champion hearing was sharp — so very sharp — and there was a gentle breeze carrying sounds from the woods back towards the house. Alex stopped, tried to listen, then returned to the window with a frown. Listening closely, she heard nothing...

But she was certain it had been his voice. Outside.

Was he out there? Why? There would be no hope of sleep with such questions in her head.

Without much thought, the younger Lady Smith opened her bedroom door and slipped quietly into the hallway. Stephanie's door was shut, and behind it Alex could detect her best friend's unsteady breathing — nightmares of her own, but hopefully not as bad. She then crept up to her parents' room door, which was also shut, and listened for her father. Caralynne was still on the new world, but the former drifter was home.

Not in his room.

Alex's heart pounded abruptly. Thoughtlessly — almost dreamily — she hurried from the hallway, through the living room and into the kitchen. She didn't think to bring her white coat; instead, she pulled on one of her dad's old denim jackets from a hook beside the door, and stepped barefoot into a pair of old shoes that sat on a mat below it.

Out into the cool night she hurried, leaving the door ajar behind her as she listened carefully for sounds in the fog. She was sure she heard her dad once again, so she continued forward with strides made awkward by the unlaced old shoes. The moisture of the fog started collecting on her borrowed coat as she entered the trees, but she was too distracted to notice the almost nightmarish dampness.

Was her father in this mist? Why was he out in such a surreal environment, and why was she following him?

Alex wandered deeper into the woods as innocently as any girl from a fairytale that ended in horror. She stepped over fallen trees, maneuvered around rocks, and stopped occasionally to listen. When she looked up, the fog was just thin enough for her to see a nearly-full moon through the treetops. All around her, the woods bore the same sickly glow.

Nothing felt natural here, and yet no terror churned within her...

Until behind her she heard a snap.

For some reason, that breaking twig did it — alerted her to the potential horror of her surroundings. Alone in the dark, misty woods, chasing voices that only she could hear? It was the cliché of a nightmare, or a bad horror film, and she was in the midst of it, wearing untied shoes, and without her coat.

She blinked once, then again, then turned in place... but her toe caught on a fallen branch. She toppled backwards in surprise, just managing to get her arms behind her to catch the trunk of the tree she'd been closest to, and slow her fall. The landing was still hard — no lasting injury, but she lost her wind.

That left her unable to gasp, or scream, when she spotted the dark shape looming in the mist. It was massive and still, standing yards away, seeming to stare at her.

At first she didn't believe it. It was impossible, of course, for there to be monsters in the woods so close to her home... monsters who traveled in fog at night. But there one stood, and as she tried to push herself upright to face it, she realized the fog was growing thicker all around.

Thicker and darker.

She hadn't woken up. Her escape before had been too easy — the supposed final element of her nightmare, her dad, was now leading her into a different kind of visceral darkness. And it felt so real — too real. How could she shake so vivid a dream?

Not without suffering first.

When the monster came forward, still concealed by the thickening mist, she struggled. None of her limbs seemed to respond the way they needed too, and as she started to feel the terror stabbing again through her pores, she screwed her eyes shut.

"Help..." she gasped. "Daddy... please!"

Some nights, even the legendary whitecoat needed her dad to chase nightmares away... but it was too late. Forcing her eyes open, Lady Alex Smith saw the shadowy figure reach down from above. She tried to scream, but without air in her lungs she couldn't. Nothing stopped it, nothing slowed it. With all the menace and inevitability of fate, it reached down to her chest...

And snorted on her.

Then it sort of nudged her.

Or maybe the word was nuzzled.

Alex froze, and every Champion sense she possessed tried to grapple with what she was feeling... and smelling. Because she knew the scent.

"Oh God, not the face," suddenly she had air enough to speak again — and strength enough to raise her hands to resist the oncoming mouth of the moose, as he tried to lick her. As she deflected him, the great big bull gave her a glare, and she frowned up at him, "Well, maybe once we know each other better."

She couldn't believe she said that, but then... it was a moose?

The fog was thinning once more — the thick patch that had concealed the moose's approach blew through. Under the moonlight, she could see him standing over her, looking rather aloof... and he snorted again.

Alex didn't know quite what to think. Obviously.

She'd worked herself up into a panic — which was embarrassing — and had been rescued from her self-inflicted terror by... a moose?

Okay. Apparently the night hadn't been surreal enough. That or her nightmares had a funny sense for plot twists.

Things became suddenly worse, because the moose lost his patience and took a step back. Alex didn't detect any menace from this move — she'd faced a moose charge before, so she knew what to look for. This was quite the opposite.

The moose put his nose on the mossy dirt in front of her, and then without lifting his chin, he lowered himself to the ground. Just like that, as if he was a dog, he lay down and fixed his big eyes on hers.

Understandably, Alex had no idea what he was trying to communicate. Perhaps had her head been clear, it would have been more obvious... but after her night so far, she was at a loss. Why would a moose lie down? The only time she'd seen one do so was when she'd forced him to, back on the Land Rover training course. Why would this guy be trying to simulate the moment that had effectively begun the legend of whitecoat? Surely moose didn't talk to each other about such things, so there was no way this one could have recognized her unless it was the same...

No.

No, that would just be ridiculous.

"You're not the same moose?" Alex asked, sounding more than a little incredulous.

The moose raised his head from the ground, and then immediately pushed himself back to his feet. Alex watched him rise and then she sniffed the air again. He did smell the same... but she figured all moose probably had that essence.

Was it... really?

"Are you actually him?" Alex's disbelief started to wane just a little, and with some difficulty she pushed herself up to her feet, then hobbled around quickly until she found her lost shoe. "Seriously?"

The moose snorted at her, and after slipping her shoe back on, she paused again and stared at him. Now that they were both standing, she could see he was about the same height as her one-time sparring partner. But here, a year later, coming literally out of the fog in the middle of the night, pretending to be a monster in the woods... really?

"Alex?"

So wrapped up in the weirdness was young Lady Smith that she didn't flinch at her father's voice. He came up behind her slowly, his Winchester '92 in hand, but held low.

"You found him," the former-drifter said to his daughter, and Alex glanced at him.

"You were looking for him?"

Smith nodded, "He's been leaving tracks around here for months, but I never catch up to him."

Alex did recall her dad's preoccupation with the woods around their house, but she set that aside as she answered, "Well this must be him. And... I think he's the one I wrestled with last year."

As she said it, she realized how daft it sounded. Wincing at the absurdity, she shook her head, "That's not possible, though, is it? I mean... he's just a moose."

Again the creature snorted, and somehow Alex got the sense that he took exception to being called 'just' anything.

Instinctively, she apologized, "Sorry. Long night."

Another snort. His apparent conversational skills were actually a bit unsettling.

Glancing again to her dad, Alex shook her head, "A moose

wouldn't be stalking me, right? I mean, if he was... why? He could have clobbered me just now if he wanted."

Smith studied the big bull for a moment, but without any suspicion on his face. Then he tilted his head slightly, and looked to his daughter, "I never told you how I met my old mare, did I?"

Presumably that question was related to the current moose situation, so Alex shook her head, "Um. No?"

"Was in mist like this, back on the new world. I was camping out, and she found me. Woke me up, and I didn't understand why until savages came. If I'd been asleep, I would have been et."

"Eaten," Alex corrected absently, and Smith nodded.

"That," he said. "But my old mare, she could have run any other way and let them feast. She stopped instead. And it was in fog like this."

Right.

Alex loved her dad dearly, but that was a weird story, and she really wasn't sure if it could possibly apply to the current situation.

Carefully, then, she asked, "So... now...?"

Smith shook his head, "Don't know. But I put stock in any creature who comes to me peaceably in fog. Maybe we should open the barn for him."

He nodded to the moose as he said it, and predictably, the fellow snorted.

Alex's eyebrows went right up, "You want me to keep him?"

Smith shrugged, "He found you for a reason. Been trying a while. Maybe there's a purpose. Only way to know is to give him a chance."

That... sort of made sense? Alex frowned at her dad, then looked back to the moose... who snorted again.

"Hey snort, quit it," she scolded him. "I'm trying to think."

With that admonishment, the big bull looked away — as if displeased by her tone... perhaps rightly, as she was sounding a bit edgier than she meant to. Because, after all, she might... keep him? Or was he keeping her? She was just tired enough, and disheveled enough, for both ideas to seem to have some merit.

"Is this a dream?" she asked quietly, looking back to her dad. "Or are we talking about... a pet moose?"

Smith could detect the beginnings of enthusiasm creeping into her voice — they'd never really had pets in the Smith house, though the former-drifter had always imagined his daughter would be good with them.

His response to his daughter was a shrug, "Let him decide. Offer the barn."

Alex began to nod slowly, and then she looked up towards the sky, and around to all the trees, "Really not a dream?"

Shaking his head, Smith continued to offer something approaching reason, "Bring him to the barn, get a bath, go to bed. If he's there when you wake up…"

"Then it wasn't a dream," Alex narrowed her eyes thoughtfully, then began to nod in appreciation of her father's wisdom. "Yes. That makes sense."

Saying it made sense was definitely pushing it, but it was as much progress as they'd manage that night.

"Alright," she turned back towards the moose. "Come on, let's get you situated. Coming, dad?"

Smith smiled at his daughter's resignation to surreality, then nodded, "Just have to get my hat. Dropped it somewhere when you called."

"Okay, see you at the barn," Alex was already busy waving to the moose, getting his attention and then heading towards the house. As planned, the big fellow followed her — something she was almost surprised to see.

Without further drama, she and the moose disappeared into another thickening mist.

As they vanished, Smith's smile did as well, and much of the air in his lungs escaped. Shoulders slumping, he turned in the opposite direction and began working his way deeper into the fog.

Stephanie was sitting on the steps to the kitchen door when she saw her friend emerge from the mist.

"Nightmare?" the young American called, but before she could explain how her own terrors had become firmly rooted in the endless corridors of a bloody Hong Kong warehouse, she watched a monster appear. Except…

"Is that a moose?" after the terrors of her sleep, Stephanie didn't even sound slightly frightened at the big beast's arrival. As monsters went, he seemed benign.

Alex looked from her friend back to her… um… moose… and then shrugged.

"My dad says we can keep him."

Right.

Stephanie closed her eyes, and opened them again. Then she held one arm out in front of herself, and carefully pinched it. That done, she looked up once more, and opened her mouth to ask another question. It took two tries.

"Keep him... for, like, supper?"

The moose snorted, and Alex winced, "Don't think he liked you saying that."

"He's a moose," Stephanie rose to her feet and quickly descended the steps, her eyes staying fixed on the tall bull. Then she stopped, turned her head slightly sideways, and considered him out of the corners of her narrowed eyes. "Wait, is he the *same* moose?"

Alex shrugged again, "I think so?"

Well somehow that just added up. Stephanie Shylock put her hands on her hips before turning her gaze back to her friend, "She wrestles a moose, and then the moose finds her later, in the middle of the night, at home, to become her pet?"

A bit sheepishly, Alex shrugged yet again. Then the moose snorted.

"I worded that pretty badly, but we can edit it, and then it's going straight into the legend of whitecoat," the Lieutenant said — apparently ready to embrace the madness. "Wait until Strong hears about this."

Alex found everything her friend said to be very awkward, so she decided to try to press on past it, "We need to open the barn for him. Come with me? This fog is creepy."

"Sure," Stephanie agreed, and joined her friend as they headed off into the mist. "But what are you wearing?"

"I literally don't even know."

"For the legend, we'll pretend it was your coat and boots," Stephanie decided thoughtfully, and the moose snorted again.

Alex really had to wonder if he had some sort of cold.

Then, with all the painfully-unfunny commentary two best friends could muster... and accompanied by a perfectly inexplicable moose... Lady Alex Smith and Second Lieutenant Stephanie Shylock disappeared into the fog.

• • •

Smith picked up his hat from the log he'd left it on, and took a deep breath. A moose in the middle of the night?

"That was close."

Closing his eyes as he heard those words, the former-drifter shook his head, "We won't have any more excuses if she sees me come out here again."

"There are always more ways."

Perhaps that was true. The past year had taught Smith there were ways to do all sorts of things: bombs could be planted, traps set, luggage smuggled... lies told. Things Smith never believed he could do could be accomplished when they had to be.

"By the way, don't ever let a Saa close to that moose with a genetic testing kit. He's not ordinary, by any means."

Alex's father didn't respond to that instruction. Instead, he stared at his hat and found himself lost in thoughts of people dead and wounded. His responsibility.

"Smith."

Suddenly, the monster was right in front of him... though perhaps 'monster' was a misleading term for an aged fellow who always arrived well-dressed in a crisp blue suit and with perfectly-combed black-and-white hair. He never seemed disheveled, though because he and Smith shared a certain connection, the former-drifter knew better than to think he was immune to worry.

Unfortunately, this monster's worries were costing lives... and costing Smith everything he valued in himself.

"Lying does not sit right on me," he said. "Especially to her."

The aged monster took a deep breath, but did not waver from his purpose, "You do what you must, Smith. And if you fail..."

He left that sentence unfinished, but Smith couldn't leave the most important part unsaid: "My daughter dies."

The monster nodded, confirming once again the gravity of the danger. Never in his life would Smith have imagined himself going against his own people, no matter what the greater cause. But this night in the fog, he could not deny the truth of his being: if his daughter was at risk, he would do whatever was necessary to save her.

And now she was at risk, and he'd become a traitor to those who trusted him most.

With that grave thought, he turned away from the monster, holding up his hand in a defeated wave goodbye. The whitehair in the blue suit said no more — simply disappeared into the fog, and left the former-drifter with his torment.

For now.

AN EXCLUSIVE LOOK AHEAD...

SHOPPING

"Do you think this is normal?"

As she asked the question, Stephanie Shylock was sitting in the driver's seat of her Land Rover, turned partway so that her boots could be up on the dash in front of the passenger seat, arms folded as she looked out through the windshield at the front door to the Randsford Coat Store.

Sitting on the bench behind the passenger seat, with his arm resting on its top and his gaze similarly directed, Sergeant Mike Strong paused to think before slowly shaking his head.

"I don't think so. What do you figure?"

When he passed along that question, it wasn't directed back at Stephanie, but at the giant face looming in the passenger-side window of the truck. That face — or more precisely his nose — snorted, and then the moose seemed to shift his weight from foot to foot, as if to say he was tired of waiting.

They all were — that was the most normal part. When Alex had agreed to help Constance Cormack choose her coat, it had seemed a great idea for the whole team to come down and show solidarity. But there was an unspoken rule about the Randsford store: it was for Champions, and Champions only. Sometimes foster parents would join the Champion they raised for a browse, but that always made people uncomfortable.

So Mike and Stephanie had agreed to wait in the truck. And that, naturally, had been two hours ago.

It was not as though either Alex or Constance were distracted shoppers; picking a coat was serious business, and it could not be rushed. But prepared as they'd been to wait, neither the Lieutenant nor the Colour had been ready for a third member of the audience to join them in the parking lot.

The moose had followed them.

Now he was standing beside the Land Rover as if his presence was the most normal thing in the world, and Stephanie shot a glare at him, "You're creepy."

Looking in the passenger side window, the big bull snorted again, then turned his gaze back to the store.

"He really thinks he's people," Strong had to make the comment, and though she wasn't sure about the grammar, Stephanie agreed with a firm nod.

"Doesn't help that we put the scarf on him."

That was probably true; the moose had been living in the barn for weeks before Smith finally suggested to his daughter that they find a way to make him identifiable, in case any hunters happened to see him when he went out into the woods during the day. Shooting moose was common enough in Newfoundland — Stephanie herself had twice implied that this fellow might make a good meal, which perhaps explained his standoffishness — so it was important to make sure Alex's bull didn't become a target.

As such, they'd made him a giant scarf that now resembled a bandana on an outlaw... but still. He was like people. At least they hadn't named him...

"Is that her moose?"

Stephanie didn't need Champion hearing to detect that question from a couple of passing students from the Lady Emily Academy. If was fortunate that Randsford's store was on the grounds of Jimmystown — if they'd been in St. John's, there would have been countless people striding by, stopping, pointing...

Instead, it was just two young Champions-in-training, so Stephanie looked out her window and waved to them, "Official business. Thanks for noticing, but nothing to see here."

The two youngsters seemed a bit giddy at the idea of spotting the legendary whitecoat moose, but they didn't mistake the dry authority in Stephanie's words. On they went, and Stephanie sighed.

"This is not normal," she said, and the moose snorted again.

They waited some more, watching the front of the store with as much patience as they could muster. Stephanie wiggled in her seat a bit, and both her feet started to fall asleep because of their elevation. Mike Strong's back was tightening up a bit too — it was October, and though there was not yet snow over Jimmystown, the air was cold. That helped his back not at all.

"I wish these seats had heaters in them," the Sergeant grumbled eventually.

A frown crossed Stephanie's brow, "Why would seats have heaters *in* them?"

"You'll understand when you're not young and invincible anymore," the Colour replied with a wince, then altered his position too. "How long now?"

Stephanie glanced at the clock in the dashboard, and was about to answer when the store's doors opened, and at last, the silhouettes of two Ladies — Constance had been granted a title as a graduate of the Lady Emily Academy, even though she was American — appeared across the parking lot.

One of them was wearing white, and carrying a bag. The other was just wearing green.

Green like the polish on Stephanie's nails.

"Isn't that the color Alex had planned to pick?" Strong spotted them immediately, and as Stephanie pulled her boots down from the dash and shifted in her seat, she tried to nod.

"That's what I thought."

The two Champions were crossing the parking lot at a relatively sedate pace, nattering to each other about the checkout, or some such thing, but as they neared the front of the Land Rover they stopped.

Alex was slightly in the lead, and she frowned and looked through the windshield at her friend, "How long has *he* been here?"

Stephanie replied, "Pretty much since you went in."

"Oh," Alex looked back to the moose. "Is that normal?"

"We don't think so," Mike Strong called, and Alex slowly began to nod.

"You really don't need to be stalking me. I'll come back home and see you. This behavior is a little possessive. I need my space."

Constance found that a little bit funny — because she was sane — so she chuckled... and the moose glared at her.

"Hey," Alex scolded him, speaking with as much apparent lucidity as she once had to a seagull. "Don't be rude."

"He's been waiting as long as we have, so we've developed camaraderie with him. Don't be mean," Stephanie called back through her window, and Alex turned her frown back towards her friend.

"You're taking his side?"

"I'm taking the 'let's stop sitting around' side. Constance found your coat?"

That was a quick pivot, and Alex blinked before looking back at the young American. Hearing the same question, the girl from Georgia smiled nervously, "It was really stuck in behind a bunch of men's coats. Mister Randsford said it was part of last year's line."

So it was the green coat that Alex had her heart set on in August of 1940... one she hadn't been able to find. Now, it was on the shoulders of another deserving Champion... and Alex was in white...

"Is that awkward?" the younger Lady Smith asked her friend, and Stephanie frowned.

"What?"

With a shrug, Alex continued to the passenger side, where the moose was waiting. With a bob of her head, she encouraged him to make enough room for her to open the door and get in... and he did so, because apparently he was better trained than many dogs. He still seemed disapproving, but as Constance gave him a wide berth and climbed into the back, Alex managed to ignore his glare.

"Do you think the green coat will be jealous of my white coat?" she asked, keeping her voice down as if the green coat would care. "Or that my white coat will be jealous that I went in there looking for that green coat?"

Stephanie stared at her, and from behind Alex's seat, Mike Strong blinked.

"I've been the source of jealousy for many women," the intrepid Colour said ruefully. "I know jealousy when I see it, but there's none here. Both coats still love you. Maybe if you get them drunk enough, you can have both... at the same time."

Of course. A smile started to spread across Strong's face as his two charges processed the rather worldly nature of his joke, but both knew better than to encourage him by providing any response.

As Constance slid up the bench facing Strong, she followed Alex's lead — didn't comment — and then she held up her hands, "So, I did okay?"

She was clearly excited by her coat, which was right. She'd have to show Vanier and George, and have some color photographs taken to send home for her mother. She was a Champion now — ready to work alongside her lover and her brother in a pursuit of villainy. Her eagerness was just barely held in check, and recognizing that, Alex had to smile.

"You know I like it."

"It matches my nail polish," Stephanie added, with a quick glance to her whitecoat, who made a sour face.

"I *know*."

Mike Strong ignored that, and instead bowed slightly towards Constance, "You are every inch a Champion, Lady Cormack. The Hospitality department will be very lucky to have you."

That was nice, and Constance smiled and shrugged a little bashfully, "Thanks Sergeant. That means a lot."

It actually did, and though they were always inclined to needle each other, neither Alex nor Stephanie undercut the compliment with a quip. It was important for Constance to feel welcomed.

But the truce ended as Alex adjusted the bag that she'd brought from the store, which was between her feet. Stephanie noticed it and nodded, "That Constance's Academy jacket?"

"Yes," Alex made a point of trying to sound too innocent, which compelled the American Lieutenant's eyes to narrow.

"And?"

"She got another white coat!" Constance spilled the news more quickly than Alex would have, but since she was right, the younger Lady Smith had to fess up to her shopping victory.

With a grin, she reached into the bag and pulled out a slightly off-white coat, holding it up for her friends to see. It had two rows of horn buttons, a belt around its waist, and it looked rather less dramatic than her own...

"It's different. And it's not as white," Stephanie frowned.

Alex nodded, "Exactly, this one will be better for when we're in places that might mess up my coat. It'll be my *field* coat."

That sounded sensible — there was no rule anywhere saying Champions could have only one coat, and while a series of miracles had kept Alex's beloved white one clean for the whole year, having a backup was probably a good idea...

"You were worried about your current coat being jealous of the *green*, but you weren't worried about it feeling threatened by a new, whiteish one?" Stephanie had to frown, and Alex shrugged.

"I guess..."

Mike Strong, being himself, had an answer: "No see, the two

white coats are like sisters. And speaking from experience, if you get two sisters drunk enough, you can—"

That's when Mike Strong fell from the bench to the floor of the Land Rover bed with a thud. He didn't so much as wheeze — just looked back in surprise as he landed. Alex had been examining her new coat, and Stephanie had been glaring at Alex, so it was only Constance who saw the nose of the moose sticking under the canvas top of the Land Rover.

Of course the bull snorted again, and then withdrew his snout.

By the time Alex and Stephanie recognized the sound of the fall and looked, Strong was already rubbing his back, "What did I say?"

"What happened?" Alex asked, and the Colour nodded towards the canvas.

"Your bull pushed me out of my seat, through the canvas."

Alex blinked, then swiveled to look back out the window at her moose. He was wandering off into the nearby trees, ignoring a couple of soldiers who had stopped to point at him.

"The moose stopped you from finishing a bad joke?" Constance Cormack wasn't sure what to make of it, and Alex let her new white coat drop into her lap as she pondered the statement.

"Maybe... maybe he's like the physical manifestation of my subconscious mind!"

She looked triumphantly back into the Land Rover, as if she expected everyone to agree.

Mike Strong was busy getting back onto his bench. Constance Cormack looked sympathetic. Stephanie Shylock looked down for a second, then turned to the steering wheel and switched on the truck.

"Because he follows me around and seems to be doing things I'd like to do — like stopping Mike's jokes?" the younger Lady Smith tried to persist, but that didn't really work.

"Deep down, you love my jokes," the Colour sounded wounded as he settled back onto his bench.

The greencoat was no more help: "If he was your subconscious, why did he seem so stern about us shopping? Were you not enjoying yourself?"

Alex started to backpedal, "No I had a lot of fun... and I do like your jokes, Mike... but..."

Her words tapered off, and as both passengers in the back of the Land Rover did a really convincing job of pretending to be offended or upset, the now-apparently-double whitecoat turned to her best friend with a slightly pouty experession, "Do you know what I mean, Stephanie?"

The Second Lieutenant who'd been born on another planet, and yet somehow appeared to be the most grounded of this bunch, took one breath as she shook her head.

"This is not normal," she decided aloud. "Everything here is weird."

Well, that *might* have been pushing it.

JOIN ALEX, STEPHANIE AND STRONG FOR THEIR NEXT MISSION:

THE CHAMPIONS OF 1942 PART 1

SNAPDRAGON

KENNETH TAM

EBOOK RELEASE: JANUARY 2014

PRINT RELEASE (AS PART OF 1942 OMNIBUS): NOVEMBER 2014

FOR THE LATEST: CHAMPIONSOF1940.COM

KENNETH TAM'S
EQUATIONS NOVELS

The Earthers evolved after humans were driven from the Earth by an intelligent bio-weapon dubbed 'Omega'. They are faster, stronger, smarter, wiser, *better* than humans, and they are the only hope for the survivors of the human race as an interstellar war between two great alien powers absorbs the galaxy. But all is not as it seems, and the humans and the Earthers face challenges that overshadow the wars of alien empires and threaten to destroy their civilizations...

The Equations Novels by Kenneth Tam
Book One: The Human Equation (Oct 2003)
Book Two: The Alien Equation (May 2004)
Book Three: The Renegade Equation (Dec 2004)
Book Four: The Earther Equation (July 2005)
Book Five: The Genesis Equation (July 2006)
Book Six: The Vengeance Equation (July 2007)
Book Seven: The Nemesis Equation (July 2008)
Book Eight: The Destiny Equation (July 2009)

The complete series is now available in both print and ebook formats. For more information, visit:

www.earther.net